The Realm of Fiction

65 Short Stories

James B. Hall

Provost of College V
University of California, Santa Cruz

The Realm of Fiction

65 Short Stories

SECOND EDITION

McGraw-Hill Book Company

New York, St. Louis, San Francisco,
Düsseldorf, London, Mexico,
Panama, Sydney, Toronto

The Realm of Fiction
65 Short Stories

Library of Congress Catalog Card Number
70-107445
1 2 3 4 5 6 7 8 9 0   MAMM 7 9 8 7 6 5 4 3 2 1 0

This book was set in Palatino by Monotype
Composition Company, Inc., and printed on
permanent paper and bound by The Maple Press
Company. The designer was Paula Tuerk.
The editors were Robert Fry,
Cheryl Kupper, and Ellen Simon. Sally R. Ellyson
supervised the production.

Preface

A definitive literary history of the short story may never be written. Nevertheless, in this second edition *The Realm of Fiction* tries once more to illuminate the topography of this demanding yet elusive art form. It has now been five years since the first publication, and both the emergence of new writers and the press of a society in revolution place new obligations on the responsible anthologist.

To help meet these demands the revised text adds a total of fifteen new stories, twelve by authors not hitherto included; Chekov, Bierce, Mann, Joyce, and Kay Boyle are now represented by stories judged to be more relevant to the times. The text itself now carries sixty-five stories, and additional changes in both arrangement and emphasis have been made. The authors and the stories are now arranged in only three large geographical areas: Russia-Europe; England-Ireland; and the United States. In the matter of chronology, however, the scheme of the first edition is largely preserved: the "older masters" give way to "the later accomplishment" and that in turn leads to the "new dimensions" which are not presented geographically.

While the stories in general still move from earlier tales to some extreme statements of the present moment, the second edition puts considerably less emphasis on the nineteenth century. Despite the diversity of their national origins, early tales may lack technical interest; too often the author who was an innovator in his own time now seems either mannered or repetitious.

Given more focus on the relevant, the contemporary, and given less emphasis on mere history and chronology, the teacher will find this edition more informal in arrangement, more suited to a newer generation of students, more flexible, and the materials not as easily exhausted. Above all, the use of this book should assist the student to become a practical critic of the short story, to learn what constitutes literary quality in the short story, and, by extension, in all literature.

As in the first edition, this text omits pedagogical apparatus except for a general introduction and brief biographical notes on each author. Included with most of the biographical notes are references for further reading, in most cases, short story collections.

The single most important addition to this second edition is its acknowledgment of the "black experience," a theme presented through the work of Charles W. Chesnutt, Langston Hughes, Kay Boyle, Saul Bellow, and James Alan McPherson. Not all those authors are black, but in their work, often written years before the awareness of the problem by the general public, they all illuminate a situation of paramount importance in America today. In passing we might note that the interesting and neglected black author Charles W. Chesnutt is here included for the first time in a text for general use. The stories direct attention to significant social and artistic issues, and they take their appropriate places in the chronology as the stories move toward more complex statement.

Thus stories involving the black experience appear alongside the memorable fiction by such writers as Kafka and Mann, Joyce and Lawrence. Other significant stories, such as those by de Alarcón, Katayev, Vasconcelos, Rosenfeld, Móricz, George Moore, Mishima, Böll, and Mrozek appear for the first time in any anthology text that I know of. Whether established, recently neglected, or new, these stories serve the same purpose: to quicken interest in all literature.

Once again, I am especially indebted to my wife, Elizabeth C. Hall, who is in fact a coeditor of this revised edition but who, too modestly, disclaims that title.

James B. Hall

Contents

The Older Masters

The Later Accomplishment

New Dimensions

x

Introduction

The short prose narrative is at once the oldest of literary forms and the newest to receive modern definition. In its primitive state the prose tale was orally realized—to entertain an audience, to chronicle history, or even to prophesy the future. Being functional, the prose tales survived; a few became the literary heritage of nations. Only about one hundred and fifty years ago, in widely separated countries, such literary artists as Hoffman, E. A. Poe, and Hawthorne began to transform the eighteenth-century prose tale into an exacting, complex art form. Today the short story is still in the process of dynamic change.

Of all literary art forms the short story is the most deceptive. Its traditional focus on a single episode, its relative lack of mass—of density of character, variety of scene, and richness of detail—and its frequently casual tone all seem to suggest ease of composition, at least to the inexperienced reader. In contrast to the panorama of the novel, the short story must strike the unwary reader as an art of limited means, of modest resources. Actually, the apparent limitations of the short story are a measure of its strength—the control of all its materials. Very possibly the deceptive nature of the short story was one reason for its wide appeal, for given conscious artists and new and more literate audiences, the form quickly became a worldwide institution. In the twentieth century the continued fecundity of short fiction is a striking fact of literary history.

The changes which came over the prose tale, on its way to becoming the modern short story, are not difficult to understand. The oldest known tale, *The Shipwrecked Sailor* (from Egyptian papyri, about 4000 B.C.), or the Book of Jonah (from the Old Testament, 350 to 750 B.C.), or tales from the *Decameron* (1353 A.D.) are not very different in literary quality from the eighteenth-century tales that immediately preceded the short story. The latest ancestors of the short story in point of time are fictional essays, such as "The Vision of Mirza" by Addison in the *Spectator* (1711) or digressions within a novel, such as "The Tale of the Old Man of the Hill" in Fielding's *Tom Jones* (1748). Typically these short prose pieces lack restraint, or an economy of means; either the moral point is obtrusive and thus the artistic effect is thin, or they lack a meaningful plot structure, and thus are discursive and flat. Perhaps the greatest difference between the prose tale and the nineteenth century short story is the consciousness of technique on the part of the nineteenth-century artist. It is precisely this consciousness, this commitment to short fiction as a demanding, distinctive art form that distinguishes Hawthorne and Poe as literary pioneers of great importance. Poe, in particular, felt that the crucial element in the short story was unity of effect—this effect coming from the artistic combination of "incident" and "tone." Poe was speaking of this necessary unity when he praised Hawthorne's stories by saying. "Every word *tells*, and there is not a word which does *not* tell. . . ." Other Americans and European writers shared a similarly lofty concept of the short story as an art form of first importance, and thus they paved the way for the modern short story of the twentieth century.

Compressed statement—the embodiment of significance at several levels of meaning—distinguishes modern short stories of the highest quality. To convey multiple meanings, the artist frequently uses language which is metaphorical or figurative—a medium of expression which is both allusive and suggestive. The story which is resourceful in its exploitation of language will most gracefully support symbolic detail and symbolic actions; in fact, the use of symbolism, justified by an adequate language, is the most interesting and useful advance in narrative technique of modern times. Because of its heightened language the short story approaches poetry in intensity. Always, however, the writer's object remains complexity with control.

If the short story has become more complex and more intense, this does not imply that the modern writer ignores the older, established demands of the form. The modern short story—as a matter of course—comments on the quality and the nature of life; but where morality is a factor, the artist recognizes that the implied or the suggested is always more moving than the easy precept easily stated. Character, namely, imaginative characterizations, continues in importance, but now the focus of narration is on the mind or on the psychic states of the protagonists. Plot structure—a story's largest unit of composition—is recognized as an integral part of the meaning of the story; details are rigorously selected for their ability to "tell." if a story can be said to have literal, allegorical, symbolic, and even mythic levels of meaning, this does not imply that modern short fiction is only an intellectual exercise for the artists and a puzzle for the reader. Close reading, critical analysis, or the brutal fragmentation of a story may be a useful prelude to rendering critical judgment. Nevertheless, both the story's intention and the author's intention remain the same: to create a unified artistic statement which may give both knowledge and pleasure.

If the short story has moved towards complexity, there is little cause for regret. After all, the roots of our short fiction are in our scientific age, in a magnificently complex world initially described by Darwin, Marx, and Freud. That is the world in which we live, and if the literary artist is to render truthfully the altered circumstances of life and morality, he must of necessity impose new demands on his art form. This is true of all imaginative writing at the present time: the novel, poetry, and drama. The short story is no exception: the artists, the art form, and new multiple audiences respond complexly.

Each story in this book, in its own way, describes a specific vision of a complex world. In "The Last Judgment" (Part 2) by Karel Čapek, the conventional notion of an all-powerful God is contradicted. "Our Father Who Art in Heaven" by Katayev also concerns God, but the title is ironic: there is no earthly salvation for the two innocent people who die in the terrible cold. In still another mode the story "Check!" by the Polish author Slawomir Mrozek dramatizes a man's relationship—or lack of it—to some "higher" power. Taken together, these three stories bring into a new kind of focus the age-old relationship of man to God. Other stories in this book raise different questions about the nature of human experience, the conflicts of man and nature, or of man with his most powerful antagonist, himself. Short stories, and all literature, are read in the faith that asking such questions is the first step to a better understanding not only of art and the world but of the self.

The final seventeen stories in New Dimensions (Part 3) are examples of recent developments in short fiction both in America and abroad. While some of these stories are more difficult than others, they are not necessarily arranged in an ascending order of complexity. In fact, the first four stories are more "open," more public, more accessible; other stories which range from "The Secret Room" by Robbe-Grillet, an example of the French "new novel" technique, to "Texts for Nothing" by Samuel Beckett, an example of a story which is virtually nonrepresentational and a final statement of its kind, may be hermetic, complex, and more demanding.

If the stories in New Dimensions at first seem strange and if certain stories in the other sections of this book at first seem difficult, the rewards of close study are great. In this volume, for example, a series of stories scattered through various sections may give insight into the "black experience." "The Web of Circumstance" by Charles W. Chesnutt and "Poor Black Fellow" by Langston Hughes are stories by talented artists who happened to be black; "Looking for Mr. Green" by Saul Bellow and "Black Boy" by Kay Boyle are stories by equally talented artists, let us say, who happen to be white. The literary and artistic issues are complex; no simple reading or quick decision will satisfy the dedicated student. And, incidentally, if these and other stories bring up the problem of the underprivileged, then should not the protagonist of "The Benefits of American Life" by James T. Farrell be considered? Rest assured that these stories will not settle the matter, nor are they intended to do so. On the other hand, this particular group of stories, including "Of Cabbages and Kings" by James Alan McPherson, is calculated to place the "black experience" and related problems in some broader, humanistic perspective. If education is the attainment not only of knowledge but also of wisdom concerning the world and ourselves, then the short story form in all its manifestations provides one useful means to that end.

The Realm of Fiction

65 Short Stories

Dostoevsky
Hoffmann
de Alarcón
Tolstoy
Verga
de Maupassant
Chekov
Moore
Bennett
Kipling
Wells
Wilde

The Older Masters

Conrad
Hawthorne
Poe
Bierce
Twain
Chesnutt
Norris
Crane

Fyodor Dostoevsky (1821–1881) was a doctor's son who left military engineering to become a writer. Arrested in 1849 for alleged conspiracy, he was sentenced to Siberia. Later, in the midst of personal tragedy and poverty, he emerged as a major creative talent with such novels as Crime and Punishment (1866), The Idiot (1868–1869), The Possessed (1871), and The Brothers Karamazov (1879–1880). For further reading: White Nights, and Other Stories, translated by Constance Garnett (1918).

A Christmas Tree and a Wedding

FYODOR DOSTOEVSKY

The other day I saw a wedding . . . but no! Better I tell you about the Christmas tree. The wedding was nice; I enjoyed it very much, but the other thing that happened was better. I do not know why, but while looking at the wedding, I thought about that Christmas tree. This was the way it happened.

On New Year's Eve, exactly five years ago, I was invited to a children's party. The host was a well-known businessman with many connections, friends and intrigues, so you might think the children's party was a pretext for the parents to meet each other and to talk things over in an innocent, casual and inadvertent manner.

I was an outsider. I did not have anything to contribute, and therefore I spent the evening on my own. There was another gentleman present who had no special family or position, but, like myself, had dropped in on this family happiness. He was the first to catch my eye. He was a tall, lean man, very serious and very properly dressed. Actually he was not enjoying this family-type party in the least. If he withdrew into a corner, he immediately stopped smiling and knit his thick bushy black eyebrows. Except for our host, the man had not a single acquaintance at the whole party. Obviously, he was terribly bored, but he was making a gallant effort to play the role of a perfectly happy, contented man. Afterwards I learned he was a gentleman from the provinces, with important, puzzling business in the capital; he had brought our host a letter of introduction, from a person our host did not patronize, so this man was invited to this children's party only out of courtesy. He didn't even play cards. They offered him no cigars; no one engaged him in conversation. Perhaps we recognized the bird by its feathers from a distance; that is why my gentleman was compelled to sit out the whole evening and stroke his whiskers merely to have something to do with his hands. His whiskers really were very fine, but he stroked them so diligently, you thought the whiskers came first, and were then fixed onto his face, the better to stroke them.

Besides this man—who had five well-fed boys—my attention was caught by a second gentleman. He was an important person. His name was Yulian Mastakovitch. With one glance, you saw he was a guest of honor. He looked down on the host much as the host looked down on the gentleman who stroked his whiskers. The host and hostess spoke to the important man from across a chasm of courtesy, waited on him, gave him drink, pampered him, and brought their guests to him for introductions. They did not take him to anyone.

When Yulian Mastakovitch commented, in regard to the evening, that he had seldom spent time in such a pleasant manner, I noticed tears sparkled in the host's eyes. In the presence of such a person, I was frightened, and, after admiring the children, I walked into a small deserted drawing-room and sat down beside an arbour of flowers which took up almost half of the room.

All the children were incredibly sweet. They absolutely refused to imitate their "elders," despite all the exhortations of their governesses and mothers. In an instant the children untwisted all the Christmas tree candy and broke half of the toys before they knew for whom they were intended. One small, black eyed, curly haired boy was especially nice. He kept wanting to shoot me with his wooden gun. But my attention was still more drawn to his sister, a girl of eleven, a quiet, pensive, pale little cupid with large thoughtful eyes. In some way, the children wounded her feelings, and so she came into the same room where I sat and busied herself in the corner—with her doll.

The guests respectfully pointed out one of the wealthy commissioned tax gatherers—her father. In a whisper someone said three hundred thousand roubles were already set aside for her dowry.

I swung around to look at those who were curious about such circumstances: my gaze fell on Yulian Mastakovitch. With his hands behind his back, with his head cocked a little to one side, he listened with extraordinary attention to the empty talk of the guests.

Later, I marveled at the wisdom of the host and hostess in the distribution of the children's gifts. The little girl—already the owner of three hundred thousand roubles—received the most expensive doll. Then followed presents lowering in value according to the class of the parents of these happy children. Finally, the last gift: a young boy, ten years-old, slender, small, freckled, red-haired, received only a book of stories about the marvels of nature and the tears of devotion—without pictures and even without engravings. He was the son of the governess of the hosts' children, a poor widow; he was a little boy, extremely oppressed and frightened. He wore a jacket made from a wretched nankeen. After he received his book, he walked around the other toys for a long time; he wanted to play with the other children, but he did not dare; he already felt and understood his position.

I love to watch children. They are extraordinarily fascinating in their first independent interests in life. I noticed the red-haired boy was so tempted by the costly toys of the other children, especially a theater in which he certainly wanted to take some kind of part, that he decided to act differently. He smiled and began playing with the other children. He gave away his apple to a puffy little boy, who had bound up a full handkerchief of sweets. He even went as far as to carry another boy on his back, so they would not turn him away from the theater. But a minute later, a kind of mischievous child gave him a considerable beating. The boy did not dare to cry. Here the governess, his mother, appeared and ordered him not to disturb the play of the other children. Then the boy went to the same room where the little girl was. She allowed him to join her. Very eagerly they both began to dress the expensive doll.

I had been already sitting in the ivy-covered arbour for a half an hour. I was almost asleep, yet listening to the little conversations of the red-haired boy and the little beauty with the dowry of three hundred thousand fussing over her doll.

Suddenly Yulian Mastakovitch walked into the room. Under cover of the quarreling children, he had noiselessly left the drawing-room. A minute before I noticed he was talking very fervently with the father of the future heiress, with whom he had just become acquainted. He discussed the advantages of one branch of the service over another. Now he stood deep in thought, as if he were calculating something on his fingers.

"Three hundred . . . three hundred," he whispered. "Eleven, twelve, thirteen," and so forth. "Sixteen—five years! Let us assume it is at four per cent—five times twelve is sixty, yes, to that sixty . . . now let us assume what it will be in five years—four hundred. Yes! Well . . . oh, but he won't hold to four per cent, the swindler. Maybe he can get eight or ten. Well, five hundred, let us assume five hundred thousand, the final measure, that's certain. Well, say a little extra for frills. H'm . . ."

He ended his reflection. He blew his nose, and intended to leave the room. Suddenly he glanced at the little girl and stopped short. He did not see me behind the pots of greenery. It seemed to me that he was really disturbed. Either his calculations had affected him, or something else. He rubbed his hands and could not stand in one place. This nervousness increased to the utmost limit. And then he stopped and threw another resolute glance at the future heiress. He was about to advance, but first he looked around. On tiptoe, as if he felt guilty, he approached the children. With a half-smile, he drew near, stooped, and kissed the little girl on the head. Not expecting the attack, she cried out, frightened.

"And what are you doing here, sweet child?" he asked in a whisper, looking around and patting the girl on the cheek.

"We are playing."

"Ah, with him?" Yulian Mastakovitch looked to one side at the boy. "And you, my dear, go into the drawing-room."

The boy kept silent and stared at him with open eyes.

Yulian Mastakovitch again looked around him and again stooped to the little girl.

"And what is this you have," he asked, "A dolly, sweet child?"

"A dolly," the little girl answered, wrinkling her face, a trifle shy.

"A dolly . . . and do you know, my sweet child, from what your dolly is made?"

"I don't know . . ." answered the little girl in a whisper, hanging her head.

"From rags, darling. You'd better go into the drawing-room to your companions, little boy," said Yulian Mastakovitch, staring severely at the child. The little girl and boy made a wry face and held onto each other's hand. They did not want to be separated.

"And do you know why they gave you that doll?" asked Yulian Mastakovitch, lowering his voice more and more.

"I don't know."

"Because you have been a sweet, well-behaved child all week."

Here Yulian Mastakovitch, emotional as could be, looked around and lowered his voice more and more, and finally asked, inaudibly, almost standing completely still from excitement and with an impatient voice:

"And will you love me, sweet little girl? When I come to visit your parents?"

Having said this, Yulian Mastakovitch tried once again to kiss the sweet girl. The red-haired boy, seeing that she wanted to cry, gripped her hand and began to whimper from sheer sympathy for her. Yulian Mastakovitch became angry, and not in jest.

"Go away. Go away from here, go away!" he said to the little boy. "Go into the drawing-room! Go in there to your companions!"

"No, he doesn't have to, doesn't have to! You go away," said the little girl, almost crying, "Leave him alone, leave him alone!"

Someone made a noise at the door.

Yulian Mastakovitch immediately raised his majestic body and became frightened. But the red-haired boy was even more startled than Yulian Mastakovitch. He left the little girl and quietly, guided by the wall, passed from the drawing-room into the dining-room. To avoid arousing suspicion, Yulian Mastakovitch also went into the dining-room. He was red as a lobster. He glanced into the mirror, as if he were disconcerted. He was perhaps annoyed with himself for his fervor and his impatience. At first perhaps he was so struck by the calculations on his fingers, so enticed and inspired that in spite of all his dignity and importance, he decided to act like a little boy, and directly pursue the object of his attentions even though she could not possibly be *his* object for at least five more years.

I followed the respectable gentleman into the dining-room. I beheld a strange sight. All red from vexation and anger, Yulian Mastakovitch frightened the red-haired boy, who was walking farther and farther, and in his fear did not know where to run.

"Go away. What are you doing here? Go away, you scamp, go away! You're stealing the fruits here, ah? You're stealing the fruits here? Go away, you reprobate. Go away. You snot-nosed boy, go away. Go to your companions!"

The frightened boy tried to get under the table. Then his persecutor, flushed as could be, took out his large batiste handkerchief and began to lash under the table at the child, who remained absolutely quiet. It must be noted that Yulian Mastakovitch was a little stout. He was a man, well-filled out, red-faced, sleek, with a paunch, with thick legs; in short, what is called a fine figure of a man, round as a nut. He was sweating, puffing and turning terribly red. Finally, he was almost in a frenzy, so great was his feelings of indignation and perhaps (who knows?) jealousy.

I burst out laughing at the top of my voice. Yulian Mastakovitch turned around, and despite all his manners, he was confounded into dust. From the opposite door at that moment came the host. The little boy climbed out from under the table and wiped his elbows and knees. Yulian Mastakovitch hurriedly blew his nose on a handkerchief, which he held in his hand by a corner.

Meanwhile, the host gave the three of us a puzzled look. But as with a man who knows life and looks at it with dead seriousness, he immediately availed himself of the chance to catch his guest in private.

"Here's the little boy," he said pointing to the red-haired boy, "for whom I was intending to intercede, your honor. . . ."

"Ah?" answered Yulian Mastakovitch, still not fully put in order.

"The son of my children's governess," the host continued with a pleading tone. "A poor woman, a widow, wife of an honest official; and therefore . . . Yulian Mastakovitch if it were possible. . . ."

"Oh, no, no," hurriedly answered Yulian Mastakovitch, "no, excuse me, Filip Alexyevitch, it's no way possible. I've asked, there are no vacancies. If there were, there are already ten candidates—all better qualified than he. . . . I'm very sorry. Very sorry. . . ."

"I am sorry," repeated the host. "The little boy is modest, quiet. . . ."

"A very mischievous boy, as I've noticed," answered Yulian Mastako-vitch, hysterically distorting his mouth. "Go away, little boy," he said addressing the child. "Why are you staying, go to your companions!"

It seemed he could not restrain himself. He glanced at me with one eye. In fun I could not restrain myself and burst out laughing directly in his face.

Yulian Mastakovitch immediately turned away, and clear enough for me to hear, he asked the host who was that strange young man. They whispered together and left the room. Afterwards, I saw Yulian Mastako-vitch listening to the host, mistrustfully shaking his head.

After laughing to my heart's content, I returned to the drawing-room. Surrounded by the fathers and mothers of the families and the host and hostess, the great man was uttering a mating call with warmth, towards a lady to whom he had just been introduced.

The lady was holding by the hand the girl, with whom ten minutes ago Yulian Mastakovitch had had the scene in the drawing-room. Now, he was showering praise and delight about the beauty, talent, grace and good manners of the sweet child. He was fawning, obviously, over the mamma; the mother listened to him almost in tears from delight. The father's lips made a smile; the host rejoiced because of the general satisfaction. All the guests were the same, and even the children stopped playing in order not to disturb the conversation. The whole atmosphere was saturated with reverence.

Later, as if touched to the depth of her heart, I heard the mother of the interesting child beg Yulian Mastakovitch to do her the special honor of presenting them his precious acquaintanceship; and I heard, with his kind of unaffected delight, Yulian Mastakovitch accepting the invitation. Afterwards, the guests all dispersed in different directions, as decency demanded; they spilled out to each other touching words of praise upon the commissioned tax gatherer who worked farmers, his wife, their daughter, and especially Yulian Mastakovitch.

"Is that gentleman married?" I asked, almost aloud, of one of my acquaintances, who was standing closest to Yulian Mastakovitch.

Yulian Mastakovitch threw at me a searching, malicious glance.

"No!" my friend answered me, chagrined to the bottom of his heart at my awkwardness, which I had displayed deliberately.

Recently, I walked by a certain church. The crowd, the congress of people startled me. All around they talked about the wedding. The day was cloudy, and it was starting to drizzle; I made my way through the crowd around the church and saw the bridegroom. He was a small, rotund, well-fed man with a slight paunch and highly dressed. He was running about, bustling, and giving orders. Finally, the voices of the crowd said that the bride was coming. I pushed my way through the crowd and saw a wonderful beauty, who had scarcely begun her first season. But the beauty was pale and sad. She looked distracted; it even seemed to me that her eyes were red from recent crying. The classical severity of every line of her face added a certain dignity and solemnity to her beauty. Through that severity and dignity, through that sadness, still appeared the first look of childish innocence—very naive, fluid, youthful, and yet neither asking nor entreating for mercy.

They were saying she was just sixteeen years-old. Glancing carefully at the bridegroom, I suddenly recognized him as Yulian Mastakovitch, whom I had not seen for five years. I took a look at her. My God!

I began to push my way quickly out of the church. The voices of the crowd said the bride was rich: a dowry of five hundred thousand . . . and a trousseau with ever so much. . . .

"It was a good calculation, though," I thought, and made my way out into the street.

Ritter Gluck

E. T. A. HOFFMANN

Late fall in Berlin usually has a few beautiful days. The sun comes
benignly out of the clouds and dries the moisture out of the tepid air
which blows through the streets. Then a long colorful column of people
comes into view, making their way through the linden trees to the park:
among them are dandies, townsmen with their wives and their dear
children in Sunday best, clergymen, Jewesses, young lawyers, prostitutes,
dancers, officers, and so on. Soon all the tables at Klaus & Weber are
occupied; the chicory coffee steams, the dandies are lighting their cigars,
there is conversation about war and about peace, about the shoes of
Madame Bethmann the actress (whether she recently wore gray ones
or green ones), about Fichte's treatise on high tariff barriers, about counter-
feit money, etc. Gradually everything blends into an aria from the light
opera *Fanchon*, with which an out of tune harp, a few discordant violins,
a consumptive flute, and a spasmodic bassoon torture themselves and
their audience. Close by the railing which separates Weber's cafe from
the Heerstrasse, there are several small round tables and garden chairs;
here one can breathe fresh air and can observe people coming and going,
but still be removed somewhat from the cacophonous din of that confounded orchestra. I take a seat there and give myself over to the light
play of my phantasy, which provides me with familiar figures with whom
I can converse about knowledge, about art, about everything which
is supposed to be dearest to man. The mass of strollers surges by me,
becoming more and more colorful, but nothing disturbs me, nothing can
frighten away my imaginary company. Only the cursed trio from a
completely worthless waltz tears me out of my dream world. I am the
only one to hear the shrill upper voice of the violins and the jarring

bass of the bassoon. They go up and down, firmly clinging to each other in octaves which pierce the ear. Instinctively, like some who is seized by a burning pain, I cry out,

"What crazy music! Those abominable octaves"—Next to me is a murmur:

"Cursed Fate! Another man who objects to octaves!"

I look up and only now become aware that, unnoticed by me, a man has taken a seat at the same table as mine. He fixes his eyes rigidly on me and my eyes cannot escape his stare.

I have never seen a head, never a figure which made such a deep impression on me so quickly. A softly curved nose was joined to a broad, open forehead, which had marked bulges above bushy, graying eyebrows, and under which the man's eyes flashed with an almost wild youthful fire. (The man was perhaps over fifty.) The delicately molded chin contrasted strangely with the tight shut mouth. A ludicrous smile, formed by the strange play of muscles in his sunken cheeks, seemed to protest against the expression of deep melancholy and seriousness lingering on his forehead. Only a few gray locks of hair lay behind the large ears which stood out from his head. A huge cloak enveloped this great lean figure. As I glanced at the man, he cast down his eyes and continued the activity which my outcry had probably interrupted. With evident pleasure he was shaking tobacco out of various small paper bags into a large snuff box which was standing before him, and wetting it with red wine from a pint-sized bottle. The music had stopped and I felt it necessary to speak to him.

"It is good that the music has stopped," I said, "I couldn't endure it."

The old man cast a fleeting glance at me and shook out the last paper bag.

"It would be better if they didn't play at all," I continued. "Do you agree with me?"

"I have no opinion," he said. "You are a musician and an expert. . . ."

"You are mistaken; I am neither. Once I did learn to play the piano and the bass fiddle as part of my general education. At that time I was told that nothing creates a more unpleasant effect than having the bass move forward with the top melody in octaves. I accepted that then as authority, and have since found it valid."

"Really?" he interrupted me, got up, walked slowly and deliberately over to the musicians, all the while gazing off into space and striking his forehead with the flat part of his hand in the manner of one who wants to awaken some kind of memory. I saw him speaking with the musicians, whom he treated with authoritative dignity. He returned, and hardly had he seated himself when they began to play the overture of *Iphigenia in Aulis.*

His eyes half-closed, his folded arms resting on the table, he listened to the Andante. Softly moving his left foot, he indicated the entrance of the instruments: now he raised his head—glanced quickly around—his left hand rested with widespread fingers on the table, as if he were striking a chord on the piano, his right hand he lifted up into the air. He was a conductor indicating the entrance of another tempo to the orchestra—the right hand falls and the Allegro begins! A burning flush spreads over his pale cheeks: his eyebrows draw together over his wrinkled forehead, an inner fury inflames his wild expression gradually consuming the smile which was hovering about his half-opened mouth. Now he leans back, his eyebrows are raised, and the play of his muscles on his cheeks resumes; his eyes gleam, a deep inner pain resolves itself into a desire which grips all of his nerves. Shaken convulsively, he draws his breath from deep in his chest—beads of sweat stand out on his forehead. He indicates the entrance of the Tutti and other main passages. His right hand maintains the beat, with his left hand he takes out a cloth and runs it over his face.—In this way he gave flesh and color to the skeleton of the piece, as presented by the two violins in the overture. I heard the soft melting lament which the flute takes up after the storm of violins and basses has abated and the thunder of the drums is silent. I heard the gentle sounding tones of the violoncello and the bassoon, which filled my heart with inexpressible sadness. The Tutti returns; like a giant the Unison moves forward majestically, the somber lament dies among its crushing steps.

The overture was over; the man let both arms drop and he sat with closed eyes like someone exhausted by too great an exertion. His bottle was empty; I filled his glass with Burgundy, which I had ordered in the meantime. He sighed deeply and seemed to awaken from a dream. I urged him to drink, which he did without hesitation. While he gulped down the full glass without stopping, he cried out: "I am satisfied with the performance! The orchestra gave a good account of itself!"

"And yet," I began to speak, "yet they only gave us the weak outlines of a masterpiece."

"Do I judge correctly? You are not a Berliner."

"Quite right. I only stay here intermittently."

"The Burgundy is good; but it is getting cold out here."

"Then let's go into the room and empty the bottle there."

"A good suggestion. I don't know you; you don't know me. We don't want to ask each other's names; names at times are troublesome. I'm drinking Burgundy, we feel comfortable with one another, and so it is good."

He said all of this with good-natured cordiality. We had entered the room and when he sat down, he opened his cloak and I noticed with amazement that he wore an embroidered waistcoat with long tails, black velvet trousers, and a small silver sword. He buttoned the cloak carefully together.

"Why did you ask me whether I was a Berliner?" I began.

"Because it would have been necessary in that case to leave you."

"That sounds puzzling."

"Not in the least, as soon as I tell you that I—I am a composer."

"I still can't guess what you mean."

"Then forgive my outcry before, for I see that you are not at all an expert on Berlin and Berliners."

He stood up and walked back and forth a few times with great agitation. Then he stepped to the window and in a voice that was barely audible sang the Chorus of the Priestesses from *Iphigenia in Tauris*, now and then beating the entrance of the Tutti on the window panes. With astonishment I noticed that he introduced certain different turns of melody which were striking for their novelty and power. I didn't interfere with him. When he had finished he returned to his place. I was silent, quite taken by his unusual behavior and the fantastic expressions of a rare musical talent. After awhile he began to speak.

"Have you never composed?"

"Yes, I tried my hand at that art, but I found everything which I had written in moments of inspiration to be insipid and boring afterwards; so I left it alone."

"You have done wrong; for the fact that you rejected your early attempts is not an indication of lack of talent. One learns music as a boy because Papa and Mamma want it that way; from that time on there is fiddling and tinkling, but imperceptibly the senses become more receptive to melody. Perhaps it was the half-forgotten theme of a little song which one now decided to sing differently—the first real idea. So this embryo, nourished with difficulty by strange powers, grew to a giant which consumed everything around it and transformed it into its marrow and blood! Ha, how is it possible to indicate the thousands of ways one comes to compose! It is a wide highway, and there everyone is bustling around, cheering and screaming: We are the chosen people! We are at the goal!—Through the ivory gates there is a way into the realm of dreams; a few see the gate only once, still fewer go through it! The place has a mysterious aspect. Peculiar figures hover here and there, but they have distinction, some more than others. They can't be found on the highway,—only on the other side of the ivory gate. It is difficult to come out of this realm, because the monsters in front of Alcina's castle block the way—it's whirling—it's turning—many dream their dreams away in this dream world—they dissolve into a dream—they no longer even cast a shadow, otherwise they would perceive in that shadow the ray of light which shines through the land of dreams—they come to the truth,—the highest moment is the contact with the Eternal, the Inexpressible! Look at the Sun, it is a triad from which chords, like stars, shoot down and entangle you with fiery threads. You are changed into a chrysalis of fire, and you lie there until Psyche soars up to the sun."

With these last words, he sprang up, glanced at me, and threw his hands up in the air. Then he sat down again, quickly emptied the glass, which had been filled. There followed a silence, which I didn't want to interrupt, in order not to divert this extraordinary man. Finally he continued more calmly:

"When I was in the realm of dreams, thousands of pains and fears tormented me! It was night and the grinning faces of monsters rushed on me. One moment they plunged me into the abyss of the sea and the next moment lifted me into the heavens. Beams of light shot through the night, and these beams were tones which surrounded me with a lovely clarity. I awakened from my torments and saw a great, bright Eye, which looked into an organ. As it looked, tones came forth and shimmered and embraced each other in marvelous chords, as I had never thought of them before. Melodies streamed up and down. I swam in this stream and wanted to drown in it. Then the Eye stared at me and held me above the roaring waves. It became night again and two Colossi in shining armor approached me: Tonic Basic Tone, and of a Fifth Interval. They lifted me up but the Eye smiled and said: 'I know what fills your heart with yearning. It is the soft, gentle youth, Interval of a Third who will step among the Colossi. You will hear his sweet voice, see me again, and my melodies will become yours.'"

He paused.

"And you saw the Eye again?"

"Yes, I saw it again! For years I lived in the realm of dreams—there—yes there! I sat in a wonderful valley and listened to the flowers singing to each other. Only one sunflower was silent and sadly bowed its closed calyx to the ground. Invisible ties drew me to it—it raised its head—the calyx opened and out of it beamed the Eye at me. Now tones went from my head to the flowers which eagerly sucked them in. The leaves of the sunflower became larger and larger—waves of fire streamed out of them —they flowed around me—the Eye had disappeared and I had disappeared into the calyx."

With these last words, he had jumped up and hurried with rapid, youthful steps out of the room. I waited in vain for his return, and decided to leave and go into the city.

I was already in the area of the Brandenburg Gate when I saw a tall figure walking in the darkness and immediately recognized my peculiar friend. I addressed him:

"Why did you leave me so suddenly?"

"It was too hot and the Euphon began to ring."

"I don't understand you."

"So much the better."

"So much the worse, for I would like to understand you completely."

"You hear nothing?"

"No."

"—It has gone by! Let us go. Usually I don't like company,—but—you are not a composer—you are not a Berliner."

"I can't understand why you are so set against Berliners. Here, where art is held in high esteem and carried on in a high degree. It is my opinion that a man of your artistic temperament should be quite happy here."

"You are mistaken! To my despair I am damned to wander here in this desolate world like a departed spirit."

"A desolate world—Berlin?"

"Yes, it is desolate here, for no congenial spirit approaches me. I stand alone."

"But the artists! The composers!"

"Away with them! They carp and carp—refine everything to the finest degree; they stir up everything in order to find one miserable idea; with their chattering about art and the meaning of art, and whatever else, they can't approach the creation of a work of art. They begin to feel happy if they have been able to bring a few ideas to light; thus this frightful coldness here shows its great distance from the sun—it is like work done in Lapland."

"Your judgment seems much too hard to me. At least the wonderful performance in the theater must satisfy you."

"Once I brought myself to go again to the theater in order to hear the opera of my young friend—what was it called? Ah, the whole world is in this opera! Through the colorful crowd of costumed people pass the spirits of the underworld, everything here is given voice and powerful sound—confound it, I mean *Don Giovanni*. But I couldn't endure the overture, which was hurried through prestissimo, without sense or understanding. So I had prepared myself through fasting and prayer, because I know that the Euphon is moved too much by these masses and it speaks then in an impure way!"

"If I am forced to admit that Mozart's works are neglected here for the most part (and it's hardly explainable) then Gluck's works on the other hand enjoy a worthy representation."

"Do you think so? Once I wanted to hear *Iphigenia in Tauris*. When I stepped into the theater, I hear that they are playing the overture to *Iphigenia in Aulis*. Hm, I think, an error. They are giving the other

Iphigenia. I am astonished, when now the Andante from *Iphigenia in Tauris* began and the storm follows. Twenty years lie between these two operas. The whole effect, the whole well-calculated exposition of the tragedy is lost. A silent Sea—a Storm—the Greeks are cast on the shore, the opera comes to life! Do you think that the composer scribbled in the overture so that it could be played just as one pleases, like a little piece for the trumpet?"

"I admit my mistake. However, everything is being done to give Gluck's works more importance."

"Oh yes!" he said abruptly and smiled then more and more bitterly. Suddenly he got up and nothing could hold him back. In a flash he had disappeared. In vain I looked for him during the next few days in the park.

A few months had passed when I found myself quite late on a cold evening in a distant part of the city and was now hurrying to my home on the Friedrichstrasse. I had to go by the theatre; the surging music, the trumpets and drums reminded me that just then Gluck's *Armida* was being performed. I was on the verge of going in, when my attention was caught by a strange monologue close by the windows of the theatre where one could hear almost every note from the orchestra.

"Now the King is coming—they are playing the march—keep on beating. It is quite lively! Yes, yes, they have to do it eleven times today—the procession is otherwise not a procession. Ha ha—*maestoso*—move back, my children. Look, there is a character with his shoe strings dangling.—Right for the twelfth time! always ending up with the dominant key—Oh you eternal powers—that never ends! Now he bows—Armida thanks him graciously. Once more? Correct, two soldiers are missing! Now they are stumbling into the recitative. What evil spirit holds me spellbound here?"

"The spell is broken," I cried. "Come!"

I took my strange acquaintance out of the park, for no one else would be talking to himself like that. I quickly grasped him by the arm and took him with me. He seemed surprised and followed me in silence. We were already in the Friedrichstrasse when he suddenly stood still. "I know you," he said. "You were in the park—we spoke about a lot of things—I drank some wine, became quite heated—afterwards the Euphon rang for two days—I have endured a great deal—but it is all past!"

"I am happy that chance has led me to you again. Let us get better acquainted. I don't live very far from here; how would it be if. . . ."

"I cannot go to anyone's house."

"No, you are not going to escape me; I am going with you."

"Then you will have to walk with me a few hundred more steps. But didn't you want to go to the theatre?"

"I wanted to hear *Armida,* but now. . . ."

"You shall now hear *Armida.* Come!"

We went up the Friedrichstrasse in silence; he turned quickly into a side street, and I was hardly able to follow him, so quickly did he walk up the street until he finally stopped before a plain-looking house. He knocked for a rather long time before the door was finally opened. Groping in the darkness we reached the stairs and climbed to a room on an upper floor, where my guide carefully unlocked the door. I heard another door being opened; soon thereafter he appeared with a lighted lamp. The sight of the strangely furnished room surprised me not a little. Old fashioned richly decorated chairs, a wall clock with gilded casing, and a ponderous mirror gave the room a sad air of past grandeur. In the middle of the room stood a small piano on which was a large ink-stand made of porcelain. Next to it lay a few pieces of ruled paper. A sharp glance at these preparations for composition convinced me, how-ever, that nothing had been written for a long time, for the paper was quite yellowed and thick cobwebs covered the inkstand. The man stepped before a cabinet in the corner of the room, which I had not yet noticed, and when he drew away the curtain, I saw a row of finely bound books with golden inscriptions: *Orfeo, Armida, Alceste, Iphigenia,* etc., in short I saw all of Gluck's masterpieces standing together.

"You have Gluck's collected works?" I cried out.

He didn't answer, but his mouth was twisted into a convulsive smile and the twitching of the muscles in his sunken cheeks, momentarily dis-torted his face into a horrible mask. With his dismal glance rigidly fixed on me, he seized one of the books—it was *Armida*—and strode to the piano. I opened the piano quickly and set up the folded music stand; he seemed to like to see that. He opened up the book—who can describe my amazement!—I saw ruled pages, but not a note written on them."

"Now I will play the overture!" he said. "Please turn the pages at the appropriate times!" I promised him that I would and he proceeded to play magnificently and masterfully, with full harmonies, the majestic Tempo die Marcia with which the overture begins, almost entirely faith-ful to the original score. The Allegro, however, was only built on Gluck's main themes. He brought in so many new, ingenious expressions, that my amazement grew more and more. In particular his modulations were quite striking without being harsh and he knew how to add so many melodic variations to the main themes that they seemed to return in a new and rejuvenated form. His face glowed. One moment his eyebrows drew together and a long-suppressed anger struggled to break loose; the next moment his eyes were filled with tears of a deep sadness. At times he sang the theme with a pleasant tenor voice as both hands worked in careful variations; at times he knew how to imitate with his voice, in a quite special way, the hollow tone of the drums. Diligently I turned the pages while following his glances. The overture had ended and with closed eyes he fell back exhausted into his chair. However, he soon pulled himself together again and while he hastily turned several empty pages of the book, said with a somber voice:

"All of this, sir, I wrote when I came from the realm of dreams. But I betrayed the sacred world to the profane. An ice cold hand gripped my glowing heart! It didn't break but I was damned to wander in the profane world, like a departed spirit—without form, so that no one knew me, until the sunflower should lift me again to the Eternal. Ha— now let us sing Armida's scene!"

He now sang the final scene of *Armida* with an expression which penetrated my innermost being. Here too, he deviated noticeably from the original score, but his altered music was a greater intensification of Gluck's scene. Everything which can express hate, love, despair, and madness was powerfully united in tones. His voice seemed to be that of a young man, for it rose from deep sombreness to penetrating strength. All my nerves trembled—I was beside myself. When he had finished, I threw myself into his arms and cried in a choked voice:

"What is that? Who are you?"

He stood up and measured me with an earnest piercing look. However, as I began to ask further questions, he escaped through a door with the lamp and left me in total darkness. Almost a quarter of an hour went by and I despaired of seeing him again. Oriented by the position of the piano, I was searching for the door when he suddenly entered with the lamp in his hand, dressed in an embroidered court costume of the 18th century, a rich waistcoat and sword at his side. I was paralyzed. Solemnly he approached me, took me by the hand and said with a strange smile: "I am the composer Gluck."

Pedro A. de Alarcón (1833–1891), Spanish author
born at Guadic, is best known for his Sombrero
de Tres Picos (1875), on which de Falla's ballet
was based. He wrote in the 1870s, a period of
transition from Romanticism to Realism—and de
Alarcón's fiction is said to combine both these elements. At one time de Alarcón served Spain as
minister to Stockholm and councillor of state.

The Nun

PEDRO A. DE ALARCÓN

I

At about eleven o'clock on a morning in March, some one hundred
years ago, the sun was as cheerful and caressing as it is now, at the outset
of this spring of 1868, and as it will be in the days of our great-grand-
children a century hence (unless the world comes to an end by then).
It came through the balconies into the main salon of an imposing manorial
house located on the banks of the Darro River in Granada; the splendid
light and pleasant warmth bathed that vast and noble room, brought
life to the ascetic paintings that covered the walls, rejuvenated the ancient
furniture and discolored tapestries, and took the place of the extinguished
brazier for three people who were alive and important at the time but
of whom there is no trace today. . . .

Near one of the balconies sat a venerable old lady whose noble and
energetic countenance, once probably very beautiful, reflected the most
austere virtue and an inordinate pride. That mouth had certainly never
smiled, and the hard folds about the lips had been formed by the long
habit of issuing orders. Although her head shook, it bowed only before
the altar of God; her eyes blazed with threats of excommunication and
as you continued gazing at her, you understood that whenever she commanded there were only two choices: to obey her or kill her. And yet
her expression was not one of cruelty or evil intent, but rather of narrow principles and an intolerance that could compromise with no person
or thing.

She wore a waist and skirt of black bombazine in imitation of the
queen and covered her thick gray hair with a cap of yellowing Belgian
lace.

On her lap she held an open prayer book, but her eyes had shifted from the book to a little boy of six or seven at play who was talking to himself and rolling on the carpet in one of the rectangles of sunlight which the balconies projected on the floor of the spacious room.

The child was as fragile, pale, blond and sickly as the children of Philip IV painted by Velázquez. Protuberant blue eyes and a network of livid veins stood out on his large head, and like all spindly children this one evinced an extraordinarily lively imagination and irritating temper, and was always on the lookout to defy authority.

He was dressed like a little man: black silk stockings, shoes with buckles, blue satin breeches, a waistcoat of the same material with abundant embroidery of many colors, and a long dress-coat of black velvet.

At the moment he was amusing himself by ripping the pages out of a magnificent book on heraldry and tearing them into tiny bits with his bony fingers; while jabbering incoherently, testily, exasperatingly: "Tomorrow I am going to do such-and-such," "Today I will not do so-and-so," "I want this and the other thing," "I will not have any such thing," as if his purpose were to defy the authority and disapproval of the terrible old woman.

The poor child was as capable as his grandmother of inspiring terror!

Finally, in a corner of the room (whence you could see the sky and the reddish towers of the Alhambra, but where you could be seen only by the birds fluttering over the bed of the Darro), a nun sat on a high-backed chair, motionless, with her gaze lost in the infinite blue of the atmosphere, and running her fingers slowly over the amber beads of a very long rosary. This nun was a member of the noble Order of Saint James; she was about thirty years old and wore the modified secular garb which the ladies of that order are wont to wear in their cells.

Her clothing consisted of cordovan shoes shaped like gaiters, a waist and skirt of serge, also black, a big linen shawl held down with pins over her shoulders, not arranged in a triangle as with laywomen, but with two ends gathered together on one side and the other two hanging down her back.

The top part of the nun's waist was, then, uncovered, and on the left side there stood out the red cross of the Holy Apostle. Since she wore neither the white mantle nor the toque her hair shone free and was combed upward and gathered together in back by that sort of bow that the Andalusian peasant women call *castaña* or chignon.

In spite of her unattractive attire, it was obvious that the woman was still very beautiful, or, more exactly, that her beauty was enhanced in good part by the carelessness of her dress which allowed greater freedom to her natural charms.

The nun was tall, vigorous, slim and proportionately built, like that noble caryatid which we stop to admire at the entrance to the Sculpture Galleries at the Vatican. Her woolen gown, clinging to her body, did not so much cover as reveal the classical form and impeccable beauty of her splendid figure.

Her hands, lusterless, white, long, dimpled, transparent, stood out bewitchingly over the black skirt, reminiscent of those hands of ancient marble, wrought by Greek chisels, which were found in Pompeii before or after the statues to which they belonged.

And to complete the picture of this sovereign beauty, imagine a tawny face, rather lean (or, more precisely, eroded by deep feeling), oval in form like Titian's Magdalen, suffused by a deep, almost yellowish pallor, and made still more interesting (since any hint of insensibility was removed and replaced by a certain intimation of passion) by two deep livid rings around her eyes, full of mysterious sadness which enveloped in melancholy twilight the ink-black suns of her magnificent eyes.

Those eyes, almost always cast down, looked up only to gaze at heaven, as if they did not dare to fix themselves on the things of this world. When she lowered them, their long lashes seemed to become the shadows of eternal night, falling over a misspent, purposeless life; when she raised them, one might think that her heart was taking flight in a luminous cloud in order to sink onto the bosom of the Lord; but if by chance they came to rest on some earthly creature or object, then those eyes blazed, trembled or wandered here and there as if inflamed by fever or flooded by tears.

Imagine, too, a smooth lofty brow, thick eyebrows, straight, strong austere, a severe, artistic nose, and an expressive, affectionate, provocative mouth, and you will have a good idea of that enchanting woman, who incorporated both the charms of pagan beauty and the mystical loveliness of Christian heroines.

II

What sort of family was this, come to life in the light of that sun which set a hundred years ago?

Let us give you a rapid summary.

The old lady was the Dowager Countess de Santos, who married to the seventh count bearing that title, had had two children, one son and one daughter. The count had died when they were very young.

But let us go back a bit.

The House of Santos had achieved great wealth and power during the lifetime of the countess's father-in-law; however, since he had had only one son and there existed no collateral branches of the family, he began to fear that his line might disappear, and he specified in his last will and testament (as new entailments were acquired from the favors Philip V bestowed upon him during the War of the Spanish Succession): "If my heir has more than one child, he will divide the fortune between the two eldest, so that my name may be propagated worthily in two branches bearing the blood of my veins. . . ."

Now, then, that clause would have been obeyed by his grandchildren, that is, the two children of the austere old lady whose acquaintance we have just made. . . . But it happened that she, in the belief that the luster of a great name is better preserved in one single, powerful branch than in two, sought to conciliate her ideas with those of the founder of the house by having her daughter renounce all earthly property and take the nun's habit; in this fashion, the entire Santos fortune would be the exclusive patrimony of her other child who, because he had been born first and was of the male sex, became the pride and joy of his aristocratic mother.

Therefore, when her unfortunate daughter was scarcely eight years old, she was put into the convent of the *comendadoras* of the Order of Saint James so that she, the second child of the Count de Santo, then called Doña Isabel, might accustom herself to the monastic life which was her inevitable fate. There the child grew up breathing the air of the cloister and was never consulted about her wishes until, with the arrival of that time of life when all rational beings trace the paths of their future on the canvas of fantasy, she took the veil of Christ's bride with the cold meekness of one who never imagined that she could claim the right to determine her own actions. We may even add this: since Doña Isabel could not at the time comprehend the full significance of the vows she had just taken (she was still so ignorant of what was in the world and in her own heart), and yet could perfectly well understand (since she, too, was proud of her lineage) the great advantages which her vocation would add to the splendor of her name, it fell out that she became a nun with a certain pride although with no obvious, outspoken joy.

But the years wore on and Sister Isabel, who had grown up languid and fragile, suddenly revealed the lush, remarkable beauty which we have admired and which was as nothing compared to the splendid spring-time which at the same time bloomed in her heart and soul. From that day on the young nun became the miracle and idol not only of her community but of all those having business with the convent whose rule was as lenient as all the others of that order. Some compared Sister Isabel with Rebecca, some with Sarah, others with Ruth, and still others with Judith. . . . The man who tuned the organ called her Saint Cecilia; the steward called her Saint Pauline; the sexton, Saint Monica. In other words, they all agreed she bore a close resemblance to other female saints, whether spinsters, widows or married.

More than once Sister Isabel went through the Bible and the *Flos Sanctorum* to find stories of those great heroines, queens, wives and mothers, with whom she was compared, and as a result of such studies, vanity, ambition and curiosity concerning life in the outside world grew in her imagination with such speed that her spiritual director was obliged to admonish her very severely that "the direction which her ideas and emotions were taking were precisely those that would lead her to eternal damnation."

When she heard these words, Sister Isabel underwent an instantaneous, absolute and definite change. From that day on she became a haughty, high-spirited noblewoman infatuated with her lineage, and a virgin of the Lord, pious, mystical, fervent to the point of ecstasy and delirium. She exerted herself to such extremes of self-mortification and was tormented by such subtle scruples that her mother superior and even her confessor were obliged to reassure her and could find no sins from which to absolve her.

What had happened, during this time, to the nun's heart and soul, that heart and soul that had blossomed so suddenly and exuberantly?

We do not really know.

We only know that after five years (during which her brother had married, sired a son, and then lost his wife), Sister Isabel, more beautiful than ever, but as languid as a fading lily, was sent home on the advice of physicians and through the influence of her mother, so that she might breathe in the healthy air of the Darro region, the only remedy to be found for the mysterious illness that was killing her. Some called her ailment *excessive religious zeal,* and others called it *dark melancholy* but no one could find a technical name for it and they could only identify it in terms of her symptoms which were extreme languor and a continuous propensity to tears.

With her removal home, health and strength, if not happiness, returned; but since at that time her brother Alfonso died, leaving a little boy of three, it was arranged for the nun to stay on and consider her home her convent, in order to be her aging mother's companion and help to take care of her little nephew, the sole and universal heir to the Santos title and estate.

And so now we know who the little lad was who was tearing the heraldry book up on the carpet, and we need only add—although it may be easily guessed—that the child was the soul, the life, the love, the pride, and at the same time, the tyrant of his grandmother and his aunt who saw in him not only a given individual but also the one hope for the perpetuation of his line.

III

Let us turn back to our three characters now that we know them inside and out.

The child suddenly stood up; he thew away what was left of the book and walked out of the room, singing loudly, doubtlessly in search of some other object to destroy. The two ladies continued where we left them some time ago; the old lady resumed her reading, but the nun stopped saying her rosary.

What was the nun thinking about?

Who knows?

Spring had begun. . . .

Canaries and nightingales in cages hanging from the balconies outside the room, were engaged in some sort of dialogue with birds of both sexes who lived freely and happily in the groves of the Alhambra; perhaps the captive creatures were telling them of that sadness and boredom attendant on loveless lives. . . .

The pots of gilliflowers, cresses and hyacinths which adorned the balconies were beginning to bloom, indicating that nature was again with child. The air, perfumed and warm, seemed to draw lovers from the city to the charming solitude of fields and the sweet mystery of forests where they could look at one another freely and confess their most secret thoughts. . . .

The streets echoed the footsteps of people going and coming, involved in the tasks of life; people who are envied for their good fortune by those who catch sight of them from the heights of their own griefs. . . .

From time to time one could hear snatches of a fandango in which some neighborhood buck referred to his Sunday adventures or with which the apprentice of some near-by shop passed away the time, while waiting for the inevitable evening, and with the evening, a certain rendezvous. . . .

In addition, there came together in philosophic converse the perpetual murmurings of the river, the confused noise of the capital, the rhythmic beat of a pendulum in the salon, and the distant clamor of bells which might have been ringing in a feast, announcing a funeral, or solemnizing the taking of vows by another nun of the Order of Saint James.

All this, plus the sun which was returning to seek out the chilly corners, or that piece of blue sky which took in the eye and the soul, and those towers of the Alhambra, full of romantic and voluptuous memories, and the trees which bloomed at their feet just as they had when Granada belonged to the Moors . . . all that must have weighed like lead on the soul of that woman of thirty whose entire existence had always been exactly as it was now, and whose future could be nothing more than a slow, endless repetition of such melancholy moments. . .

The return of the little boy to the salon drew the nun out of her abstractions and again interrupted the countess's reading.

"Grandmother!" the child shouted shrilly. "The Italian who is fixing the stone shield on the staircase downstairs has just said something very funny to the old man painting the roof. I heard him, but they didn't see me; and since I already understand the broken Spanish the sculptor speaks to the painter, I understood everything! If you only knew what he said!"

"Carlos," answered the old lady with the equivocal delicacy that denotes cowardice, "I have told you never to have anything to do with men like that. Remember that you are the Count de Santos!"

"But I like them!" the child replied. "I like painters and sculptors, and I am going right back to them now!"

"Carlos," the nun murmured sweetly, "you are addressing your father's mother. You must respect her as he did and as I do. . . ."

The child burst out laughing and continued: "But if you only knew, auntie, what the sculptor said. . . . He was talking about you!"

"About me?"

"Keep still, Carlos!" the old woman exclaimed severely.

The child kept on in the same tone of voice and with the same sly gestures: "The sculptor said to the painter: 'Friend, how beautiful the nun must be all naked! She must look like a Greek statue!' What is a Greek statue, Aunt Isabel?"

Sister Isabel turned livid, seized the little count by the arm and said, with ill-contained anger: "Little boys do not listen to such things and don't repeat them either! The sculptor will leave this house at once. And as for you, the chaplain will explain to you what a sin you have committed, and will impose a fitting penance. . . ."

"Who, the priest? The priest will do that to me? I'm braver than he is and I'll throw him out into the street. But the sculptor will remain right here!"

Then, turning to the nun, the boy continued: "Auntie! I want to see you all naked. . . ."

"Holy Lord in Heaven!" exclaimed the grandmother, covering her face with her hands.

Sister Isabel showed no emotion.

"Yes, I want to see auntie all naked!" the child repeated facing the old lady.

"Insolent boy!" she shouted, raising her hand to her grandson.

At that moment, the boy turned red as a beet, and stamping his feet in fury, looked as if he were going to attack the countess. Then he again exclaimed in dull tones: "I said I want to see my aunt all naked! Hit me, if you dare!"

The nun rose with an air of contempt and made her way to the door, paying no heed to the child.

Carlos jumped up, threw himself in her way and repeated his frightening command with voice and gesture of true madness.

Sister Isabel did not stop.

The child struggled to hold her, was unsuccessful and fell to the floor, prey to a violent convulsion.

The grandmother let out a mortal cry at which the nun turned her head.

She had stopped in her tracks, terrified, as she became aware of her nephew lying on the ground, with his eyes rolling in his head, foaming at the mouth and stammering fiercely: ". . . auntie all naked. . . ."

"Satan! . . ." stammered the nun, staring wildly at her mother.

The child writhed like a snake on the floor, turned purple, called out to his aunt again, and then froze, choking, breathless.

"The heir to the Santos family is dying!" the grandmother cried with indescribable terror. "Water, water! A doctor!"

The servants came running with water and vinegar. The countess sprinkled the child's face with one and then the other; she kissed him frantically, called him *angel*, wept, prayed. . . . But it was all in vain. The child shook like one possessed, opened his crazed, sightless, terrifying eyes and then turned stiff once more. . . .

The nun stood frozen in the middle of the room, looking as if she were about to leave, but with her head turned back, staring fixedly at her brother's child.

The boy finally released some breath and vague words escaped from between his clenched, gritting teeth. . . . The words were "Naked . . . auntie. . . ."

The nun raised her hands to heaven, and took a few more steps.

The grandmother, fearing that the servants would make out what the child was saying, shouted imperiously: "Everyone get out! You stay, Isabel!"

Filled with amazement, the servants obeyed.

The nun fell to her knees.

"My child! Carlos! Adored one!" the old lady groaned, embracing what she thought was already the corpse of her grandson. "Weep! Weep! Do not be angry! We shall do whatever you wish!"

"Naked!" Carlos said hoarsely as if the death rattle had already begun.

"Daughter," the old lady began, looking at the nun strangely. "The Santos heir is dying and with him our line comes to an end!"

The nun's entire body shook. As aristocratic, pious and chaste as her mother, she understood the enormity of the situation.

At this, Carlos came to a bit, looked at both women, tried to pick himself up, let out a furious cry and fell into another attack even more terrible than the first.

". . . see auntie all naked . . . !" he roared before stiffening again. And his fists were clenched in a theatening gesture.

The old lady crossed herself; then, seizing her prayerbook, she made her way to the door, and as she passed the nun, she said, raising her hand to heaven with grievous solemnity: "Daughter, it is God's will!"

And she disappeared, shutting the door behind her.

IV

Half an hour later, the Count of Santos entered his grandmother's room, panting, laughing and sucking on a sweet (still moistened by the teardrops of his tantrum); and, without looking at the old lady, but nudging her with his elbow, he said in a hoarse, savage voice: "My, auntie is so fat!"

The countess, who had been kneeling in prayer at an old priedieu, let her head fall on her prayer-book and made no answer.

The child walked out to look for the sculptor and found him surrounded by authorities of the Holy Office who had brought an order for him to follow them to the prisons of the Inquisitions "for being a pagan and blasphemer," according to the accusation made by the Dowager Countess de Santos.

Despite all his audicity, at the sight of the bailiffs of the formidable Tribunal, Carlos said and did nothing.

V

At nightfall, before the lights were put on, the countess made her way to her daughter's room; she did not want to look at her, but simply offer her consolation. There she found the following letter which Sister Isabel's maid handed to her:

Very beloved mother:

Forgive me for making the only decision in my life in which I did not consult you, but my heart tells me that you will not disapprove.

I am returning to the convent which I should never have left and which I shall never again leave. I go without bidding you good-by in order to spare you any further grief.

God keep you and shed His mercy upon your very devoted daughter,

Sister Isabel de los Angeles.

No sooner had the old lady read those unhappy lines when she heard the sound of carriage wheels roll out of the courtyard of the house and then slowly die away in the direction of the Plaza Nueva . . .

It was the carriage that was bearing her daughter away.

VI

Four years later, the bells of the Convent of Saint James rang out for the soul of Sister Isabel de los Angeles, as her body was given back to mother earth.

The countess died shortly thereafter.

Count Carlos perished without succession fifteen or twenty years later, during the siege of Menorca, and with him the noble line of the Counts of Santos came to an end.

Leo Tolstoy (1828–1910) was born a nobleman, and after a carefree life in St. Petersburg and Moscow, he began to write fiction while on duty as an artillery officer in the Crimea. After marriage, he managed his estate and wrote some of the world's most remarkable novels, War and Peace **(1866) and** Anna Karenina **(1877). Before his death, Tolstoy renounced his work and his world, including his material possessions, in favor of the simple Christian existence of a Russian peasant. For further reading:** A Russian Proprietor, The Invaders, The Death of Ivan Ilyitch, The Long Exile **(1899–1902).**

The Story of Yemilyan and the Empty Drum

LEO TOLSTOY

Yemilyan lived out as a day-laborer. Once upon a time he was on his way to the meadow where his work was, and lo and behold! a frog leaped out before him. He almost set his foot on it. But he stepped over it. Suddenly he heard some one calling to him from behind. He looked round and saw a beautiful girl standing there, and she said to him:—

"Yemilyan, why are you not married?"

"How could I be married, my pretty maid? Look at me; I have nothing at all. No one would take me."

"Well," said the girl, "take me for a wife."

The girl greatly pleased Yemilyan; said he:—

"I should like to; but where should we live?"

"That is something to think about," said the girl. "Hard work and little sleep is all that is required; but we can find clothes and food anywhere."

"Very good, I'm agreed; let us get married. Where shall we go?"

"Let us go to the city."

Yemilyan and the girl went to the city. The girl took him to a little cottage at the farther end of the city, and they were married and lived there.

One time the voyevode came to the city. He passed by Yemilyan's cottage, and Yemilyan's wife went out to look at him. When the voyevode saw her he was amazed.

"Where did such a beauty as that come from?"

He reined in his horse, and summoned Yemilyan's wife, and began to question her.

"Who are you?" he asked.

"The wife of the peasant Yemilyan," said she.

"How did it happen," said he, "that such a beautiful woman as you married a peasant? You ought to be a princess."

"Thank you," said she, "for your flattering remark, but I am satisfied with my husband."

The voyevode talked with her awhile, and then rode on his way. He reached his palace. But he could not help thinking of Yemilyan's wife. He lay awake all night long, planning how he might get her away from Yemilyan. He could not think of any way of doing it. He summoned his servants, and bade them devise some way. And the voyevode's servants said to him:—

"Take Yemilyan as your workman," said they. "We'll work him to death; his wife will be a widow, and then you can have her."

So the voyevode did; he sent for Yemilyan to come to him as a dvornik, and offered him a house for him and his wife.

The messengers came and told Yemilyan their story. But Yemilyan's wife said:—

"Very good," said she. "Go. Work there during the daytime, but at night return to me."

Yemilyan went. When he reached the palace, the voyevode's steward said to him:—

"Why have you come alone, without your wife?"

"Why should I bring her? Her place is at home."

In the voyevode's courtyard they gave him so much work to do that two men could not have accomplished it. Yemilyan took hold of the work, but it seemed hopeless for him to finish it. But lo and behold! when evening came it was all done. The steward saw that he had finished it, and gave him four times as much for the next day. Yemilyan went home and found the house all neatly swept and in order; the fire was burning in the stove, the baking and boiling were under way. His wife was sitting at the table sewing and waiting for her husband. When he entered she met him, got supper ready, and, after he had had all he wanted to eat and drink, she began to ask him about his work.

"Well," said he, "it went badly. They gave me more than I had strength to do. They are going to kill me with work."

"Now, then," said she, "don't you worry about your work, and don't look back and don't look forward to see if much has been done and much remains to be done. Only work. All will come out right."

Yemilyan went to bed. The next morning he went to his work again. He took hold of it, and not once did he look round. And lo and behold! it was all done by four o'clock, and while it was still light he went home for the night. And though they kept adding to his tasks, still Yemilyan always managed to finish it up and go home for the night.

Thus passed a week. The voyevode's servants perceived that they could not overcome the muzhik by "black work." They began to impose handiwork upon him, but this also proved vain. Carpentry work and mason work and the art of thatching—whatever they imposed upon him, that Yemilyan got done in ample time for him to go home and spend the night with his wife. Thus passed a second week. The voyevode summoned his servants, and said:—

"I should like to know if I feed you for doing nothing? Here two weeks have passed and I can't see that you have done anything at all. You were going to put Yemilyan out of the way for me, but from the window I see him going home every afternoon, singing songs. I should like to know if you are scheming to turn me into ridicule?"

The servants began to justify themselves:—

"We tried with all our might," said they, "to kill him off by 'black work,' but we could not do anything with him. Everything we gave him to work at he worked out, and we could not tire him. Then we gave him handiwork to do, thinking he would not have wit enough to do it, but in this too we failed to get him. It is like magic. As soon as he touches anything it is done. It must be that either he or his wife practices some witchcraft. We are tired to death of him. And now we are trying to think of something that he can't do. We have decided to make him build a new cathedral in one day. So will you summon Yemilyan and command him to build a new cathedral opposite your palace in one day? And if he does not have it done, then we will have his head cut off as a punishment."

The voyevode sent for Yemilyan.

"Well," said he, "this is my command. Build me a new cathedral on the square opposite my palace, so that it shall be all done to-morrow evening. If you get it built, I will reward you; if you fail, I shall punish you."

Yemilyan heard the command, he turned round and went home.

"Well," said he to himself, "that's the end of me."

He went to his wife and said:—

"Get yourself ready, wife; we must make our escape somewhere or other, else we shall be ruined."

"Why," she said, "are you such a coward that you must run away?"

"How can I help being?" said he. "The voyevode has ordered me to come to-morrow and build a new cathedral all in one day. And if I don't get it built, he threatens to cut off my head. The only thing left to do is to escape while there is time."

But his wife would not hear to this.

"The voyevode has many servants. They will catch us anywhere. You can't escape from him. But since you have the power, you must obey him."

"Yes, but how can one obey him, if one has not the power?"

"Listen, batyushka. Don't you worry. Eat your supper and go to bed. In the morning get up a little earlier than usual; you'll have it all done."

Yemilyan went to bed; his wife wakened him.

"Go," said she, "build your cathedral as quickly as possible. Here are nails and a hammer; there'll be work enough for you for the day."

Yemilyan went to the city; when he got there the new cathedral was already standing in the midst of the square, almost finished. Yemilyan went to work to finish it; by evening it was all complete.

The voyevode woke up, he looked out of his palace window, and saw that the cathedral was already built. Yemilyan was walking up and down, here and there driving in nails. And the voyevode was not pleased to see the cathedral; he was vexed because he had nothing to punish Yemilyan for, and could not take away his wife. So he called his servants again.

"Yemilyan has accomplished his task; there is nothing to punish him for. This task," said he, "was too small for him. Something craftier must be thought up. Put your wits to work, or else I will punish you instead of him."

And the voyevode's servants suggested that he should command Yemilyan to make a river which should flow round the palace, and that ships should be sailing on it. The voyevode summoned Yemilyan, and laid before him the new task.

"If you are able," said he, "in one night to build a cathedral, then you will be able to do this also. See to it that to-morrow everything be as I have commanded. And if it is not ready, then I will cut off your head."

Yemilyan was more than ever discouraged, and he returned to his wife in a very gloomy frame of mind.

"Why," said his wife, "are you so discouraged? Have you some new task imposed on you?"

Yemilyan told her.

"We must make our escape," said he.

But his wife said:—

"You can't run away; they will catch you everywhere; you must obey."

"Yes, but how can I obey?"

"Well, batyushka, there is nothing to be discouraged about. Eat your supper and go to bed. But get up earlier than usual; everything will be in order."

Yemilyan went to bed and slept. Early in the morning his wife waked him.

"Go," said she, "go to the city, all is ready. You will find one mound only at the harbor. Take your spade and level it off."

Yemilyan started. He reached the city; round the palace was a river, ships were sailing on it. Yemilyan reached the harbor, he saw the uneven place, and began to level it.

The voyevode woke up, he saw a river where no river had been; ships were sailing on it and Yemilyan was leveling a mound with his spade. The voyevode was horror-struck and was not rejoiced at the sight of the river and the ships; but he was vexed because he could not punish Yemilyan. He said to himself:—

"There is no task that he cannot accomplish it. What shall we try now?"

He summoned his servants and proceeded to consult with them.

"Think up some task," said he, "that will be above Yemilyan's powers. For whatever you have so far devised for him, he has done at once, and it is impossible to take his wife from him."

The servants cudgeled their brains, and at last had a bright idea. They came to the voyevode and said:—

"You must summon Yemilyan and say to him:—

"'Go somewhere, you know not where, and bring back something, you know not what.' He won't be able to escape from this. Wherever he goes you will say that he went to the wrong place, and whatever he brings back you will say that he brought back the wrong thing. Then you will be able to punish him and take away his wife."

This pleased the voyevode.

"This time," said he, "you have had a bright idea."

He sent for Yemilyan and said to him:—

"Go somewhere, you know not where, and bring back something, you know not what, and if you don't bring it, I will cut your head off."

Yemilyan went to his wife, and told her what the voyevode had said. His wife put on her thinking-cap.

"Well," said she, "they've been teaching the voyevode something to his own ruin. We must work now wisely."

She sat down, pondered for a while and then said to her husband:—

"You will have to take a long journey—to our babushka, our grand-mother—to the ancient peasant mother—and you must ask for her good-will. And from her you will receive an object; then go straightway to the voyevode, and I shall be there. For now I shall not get out of their hands. They will take me by force, but not for long. If you do all the old babushka commands, you will speedily rescue me."

The wife got her husband ready; she gave him a wallet and gave him a spindle.

"Here, take this," said she, "and give it to her. By this she will know that you are my husband."

She showed him the way. Yemilyan started; he went beyond the city, and he saw some bowmen drilling. Yemilyan stopped and watched them. After the bowmen had practised, they sat down to rest. Yemilyan approached them and asked:—

"Do you know, my brethren, where I must go, not knowing where, to get something, not knowing what?"

The bowmen listed to what he had to say, and they were filled with wonder.

"Who sent you to find out?" they inquired.

"The voyevode," said he.

"No," said they, "we cannot help you."

After Yemilyan had sat a little while, he proceeded on his way.

He went and he went, and at last he came to a forest. In the forest lived the old babushka.

The old woman was sitting in a cottage—the ancient peasant mother— she was spinning flax—and she was weeping. When the old woman saw Yemilyan, she cried out to him:—

"What have you come for?"

Yemilyan gave her the distaff, and told her his wife had sent it to her. And Yemilyan began to tell her all about his life, how he had married the girl, how he had gone to the city to live, how he had been taken as a dvornik, how he had served the voyevode, how he had built the cathedral and made the river with the ships, and how now the voyevode had commanded him to go somewhere, not knowing where, to get something, he knew not what.

The old woman listened to him and ceased to weep. She began to mutter to herself.

"That is very good," said she, "but sit down, little son, and eat."

Yemilyan ate his fill, and the old woman began to talk with him.

"Here is a little ball," said she; "roll it before you and follow it, wherever it may roll. You will have to go far, even to the sea. When you reach the sea, you will find there a great city. When you enter the city, ask for a night's lodgings at the last house. There you will find what you need."

"But how shall I know it, babushka?"

"Well, when you see what men obey sooner than father and mother, that is what you want; seize on it and take it with you. You will take it to the voyevode, but he will say to you that you have not brought the thing that was required, and then do you say to him: "Well, if it is not what is wanted it must be broken; then hit the thing a blow and take it down to the river, break it, and fling it into the water, and then you will recover your wife."

Yemilyan bade the old woman good-by, rolled the little ball ahead of him; it rolled and it rolled, and it took him to the sea, and by the sea was a great city. At the border of the city was a large house. Yemilyan there demanded hospitality for the night; it was granted, and he went to bed. He woke early in the morning and listened; the father was getting up, he called his son and sent him to split kindlings. But the son would not heed; "It is too early as yet," said he, "I shall have time enough." Yemilyan heard the mother get down from the oven and say:—

"Go, little son, your father's bones pain him; would you make him go?"

"There's plenty of time."

The son made a smacking noise with his lips, and dropped off to sleep again. As soon as he had fallen asleep there was a noise like thunder, and a loud crash in the street. The son leaped down, put on his clothes, and ran down into the street. Yemilyan also jumped down and followed him to see what the son obeyed better than his parents. Yemilyan ran down and saw a man going along the street, carrying a round object and beating on it with sticks, and it rumbled, and the son listened to it. Yemilyan ran closer and examined the object, and saw that it was round like a small tub, and both ends were covered with skin. And he insisted on knowing what it was called.

"A drum," they told him.

Yemilyan was amazed, and asked them to give it to him. They refused to give it to him. So Yemilyan ceased to ask for it, but he walked along following it. He walked all that day, and when the man that had it lay down to sleep, Yemilyan seized his drum and ran off with it.

He ran and he ran, and at last came back to his own city. He expected to see his wife at home, but she was not there.

On the next day they had brought her to the voyevode. Yemilyan went to the voyevode's, and bade them announce him in these words:—

"Here! the man who went he knew not where, has come back, bringing he knows not what."

The voyevode bade Yemilyan to return the next day.

Yemilyan then ordered them to say to the voyevode:—

"I," said he, "have come to-day. I have brought what he bade me bring; let the voyevode come to me or I will come to him."

The voyevode replied:—

"Where did you go?" he asked.

"I don't know," said he.

"And what did you bring with you?"

Yemilyan was about to show it to him, but the voyevode refused to look at it:—

"It's nothing," said he.

"Yes, it's nothing," said Yemilyan; "but then one must beat on it, and the devil is in it."

Yemilyan came with the drum and beat on it.

As soon as he began to beat on it, all the voyevode's army came and joined Yemilyan. They saluted him and waited till he should give the word of command.

The voyevode began to shout to his bowmen from the window of his palace, forbidding them to follow Yemilyan. They refused to obey him, and followed Yemilyan. The voyevode perceived this, and ordered them to restore his wife to Yemilyan, and then asked him to give him the drum.

"I cannot," said Yemilyan. "I must beat it," said he, "and throw the scrapings into the river."

Yemilyan went with the drum to the river, and the bowmen followed him. Yemilyan beat the drum by the river, broke it into pieces, and flung them into the river. And all the bowmen scattered in all directions. But Yemilyan took his wife and brought her home. And from that time forth the voyevode ceased to bother him, and he lived long and happily ever after.

Giovanni Verga (1840–1922) was born in Catania, Sicily. An early realist, he wrote of suffering and poverty, but always with the sense of the continuity of life despite individual reversal and tragedy. One of the giants of Italian literature, he has greatly influenced twentieth-century imaginative writing. One of his celebrated novels is The House by the Medlar Tree (1881). For further reading: The She Wolf, and Other Stories, translated by Giovanni Cecchetti (1958).

Consolation

GIOVANNI VERGA

"**Y**ou'll be happy but first you'll have troubles," the fortuneteller had told Arlia.

Who would have imagined it when she married Manica, who had his fine barbershop on Fabbri Street, and she was a hairdresser too—both of them young and healthy? Only Father Calogero, her uncle, hadn't wanted to bless that marriage—had washed his hands of it like Pilate, as he said. He knew they were all consumptive in his own family, from father to son, and he had been able to put a little fat on himself by choosing the quiet life of a parish rector.

"The world is full of troubles," Father Calogero preached. "It's best to keep away from it."

The troubles had come, in fact, little by little. Arlia was always pregnant, year after year, so that her clients deserted her shop, because it was sad to see her come all out of breath and cursed with that big belly. Besides, she didn't have time to keep up to date with fashions. Her husband had dreamed of a big barbershop on the Avenue, with perfumes in the window, but in vain he could go on and on shaving beards at three *soldi* each. The children became consumptive one after the other, and before going to the cemetery gobbled up the small profit of the year.

Angiolino, who didn't want to die so young, complained during his fever: "Mamma, why did you bring me into the world?" Just like his brothers who had died before him. The mother, thin and wan, standing before the little bed, didn't know what to answer. They had done the impossible; the children had eaten all kinds of things, cooked and raw: broths, medicines, pills as small as the head of a pin. Arlia had spent three *lire* for a Mass, and had gone to hear it on her knees in Saint Lawrence's, beating her breast for her sins. The Virgin in the picture seemed to be winking yes to her. But Manica, more sensible, would laugh with his crooked mouth, scratching his beard. Finally, the poor mother grabbed her veil like a crazy woman and ran to the fortuneteller. A countess, who had wanted to have her hair cut off out of desperation over her lover, had found consolation there.

"You'll be happy, but first you'll have troubles," answered the fortune-teller.

In vain her uncle, the priest, could say over and over again:

"It's all a fraud of Satan!"

You have to feel what it is like to have your heart black with bitterness as you wait for the verdict, while that old woman reads your whole destiny in the white of an egg. Afterward, it seemed to her that at home she would find her boy up, saying to her happily: "Mamma, I'm all better."

Instead, the boy was slowly wasting away, all skin and bones in his little bed, his eyes getting bigger and bigger. When Father Calogero, who knew about dead people, came to see his nephew, he called the mother aside and said:

"I'll take care of the funeral myself. Don't worry!"

But the unfortunate woman, beside the bed, went on hoping. Some-times, when also Manica, with an eight-day beard and his back bent, came upstairs to see how his boy was doing, she pitied him because he didn't believe. How the poor man must have suffered! She, at least, had the words of the fortuneteller in her heart, like a burning lamp, till the moment when her uncle, the priest, sat at the foot of the bed with his stole on. Then when they carried her hope away inside her son's coffin, she felt a great darkness in her breast, and mumbled before the empty little bed:

"And what did the fortuneteller promise me?"

Because of all the heartache, her husband had taken to drinking. Finally, a great calm came slowly into her heart. Just like before. Now that all the troubles had fallen on her shoulders, happiness would come. That's the way it often is with the poor!

Fortunata, the last one of so many children, got up in the morning, pale and with rings the color of mother-of-pearl under her eyes, like her brothers who had died of consumption. The clients deserted Arlia one by one, the debts piled up, the shop became empty. Manica, her husband, waited for customers all day long, his nose against the clouded window.

Arlia asked her daughter:

"Does your heart tell you that what fate promised us will really come true?"

Fortunata didn't say anything, her eyes circled with black like her brothers', and fixed on a point that only she could see. One day her mother caught her on the stairs with a young man, who slipped away quickly when he saw somebody come, and the girl was left there all red in the face.

"Oh, poor me! . . . What are you doing here?"

Fortunata lowered her head.

"Who was that young man? What did he want?"

"Nothing."

"Tell your mother, who's your own flesh and blood. If your father knew! . . ."

The girl's only answer was to raise her forehead and fix her blue eyes on her mother's face.

"Mamma, I don't want to die like the others!"

May was in flower, but the girl wore a different look on her face and had become uneasy under the anxious eyes of her mother. The neighbors warned:

"Arlia, watch your girl."

Even her husband, frowning, one day had taken her aside face to face, in the dark little shop, in order to repeat:

"Watch your daughter, understand? Let's at least not have our flesh and blood disgraced!"

The poor woman, seeing her daughter so wild-eyed, didn't dare question her. She only fixed her eyes on her with looks that went through to the heart. One night, in front of the open window, while the song of spring came up from the street, the girl buried her face in her mother's breast and confessed everything, crying bitter tears.

The poor mother fell into a chair, as if her legs had been cut off. And she kept stammering with her colorless lips:

"Ah, what'll we do now?"

She seemed to see Manica warmed by wine, his heart hardened by misfortune. But worst of all were the eyes of the girl when she answered:

"See that window, Mamma? . . . See how high it is? . . ."

The young man, who was an honest fellow, had sent someone to see the uncle, the priest, to sound him out in order to know which way to turn. Father Calogero had purposely become a priest so that he wouldn't have to listen to the troubles of the world. It was no secret that Manica wasn't rich. The young man understood the refrain and sent word that he was sorry that he wasn't rich himself and wouldn't be able to do without a dowry.

Then Fortunata became really sick and began to cough as her brothers

had done. Holding her arm around her mother, she often whispered,
with her face red, and repeated:

"See how high that window is? . . ."

And her mother had to run here and there, to comb rich women's
hair for the theater, the terror of that window always before her eyes
if she couldn't find a dowry for her daughter, or if her husband learned
about the blunder.

From time to time the fortuneteller's words came back into her mind,
like a ray of light. One evening, passing before a lottery window as she
was going back home tired and discouraged, the printed numbers fell
under her eyes, and for the first time she got the idea of gambling.
Then, with the little yellow slip in her pocket, it seemed to her as if
she had her daughter healthy, her husband rich and her home peaceful.
She also thought with tenderness of Angiolino and the other children
who had long been underground in the Porta Magenta cemetery. It was
a Friday, a day of the afflicted, and the spring twilight was serene.

And so it was every week. By going without food, she got together
the few cents needed for the lottery ticket, so that she could live with the
hope of the great happiness which was to come to her all at once. The
blessed souls of her children would take care of it from up above. Manica,
one day when the little yellow slips jumped out of the drawer as he was
secretly looking for a few *lire* to drown his ill-humor at the tavern, flew
into a terrible rage:

"So that's the way the money's been going! . . ."

His wife, trembling all over, didn't know what to answer.

"But listen, what if the Lord should send us the right numbers? . . .
We have to leave the door open to luck."

And in her heart she was thinking of the words of the fortuneteller.

"If that's the only hope you've got . . . ," muttered Manica with a
bitter smile.

"And what hope have you got?"

"Give me two *lire*!" he answered bluntly.

"Two *lire*! Holy Virgin! . . . What do you want them for?"

"Give me just one!" insisted Manica, his face distorted.

It was a dark day with snow everywhere and dampness that you felt
in your bones. That night Manica came back home with his face shining
and gay. Fortunata instead kept saying:

"I'm the only one who can't find any consolation."

At times, she would have liked to have been under the grass in the
cemetery, like her brothers. They, at least, weren't suffering any more,
and even their parents, poor people, had become hardened.

"The Lord won't abandon us completely," stammered Arlia. "The
fortuneteller told me so. And I've got an idea."

On Christmas Day they set the table with flowers and their best tablecloth, and this time they had invited her uncle, the priest, who was the only hope they had left. Manica rubbed his hands together and said:

"Today we've got to be happy and gay."

But the lamp hanging on the ceiling swayed sadly.

They had beef, roast turkey, and even a *panettone* that had a picture of the Cathedral of Milan. At dessert, the poor uncle, a good glass of *barbera* wine in his hand, seeing them lament on such a day, couldn't resist any more and had to promise the girl a dowry. The lover—Silvio Liotti, a clerk in a store, and well-informed—was heard from again: he was ready to make amends for the wrong he had done.

Manica, holding up a glass in his hand, said to Father Calogero:

"See this, sir? It cures many ills."

It was destiny, though, that where Arlia was, happiness didn't last. The son-in-law, a really fine fellow, ate up his wife's dowry, and after six months Fortunata, hungry and beaten, went back to her parents' home to tell her troubles and to show her bruises. Every year she too had a baby, just like her mother, and each one was bursting with health and ate like a horse. To the grandmother it seemed as if she were having babies again herself, because each one brought more trouble, even without dying of consumption. Having become old now, she had to run as far as Borgo Degli Ortolani and to Porta Garibaldi in order to earn four *lire* a month doing little jobs for the shopkeepers. Her husband, whose hands trembled, made hardly ten *lire* on Saturday, by cutting his customers and using spider webs to stop the blood. The rest of the week, he either sulked behind the dirty window or was at the tavern with his hat slanted over his ear.

And Arlia now spent the lottery money on brandy, drinking it secretly and hiding it under her apron; her consolation was to feel it warm her heart, as she sat before the window thinking of nothing, looking out at the wet, dripping roofs.

Guy de Maupassant (1850–1893) was born in Normandy and learned to write under a master novelist, Flaubert. A man of prodigious energy, de Maupassant wrote about sixteen volumes of short stories during his brief lifetime. Generally, his work is marked by sensuality and a combination of both the comic and the tragic aspects of the human condition. For further reading: The House of Madam Tellier (1881), Mademoiselle Fifi (1882), Miss Harriet (1884).

The Piece of String

GUY DE MAUPASSANT

It was market-day, and over all the roads round Goderville the peasants and their wives were coming towards the town. The men walked easily, lurching the whole body forward at every step. Their long legs were twisted and deformed by the slow, painful labors of the country:—by bending over to plough, which is what also makes their left shoulders too high and their figures crooked; and by reaping corn, which obliges them for steadiness' sake to spread their knees too wide. Their starched blue blouses, shining as though varnished, ornamented at collar and cuffs with little patterns of white stitch-work, and blown up big around their bony bodies, seemed exactly like balloons about to soar, but putting forth a head, two arms, and two feet.

Some of these fellows dragged a cow or a calf at the end of a rope. And just behind the animal, beating it over the back with a leaf-covered branch to hasten its pace, went their wives, carrying large baskets from which came forth the heads of chickens or the heads of ducks. These women walked with steps far shorter and quicker than the men; their figures, withered and upright, were adorned with scanty little shawls pinned over their flat bosoms; and they enveloped their heads each in a white cloth, close fastened round the hair and surmounted by a cap.

Now a char-à-banc passed by, drawn by a jerky-paced nag. It shook up strangely the two men on the seat. And the woman at the bottom of the cart held fast to its sides to lessen the hard joltings.

In the market-place at Goderville was a great crowd, a mingled multitude of men and beasts. The horns of cattle, the high and long-napped hats of wealthy peasants, the head-dresses of the women, came to the surface of that sea. And voices clamorous, sharp, shrill, made a continuous and savage din. Above it a huge burst of laughter from the sturdy lungs of a merry yokel would sometimes sound, and sometimes a long bellow from a cow tied fast to the wall of a house.

It all smelled of the stable, of milk, of hay, and of perspiration, giving off that half-human, half-animal odor which is peculiar to the men of the fields.

Maître Hauchecorne, of Bréauté, had just arrived at Goderville, and was taking his way towards the square, when he perceived on the ground a little piece of string. Maître Hauchecorne, economical, like all true Normans, reflected that everything was worth picking up which could be of any use; and he stooped down—but painfully, because he suffered from rheumatism. He took the bit of thin cord from the ground, and was carefully preparing to roll it up when he saw Maître Malandain, the harness-maker, on his door-step, looking at him. They had once had a quarrel about a halter, and they had remained angry, bearing malice on both sides. Maître Hauchecorne was overcome with a sort of shame at being seen by his enemy looking in the dirt so for a bit of string. He quickly hid his find beneath his blouse; then in the pocket of his breeches; then pretended to be still looking for something on the ground which he did not discover; and at last went off towards the market-place, with his head bent forward, and a body almost doubled in two by rheumatic pains.

He lost himself immediately in the crowd, which was clamorous, slow, and agitated by interminable bargains. The peasants examined the cows, went off, came back, always in great perplexity and fear of being cheated, never quite daring to decide, spying at the eye of the seller, trying ceaselessly to discover the tricks of the man and the defect in the beast.

The women, having placed their great baskets at their feet, had pulled out the poultry, which lay upon the ground, tied by the legs, with eyes scared, with combs scarlet.

They listened to propositions, maintaining the prices, with a dry manner, with an impassible face; or, suddenly, perhaps, deciding to take the lower price which was offered, they cried out to the customer, who was departing slowly:

"All right, I'll let you have them, Mâit' Anthime."

Then, little by little, the square became empty, and when the *Angelus* struck midday those who lived at a distance poured into the inns.

At Jourdain's the great room was filled with eaters, just as the vast court was filled with vehicles of every sort—wagons, gigs, char-à-bancs, tilburys, tilt-carts which have no name, yellow with mud, misshapen, pieced together, raising their shafts to heaven like two arms, or it may be with their nose in the dirt and their rear in the air.

Just opposite to where the diners were at table the huge fireplace, full of clear flame, threw a lively heat on the backs of those who sat along the right. Three spits were turning, loaded with chickens, with pigeons, and with joints of mutton; and a delectable odor of roast meat, and of gravy gushing over crisp brown skin, took wing from the hearth, kindled merriment, caused mouths to water.

All the aristocracy of the plough were eating there, at Maît' Jourdain's, the innkeeper's, a dealer in horses also, and a sharp fellow who had made a pretty penny in his day.

The dishes were passed round, were emptied, with jugs of yellow cider. Every one told of his affairs, of his purchases and his sales. They asked news about the crops. The weather was good for green stuffs, but a little wet for wheat.

All of a sudden the drum rolled in the court before the house. Every one, except some of the most indifferent, was on his feet at once, and ran to the door, to the windows, with his mouth still full and his napkin in his hand.

When the public crier had finished his tattoo he called forth in a jerky voice, making his pauses out of time:

"Be it known to the inhabitants of Goderville, and in general to all—persons present at the market, that there has been lost this morning, on the Beuzeville road between—nine and ten o'clock, a pocket-book of black leather, containing five hundred francs and business papers. You are requested to return it—to the mayor's office, at once, or to Maître Fortuné Houlbrèque, of Manneville. There will be twenty francs reward."

Then the man departed. They heard once more at a distance the dull beatings of the drum and the faint voice of the crier.

Then they began to talk of this event, reckoning up the chances which Maître Houlbrèque had of finding or of not finding his pocket-book again.

And the meal went on.

They were finishing their coffee when the corporal of gendarmes appeared on the threshold.

He asked:

"Is Maître Hauchecorne, of Bréauté, here?"

Maître Hauchecorne, seated at the other end of the table, answered:

"Here I am."

And the corporal resumed:

"Maître Houchecorne, will you have the kindness to come with me to the mayor's office? M. le Maire would like to speak to you."

The peasant, surprised and uneasy, gulped down his little glass of cognac, got up, and, even worse bent over than in the morning since the first steps after a rest were always particularly difficult, started off, repeating:

"Here I am, here I am."

And he followed the corporal.

The mayor was waiting for him, seated in an arm-chair. He was the notary of the place, a tall, grave man of pompous speech.

"Maître Hauchecorne," said he, "this morning, on the Beuzeville road, you were seen to pick up the pocket-book lost by Maître Houlbréque, of Manneville."

The countryman, speechless, regarded the mayor, frightened already by this suspicion which rested on him he knew not why.

"I, I picked up that pocket-book?"

"Yes, you."

"I swear I didn't even know nothing about it at all."

"You were seen."

"They saw me, me? Who is that who saw me?"

"M. Malandain, the harness-maker."

Then the old man remembered, understood, and reddening with anger:

"Ah, he saw me, did he, the rascal? He saw me picking up this string here, M'sieu' le Maire."

And, fumbling at the bottom of his pocket, he pulled out of it the little end of string.

But the mayor incredulously shook his head:

"You will not make me believe, Maître Hauchecorne, that M. Malandain, who is a man worthy of credit, has mistaken this string for a pocket-book."

The peasant, furious, raised his hand and spit as if to attest his good faith, repeating:

"For all that, it is the truth of the good God, the blessed truth, M'sieu' le Maire. There! on my soul and my salvation I repeat it."

The mayor continued:

"After having picked up the thing in question, you even looked for some time in the mud to see if a piece of money had not dropped out of it."

The good man was suffocated with indignation and with fear:

"If they can say!—if they can say . . . such lies as that to slander an honest man! If they can say!—"

He might protest, he was not believed.

He was confronted with M. Malandain, who repeated and sustained his testimony. They abused one another for an hour. At his own request Maître Hauchecorne was searched. Nothing was found upon him.

At last, the mayor, much perplexed, sent him away, warning him that he would inform the public prosecutor, and ask for orders.

The news had spread. When he left the mayor's office, the old man was surrounded, interrogated with a curiosity which was serious or mocking as the case might be, but into which no indignation entered. And he began to tell the story of the string. They did not believe him. They laughed.

He passed on, button-holed by every one, himself button-holing his acquaintances, beginning over and over again his tale and his protestations, showing his pockets turned inside out to prove that he had nothing.

They said to him:

"You old rogue, *va!*"

And he grew angry, exasperated, feverish, in despair at not being believed, and always telling his story.

The night came. It was time to go home. He set out with three of his neighbors, to whom he pointed out the place where he had picked up the end of string; and all the way he talked of his adventure.

That evening he made the round in the village of Bréauté, so as to tell every one. He met only unbelievers.

He was ill of it all night long.

The next day, about one in the afternoon, Marius Paumelle, a farm hand of Maître Breton, the market-gardener at Ymauville, returned the pocket-book and its contents to Maître Houlbrèque, of Manneville.

This man said, indeed, that he had found it on the road; but not knowing how to read, he had carried it home and given it to his master.

The news spread to the environs. Maître Hauchecorne was informed. He put himself at once upon the go, and began to relate his story as completed by the *dénouement*. He triumphed.

"What grieved me," said he, "was not the thing itself, do you understand; but it was the lies. There's nothing does you so much harm as being in disgrace for lying."

All day he talked of his adventure, he told it on the roads to the people who passed; at the cabaret to the people who drank; and the next Sunday, when they came out of church. He even stopped strangers to tell them about it. He was easy, now, and yet something worried him without his knowing exactly what it was. People had a joking manner while they listened. They did not seem convinced. He seemed to feel their tittle-tattle behind his back.

On Tuesday of the next week he went to market at Goderville, prompted entirely by the need of telling his story.

Malandain, standing on his door-step, began to laugh as he saw him pass. Why?

He accosted a farmer of Criquetot, who did not let him finish, and, giving him a punch in the pit of his stomach, cried in his face: "Oh you great rogue, *va!*" Then turned his heel upon him.

Maître Hauchecorne remained speechless, and grew more and more uneasy. Why had they called him "great rogue?"

When seated at table in Jourdain's tavern he began again to explain the whole affair.

A horse-dealer of Montivilliers shouted at him:

"Get out, get out, you old scamp; I know all about your string!"

Hauchecorne stammered:

"But since they found it again, the pocket-book!"

But the other continued:

"Hold your tongue, daddy; there's one who finds it and there's another who returns it. And no one the wiser."

The peasant was choked. He understood at last. They accused him of having had the pocket-book brought back by an accomplice, by a confederate.

He tried to protest. The whole table began to laugh.

He could not finish his dinner, and went away amid a chorus of jeers.

He went home, ashamed and indignant, choked with rage, with confusion, the more cast-down since from his Norman cunning, he was, perhaps, capable of having done what they accused him of, and even of boasting of it as a good trick. His innocence dimly seemed to him impossible to prove, his craftiness being so well known. And he felt himself struck to the heart by the injustice of the suspicion.

Then he began anew to tell of his adventure, lengthening his recital every day, each time adding new proofs, more energetic protestations, and more solemn oaths which he thought of, which he prepared in his hours of solitude, his mind being entirely occupied by the story of the string. The more complicated his defence, the more artful his arguments, the less he was believed.

"Those are liars' proofs," they said behind his back.

He felt this; it preyed upon his heart. He exhausted himself in useless efforts.

He was visibly wasting away.

The jokers now made him tell the story of "The Piece of String" to amuse them, just as you make a soldier who has been on a campaign tell his story of the battle. His mind, struck at the root, grew weak.

About the end of December he took to his bed.

He died early in January, and, in the delirium of the death-agony, he protested his innocence, repeating:

"A little bit of string—a little bit of string—see, here it is, M'sieu' le Maire."

Anton Pavlovich Chekov (1860–1904) was the son of an unsuccessful grocery store owner in Taganrog on the Sea of Azov. While earning a degree in medicine at the University of Moscow, he began to write humorous sketches. He died of tuberculosis at the age of forty-four, but not before he had become one of the world's most influential short-story writers. For further reading: The Tales of Chekov, translated by Constance Garnett (1916–1922); specifically, The Chorus Girl (1886), The Party (1888), The Darling (1898).

The Man in a Shell

ANTON CHEKOV

On the outskirts of the village of Mironositzkoe two belated huntsmen had settled for the night in the barn belonging to the Elder, Prokofy. They were the veterinary, Ivan Ivanych, and the high school teacher, Burkin. Ivan Ivanych had a rather queer double surname—Chimsha-Himalaisky— which did not suit him at all, and he was known as Ivan Ivanych all over the province. He lived on a stud-farm near the town, and had gone out shooting to breathe some fresh air. As for Burkin, the high school teacher, he spent every summer at Count P———'s, and had long been thoroughly at home in the district.

They did not sleep. Ivan Ivanych, a tall, spare old man with long mustaches, was sitting outside the door, smoking a pipe in the moonlight. Burkin was lying inside on the hay, and could not be seen for the darkness.

They were telling each other stories. Among other things, they spoke of the Elder's wife, Mavra, a healthy and by no means stupid woman, observing that she had never been beyond her native village, had never seen a city or a railway in her life, and had spent the last ten years hugging the stove and only going out into the street at night.

"There's nothing remarkable about that!" said Burkin. "There are not a few people in the world, temperamentally unsociable, who try to withdraw into a shell like a hermit crab or a snail. Perhaps it is a manifestation of atavism, a return to the time when man's ancestor was not yet a gregarious animal and lived alone in his lair, or perhaps it is only one

47

of the varieties of human character—who knows? I am no naturalist, and it is not my business to settle such questions; I only mean to say that people like Mavra are by no means rare. Why, not to go far afield, there was Belikov, a colleague of mine, a teacher of Greek, who died in our town two months ago. You have heard of him, no doubt. The curious thing about him was that he wore rubbers, and a warm coat with an interlining, and carried an umbrella even in the finest weather. And he kept his umbrella in its cover and his watch in a gray chamois case, and when he took out his penknife to sharpen his pencil, his penknife, too, was in a little case; and his face seemed to be in a case too, because it was always hidden in his turned-up collar. He wore dark spectacles and a sweater, stuffed his ears with cotton-wool, and when he got into a cab always told the driver to put up the hood. In short, the man showed a constant and irrepressible inclination to keep a covering about himself, to create for himself a membrane, as it were, which would isolate him and protect him from outside influences. Actuality irritated him, frightened him, kept him in a state of continual agitation, and, perhaps to justify his timidity, his aversion for the present, he would always laud the past and things that had never existed, and the dead languages that he taught were in effect for him the same rubbers and umbrella in which he sought concealment from real life.

" 'Oh, how sonorous, how beautiful the Greek language is!' he would say, with a saccharine expression; and as though to prove his point, he would screw up his eyes and, raising one finger, utter: 'Anthropos!'

"His thoughts, too, Belikov tried to tuck away in a sheath. The only things that were clear to him were Government regulations and newspaper notices in which something was forbidden. When some ruling prohibited high school students from appearing on the streets after nine o'clock at night, or some article censured carnal love, this he found clear and definite: it was forbidden, and that was that. But there was always a doubtful element for him, something vague and not fully expressed in any sanction or permission. When a dramatic club or a reading-room or a teahouse was licensed in the town, he would shake his head and say in a low voice:

" 'Of course, it's all very well, but you can't tell what may come of it.'

"Any infringement of the rules, any deviation or departure from them, plunged him into gloom, though one would have thought it was no concern of his. If one of his colleagues was late for the thanksgiving service, or if rumors reached him of some prank of the high school boys, or if one of the female members of the staff had been seen late in the evening in the company of an officer, he would become very much agitated and keep saying that one couldn't tell what might come of it. At faculty meetings he simply crushed us with his cautiousness, his suspiciousness, and his typical remarks to the effect that the young people in the girls' as well as in the boys' high school were unruly, that there was much noise in the classrooms, that it might reach the ears of the authorities, that one couldn't tell what might come of it, and that it would be a good thing if Petrov were expelled from the second form and Yegorov from the fourth. And what do you think, with his sighs, his moping, the dark spectacles on his pale little face, a little face like a polecat's, you know, he weighed us all down, and we submitted, reduced Petrov's and Yegorov's marks for conduct, detained them, and in the end expelled them both.

"He had a peculiar habit of visiting our lodgings. He would call on some teacher, would sit down, and remain silently staring, as though he were trying to detect something. He would sit like this in silence for an hour or two and then leave. This he called 'maintaining good relations with his colleagues'; and it was obvious that making these calls and sitting there like that was painful to him, and that he went to see us simply because he considered it his duty to his colleagues. We teachers were afraid of him. And even the principal was afraid of him. Would you believe it, our teachers were all thoughtful, decent people, brought up on Turgenev and Shchedrin, yet this little man, who always wore rubbers and carried an umbrella, had the whole high school under his thumb for fully fifteen years! The high school? The whole town! Our ladies did not get up private theatricals on Saturdays for fear he should find it out, and the clergy dared not eat meat in Lent or play cards in his presence. Under the influence of people like Belikov the whole town spent ten to fifteen frightened years. We were afraid to speak out loud, to write letters, to make acquaintances, to read books, to help the poor, to teach people how to read and write . . ."

Ivan Ivanych coughed, as a preliminary to making some remark, but first lighted his pipe, gazed at the moon, and then said, between pauses:

"Yes, thoughtful, decent people, readers of Shchedrin and Turgenev, of Buckle and all the rest of them, yet they knuckled under and put up with it—that's just how it is."

"Belikov and I lived in the same house," Burkin went on, "on the same floor, his door facing mine; we often saw each other, and I was acquainted with his domestic arrangements. It was the same story: dressing-gown, nightcap, blinds, bolts, prohibitions and restrictions of all sorts, and, 'Oh, you can't tell what may come of it!' Lenten fare didn't agree with him, yet he could not eat meat, as people might say that Belikov did not keep the fasts, and he ate perch fried in butter—not a Lenten dish, yet one could not call it meat. He did not keep a female servant for fear people might think evil of him, but instead employed an old man of sixty, called Afanasy, half-witted and given to drinking, who had once been an orderly and could cook after a fashion. This Afanasy was usually standing at the door with folded arms; he would sigh deeply and always mutter the same thing:

" 'The likes of *them* is thick as hops hereabouts!' "

"Belikov's bedroom was tiny and boxlike; his bed was curtained. When he went to bed he drew the bed-clothes over his head; it was hot and stuffy; the wind rattled the closed doors; a humming noise came from the stove and the sound of sighs from the kitchen, ominous sighs— And he lay under the quilt, terrified. He was afraid that something might happen, that Afanasy would murder him, that thieves would break in, and he had bad dreams all night long, and in the morning when we went to school together, he was downcast and pale, and it was plain that the place, swarming with people, towards which he was going, filled his whole being with dread and aversion, and that walking beside me was disagreeable to a man of his unsociable temperament.

" 'How noisy the classrooms are, he used to say, as though trying to find an explanation for his distress. 'It's an outrage.'

"And imagine, this teacher of Greek—this man in a shell—came near to getting married."

Ivan Ivanych glanced rapidly into the barn, and said, "You are joking!"

"Yes, strange as it seems, he nearly got married. A new teacher of geography and history, a certain Mihail Savvich Kovalenko, a Ukrainian, was assigned to our school. He did not come alone, but with his sister, Varenka. He was a tall, dark young man with huge hands, and one could see from his face that he spoke in a deep voice, and, in fact, his voice seemed to come out of a barrel: 'Boom, boom, boom!' She was not so young, about thirty, but she too was tall, well built, with black eyebrows and red cheeks—in a word, she was not a girl but a peach, and so lively, so noisy; she was always singing Little Russian songs and laughing. At the least provocation, she would go off into ringing laughter: 'Ha-ha-ha!' We first got well acquainted with the Kovalenkos, I remember, at the principal's name-day party. Among the morose, emphatically dull pedagogues who attend even a name-day party as a duty, we suddenly saw a new Aphrodite risen from the foam; she walked with her arms akimbo, laughed, sang, danced. She sang with feeling 'The Winds Are Blowing' and then another Ukrainian song and another, and she fascinated us all, all, even Belikov. He sat down beside her and said with a saccharine smile:

" 'The Little Russian tongue reminds one of ancient Greek in its softness and agreeable sonority.'

"That flattered her, and she began telling him with feeling and persuasiveness that they had a farm in the Gadyach district, and that her Mummy lived there, and that they had such pears, such melons, such *kabaki!* The Little Russians call a pumpkin *kabak* [Russian for tavern], while their taverns they call *shinki*, and they make a *borshch* with tomatoes and eggplant in it, 'which is so delicious—ever so delicious!'

"We listened, and listened, and suddenly the same idea occurred to all of us:

" 'It would be a good thing to marry them off,' the principal's wife whispered to me.

"For some reason we all recalled that our friend Belikov was unmarried, and it seemed strange to us now that we had failed to notice it before, and in fact had completely lost sight of so important a detail in his life. What was his attitude towards women? How had he settled for himself this vital problem? Until then we had had no interest in the matter; perhaps we had not even admitted the idea that a man who wore rubbers in all weathers and slept behind curtains was capable of love.

" 'He is way past forty and she is thirty,' the principal's wife clarified her idea. 'I believe she would marry him.'

"What isn't done in the provinces out of boredom, how many useless and foolish things! And that is because what is necessary isn't done at all. What need was there, for instance, for us to make a match for this Belikov, whom one could not even imagine as a married man? The principal's wife, the inspector's wife, and all our high school ladies, grew livelier and even better looking, as though they had suddenly found an object in life. The principal's wife would take a box at the theater, and lo and behold! Varenka would be sitting in it, fanning herself, beaming and happy, and beside her would be Belikov, a twisted little man, looking as though he had been pulled out of his lodging by pincers. I would give an evening party and the ladies would insist on my inviting Belikov and Varenka. In short, the machine was set in motion. It turned out that Varenka was not averse to matrimony. Her life with her brother was not very cheerful: they did nothing but argue and quarrel with one another for days on end. Here is a typical scene: Kovalenko strides down the street, a tall, husky fellow, in an embroidered shirt, a lock of hair falling over his forehead from under his cap, in one hand a bundle of books, in the other a thick, knotted stick; he is followed by his sister, also carrying books.

" 'But you haven't read it, Mihailik!' she is arguing loudly. 'I tell you, I swear you haven't read it at all!'

" 'And I tell you I have read it,' bellows Kovalenko, banging his stick on the sidewalk.

" 'Oh, my goodness, Mihailik, why are you so cross? We are only discussing principles.'

" 'I tell you that I have read it!' Kovalenko shouts, more loudly than ever.

"And at home, if there was an outsider present, there was sure to be a fusillade. She must have been fed up with such a life and longed for a home of her own. Besides, there was her age; there was no time left to pick and choose; she was apt to marry anybody, even a teacher of Greek. Come to think of it, most of our young ladies don't care whom they marry so long as they do marry. Be that as it may, Varenka began to show an unmistakable inclination for Belikov.

"And Belikov? He used to call on Kovalenko just as he did on the rest of us. He would arrive, sit down, and go on sitting there in silence. He would sit quietly, and Varenka would sing to him 'The Winds Are Blowing' or would stare at him pensively with her dark eyes, or would suddenly go off into a peal of laughter—'Ha-ha-ha!'

"In amorous affairs and in marrying, suggestion plays a great part. Everybody—both his colleagues and the ladies—began assuring Belikov that he ought to get married, that there was nothing left for him in life but to get married; we all felicitated him, and with solemn faces delivered ourselves of various platitudes, such as 'Marriage is a serious step.' Besides, Varenka was good-looking and attractive; she was the daughter of a civil councilor, and she owned a farm; above all, she was the first woman who had treated him cordially and affectionately. His head was turned, and he decided that he really ought to get married."

"Well, at that point," said Ivan Ivanych, "you should have taken away his rubbers and umbrella."

"Just fancy, that proved to be impossible. He put Varenka's portrait on his table, kept calling on me and talking about Varenka, and about family life, saying that marriage was a serious step. He went frequently to the Kovalenkos, but he did not alter his habits in the least. On the contrary, his decision to get married seemed to have a deleterious effect on him. He grew thinner and paler and seemed to retreat further into his shell.

" 'I like Varvara Savvishna,' he would say to me, with a faint and crooked smile, 'and I know that everyone ought to get married, but—you know, all this has happened so suddenly—One must think it over a little.'

" 'What is there to think over?' I would say to him. 'Get married—that's all.'

" 'No; marriage is a serious step; one must first weigh the impending duties and responsibilities—so that nothing untoward may come of it. It worries me so much that I don't sleep nights. And I must confess I am afraid: she and her brother have such a peculiar way of thinking; they reason so strangely, you know, and she has a very impetuous disposition. You get married, and then, there is no telling, you may get into trouble.'

"And he did not propose; he kept putting if off, to the great vexation of the principal's wife and all our ladies; he kept weighing his future duties and responsibilities, and meanwhile he went for a walk with Varenka almost every day—possibly he thought that this was the proper thing under the circumstances—and came to see me to talk about family life. And in all probability he would have ended by proposing to her, and would have made one of those needless, stupid marriages thousands of which are made among us out of sheer boredom and idleness, if it had not been for a *kolossalischer Skandal*.

"I must tell you that Varenka's brother conceived a hatred of Belikov from the first day of their acquaintance and couldn't endure him.

" 'I don't understand,' he used to say to us, shrugging his shoulders, 'I don't understand how you can put up with that informer, that nasty mug. Ugh! how can you live here? The atmosphere you breathe is vile, stifling! Are you pedagogues, teachers? No, you are piddling functionaries; yours is not a temple of learning but a police station, and it has the same sour smell. No, brothers, I will stay with you for a while, and then I will go to my farm and catch crayfish there and teach Ukrainian brats. I will go, and you can stay here with your Judas—blast him!'

"Or he would laugh till tears came to his eyes, his laughter now deep, now shrill, and ask me, throwing up his hands, 'What does he come here for? What does he want? He sits and stares.'

"He even gave Belikov a nickname, 'The Spider.' Of course, we avoided talking to him about his sister's planning to marry 'The Spider.' And when, on one occasion, the principal's wife hinted to him what a good thing it would be if his sister settled down with such a substantial, universally respected man as Belikov, he frowned and grumbled:

" 'It's none of my business; let her marry a viper if she likes. I don't care to meddle in other people's affairs.'

"Now listen to what happened next. Some wag drew a caricature of Belikov walking along under his umbrella, wearing his rubbers, his trousers tucked up, with Varenka on his arm; below there was the legend 'Anthropos in love.' The artist got the expression admirably, you know. He must have worked more than one night, for the teachers of both the boys' and girls' high schools, the teachers of the theological seminary, and the government officials all received copies. Belikov received one, too. The caricature made a very painful impression on him.

"We left the house together; it was the first of May, a Sunday, and all of us, the boys and the teachers, had agreed to meet at the high school and then to walk to a grove on the outskirts of the town. We set off, and he was green in the face and gloomier than a thundercloud.

" 'What wicked, malicious people there are!' he said, and his lips quivered.

"I couldn't help feeling sorry for him. We were walking along, and all of a sudden—imagine!—Kovalenko came rolling along on a bicycle, and after him, also on a bicycle, Varenka, flushed and exhausted, but gay and high-spirited.

" 'We are going on ahead,' she shouted. 'What lovely weather! Just too lovely!'

"And they both vanished. Belikov turned from green to white, and seemed petrified. He stopped short and stared at me.

" 'Good heavens, what is this?' he asked. 'Can my eyes be deceiving me? Is it proper for high school teachers and ladies to ride bicycles?'

" 'What's improper about it?' I asked. 'Let them ride and may it do them good.'

" 'But you can't mean it,' he cried, amazed at my calm. 'What are you saying?'

"And he was so shocked that he refused to go farther, and returned home.

"Next day he was continually twitching and rubbing his hands nervously, and it was obvious from the expression of his face that he was far from well. And he left before the school day was over, for the first time in his life. And he ate no dinner. Towards evening he wrapped himself up warmly, though it was practically summer weather, and made his way to the Kovalenkos'. Varenka was out; he found only her brother at home.

" 'Please sit down,' Kovalenko said coldly, frowning. He had a sleepy look; he had just taken an after-dinner nap and was in a very bad humor.

"Belikov sat in silence for about ten minutes, and then began, 'I have come to you to relieve my mind. I am very, very much troubled. Some malicious fellow has drawn a caricature of me and of another person who is close to both of us. I regard it as my duty to assure you that I had nothing to do with it. I have given no grounds for such an attack—on the contrary, I have always behaved as a respectable person would.'

"Kovalenko sat there sulking without a word. Belikov waited a while, and then went on in a low, mournful voice, 'And I have something else to say to you. I have been in the service for years, while you have entered it only lately, and I consider it my duty as an older colleague to give you a warning. You ride a bicycle, and that pastime is utterly improper for an educator of youth.'

" 'Why so?' asked Kovalenko in his deep voice.

" 'Surely that needs no explanation, Mihail Savvich—surely it is self-evident! If the teacher rides a bicycle, what can one expect of the pupils? The only thing left them is to walk on their heads! And so long as it is not explicitly permitted, it should not be done. I was horrified yesterday! When I saw your sister, everything went black before my eyes. A lady or a young girl on a bicycle—it's terrible!'

" 'What is it you wish exactly?'

" 'All I wish to do is to warn you, Mihail Savvich. You are a young man, you have a future before you, you must be very careful of your behavior, and you are so neglectful, oh, so neglectful! You go about in an embroidered shirt, are constantly seen in the street carrying books, and now the bicycle, too. The principal will learn that you and your sister ride bicycles, and then it will reach the Trustee's ears. No good can come of that.'

" 'It's nobody's business if my sister and I do bicycle,' said Kovalenko, and he turned crimson. 'And whoever meddles in my private affairs can go to the devil!'

"Belikov turned pale and got up.

" 'If you speak to me in that tone, I cannot continue,' he said. 'And I beg you never to express yourself in that manner about our superiors in my presence; you should be respectful to the authorities.'

" 'Have I said anything offensive about the authorities?' asked Kovalenko, looking at him angrily. 'Please leave me in peace. I am an honorable man, and do not care to talk to gentlemen of your stripe. I hate informers!'

"Belikov fidgeted nervously and hurriedly began putting on his coat, with an expression of horror on his face. It was the first time in his life he had been spoken to so rudely.

" 'You can say what you please,' he declared, as he stepped out of the entry onto the staircase landing. 'Only I must warn you: someone may have overheard us, and lest our conversation be misinterpreted and harm come of it, I shall have to inform the principal of the contents of our conversation—in a general way. I am obliged to do so.'

" 'Inform him? Go, make your report and be damned to you!'

"Kovalenko seized him from behind by the collar and gave him a shove, and Belikov rolled noisily downstairs, rubbers and all. The staircase was high and steep, but he arrived at the bottom safely, got up, and felt his nose to see whether his spectacles were intact. But just as he was rolling down the stairs, Varenka came in, accompanied by two ladies; they stood below, staring, and this was more dreadful to Belikov than anything else. I believe he would rather have broken his neck or both legs than have been an object of ridicule. Why, now the whole town would hear of it; it would come to the principal's ears, it would reach the Trustee. Oh, there was no telling what might come of it! There would be another caricature, and it would all end in his being ordered to retire from his post.

"When he go up, Varenka recognized him and, looking at his ludicrous face, his crumpled overcoat, and his rubbers, not grasping the situation and supposing that he had fallen by accident, could not restrain herself and burst into laughter that resounded throughout the house:

" 'Ha-ha-ha!'

"And this reverberant, ringing 'Ha-ha-ha! put an end to everything: to the expected match and to Belikov's earthly existence. He did not hear what Varenka was saying; he saw nothing. On reaching home, the first thing he did was to remove Varenka's portrait from the table; then he went to bed, and he never got up again.

"Two or three days later Afanasy came to me and asked whether the doctor should not be sent for, as there was something wrong with his master. I went in to see Belikov. He lay silent behind the curtains, covered with a quilt; when you questioned him, he answered 'yes' and 'no' and nothing more. He lay there while Afanasy, gloomy and scowling, hovered about him, sighing heavily and reeking of vodka like a tavern.

"A month later Belikov died. We all went to his funeral—that is, all connected with both high schools and with the theological seminary. Now when he was lying in his coffin his expression was mild, pleasant, even cheerful, as though he were glad that he had at last been put into a case that he would never leave again. Yes, he had attained his ideal! And as though in his honor, it was cloudy, rainy weather on the day of his funeral, and we all wore rubbers and carried umbrellas. Varenka, too, was at the funeral, and when the coffin was lowered into the grave, she dropped a tear. I have noticed that Ukrainian women always laugh or cry—there is no intermediate state for them.

"I confess, it is a great pleasure to bury people like Belikov. As we were returning from the cemetery we wore discreet Lenten faces; no one wanted to display this feeling of pleasure—a feeling like that we had experienced long, long ago as children when the grownups had gone out and we ran about the garden for an hour or two, enjoying complete freedom. Ah, freedom, freedom! A mere hint, the faintest hope of its possibility, gives wings to the soul, isn't that true?

"We returned from the cemetery in good humor. But not more than a week had passed before life dropped into its old rut, and was as gloomy, tiresome, and stupid as before, the sort of life that is not explicitly forbidden, but on the other hand is not fully permitted; things were no better. And, indeed, though we had burried Belikov, how many such men in shells were left, how many more of them there will be!"

"That's the way it is," said Ivan Ivanych, and lit his pipe.

"How many more of them there will be!" repeated Burkin.

The high school teacher came out of the barn. He was a short, stout man, completely bald, with a black beard that nearly reached his waist; two dogs came out with him.

"What a moon!" he said, looking up.

It was already midnight. On the right could be seen the whole village, a long street stretching far away for some three miles. Everything was sunk in deep, silent slumber; not a movement, not a sound; one could hardly believe that nature could be so still. When on a moonlight night you see a wide village street, with its cottages, its haystacks, and its willows that have dropped off to sleep, a feeling of serenity comes over the soul; as it rests thus, hidden from toil, care, and sorrow by the nocturnal shadows, the street is gentle, sad, beautiful, and it seems as though the stars look down upon it kindly and tenderly, and as if there were no more evil on earth, and all were well. On the left, where the village ended, the open country began; the fields could be seen stretching far away to the horizon, and there was no movement, no sound in that whole expanse drenched with moonlight.

"Yes, that's the way it is," repeated Ivan Ivanych; "and isn't our living in the airless, crowded town, our writing useless papers, our playing vint— isn't all that a sort of shell for us? And this spending our lives among pettifogging, idle men and silly, unoccupied women, our talking and our listening to all sorts of poppycock—isn't that a shell, too? If you like, I will tell you a very instructive story."

"No; it's time to turn in," said Burkin. "Tomorrow's another day."

They went into the barn and lay down on the hay. And they were both covered up and had dozed off when suddenly there was the sound of light footsteps—tap, tap. Someone was walking near the barn, walking a little and stopping, and a minute later, tap tap again. The dogs began to growl.

"That's Mavra," said Burkin.

The footsteps died away.

"To see and hear them lie," said Ivan Ivanych, turning over on the other side, "and to be called a fool for putting up with their lies; to endure insult and humiliation, and not dare say openly that you are on the side of the honest and the free, and to lie and smile yourself, and all for the sake of a crust of bread, for the sake of a warm nook, for the sake of a mean, worthless rank in the service—no, one cannot go on living like that!"

"Come, now, that's a horse of another color, Ivan Ivanych," said the teacher. "Let's go to sleep."

And ten minutes later Burkin was asleep. But Ivan Ivanych kept sighing and turning from one side to the other; then he got up, went outside again, and seating himself near the door, lighted his pipe.

George Moore (1852–1933) was born in Ireland
but lived most of his adult life in Paris and London; he studied as a painter and later established
a firm literary reputation as a novelist and critic.
He helped found the new Irish theater and spent
a period in Dublin from 1901 until 1910 writing
in Gaelic. Through Moore, the influence of major
European and Russian writers came to Ireland. For
further reading, see his novels: Esther Waters (1894)
and The Lake (1905). His influential book of short
stories is The Untilled Field. Hail and Farewell
(1911–1914) is his three-volume history of the Irish
literary revival.

Home Sickness

GEORGE MOORE

He told the doctor he was due in the bar-room at eight o'clock in the
morning; the bar-room was in a slum in the Bowery; and he had only
been able to keep himself in health by getting up at five o'clock and going
for long walks in the Central Park.

"A sea voyage is what you want," said the doctor. "Why not go to
Ireland for two or three months? You will come back a new man."

"I'd like to see Ireland again."

And then he began to wonder how the people at home were getting on.
The doctor was right. He thanked him, and three weeks afterwards he
landed in Cork.

As he sat in the railway carriage he recalled his native village—he
could see it and its lake, and then the fields one by one, and the roads.
He could see a large piece of rocky land—some three or four hundred
acres of headland stretching out into the winding lake. Upon this headland
the peasantry had been given permission to build their cabins by former
owners of the Georgian house standing on the pleasant green hill. The
present owners considered the village a disgrace, but the villagers paid
high rents for their plots of ground, and all the manual labour that the
Big House required came from the village: the gardeners, the stable helpers,
the house and the kitchen maids.

He had been thirteen years in America, and when the train stopped at his station, he looked round to see if there were any changes in it. It was just the same blue limestone station-house as it was thirteen years ago. The platform and the sheds were the same, and there were five miles of road from the station to Duncannon. The sea voyage had done him good, but five miles were too far for him to-day; the last time he had walked the road, he had walked it in an hour and a half, carrying a heavy bundle on a stick.

He was sorry he did not feel strong enough for the walk; the evening was fine, and he would meet many people coming home from the fair, some of whom he had known in his youth, and they would tell him where he could get a clean lodging. But the carman would be able to tell him that; he called the car that was waiting at the station, and soon he was answering questions about America. But Bryden wanted to hear of those who were still living in the old country, and after hearing the stories of many people he had forgotten, he heard that Mike Scully, who had been away in a situation for many years as a coachman in the King's County, had come back and built a fine house with a concrete floor. Now there was a good loft in Mike Scully's house, and Mike would be pleased to take in a lodger.

Bryden remembered that Mike had been in a situation at the Big House; he had intended to be a jockey, but had suddenly shot up into a fine tall man, and had had to become a coachman instead. Bryden tried to recall the face, but he could only remember a straight nose, and a somewhat dusky complexion. Mike was one of the heroes of his childhood, and his youth floated before him, and he caught glimpses of himself, something that was more than a phantom and less than a reality. Suddenly his reverie was broken: the carman pointed with his whip, and Bryden saw a tall, finely-built, middle-aged man coming through the gates, and the driver said:—

"There's Mike Scully."

Mike had forgotten Bryden even more completely than Bryden had forgotten him, and many aunts and uncles were mentioned before he began to understand.

"You've grown into a fine man, James," he said, looking at Bryden's great width of chest. "But you are thin in the cheeks, and you're sallow in the cheeks too."

"I haven't been very well lately—that is one of the reasons I have come back; but I want to see you all again."

Bryden paid the carman, wished him "God-speed," and he and Mike divided the luggage between them, Mike carrying the bag and Bryden the bundle, and they walked round the lake, for the townland was at the back of the demesne; and while they walked, James proposed to pay Mike ten shillings a week for his board and lodging.

He remembered the woods thick and well-forested; now they were wind-worn, the drains were choked, and the bridge leading across the lake inlet was falling away. Their way led between long fields where herds of cattle were grazing; the road was broken—Bryden wondered how the villagers drove their carts over it, and Mike told him that the land-lord could not keep it in repair, and he would not allow it to be kept in repair out of the rates, for then it would be a public road, and he did not think there should be a public road through his property.

At the end of many fields they came to the village, and it looked a deso-late place, even on this fine evening, and Bryden remarked that the county did not seem to be as much lived in as it used to be. It was at once strange and familiar to see the chickens in the kitchen; and, wishing to re-knit himself to the old habits, he begged of Mrs. Scully not to drive them out, saying he did not mind them. Mike told his wife that Bryden was born in Duncannon, and when he mentioned Bryden's name she gave him her hand, after wiping it in her apron, saying he was heartily welcome, only she was afraid he would not care to sleep in a loft.

"Why wouldn't I sleep in a loft, a dry loft! You're thinking a good deal of America over here," said he, "but I reckon it isn't all you think it. Here you work when you like and you sit down when you like; but when you have had a touch of blood-poisoning as I had, and when you have seen young people walking with a stick, you think that there is something to be said for old Ireland."

"Now won't you be taking a sup of milk? You'll be wanting a drink after travelling," said Mrs. Scully.

And when he had drunk the milk Mike asked him if he would like to go inside or if he would like to go for a walk.

"Maybe it is sitting down you would like to be."

And they went into the cabin, and started to talk about the wages a man could get in America, and the long hours of work.

And after Bryden had told Mike everything about America that he thought would interest him, he asked Mike about Ireland. But Mike did not seem to be able to tell him much that was of interest. They were all very poor—poorer, perhaps, than when he left them.

"I don't think anyone except myself has a five pound note to his name."

Bryden hoped he felt sufficiently sorry for Mike. But after all Mike's life and prospects mattered little to him. He had come back in search of health; and he felt better already; the milk had done him good, and the bacon and cabbage in the pot sent forth a savoury odour. The Scullys were very kind, they pressed him to make a good meal; a few weeks of country air and food, they said, would give him back the health he had lost in the Bowery; and when Bryden said he was longing for a smoke, Mike said there was no better sign than that. During his long illness he had never wanted to smoke, and he was a confirmed smoker.

It was comfortable to sit by the mild peat fire watching the smoke of their pipes drifting up the chimney, and all Bryden wanted was to be let alone; he did not want to hear of anyone's misfortunes, but about nine o'clock a number of villagers came in, and their appearance was depressing. Bryden remembered one or two of them—he used to know them very well when he was a boy; their talk was as depressing as their appearance, and he could feel no interest whatever in them. He was not moved when he heard that Higgins the stone-mason was dead; he was not affected when he heard that Mary Kelly, who used to go to do the laundry at the Big House, had married; he was only interested when he heard she had gone to America. No, he had not met her there, America is a big place. Then one of the peasants asked him if he remembered Patsy Carabine, who used to do the gardening at the Big House. Yes, he remembered Patsy well. Patsy was in the poor-house. He had not been able to do any work on account of his arm; his house had fallen in; he had given up his holding and gone into the poor-house. All this was very sad, and to avoid hearing any further unpleasantness, Bryden began to tell them about America. And they sat round listening to him; but all the talking was on his side; he wearied of it; and looking round the group he recognised a ragged hunchback with grey hair; twenty years ago he was a young hunchback, and, turning to him, Bryden asked him if he were doing well with his five acres.

"Ah, not much. This has been a bad season. The potatoes failed; they were watery—there is no diet in them."

These peasants were all agreed that they could make nothing out of their farms. Their regret was that they had not gone to America when they were young; and after striving to take an interest in the fact that O'Connor had lost a mare and foal worth forty pounds Bryden began to wish himself back in the slum. And when they left the house he wondered if every evening would be like the present one. Mike piled fresh sods on the fire, and he hoped it would show enough light in the loft for Bryden to undress himself by.

The cackling of some geese in the road kept him awake, and the loneliness of the country seemed to penetrate to his bones, and to freeze the marrow in them. There was a bat in the loft—a dog howled in the distance —and then he drew the clothes over his head. Never had he been so unhappy, and the sound of Mike breathing by his wife's side in the kitchen added to his nervous terror. Then he dozed a little; and lying on his back he dreamed he was awake, and the men he had seen sitting round the fireside that evening seemed to him like spectres come out of some unknown region of morass and reedy tarn. He stretched out his hands for his clothes, determined to fly from this house, but remembering the lonely road that led to the station he fell back on his pillow. The geese still cackled, but he was too tired to be kept awake any longer. He seemed to have been asleep only a few minutes when he heard Mike calling him. Mike had come half way up the ladder and was telling him that breakfast was ready. "What kind of breakfast will he give me?" Bryden asked himself as he pulled on his clothes. There were tea and hot griddle cakes for breakfast, and there were fresh eggs; there was sunlight in the kitchen and he liked to hear Mike tell of the work he was going to do in the fields. Mike rented a farm of about fifteen acres, at least ten of it was grass; he grew an acre of potatoes and some corn, and some turnips for his sheep. He had a nice bit of meadow, and he took down his scythe, and as he put the whetstone in his belt Bryden noticed a second scythe, and he asked Mike if he should go down with him and help him to finish the field.

"You haven't done any mowing this many a year; I don't think you'd be of much help. You'd better go for a walk by the lake, but you may come in the afternoon if you like and help to turn the grass over."

Bryden was afraid he would find the lake shore very lonely, but the magic of returning health is the sufficient distraction for the convalescent, and the morning passed agreeably. The weather was still and sunny. He could hear the ducks in the reeds. The hours dreamed themselves away, and it became his habit to go to the lake every morning. One morning he met the landlord, and they walked together, talking of the country, of what it had been, and the ruin it was slipping into. James Bryden told him that ill health had brought him back to Ireland; and the landlord lent him his boat, and Bryden rowed about the islands, and resting upon his oars he looked at the old castles, and remembered the pre-historic raiders that the landlord had told him about. He came across the stones to which the lake dwellers had tied their boats, and these signs of ancient Ireland were pleasing to Bryden in his present mood.

As well as the great lake there was a smaller lake in the bog where the villagers cut their turf. This lake was famous for its pike, and the landlord allowed Bryden to fish there, and one evening when he was looking for a frog with which to bait his line he met Margaret Dirken driving home the cows for the milking. Margaret was the herdsman's daughter, and she lived in a cottage near the Big House; but she came up to the village whenever there was a dance, and Bryden had found himself opposite to her in the reels. But until this evening he had had little opportunity of speaking to her, and he was glad to speak to someone, for the evening was lonely, and they stood talking together.

"You're getting your health again," she said. "You'll soon be leaving us."

"I'm in no hurry."

"You're grand people over there; I hear a man is paid four dollars a day for his work."

"And how much," said James, "has he to pay for his food and for his clothes?"

Her cheeks were bright and her teeth small, white and beautifully even; and a woman's soul looked at Bryden out of her soft Irish eyes. He was troubled and turned aside, and catching sight of a frog looking at him out of a tuft of grass he said:—

"I have been looking for a frog to put upon my pike line."

The frog jumped right and left, and nearly escaped in some bushes, but he caught it and returned with it in his hand.

"It is just the kind of frog a pike will like," he said. "Look at its great white belly and its bright yellow back."

And without more ado he pushed the wire to which the hook was fastened through the frog's fresh body, and dragging it through the mouth he passed the hooks through the hind legs and tied the line to the end of the wire.

"I think," said Margaret, "I must be looking after my cows; it's time I got them home."

"Won't you come down to the lake while I set my line?"

She thought for a moment and said:—

"No, I'll see you from here."

He went down to the reedy tarn, and at his approach several snipe got up, and they flew above his head uttering sharp cries. His fishing-rod was a long hazel stick, and he threw the frog as far as he could into the lake. In doing this he roused some wild ducks; a mallard and two ducks got up, and they flew towards the larger lake. Margaret watched them; they flew in a line with an old castle; and they had not disappeared from view when Bryden came towards her, and he and she drove the cows home together that evening.

They had not met very often when she said, "James, you had better not come here so often calling to me."

"Don't you wish me to come?"

"Yes, I wish you to come well enough, but keeping company is not the custom of the country, and I don't want to be talked about."

"Are you afraid the priest would speak against us from the altar?"

"He has spoken against keeping company, but it is not so much what the priest says, for there is no harm in talking."

"But if you are going to be married there is no harm in walking out together."

"Well, not so much, but marriages are made differently in these parts; there is not much courting here."

And the next day it was known in the village that James was going to marry Margaret Dirken.

His desire to excel the boys in dancing had aroused much gaiety in the parish, and for some time past there had been dancing in every house where there was a floor fit to dance upon; and if the cottager had no money to pay for a barrel of beer, James Bryden, who had money, sent him a barrel, so that Margaret might get her dance. She told him that they sometimes crossed over into another parish where the priest was not so adverse to dancing, and James wondered. And next morning at Mass he wondered at their simple fervour. Some of them held their hands above their heads as they prayed, and all this was very new and very old to James Bryden. But the obedience of these people to their priest surprised him. When he was a lad they had not been so obedient, or he had forgotten their obedience; and he listened in mixed anger and wonderment to the priest who was scolding his parishioners, speaking to them by name, saying that he had heard there was dancing going on in their homes. Worse than that, he said he had seen boys and girls loitering about the roads, and the talk that went on was of one kind—love. He said that newspapers containing love-stories were finding their way into the people's houses, stories about love, in which there was nothing elevating or ennobling. The people listened, accepting the priest's opinion without question. And their submission was pathetic. It was the submission of a primitive people clinging to religious authority, and Bryden contrasted the weakness and incompetence of the people about him with the modern restlessness and cold energy of the people he had left behind him.

One evening, as they were dancing, a knock came to the door, and the piper stopped playing, and the dancers whispered:—

"Some one has told on us; it is the priest."

And the awe-stricken villagers crowded round the cottage fire, afraid to open the door. But the priest said that if they did not open the door he would put his shoulder to it and force it open. Bryden went towards the door, saying he would allow no one to threaten him, priest or no priest, but Margaret caught his arm and told him that if he said anything to the priest, the priest would speak against them from the altar, and they would be shunned by the neighbours. It was Mike Scully who went to the door and let the priest in, and he came in saying they were dancing their souls into hell.

"I've heard of your goings on," he said—"of your beer-drinking and dancing. I will not have it in my parish. If you want that sort of thing you had better go to America."

"If that is intended for me, sir, I will go back tomorrow. Margaret can follow."

"It isn't the dancing, it's the drinking I'm opposed to," said the priest, turning to Bryden.

"Well, no one has drunk too much, sir," said Bryden.

"But you'll sit here drinking all night," and the priest's eyes went towards the corner where the women had gathered, and Bryden felt that
the priest looked on the women as more dangerous than the porter.

"It's after midnight," he said, taking out his watch.

By Bryden's watch it was only half-past eleven, and while they were
arguing about the time Mrs. Scully offered Bryden's umbrella to the
priest, for in his hurry to stop the dancing the priest had gone out
without his; and, as if to show Bryden that he bore him no ill-will, the
priest accepted the loan of the umbrella, for he was thinking of the big
marriage fee that Bryden would pay him.

"I shall be badly off for the umbrella to-morrow," Bryden said, as soon
as the priest was out of the house. He was going with his father-in-law
to a fair. His father-in-law was learning him how to buy and sell cattle.
And his father-in-law was saying that the country was mending, and that
a man might become rich in Ireland if he only had a little capital. Bryden
had the capital, and Margaret had an uncle on the other side of the lake
who would leave her all he had, that would be fifty pounds, and never in
the village of Duncannon had a young couple begun life with so much
prospect of success as would James Bryden and Margaret Dirken.

Some time after Christmas was spoken of as the best time for the
marriage; James Bryden said that he would not be able to get his money out
of America before the spring. The delay seemed to vex him, and he seemed
anxious to be married, until one day he received a letter from America,
from a man who had served in the bar with him. This friend wrote to ask
Bryden if he were coming back. The letter was no more than a passing
wish to see Bryden again. Yet Bryden stood looking at it, and everyone
wondered what could be in the letter. It seemed momentous, and they
hardly believed him when he said it was from a friend who wanted to
know if his health were better. He tried to forget the letter, and he looked
at the worn fields, divided by walls of loose stones, and a great longing
came upon him.

The smell of the Bowery slum had come across the Atlantic, and had
found him out in this western headland; and one night he awoke from
a dream in which he was hurling some drunken customer through the
open doors into the darkness. He had seen his friend in his white duck
jacket throwing drink from glass into glass amid the din of voices and
strange accents; he had heard the clang of money as it was swept into
the till, and his sense sickened for the bar-room. But how should he tell
Margaret Dirken that he could not marry her? She had built her life
upon this marriage. He could not tell her that he would not marry her . . .
yet he must go. He felt as if he were being hunted; the thought that he
must tell Margaret that he could not marry her hunted him day after
day as a weasel hunts a rabbit. Again and again he went to meet her with

the intention of telling her that he did not love her, that their lives were not for one another, that it had all been a mistake, and that happily he had found out it was a mistake soon enough. But Margaret, as if she guessed what he was about to speak of, threw her arms about him and begged him to say he loved her, and that they would be married at once. He agreed that he loved her, and that they would be married at once. But he had not left her many minutes before the feeling came upon him that he could not marry her—that he must go away. The smell of the bar-room hunted him down. Was it for the sake of the money that he might make there that he wished to go back? No, it was not the money. What then? His eyes fell on the bleak country, on the little fields divided by bleak walls; he remembered the pathetic ignorance of the people, and it was these things he could not endure. It was the priest who came to forbid the dancing. Yes, it was the priest. As he stood looking at the line of the hills the bar-room seemed by him. He heard the politicians, and the excitement of politics was in his blood again. He must go away from this place—he must get back to the bar-room. Looking up he saw the scanty orchard, and he hated the spare road that led to the village, and he hated the little hill at the top of which the village began, and he hated more than all other places the house where he was to live with Margaret Dirken— if he married her. He could see it from where he stood—by the edge of the lake, with twenty acres of pasture land about it, for the landlord had given up part of his demesne land to them.

He caught sight of Margaret, and he called to her to come through the stile.

"I have just had a letter from America."

"About the money?" she said.

"Yes, about the money. But I shall have to go over there."

He stood looking at her, seeking for words; and she guessed from his embarrassment that he would say to her that he must go to America before they were married.

"Do you mean, James, you will have to go at once?"

"Yes," he said, "at once. But I shall come back in time to be married in August. It will only mean delaying our marriage a month."

They walked on a little way talking; every step he took James felt that he was a step nearer the Bowery slum. And when they came to the gate Bryden said:—

"I must hasten or I shall miss the train."

"But," she said, "you are not going now—you are not going to-day?"

"Yes, this morning. It is seven miles. I shall have to hurry not to miss the train."

And then she asked him if he would ever come back.

"Yes," he said, "I am coming back."

"If you are coming back, James, why not let me go with you?"

"You could not walk fast enough. We should miss the train."

"One moment, James. Don't make me suffer; tell me the truth. You are not coming back. Your clothes—where shall I send them?"

He hurried away, hoping he would come back. He tried to think that he liked the country he was leaving, that it would be better to have a farmhouse and live there with Margaret Dirken than to serve drinks behind a counter in the Bowery. He did not think he was telling her a lie when he said he was coming back. Her offer to forward his clothes touched his heart, and at the end of the road he stood and asked himself if he should go back to her. He would miss the train if he waited another minute, and he ran on. And he would have missed the train if he had not met a car. Once he was on the car he felt himself safe—the country was already behind him. The train and the boat at Cork were mere formulae; he was already in America.

The moment he landed he felt the thrill of home that he had not found in his native village, and he wondered how it was that the smell of the bar seemed more natural than the smell of the fields, and the roar of crowds more welcome than the silence of the lake's edge. However, he offered up a thanksgiving for his escape, and entered into negotiations for the purchase of the bar-room.

He took a wife, she bore him sons and daughters, the bar-room prospered, property came and went; he grew old, his wife died, he retired from business, and reached the age when a man begins to feel there are not many years in front of him, and that all he has had to do in life has been done. His children married, lonesomeness began to creep about him; in the evening, when he looked into the fire-light, a vague, tender reverie floated up, and Margaret's soft eyes and name vivified the dusk. His wife and children passed out of mind, and it seemed to him that a memory was the only real thing he possessed, and the desire to see Margaret again grew intense. But she was an old woman, she had married, maybe she was dead. Well, he would like to be buried in the village where he was born.

There is an unchanging, silent life within every man that none knows but himself, and his unchanging, silent life was his memory of Margaret Dirken. The bar-room was forgotten and all that concerned it, and the things he saw most clearly were the green hillside, and the bog lake and the rushes about it, and the greater lake in the distance, and behind it the blue lines of wandering hills.

Arnold Bennett (1867–1931) was born in Hanley, in the center of England's Staffordshire pottery industry. A thoroughly professional author, Bennett turned his talents to journalism and the theater as well as to novels and short stories. He is best known for his novels Clayhanger (1910) and The Old Wives' Tale (1908). For further reading: Tales of the Five Towns (1905).

The Sisters Qita

ARNOLD BENNETT

The manuscript ran thus:

W hen I had finished my daily personal examination of the ropes and trapezes, I hesitated a moment, and then climbed up again, to the roof, where the red and the blue long ropes were fastened. I took my sharp scissors from my chatelaine, and gently fretted the blue rope with one blade of the scissors until only a single strand was left intact. I gazed down at the vast floor a hundred feet below. The afternoon varieties were over, and a phrenologist was talking to a small crowd of gapers in a corner. The rest of the floor was pretty empty save for the chairs and the fancy stalls, and the fatigued stall-girls in their black dresses. I too, had once almost been a stall-girl at the Aquarium! I descended. Few observed me in my severe street dress. Our secretary, Charles, attended me on the stage.

"Everything right, Miss Paquita?" he said, handing me my hat and gloves, which I had given him to hold.

I nodded. I could see that he thought I was in one of my stern, far-away moods.

"Miss Mariquita is waiting for you in the carriage," he said.

We drove away in silence—I with my inborn melancholy too sad, Sally (Mariquita) too happy to speak. This daily afternoon drive was really part of our "turn"! A team of four mules driven by a negro will make a sensation even in Regent Street. All London looked at us, and contrasted our impassive beauty—Mine mature (too mature!) and dark, Sally's so blonde and youthful, our simple costumes, and the fact that we stayed at an exclusive Mayfair hotel, with the stupendous flourish of

our turnout. The renowned Sisters Qita—Paquita and Mariquita Qita—
and the renowned mules of the Sisters Qita! Two hundred pounds a week
at the Aquarium! Twenty-five thousand francs for one month at the
Casino de Paris! Twelve thousand five hundred dollars for a tour of fifty
performances in the States! Fifteen hundred pesos a night and a special
train *de luxe* in Argentina and Brazil! I could see the loungers and the
drivers talking and pointing as usual. The gilded loungers in Verrey's
café got up and watched us through the windows as we passed. This
was fame. For nearly twenty years I had been intimate with fame, and with
the envy of women and the foolish homage of men.

We saw dozens of omnibuses bearing the legend "Qita." Then we met
one which said: "Empire Theatre. Valdès, the matchless juggler," and Sally
smiled with pleasure.

"He's coming to see our turn to-night, after his," she remarked, blushing.

"Valdès? Why?" I asked, without turning my head.

"He wants us to sup with him, to celebrate our engagement."

"When do you mean to get married?" I asked her shortly. I felt quite
calm.

"I guess you're a Tartar to-day," said the pretty thing, with a touch of
her American sauciness. "We haven't studied it out yet. It was only
yesterday afternoon he kissed me for the first time." Then she bent
towards me with her characteristic plaintive, wistful appeal. "Say! You
aren't vexed, Selina, are you, because of this? Of course, he wants me
to tour with him after we're married, and do a double act. He's got lots of
dandy ideas for a double act. But I won't, I won't, Selina, unless you say
the word. Now, don't you go and be cross, Selina."

I let myself expand generously.

"My darling girl!" I said, glancing at her kindly. "You ought to know
me better. Of course I'm not cross. And of course you must tour with
Valdès. I shall be all right. How do you suppose I managed before I invented you?" I smiled like an indulgent mother.

"Oh! I didn't mean that," she said. "I know you're frightfully clever. I'm
nothing——"

"I hope you'll be awfully happy," I whispered, squeezing her hand.
"And don't forget that I introduced him to you—I knew him years before
you did. I'm the cause of this bliss—— Do you remember that cold morning
in Berlin?"

"Oh! well, I should say!" she exclaimed in ecstasy.

When we reached our rooms in the hotel I kissed her warmly. Women do
that sort of thing.

Then a card was brought to me. "George Capey," it said; and in pencil,
"Of the Five Towns."

I shrugged my shoulders. Sally had gone to scribble a note to her Valdès.

"Show Mr. Capey in," I said, and a natty young man entered, half nervousness, half audacity.

"How did you know I came from the Five Towns?" I questioned him.

"I am on the *Evening Mail*," he said, "where they know everything, madam."

I was annoyed. "Then they know, on the *Evening Mail* that Paquita Qita has never been interviewed, and never will be," I said.

"Besides," he went on, "I come from the Five Towns myself."

"Bursley?" I asked mechanically.

"Bursley," he ejaculated; then added, "you haven't been near old Bosley since——"

It was true.

"No," I said hastily. "It is many years since I have been in England, even. Do they know down there who Qita is?"

"Not they!" he replied.

I grew reflective. Stars such as I have no place of origin. We shoot up out of a void, and sink back into a void. I had forgotten Bursley and Bursley folk. Recollections rushed in upon me. . . . I felt beautifully sad. I drew off my gloves, and flung my hat on a chair with a movement that would have bewitched a man of the world, but Mr. George Capey was unimpressed. I laughed.

"What's the joke?" he inquired. I adored him for his Bursliness.

"I was just thinking of fat Mrs. Cartledge, who used to keep that fishmonger's shop in Oldcastle Street, opposite Bates's. I wonder if she's still there?"

"She is," he said. "And fatter than ever! She's getting on in years now."

I broke the rule of a lifetime, and let him interview me.

"Tell them I'm thirty-seven," I said. "Yes, I mean it. Tell them."

And then for another tit-bit I explained to him how I had discovered Sally at Koster and Bial's, in New York, five years ago, and made her my sister for stage purposes because I was lonely, and liked her American simplicity and twang. He departed full of tea and satisfaction.

It was our last night at the Aquarium. The place was crammed. The houses where I performed were always crammed. Our turn was in three parts, and lasted half an hour. The first part was a skirt dance in full afternoon dress (*danse de modernité*, I called it); the second was a double horizontal bar act; the third was the famous act of the red and blue ropes, in full evening dress. It was 10:45 when we climbed the silk ladders for the third part. High up in the roof, separated from each other by nearly the length of the great hall, Sally and I stood on two little platforms. I held the ends of the red and the blue ropes. I had to let the blue rope swing across the hall to her. She would seize it, and clutching it, sweep like the ball of an enormous pendulum from her platform to mine. (But would she?) I should then swing on the red rope to the platform she had left.

Then the band would stop for the thrilling moment, and the lights would be lowered. Each lighting and holding a powerful electric hand-light—one red, one blue—we should signal the drummer and plunge simultaneously into space, flash past each other in mid-flight, exchanging lights as we passed (this was the trick), and soar to opposite platforms again, amid frenzied applause. There were no nets.

That was what ought to occur.

I stood bowing to the floor of tiny upturned heads, and jerking the ropes a little. Then I let Sally's rope go with a push, and it dropped away from me, and in a few seconds she had it safe in her strong hand. She was taller than me, with a fuller figure, yet she looked quite small on her distant platform. All the evening I had been thinking of fat old Mrs. Cartledge messing and slopping among cod and halibut on white tiles. I could not get Bursley and my silly infancy out of my head. I followed my feverish career from the age of fifteen, when that strange Something in me, which makes an artist, had first driven me forth to conquer two continents. I thought of all the golden loves I had scorned, and my own love, which had been ignored, unnoticed, but which still obstinately burned. I glanced downwards and descried Valdès precisely where Sally had said he would be. Valdès, what a fool you were! And I hated a fool. I am one of those who can love and hate, who can love and despise, who can love and loathe the same object in the same moment. Then I signalled to Sally to plunge, and my eyes filled with tears. For, you see, somehow, in some senseless sentimental way, the thought of fat Mrs. Cartledge and my silly infancy had forced me to send Sally the red rope, not the blue one. We exchanged ropes on alternate nights, but this was her night for the blue one.

She swung over, alighting accurately at my side with that exquisite outward curve of the spine which had originally attracted me to her.

"You sent me the red one," she said to me, after she had acknowledged the applause.

"Yes," I said. "Never mind; stick to it now you've got it. Here's the red light. Have you seen Valdès?"

She nodded.

I took the blue light and clutched the blue rope. Instead of murder—suicide, since it must be one or the other. And why not? Indeed, I censured myself in that second for having meant to kill Sally. Not because I was ashamed of the sin, but because the revenge would have been so pitiful and weak. If Valdès the matchless was capable of passing me over and kneeling to the pretty thing——

I stood ready. The world was to lose that fineness, that distinction, that originality, that disturbing subtlety, which constituted Paquita Qita. I plunged.

. . . I was on the other platform. The rope had held, then. I remembered nothing of the flight except that I had passed near the upturned, pleasant face of Valdès.

The band stopped. The lights of the hall were lowered. All was dark. I switched on my dazzling blue light; Sally switched on her red one. I stood ready. The rope could not possibly endure a second strain. I waved to Sally and signalled to the conductor. The world was to lose Paquita. The drum began its formidable roll. Whirrr! I plunged, and saw the red star rushing towards me. I snatched it and soared upwards. The blue rope seemed to tremble. As I came near the platform at decreasing speed, it seemed to stretch like elastic. It broke! The platform jumped up suddenly over my head, but I caught at the silk ladder. I was saved! There was a fearful silence, and then the appalling shock of hysterical applause from seven thousand throats. I slid down the ladder, ran across the stage into my dressing-room for a cloak, out again into the street. In two days I was in Buda-Pesth.

Rudyard Kipling (1865–1936) was born in Bombay, India, and educated in England. After working as a journalist in India, he returned to England to begin his meteoric rise to fame as a poet, novelist, and short-story writer. He was awarded the Nobel Prize for literature in 1907. For further reading: Plain Tales from the Hills (1888), Life's Handicap (1891), Under the Deodars (1899).

The Story of Muhammad Din

RUDYARD KIPLING

> Who is the happy man? He that sees in his own house at home, little children crowned with dust, leaping and falling and crying.
> Munichandra, translated by Professor Peterson

The polo-ball was an old one, scarred, chipped, and dinted. It stood on the mantelpiece among the pipe-stems which Imam Din, *khitmatgar*, was cleaning for me.

"Does the Heaven-born want this ball?" said Imam Din, deferentially.

The Heaven-born set no particular store by it; but of what use was a polo-ball to a *khitmatgar*?

"By your Honor's favor, I have a little son. He has seen this ball, and desires it to play with. I do not want it for myself."

No one would for an instant accuse portly old Imam Din of wanting to play with polo-balls. He carried out the battered thing into the veranda; and there followed a hurricane of joyful squeaks, a patter of small feet, and the *thud-thud-thud* of the ball rolling along the ground. Evidently the little son had been waiting outside the door to secure his treasure. But how had he managed to see that polo-ball?

Next day, coming back from office half an hour earlier than usual, I was aware of a small figure in the dining-room—a tiny, plump figure in a ridiculously inadequate shirt which came, perhaps, half-way down the tubby stomach. It wandered round the room, thumb in mouth, crooning to itself as it took stock of the pictures. Undoubtedly this was the "little son."

73

He had no business in my room, of course; but was so deeply absorbed in his discoveries that he never noticed me in the doorway. I stepped into the room and startled him nearly into a fit. He sat down on the ground with a gasp. His eyes opened, and his mouth followed suit. I knew what was coming, and fled, followed by a long, dry howl which reached the servants' quarters far more quickly than any command of mine had ever done. In ten seconds Imam Din was in the dining-room. Then despairing sobs arose, and I returned to find Imam Din admonishing the small sinner who was using most of his shirt as a handkerchief.

"This boy," said Imam Din, judicially, "is a *budmash*—a big *budmash*. He will, without doubt, go to the *jail-khana* for his behavior." Renewed yells from the penitent, and an elaborate apology to myself from Imam Din.

"Tell the baby," said I, "that the *Sahib* is not angry, and take him away." Imam Din conveyed my forgiveness to the offender, who had now gathered all his shirt round his neck, stringwise, and the yell subsided into a sob. The two set off for the door. "His name," said Imam Din, as though the name were part of the crime, "is Muhammad Din, and he is a *budmash*." Freed from present danger, Muhammad Din turned round in his father's arms, and said gravely, "It is true that my name is Muhammad Din, *Tahib*, but I am not a *budmash*. I am a *man*!"

From that day dated my acquaintance with Muhammad Din. Never again did he come into my dining-room, but on the neutral ground of the garden, we greeted each other with much state, though our conversation was confined to "*Talaam, Tahib*" from his side, and "*Salaam, Muhammad Din*" from mine. Daily on my return from office, the little white shirt, and the fat little body used to rise from the shade of the creeper-covered trellis where they had been hid; and daily I checked my horse here, that my salutation might not be slurred over or given unseemly.

Muhammad Din never had any companions. He used to trot about the compound, in and out of the castor-oil bushes, on mysterious errands of his own. One day I stumbled upon some of his handiwork far down the grounds. He had half buried the polo-ball in dust, and stuck six shriveled old marigold flowers in a circle round it. Outside that circle again was a rude square, traced out in bits of red brick alternating with fragments of broken china; the whole bounded by a little bank of dust. The water-man from the well-curb put in a plea for the small architect, saying that it was only the play of a baby and did not much disfigure my garden.

Heaven knows that I had no intention of touching the child's work then or later; but, that evening, a stroll through the garden brought me unawares full on it; so that I trampled, before I knew, marigold-heads, dust-bank, and fragments of broken soap-dish into confusion past all hope of mending. Next morning, I came upon Muhammad Din crying softly to himself over the ruin I had wrought. Some one had cruelly told him that the *Sahib* was very angry with him for spoiling the garden, and had scattered his rubbish, using bad language the while. Muhammad Din labored for an hour at effacing every trace of the dust-bank and pottery fragments, and it was with a tearful and apologetic face that he said *"Talaam, Tahib,"* when I came home from office. A hasty inquiry resulted in Imam Din informing Muhammad Din that, by my singular favor, he was permitted to disport himself as he pleased. Whereat the child took heart and fell to tracing the ground-plan of an edifice which was to eclipse the marigold-polo-ball creation.

For some months, the chubby little eccentricity revolved in his humble orbit among the castor-oil bushes and in the dust; always fashioning magnificent palaces from the stale flowers thrown away by the bearer, smooth water-worn pebbles, bits of broken glass, and feathers pulled, I fancy, from my fowls—always alone, and always crooning to himself.

A gaily-spotted sea-shell was dropped one day close to the last of his little buildings; and I looked that Muhammad Din should build something more than ordinarily splendid on the strength of it. Nor was I disappointed. He meditated for the better part of an hour, and his crooning rose to a jubilant song. Then he began tracing in the dust. It would certainly be a wondrous palace, this one, for it was two yards long and a yard broad in ground-plan. But the palace was never completed.

Next day there was no Muhammad Din at the head of the carriage-drive, and no *"Talaam, Tahib"* to welcome my return. I had grown accustomed to the greeting, and its omission troubled me. Next day Imam told me that the child was suffering slightly from fever and needed quinine. He got the medicine, and an English Doctor.

"They have no stamina, these brats," said the Doctor, and he left Imam Din's quarters.

A week later, though I would have given much to have avoided it, I met on the road to the Mussulman burying-ground Imam Din, accompanied by one other friend, carrying in his arms, wrapped in a white cloth, all that was left of little Muhammad Din.

Herbert George Wells (1866–1946) was born in
Bromley and educated at the Royal College of Science, South Kensington. Wells became a teacher,
but soon turned to the writing of fiction. His
novels often make use of his training and interest
in science—for example, The Time Machine and
The War of the Worlds. His stories tend toward
the fantastic and the extreme and are often laid
centuries in the future. For further reading: Short
Stories of H. G. Wells (1927).

The Lord of the Dynamos

H. G. WELLS

The chief attendant of the three dynamos that buzzed and rattled at
Camberwell, and kept the electric railway going, came out of Yorkshire,
and his name was James Holroyd. He was a practical electrician, but
fond of whiskey, a heavy red-haired brute with irregular teeth. He doubted
the existence of the deity, but accepted Carnot's cycle, and he had read
Shakespeare and found him weak in chemistry. His helper came out
of the mysterious East, and his name was Azuma-zi. But Holroyd called
him Pooh-bah. Holroyd liked a nigger help because he could stand kicking—a habit with Holroyd—and did not pry into the machinery and try
to learn the ways of it. Certain odd possibilities of the negro mind brought
into abrupt contact with the crown of our civilisation Holroyd never fully
realised, though just at the end he got some inkling of them.

To define Azuma-zi was beyond ethnology. He was, perhaps, more ne-
groid than anything else, though his hair was curly rather than frizzy,
and his nose had a bridge. Moreover, his skin was brown rather than black,
and the whites of his eyes were yellow. His broad cheek-bones and narrow
chin gave his face something of the viperine V. His head, too, was broad
behind, and low and narrow at the forehead, as if his brain had been
twisted round in the reverse way to a European's. He was short of stature
and still shorter of English. In conversation he made numerous odd noises
of no known marketable value, and his infrequent words were carved and
wrought into heraldic grotesqueness. Holroyd tried to elucidate his religious beliefs, and—especially after whiskey—lectured to him against

superstition and missionaries. Azuma-zi, however, shirked the discussion of his gods, even though he was kicked for it.

Azuma-zi had come, clad in white but insufficient raiment, out of the stoke-hole of the *Lord Clive*, from the Straits Settlements, and beyond, into London. He had heard even in his youth of the greatness and riches of London, where all the women are white and fair, and even the beggars in the streets are white; and he had arrived, with newly earned gold coins in his pocket, to worship at the shrine of civilisation. The day of his landing was a dismal one; the sky was dun, and a wind-worried drizzle filtered down to the greasy streets, but he plunged boldly into the delights of Shadwell, and was presently cast up, shattered in health, civilised in costume, penniless, and, except in matters of the direst necessity, practically a dumb animal, to toil for James Holroyd and to be bullied by him in the dynamo shed at Camberwell. And to James Holroyd bullying was a labour of love.

There were three dynamos with their engines at Camberwell. The two that have been there since the beginning are small machines; the larger one was new. The smaller machines made a reasonable noise; their straps hummed over the drums, every now and then the brushes buzzed and fizzled, and the air churned steadily, whoo! whoo! whoo! between their poles. One was loose in its foundations and kept the shed vibrating. But the big dynamo drowned these little noises altogether with the sustained drone of its iron core, which somehow set part of the iron-work humming. The place made the visitor's head reel with the throb, throb, throb of the engines, the rotation of the big wheels, the spinning ball valves, the occasional spittings of the steam, and over all the deep, unceasing, surging note of the big dynamo. This last noise was from an engineering point of view a defect; but Azuma-zi accounted it unto the monster for mightiness and pride.

If it were possible we would have the noises of that shed always about the reader as he reads, we would tell all our story to such an accompaniment. It was a steady stream of din, from which the ear picked out first one threat and then another; there was the intermittent snorting, panting, and seething of the steam-engines, the suck and thud of their pistons, the dull beat on the air as the spokes of the great driving-wheels came round, a note the leather straps made as they ran tighter and looser, and a fretful tumult from the dynamos; and, over all, sometimes inaudible, as the ear tired of it, and then creeping back upon the senses again, was this trombone note of the big machine. The floor never felt steady and quiet beneath one's feet, but quivered and jarred. It was a confusing, unsteady place, and enough to send any one's thoughts jerking into odd zigzags. And for three months, while the big strike of the engineers was in progress, Holroyd, who was a blackleg, and Azuma-zi, who was a mere black, were never out of the stir and eddy of it, but slept and fed in the little wooden shanty between the shed and the gates.

Holroyd delivered a theological lecture on the text of his big machine soon after Azuma-zi came. He had to shout to be heard in the din. "Look at that," said Holroyd; "where's your 'eathen idol to match 'im?" And Azuma-zi looked. For a moment Holroyd was inaudible, and then Azuma-zi heard: "Kill a hundred men. Twelve per cent on the ordinary shares," said Holroyd, "and that's something like a Gord!"

Holroyd was proud of his big dynamo, and expatiated upon its size and power to Azuma-zi until heaven knows what odd currents of thought that, and the incessant whirling and shindy, set up within the curly, black cranium. He would explain in the most graphic manner the dozen or so ways in which a man might be killed by it, and once he gave Azuma-zi a shock as a sample of its quality. After that, in the breathing-times of his labour—it was heavy labour, being not only his own but most of Holroyd's—Azuma-zi would sit and watch the big machine. Now and then the brushes would sparkle and spit blue flashes, at which Holroyd would swear, but all the rest was as smooth and rhythmic as breathing. The band ran shouting over the shaft, and ever behind one as one watched was the complacent thud of the piston. So it lived all day in this big airy shed, with him and Holroyd to wait upon it; not prisoned up and slaving to drive a ship as the other engines he knew—mere captive devils of the British Solomon—had been, but a machine en-throned. Those two smaller dynamos, Azuma-zi by force of contrast despised; the large one he privately christened the Lord of the Dynamos. They were fretful and irregular, but the big dynamo was steady. How great it was! How serene and easy in its working! Greater and calmer even than the Buddahs he had seen at Rangoon, and yet not motionless, but living! The great block coils spun, spun, spun, the rings ran round under the brushes, and the deep note of its coil steadied the whole. It affected Azuma-zi queerly.

Azuma-zi was not fond of labour. He would sit about and watch the Lord of the Dynamos while Holroyd went away to persuade the yard porter to get whiskey, although his proper place was not in the dynamo shed but behind the engines, and, moreover, if Holroyd caught him skulking he got hit for it with a rod of stout copper wire. He would go and stand close to the colossus and look up at the great leather band running overhead. There was a black patch on the band that came round, and it pleased him somehow among all the clatter to watch this return again and again. Odd thoughts spun with the whirl of it. Scientific people tell us that savages give souls to rocks and trees—and a machine is a thousand times more alive than a rock or a tree. And Azuma-zi was practically a savage still; the veneer of civilisation lay no deeper than his slop suit, his bruises and the coal grime on his face and hands. His father before him had worshipped a meteoric stone, kindred blood, it may be, had splashed the broad wheels of Juggernaut.

He took every opportunity Holroyd gave him of touching and handling the great dynamo that was fascinating him. He polished and cleaned it until the metal parts were blinding in the sun. He felt a mysterious sense of service in doing this. He would go up to it and touch its spinning coils gently. The gods he had worshipped were all far away. The people in London hid their gods.

At last his dim feelings grew more distinct, and took shape in thoughts and acts. When he came into the roaring shed one morning he salaamed to the Lord of the Dynamos; and then, when Holroyd was away, he went and whispered to the thundering machine that he was its servant, and prayed it to have pity on him and save him from Holroyd. As he did so a rare gleam of light came in through the open archway of the throbbing machine-shed, and the Lord of the Dynamos, as he whirled and roared, was radiant with pale gold. Then Azuma-zi knew that his service was acceptable to his Lord. After that he did not feel so lonely as he had done, and he had indeed been very much alone in London. And even when his work time was over, which was rare, he loitered about the shed.

Then, the next time Holroyd maltreated him, Azuma-zi went presently to the Lord of the Dynamos and whispered, "Thou seest, O my Lord!" and the angry whirr of the machinery seemed to answer him. Thereafter it appeared to him that whenever Holroyd came into the shed a different note came into the sounds of the great dynamo. "My Lord bides his time," said Azuma-zi to himself. "The iniquity of the fool is not yet ripe." And he waited and watched for the day of reckoning. One day there was evidence of short circuiting, and Holroyd, making an unwary examina-tion—it was in the afternoon—got a rather severe shock. Azuma-zi from behind the engine saw him jump off and curse at the peccant coil.

"He is warned," said Azuma-zi to himself. "Surely my Lord is very patient."

Holroyd had at first initiated his "nigger" into such elementary con-ceptions of the dynamo's working as would enable him to take temporary charge of the shed in his absence. But when he noticed the manner in which Azuma-zi hung about the monster, he became suspicious. He dimly per-ceived his assistant was "up to something," and connecting him with the anointing of the coils with oil that had rotted the varnish in one place, he issued an edict, shouted above the confusion of the machinery, "Don't 'ee go nigh that big dynamo any more, Pooh-bah, or a'll take thy skin off!" Besides, if it pleased Azuma-zi to be near the big machine, it was plain sense and decency to keep him away from it.

Azuma-zi obeyed at the time, but later he was caught bowing before the Lord of the Dynamos. At which Holroyd twisted his arm and kicked him as he turned to go away. As Azuma-zi presently stood behind the engine and glared at the back of the hated Holroyd, the noises of the machinery took a new rhythm, and sounded like four words in his native tongue.

It is hard to say exactly what madness is. I fancy Azuma-zi was mad. The incessant din and whirl of the dynamo shed may have churned up his little store of knowledge and big store of superstitious fancy, at last, into something akin to frenzy. At any rate, when the idea of making Holroyd a sacrifice to the Dynamo Fetich was thus suggested to him, it filled him with a strange tumult of exultant emotion.

That night the two men and their black shadows were alone in the shed together. The shed was lit with one big arc light that winked and flickered purple. The shadows lay black behind the dynamos, the ball governors of the engines whirled from light to darkness, and their pistons beat loud and steady. The world outside seen through the open end of the shed seemed incredibly dim and remote. It seem absolutely silent, too, since the riot of the machinery drowned every external sound. Far away was the black fence of the yard with grey, shadowy houses behind, and above was the deep blue sky and the pale little stars. Azuma-zi suddenly walked across the centre of the shed above which the leather bands were running, and went into the shadow by the big dynamo. Holroyd heard a click, and the spin of the armature changed.

"What are you dewin' with that switch?" he bawled in surprise. "Ha'n't I told you—"

Then he saw the set expression of Azuma-zi's eyes as the Asiatic came out of the shadow towards him.

In another moment the two men were grappling fiercely in front of the great dynamo.

"You coffee-headed fool!" gasped Holroyd, with a brown hand at his throat. "Keep off those contact rings." In another moment he was tripped and reeling back upon the Lord of the Dynamos. He instinctively loosened his grip upon his antagonist to save himself from the machine.

The messenger, sent in furious haste from the station to find out what had happened in the dynamo shed, met Azuma-zi at the porter's lodge by the gate. Azuma-zi tried to explain something, but the messenger could make nothing of the black's incoherent English, and hurried on to the shed. The machines were all noisily at work, and nothing seemed to be disarranged. There was, however, a queer smell of singed hair. Then he saw an odd-looking, crumpled mass clinging to the front of the big dynamo, and, approaching, recognised the distorted remains of Holroyd.

The man stared and hesitated a moment. Then he saw the face and shut his eyes convulsively. He turned on his heel before he opened them, so that he should not see Holroyd again, and went out of the shed to get advice and help.

When Azuma-zi saw Holroyd die in the grip of the Great Dynamo he had been a little scared about the consequences of his act. Yet he felt strangely elated, and knew that the favour of the Lord Dynamo was upon him. His plan was already settled when he met the man coming from the station, and the scientific manager who speedily arrived on the scene jumped at the obvious conclusion of suicide. This expert scarcely noticed Azuma-zi except to ask a few questions. Did he see Holroyd kill himself? Azuma-zi explained he had been out of sight at the engine furnace until he heard a difference in the noise from the dynamo. It was not a difficult examination, being untinctured by suspicion.

The distorted remains of Holroyd, which the electrician removed from the machine, were hastily covered by the porter with a coffee-stained tablecloth. Somebody, by a happy inspiration, fetched a medical man. The expert was chiefly anxious to get the machine at work again, for seven or eight trains had stopped midway in the stuffy tunnels of the electric railway. Azuma-zi, answering or misunderstanding the questions of the people who had by authority or impudence come into the shed, was presently sent back to the stoke-hole by the scientific manager. Of course a crowd collected outside the gates of the yard,—a crowd, for no known reason, always hovers for a day or two near the scene of a sudden death in London; two or three reporters percolated somehow into the engine-shed, and one even got to Azuma-zi; but the scientific expert cleared them out again, being himself an amateur journalist.

Presently the body was carried away, and public interest departed with it. Azuma-zi remained very quiety at his furnace, seeing over and over again in the coals a figure that wriggled violently and became still. An hour after the murder, to any one coming into the shed it would have looked exactly as if nothing remarkable had ever happened there. Peeping presently from his engine-room the black saw the Lord Dynamo spin and whirl beside his little brothers, the driving wheels were beating round, and the steam in the pistons went thud, thud, exactly as it had been earlier in the evening. After all, from the mechanical point of view, it had been a most insignificant incident—the mere temporary deflection of a current. But now the slender form and slender shadow of the scientific manager replaced the sturdy outline of Holroyd travelling up and down the lane of light upon the vibrating floor under the straps between the engines and the dynamos.

"Have I not served my Lord?" said Azuma-zi, inaudibly, from his shadow, and the note of the great dynamo rang out full and clear. As he looked at the big, whirling mechanism the strange fascination of it that had been a little in abeyance since Holroyd's death resumed its sway.

Never had Azuma-zi seen a man killed so swiftly and pitilessly. The big, humming machine had slain its victim without wavering for a second from it steady beating. It was indeed a mighty god.

The unconscious scientific manager stood with his back to him, scribbling on a piece of paper. His shadow lay at the foot of the monster.

"Was the Lord Dynamo still hungry? His servant was ready."

Azuma-zi made a stealthy step forward, then stopped. The scientific manager suddenly stopped writing, and walked down the shed to the end-most of the dynamos, and began to examine the brushes.

Azuma-zi hesitated, and then slipped across noiselessly into the shadow by the switch. There he waited. Presently the manager's footsteps could be heard returning. He stopped in his old position, unconscious of the stoker crouching ten feet away from him. Then the big dynamo suddenly fizzled, and in another moment Azuma-zi had sprung out of the darkness upon him.

First, the scientific manager was gripped round the body and swung towards the big dynamo, then, kicking with his knee and forcing his antagonist's head down with his hands, he loosened the grip on his waist and swung round away from the machine. Then the black grasped him again, putting a curly head against his chest, and they swayed and panted as it seemed for an age or so. Then the scientific manager was impelled to catch a black ear in his teeth and bite furiously. The black yelled hideously.

They rolled over on the floor, and the black, who had apparently slipped from the vice of the teeth or parted with some ear—the scientific manager wondered which at the time—tried to throttle him. The scientific manager was making some ineffectual efforts to claw something with his hands and to kick, when the welcome sound of quick footsteps sounded on the floor. The next moment Azuma-zi had left him and darted towards the big dynamo. There was a splutter amid the roar.

The officer of the company, who had entered, stood staring as Azuma-zi caught the naked terminals in his hands, gave one horrible convulsion, and then hung motionless from the machine, his face violently distorted.

"I'm jolly glad you came in when you did," said the scientific manager, still sitting on the floor.

He looked at the still quivering figure. "It is not a nice death to die, apparently—but it is quick."

The official was still staring at the body. He was a man of slow apprehension.

There was a pause.

The scientific manager got up on his feet rather awkwardly. He ran his fingers along his collar thoughtfully, and moved his head to and fro several times.

"Poor Holroyd! I see now." Then almost mechanically he went towards the switch in the shadow and turned the current into the railway circuit again. As he did so the singed body loosened its grip upon the machine and fell forward on its face. The cone of the dynamo roared out loud and clear, and the armature beat the air.

So ended prematurely the Worship of the Dynamo Deity, perhaps the most short-lived of all religions. Yet withal it could boast a Martyrdom and a Human Sacrifice.

Oscar Wilde (1854–1900) was born in Dublin and educated at Trinity College, Dublin, and at Magdalen College, Oxford. A versatile genius, he wrote poems, fairy tales, plays, a novel (The Picture of Dorian Gray), and a number of short stories. His private life was London scandal; after a celebrated trial (1895) he was committed to prison for two years. For further reading: The Writings of Oscar Wilde (1931).

The Remarkable Rocket

OSCAR WILDE

The King's son was going to be married, so there were general rejoicings. He had waited a whole year for his bride, and at last she had arrived. She was a Russian Princess, and had driven all the way from Finland in a sledge drawn by six reindeer. The sledge was shaped like a great golden swan, and between the swan's wings lay the little Princess herself. Her long ermine cloak reached right down to her feet, on her head was a tiny cap of silver tissue, and she was as pale as the Snow Palace in which she had always lived. So pale was she that as she drove through the streets all the people wondered. "She is like a white rose!" they cried, and they threw down flowers on her from the balconies.

At the gate of the Castle the Prince was waiting to receive her. He had dreamy violet eyes, and his hair was like fine gold. When he saw her he sank upon one knee, and kissed her hand.

"Your picture was beautiful," he murmured, "but you are more beautiful than your picture;" and the little Princess blushed.

"She was like a white rose before," said a young page to his neighbour, "but she is like a red rose now;" and the whole Court was delighted.

For the next three days everybody went about saying "White rose, Red rose, Red rose, White rose," and the King gave orders that the Page's salary was to be doubled. As he received no salary at all this was not of much use to him, but it was considered a great honour and was duly published in the Court Gazette.

When the three days were over the marriage was celebrated. It was a magnificent ceremony, and the bride and bridegroom walked hand in hand under a canopy of purple velvet embroidered with little pearls. Then there was a State Banquet, which lasted for five hours. The Prince and Princess sat at the top of the Great Hall and drank out of a cup of clear crystal. Only true lovers could drink out of this cup, for if false lips touched it, it grew grey and dull and cloudy.

"It is quite clear that they love each other," said the little Page, "as clear as crystal!" and the King doubled his salary a second time.

"What an honour!" cried all the courtiers.

After the banquet there was to be a Ball. The bride and bridegroom were to dance the Rose-dance together, and the King had promised to play the flute. He played very badly, but no one had ever dared to tell him so, because he was the King. Indeed, he knew only two airs, and was never quite certain which one he was playing; but it made no matter, for, whatever he did, everybody cried out, "Charming! charming!"

The last item on the programme was a grand display of fireworks, to be let off exactly at midnight. The little Princess had never seen a firework in her life, so the King had given orders that the Royal Pyrotechnist should be in attendance on the day of her marriage.

"What are fireworks like?" she had asked the Prince, one morning, as she was walking on the terrace.

"They are like the Aurora Borealis," said the King, who always answered questions that were addressed to other people, "only much more natural. I prefer them to stars myself, as you always know when they are going to appear, and they are as delightful as my own flute-playing. You must certainly see them."

So at the end of the King's garden a great stand had been set up, and as soon as the Royal Pyrotechnist had put everything in its proper place, the fireworks began to talk to each other.

"The world is certainly very beautiful," cried a little Squib. "Just look at those yellow tulips. Why! if they were real crackers they could not be lovelier. I am very glad I have travelled. Travel improves the mind wonderfully, and does away with all one's prejudices."

"The King's garden is not the world, you foolish Squib," said a big Roman Candle; "the world is an enormous place, and it would take you three days to see it thoroughly."

"Any place you love is the world to you," exclaimed the pensive Catherine Wheel, who had been attached to an old deal box in early life, and prided herself on her broken heart; "but love is not fashionable any more, the poets have killed it. They wrote so much about it that nobody believed them, and I am not surprised. True love suffers, and is silent. I remember myself once—— But no matter now. Romance is a thing of the past."

"Nonsense!" said the Roman Candle, "Romance never dies. It is like the moon, and lives for ever. The bride and bridegroom, for instance, love each other very dearly. I heard all about them this morning from a brown-paper cartridge, who happened to be staying in the same drawer as myself, and he knew the latest Court news."

But the Catherine Wheel shook her head. "Romance is dead, Romance is dead, Romance is dead," she murmured. She was one of those people who think that, if you say the same thing over and over a great many times, it becomes true in the end.

Suddenly, a sharp, dry cough was heard, and they all looked round.

It came from a tall, supercilious-looking Rocket, who was tied to the end of a long stick. He always coughed before he made any observations, so as to attract attention.

"Ahem! ahem!" he said, and everybody listened except the poor Catherine Wheel, who was still shaking her head, and murmuring, "Romance is dead."

"Order! order!" cried out a Cracker. He was something of a politician, and had always taken a prominent part in the local elections, so he knew the proper Parliamentary expressions to use.

"Quite dead," whispered the Catherine Wheel, and she went off to sleep.

As soon as there was perfect silence, the Rocket coughed a third time and began. He spoke with a very slow, distinct voice, as if he were dictating his memoirs, and always looked over the shoulder of the person to whom he was talking. In fact, he had a most distinguished manner.

"How fortunate it is for the King's son," he remarked, "that he is to be married on the very day on which I am to be let off! Really, if it had not been arranged beforehand, it could not have turned out better for him; but Princes are always lucky."

"Dear me!" said the little Squib, "I thought it was quite the other way, and that we were to be let off in the Prince's honour."

"It may be so with you," he answered; "indeed, I have no doubt that it is, but with me it is different. I am a very remarkable Rocket, and come of remarkable parents. My mother was the most celebrated Catherine Wheel of her day, and was renowned for her graceful dancing. When she made her great public appearance she spun round nineteen times before she went out, and each time that she did so she threw into the air seven pink stars. She was three feet and a half in diameter, and made of the very best gunpowder. My father was a Rocket like myself, and of French extraction. He flew so high that the people were afraid that he would never come down again. He did, though, for he was of a kindly disposition, and he made a most brilliant descent in a shower of golden rain. The newspapers wrote about his performance in very flattering terms. Indeed, the Court Gazette called him a triumph of Pylotechnic art."

"Pyrotechnic, Pyrotechnic, you mean," said a Bengal Light; "I know it is Pyrotechnic, for I saw it written on my own canister."

"Well, I said Pylotechnic," answered the Rocket, in a severe tone of voice, and the Bengal Light felt so crushed that he began at once to bully the little squibs, in order to show that he was still a person of some importance.

"I was saying," continued the Rocket, "I was saying—— What was I saying?"

"You were talking about yourself," replied the Roman Candle.

"Of course; I knew I was discussing some interesting subject when I was so rudely interrupted. I hate rudeness and bad manners of every kind, for I am extremely sensitive. No one in the whole world is so sensitive as I am, I am quite sure of that."

"What is a sensitive person?" said the Cracker to the Roman Candle.

"A person who, because he has corns himself, always treads on other people's toes," answered the Roman Candle in a low whisper; and the Cracker nearly exploded with laughter.

"Pray, what are you laughing at?" inquired the Rocket; "I am not laughing."

"I am laughing because I am happy," replied the Cracker.

"That is a very selfish reason," said the Rocket angrily. "What right have you to be happy? You should be thinking about others. In fact, you should be thinking about me. I am always thinking about myself, and I expect everybody else to do the same. That is what is called sympathy. It is a beautiful virtue, and I possess it in a high degree. Suppose, for instance, anything happened to me to-night, what a misfortune that would be for every one! The Prince and Princess would never be happy again, their whole married life would be spoiled; and as for the King, I know he would not get over it. Really, when I begin to reflect on the importance of my position, I am almost moved to tears."

"If you want to give pleasure to others," cried the Roman Candle, "you had better keep yourself dry."

"Certainly," exclaimed the Bengal Light, who was now in better spirits; "that is only common sense."

"Common sense, indeed!" said the Rocket indignantly; "you forget that I am very uncommon, and very remarkable. Why, anybody can have common sense, provided that they have no imagination. But I have imagination, for I never think of things as they really are; I always think of them as being quite different. As for keeping myself dry, there is evidently no one here who can at all appreciate an emotional nature. Fortunately for myself, I don't care. The only thing that sustains one through life is the consciousness of the immense inferiority of everybody else, and this is a feeling I have always cultivated. But none of you have any hearts. Here you are laughing and making merry just as if the Prince and Princess had not just been married."

"Well, really," exclaimed a small Fire-balloon, "why not? It is a most joyful occasion, and when I soar up into the air I intend to tell the stars all about it. You will see them twinkle when I talk to them about the pretty bride."

"Ah, what a trivial view of life!" said the Rocket; "but it is only what I expected. There is nothing in you; you are hollow and empty. Why, perhaps the Prince and Princess may go to live in a country where there is a deep river, and perhaps they may have one only son, a little fair-haired boy with violet eyes like the Prince himself; and perhaps some day he may go out to walk with his nurse; and perhaps the nurse may go to sleep under a great elder-tree; and perhaps the little boy may fall into the deep river and be drowned. What a terrible misfortune! Poor people, to lose their only son! It is really too dreadful! I shall never get over it."

"But they have not lost their only son," said the Roman Candle; "no misfortune has happened to them at all."

"I never said that they had," replied the Rocket; "I said that they might. If they had lost their only son there would be no use in saying any more about the matter. I hate people who cry over spilt milk. But when I think that they might lose their only son, I certainly am very much affected."

"You certainly are!" cried the Bengal Light. "In fact, you are the most affected person I ever met."

"You are the rudest person I ever met," said the Rocket, "and you cannot understand my friendship for the Prince."

"Why, you don't even know him," growled the Roman Candle.

"I never said I knew him," answered the Rocket. "I dare say that if I knew him I should not be his friend at all. It is a very dangerous thing to know one's friends."

"You had really better keep yourself dry," said the Fire-balloon. "That is the important thing."

"Very important for you, I have no doubt," answered the Rocket, "but I shall weep if I choose;" and he actually burst into real tears, which flowed down his stick like raindrops, and nearly drowned two little beetles, who were just thinking of setting up house together, and were looking for a nice dry spot to live in.

"He must have a truly romantic nature," said the Catherine Wheel, "for he weeps when there is nothing at all to weep about;" and she heaved a deep sigh and thought about the deal box.

But the Roman Candle and the Bengal Light were quite indignant, and kept saying, "Humbug! humbug!" at the top of their voices. They were extremely practical, and whenever they objected to anything they called it humbug.

Then the moon rose like a wonderful silver shield; and the stars began to shine, and a sound of music came from the palace.

The Prince and Princess were leading the dance. They danced so beautifully that the tall white lilies peeped in at the window and watched them, and the great red poppies nodded their heads and beat time.

Then ten o'clock struck, and then eleven, and then twelve, and at the last stroke of midnight every one came out on the terrace, and the King sent for the Royal Pyrotechnist.

"Let the fireworks begin," said the King; and the Royal Pyrotechnist made a low bow, and marched down to the end of the garden. He had six attendants with him, each of whom carried a lighted torch at the end of a long pole.

It was certainly a magnificent display.

Whizz! Whizz! went the Catherine Wheel, as she spun round and round. Boom! Boom! went the Roman Candle. Then the Squibs danced all over the place, and the Bengal Lights made everything look scarlet. "Good-bye," cried the Fire-balloon, as he soared away, dropping tiny blue sparks. Bang! Bang! answered the Crackers, who were enjoying themselves immensely. Every one was a great success except the Remarkable Rocket. He was so damped with crying that he could not go off at all. The best thing in him was the gunpowder, and that was so wet with tears that it was of no use. All his poor relations, to whom he would never speak, except with a sneer, shot up into the sky like wonderful golden flowers with blossoms of fire. Huzza! Huzza! cried the Court; and the little Princess laughed with pleasure.

"I suppose they are reserving me for some grand occasion," said the Rocket; "no doubt that is what it means," and he looked more supercilious than ever.

The next day the workmen came to put everything tidy. "This is, evidently, a deputation," said the Rocket; "I will receive them with becoming dignity:" so he put his nose in the air, and began to frown severely, as if he were thinking about some very important subject. But they took no notice of him at all till they were just going away. Then one of them caught sight of him. "Hallo!" he cried, "what a bad rocket!" and he threw him over the wall into the ditch.

"BAD ROCKET? BAD ROCKET?" he said, as he whirled through the air; "impossible! GRAND ROCKET, that is what the man said. BAD and GRAND sound very much the same, indeed they often are the same;" and he fell into the mud.

"It is not comfortable here," he remarked, "but no doubt it is some fashionable watering-place, and they have sent me away to recruit my health. My nerves are certainly very much shattered, and I require rest."

Then a little Frog, with bright jewelled eyes, and a green mottled coat, swam up to him.

"A new arrival, I see!" said the Frog. "Well, after all there is nothing like mud. Give me rainy weather and a ditch, and I am quite happy. Do you think it will be a wet afternoon? I am sure I hope so, but the sky is quite blue and cloudless. What a pity!"

"Ahem! Ahem!" said the Rocket, and he began to cough.

"What a delightful voice you have!" cried the Frog. "Really it is quite like a croak, and croaking is, of course, the most musical sound in the world. You will hear our glee-club this evening. We sit in the old duck-pond close by the farmer's house, and as soon as the moon rises we begin. It is so entrancing that everybody lies awake to listen to us. In fact, it was only yesterday that I heard the farmer's wife say to her mother that she could not get a wink of sleep at night on account of us. It is most gratifying to find oneself so popular."

"Ahem! ahem!" said the Rocket angrily. He was very much annoyed that he could not get a word in.

"A delightful voice, certainly," continued the Frog; "I hope you will come over to the duck-pond. I am off to look for my daughters. I have six beautiful daughters, and I am so afraid the Pike may meet them. He is a perfect monster, and would have no hesitation in breakfasting off them. Well, good-bye; I have enjoyed our conversation very much, I assure you."

"Conversation, indeed!" said the Rocket. "You have talked the whole time yourself. That is not conversation."

"Somebody must listen," answered the Frog, "and I like to do all the talking myself. It saves time, and prevents arguments."

"But I like arguments," said the Rocket.

"I hope not," said the Frog complacently. "Arguments are extremely vulgar, for everybody in good society holds exactly the same opinions. Good-bye a second time; I see my daughters in the distance;" and the little Frog swam away.

"You are a very irritating person," said the Rocket, "and very ill-bred. I hate people who talk about themselves, as you do, when one wants to talk about oneself, as I do. It is what I call selfishness, and selfishness is a most detestable thing, especially to any one of my temperament, for I am well known for my sympathetic nature. In fact, you should take example by me; you could not possibly have a better model. Now that you have the chance you had better avail yourself of it, for I am going back to Court almost immediately. I am a great favourite at Court; in fact, the Prince and Princess were married yesterday in my honour. Of course, you know nothing of these matters, for you are a provincial."

"There is no good talking to him," said a Dragonfly, who was sitting on the top of a large brown bulrush; "no good at all, for he has gone away."

"Well, that is his loss, not mine," answered the Rocket. "I am not going to stop talking to him merely because he pays no attention. I like hearing myself talk. It is one of my greatest pleasures. I often have long conversations all by myself, and I am so clever that sometimes I don't understand a single word of what I am saying."

"Then you should certainly lecture on Philosophy," said the Dragonfly, and he spread a pair of lovely gauze wings and soared away into the sky.

"How very silly of him not to stay here!" said the Rocket. "I am sure that he has not often got such a chance of improving his mind. However, I don't care a bit. Genius like mine is sure to be appreciated some day;" and he sank down a little deeper into the mud.

After some time a large White Duck swam up to him. She had yellow legs, and webbed feet, and was considered a great beauty on account of her waddle.

"Quack, quack, quack," she said. "What a curious shape you are! May I ask were you born like that, or is it the result of an accident?"

"It is quite evident that you have always lived in the country," answered the Rocket, "otherwise you would know who I am. However, I excuse your ignorance. It would be unfair to expect other people to be as remarkable as oneself. You will no doubt be surprised to hear that I can fly up into the sky, and come down in a shower of golden rain."

"I don't think much of that," said the Duck, "as I cannot see what use it is to any one. Now, if you could plough the fields like the ox, or draw a cart like the horse, or look after the sheep like the collie-dog, that would be something."

"My good creature," cried the Rocket in a very haughty tone of voice, "I see that you belong to the lower orders. A person of my position is never useful. We have certain accomplishments, and that is more than sufficient. I have no sympathy myself with industry of any kind, least of all with such industries as you seem to recommend. Indeed, I have always been of opinion that hard work is simply the refuge of people who have nothing whatever to do."

"Well, well," said the Duck, who was of a very peaceful disposition, and never quarrelled with any one, "everybody has different tastes. I hope, at any rate, that you are going to take up your residence here."

"Oh! dear no," cried the Rocket. "I am merely a visitor, a distinguished visitor. The fact is that I find this place rather tedious. There is neither society here, nor solitude. In fact, it is essentially suburban. I shall probably go back to Court, for I know that I am destined to make a sensation in the world."

"I had thoughts of entering public life once myself," remarked the Duck; "there are so many things that need reforming. Indeed, I took the chair at a meeting some time ago, and we passed resolutions condemning everything that we did not like. However, they did not seem to have much effect. Now I go in for domesticity, and look after my family."

"I am made for public life," said the Rocket, "and so are all my relations, even the humblest of them. Whenever we appear we excite great attention. I have not actually appeared myself, but when I do so it will be a magnificent sight. As for domesticity, it ages one rapidly, and distracts one's mind from higher things."

"Ah! the higher things of life, how fine they are!" said the Duck; "and that reminds me how hungry I feel:" and she swam away down the stream, saying, "Quack, quack, quack."

"Come back! come back!" screamed the Rocket, "I have a great deal to say to you;" but the Duck paid no attention to him. "I am glad that she has gone," he said to himself, "she had a decidedly middle-class mind;" and he sank a little deeper still into the mud, and began to think about the loneliness of genius, when suddenly two little boys in white smocks came running down the bank, with a kettle and some faggots.

"This must be the deputation," said the Rocket, and he tried to look very dignified.

"Hallo!" cried one of the boys, "look at this old stick; I wonder how it came here:" and he picked the Rocket out of the ditch.

"Old Stick!" said the Rocket, "impossible! Gold Stick, that is what he said. Gold Stick is very complimentary. In fact, he mistakes me for one of the Court dignitaries!"

"Let us put it into the fire!" said the other boy, "it will help to boil the kettle."

So they piled the faggots together, and put the Rocket on top, and lit the fire.

"This is magnificent," cried the Rocket, "they are going to let me off in broad daylight, so that every one can see me."

"We will go to sleep now," they said, "and when we wake up the kettle will be boiled;" and they lay down on the grass, and shut their eyes.

The Rocket was very damp, so he took a long time to burn. At last, however, the fire caught him.

"Now I am going off!" he cried, and he made himself very stiff and straight. "I know I shall go much higher than the stars, much higher than the moon, much higher than the sun. In fact, I shall go so high that——"

Fizz! Fizz! Fizz! and he went straight up into the air.

"Delightful!" he cried, "I shall go on like this for ever. What a success I am!"

But nobody saw him.

Then he began to feel a curious tingling sensation all over him.

"Now I am going to explode," he cried. "I shall set the whole world on fire, and make such a noise that nobody will talk about anything else for a whole year." And he certainly did explode. Bang! Bang! Bang! went the gunpowder. There was no doubt about it.

But nobody heard him, not even the two little boys, for they were sound asleep.

Then all that was left of him was the stick, and this fell down on the back of a Goose who was taking a walk by the side of the ditch.

"Good heavens!" cried the Goose. "It is going to rain sticks;" and she rushed into the water.

"I knew I should create a great sensation," gasped the Rocket, and he went out.

Joseph Conrad (1857–1924) was born in the Ukraine
of Polish parents. He shipped as a sailor for twenty
years before finally settling in England as a British
citizen. Although he did not learn English until
he was twenty-one, he is one of the great masters
of English prose; his novels, such as Lord Jim (1900),
Nostromo (1904), and Victory (1905), continue to
engage our best literary minds. For further reading:
Tales of Unrest (1898), Youth, and Other Tales
(1902).

An Outpost of Progress

JOSEPH CONRAD

I

There were two white men in charge of the trading station. Kayerts,
the chief, was short and fat; Carlier, the assistant, was tall, with a large
head and a very broad trunk perched upon a long pair of thin legs. The
third man on the staff was a Sierra Leone nigger, who maintained that
his name was Henry Price. However, for some reason or other, the
natives down the river had given him the name of Makola, and it stuck
to him through all his wanderings about the country. He spoke English
and French with a warbling accent, wrote a beautiful hand, understood
bookkeeping, and cherished in his innermost heart the worship of evil
spirits. His wife was a negress from Loanda, very large and very noisy.
Three children rolled about in sunshine before the door of his low, shed-
like dwelling. Makola, taciturn and impenetrable, despised the two white
men. He had charge of a small clay storehouse with a dried-grass roof, and
pretended to keep a correct account of beads, cotton cloth, red kerchiefs,
brass wire, and other trade goods it contained. Besides the storehouse
and Makola's hut, there was only one large building in the cleared ground
of the station. It was built neatly of reeds, with a verandah on all the
four sides. There were three rooms in it. The one in the middle was the
living-room, and had two rough tables and a few stools in it. The other
two were the bedrooms for the white men. Each had a bedstead and a
mosquito net for all furniture. The plank floor was littered with the
belongings of the white men; open half-empty boxes, torn wearing apparel,
old boots; all the things dirty, and all the things broken, that accumulate
mysteriously round untidy men. There was also another dwelling-place

some distance away from the buildings. In it, under a tall cross much out of the perpendicular, slept the man who had seen the beginning of all this; who had planned and had watched the construction of this outpost of progress. He had been, at home, an unsuccessful painter who, weary of pursuing fame on an empty stomach, had gone out there through high protections. He had been the first chief of that station. Makola had watched the energetic artist die of fever in the just finished house with his usual kind of "I told you so" indifference. Then, for a time, he dwelt alone with his family, his account books, and the Evil Spirit that rules the lands under the equator. He got on very well with his god. Perhaps he had propitiated him by a promise of more white men to play with, by and by. At any rate the director of the Great Trading Company, coming up in a steamer that resembled an enormous sardine box with a flat-roofed shed erected on it, found the station in good order, and Makola as usual quietly diligent. The director had the cross put up over the first agent's grave, and appointed Kayerts to the post. Carlier was told off as second in charge. The director was a man ruthless and efficient, who at times, but very imperceptibly, indulged in grim humour. He made a speech to Kayerts and Carlier, pointing out to them the promising aspect of this station. The nearest trading-post was about three hundred miles away. It was an exceptional opportunity for them to distinguish themselves and to earn percentages on the trade. This appointment was a favour done to beginners. Kayerts was moved almost to tears by his director's kindness. He would, he said, by doing his best, try to justify the flattering confidence, &c., &c. Kayerts had been in the Administration of the Telegraphs, and knew how to express himself correctly. Carlier, an ex-non-commissioned officer of cavalry in an army guaranteed from harm by several European Powers, was less impressed. If there were commissions to get, so much the better, and, trailing a sulky glance over the river, the forests, the impenetrable bush that seemed to cut off the station from the rest of the world, he muttered between his teeth, "We shall see, very soon."

Next day, some bales of cotton goods and a few cases of provisions having been thrown on shore, the sardine-box steamer went off, not to return for another six months. On the deck the director touched his cap to the two agents, who stood on the bank waving their hats, and turning to an old servant of the Company on his passage to headquarters, said, "Look at those two imbeciles. They must be mad at home to send me such specimens. I told those fellows to plant a vegetable garden, build new storehouses and fences, and construct a landing-stage. I bet nothing will be done! They won't know how to begin. I always thought the station on this river useless, and they just fit the station!"

"They will form themselves there," said the old stager with a quiet smile.

"At any rate, I am rid of them for six months," retorted the director.

The two men watched the steamer round the bend, then, ascending arm in arm the slope of the bank, returned to the station. They had been in this vast and dark country only a very short time, and as yet always in the midst of other white men, under the eye and guidance of their superiors. And now, dull as they were to the subtle influences of surroundings, they felt themselves very much alone, when suddenly left unassisted to face the wilderness; a wilderness rendered more strange, more incomprehensible by the mysterious glimpses of the vigorous life it contained. They were two perfectly insignificant and incapable individuals, whose existence is only rendered possible through the high organization of civilized crowds. Few men realize that their life, the very essence of their character, their capabilities and their audacities, are only the expression of their belief in the safety of their surroundings. The courage, the composure, the confidence; the emotions and principles; every great and every insignificant thought belongs not to the individual but to the crowd: to the crowd that believes blindly in the irresistible force of its institutions and of its morals, in the power of its police and of its opinion. But the contact with pure unmitigated savagery, with primitive nature and primitive man, brings sudden and profound trouble into the heart. To the sentiment of being alone of one's kind, to the clear perception of the loneliness of one's thoughts, of one's sensations—to the negation of the habitual, which is safe, there is added the affirmation of the unusual, which is dangerous; a suggestion of things vague, uncontrollable, and repulsive, whose discomposing intrusion excites the imagination and tries the civilized nerves of the foolish and the wise alike.

Kayerts and Carlier walked arm in arm, drawing close to one another as children do in the dark; and they had the same, not altogether unpleasant, sense of danger which one half suspects to be imaginary. They chatted persistently in familiar tones. "Our station is prettily situated," said one. The other assented with enthusiasm, enlarging volubly on the beauties of the situation. Then they passed near the grave. "Poor devil!" said Kayerts. "He died of fever, didn't he?" muttered Carlier, stopping short. "Why," retorted Kayerts, with indignation, "I've been told that the fellow exposed himself recklessly to the sun. The climate here, everybody says, is not all worse than at home, as long as you keep out of the sun. Do you hear that, Carlier? I am chief here, and my orders are that you should not expose yourself to the sun!" He assumed his superiority jocularly, but his meaning was serious. The idea that he would, perhaps, have to bury Carlier and remain alone, gave him an inward shiver. He felt suddenly that this Carlier was more precious to him here, in the centre of Africa, than a brother could be anywhere else. Carlier, entering into the spirit of the thing, made a military salute and answered in a brisk tone, "Your orders shall be attended to, chief!" Then he burst out laughing, slapped Kayerts on the back and shouted, "We shall let life run easily here! Just sit still and gather in the ivory those savages will bring. This country has its good points, after all!" They both laughed loudly while Carlier thought: "That poor Kayerts, he is so fat and unhealthy. It would be awful if I had to bury him here. He is a man I respect." . . . Before they reached the verandah of their house they called one another "my dear fellow."

The first day they were very active, pottering about with hammers and nails and red calico, to put up curtains, make their house habitable and pretty; resolved to settle down comfortably to their new life. For them an impossible task. To grapple effectually with even purely material problems requires more serenity of mind and more lofty courage than people generally imagine. No two beings could have been more unfitted for such a struggle. Society, not from any tenderness, but because of its strange needs, had taken care of those two men, forbidding them all independent thought, all initiative, all departure from routine; and forbidding it under pain of death. They could only live on condition of being machines. And now, released from the fostering care of men with pens behind the ears, or of men with gold lace on the sleeves, they were like those lifelong prisoners who, liberated after many years, do not know what use to make of their freedom. They did not know what use to make of their faculties, being both, through want of practice, incapable of independent thought.

At the end of two months Kayerts often would say, "If it was not for my Melie, you wouldn't catch me here." Melie was his daughter. He had thrown up his post in the Administration of the Telegraphs, though he had been for seventeen years perfectly happy there, to earn a dowry for his girl. His wife was dead; and the child was being brought up by his sisters. He regretted the streets, the pavements, the cafés, his friends of many years; all the things he used to see, day after day; all the thoughts suggested by familiar things—the thoughts effortless, monotonous, and soothing of a Government clerk; he regretted all the gossip, the small enmities, the mild venom, and the little jokes of Government offices. "If I had had a decent brother-in-law," Carlier would remark, "a fellow with a heart, I would not be here." He had left the army and had made himself so obnoxious to his family by his laziness and impudence, that an exasperated brother-in-law had made superhuman efforts to procure him an appointment in the Company as a second-class agent. Having not a penny in the world he was compelled to accept this means of livelihood as soon as it became quite clear to him that there was nothing more to squeeze out of his relations. He, like Kayerts, regretted his old life. He regretted the clink of sabre and spurs on a fine afternoon, the barrack-room witticisms, the girls of garrison towns; but, besides, he had also a sense of grievance. He was evidently a much ill-used man. This made him moody, at times. But the two men got on well together in the fellowship of their stupidity and laziness. Together they did nothing, absolutely nothing, and enjoyed the sense of the idleness for which they were paid. And in time they came to feel something resembling affection for one another.

They lived like blind men in a large room, aware only of what came in contact with them (and of that only imperfectly), but unable to see the general aspect of things. The river, the forest, all the great land throbbing with life, were like a great emptiness. Even the brilliant sunshine disclosed nothing intelligible. Things appeared and disappeared before their eyes in an unconnected and aimless kind of way. The river seemed to come from nowhere and flow nowhither. It flowed through a void. Out of that void, at times, came canoes, and men with spears in their hands would suddenly crowd the yard of the station. They were naked, glossy black, ornamented with snowy shells and glistening brass wire, perfect of limb. They made an uncouth babbling noise when they spoke, moved in a stately manner, and sent quick, wild glances out of their startled, never-resting eyes. Those warriors would squat in long rows, four or more deep, before the verandah, while their chiefs bargained for hours with Makola over an elephant tusk. Kayerts sat on his chair and looked down on the proceedings, understanding nothing. He stared at them with his round blue eyes, called out to Carlier, "Here, look! look at that fellow there—and that other one, to the left. Did you ever see such a face? Oh, the funny brute!"

Carlier, smoking native tobacco in a short wooden pipe, would swagger up twirling his moustaches, and surveying the warriors with haughty indulgence, would say—

"Fine animals. Brought any bone? Yes? It's not any too soon. Look at the muscles of that fellow—third from the end. I wouldn't care to get a punch on the nose from him. Fine arms, but legs no good below the knee. Couldn't make cavalry men of them." And after glancing down complacently at his own shanks, he always concluded: "Pah! Don't they stink! You, Makola! Take that herd over to the fetish" (the storehouse was in every station called the fetish, perhaps because of the spirit of civilization it contained) "and give them up some of the rubbish you keep there. I'd rather see it full of bone than full of rags."

Kayerts approved.

"Yes, yes! Go and finish that palaver over there, Mr. Makola. I will come round when you are ready, to weigh the tusk. We must be careful." Then turning to his companion: "This is the tribe that lives down the river; they are rather aromatic. I remember, they had been once before here. D'ye hear that row? What a fellow has got to put up with in this dog of a country! My head is split."

Such profitable visits were rare. For days the two pioneers of trade and progress would look on their empty courtyard in the vibrating brilliance of vertical sunshine. Below the high bank, the silent river flowed on glittering and steady. On the sands in the middle of the stream, hippos and alligators sunned themselves side by side. And stretching away in all directions, surrounding the insignificant cleared spot of the trading post, immense forests, hiding fateful complications of fantastic life, lay in the eloquent silence of mute greatness. The two men understood nothing, cared for nothing but for the passage of days that separated them from the steamer's return. Their predecessor had left some torn books. They took up these wrecks of novels, and, as they had never read anything of the kind before, they were surprised and amused. Then during long days there were interminable and silly discussions about plots and personages. In the centre of Africa they made acquaintance of Richelieu and of d'Artagnan, of Hawkeye and of Father Goriot, and of many other people. All these imaginary personages became subjects for gossip as if they had been living friends. They discounted their virtues, suspected their motives, decried their successes; were scandalized at their duplicity or were doubtful about their courage. The accounts of crimes filled them with indignation, while tender or pathetic passages moved them deeply. Carlier clear his throat and said in a soldierly voice, "What nonsense!" Kayerts, his round eyes suffused with tears, his fat cheeks quivering, rubbed his bald head, and declared, "This is a splendid book. I had no idea there were such clever fellows in the world." They also found some old copies of a home paper. The print discussed what it was pleased to call "Our Colonial Expansion" in high-flown language. It spoke much of the rights and duties of civilization, of the sacredness of the civilizing work, and extolled the merits of those who went about bringing light, and faith and commerce to the dark places of the earth. Carlier and Kayerts read, wondered, and began to think better of themselves. Carlier said one evening, waving his hand about "In a hundred years, there will be perhaps a town here. Quays, and warehouses, and barracks, and—and—billiard-rooms. Civilization, my boy, and virtue—and all. And then, chaps will read that two good fellows, Kayerts and Carlier, were the first civilized men to live in this very spot!" Kayerts nodded, "Yes, it is a consolation to think of that." They seemed to forget their dead predecessor; but, early one day, Carlier went out and replanted the cross firmly. "It used to make me squint whenever I walked that way," he explained to Kayerts over the morning coffee. "It made me squint, leaning over so much. So I planted it upright. And solid, I promise you! I suspended myself with both hands to the cross-piece. Not a move. Oh, I did that properly."

At times Gobila came to see them. Gobila was the chief of the neighboring villages. He was a gray-headed savage, thin and black, with a white cloth round his loins and a mangy panther skin hanging over his back. He came up with long strides of his skeleton legs, swinging a staff as tall as himself, and entering the common room of the station, would squat on his heels to the left of the door. There he sat, watching Kayerts, and now and then making a speech which the other did not understand. Kayerts, without interrupting his occupation, would from time to time say in a friendly manner: "How goes it, you old image?" and they would smile at one another. The two whites had a liking for that old and incomprehensible creature, and called him Father Gobila. Gobila's manner was paternal, and he seemed really to love all white men. They all appeared to him very young, indistinguishably alike (except for stature), and he knew that they were all brothers, and also immortal. The death of the artist, who was the first white man whom he knew intimately, did not disturb this belief, because he was firmly convinced that the white stranger had pretended to die and got himself buried for some mysterious purpose of his own, into which it was useless to inquire. Perhaps it was his way of going home to his own country? At any rate, these were his brothers, and he transferred his absurd affection to them. They returned it in a way. Carlier slapped him on the back, and recklessly struck off matches for his amusement. Kayerts was always ready to let him have a sniff at the ammonia bottle. In short, they behaved just like that other white creature that had hidden itself in a hole in the ground. Gobilia considered them attentively. Perhaps they were the same being with the other—or one of them was. He couldn't decide—clear up that mystery; but he remained always very friendly. In consequence of that friendship the women of Gobila's village walked in single file through the reedy grass, bringing every morning to the station, fowls, and sweet potatoes, and palm wine, and sometimes a goat. The Company never provisions the stations fully, and the agents required those local supplies to live. They had them through the good-will of Gobila, and lived well. Now and then one of them had a bout of fever, and the other nursed him with gentle devotion. They did not think much of it. It left them weaker, and their appearance changed for the worse. Carlier was hollow-eyed and irritable. Kayerts showed a drawn, flabby face above the rotundity of his stomach, which gave him a weird aspect. But being constantly together, they did not notice the change that took place gradually in their appearance, and also in their dispositions.

Five months passed in that way.

Then, one morning, as Kayerts and Carlier, lounging in their chairs under the verandah, talked about the approaching visit of the steamer, a knot of armed men came out of the forest and advanced towards the station. They were strangers to that part of the country. They were tall, slight, draped classically from neck to heel in blue fringed cloths, and carried percussion muskets over their bare right shoulders. Makola showed signs of excitement, and ran out of the storehouse (where he spent all his days) to meet these visitors. They came into the courtyard and looked about them with steady, scornful glances. Their leader, a powerful and determined-looking negro with bloodshot eyes, stood in front of the verandah and made a long speech. He gesticulated much, and ceased very suddenly.

There was something in his intonation, in the sounds of the long sentences he used, that startled the two whites. It was like a reminiscence of something not exactly familiar, and yet resembling the speech of civilized men. It sounded like one of those impossible languages which sometimes we hear in our dreams.

"What lingo is that?" said the amazed Carlier. "In the first moment I fancied the fellow was going to speak French. Anyway, it is a different kind of gibberish to what we ever heard."

"Yes," replied Kayerts. "Hey, Makola, what does he say? Where do they come from? Who are they?"

But Makola, who seemed to be standing on hot bricks, answered hurriedly, "I don't know. They come from very far. Perhaps Mrs. Price will understand. They are perhaps bad men."

The leader, after waiting for a while, said something sharply to Makola, who shook his head. Then the man, after looking round, noticed Makola's hut and walked over there. The next moment Mrs. Makola was heard speaking with great volubility. The other strangers—they were six in all—strolled about with an air of ease, put their heads through the door of the storeroom, congregated round the grave, pointed understandingly at the cross, and generally made themselves at home.

"I don't like those chaps—and, I say, Kayerts, they must be from the coast; they've got firearms," observed the sagacious Carlier.

Kayerts also did not like those chaps. They both, for the first time, became aware that they lived in conditions where the unusual may be dangerous, and that there was no power on earth outside of themselves to stand between them and the unusual. They became uneasy, went in and loaded their revolvers. Kayerts said, "We must order Makola to tell them to go away before dark."

The strangers left in the afternoon, after eating a meal prepared for them by Mrs. Makola. The immense woman was excited, and talked much with the visitors. She rattled away shrilly, pointing here and there at the forests and at the river. Makola sat apart and watched. At times he got up and whispered to his wife. He accompanied the strangers across the ravine at the back of the station-ground, and returned slowly looking very thoughtful. When questioned by the white men he was very strange, seemed not to understand, seemed to have forgotten French—seemed to have forgotten how to speak altogether. Kayerts and Carlier agreed that the nigger had had too much palm wine.

There was some talk about keeping a watch in turn, but in the evening everything seemed so quiet and peaceful that they retired as usual. All night they were disturbed by a lot of drumming in the villages. A deep, rapid roll near by would be followed by another far off—then all ceased. Soon short appeals would rattle out here and there, then all mingle together, increase, become vigorous and sustained, would spread out over the forest, roll through the night, unbroken and ceaseless, near and far, as if the whole land had been one immense drum booming out steadily an appeal to heaven. And through the deep and tremendous noise sudden yells that resembled snatches of songs from a madhouse darted shrill and high in discordant jets of sound which seemed to rush far above the earth and drive all peace from under the stars.

Carlier and Kayerts slept badly. They both thought they had heard shots fired during the night—but they could not agree as to the direction. In the morning Makola was gone somewhere. He returned about noon with one of yesterday's strangers, and eluded all Kayerts' attempts to close with him: had become deaf apparently. Kayerts wondered. Carlier, who had been fishing off the bank, came back and remarked while he showed his catch, "The niggers seem to be in a deuce of a stir; I wonder what's up. I saw about fifteen canoes cross the river during the two hours I was there fishing." Kayerts, worried, said, "Isn't this Makola very queer to-day?" Carlier advised, "Keep all our men together in case of some trouble."

II

There were ten station men who had been left by the Director. Those fellows, having engaged themselves to the Company for six months (without having any idea of a month in particular and only a very faint notion of time in general), had been serving the cause of progress for upwards of two years. Belonging to a tribe from a very distant part of the land of darkness and sorrow, they did not run away, naturally supposing that as wandering strangers they would be killed by the inhabitants of the country; in which they were right. They lived in straw huts on the slope of a ravine over-grown with reedy grass, just behind the station buildings.

They were not happy, regretting the festive incantations, the sorceries, the human sacrifices of their own land; where they also had parents, brothers, sisters, admired chiefs, respected magicians, loved friends, and other ties supposed generally to be human. Besides, the rice rations served out by the Company did not agree with them, being a food unknown to their land, and to which they could not get used. Consequently they were unhealthy and miserable. Had they been of any other tribe they would have made up their minds to die—for nothing is easier to certain savages than suicide—and so have escaped from the puzzling difficulties of existence. But belonging, as they did to a warlike tribe with filed teeth, they had more grit, and went on stupidly living through disease and sorrow. They did very little work, and had lost their splendid physique. Carlier and Kayerts doctored them assiduously without being able to bring them back into condition again. They were mustered every morning and told off to different tasks—grass-cutting, fence-building, tree-felling, &c., &c., which no power on earth could induce them to execute efficiently. The two whites had practically very little control over them.

In the afternoon Makola came over to the big house and found Kayerts watching three heavy columns of smoke rising above the forests. "What is that?" asked Kayerts. "Some villages burn," answered Makola, who seemed to have regained his wits. Then he said abruptly: "We have got very little ivory; bad six months' trading. Do you like get a little more ivory?"

"Yes," said Kayerts, eagerly. He thought of percentages which were low.

"Those men who came yesterday are traders from Loanda who have got more ivory than they can carry home. Shall I buy? I know their camp."

"Certainly," said Kayerts. "What are those traders?"

"Bad fellows," said Makola, indifferently. "They fight with people, and catch women and children. They are bad men, and got guns. There is a great disturbance in the country. Do you want ivory?"

"Yes," said Kayerts. Makola said nothing for a while. Then: "Those workmen of ours are no good at all," he muttered, looking round. "Station in very bad order, sir. Director will growl. Better get a fine lot of ivory, then he say nothing."

"I can't help it; the men won't work," said Kayerts. "When will you get that ivory?"

"Very soon," said Makola. "Perhaps to-night. You leave it to me and keep indoors, sir. I think you had better give some palm wine to our men to make a dance this evening. Enjoy themselves. Work better to-morrow. There's plenty palm wine—gone a little sour."

Kayerts said "yes," and Makola, with his own hands carried big cala-bashes to the door of his hut. They stood there till the evening, and Mrs. Makola looked into every one. The men got them at sunset. When Kayerts and Carlier retired, a big bonfire was flaring before the men's huts. They could hear their shouts and drumming. Some men from Gobila's vil-lage had joined the station hands, and the entertainment was a great success.

In the middle of the night, Carlier, waking suddenly, heard a man shout loudly; then a shot was fired. Only one. Carlier ran out and met Kayerts on the verandah. They were both startled. As they went across the yard to call Makola, they saw shadows moving in the night. One of them cried, "Don't shoot! It's me, Price." Then Makola appeared close to them. "Go back, go back, please," he urged, "you spoil all." "There are strange men about," said Carlier. "Never mind; I know," said Makola. Then he whispered, "All right. Bring ivory. Say nothing! I know my business." The two white men reluctantly went back to the house, but did not sleep. They heard footsteps, whispers, some groans. It seemed as if a lot of men came in, dumped heavy things on the ground, squabbled a long time, then went away. They lay on their hard beds and thought: "This Makola is invaluable." In the morning Carlier came out, very sleepy, and pulled at the cord of the big bell. The station hands mustered every morning to the sound of the bell. That morning nobody came. Kayerts turned out also, yawning. Across the yard they saw Makola came out of his hut, a tin basin of soapy water in his hand. Makola, a civilized nigger, was very neat in his person. He threw the soapsuds skillfully over a wretched little yellow cur he had, then turning his face to the agent's house, he shouted from the distance, "All the men gone last night!"

They heard him plainly, but in their surprise they both yelled out to-gether: "What!" Then they stared at one another. "We are in a proper fix now," growled Carlier. "It's incredible!" muttered Kayerts. "I will go to the huts and see," said Carlier, striding off. Makola coming up found Kayerts standing alone.

"I can hardly believe it," said Kayerts, tearfully. "We took care of them as if they had been our children."

"They went with the coast people," said Makola after a moment of hesitation.

"What do I care with whom they went—the ungrateful brutes!" ex-claimed the other. Then with sudden suspicion, and looking hard at Makola, he added: "What do you know about it?"

Makola moved his shoulders, looking down on the ground. "What do I know? I think only. Will you come and look at the ivory I've got there? It is a fine lot. You never saw such."

He moved towards the store. Kayerts followed him mechanically, thinking about the incredible desertion of the men. On the ground before the door of the fetish lay six splendid tusks.

"What did you give for it?" asked Kayerts, after surveying the lot with satisfaction.

"No regular trade," said Makola. "They brought the ivory and gave it to me. I told them to take what they most wanted in the station. It is a beautiful lot. No station can show such tusks. Those traders wanted carriers badly, and our men were no good here. No trade, no entry in books; all correct."

Kayerts nearly burst with indignation. "Why!" he shouted, "I believe you have sold our men for these tusks!" Makola stood impassive and silent. "I—I—will—I," stuttered Kayerts. "You fiend!" he yelled out.

"I did the best for you and the Company," said Makola, imperturbably. "Why you shout so much? Look at this tusk."

"I dismiss you! I will report you—I won't look at the tusk. I forbid you to touch them. I order you to throw them into the river. You— you!"

"You very red, Mr. Kayerts. If you are so irritable in the sun, you will get fever and die—like the first chief!" pronounced Makola impressively.

They stood still, contemplating one another with intense eyes, as if they had been looking with effort across immense distances. Kayerts shivered. Makola had meant no more than he said, but his words seemed to Kayerts full of ominous menace! He turned sharply and went away to the house. Makola retired into the bosom of his family; and the tusks, left lying before the store, looked very large and valuable in the sunshine.

Carlier came back on the verandah. "They're all gone, hey? asked Kayerts from the far end of the common room in a muffled voice. "You did not find anybody?"

"Oh yes," said Carlier, "I found one of Gobila's people lying dead before the huts—shot through the body. We heard that shot last night."

Kayerts came out quickly. He found his companion staring grimly over the yard at the tusks, away by the store. They both sat in silence for a while. Then Kayerts related his conversation with Makola. Carlier said nothing. At the midday meal they ate very little. They hardly exchanged a word that day. A great silence seemed to lie heavily over the station and press on their lips. Makola did not open the store; he spent the day playing with his children. He lay full-length on a mat outside his door, and the youngsters sat on his chest and clambered all over him. It was a touching picture. Mrs. Makola was busy cooking all day as usual. The white men made a somewhat better meal in the evening. Afterwards, Carlier smoking his pipe strolled over to the store;

he stood for a long time over the tusks, touched one or two with his foot, even tried to lift the largest one by its small end. He came back to his chief, who had not stirred from the verandah, threw himself in the chair and said—

"I can see it! They were pounced upon while they slept heavily after drinking all that palm wine you've allowed Makola to give them. A put-up job! See? The worst is, some of Gobila's people were there, and got carried off too, no doubt. The least drunk woke up, and got shot for his sobriety. This is a funny country. What will you do now?"

"We can't touch it, of course," said Kayerts.

"Of course not," assented Carlier.

"Slavery is an awful thing," stammered out Kayerts in an unsteady voice.

"Frightful—the sufferings," grunted Carlier with conviction.

They believed their words. Everybody shows a respectful deference to certain sounds that he and his fellows can make. But about feelings people really know nothing. We talk with indignation or enthusiasm; we talk about oppression, cruelty, crime, devotion, self-sacrifice, virtue, and we know nothing real beyond the words. Nobody knows what suffering or sacrifice mean—except, perhaps the victims of the mysterious purpose of these illusions.

Next morning they saw Makola very busy setting up in the yard the big scales used for weighing ivory. By and by Carlier said: "What's that filthy scoundrel up to?" and lounged out into the yard. Kayerts followed. They stood watching. Makola took no notice. When the balance was swung true, he tried to lift a tusk into the scale. It was too heavy. He looked up helplessly without a word, and for a minute they stood round that balance as mute and still as three statues. Suddenly Carlier said: "Catch hold of the other end, Makola—you beast!" and together they swung the tusk up. Kayerts trembled in every limb. He muttered, "I say! O! I say!" and putting his hand in his pocket found there a dirty bit of paper and the stump of a pencil. He turned his back on the others, as if about to do something tricky, and noted stealthily the weights which Carlier shouted out to him with unnecessary loudness. When all was over Makola whispered to himself: "The sun's very strong here for the tusks." Carlier said to Kayerts in a careless tone: "I say, chief, I might just as well give him a lift with this lot into the store."

As they were going back to the house Kayerts observed with a sigh: "It had to be done." And Carlier said: "It's deplorable, but, the men being Company's men the ivory is Company's ivory. We must look after it." "I will report to the Director, of course," said Kayerts. "Of course; let him decide," approved Carlier.

At midday they made a hearty meal. Kayerts sighed from time to time. Whenever they mentioned Makola's name they always added to it an opprobrious epithet. It eased their conscience. Makola gave himself a half-holiday, and bathed his children in the river. No one from Gobila's villages came near the station that day. No one came the next day, and the next, nor for a whole week. Gobila's people might have been dead and buried for any sight of life they gave. But they were only mourning for those they had lost by the witchcraft of white men, who had brought wicked people into their country. The wicked people were gone, but fear remained. Fear always remains. A man may destroy everything within himself, love and hate and belief, and even doubt; but as long as he clings to life he cannot destroy fear: the fear, subtle, indestructible, and terrible, that pervades his being; that tinges his thoughts; that lurks in his heart; that watches on his lips the struggle of his last breath. In his fear, the mild old Gobila offered extra human sacrifices to all the Evil Spirits that had taken possession of his white friends. His heart was heavy. Some warriors spoke about burning and killing, but the cautious old savage dissuaded them. Who could foresee the woe those mysterious creatures, if irritated, might bring? They should be left alone. Perhaps in time they would disappear into the earth as the first one had disappeared. His people must keep away from them, and hope for the best.

Kayerts and Carlier did not disappear, but remained above on this earth, that, somehow, they fancied had become bigger and very empty. It was not the absolute and dumb solitude of the post that impressed them so much as an inarticulate feeling that something from within them was gone, something that worked for their safety, and had kept the wilderness from interfering with their hearts. The images of home; the memory of people like them, of men that thought and felt as they used to think and feel, receded into distances made indistinct by the glare of unclouded sunshine. And out of the great silence of the surrounding wilderness, its very hopelessness and savagery seemed to approach them nearer, to draw them gently, to look upon them, to envelop them with a solicitude irresistible, familiar, and disgusting.

Days lengthened into weeks, then into months. Gobila's people drummed and yelled to every new moon, as of yore, but kept away from the station. Makola and Carlier tried once in a canoe to open communications, but were received with a shower of arrows, and had to fly back to the station for dear life. That attempt set the country up and down the river into an uproar that could be very distinctly heard for days. The steamer was late. At first they spoke of delay jauntily, then anxiously, then gloomily. The matter was becoming serious. Stores were running short. Carlier cast his lines off the bank, but the river was low, and the fish kept out in the stream. They dared not stroll far way from the station to shoot.

Moreover, there was no game in the impenetrable forest. Once Carlier shot a hippo in the river. They had no boat to secure it, and it sank. When it floated up it drifted away, and Gobila's people secured the carcase. It was the occasion for a national holiday, but Carlier had a fit of rage over it and talked about the necessity of exterminating all the niggers before the country could be made habitable. Kayerts mooned about silently; spent hours looking at the portrait of his Melie. It represented a little girl with long bleached tresses and a rather sour face. His legs were much swollen, and he could hardly walk. Carlier, undermined by fever, could not swagger any more, but kept tottering about, still with a devil-may-care air, as became a man who remembered his crack regiment. He had become hoarse, sarcastic, and inclined to say unpleasant things. He called it "being frank with you." They had long ago reckoned their percentages on trade, including in them that last deal of "this infamous Makola." They had also concluded not to say anything about it. Kayerts hesitated at first—was afraid of the Director.

"He has seen worse things done on the quiet," maintained Carlier, with a hoarse laugh. "Trust him! He won't thank you if you blab. He is no better than you or me. Who will talk if we hold our tongues? There is nobody here."

That was the root of the trouble! There was nobody there; and being left there alone with their weakness, they became daily more like a pair of accomplices than like a couple of devoted friends. They had heard nothing from home for eight months. Every evening they said, "To-morrow we shall see the steamer." But one of the Company's steamers had been wrecked, and the Director was busy with the other, relieving very distant and important stations on the main river. He thought that the useless station, and the useless men, could wait. Meantime Kayerts and Carlier lived on rice boiled without salt, and cursed the Company, all Africa, and the day they were born. One must have lived on such diet to discover what ghastly trouble the necessity of swallowing one's food may become. There was literally nothing else in the station but rice and coffee; they drank the coffee without sugar. The last fifteen lumps Kayerts had solemnly locked away in his box, together with a half-bottle of Cognâc, "in case of sickness," he explained. Carlier approved. "When one is sick," he said, "any little extra like that is cheering."

They waited. Rank grass began to sprout over the courtyard. The bell never rang now. Days passed, silent, exasperating, and slow. When the two men spoke, they snarled; and their silences were bitter, as if tinged by the bitterness of their thoughts.

One day after a lunch of boiled rice, Carlier put down his cup untasted, and said: "Hang it all!" Let's have a decent cup of coffee for once. Bring out that sugar, Kayerts!"

"For the sick," muttered Kayerts, without looking up.

"For the sick," mocked Carlier. "Bosh! . . . Well! I am sick."

"You are no more sick than I am, and I go without," said Kayerts in a peaceful tone.

"Come! out with that sugar, you stingy old slave-dealer."

Kayerts looked up quickly. Carlier was smiling with marked insolence. And suddenly it seemed to Kayerts that he had never seen that man before. Who was he? He knew nothing about him. What was he capable of? There was a surprising flash of violent emotion within him, as if in the presence of something undreamt-of, dangerous, and final. But he managed to pronounce with composure—

"That joke is in very bad taste. Don't repeat it."

"Joke!" said Carlier, hitching himself forward on his seat. "I am hungry—I am sick—I don't joke! I hate hypocrites. You are a hypocrite. You are a slave-dealer. I am a slave-dealer. There's nothing but slave-dealers in this cursed country. I mean to have sugar in my coffee to-day, anyhow!"

"I forbid you to speak to me in that way," said Kayerts with a fair show of resolution.

"You!—What?" shouted Carlier, jumping up.

Kayerts stood up also. "I am your chief," he began, trying to master the shakiness of his voice.

"What?" yelled the other. "Who's chief? There's no chief here. There's nothing here: there's nothing but you and I. Fetch the sugar—you pot-bellied ass."

"Hold your tongue. Go out of this room," screamed Kayerts. "I dismiss you—you scoundrel!"

Carlier swung a stool. All at once he looked dangerously in earnest. "You flabby, good-for-nothing civilian—take that!" he howled.

Kayerts dropped under the table, and the stool struck the grass inner wall of the room. Then, as Carlier was trying to upset the table, Kayerts in desperation made a blind rush, head low, like a cornered pig would do, and over-turning his friend, bolted along the verandah, and into his room. He locked the door, snatched his revolver, and stood panting. In less than a minute Carlier was kicking at the door furiously, howling, "If you don't bring out that sugar, I will shoot you at sight, like a dog. Now then—one—two—three. You won't? I will show you who's the master."

Kayerts thought the door would fall in, and scrambled through the square hole that served for a window in his room. There was then the whole breadth of the house between them. But the other was apparently not strong enough to break in the door, and Kayerts heard him running round. Then he also began to run laboriously on his swollen legs. He ran as quickly as he could, grasping the revolver, and unable yet to understand what was happening to him. He saw in succession Makola's house, the store, the river, the ravine, and the low bushes; and he saw all those things again as he ran for the second time round the house. Then again they flashed past him. That morning he could not have walked a yard without a groan.

And now he ran. He ran fast enough to keep out of sight of the other man.

Then as, weak and desperate, he thought, "Before I finish the next round I shall die," he heard the other man stumble heavily, then stop. He stopped also. He had the back and Carlier the front of the house, as before. He heard him drop into a chair cursing, and suddenly his own legs gave way, and he slid down into a sitting posture with his back to the wall. His mouth was as dry as a cinder, and his face was wet with perspiration—and tears. What was it all about? He thought it must be a horrible illusion; he thought he was dreaming; he thought he was going mad! After a while he collected his senses. What did they quarrel about? That sugar! How absurd! He would give it to him—didn't want it himself. And he began scrambling to his feet with a sudden feeling of security. But before he had fairly stood upright, a common-sense reflection occurred to him and drove him back into despair. He thought: "If I give way now to that brute of a soldier, he will begin this horror again tomorrow—and the day after—every day—raise other pretensions, trample on me, torture me, make me his slave—and I will be lost! Lost! The steamer may not come for days—may never come." He shook so that he had to sit down on the floor again. He shivered forlornly. He felt he could not, would not move any more. He was completely distracted by the sudden perception that the position was without issue—that death and life had in a moment become equally difficult and terrible.

All at once he heard the other push his chair back; and he leaped to his feet with extreme facility. He listened and got confused. Must run again! Right or left? He heard footsteps. He darted to the left, grasping his revolver, and at the very same instant, as it seemed to him, they came into violent collision. Both shouted with surprise. A loud explosion took place between them; a roar of red fire, thick smoke; and Kayerts, deafened and blinded, rushed back thinking: "I am hit—it's all over." He expected the other to come round—to gloat over his agony. He caught hold of an upright of the roof—"All over!" Then he heard a crashing fall on the other side of the house, as if somebody had tumbled headlong over a chair—then silence. Nothing more happened. He did not die. Only his shoulder felt as if it had been badly wrenched, and he had lost his revolver. He was disarmed and helpless! He waited for his fate. The other man made no sound.

It was a stratagem. He was stalking him now! Along what side? Perhaps he was taking aim this very minute!

After a few moments of an agony frightful and absurd, he decided to go and meet his doom. He was prepared for every surrender. He turned the corner, steadying himself with one hand on the wall; made a few paces, and nearly swooned. He had seen on the floor, protruding past the other corner, a pair of turned-up feet. A pair of white naked feet in red slippers. He felt deadly sick, and stood for a time in profound darkness. Then Makola appeared before him, saying quietly: "Come along, Mr. Kayerts. He is dead." He burst into tears of gratitude; a loud, sobbing fit of crying. After a time he found himself sitting in a chair and looking at Carlier, who lay stretched on his back. Makola was kneeling over the body.

"Is this your revolver?" asked Makola, getting up.

"Yes," said Kayerts; then he added very quickly, "He ran after me to shoot me—you saw!"

"Yes, I saw," said Makola. "There is only one revolver; where's his?"

"Don't know," whispered Kayerts in a voice that had become suddenly very faint.

"I will go and look for it," said the other, gently. He made the round along the verandah, while Kayerts sat still and looked at the corpse. Makola came back empty-handed, stood in deep thought, then stepped quietly into the dead man's room, and came out directly with a revolver, which he held up before Kayerts. Kayerts shut his eyes. Everything was going round. He found life more terrible and difficult than death. He had shot an unarmed man.

After meditating for a while, Makola said softly, pointing at the dead man who lay there with his right eye blown out—

"He died of fever." Kayerts looked at him with a stony stare. "Yes," repeated Makola, thoughtfully, stepping over the corpse, "I think he died of fever. Bury him to-morrow."

And he went away slowly to his expectant wife, leaving the two white men alone on the verandah.

Night came, and Kayerts sat unmoving on his chair. He sat quiet as if he had taken a dose of opium. The violence of the emotions he had passed through produced a feeling of exhausted serenity. He had plumbed in one short afternoon the depths of horror and despair, and now found repose in the conviction that life had no more secrets for him: neither had death! He sat by the corpse thinking; thinking very actively, thinking very new thoughts. He seemed to have broken loose from himself altogether. His old thoughts, convictions, likes and dislikes, things he respected and things abhorred, appeared in their true light at last! Appeared contemptible and childish, false and ridiculous. He revelled in his new wisdom while he sat by the man he had killed. He argued with himself about all things under heaven with that kind of wrong-headed lucidity which may be observed in some lunatics. Incidentally he reflected that the fellow dead there had been a noxious beast anyway; that men died every day in thousands; perhaps in hundreds of thousands—who could tell?—and that in the number, that one death could not possibly make any difference; couldn't have any importance, at least to a thinking creature. He, Kayerts, was a thinking creature. He had been all his life, till that moment, a believer in a lot of nonsense like the rest of mankind—who are fools; but now he thought! He knew! He was at peace; he was familiar with the highest wisdom! Then he tried to imagine himself dead, and Carlier sitting in his chair watching him; and his attempt met with such unexpected success, that in a very few moments he became not at all sure who was dead and who was alive. This extraordinary achievement of his fancy startled him, however, and by a clever and timely effort of mind he saved himself just in time from becoming Carlier. His heart thumped, and he felt hot all over at the thought of the danger. Carlier! What a beastly thing! To compose his now disturbed nerves—and no wonder!—he tried to whistle a little. Then, suddenly, he fell asleep, or thought he had slept; but at any rate there was a fog, and somebody had whistled in the fog.

He stood up. The day had come, and a heavy mist had descended upon the land: the mist penetrating, enveloping, and silent; the morning mist of tropical lands; the mist that clings and kills; the mist white and deadly, immaculate and poisonous. He stood up, saw the body, and threw his arms above his head with a cry like that of a man who, waking from a trance, finds himself immured forever in a tomb. "Help! . . . My God!"

A shriek inhuman, vibrating and sudden, pierced like a sharp dart the white shroud of that land of sorrow. Three short, impatient screeches followed, and then, for a time, the fog-wreaths rolled on, undisturbed, through a formidable silence. Then many more shrieks, rapid and piercing, like the yells of some exasperated and ruthless creature, rent the air. Progress was calling to Kayerts from the river. Progress and civilization and all the virtues. Society was calling to its accomplished child to come, to be taken care of, to be instructed, to be judged, to be comdemned, it called him to return to that rubbish heap from which he had wandered away, so that justice could be done.

Kayerts heard and understood. He stumbled out of the verandah, leaving the other man quite alone for the first time since they had been thrown there together. He groped his way through the fog, calling in his ignorance upon the invisible heaven to undo its work. Makola flitted by in the mist, shouting as he ran—

"Steamer! Steamer! They can't see. They whistle for the station. I go ring the bell. Go down to the landing, sir. I ring."

He disappeared. Kayerts stood still. He looked upwards; the fog rolled low over his head. He looked round like a man who has lost his way; and he saw a dark smudge, a cross-shaped stain, upon the shifting purity of the mist. As he began to stumble toward it, the station bell rang in a tumultuous peal its answer to the impatient clamour of the steamer.

The Managing Director of the Great Civilizing Company (since we know that civilization follows trade) landed first, and incontinently lost sight of the steamer. The fog down by the river was exceedingly dense; above, at the station, the bell rang unceasing and brazen.

The Director shouted loudly to the steamer:

"There is nobody down to meet us; there may be something wrong; though they are ringing. You had better come, too!"

And he began to toil up the steep bank. The captain and the engine-driver of the boat followed behind. As they scrambled up the fog thinned, and they could see their Director a good way ahead. Suddenly they saw him start forward, calling to them over his shoulder:—"Run! Run to the house! I've found one of them. Run, look for the other!"

He had found one of them! And even he, the man of varied and startling experience, was somewhat discomposed by the manner of this finding. He stood and fumbled in his pockets (for a knife) while he faced Kayerts, who was hanging by a leather strap from the cross. He had evidently climbed the grave, which was high and narrow, and after tying the end of the strap to the arm, had swung himself off. His toes were only a couple of inches above the ground; his arms hung stiffly down; he seemed to be standing rigidly at attention, but with one purple cheek playfully posed on the shoulder. And, irreverently, he was putting out a swollen tongue at his Managing Director.

Nathaniel Hawthorne (1804–1864) was born in Salem, Massachusetts. After college he spent a dozen years in relative obscurity before gaining recognition with his first collection of tales. His work characteristically blends realism, melodrama, and the Gothic conventions; his themes center on the mysteries of the human heart, the nature of sin, and the meaning of "darkness." For further reading: Twice-told Tales (1837 and 1842); The Snow Image and Other Twice-told Tales (1852); Tales by Hawthorne, edited by Carl Van Doren (1921).

Young Goodman Brown

NATHANIEL HAWTHORNE

Young Goodman Brown came forth at sunset into the street at Salem village; but put his head back, after crossing the threshold, to exchange a parting kiss with his young wife. And Faith, as the wife was aptly named, thrust her own pretty head into the street, letting the wind play with the pink ribbons of her cap while she called to Goodman Brown.

"Dearest heart," whispered she, softly and rather sadly, when her lips were close to his ear, "prithee put off your journey until sunrise and sleep in your own bed to-night. A lone woman is troubled with such dreams and such thoughts that she's afeard of herself sometimes. Pray tarry with me this night, dear husband, of all nights in the year."

"My love and my Faith," replied young Goodman Brown, "of all nights in the year, this one night must I tarry away from thee. My journey, as thou callest it, forth and back again, must needs be done 'twixt now and sunrise. What, my sweet, pretty wife, dost thou doubt me already, and we but three months married?"

"Then God bless you!" said Faith, with the pink ribbons; "and may you find all well when you come back."

"Amen!" cried Goodman Brown. "Say thy prayers, dear Faith, and go to bed at dusk, and no harm will come to thee."

So they parted; and the young man pursued his way until, being about to turn the corner by the meeting-house, he looked back and saw the head of Faith still peeping after him with a melancholy air, in spite of her pink ribbons.

"Poor little Faith!" thought he, for his heart smote him. "What a wretch am I to leave her on such an errand! She talks of dreams, too. Methought as she spoke there was trouble in her face, as if a dream had warned her what work is to be done to-night. But no, no; 't would kill her to think it. Well, she's a blessed angel on earth; and after this one night I'll cling to her skirts and follow her to heaven."

With this excellent resolve for the future, Goodman Brown felt himself justified in making more haste on his present evil purpose. He had taken a dreary road, darkened by all the gloomiest trees of the forest, which barely stood aside to let the narrow path creep through, and closed immediately behind. It was all as lonely as could be; and there is this peculiarity in such a solitude, that the traveller knows not who may be concealed by the innumerable trunks and the thick boughs overhead; so that with lonely footsteps he may yet be passing through an unseen multitude.

"There may be a devilish Indian behind every tree," said Goodman Brown to himself; and he glanced fearfully behind him as he added, "What if the devil himself should be at my very elbow!"

His head being turned back, he passed a crook of the road, and, looking forward again, beheld the figure of a man, in grave and decent attire, seated at the foot of an old tree. He arose at Goodman Brown's approach and walked onward side by side with him.

"You are late, Goodman Brown," said he. "The clock of the Old South was striking as I came through Boston, and that is full fifteen minutes agone."

"Faith kept me back a while," replied the young man, with a tremor in his voice, caused by the sudden appearance of his companion, though not wholly unexpected.

It was now deep dusk in the forest, and deepest in that part of it where these two were journeying. As nearly as could be discerned, the second traveller was about fifty years old, apparently in the same rank of life as Goodman Brown, and bearing a considerable resemblance to him, though perhaps more in expression than features. Still they might have been taken for father and son. And yet, though the elder person was as simply clad as the younger, and as simple in manner too, he had an indescribable air of one who knew the world, and who would not have felt abashed at the governor's dinner table or in King William's court, were it possible that his affairs should call him thither. But the only thing about him that could be fixed upon as remarkable was his staff, which bore the likeness of a great black snake, so curiously wrought that it might almost be seen to twist and wriggle itself like a living serpent.

This, of course, must have been an ocular deception, assisted by the uncertain light.

"Come, Goodman Brown," cried his fellow-traveller, "this is a dull pace for the beginning of a journey. Take my staff, if you are so soon weary."

"Friend," said the other, exchanging his slow pace for a full stop, "having kept covenant by meeting thee here, it is my purpose now to return whence I came. I have scruples touching the matter thou wot'st of."

"Sayest thou so?" replied he of the serpent, smiling apart. "Let us walk on, nevertheless, reasoning as we go; and if I convince thee not thou shalt turn back. We are but a little way in the forest yet."

"Too far! too far!" exclaimed the goodman, unconsciously resuming his walk. "My father never went into the woods on such an errand, nor his father before him. We have been a race of honest men and good Christians since the days of the martyrs; and shall I be the first of the name of Brown that ever took this path and kept"—

"Such company, thou wouldst say," observed the elder person, interpreting his pause. "Well said, Goodman Brown! I have been as well acquainted with your family as with ever a one among the Puritans; and that's no trifle to say. I helped your grandfather, the constable, when he lashed the Quaker woman so smartly through the streets of Salem; and it was I that brought your father a pitch-pine knot, kindled at my own hearth, to set fire to an Indian village, in King Philip's war. They were my good friends, both; and many a pleasant walk have we had along this path, and returned merrily after midnight. I would fain be friends with you for their sake."

"If it be as thou sayest," replied Goodman Brown, "I marvel they never spoke of these matters; or, verily, I marvel not, seeing that the least rumor of the sort would have driven them from New England. We are a people of prayer, and good works to boot, and abide no such wickedness."

"Wickedness or not," said the traveller with the twisted staff, "I have a very general acquaintance here in New England. The deacons of many a church have drunk the communion wine with me; the selectmen of divers towns make me their chairman; and a majority of the Great and General Court are firm supporters of my interest. The governor and I, too—But these are state secrets."

"Can this be so?" cried Goodman Brown, with a stare of amazement at his undisturbed companion. "Howbeit, I have nothing to do with the governor and council; they have their own ways, and are no rule for a simple husbandman like me. But, were I to go on with thee, how should I meet the eye of that good old man, our minister, at Salem village? Oh, his voice would make me tremble both Sabbath day and lecture day."

Thus far the elder traveller has listened with due gravity; but now burst into a fit of irrepressible mirth, shaking himself so violently that his snake-like staff actually seemed to wriggle in sympathy.

"Ha! ha! ha!" shouted he again and again; then composing himself "Well, go on, Goodman Brown, go on; but, prithee, don't kill me with laughing."

"Well, then, to end the matter at once," said Goodman Brown, considerably nettled, "there is my wife, Faith. It would break her dear little heart; and I'd rather break my own."

"Nay, if that be the case," answered the other, "e'en go thy ways, Goodman Brown. I would not for twenty old women like the one hobbling before us that Faith should come to any harm."

As he spoke he pointed his staff at a female figure on the path, in whom Goodman Brown recognized a very pious and exemplary dame, who had taught him his catechism in youth, and was still his moral and spiritual adviser, jointly with the minister and Deacon Gookin.

"A marvel, truly, that Goody Cloyse should be so far in the wilderness at nightfall," said he. "But with your leave, friend, I shall take a cut through the woods until we have left this Christian woman behind. Being a stranger to you, she might ask whom I was consorting with and whither I was going."

"Be it so," said his fellow-traveller. "Betake you to the woods, and let me keep the path."

Accordingly the young man turned aside, but took care to watch his companion, who advanced softly along the road until he had come within a staff's length of the old dame. She, meanwhile, was making the best of her way, with singular speed for so aged a woman, and mumbling some indistinct words—a prayer, doubtless—as she went. The traveller put forth his staff and touched her withered neck with what seemed the serpent's tail.

"The devil!" screamed the pious old lady.

"Then Goody Cloyse knows her old friend?" observed the traveller, confronting her and leaning on his writhing stick.

"Ah, forsooth, and is it your worship indeed?" cried the good dame. "Yea, truly is it, and in the very image of my old gossip, Goodman Brown, the grandfather of the silly fellow that now is. But—would your worship believe it?—my broomstick hath strangely disappeared, stolen, as I suspect, by the unhanged witch, Goody Cory, and that, too, when I was all anointed with the juice of smallage, and cinquefoil, and wolf's bane"—

"Mingled with fine wheat and the fat of a new-born babe," said the shape of old Goodman Brown.

"Ah, your worship knows the recipe," cried the old lady, cackling aloud. "So, as I was saying, being all ready for the meeting, and no horse to ride on, I made up my mind to foot it; for they tell me there is a nice young man to be taken into communion to-night. But now your good worship will lend me your arm, and we shall be there in a twinkling."

"That can hardly be," answered her friend. "I may not spare you my arm, Goody Cloyse; but here is my staff, if you will."

So saying, he threw it down at her feet, where, perhaps, it assumed life, being one of the rods which its owner had formerly lent to the Egyptian magi. Of this fact, however, Goodman Brown could not take cognizance. He had cast up his eyes in astonishment, and, looking down again, beheld neither Goody Cloyse nor the serpentine staff, but his fellow-traveller alone, who waited for him as calmly as if nothing had happened.

"That old woman taught me my catechism," said the young man; and there was a world of meaning in this simple comment.

They continued to walk onward, while the elder traveller exhorted his companion to make good speed and persevere in the path, discoursing so aptly that his arguments seemed rather to spring up in the bosom of his auditor than to be suggested by himself. As they went, he plucked a branch of maple to serve for a walking stick, and began to strip it of the twigs and little boughs, which were wet with evening dew. The moment his fingers touched them they became strangely withered and dried up as with a week's sunshine. Thus the pair proceeded, at a good free pace, until suddenly, in a gloomy hollow of the road, Goodman Brown sat himself down on the stump of a tree and refused to go any farther.

"Friend," said he, stubbornly, "my mind is made up. Not another step will I budge on this errand. What if a wretched old woman do choose to go to the devil when I thought she was going to heaven: is that any reason why I should quit my dear Faith and go after her?"

"You will think better of this by and by," said his acquaintance, composedly. "Sit here and rest yourself a while; and when you feel like moving again, there is my staff to help you along."

Without more words, he threw his companion the maple stick, and was as speedily out of sight as if he had vanished into the deepening gloom. The young man sat a few moments by the roadside, applauding himself greatly, and thinking with how clear a conscience he should meet the minister in his morning walk, nor shrink from the eye of good old Deacon Gookin. And what calm sleep would be his that very night, which was to have been spent so wickedly, but so purely and sweetly now, in the arms of Faith! Amidst these pleasant and praiseworthy meditations, Goodman Brown heard the tramp of horses along the road, and deemed it advisable to conceal himself within the verge of the forest, conscious of the guilty purpose that had brought him thither, though now so happily turned from it.

On came the hoof tramps and the voices of the riders, two grave old voices, conversing soberly as they drew near. These mingled sounds appeared to pass along the road, within a few yards of the young man's hiding-place; but, owing doubtless to the depth of the gloom at that particular spot, neither the travellers nor their steeds were visible. Though their figures brushed the small boughs by the wayside, it could not be seen that they intercepted, even for a moment, the faint gleam from the strip of bright sky athwart which they might have passed. Goodman Brown alternately crouched and stood on tiptoe, pulling aside the branches and thrusting forth his head as far as he durst without discerning so much as a shadow. It vexed him the more because he could have sworn, were such a thing possible that he recognized the voices of the minister and Deacon Gookin, jogging along quietly, as they were wont to do, when bound to some ordination or ecclesiastical council. While yet within hearing, one of the riders stopped to pluck a switch.

"Of the two, reverend sir," said the voice like the deacon's, "I had rather miss an ordination dinner than to-night's meeting. They tell me that some of our community are to be here from Falmouth and beyond, and others from Connecticut and Rhode Island, besides several of the Indian powwows, who, after their fashion, know almost as much deviltry as the best of us. Moreover, there is a goodly young woman to be taken into communion."

"Mighty well, Deacon Gookin!" replied the solemn old tones of the minister. "Spur up, or we shall be late. Nothing can be done, you know, until I get on the ground."

The hoofs clattered again; and the voices, talking so strangely in the empty air, passed on through the forest, where no church had ever been gathered or solitary Christian prayed. Whither, then, could these holy men be journeying so deep into the heathen wilderness? Young Goodman Brown caught hold of a tree for support, being ready to sink down on the ground, faint and overburdened with the heavy sickness of his heart. He looked up to the sky, doubting whether there really was a heaven above him. Yet there was the blue arch, and the stars brightening in it.

"With heaven above and Faith below, I will yet stand firm against the devil!" cried Goodman Brown.

While he still gazed upward into the deep arch of the firmament and had lifted his hands to pray, a cloud, though no wind was stirring, hurried across the zenith and hid the brightening stars. The blue sky was still visible, except directly overhead, where this black mass of cloud was sweeping swiftly northward. Aloft in the air, as if from the depths of the cloud, came a confused and doubtful sound of voices. Once the listener fancied that he could distinguish the accents of towns-people of his own, men and women, both pious and ungodly, many of whom he had met at the communion table, and had seen others rioting at the tavern. The next moment, so indistinct were the sounds, he doubted whether he had heard aught but the murmur of the old forest, whispering without a wind. Then came a stronger swell of those familiar tones, heard daily in the sunshine at Salem village, but never until now from a cloud of night. There was one voice, of a young woman, uttering lamentations, yet with an uncertain sorrow, and entreating for some favor, which, perhaps, it would grieve her to obtain; and all the unseen multitude, both saints and sinners, seemed to encourage her onward.

"Faith!" shouted Goodman Brown, in a voice of agony and desperation; and the echoes of the forest mocked him, crying "Faith! Faith!" as if bewildered wretches were seeking her all through the wilderness.

The cry of grief, rage, and terror was yet piercing the night, when the unhappy husband held his breath for a response. There was a scream, drowned immediately in a louder murmur of voices, fading into far-off laughter, as the dark cloud swept away, leaving the clear and silent sky above Goodman Brown. But something fluttered lightly down through the air and caught on the branch of a tree. The young man seized it, and beheld a pink ribbon.

"My Faith is gone!" cried he, after one stupefied moment. "There is no good on earth; and sin is but a name. Come, devil; for to thee is this world given."

And, maddened with despair, so that he laughed loud and long, did Goodman Brown grasp his staff and set forth again, at such a rate that he seemed to fly along the forest path rather than to walk or run. The road grew wilder and drearier and more faintly traced, and vanished at length, leaving him in the heart of the dark wilderness, still rushing onward with the instinct that guides mortal man to evil. The whole forest was peopled with frightful sounds—the creaking of the trees, the howling of wild beasts, and the yell of Indians; while sometimes the wind tolled like a distant church bell, and sometimes gave a broad roar around the traveller, as if all Nature were laughing him to scorn. But he was himself the chief horror of the scene, and shrank not from its other horrors.

"Ha! ha! ha!" roared Goodman Brown when the wind laughed at him. "Let us hear which will laugh loudest. Think not to frighten me with your deviltry. Come witch, come wizard, come Indian powwow, come devil himself, and here comes Goodman Brown. You may as well fear him as he fear you."

In truth, all through the haunted forest there could be nothing more frightful than the figure of Goodman Brown. On he flew among the black pines, brandishing his staff with frenzied gestures, now giving vent to an inspiration of horrid blasphemy, and now shouting forth such laughter as set all the echoes of the forest laughing like demons around him. The fiend in his own shape is less hideous than when he rages in the breast of man. Thus sped the demoniac on his course, until, quivering among the trees, he saw a red light before him, as when the felled trunks and branches of a clearing have been set on fire, and throw up their lurid blaze against the sky, at the hour of midnight. He paused, in a lull of the tempest that had driven him onward, and heard the swell of what seemed a hymn, rolling solemnly from a distance with the weight of many voices. He knew the tune; it was a familiar one in the choir of the village meeting-house. The verse died heavily away, and was lengthened by a chorus, not of human voices, but of all the sounds of the benighted wilderness pealing in awful harmony together. Goodman Brown cried out, and his cry was lost to his own ear by its unison with the cry of the desert.

In the interval of silence he stole forward until the light glared full upon his eyes. At one extremity of an open space, hemmed in by the dark wall of the forest, arose a rock, bearing some rude, natural resemblance either to an altar or a pulpit, and surrounded by four blazing pines, their tops aflame, their stems untouched, like candles at an evening meeting. The mass of foliage that had overgrown the summit of the rock was all on fire, blazing high into the night and fitfully illuminating the whole field. Each pendent twig and leafy festoon was in a blaze. As the red light arose and fell, a numerous congregation alternately shone forth, then disappeared in shadow, and again grew, as it were, out of the darkness, peopling the heart of the solitary woods at once.

"A grave and dark-clad company," quoted Goodman Brown.

In truth they were such. Among them, quivering to and fro between gloom and splendor, appeared faces that would be seen next day at the council board of the province, and others which, Sabbath after Sabbath, looked devoutly heavenward, and benignantly over the crowded pews, from the holiest pulpits in the land. Some affirm that the lady of the governor was there. At least there were high dames well known to her, and wives of honored husbands, and widows, a great multitude, and ancient maidens, all of excellent repute, and fair young girls, who trembled lest their mothers should espy them. Either the sudden gleams of light flashing over the obscure field bedazzled Goodman Brown, or he recognized a score of the church members of Salem village famous for their especial sanctity. Good old Deacon Gookin had arrived, and waited at the skirts of that venerable saint, his revered pastor. But, irreverently consorting with these grave, reputable, and pious people, these elders of the church, these chaste dames and dewy virgins, there were men of dissolute lives and women of spotted fame, wretches given over to all mean and filthy vice, and suspected even of horrid crimes. It was strange to see that the good shrank not from the wicked, nor were the sinners abashed by the saints. Scattered also among their pale-faced enemies were the Indian priests, or powwows, who had often scared their native forest with more hideous incantations than any known to English witchcraft.

"But where is Faith?" thought Goodman Brown, and, as hope came into his heart, he trembled.

Another verse of the hymn arose, a slow and mournful strain, such as the pious love, but joined to words which expressed all that our nature can conceive of sin, and darkly hinted at far more. Unfathomable to mere mortals is the lore of fiends. Verse after verse was sung; and still the chorus of the desert swelled between like the deepest tone of a mighty organ; and with the final peal of that dreadful anthem there came a sound, as if the roaring wind, the rushing streams, the howling beasts, and every other voice of the unconcerted wilderness were mingling and according with the voice of guilty man in homage to the prince of all. The four blazing pines threw up a loftier flame, and obscurely discovered shapes and visages of horror on the smoke wreaths above the impious assembly. At the same moment the fire on the rock shot redly forth and formed a glowing arch above its base, where now appeared a figure. With reverence be it spoken, the figure bore no slight similitude, both in garb and manner, to some grave divine of the New England churches.

"Bring forth the converts!" cried a voice that echoed through the field and rolled into the forest.

At the word, Goodman Brown stepped forth from the shadow of the trees and approached the congregation, with whom he felt a loathful brotherhood by the sympathy of all that was wicked in his heart. He could have well-nigh sworn that the shape of his own dead father beckoned him to advance, looking downward from a smoke wreath, while a woman, with dim features of despair, threw out her hand to warn him back. Was it his mother? But he had no power to retreat one step, nor to resist, even in thought, when the minister and good old Deacon Gookin seized his arms and led him to the blazing rock. Thither came also the slender form of a veiled female, led between Goody Cloyse, that pious teacher of the catechism, and Martha Carrier, who had received the devil's promise to be queen of hell. A rampant hag was she. And there stood the proselytes beneath the canopy of fire.

"Welcome, my children," said the dark figure, "to the communion of your race. Ye have found thus young your nature and your destiny. My children, look behind you!"

They turned; and flashing forth, as it were, in a sheet of flame, the fiend worshippers were seen; the smile of welcome gleamed darkly on every visage.

"There," resumed the sable form, "are all whom ye have reverenced from youth. Ye deemed them holier than yourselves, and shrank from your own sin, contrasting it with their lives of righteousness and prayerful aspirations heavenward. Yet here are they all in my worshipping assembly. This night it shall be granted you to know their secret deeds: how hoary-bearded elders of the church have whispered wanton words to the young maids of their households; how many a woman, eager for widows' weeds, has given her husband a drink at bedtime and let him sleep his last sleep in her bosom; how beardless youths have made haste to inherit their fathers' wealth; and how fair damsels—blush not, sweet ones—have dug little graves in the garden, and bidden me, the sole guest, to an infant's funeral. By the sympathy of your human hearts for sin ye shall scent out all the places—whether in church, bed-chamber, street, field, or forest—where crime has been committed, and shall exult to behold the whole earth one stain of guilt, one mighty blood spot. Far more than this. It shall be yours to penetrate, in every bosom, the deep mystery of sin, the fountain of all wicked arts, and which inexhaustibly supplies more evil impulses than human power—than my power at its utmost—can make manifest in deeds. And now, my children, look upon each other."

They did so; and, by the blaze of the hell-kindled torches, the wretched man beheld his Faith, and the wife her husband, trembling before that unhallowed altar.

"Lo, there ye stand, my children," said the figure, in a deep and solemn tone, almost sad with its despairing awfulness, as if his once angelic nature could yet mourn for our miserable race. "Depending upon one another's hearts, ye had still hoped that virtue were not all a dream. Now are ye undeceived. Evil is the nature of mankind. Evil must be your only happiness. Welcome again, my children, to the communion of your race."

"Welcome," repeated the fiend worshippers, in one cry of despair and triumph.

And there they stood, the only pair, as it seemed, who were yet hesitating on the verge of wickedness in this dark world. A basin was hollowed, naturally, in the rock. Did it contain water, reddened by the lurid light? or was it blood? or, perchance, a liquid flame? Herein did the shape of evil dip his hand and prepare to lay the mark of baptism upon their foreheads, that they might be partakers of the mystery of sin, more conscious of the secret guilt of others, both in deed and thought, than they could now be of their own. The husband cast one look at his pale wife, and Faith at him. What polluted wretches would the next glance show them to each other, shuddering alike at what they disclosed and what they saw!

"Faith! Faith!" cried the husband, "look up to heaven, and resist the wicked one."

Whether Faith obeyed he knew not. Hardly had he spoken when he found himself amid calm night and solitude, listening to a roar of the wind which died heavily away through the forest. He staggered against the rock, and felt it chill and damp; while a hanging twig, that had been all on fire, besprinkled his cheek with the coldest dew.

The next morning young Goodman Brown came slowly into the street of Salem village, staring around him like a bewildered man. The good old minister was taking a walk along the graveyard to get an appetite for breakfast and meditate his sermon, and bestowed a blessing, as he passed, on Goodman Brown. He shrank from the venerable saint as if to avoid an anathema. Old Deacon Gookin was at domestic worship, and the holy words of his prayer were heard through the open window. "What God doth the wizard pray to?" quoth Goodman Brown. Goody Cloyse, that excellent old Christian, stood in the early sunshine at her own lattice, catechizing a little girl who had brought her a pint of morning's milk. Goodman Brown snatched away the child as from the grasp of the fiend himself. Turning the corner by the meeting-house, he spied the head of Faith, with the pink ribbons, gazing anxiously forth, and bursting into such joy at sight of him that she skipped along the street and almost kissed her husband before the whole village. But Goodman Brown looked sternly and sadly into her face, and passed on without a greeting.

Had Goodman Brown fallen asleep in the forest and only dreamed a wild dream of a witch-meeting?

Be it so if you will; but, alas! it was a dream of evil omen for young Goodman Brown. A stern, a sad, a darkly meditative, a distrustful, if not a desperate man did he become from the night of that fearful dream. On the Sabbath day, when the congregation were singing a holy psalm, he could not listen because an anthem of sin rushed loudly upon his ear and drowned all the blessed strain. When the minister spoke from the pulpit with power and fervid eloquence, and, with his hand on the open Bible, of the sacred truths of our religion, and of saint-like lives and triumphant deaths, and of future bliss or misery unutterable, then did Goodman Brown turn pale, dreading lest the roof should thunder down upon the gray blasphemer and his hearers. Often, awaking suddenly at midnight, he shrank from the bosom of Faith; and at morning or eventide, when the family knelt down at prayer, he scowled and muttered to himself, and gazed sternly at his wife, and turned away. And when he had lived long, and was borne to his grave a hoary corpse, followed by Faith, an aged woman, and children and grandchildren, a goodly procession, besides neighbors not a few, they carved no hopeful verse upon his tombstone, for his dying hour was gloom.

Edgar Allan Poe (1809–1849) was the son of an actor and an actress, both of whom died when he was a child; he later lived with John Allan, a wealthy businessman from Virginia. Poe left the Military Academy at West Point without a commission and became a poet, a critic, and a celebrated—if unstable—writer of short stories. He died in Baltimore—under somewhat mysterious circumstances—probably by violence. For further reading: Tales of the Grotesque and Arabesque (1840); Poe's Short Stories, edited by Killis Campbell (1927).

The Black Cat

EDGAR ALLAN POE

For the most wild, yet most homely narrative which I am about to pen, I neither expect nor solicit belief. Mad indeed would I be to expect it, in a case where my very senses reject their own evidence. Yet, mad am I not—and very surely do I not dream. But to-morrow I die, and to-day I would unburthen my soul. My immediate purpose is to place before the world, plainly, succinctly, and without comment, a series of mere household events. In their consequences, these events have terrified—have tortured—have destroyed me. Yet I will not attempt to expound them. To me, they have presented little but Horror—to many they will seem less terrible than *baroques*. Hereafter, perhaps, some intellect may be found which will reduce my phantasm to the common-place—some intellect more calm, more logical and far less excitable than my own, which will perceive, in the circumstances I detail with awe, nothing more than an ordinary succession of very natural causes and effects.

From my infancy I was noted for the docility and humanity of my disposition. My tenderness of heart was even so conspicuous as to make me the jest of my companions. I was especially fond of animals, and was indulged by my parents with a great variety of pets. With these I spent most of my time, and never was so happy as when feeding and caressing them. This peculiarity of character grew with my growth, and, in my manhood, I derived from it one of my principal sources of pleasure. To those who have cherished an affection for a faithful and sagacious dog, I need hardly

be at the trouble of explaining the nature or the intensity of the gratification thus derivable. There is something in the unselfish and self-sacri-
ficing love of a brute, which goes directly to the heart of him who has
had frequent occasion to test the paltry friendship and gossamer fidelity of
mere *Man*.

I married early, and was happy to find in my wife a disposition not
uncongenial with my own. Observing my partiality for domestic pets, she
lost no opportunity of procuring those of the most agreeable kind. We had
birds, gold fish, a fine dog, rabbits, a small monkey, and *a cat*.

This latter was a remarkably large and beautiful animal, entirely black,
and sagacious to an astonishing degree. In speaking of his intelligence, my
wife, who at heart was not a little tinctured with superstition, made frequent
allusion to the ancient popular notion, which regarded all black cats as
witches in disguise. Not that she was ever *serious* upon this point—and
I mention the matter at all for no better reason than that it happens, just
now, to be remembered.

Pluto—this was the cat's name—was my favorite pet and playmate.
I alone fed him, and he attended me wherever I went about the house.
It was even with difficulty that I could prevent him from following me
through the streets.

Our friendship lasted, in this manner, for several years, during which
my general temperament and character—through the instrumentality of
the Fiend Intemperance—had (I blush to confess it) experienced a radical alteration for the worse. I grew, day by day, more moody, more
irritable, more regardless of the feelings of others. I suffered myself
to use intemperate language to my wife. At length, I even offered her
personal violence. My pets, of course, were made to feel the change in
my disposition. I not only neglected, but ill-used them. For Pluto, however, I still retained sufficient regard to restrain me from maltreating
him, as I made no scruple of maltreating the rabbits, the monkey, or
even the dog, when by accident, or through affection, they came in my
way. But my disease grew upon me—for what disease is like Alcohol!—
and at length even Pluto, who was now becoming old, and consequently
somewhat peevish—even Pluto began to experience the effects of my ill
temper.

One night, returning home, much intoxicated, from one of my haunts
about town, I fancied that the cat avoided my presence. I seized him; when,
in his fright at my violence, he inflicted a slight wound upon my hand
with his teeth. The fury of a demon instantly possessed me. I knew myself no longer. My original soul seemed, at once, to take its flight from
my body; and a more than fiendish malevolence, gin-nurtured, thrilled every
fibre of my frame. I took from my waistcoat-pocket a pen-knife, opened
it, grasped the poor beast by the throat, and deliberately cut one of its

eyes from the socket! I blush, I burn, I shudder, while I pen the damnable atrocity.

When reason returned with the morning—when I had slept off the fumes of the night's debauch—I experienced a sentiment half of horror, half of remorse, for the crime of which I had been guilty; but it was, at best, a feeble and equivocal feeling, and the soul remained untouched. I again plunged into excess, and soon drowned in wine all memory of the deed.

In the meantime the cat slowly recovered. The socket of the lost eye presented, it is true, a frightful appearance, but he no longer appeared to suffer any pain. He went about the house as usual, but, as might be expected, fled in extreme terror at my approach. I had so much of my old heart left, as to be at first grieved by this evident dislike on the part of a creature which had once so loved me. But this feeling soon gave place to irritation. And then came, as if to my final and irrevocable overthrow, the spirit of PERVERSENESS. Of this spirit philosophy takes no account. Yet I am not more sure that soul lives, than I am that perverseness is one of the primitive impulses of the human heart—one of the indivisible primary faculties, or sentiments, which give direction to the character of Man. Who has not, a hundred times, found himself committing a vile or a silly action, for no other reason than because he knows he should *not*? Have we not a perpetual inclination, in the teeth of our best judgment, to violate that which is *Law*, merely because we understand it to be such? This spirit of perverseness, I say, came to my final overthrow. It was this unfathomable longing of the soul *to vex itself* —to offer violence to its own nature—to do wrong for the wrong's sake only—that urged me to continue and finally consummate the injury I had inflicted upon the unoffending brute. One morning, in cold blood, I slipped a noose about his neck and hung it to the limb of a tree;—hung it with the tears streaming from my eyes, and with the bitterest remorse at my heart;—hung it *because* I knew that it had loved me, and *because* I felt it had given me no reason of offense;—hung it *because* I knew that in so doing I was committing a sin—a deadly sin that would so jeopardize my immortal soul as to place it—if such a thing were possible—even beyond the reach of the infinite mercy of the Most Merciful and Most Terrible God.

On the night of the day on which this cruel deed was done, I was aroused from sleep by the cry of fire. The curtains of my bed were in flames. The whole house was blazing. It was with great difficulty that my wife, a servant, and myself, made our escape from the conflagration. The destruction was complete. My entire wordly wealth was swallowed up, and I resigned myself thenceforward to despair.

I am above the weakness of seeking to establish a sequence of cause and effect, between the disaster and the atrocity. But I am detailing a chain of facts—and wish not to leave even a possible link imperfect. On the day succeeding the fire, I visited the ruins. The walls, with one exception, had fallen in. This exception was found in a compartment wall, not very thick, which stood about the middle of the house, and against which had rested the head of my bed. The plastering had here, in great measure, resisted the action of the fire—a fact which I attributed to its having been recently spread. About this wall a dense crowd were collected, and many persons seemed to be examining a particular portion of it with very minute and eager attention. The words "strange!" "singular!" and other similar expressions, excited my curiosity. I approached and saw, as if graven in *bas relief* upon the the white surface, the figure of a gigantic *cat*. The impression was given with an accuracy truly marvellous. There was a rope about the animal's neck.

When I first beheld this apparition—for I could scarcely regard it as less —my wonder and my terror were extreme. But at length reflection came to my aid. The cat, I remembered, had been hung in a garden adjacent to the house. Upon the alarm of fire, this garden had been immediately filled by the crowd—by some one of whom the animal must have been cut from the tree and thrown, through an open window, into my chamber. This had probably been done with the view of arousing me from sleep. The falling of other walls had compressed the victim of my cruelty into the substance of the freshly-spread plaster; the lime of which, with the flames, and the *ammonia* from the carcass, had then accomplished the portraiture as I saw it.

Although I thus readily accounted to my reason, if not altogether to my conscience, for the startling fact just detailed, it did not the less fail to make a deep impression upon my fancy. For months I could not rid myself of the phantasm of the cat; and, during this period, there came back into my spirit a half-sentiment that seemed, but was not, remorse. I went so far as to regret the loss of the animal, and look about me, among the vile haunts which I now habitually frequented, for another pet of the same species, and of somewhat similar appearance, with which to supply its place.

One night as I sat, half stupified, in a den of more than infamy, my attention was suddenly drawn to some black object, reposing upon the head of one of the immense hogheads of Gin, or of Rum, which constituted the chief furniture of the apartment. I had been looking steadily at the top of this hogshead for some minutes, and what now caused me surprise was the fact that I had not sooner perceived the object thereupon. I approached it, and touched it with my hand. It was a black cat—a very large one—fully as large as Pluto, and closely resembling him in every respect but one. Pluto had not a white hair upon any portion of his body; but this cat had a large, although indefinite splotch of white, covering nearly the whole region of the breast.

Upon my touching him, he immediately arose, purred loudly, rubbed against my hand, and appeared delighted with my notice. This, then, was the very creature of which I was in search. I at once offered to purchase it of the landlord; but this person made no claim to it—knew nothing of it—had never seen it before.

I continued my caresses, and, when I prepared to go home, the animal evinced a disposition to accompany me. I permitted it to do so; occasionally stooping and patting it as I proceeded. When it reached the house it domesticated itself at once, and became immediately a great favorite with my wife.

For my own part, I soon found a dislike to it arising within me. This was just the reverse of what I had anticipated; but I know not how or why it was—its evident fondness for myself rather disgusted and annoyed. By slow degrees, these feelings of disgust and annoyance rose into the bitterness of hatred. I avoided the creature; a certain sense of shame, and the remembrance of my former deed of cruelty, preventing me from physically abusing it. I did not, for some weeks, strike, or otherwise violently ill use it; but gradually—very gradually—I came to look upon it with unutterable loathing, and to flee silently from its odious presence, as from the breath of a pestilence.

What added, no doubt, to my hatred of the beast, was the discovery, on the morning after I brought it home, that, like Pluto, it also had been deprived of one of its eyes. This circumstance, however, only endeared it to my wife, who, as I have already said, possessed, in a high degree, that humanity of feeling which had once been my distinguishing trait, and the source of many of my simplest and purest pleasures.

With my aversion to this cat, however, its partiality for myself seemed to increase. It followed my footsteps with a pertinacity which it would be difficult to make the reader comprehend. Whenever I sat, it would crouch beneath my chair, or spring upon my knees, covering me with its loathsome caresses. If I arose to walk it would get between my feet and thus nearly throw me down, or, fastening its long and sharp claws in my dress, clamber, in this manner, to my breast. At such times, although I longed to destroy it with a blow, I was yet withheld from so doing, partly by a memory of my former crime, but chiefly—let me confess it at once—by absolute *dread* of the beast.

This dread was not exactly a dread of physical evil—and yet I should be at a loss how otherwise to define it. I am almost ashamed to own—yes, even in this felon's cell, I am almost ashamed to own—that the terror and horror with which the animal inspired me, had been heightened by one of the merest chimæras it would be possible to conceive. My wife had called my attention, more than once, to the character of the mark of white hair, of which I have spoken, and which constituted the sole visible difference between the strange beast and the one I had destroyed. The reader will remember that this mark, although large, had been originally very indefinite; but, by slow degrees—degrees nearly imperceptible, and which for a long time my Reason struggled to reject as fanciful—it had, at length, assumed a rigorous distinctness of outline. It was now the representation of an object that I shudder to name—and for this, above all, I loathed, and dreaded, and would have rid myself of the monster *had I dared* —it was now, I say, the image of a hideous—ghastly thing—of the GALLOWS!—oh, mournful and terrible engine of Horror and of Crime—of Agony and of Death!

And now was I indeed wretched beyond the wretchedness of mere Humanity. And *a brute beast*—whose fellow I had contemptuously destroyed —*a brute beast* to work out for *me*—for me a man, fashioned in the image of the High God—so much of insufferable woe! Alas! neither by day nor by night knew I the blessing of Rest any more! During the former the creature left me no moment alone; and, in the latter, I started, hourly, from dreams of unutterable fear, to find the hot breath of *the thing* upon my face, and its vast weight—an incarnate Night-Mare that I had no power to shake off —incumbent eternally upon my *heart!*

Beneath the pressure of torments such as these, the feeble remnant of the good within me succumbed. Evil thoughts became my sole intimates— the darkest and most evil of thoughts. The moodiness of my usual temper increased to hatred of all things and of all mankind; while, from the sudden, frequent, and ungovernable outbursts of a fury to which I now blindly abandoned myself, my uncomplaining wife, alas! was the most usual and the most patient of sufferers.

One day she accompanied me, upon some household errand, into the cellar of the old building which our poverty compelled us to inhabit. The cat followed me down the steep stairs, and, nearly throwing me headlong, exasperated me to madness. Uplifting an axe, and forgetting, in my wrath, the childish dread which had hitherto stayed my hand, I aimed a blow at the animal which, of course, would have proved instantly fatal had it descended as I wished. But this blow was arrested by the hand of my wife. Goaded, by the interference, into a rage more than demoniacal, I withdrew my arm from her grasp and buried the axe in her brain. She fell dead upon the spot, without a groan.

This hideous murder accomplished, I sat myself forthwith, and with entire deliberation, to the task of concealing the body. I knew that I could not remove it from the house, either by day or by night, without the risk of being observed by the neighbors. Many projects entered my mind. At one period I thought of cutting the corpse into minute fragments, and destroying them by fire. At another, I resolved to dig a grave for it in the floor of the cellar. Again, I deliberated about casting it in the well in the yard—about packing it in a box, as if merchandize, with the usual arrangements, and so getting a porter to take it from the house. Finally I hit upon what I considered a far better expedient than either of these. I determined to wall it up in the cellar—as the monks of the middle ages are recorded to have walled up their victims.

For a purpose such as this the cellar was well adapted. Its walls were loosely constructed, and had lately been plastered throughout with a rough plaster, which the dampness of the atmosphere had prevented from hardening. Moreover, in one of the walls was a projection, caused by a false chimney, or fireplace, that had been filled up, and made to resemble the rest of the cellar. I made no doubt that I could readily displace the bricks at this point, insert the corpse, and wall the whole up as before, so that no eye could detect anything suspicious.

And in this calculation I was not deceived. By means of a crow-bar I easily dislodged the bricks, and, having carefully deposited the body against the inner wall, I propped it in that position, while, with little trouble, I relaid the whole structure as it originally stood. Having procured mortar, sand, and hair, with every possible precaution, I prepared a plaster which could not be distinguished from the old, and with this I very carefully went over the new brick-work. When I had finished, I felt satisfied that all was right. The wall did not present the slightest appearance of having been disturbed. The rubbish on the floor was picked up with the minutest care. I looked around triumphantly, and said to myself—"Here at least, then, my labor has not been in vain."

My next step was to look for the beast which had been the cause of so much wretchedness; for I had, at length, firmly resolved to put it to death. Had I been able to meet with it, at the moment, there could have been no doubt of its fate; but it appeared that the crafty animal had been alarmed at the violence of my previous anger, and forebore to present itself in my present mood. It is impossible to describe, or to imagine, the deep, the blissful sense of relief which the absence of the detested creature occasioned in my bosom. It did not make its appearance during the night —and thus for one night at least, since its introduction into the house, I soundly and tranquilly slept; aye, *slept* even with the burden of murder upon my soul!

The second and third day passed, and still my tormentor came not. Once again I breathed as a freeman. The monster, in terror, had fled the premises forever! I should behold it no more! My happiness was supreme! The guilt of my dark deed disturbed me but little. Some few inquiries had been made, but these had been readily answered. Even a search had been instituted —but of course nothing was to be discovered. I looked upon my future felicity as secured.

Upon the fourth day of the assassination, a party of the police came, very unexpectedly, into the house, and proceeded again to make rigorous investigation of the premises. Secure, however, in the inscrutability of my place of concealment, I felt no embarrassment whatever. The officers bade me accompany them in their search. They left no nook or corner unexplored. At length, for the third or fourth time, they descended into the cellar. I quivered not in a muscle. My heart beat calmly as that of one who slumbers in innocence. I walked the cellar from end to end. I folded my arms upon my bosom, and roamed easily to and fro. The police were thoroughly satisfied and prepared to depart. The glee at my heart was too strong to be restrained. I burned to say if but one word, by way of triumph, and to render doubly sure their assurance of my guiltlessness.

"Gentlemen," I said at last, as the party ascended the steps, "I delight to have allayed your suspicions. I wish you all health, and a little more courtesy. By the bye, gentlemen, this—this is a very well constructed house." [In the rabid desire to say something easily, I scarcely knew what I uttered at all.]—"I may say an *excellently* well constructed house. These walls—are you going, gentlemen—these walls are solidly put together;" and here, through the mere phrenzy of bravado, I rapped heavily, with a cane which I held in my hand, upon that very portion of the brick-work behind which stood the corpse of the wife of my bosom.

But may God shield and deliver me from the fangs of the Arch-Fiend! No sooner had the reverberation of my blows sunk into silence, than I was answered by a voice from within the tomb!—by a cry, at first muffled and broken, like the sobbing of a child, and then quickly swelling into one long, loud, and continuous scream, utterly anomalous and in- human—a howl—a wailing shriek, half of horror and half of triumph, such as might have arisen only out of hell, conjointly from the throats of the damned in their agony and of the demons that exult in the damnation.

Of my own thoughts it is folly to speak. Swooning, I staggered to the opposite wall. For one instant the party upon the stairs remained motion- less, through extremity of terror and of awe. In the next, a dozen stout arms were toiling at the wall. It fell bodily. The corpse, already greatly decayed and clotted with gore, stood erect before the eyes of the spectators. Upon its head, with red extended mouth and solitary eye of fire, sat the hideous beast whose craft had seduced me into murder, and whose informing voice had consigned me to the hangman. I had walled the monster up within the tomb!

Ambrose Bierce (1842–1914) was born in Ohio and
served as a staff officer in the Civil War. Later,
in San Francisco, he became an editor, a journalist, and a writer of polemics and short fiction.
His work deals with the macabre, the supernatural,
and the malevolent; his heroes are victims—often
lonely men, the doomed. Bierce went to Mexico and
was probably shot by one or another revolutionary
faction. For further reading: Tales of Soldiers and
Civilians (1891)—also published as In the Midst of
Life (1898).

One Kind of Officer

AMBROSE BIERCE

I   Of the uses of civility

Captain Ransome, it is not permitted to you to know *anything*. It is
sufficient that you obey my order—which permit me to repeat. If you
perceive any movement of troops in your front you are to open fire, and
if attacked hold this position as long as you can. Do I make myself understood, sir?"

"Nothing could be plainer. Lieutenant Price,"—this to an officer of his
own battery, who had ridden up in time to hear the order—"the general's
meaning is clear, is it not?"

"Perfectly."

The lieutenant passed on to his post. For a moment General Cameron
and the commander of the battery sat in their saddles, looking at each
other in silence. There was no more to say; apparently too much had
already been said. Then the superior officer nodded coldly and turned
his horse to ride away. The artillerist saluted slowly, gravely, and with
extreme formality. One acquainted with the niceties of military etiquette
would have said that by his manner he attested a sense of the rebuke
that he had incurred. It is one of the important uses of civility to signify
resentment.

When the general had joined his staff and escort, awaiting him at a
little distance, the whole cavalcade moved off toward the right of the
guns and vanished in the fog. Captain Ransome was alone, silent, motionless as an equestrian statue. The gray fog, thickening every moment,
closed in about him like a visible doom.

II   Under what circumstances men do not wish to be shot

The fighting of the day before had been desultory and indecisive. At the points of collision the smoke of battle had hung in blue sheets among the branches of the trees till beaten into nothing by the falling rain. In the softened earth the wheels of cannon and ammunition wagons cut deep, ragged furrows, and movements of infantry seemed impeded by the mud that clung to the soldiers' feet as, with soaken garments and rifles imperfectly protected by capes of overcoats they went dragging in sinuous lines hither and thither through dripping forest and flooded field. Mounted officers, their heads protruding from rubber ponchos that glittered like black armor, picked their way, singly and in loose groups, among the men, coming and going with apparent aimlessness and commanding attention from nobody but one another. Here and there a dead man, his clothing defiled with earth, his face covered with a blanket or showing yellow and claylike in the rain, added his dispiriting influence to that of the other dismal features of the scene and augmented the general discomfort with a particular dejection. Very repulsive these wrecks looked—not at all heroic, and nobody was accessible to the infection of their patriotic example. Dead upon the field of honor, yes; but the field of honor was so very wet! It makes a difference.

The general engagement that all expected did not occur, none of the small advantages accruing, now to this side and now to that, in isolated and accidental collisions being followed up. Half-hearted attacks provoked a sullen resistance which was satisfied with mere repulse. Orders were obeyed with mechanical fidelity; no one did any more than his duty.

"The army is cowardly to-day," said General Cameron, the commander of a Federal brigade, to his adjutant-general.

"The army is cold," replied the officer addressed, "and—yes, it doesn't wish to be like that."

He pointed to one of the dead bodies, lying in a thin pool of yellow water, its face and clothing bespattered with mud from hoof and wheel.

The army's weapons seemed to share its military delinquency. The rattle of rifles sounded flat and contemptible. It had no meaning and scarcely roused to attention and expectancy the unengaged parts of the line-of-battle and the waiting reserves. Heard at a little distance, the reports of cannon were feeble in volume and *timbre:* they lacked sting and resonance. The guns seemed to be fired with light charges, unshotted. And so the futile day wore on to its dreary close, and then to a night of discomfort succeeded a day of apprehension.

An army has a personality. Beneath the individual thoughts and emotions of its component parts it thinks and feels as a unit. And in this large, inclusive sense of things lies a wiser wisdom than the mere sum of all that it knows. On that dismal morning this great brute force, groping at the bottom of a white ocean of fog among trees that seemed as sea weeds, had a dumb consciousness that all was not well; that a day's manœuvring had resulted in a faulty disposition of its parts, a blind diffusion of its strength. The men felt insecure and talked among themselves of such tactical errors as with their meager military vocabulary they were able to name. Field and line officers gathered in groups and spoke more learnedly of what they apprehended with no greater clearness. Commanders of brigades and divisions looked anxiously to their connections on the right and on the left, sent staff officers on errands of inquiry and pushed skirmish lines silently and cautiously forward into the dubious region between the known and the unknown. At some points on the line the troops, apparently of their own volition, constructed such defenses as they could without the silent spade and the noisy ax.

One of these points was held by Captain Ransome's battery of six guns. Provided always with intrenching tools, his men had labored with diligence during the night, and now his guns thrust their black muzzles through the embrasures of a really formidable earthwork. It crowned a slight acclivity devoid of undergrowth and providing an unobstructed fire that would sweep the ground for an unknown distance in front. The position could hardly have been better chosen. It had this peculiarity, which Captain Ransome, who was greatly addicted to the use of the compass, had not failed to observe: it faced northward, whereas he knew that the general line of the army must face eastward. In fact, that part of the line was "refused"— that is to say, bent backward, away from the enemy. This implied that Captain Ransome's battery was somewhere near the left flank of the army; for an army in line of battle retires its flanks if the nature of the ground will permit, they being its vulnerable points. Actually, Captain Ransome appeared to hold the extreme left of the line, no troops being visible in that direction beyond his own. Immediately in rear of his guns occurred that conversation between him and his brigade commander, the concluding and more picturesque part of which is reported above.

III   How to play the cannon without notes

Captain Ransome sat motionless and silent on horseback. A few yards away his men were standing at their guns. Somewhere—everywhere within a few miles—were a hundred thousand men, friends and enemies. Yet he was alone. The mist had isolated him as completely as if he had been in the heart of a desert. His world was a few square yards of wet and trampled earth about the feet of his horse. His comrades in that ghostly domain were invisible and inaudible. These were conditions favorable to thought, and he was thinking. Of the nature of his thoughts his clear-cut handsome features yielded no attesting sign. His face was as inscrutable as that of the sphinx. Why should it have made a record which there was none to observe? At the sound of a footstep he merely turned his eyes in the direction whence it came; one of his sergeants, looking a giant in stature in the false perspective of the fog, approached, and when clearly defined and reduced to his true dimensions by propinquity, saluted and stood at attention.

"Well, Morris," said the officer, returning his subordinate's salute.

"Lieutenant Price directed me to tell you, sir, that most of the infantry has been withdrawn. We have not sufficient support."

"Yes, I know."

"I am to say that some of our men have been out over the works a hundred yards and report that our front is not picketed."

"Yes."

"They were so far forward that they heard the enemy."

"Yes."

"They heard the rattle of the wheels of artillery and the commands of officers."

"Yes."

"The enemy is moving toward our works."

Captain Ransome, who had been facing to the rear of his line—toward the point where the brigade commander and his cavalcade had been swallowed up by the fog—reined his horse about and faced the other way. Then he sat motionless as before.

"Who are the men who made that statement?" he inquired, without looking at the sergeant; his eyes were directed straight into the fog over the head of his horse.

"Corporal Hassman and Gunner Manning."

Captain Ransome was a moment silent. A slight pallor came into his face, a slight compression affected the lines of his lips, but it would have required a closer observer than Sergeant Morris to note the change. There was none in the voice.

"Sergeant, present my compliments to Lieutenant Price and direct him to open fire with all the guns. Grape."

The sergeant saluted and vanished in the fog.

IV   To introduce General Masterson

Searching for his division commander, General Cameron and his escort had followed the line of battle for nearly a mile to the right of Ransome's battery, and there learned that the division commander had gone in search of the corps commander. It seemed that everybody was looking for his immediate superior — an ominous circumstance. It meant that nobody was quite at ease. So General Cameron rode on for another half-mile, where by good luck he met General Masterson, the division commander, returning.

"Ah, Cameron," said the higher officer, reining up, and throwing his right leg cross the pommel of his saddle in a most unmilitary way—"anything up? Found a good position for your battery, I hope—if one place is better than another in a fog."

"Yes, general," said the other, with the greater dignity appropriate to his less exalted rank, "my battery is very well placed.. I wish I could say that it is as well commanded."

"Eh, what's that? Ransome? I think him a fine fellow. In the army we should be proud of him."

It was customary for officers of the regular army to speak of it as "the army." As the greatest cities are most provincial, so the self-complacency of aristocracies is most frankly plebeian.

"He is too fond of his opinion. By the way, in order to occupy the hill that he holds I had to extend my line dangerously. The hill is on my left—that is to say the left flank of the army."

"Oh, no, Hart's brigade is beyond. It was ordered up from Drytown during the night and directed to hook on to you. Better go and—"

The sentence was unfinished: a lively cannonade had broken out on the left, and both officers, followed by their retinues of aides and orderlies making a great jingle and clank, rode rapidly toward the spot. But they were soon impeded, for they were compelled by the fog to keep within sight of the line-of-battle, behind which were swarms of men, all in motion across their way. Everywhere the line was assuming a sharper and harder definition, as the men sprang to arms and the officers, with drawn swords, "dressed" the ranks. Color-bearers unfurled the flags, buglers blew the "assembly," hospital attendants appeared with stretchers. Field officers mounted and sent their impedimenta to the rear in care of negro servants. Back in the ghostly spaces of the forest could be heard the rustle and murmur of the reserves, pulling themselves together.

Nor was all this preparation vain, for scarcely five minutes had passed since Captain Ransome's guns had broken the truce of doubt before the whole region was aroar: the enemy had attacked nearly everywhere.

V   How sounds can fight shadows

Captain Ransome walked up and down behind his guns, which were firing rapidly but with steadiness. The gunners worked alertly, but without haste or apparent excitement. There was really no reason for excitement;

it is not much to point a cannon into a fog and fire it. Anybody can do as much as that.

The men smiled at their noisy work, performing it with a lessening alacrity. They cast curious regards upon their captain, who had now mounted the banquette of the fortification and was looking across the parapet as if observing the effect of his fire. But the only visible effect was the substitution of wide, low-lying sheets of smoke for their bulk of fog. Suddenly out of the obscurity burst a great sound of cheering, which filled the intervals between the reports of the guns with startling distinctness! To the few with leisure and opportunity to observe, the sound was inexpressibly strange—so loud, so near, so menacing, yet nothing seen! The men who had smiled at their work smiled no more, but performed it with a serious and feverish activity.

From his station at the parapet Captain Ransome now saw a great multitude of dim gray figures taking shape in the mist below him and swarming up the slope. But the work of the guns was now fast and furious. They swept the populous declivity with gusts of grape and canister, the whirring of which could be heard through the thunder of the explosions. In this awful tempest of iron the assailants struggled forward foot by foot across their dead, firing into the embrasures, reloading, firing again, and at last falling in their turn, a little in advance of those who had fallen before. Soon the smoke was dense enough to cover all. It settled down upon the attack and, drifting back, involved the defense. The gunners could hardly see to serve their pieces, and when occasional figures of the enemy appeared upon the parapet—having had the good luck to get near enough to it, between two embrasures, to be protected from the guns—they looked so unsubstantial that it seemed hardly worth while for the few infantrymen to go to work upon them with the bayonet and tumble them back into the ditch.

As the commander of a battery in action can find something better to do than cracking individual skulls, Captain Ransome had retired from the parapet to his proper post in rear of his guns, where he stood with folded arms, his bugler beside him. Here, during the hottest of the fight, he was approached by Lieutenant Price, who had just sabred a daring assailant inside the work. A spirited colloquy ensued between the two officers—spirited, at least, on the part of the lieutenant, who gesticulated with energy and shouted again and again into his commander's ear in the attempt to make himself heard above the infernal din of the guns. His gestures, if coolly noted by an actor, would have been pronounced to be those of protestation: one would have said that he was opposed to the proceedings. Did he wish to surrender?

Captain Ransome listened without a change of countenance or attitude, and when the other man had finished his harangue, looked him coldly in the eyes and during a seasonable abatement of the uproar said:

"Lieutenant Price, it is not permitted to you to know *anything*. It is sufficient that you obey my orders."

The lieutenant went to his post, and the parapet being now apparently clear Captain Ransome returned to it to have a look over. As he mounted the banquette a man sprang upon the crest, waving a great brilliant flag. The captain drew a pistol from his belt and shot him dead. The body, pitching forward, hung over the inner edge of the embankment, the arms straight downward, both hands still grasping the flag. The man's few followers turned and fled down the slope. Looking over the parapet, the captain saw no living thing. He observed also that no bullets were coming into the work.

He made a sign to the bugler, who sounded the command to cease firing. At all other points the action had already ended with a repulse of the Confederate attack; with the cessation of this cannonade the silence was absolute.

VI Why, being affronted by A, it is not best to affront B

General Masterson rode into the redoubt. The men, gathered in groups, were talking loudly and gesticulating. They pointed at the dead, running from one body to another. They neglected their foul and heated guns and forgot to resume their outer clothing. They ran to the parapet and looked over, some of them leaping down into the ditch. A score were gathered about a flag rigidly held by a dead man.

"Well, my men," said the general cheerily, "you have had a pretty fight of it."

They stared; nobody replied; the presence of the great man seem to embarrass and alarm.

Getting no response to his pleasant condescension, the easy-mannered officer whistled a bar or two of a popular air, and riding 'forward to the parapet, looked over at the dead. In an instant he had whirled his horse about and was spurring along in rear of the guns, his eyes everywhere at once. An officer sat on the trail of one of the guns, smoking a cigar. As the general dashed up he rose and tranquilly saluted.

"Captain Ransome!"—the words fell sharp and harsh, like the clash of steel blades—"you have been fighting our own men—our own men, sir; do your hear? Hart's brigade!"

"General, I know that."

"You know it—you know that, and you sit here smoking? Oh, damn it, Hamilton, I'm losing my temper,"—this to his provost-marshal. "Sir—Captain Ransome, be good enough to say—to say why you fought our own men."

"That I am unable to say. In my orders that information was withheld."

Apparently the general did not comprehend.

"Who was the aggressor in this affair, you or General Hart?" he asked.

"I was."

"And could you not have known—could you not see, sir, that you were attacking our own men?"

The reply was astounding!

"I knew that, general. It appeared to be none of my business."

Then, breaking the dead silence that followed his answer, he said:

"I must refer you to General Cameron."

"General Cameron is dead, sir—as dead as he can be—as dead as any man in this army. He lies back yonder under a tree. Do you mean to say that he had anything to do with this horrible business?"

Captain Ransome did not reply. Observing the altercation his men had gathered about to watch the outcome. They were greatly excited. The fog, which had been partly dissipated by the firing, had again closed in so darkly about them that they drew more closely together till the judge on horseback and the accused standing calmly before him had but a narrow space free from intrusion. It was the most informal of courts-martial, but all felt that the formal one to follow would but affirm its judgment. It had no jurisdiction, but it had the significance of prophecy.

"Captain Ransome," the general cried impetuously, but with something in his voice that was almost entreaty, "if you can say anything to put a better light upon your incomprehensible conduct I beg you will do so."

Having recovered his temper this generous soldier sought for something to justify his naturally sympathetic attitude toward a brave man in the imminence of a dishonorable death.

"Where is Lieutenant Price?" the captain said.

The officer stood forward, his dark saturnine face looking somewhat forbidding under a bloody handkerchief bound about his brow. He understood the summons and needed no invitation to speak. He did not look at the captain, but addressed the general:

"During the engagement I discovered the state of affairs, and apprised the commander of the battery. I ventured to urge that the firing cease. I was insulted and ordered to my post."

"Do you know anything of the orders under which I was acting?" asked the captain.

"Of any orders under which the commander of the battery was acting," the lieutenant continued, still addressing the general, "I know nothing."

Captain Ransome felt his world sink away from his feet. In those cruel words he heard the murmur of the centuries breaking upon the shore of eternity. He heard the voice of doom; it said, in cold, mechanical, and measured tones: "Ready, aim, fire!" and he felt the bullets tear his heart to shreds. He heard the sound of the earth upon his coffin and (if the good God was so merciful) the song of a bird above his forgotten grave. Quietly detaching his sabre from its supports, he handed it up to the provost-marshal.

Samuel Langhorne Clemens (1835–1910) grew up in Hannibal, Missouri. He became a steamboat pilot, but left for the West when river traffic was disrupted by the Civil War. He achieved fame as a journalist, lecturer, and humorist. His novels are landmarks in American literature; his sketches and stories frequently exploit folk materials—the tall story, the practical joke. For further reading: A Tramp Abroad (1880), The Celebrated Jumping Frog of Calaveras County (1867).

Jim Baker's Blue-jay Yarn

MARK TWAIN

Animals talk to each other, of course. There can be no question about that; but I suppose there are very few people who can understand them. I never knew but one man who could. I knew he could, however, because he told me so himself. He was a middle-aged, simple-hearted miner who lived in a lonely corner of California, among the woods and mountains, a good many years, and had studied the ways of his only neighbors, the beasts and the birds, until he believed he could accurately translate any remark which they made. This was Jim Baker. According to Jim Baker, some animals have only a limited education, and use only very simple words, and scarcely ever a comparison or a flowery figure; whereas, certain other animals have a large vocabulary, a fine command of language and a ready and fluent delivery; consequently these latter talk a great deal; they like it; they are conscious of their talent, and they enjoy "showing off." Baker said, that after long and careful observation, he had come to the conclusion that the blue-jays were the best talkers he had found among birds and beasts. Said he:—

"There's more *to* a blue-jay than any other creature. He has got more moods, and more different kinds of feelings than other creature; and mind you, whatever a blue-jay feels, he can put into language. And no mere common-place language, either, but rattling, out-and-out book talk—and bristling with metaphor, too—just bristling! And as for command of language—why *you* never see a blue-jay get stuck for a word. No man ever did. They just boil out of him! And another thing: I've noticed a good deal, and there's no bird, or cow, or anything that uses as good grammar as a blue-jay. You may say a cat uses good grammar. Well, a cat does—but you let a cat get excited, once; you let a cat get to pulling fur with another cat on a shed, nights, and you'll hear grammar that will give you the lockjaw. Ignorant people think it's the *noise* which fighting cats make that is so aggravating, but it ain't so; it's the sickening grammar they use. Now I've never heard a jay use bad grammar but very seldom; and when they do, they are as ashamed as a human; they shut right down and leave.

"You may call a jay a bird. Well, so he is, in a measure—because he's got feathers on him, and don't belong to no church, perhaps; but otherwise he is just as much a human as you be. And I'll tell you for why. A jay's gifts, and instincts, and feelings, and interests, cover the whole ground. A jay hasn't got any more principle than a Congressman. A jay will lie, a jay will steal, a jay will deceive, a jay will betray; and four times out of five, a jay will go back on his solemnest promise. The sacredness of an obligation is a thing which you can't cram into no blue-jay's head. Now on top of all this, there's another thing: a jay can outswear any gentleman in the mines. You think a cat can swear. Well, a cat can; but you give a blue-jay a subject that calls for his reserve-powers, and where is your cat? Don't talk to *me*— I know too much about this thing. And there's yet another thing: in the one little particular of scolding—just good, clean, out-and-out scolding—a blue-jay can lay over anything, human or divine. Yes, sir, a jay is everything that a man is. A jay can cry, a jay can laugh, a jay can feel shame, a jay can reason and plan and discuss, a jay likes gossip and scandal, a jay has got a sense of humor, a jay knows when he is an ass just as well as you do —maybe better. If a jay ain't human, he better take in his sign, that's all. Now I'm going to tell you a perfectly true fact about some blue-jays."

"When I first begun to understand jay language correctly, there was a little incident happened here. Seven years ago, the last man in this region but me, moved away. There stands his house,—been empty ever since; a log house, with a plank roof—just one big room, and no more; no ceiling—nothing between the rafters and the floor. Well, one Sunday morning I was sitting out here in front of my cabin, with my cat, taking the sun, and looking at the blue hills, and listening to the leaves rustling; so lonely in the trees, and thinking of the home away yonder in the States, that I hadn't heard from in thirteen years, when a blue jay lit on that house, with an acorn in his mouth, and says, 'Hello, I reckon I've struck something.' When he spoke, the acorn dropped out of his mouth and rolled down the roof, of course, but he didn't care; his mind was all on the thing he had struck. It was a knot-hole in the roof. He cocked his head to one side, shut one eye and put the other to the hole, like a 'possum looking down a jug; then he glanced up with his bright eyes, gave a wink or two with his wings—which signifies gratification, you understand,—and says, 'It looks like a hole, it's located like a hole,—blamed if I don't believe it *is* a hole!'

"Then he cocked his head down and took another look, he glances up perfectly joyful, this time; winks his wings and his tail both, and says, 'O, no, this ain't no fat thing, I reckon! If I ain't in luck!—why it's a perfectly elegant hole!' So he flew down and got that acorn, and fetched it up and dropped it in, and was just tilting his head back, with the heavenliest smile on his face, when all of a sudden he was paralyzed into a listening attitude and that smile faded gradually out of his countenance like breath off'n a razor, and the queerest look of surprise took its place. Then he says, 'Why I didn't hear it fall!' He cocked his eye at the hole again, and took a long look; raised up and shook his head; stepped around to the other side of the hole and took another look from that side; shook his head again. He studied a while, then he just went into the *details*—walked round and round the hole and spied into it from every point of the compass. No use. Now he took a thinking attitude on the comb of the roof and scratched the back of his head with his right foot a minute, and finally says, 'Well, it's too many for *me*, that's certain; must be a mighty long hole; however, I ain't got no time to fool around here, I got to 'tend to business; I reckon it's all right—chance it, anyway.'

"So he flew off and fetched another acorn and dropped it in, and tried to flirt his eye to the hole quick enough to see what become of it, but he was too late. He held his eye there as much as a minute; then he raised up and sighed, and says, 'Consound it, I don't seem to understand this thing, no way; however, I'll tackle her again.' He fetched another acorn, and done his level best to see what become of it, but he couldn't. He says, 'Well,

I never struck no such a hole as this, before; I'm of the opinion it's a totally new kind of a hole.' Then he begun to get mad. He held in for a spell, walking up and down the comb of the roof and shaking his head and muttering to himself; but his feelings got the upper hand of him, presently, and he broke loose and cussed himself black in the face. I never see a bird take on so about a little thing. When he got through he walks to the hole and looks in again for half a minute; then he says, 'Well, you're a long hole, and a deep hole, and a mighty singular hole altogether—but I've started in to fill you, and I'm d—d if I *don't* fill you if it takes a hundred years!'

"And with that, away he went. You never see a bird work so since you was born. He laid into his work like a nigger, and the way he hove acorns into that hole for about two hours and a half was one of the most exciting and astonishing spectacles I ever struck. He never stopped to take a look any more—he just hove 'em in and went for more. Well at last he could hardly flop his wings, he was so tuckered out. He comes a-drooping down, once more, sweating like an ice-pitcher, drops his acorn in and says, '*Now* I guess I got the bulge on you by this time!' So he bent down for a look. If you'll believe me, when his head come up again he was just pale with rage. He says 'I've shoveled acorns enough in there to keep the family thirty years, and if I can see a sign of one of 'em I wish I may land in a museum with a belly full of sawdust in two minutes!'

"He just had strength enough to crawl up on to the comb and lean his back agin the chimbly, and then he collected his impressions and begun to free his mind. I see in a second that what I had mistook for profanity in the mines was only just the rudiments, as you may say.

"Another jay was going by, and heard him doing his devotions, and stops to inquire what was up. The sufferer told him the whole circumstance, and says, 'Now yonder's the hole, and if you don't believe me, go and look for yourself.' So this fellow went and looked, and comes back and says, 'How many did you say you put in there?' 'Not any less than two tons, says the sufferer. The other jay went and looked again. He couldn't seem to make it out, so he raised a yell, and three more jays come. They all examined the hole, they all made the sufferer tell it over again, then they all discussed it, and got off as many leather-headed opinions about it as an average crowd of humans could have done.

"They called in more jays; then more and more, till pretty soon this whole region 'peared to have a blue flush about it. There must have been five thousand of them; and such another jawing and disputing and ripping and cussing, you never heard. Every jay in the whole lot put his eye to the hole and delivered a more chuckle-headed opinion about the mystery than the jay that went there before him. They examined the house all over, too. The door was standing half open, and at last one old jay happened to go and light on it and look in. Of course that knocked the mystery galley-west in a second. There lay the acorns, scattered all over the floor. He flopped his wings and raised a whoop. 'Come here!' he says, 'Come here, everybody; hang'd if this fool hasn't been trying to fill up a house with acorns!' They all came a-swooping down like a blue cloud, and as each fellow lit on the door and took a glance, the whole absurdity of the contract that the first jay had tackled hit him home and he fell over backwards suffocating with laughter, and the next jay took his place and done the same.

"Well, sir, they roosted around here on the house-top and the trees for an hour, and guffawed over that thing like human beings. It ain't any use to tell me a blue-jay hasn't got a sense of humor, because I know better. And memory, too. They brought jays here from all over the United States to look down that hole, every summer for three years. Other birds too. And they could all see the point, except an owl that come from Nova Scotia to visit the Yo Semite, and he took this thing in on his way back. He said he couldn't see anything funny in it. But then he was a good deal disappointed about Yo Semite, too."

Charles W. Chesnutt (1858–1932), teacher, journalist, and practicing attorney, was the first American Negro recognized as a master of the short story. Born in Ohio, he was taken early in life to North Carolina. The Conjure Woman (1899) is a collection of stories told by "Uncle Julius"; other stories in The Wife of His Youth (1899) deal with black social problems after the Civil War. His novels are The House Behind the Cedars (1900), The Marrow of Tradition (1901), and The Colonel's Dream (1905).

The Web of Circumstance

C. W. CHESNUTT

I

W ithin a low clapboarded hut, with an open front, a forge was glowing. In front a blacksmith was shoeing a horse, a sleek, well-kept animal with the signs of good blood and breeding. A young mulatto stood by and handed the blacksmith such tools as he needed from time to time. A group of negroes were sitting around, some in the shadow of the shop, one in the full glare of the sunlight. A gentleman was seated in a buggy a few yards away, in the shade of a spreading elm. The horse had loosened a shoe, and Colonel Thornton, who was a lover of fine horse-flesh, and careful of it, had stopped at Ben Davis's blacksmith shop, as soon as he discovered the loose shoe, to have it fastened on.

"All right, Kunnel," the blacksmith called out. "Tom," he said, addressing the young man, "he'p me hitch up."

Colonel Thornton alighted from the buggy, looked at the shoe, signified his approval of the job, and stood looking on while the blacksmith and his assistant harnessed the horse to the buggy.

"Dat's a mighty fine whip yer got dere, Kunnel," said Ben, while the young man was tightening the straps of the harness on the opposite side of the horse. "I wush I had one like it. Where kin yer git dem whips?"

"My brother brought me this from New York," said the Colonel. "You can't buy them down here."

The whip in question was a handsome one. The handle was wrapped with interlacing threads of variegated colors, forming an elaborate pat-

145

tern, the lash being dark green. An octagonal ornament of glass was set in the end of the handle. "It cert'n'y is fine," said Ben; "I wish I had one like it." He looked at the whip longingly as Colonel Thornton drove away.

" 'Pears ter me Ben gittin mighty blooded," said one of the bystanders, "drivin' a hoss an' buggy, an' wantin' a whip like Colonel Thornton's."

"What's de reason I can't hab a hoss an' buggy an' a whip like Kunnel Tho'nton's, ef I pay fer em?" asked Ben. "We colored folks never had no chance ter git nothin' befo' de wah, but ef eve'y nigger in dis town had a tuck keer er his money sence de wah, like I has, an' bought as much lan' as I has, de niggers might 'a' got half de lan' by dis time," he went on, giving a finishing blow to a horseshoe, and throwing it on the ground to cool.

Carried away by his own eloquence, he did not notice the approach of two white men who came up the street from behind him.

"An' ef you niggers," he continued, raking the coals together over a fresh bar of iron, "would stop wastin' yo' money on 'scursions to put money in w'ite folks' pockets, an' stop buildin' fine chu'ches, an' buil' houses fer yo'se'ves, you'd git along much faster."

"You're talkin' sense, Ben," said one of the white men. "Yo'r people will never be respected till they've got property."

The conversation took another turn. The white men transacted their business and went away. The whistle of a neighboring steam sawmill blew a raucous blast for the hour of noon, and the loafers shuffled away in different directions.

"You kin go ter dinner, Tom," said the blacksmith. "An' stop at de gate w'en yer go by my house, and tell Nancy I'll be dere in 'bout twenty minutes. I got ter finish dis yer plough p'int fus'."

The young man walked away. One would have supposed, from the rapidity with which he walked, that he was very hungry. A quarter of an hour later the blacksmith dropped his hammer, pulled off his leather apron, shut the front door of the shop, and went home to dinner. He came into the house out of the fervent heat, and, throwing off his straw hat, wiped his brow vigorously with a red cotton handkerchief.

"Dem collards smells good," he said, sniffing the odor that came in through the kitchen door, as his good-looking yellow wife opened it to enter the room where he was. "I've got a monst'us good appetite ter-day. I feels good, too. I paid Majah Ransom de intrus' on de mortgage dis mawnin' an' a hund'ed dollahs besides, an' I spec's ter hab de balance ready by de fust of nex' Jiniwary; an' den we won't owe nobody a cent. I tell yer dere ain' nothin' like propputy ter make a pusson feel like a man. But w'at's de matter wid yer, Nancy? Is sump'n' skeered yer?"

The woman did seem excited and ill at ease. There was a heaving of the full bust, a quickened breathing that betokened suppressed excitement.

"I—I—jes' seen a rattlesnake out in de gyahden," she stammered.

The blacksmith ran to the door. "Which way? Whar wuz he?" he cried.

He heard a rustling in the bushes at one side of the garden, and the sound of a breaking twig, and, seizing a hoe which stood by the door, he sprang toward the point from which the sound came.

"No, no," said the woman hurriedly, "it wuz over here," and she directed her husband's attention to the other side of the garden.

The blacksmith, with the uplifted hoe, its sharp blade gleaming in the sunlight, peered cautiously among the collards and tomato plants, listening all the while for the ominous rattle, but found nothing.

"I reckon he's got away," he said, as he set the hoe up again by the door. "Whar's de chillen?" he asked with some anxiety. "Is dey playin' in de woods?"

"No," answered his wife, "dey've gone ter de spring."

The spring was on the opposite side of the garden from that on which the snake was said to have been seen, so the blacksmith sat down and fanned himself with a palm-leaf fan until the dinner was served.

"Yer ain't quite on time ter-day, Nancy," he said, glancing up at the clock on the mantel, after the edge of his appetite had been taken off. "Got ter make time ef yer wanter make money. "Did n' Tom tell yer I'd be heah in twenty minutes?"

"No," she said; "I seen him goin' pas'; he did n' say nothin'."

"I dunno w'at's de matter wid dat boy," mused the blacksmith over his apple dumpling. "He's gittin' mighty keerless heah lately; mus' hab sump'n' on 'is min',—some gal, I reckon."

The children had come in while he was speaking,—a slender, shapely boy, yellow like his mother, a girl several years younger, dark like her father: both bright-looking children and neatly dressed.

"I seen cousin Tom down by de spring," said the little girl, as she lifted off the pail of water that had been balanced on her head. "He come out er de woods jest ez we wuz fillin' our buckets."

"Yas," insisted the blacksmith, "he's got some gal on his min'."

II

The case of the State of North Carolina *vs.* Ben Davis was called. The accused was led into court, and took his seat in the prisoner's dock.

"Prisoner at the bar, stand up."

The prisoner, pale and anxious, stood up. The clerk read the indictment, in which it was charged that the defendant by force and arms had entered the barn of one G. W. Thornton, and feloniously taken therefrom one whip, of the value of fifteen dollars.

"Are you guilty or not guilty?" asked the judge.

"Not guilty, yo' Honah; not guilty, Jedge. I never tuck de whip."

The State's attorney opened the case. He was young and zealous. Recently elected to the office, this was his first batch of cases, and he was anxious to make as good a record as possible. He had no doubt of the prisoner's guilt. There had been a great deal of petty thieving in the county, and several gentlemen had suggested to him the necessity for greater severity in punishing it. The jury were all white men. The prosecuting attorney stated the case.

"We expect to show, gentlemen of the jury, the facts set out in the indictment,—not altogether by direct proof, but by a chain of circumstantial evidence which is stronger even than the testimony of eye-witnesses. Men might lie, but circumstances cannot. We expect to show that the defendant is a man of dangerous character, a surly, impudent fellow; a man whose views of property are prejudicial to the welfare of society, and who has been heard to assert that half the property which is owned in this county has been stolen, and that, if justice were done, the white people ought to divide up the land with the negroes; in other words, a negro nihilist, a communist, a secret devotee of Tom Paine and Voltaire, a pupil of the anarchist propaganda, which, if not checked by the stern hand of the law, will fasten its insidious fangs on our social system, and drag it down to ruin."

"We object, may it please your Honor," said the defendant's attorney. "The prosecutor should defer his argument until the testimony is in."

"Confine yourself to the facts, Major," said the court mildly.

The prisoner sat with half-open mouth, overwhelmed by this flood of eloquence. He had never heard of Tom Paine or Voltaire. He had no conception of what a nihilist or an anarchist might be, and could not have told the difference between a propaganda and a potato.

"We expect to show, may it please the court, that the prisoner had been employed by Colonel Thornton to shoe a horse; that the horse was taken to the prisoner's blacksmith shop by a servant of Colonel Thornton's; that, this servant expressing a desire to go somewhere on an errand before the horse had been shod, the prisoner volunteered to return the horse to Colonel Thornton's stable; that he did so, and the following morning the whip in question was missing; that, from circumstances, suspicion naturally fell upon the prisoner, and a search was made of his shop, where the whip was found secreted; that the prisoner denied that the whip was there, but when confronted with the evidence of his crime, showed by his confusion that he was guilty beyond a peradventure."

The prisoner looked more anxious; so much eloquence could not but be effective with the jury.

The attorney for the defendant answered briefly, denying the defendant's guilt, dwelling upon his previous good character for honesty, and begging the jury not to prejudge the case, but to remember that the law is merciful, and that the benefit of the doubt should be given to the prisoner.

The prisoner glanced nervously at the jury. There was nothing in their faces to indicate the effect upon them of the opening statements. It seemed to the disinterested listeners as if the defendant's attorney had little confidence in his client's cause.

Colonel Thornton took the stand and testified to his ownership of the whip, the place where it was kept, its value, and the fact that it had disappeared. The whip was produced in court and identified by the witness. He also testified to the conversation at the blacksmith shop in the course of which the prisoner had expressed a desire to possess a similar whip. The cross-examination was brief, and no attempt was made to shake the Colonel's testimony.

The next witness was the constable who had gone with a warrant to search Ben's shop. He testified to the circumstances under which the whip was found.

"He wuz brazen as a mule at fust, an' wanted ter git mad about it. But when we begun ter turn over that pile er truck in the cawner, he kinder begun ter trimble; when the whip-handle stuck out, his eyes commenced ter grow big, an' when we hauled the whip out he turned pale ez ashes, an' begun to swear he did n' take the whip an' did n' know how it got thar."

"You may cross-examine," said the prosecuting attorney triumphantly.

The prisoner felt the weight of the testimony, and glanced furtively at the jury, and then appealingly at his lawyer.

"You say that Ben denied that he had stolen the whip," said the prisoner's attorney, on cross-examination. "Did it not occur to you that what you took for brazen impudence might have been the evidence of conscious innocence?"

The witness grinned incredulously, revealing thereby a few blackened fragments of teeth.

"I've tuck up more 'n a hundred niggers fer stealin', Kurnel, an' I never seed one yit that did n' 'ny it ter the las'."

"Answer my question. Might not the witness's indignation have been a manifestation of conscious innocence? Yes or no?"

"Yes, it mought, an' the moon mought fall—but it don't."

Further cross-examination did not weaken the witness's testimony, which was very damaging, and every one in the court room felt instinctively that a strong defense would be required to break down the State's case.

"The State rests," said the prosecuting attorney, with a ring in his voice which spoke of certain victory.

There was a temporary lull in the proceedings, during which a bailiff passed a pitcher of water and a glass along the line of jurymen. The defense was then begun.

The law in its wisdom did not permit the defendant to testify in his own behalf. There were no witnesses to the facts, but several were called to testify to Ben's good character. The colored witnesses made him out possessed of all the virtues. One or two white men testified that they had never known anything against his reputation for honesty.

The defendant rested his case, and the State called its witnesses in rebuttal. They were entirely on the point of character. One testified that he had heard the prisoner say that, if the negroes had their rights, they would own at least half the property. Another testified that he had heard the defendant say that the negroes spent too much money on churches, and that they cared a good deal more for God than God had ever seemed to care for them.

Ben Davis listened to this testimony with half-open mouth and staring eyes. Now and then he would lean forward and speak perhaps a word, when his attorney would shake a warning finger at him, and he would fall back helplessly, as if abandoning himself to fate; but for a moment only, when he would resume his puzzled look.

The arguments followed. The prosecuting attorney briefly summed up the evidence, and characterized it as almost a mathematical proof of the prisoner's guilt. He reserved his eloquence for the closing argument.

The defendant's attorney had a headache, and secretly believed his client guilty. His address sounded more like an appeal for mercy than a demand for justice. Then the State's attorney delivered the maiden argument of his office, the speech that made his reputation as an orator, and opened up to him a successful political career.

The judge's charge to the jury was a plain, simple statement of the law as applied to circumstantial evidence, and the mere statement of the law foreshadowed the verdict.

The eyes of the prisoner were glued to the jury-box, and he looked more and more like a hunted animal. In the rear of the crowd of blacks who filled the back part of the room, partly concealed by the projecting angle of the fireplace, stood Tom, the blacksmith's assistant. If the face is the mirror of the soul, then this man's soul, taken off its guard in this moment of excitement, was full of lust and envy and all evil passions.

The jury filed out of their box, and into the jury room behind the judge's stand. There was a moment of relaxation in the court room. The lawyers fell into conversation across the table. The judge beckoned to Colonel Thornton, who stepped forward, and they conversed together a few moments. The prisoner was all eyes and ears in this moment of waiting, and from an involuntary gesture on the part of the judge he divined that they were speaking of him. It is a pity he could not hear what was said.

"How do you feel about the case, Colonel?" asked the judge.

"Let him off easy," replied Colonel Thornton. "He's the best blacksmith in the county."

The business of the court seemed to have halted by tacit consent, in anticipation of a quick verdict. The suspense did not last long. Scarcely ten minutes had elapsed when there was a rap on the door, the officer opened it, and the jury came out.

The prisoner, his soul in his eyes, sought their faces, but met no reassuring glance; they were all looking away from him.

"Gentlemen of the jury, have you agreed upon a verdict?"

"We have," responded the foreman. The clerk of the court stepped forward and took the fateful slip from the foreman's hand.

The clerk read the verdict: "We, the jury impaneled and sworn to try the issues in this cause, do find the prisoner guilty as charged in the indictment."

There was a moment of breathless silence. Then a wild burst of grief from the prisoner's wife, to which his two children, not understanding it all, but vaguely conscious of some calamity, added their voices in two long, discordant wails, which would have been ludicrous had they not been heart-rending.

The face of the young man in the back of the room expressed relief and badly concealed satisfaction. The prisoner fell back upon the seat from which he had half risen in his anxiety, and his dark face assumed an ashen hue. What he thought could only be surmised. Perhaps, knowing his innocence, he had not believed conviction possible; perhaps, conscious of guilt, he dreaded the punishment, the extent of which was optional with the judge, within very wide limits. Only one other person present knew whether or not he was guilty, and that other had slunk furtively from the court room.

Some of the spectators wondered why there should be so much ado about convicting a negro of stealing a buggy-whip. They had forgotten their own interest of the moment before. They did not realize out of what trifles grow the tragedies of life.

It was four o'clock in the afternoon, the hour for adjournment, when the verdict was returned. The judge nodded to the bailiff.

"Oyez, oyez! this court is now adjourned until ten o'clock to-morrow morning," cried the bailiff in a singsong voice. The judge left the bench, the jury filed out of the box, and a buzz of conversation filled the court room.

"Brace up, Ben, brace up, my boy," said the defendant's lawyer, half apologetically. "I did what I could for you, but you can never tell what a jury will do. You won't be sentenced till to-morrow morning. In the meantime I'll speak to the judge and try to get him to be easy with you. He may let you off with a light fine."

The negro pulled himself together, and by an effort listened.

"Thanky, Majah," was all he said. He seemed to be thinking of something far away.

He barely spoke to his wife when she frantically threw herself on him, and clung to his neck, as he passed through the side room on his way to jail. He kissed his children mechanically, and did not reply to the soothing remarks made by the jailer.

III

There was a good deal of excitement in town the next morning. Two white men stood by the post office talking.

"Did yer hear the news?"

"No, what wuz it?"

"Ben Davis tried ter break jail las' night."

"You don't say so! What a fool! He ain't be'n sentenced yit."

"Well, now," said the other, "I've knowed Ben a long time, an' he wuz a right good nigger. I kinder found it hard ter b'lieve he did steal that whip. But what's a man's feelin's ag'in' the proof?"

They spoke on awhile, using the past tense as if they were speaking of a dead man.

"Ef I know Jedge Hart, Ben 'll wish he had slep' las' night, 'stidder tryin' ter break out'n jail."

At ten o'clock the prisoner was brought into court. He walked with shambling gait, bent at the shoulders, hopelessly, with downcast eyes, and took his seat with several other prisoners who had been brought in for sentence. His wife, accompanied by the children, waited behind him, and a number of his friends were gathered in the court room.

The first prisoner sentenced was a young white man, convicted several days before of manslaughter. The deed was done in the heat of passion, under circumstances of great provocation, during a quarrel about a woman. The prisoner was admonished of the sanctity of human life, and sentenced to one year in the penitentiary.

The next case was that of a young clerk, eighteen or nineteen years of age, who had committed a forgery in order to procure the means to buy lottery tickets. He was well connected, and the case would not have been prosecuted if the judge had not refused to allow it to be nolled, and, once brought to trial, a conviction could not have been avoided.

"You are a young man," said the judge gravely, yet not unkindly, "and your life is yet before you. I regret that you should have been led into evil courses by the lust for speculation, so dangerous in its tendencies, so fruitful of crime and misery. I am led to believe that you are sincerely penitent, and that, after such punishment as the law cannot remit without bringing itself into contempt, you will see the error of your ways and follow the strict path of rectitude. Your fault has entailed distress not only upon yourself, but upon your relatives, people of good name and good family, who suffer as keenly from your disgrace as you yourself. Partly out of consideration for their feelings, and partly because I feel that, under the circumstances, the law will be satisfied by the penalty I shall inflict, I sentence you to imprisonment in the county jail for six months, and a fine of one hundred dollars and the costs of this action."

"The jedge talks well, don't he?" whispered one spectator to another.

"Yes, and kinder likes ter hear hisse'f talk," answered the other.

"Ben Davis, stand up," ordered the judge.

He might have said "Ben Davis, wake up," for the jailer had to touch the prisoner on the shoulder to rouse him from his stupor. He stood up, and something of the hunted look came again into his eyes, which shifted under the stern glance of the judge.

"Ben Davis, you have been convicted of larceny, after a fair trial before twelve good men of this county. Under the testimony, there can be no doubt of your guilt. The case is an aggravated one. You are not an ignorant, shiftless fellow, but a man of more than ordinary intelligence among your people, and one who ought to know better. You have not even the poor excuse of having stolen to satisfy hunger or a physical appetite. Your conduct is wholly without excuse, and I can only regard your crime as the result of a tendency to offenses of this nature, a tendency which is only too common among your people; a tendency which is a menace to civilization, a menace to society itself, for society rests upon the sacred right of property. Your opinions, too, have been given a wrong turn; you have been heard to utter sentiments which, if disseminated among an ignorant people, would breed discontent, and give rise to strained relations between them and their best friends, their old masters, who understand their real nature and their real needs, and to whose justice and enlightened guidance they can safely trust. Have you anything to say why sentence should not be passed upon you?"

"Nothin', suh, cep'n dat I did 'n take de whip."

"The law, largely, I think, in view of the peculiar circumstances of your unfortunate race, has vested a large discretion in courts as to the extent of the punishment for offenses of this kind. Taking your case as a whole, I am convinced that it is one which, for the sake of example, deserves a severe punishment. Nevertheless, I do not feel disposed to give you the full extent of the law, which would be twenty years in the penitentiary,[1] but, considering the fact that you have a family, and have heretofore borne a good reputation in the community, I will impose upon you the light sentence of imprisonment for five years in the penitentiary at hard labor. And I hope that this will be a warning to you and others who may be similarly disposed, and that after your sentence has expired you may lead the life of a law-abiding citizen."

"O Ben! O my husband! O God!" moaned the poor wife, and tried to press forward to her husband's side.

"Keep back, Nancy, keep back," said the jailer. "You can see him in jail."

Several people were looking at Ben's face. There was one flash of despair, and then nothing but a stony blank, behind which he masked his real feelings, whatever they were.

Human character is a compound of tendencies inherited and habits acquired. In the anxiety, the fear of disgrace, spoke the nineteenth century civilization with which Ben Davis had been more or less closely in touch during twenty years of slavery and fifteen years of freedom. In the stolidity with which he received this sentence for a crime which he had not committed, spoke who knows what trait of inherited savagery? For stoicism is a savage virtue.

IV

One morning in June, five years later, a black man limped slowly along the old Lumberton plank road; a tall man, whose bowed shoulders made him seem shorter than he was, and a face from which it was difficult to guess his years, for in it the wrinkles and flabbiness of age were found side by side with firm white teeth, and eyes not sunken,—eyes bloodshot, and burning with something, either fever or passion. Though he limped painfully with one foot, the other hit the ground impatiently, like the good horse in a poorly matched team. As he walked along, he was talking to himself:—

"I wonder what dey'll do w'en I git back? I wonder how Nancy's s'ported the fambly all dese years? Tuck in washin', I s'ppose,— she was a monst'us good washer an' ironer. I wonder ef de chillun'll be too proud ter reco'nize deir daddy come back f'um de penetenchy? I 'spec' Billy must be a big boy by dis time. He won' b'lieve his daddy ever stole anything. I'm gwine ter slip round' an' s'prise 'em."

Five minutes later a faced peered cautiously into the window of what

---

[1] There are no degrees of larceny in North Carolina, and the penalty for any offense lies in the discretion of the judge, to the limit of twenty years.

had once been Ben Davis's cabin,—at first an eager face, its coarseness lit up with the fire of hope; a moment later a puzzled face; then an anxious, fearful face as the man stepped away from the window and rapped at the door.

"Is Mis' Davis home?" he asked of the woman who opened the door.

"Mis' Davis don' live here. You er mistook in de house."

"Whose house is dis?"

"It b'longs ter my husban', Mr. Smith,— Primus Smith."

" 'Scuse me, but I knowed de house some years ago w'en I wuz here oncet on a visit, an' it b'longed ter a man name' Ben Davis."

"Ben Davis—Ben Davis?—oh yes, I 'member now. Dat wuz de gen'man w'at wuz sent ter de penitenchy fer sump'n er nuther,—sheep-stealin', I b'lieve. Primus," she called, "w'at wuz Ben Davis, w'at useter own dis yer house, sent ter de penitenchy fer?"

"Hoss-stealin'," came back the reply in sleepy accents, from the man seated by the fireplace.

The traveler went on to the next house. A neat-looking yellow woman came to the door when he rattled the gate, and stood looking suspiciously at him.

"W'at you want?" she asked.

"Please, ma'am, will you tell me whether a man name' Ben Davis useter live in dis neighborhood?"

"Useter live in de nex' house; wuz sent ter de penitenchy fer killin' a man."

"Kin yer tell me w'at went wid Mis' Davis?"

"Uuph! I's a 'spectable 'oman, I is, en don' mix wid dem kind er people. She wuz 'n' no better'n her husban'. She tuk up wid a man dat useter wuk for Ben, an' dey're livin' down by de ole wagon-ya'd, where no 'spectable 'oman ever puts her foot."

"An' de chillen?"

"De gal's dead. Wuz'n no better'n she oughter be'n. She fell in de crick an' got drown'; some folks say she wuz'n' sober w'en it happen'. De boy tuck atter his pappy. He wuz 'rested las' week fer shootin' a w'ite man, an' wuz lynch' de same night. Dey wa'n't none of 'em no 'count after deir pappy went ter de penitenchy."

"What went wid de proputty?"

"Hit wuz sol' fer de mortgage, er de taxes, er de lawyer, er sump'n,—I don' know w'at. A w'ite man got it."

The man with the bundle went on until he came to a creek that crossed the road. He descended the sloping bank, and, sitting on a stone in the shade of a water-oak, took off his coarse brogans, unwound the rags that served him in lieu of stockings, and laved in the cool water the feet that were chafed with many a weary mile of travel.

After five years of unrequited toil, and unspeakable hardship in convict camps,— five years of slaving by the side of human brutes, and of nightly herding with them in vermin-haunted huts,—Ben Davis had become like them. For a while he had received occasional letters from home, but in the shifting life of the convict camp they had long since ceased to reach him, if indeed they had been written. For a year or two, the consciousness of his innocence had helped to make him resist the debasing influences that surrounded him. The hope of shortening his sentence by good behavior, too, had worked a similar end. But the transfer from one contractor to another, each interested in keeping as long as possible a good worker, had speedily dissipated any such hope. When hope took flight, its place was not long vacant. Despair followed, and black hatred of all mankind, hatred especially of the man to whom he attributed all his misfortunes. One who is suffering unjustly is not apt to indulge in fine abstractions, nor to balance probabilities. By long brooding over his wrongs, his mind became, if not unsettled, at least warped, and he imagined that Colonel Thornton had deliberately set a trap into which he had fallen. The Colonel, he convinced himself, had disapproved of his prosperity, and had schemed to destroy it. He reasoned himself into the belief that he represented in his person the accumulated wrongs of a whole race, and Colonel Thornton the race who had oppressed them. A burning desire for revenge sprang up in him, and he nursed it until his sentence expired and he was set at liberty. What he had learned since reaching home had changed his desire into a deadly purpose.

When he had again bandaged his feet and slipped them into his shoes, he looked around him, and selected a stout sapling from among the undergrowth that covered the bank of the stream. Taking from his pocket a huge clasp-knife, he cut off the length of an ordinary walking stick and trimmed it. The result was an ugly-looking bludgeon, a dangerous weapon when in the grasp of a strong man.

With the stick in his hand, he went on down the road until he approached a large white house standing some distance back from the street. The grounds were filled with a profusion of shrubbery. The negro entered the gate and secreted himself in the bushes, at a point where he could hear any one that might approach.

It was near midday, and he had not eaten. He had walked all night, and had not slept. The hope of meeting his loved ones had been meat and drink and rest for him. But as he sat waiting, outraged nature asserted itself, and he fell asleep, with his head on the rising foot of a tree, and his face upturned.

And as he slept, he dreamed of his childhood; of an old black mammy taking care of him in the daytime, and of a younger face, with soft eyes, which bent over him sometimes at night, and a pair of arms which clasped him closely. He dreamed of his past,—of his young wife, of his bright children. Somehow his dreams all ran to pleasant themes for a while.

Then they changed again. He dreamed that he was in the convict camp, and, by an easy transition, that he was in hell, consumed with hunger, burning with thirst. Suddenly the grinning devil who stood over him with a barbed whip faded away, and a little white angel came and handed him a drink of water. As he raised it to his lips the glass slipped, and he struggled back to consciousness.

"Poo' man! Poo' man sick, an' sleepy. Dolly b'ing f'owers to cover poo' man up. Poo' man mus' be hungry. W'en Dolly get him covered up, she go b'ing poo' man some cake."

A sweet little child, as beautiful as a cherub escaped from Paradise, was standing over him. At first he scarcely comprehended the words the baby babbled out. But as they became clear to him, a novel feeling crept slowly over his heart. It had been so long since he had heard anything but curses and stern words of command, or the ribald songs of obscene merriment, that the clear tones of this voice from heaven cooled his calloused heart as the water of the brook had soothed his blistered feet. It was so strange, so unwonted a thing, that he lay there with half-closed eyes while the child brought leaves and flowers and laid them on his face and on his breast, and arranged them with little caressing taps.

She moved away, and plucked a flower. And then she spied another farther on, and then another, and, as she gathered them, kept increasing the distance between herself and the man lying there, until she was several rods away.

Ben Davis watched her through eyes over which had come an unfamiliar softness. Under the lingering spell of his dream, her golden hair, which fell in rippling curls, seemed like a halo of purity and innocence and peace, irradiating the atmosphere around her. It is true the thought occurred to Ben, vaguely, that through harm to her he might inflict the greatest punishment upon her father; but the idea came like a dark shape that faded away and vanished into nothingness as soon as it came within the nimbus that surrounded the child's person.

The child was moving on to pluck still another flower, when there came the sound of hoof-beats, and Ben was aware that a horseman, visible through the shrubbery, was coming along the curved path that led from the gate to the house. It must be the man he was waiting for, and now was the time to wreak his vengeance. He sprang to his feet, grasped his club, and stood for a moment irresolute. But either the instinct of the convict, beaten, driven, and debased, or the influence of the child, which was still strong upon him, impelled him, after the first momentary pause, to flee as though seeking safety.

His flight led him toward the little girl, whom he must pass in order to make his escape, and as Colonel Thornton turned the corner of the path he saw a desperate-looking negro, clad in filthy rags, and carrying in his hand a murderous bludgeon, running toward the child, who, startled by the sound of footsteps, had turned and was looking toward the approaching man with wondering eyes. A sickening fear came over the father's heart, and drawing the ever-ready revolver, which according to the Southern custom he carried always upon his person, he fired with unerring aim. Ben Davis ran a few yards farther, faltered, threw out his hands, and fell dead at the child's feet.

Some time, we are told, when the cycle of years has rolled around, there is to be another golden age, when all men will dwell together in love and harmony, and when peace and righteousness shall prevail for a thousand years. God speed the day, and let not the shining thread of hope become so enmeshed in the web of circumstance that we lose sight of it; but give us here and there, and now and then, some little foretaste of this golden age, that we may the more patiently and hopefully await its coming!

Frank Norris (1870–1902) left Chicago to become an art student in Paris. He returned to America to study and later worked as a magazine editor and journalist, most notably as a foreign correspondent in Cuba during the Spanish-American War. He is widely recognized for his novels of social problems and corruption in business, his most famous works being The Octopus (1901) and The Pit (1903). For further reading: A Deal in Wheat and Other Stories (1903).

A Deal in Wheat

FRANK NORRIS

I   The bear—wheat at sixty-two

As Sam Lewiston backed the horse into the shafts of his buckboard and began hitching the tugs to the whiffletree, his wife came out from the kitchen door of the house and drew near, and stood for some time at the horse's head, her arms folded and her apron rolled around them. For a long moment neither spoke. They had talked over the situation so long and so comprehensively the night before that there seemed to be nothing more to say.

The time was late in the summer, the place a ranch in southwestern Kansas, and Lewiston and his wife were two of a vast population of farmers, wheat growers, who at that moment were passing through a crisis—a crisis that at any moment might culminate in tragedy. Wheat was down to sixty-six.

At length Emma Lewiston spoke.

"Well," she hazarded, looking vaguely out across the ranch toward the horizon, leagues distant; "well, Sam, there's always that offer of brother Joe's. We can quit—and go to Chicago—if the worst comes."

"And give up!" exclaimed Lewiston, running the lines through the torets. "Leave the ranch! Give up! After all these years!"

His wife made no reply for the moment. Lewiston climbed into the buckboard and gathered up the lines. "Well, here goes for the last try, Emmie," he said. "Good-by, girl. Maybe things will look better in town to-day."

"Maybe," she said gravely. She kissed her husband good-by and stood for some time looking after the buckboard traveling toward the town in a moving pillar of dust.

"I don't know," she murmured at length; "I don't know just how we're going to make out."

When he reached town, Lewiston tied the horse to the iron railing in front of the Odd Fellows' Hall, the ground floor of which was occupied by the post-office, and went across the street and up the stairway of a building of brick and granite—quite the most pretentious structure of the town—and knocked at a door upon the first landing. The door was furnished with a pane of frosted glass, on which, in gold letters, was inscribed, "Bridges & Co., Grain Dealers."

Bridges himself, a middle-aged man who wore a velvet skull-cap and who was smoking a Pittsburgh stogie, met the farmer at the counter and the two exchanged perfunctory greetings.

"Well," said Lewiston, tentatively, after awhile.

"Well, Lewiston," said the other, "I can't take that wheat of yours at any better than sixty-two."

"Sixty-*two*."

"It's the Chicago price that does it, Lewiston. Truslow is bearing the stuff for all he's worth. It's Truslow and the bear clique that stick the knife into us. The price broke again this morning. We've just got a wire."

"Good heavens," murmured Lewiston, looking vaguely from side to side. "That—that ruins me. I *can't* carry my grain any longer—what with storage charges and—and——Bridges, I don't see just how I'm going to make out. Sixty-two cents a bushel! Why, man, what with this and with that it's cost me nearly a dollar a bushel to raise that wheat, and now Truslow——"

He turned away abruptly with a quick gesture of infinite discouragement.

He went down the stairs, and making his way to where his buckboard was hitched, got in, and, with eyes vacant, the reins slipping and sliding in his limp, half-open hands, drove slowly back to the ranch. His wife had seen him coming, and met him as he drew up before the barn.

"Well?" she demanded.

"Emmie," he said as he got out of the buckboard, laying his arm across her shoulder, "Emmie, I guess we'll take up with Joe's offer. We'll go to Chicago. We're cleaned out!"

II   The bull—wheat at a dollar-ten

. . . —— *and said Party of the Second Part further covenants and agrees to merchandise such wheat in foreign ports, it being understood and agreed between the Party of the First Part and the Party of the Second Part that the wheat hereinbefore mentioned is released and sold to the Party of the*

*Second Part for export purposes only, and not for consumption or distribu-
tion within the boundaries of the United States of America or of Canada.*

"Now, Mr. Gates, if you will sign for Mr. Truslow I guess that'll be all,"
remarked Hornung when he had finished reading.

Hornung affixed his signature to the two documents and passed them
over to Gates, who signed for his principal and client, Truslow—or, as he
had been called ever since he had gone into the fight against Hornung's
corner—the Great Bear. Hornung's secretary was called in and witnessed
the signatures, and Gates thrust the contract into his Gladstone bag and
stood up, smoothing his hat.

"You will deliver the warehouse receipts for the grain," began Gates.

"I'll send a messenger to Truslow's office before noon," interrupted
Hornung. "You can pay by certified check through the Illinois Trust
people."

When the other had taken himself off, Hornung sat for some moments
gazing abstractedly toward his office windows, thinking over the whole
matter. He had just agreed to release to Truslow, at the rate of one dollar
and ten cents per bushel, one hundred thousand out of the two million and
odd bushels of wheat that he, Hornung, controlled, or actually owned. And
for the moment he was wondering if, after all, he had done wisely in not
goring the Great Bear to actual financial death. He had made him pay one
hundred thousand dollars. Truslow was good for this amount. Would it not
have been better to have put a prohibitive figure on the grain and forced
the Bear into bankruptcy? True, Hornung would then be without his
enemy's money, but Truslow would have been eliminated from the situation, and that—so Hornung told himself—was always a consummation most
devoutly, strenuously and diligently to be striven for. Truslow once dead
was dead, but the Bear was never more dangerous than when desperate.

"But so long as he can't get *wheat*," muttered Hornung at the end of his
reflections, "he can't hurt me. And he can't get it. That I *know*."

For Hornung controlled the situation. So far back as the February of that
year an "unknown bull" had been making his presence felt on the floor of
the Board of Trade. By the middle of March the commercial reports of the
daily press had begun to speak of "the powerful bull clique"; a few weeks
later that legendary condition of affairs implied and epitomized in the magic
words "Dollar Wheat" had been attained, and by the first of April, when
the price had been boosted to one dollar and ten cents a bushel, Hornung
had disclosed his hand, and in place of mere rumours, the definite and
authoritative news that May wheat had been cornered in the Chicago pit
went flashing around the world from Liverpool to Odessa and from Duluth
to Buenos Ayres.

It was—so the veteran operators were persuaded—Truslow himself who
had made Hornung's corner possible. The Great Bear had for once over-

reached himself, and, believing himself all-powerful, had hammered the price just the fatal fraction too far down. Wheat had gone to sixty-two—for the time, and under the circumstances, an abnormal price. When the reaction came it was tremendous. Hornung saw his chance, seized it, and in a few months had turned the tables, had cornered the product, and virtually driven the bear clique out of the pit.

On the same day that the delivery of the hundred thousand bushels was made to Truslow, Hornung met his broker at his lunch club.

"Well," said the latter, "I see you let go that line of stuff to Truslow."

Hornung nodded; but the broker added:

"Remember, I was against it from the very beginning. I know we've cleared up over a hundred thou'. I would have fifty times preferred to have lost twice that and *smashed Truslow dead*. Bet you what you like he makes us pay for it somehow."

"Huh!" grunted his principal. "How about insurance, and warehouse charges, and carrying expenses on that lot? Guess we'd have had to pay those, too, if we'd held on."

But the other put up his chin, unwilling to be persuaded. "I won't sleep easy," he declared, "till Truslow is busted."

III   The pit

Just as Going mounted the steps on the edge of the pit the great gong struck, a roar of a hundred voices developed with the swiftness of successive explosions, the rush of a hundred men surging downward to the centre of the pit filled the air with the stamp and grind of feet, a hundred hands in eager strenuous gestures tossed upward from out of the brown of the crowd, the official reporter in his cage on the margin of the pit leaned far forward with straining ear to catch the opening bid, and another day of battle was begun.

Since the sale of the hundred thousand bushels of wheat to Truslow the "Hornung crowd" had steadily shouldered the price higher until on this particular morning it stood at one dollar and a half. That was Hornung's price. No one else had any grain to sell.

But not ten minutes after the opening, Going was surprised out of all countenance to hear shouted from the other side of the pit these words:

"Sell May at one-fifty."

Going was for the moment touching elbows with Kimbark on one side and with Merriam on the other, all three belonging to the "Hornung crowd." Their answering challenge of *"Sold"* was as the voice of one man. They did not pause to reflect upon the strangeness of the circumstance. (That was for afterward.) Their response to the offer was as unconscious as reflex action and almost as rapid, and before the pit was well aware of what had happened the transaction of one thousand bushels was down upon Going's trading-card and fifteen hundred dollars had changed hands. But here was a marvel—the whole available supply of wheat cornered, Hornung master of the situation, invincible, unassailable; yet behold a man willing to sell, a Bear bold enough to raise his head.

"That was Kennedy, wasn't it, who made that offer?" asked Kimbark, as Going noted down the trade—"Kennedy, that new man?"

"Yes; who do you suppose he's selling for; who's willing to go short at this stage of the game?"

"Maybe he ain't short."

"Short! Great heavens, man; where'd he get the stuff?"

"Blamed if I know. We can account for every handful of May. Steady! Oh, there he goes again."

"Sell a thousand May at one-fifty," vociferated the bear-broker, throwing out his hand, one finger raised to indicate the number of "contracts" offered. This time it was evident that he was attacking the Hornung crowd deliberately, for, ignoring the jam of traders that swept toward him, he looked across the pit to where Going and Kimbark were shouting "Sold! Sold!" and nodded his head.

A second time Going made memoranda of the trade, and either the Hornung holdings were increased by two thousand bushels of May wheat or the Hornung bank account swelled by at least three thousand dollars of some unknown short's money.

Of late—so sure was the bull crowd of its position—no one had even thought of glancing at the inspection sheet on the bulletin board. But now one of Going's messengers hurried up to him with the announcement that this sheet showed receipts at Chicago for that morning of twenty-five thousand bushels, and not credited to Hornung. Some one had got hold of a line of wheat overlooked by the "clique" and was dumping it upon them.

"Wire the Chief," said Going over his shoulder to Merriam. This one struggled out of the crowd, and on a telegraph blank scribbled:

"Strong bear movement—New man—Kennedy—Selling in lots of five contracts—Chicago receipts twenty-five thousand."

The message was despatched, and in a few moments the answer came back, laconic, of military terseness:

"Support the market."

And Going obeyed, Merriam and Kimbark following, the new broker fairly throwing the wheat at them in thousand-bushel lots.

"Sell May at 'fifty; sell May; sell May." A moment's indecision, an instant's hesitation, the first faint suggestion of weakness, and the market would have broken under them. But for the better part of four hours they stood their ground, taking all that was offered, in constant communication with the Chief, and from time to time stimulated and steadied by his brief, unvarying command:

"Support the market."

At the close of the session they had bought in the twenty-five thousand bushels of May. Hornung's position was as stable as a rock, and the price closed even with the opening figure—one dollar and a half.

But the morning's work was the talk of all La Salle Street. Who was back of the raid? What was the meaning of this unexpected selling? For weeks the pit trading had been merely nominal. Truslow, the Great Bear, from whom the most serious attack might have been expected, had gone to his country seat at Geneva Lake, in Wisconsin, declaring himself to be out of the market entirely. He went bass-fishing every day.

IV   The belt line

On a certain day toward the middle of the month, at a time when the mysterious Bear had unloaded some eighty thousand bushels upon Hornung, a conference was held in the library of Hornung's home. His broker attended it, and also a clean-faced, bright-eyed individual whose name of Cyrus Ryder might have been found upon the pay-roll of a rather well-known detective agency. For upward of half an hour after the conference began the detective spoke, the other two listening attentively, gravely.

"Then, last of all," concluded Ryder, "I made out I was a hobo, and began stealing rides on the Belt Line Railroad. Know the road? It just circles Chicago. Truslow owns it. Yes? Well, then I began to catch on. I noticed that cars of certain numbers—thirty-one nought thirty-four, thirty-two one ninety—well, the numbers don't matter, but anyhow, these cars were always switched onto the sidings by Mr. Truslow's main elevator D soon as they came in. The wheat was shunted in, and they were pulled out again. Well, I spotted one car and stole a ride on her. Say, look here, *that car went right around the city on the Belt, and came back to D again, and the same wheat in her all the time.* The grain was reinspected—it was raw, I tell you—and the warehouse receipts made out just as though the stuff had come in from Kansas or Iowa."

"The same wheat all the time!" interrupted Hornung.

"The same wheat—your wheat, that you sold to Truslow."

"Great snakes!" ejaculated Hornung's broker. "Truslow never took it abroad at all."

"Took it abroad! Say, he's just been running it around Chicago, like the supers in 'Shenandoah,' round an' round, so you'd think it was a new lot, an' selling it back to you again."

"No wonder we couldn't account for so much wheat."

"Bought it from us at one-ten, and made us buy it back—our own wheat
—at one-fifty."

Hornung and his broker looked at each other in silence for a moment.
Then all at once Hornung struck the arm of his chair with his fist and exploded in a roar of laughter. The broker stared for one bewildered moment,
then followed his example.

"Sold! Sold!" shouted Hornung almost gleefully. "Upon my soul it's as
good as a Gilbert and Sullivan show. And we—— Oh, Lord! Billy, shake
on it, and hats off to my distinguished friend, Truslow. He'll be President
some day. Hey! What? Prosecute him? Not I."

"He's done us out of a neat hatful of dollars for all that," observed the
broker, suddenly grave.

"Billy, it's worth the price."

"We've got to make it up somehow."

"Well, tell you what. We were going to boost the price to one seventy-
five next week, and make that our settlement figure."

"Can't do it now. Can't afford it."

"No. Here; we'll let out a big link; we'll put wheat at two dollars, and
let it go at that."

"Two it is, then," said the broker.

V   The bread line

The street was very dark and absolutely deserted. It was a district on the
"South Side," not far from the Chicago River, given up largely to wholesale
stores, and after nightfall was empty of all life. The echoes slept but lightly
hereabouts, and the slightest footfall, the faintest noise, woke them upon
the instant and sent them clamouring up and down the length of the pavement between the iron shuttered fronts. The only light visible came from
the side door of a certain "Vienna" bakery, where at one o'clock in the
morning loaves of bread were given away to any who should ask. Every
evening about nine o'clock the outcasts began to gather about the side door.
The stragglers came in rapidly, and the line—the "bread line," as it was
called—began to form. By midnight it was usually some hundred yards in
length, stretching almost the entire length of the block.

Toward ten in the evening, his coat collar turned up against the fine
drizzle that pervaded the air, his hands in his pockets, his elbows gripping
his sides, Sam Lewiston came up and silently took his place at the end of
the line.

Unable to conduct his farm upon a paying basis at the time when
Truslow, the "Great Bear," had sent the price of grain down to sixty-two
cents a bushel, Lewiston had turned over his entire property to his creditors,

and, leaving Kansas for good, had abandoned farming, and had left his wife at her sister's boarding-house in Topeka with the understanding that she was to join him in Chicago so soon as he had found a steady job. Then he had come to Chicago and had turned workman. His brother Joe conducted a small hat factory on Archer Avenue, and for a time he found there a meager employment. But difficulties had occurred, times were bad, the hat factory was involved in debts, the repealing of a certain import duty on manufactured felt overcrowded the home market with cheap Belgian and French products, and in the end his brother had assigned and gone to Milwaukee.

Thrown out of work, Lewiston drifted aimlessly about Chicago, from pillar to post, working a little, earning here a dollar, there a dime, but always sinking, sinking, till at last the ooze of the lowest bottom dragged at his feet and the rush of the great ebb went over him and engulfed him and shut him out from the light, and a park bench became his home and the "bread line" his chief makeshift of subsistence.

He stood now in the enfolding drizzle, sodden, stupefied with fatigue. Before and behind stretched the line. There was no talking. There was no sound. The street was empty. It was so still that the passing of a cable-car in the adjoining thoroughfare grated like prolonged rolling explosions, beginning and ending at immeasurable distances. The drizzle descended incessantly. After a long time midnight struck.

There was something ominous and gravely impressive in this interminable line of dark figures, close-pressed, soundless; a crowd, yet absolutely still; a close-packed, silent file, waiting, waiting in the vast deserted night-ridden street; waiting without a word, without a movement, there under the night and under the slow-moving mists of rain.

Few in the crowd were professional beggars. Most of them were workmen, long since out of work, forced into idleness by long-continued "hard times," by ill luck, by sickness. To them the "bread line" was a godsend. At least they could not starve. Between jobs here in the end was something to hold them up—a small platform, as it were, above the sweep of black water, where for a moment they might pause and take breath before the plunge.

The period of waiting on this night of rain seemed endless to those silent, hungry men; but at length there was a stir. The line moved. The side door opened. Ah, at last! They were going to hand out the bread.

But instead of the usual white-aproned undercook with his crowded hampers there now appeared in the doorway a new man—a young fellow who looked like a bookkeeper's assistant. He bore in his hand a placard, which he tacked to the outside of the door. Then he disappeared within the bakery, locking the door after him.

A shudder of poignant despair, an unformed, inarticulate sense of calamity, seemed to run from end to end of the line. What had happened? Those in the rear, unable to read the placard, surged forward, a sense of bitter disappointment clutching at their hearts.

The line broke up, disintegrated into a shapeless throng—a throng that crowded forward and collected in front of the shut door whereon the placard was affixed. Lewiston, with the others, pushed forward. On the placard he read these words:

"Owing to the fact that the price of grain has been increased to two dollars a bushel, there will be no distribution of bread from this bakery until further notice."

Lewiston turned away, dumb, bewildered. Till morning he walked the streets, going on without purpose, without direction. But now at last his luck had turned. Overnight the wheel of his fortunes had creaked and swung upon its axis, and before noon he had found a job in the street-cleaning brigade. In the course of time he rose to be first shift-boss, then deputy inspector, then inspector, promoted to the dignity of driving in a red wagon with rubber tires and drawing a salary instead of mere wages. The wife was sent for and a new start made.

But Lewiston never forgot. Dimly he began to see the significance of things. Caught once in the cogs and wheels of a great and terrible engine, he had seen—none better—its workings. Of all the men who had vainly stood in the "bread line" on that rainy night in early summer, he, perhaps, had been the only one who had struggled up to the surface again. How many others had gone down in the great ebb? Grim question; he dared not think how many.

He had seen the two ends of a great wheat operation—a battle between Bear and Bull. The stories (subsequently published in the city's press) of Truslow's countermove in selling Hornung his own wheat, supplied the unseen section. The farmer—he who raised the wheat—was ruined upon one hand; the working-man—he who consumed it—was ruined upon the other. But between the two, the great operators, who never saw the wheat they traded in, bought and sold the world's food, gambled in the nourishment of entire nations, practised their tricks, their chicanery and oblique shifty "deals," were reconciled in their differences, and went on through their appointed way, jovial, contented, enthroned, and unassailable.

The Bride Comes to Yellow Sky

STEPHEN CRANE

I

The great Pullman was whirling onward with such dignity of motion
that a glance from the window seemed simply to prove that the plains of
Texas were pouring eastward. Vast flats of green grass, dull-hued spaces
of mesquit and cactus, little groups of frame houses, woods of light and
tender trees, all were sweeping into the east, sweeping over the horizon, a
precipice.

A newly married pair had boarded this coach at San Antonio. The man's
face was reddened from many days in the wind and sun, and a direct
result of his new black clothes was that his brick-colored hands were constantly performing in a most conscious fashion. From time to time he looked
down respectfully at his attire. He sat with a hand on each knee, like a man
waiting in a barber's shop. The glances he devoted to other passengers were
furtive and shy.

The bride was not pretty, nor was she very young. She wore a dress of
blue cashmere, with small reservations of velvet here and there, and with
steel buttons abounding. She continually twisted her head to regard her puff
sleeves, very stiff, straight, and high. They embarrassed her. It was quite
apparent that she had cooked, and that she expected to cook, dutifully. The
blushes caused by the careless scrutiny of some passengers as she had entered the car were strange to see upon this plain, underclass countenance,
which was drawn in placid, almost emotionless lines.

They were evidently very happy. "Ever been in a parlor-car before?" he asked, smiling with delight.

"No," she answered; "I never was. It's fine, ain't it?"

"Great! And then after a while we'll go forward to the diner, and get a big lay-out. Finest meal in the world. Charge a dollar."

"Oh, do they?" cried the bride. "Charge a dollar? Why, that's too much —for us—ain't it, Jack?"

"Not this trip, anyhow," he answered bravely. "We're going to go the whole thing."

Later he explained to her about the trains. "You see, it's a thousand miles from one end of Texas to the other; and this train runs right across it, and never stops but four times." He had the pride of an owner. He pointed out to her the dazzling fittings of the coach; and in truth her eyes opened wider as she contemplated the sea-green figured velvet, the shining brass, silver, and glass, the wood that gleamed as darkly brilliant as the surface of a pool of oil. At one end a bronze figure sturdily held a support for a separated chamber, and at convenient places on the ceiling were frescos in olive and silver.

To the minds of the pair, their surroundings reflected the glory of their marriage that morning in San Antonio; this was the environment of their new estate; and the man's face in particular beamed with an elation that made him appear ridiculous to the negro porter. The individual at times surveyed them from afar with an amused and superior grin. On other occasions he bullied them with skill in ways that did not make it exactly plain to them that they were being bullied. He subtly used all the manners of the most unconquerable kind of snobbery. He oppressed them; but of this oppression they had small knowledge, and they speedily forgot that infrequently a number of travelers covered them with stares of derisive enjoyment. Historically there was supposed to be something infinitely humorous in their situation.

"We are due in Yellow Sky at 3:42," he said, looking tenderly into her eyes.

"Oh, are we?" she said, as if she had not been aware of it. To evince surprise at her husband's statement was part of her wifely amiability. She took from a pocket a little silver watch; and as she held it before her, and stared at it with a frown of attention, the new husband's face shone.

"I bought it in San Anton' from a friend of mine," he told her gleefully.

"It's seventeen minutes past twelve," she said, looking up at him with a kind of shy and clumsy coquetry. A passenger, noting this play, grew excessively sardonic, and winked at himself in one of the numerous mirrors.

At last they went to the dining-car. Two rows of negro waiters, in glowing white suits, surveyed their entrance with the interest, and also the equanimity, of men who had been forewarned. The pair fell to the lot of a waiter who happened to feel pleasure in steering them through their meal. He viewed them with the manner of a fatherly pilot, his countenance radiant with benevolence. The patronage, entwined with the ordinary deference, was not plain to them. And yet, as they returned to their coach, they showed in their faces a sense of escape.

To the left, miles down a long purple slope, was a little ribbon of mist where moved the keening Rio Grande. The train was approaching it at an angle, and the apex was Yellow Sky. Presently it was apparent that, as the distance from Yellow Sky grew shorter, the husband became commensurately restless. His brick-red hands were more insistent in their prominence. Occasionally he was even rather absent-minded and far-away when the bride leaned forward and addressed him.

As a matter of truth, Jack Potter was beginning to find the shadow of a deed weigh upon him like a leaden slab. He, the town marshal of Yellow Sky, a man known, liked, and feared in his corner, a prominent person, had gone to San Antonio to meet a girl he believed he loved, and there, after the usual prayers, had actually induced her to marry him, without consulting Yellow Sky for any part of the transaction. He was now bringing his bride before an innocent and unsuspecting community.

Of course people in Yellow Sky married as it pleased them, in accordance with a general custom; but such was Potter's thought of his duty to his friends, or of their idea of his duty, or of an unspoken form which does not control men in these matters, that he felt he was heinous. He had committed an extraordinary crime. Face to face with this girl in San Antonio, and spurred by his sharp impulse, he had gone headlong over all the social hedges. At San Antonio he was like a man hidden in the dark. A knife to sever any friendly duty, any form, was easy to his hand in that remote city. But the hour of Yellow Sky—the hour of daylight —was approaching.

He knew full well that his marriage was an important thing to his town. It could only be exceeded by the burning of the new hotel. His friends could not forgive him. Frequently he had reflected on the advisability of telling them by telegraph, but a new cowardice had been upon him. He feared to do it. And now the train was hurrying him toward a scene of amazement, glee, and reproach. He glanced out of the window at the line of haze swingingly slowly in toward the train.

Yellow Sky had a kind of brass band, which played painfully, to the delight of the populace. He laughed without heart as he thought of it. If the citizens could dream of his prospective arrival with his bride, they would parade the band at the station and escort them, amid cheers and laughing congratulations, to his adobe home.

He resolved that he would use all the devices of speed and plains-craft in making the journey from the station to his house. Once within that safe citadel, he could issue some sort of a vocal bulletin, and then not go among the citizens until they had time to wear off a little of their enthusiasm.

The bride look anxiously at him. "What's worrying you, Jack?"

He laughed again. "I'm not worrying, girl; I'm only thinking of Yellow Sky."

She flushed in comprehension.

A sense of mutual guilt invaded their minds and developed a finer tenderness. They looked at each other with eyes softly aglow. But Potter often laughed the same nervous laugh; the flush upon the bride's face seemed quite permanent.

The traitor to the feelings of Yellow Sky narrowly watched the speeding landscape. "We're nearly there," he said.

Presently the porter came and announced the proximity of Potter's home. He held a brush in his hand, and, with all his airy superiority gone, he brushed Potter's new clothes as the latter slowly turned this way and that way. Potter fumbled out a coin and gave it to the porter, as he had seen others do. It was a heavy and muscle-bound business, as that of a man shoeing his first horse.

The porter took their bag, and as the train began to slow they moved forward to the hooded platform of the car. Presently the two engines and their long string of coaches rushed into the station of Yellow Sky.

"They have to take water here," said Potter, from a constricted throat and in mournful cadence, as one announcing death. Before the train stopped his eye had swept the length of the platform, and he was glad and astonished to see there was none upon it but the station-agent, who, with a slightly hurried and anxious air, was walking toward the watertanks. When the train had halted, the porter alighted first, and placed in position a little temporary step.

"Come on, girl," said Potter, hoarsely. As he helped her down they each laughed on a false note. He took the bag from the negro, and bade his wife cling to his arm. As they slunk rapidly away, his hang-dog glance perceived that they were unloading the two trunks, and also that the station-agent, far ahead near the baggage-car, had turned and was running toward him, making gestures. He laughed, and groaned as he laughed, when he noted the first effect of his marital bliss upon Yellow Sky. He gripped his wife's arm firmly to his side, and they fled. Behind them the porter stood, chuckling fatuously.

II

The California express on the Southern Railway was due at Yellow Sky in twenty-one minutes. There were six men at the bar of the Weary Gentleman Saloon. One was a drummer, who talked a great deal and rapidly; three were Texans, who did not care to talk at that time; and two were Mexican sheep-herders, who did not talk as a general practice in the Weary Gentleman Saloon. The barkeeper's dog lay on the board walk that crossed in front of the door. His head was on his paws, and he glanced drowsily here and there with the constant vigilance of a dog that is kicked on occasion. Across the sandy street were some vivid green grass-plots, so wonderful in appearance, amid the sands that burned near them in a blazing sun, that they caused a doubt in the mind. They exactly resembled the grass mats used to represent lawns on the stage. At the cooler end of the railway station, a man without a coat sat in a tilted chair and smoked his pipe. The fresh-cut bank of the Rio Grande circled near the town, and there could be seen beyond it a great plum-colored plain of mesquit.

Save for the busy drummer and his companions in the saloon, Yellow Sky was dozing. The new-comer leaned gracefully upon the bar, and recited many tales with the confidence of a bard who has come upon a new field.

"—and at the moment that the old man fell down-stairs with the bureau in his arms, the old woman was coming up with two scuttles of coal, and of course—"

The drummer's tale was interrupted by a young man who suddenly appeared in the open door. He cried: "Scratchy Wilson's drunk, and has turned loose with both hands." The two Mexicans at once set down their glasses and faded out of the rear entrance of the saloon.

The drummer, innocent and jocular, answered: "All right, old man. S'pose he has? Come in and have a drink, anyhow."

But the information had made such an obvious cleft in every skull in the room that the drummer was obliged to see its importance. All had become instantly solemn. "Say," said he, mystified, "what is this?" His three companions made the introductory gesture of eloquent speech; but the young man at the door forestalled them.

"It means, my friend," he answered, as he came into the saloon, "that for the next two hours this town won't be a health resort."

The barkeeper went to the door, and locked and barred it; reaching out of the window, he pulled in heavy wooden shutters, and barred them. Immediately a solemn, chapel-like gloom was upon the place. The drummer was looking from one to another.

"But say," he cried, "what is this, anyhow? You don't mean there is going to be a gun-fight?"

"Don't know whether there'll be a fight or not," answered one man, grimly; "but there'll be some shootin'—some good shootin'."

The young man who had warned them waved his hand. "Oh, there'll be a fight fast enough, if any one wants it. Anybody can get a fight out there in the street. There's a fight just waiting."

The drummer seemed to be swayed between the interest of a foreigner and a perception of personal danger.

"What did you say his name was?" he asked.

"Scratchy Wilson," they answered in chorus.

"And will he kill anybody? What are you going to do? Does this happen often? Does he rampage around like this once a week or so? Can he break in that door?"

"No; he can't break down that door," replied the barkeeper. "He's tried three times. But when he comes you'd better lay down on the floor, stranger. He's dead sure to shoot at it, and a bullet may come through."

Thereafter the drummer kept a strict eye upon the door. The time had not yet been called for him to hug the floor, but, as a minor precaution, he sidled near to the wall. "Will he kill anybody?" he said again.

The men laughed low and scornfully at the question.

"He's out to shoot, and he's out for trouble. Don't see any good in experimentin' with him."

"But what do you do in a case like this? What do you do?"

A man responded: "Why, he and Jack Potter—"

"But," in chorus the other men interrupted, "Jack Potter's in San Anton'."

"Well, who is he? What's he got to do with it?"

"Oh, he's the town marshal. He goes out and fights Scratchy when he gets on one of these tears."

"Wow!" said the drummer, mopping his brow. "Nice job he's got."

The voices had toned away to mere whisperings. The drummer wished to ask further questions, which were born of an increasing anxiety and bewilderment; but when he attempted them, the men merely looked at him in irritation and motioned him to remain silent. A tense waiting hush was upon them. In the deep shadows of the room their eyes shone as they listened for sounds from the street. One man made three gestures at the barkeeper; and the latter, moving like a ghost, handed him a glass and a bottle. The man poured a full glass of whisky, and set down the bottle noiselessly. He gulped the whisky in a swallow, and turned again toward the door in immovable silence. The drummer saw that the barkeeper, without a sound, had taken a Winchester from beneath the

bar. Later he saw this individual beckoning to him, so he tiptoed across th
room.

"You better come with me back of the bar."

"No, thanks," said the drummer, perspiring; "I'd rather be where I ca
make a break for the back door."

Whereupon the man of bottles made a kindly but peremptory gestur.
The drummer obeyed it, and, finding himself seated on a box with hi
head below the level of the bar, balm was laid upon his soul at sight o
various zinc and copper fittings that bore a resemblance to armor-plate. Th
barkeeper took a seat comfortably upon an adjacent box.

"You see," he whispered, "this here Scratchy Wilson is a wonder with
gun—a perfect wonder; and when he goes on the war-trail, we hunt ou
holes—naturally. He's about the last one of the old gang that used to han,
out along the river here. He's a terror when he's drunk. When he's sobe
he's all right—kind of simple—would n't hurt a fly—nicest fellow in towr
But when he's drunk—whoo!"

There were periods of stillness. "I wish Jack Potter was back from Sa.
Anton'," said the barkeeper. "He shot Wilson up once,—in the leg,—an.
he would sail in and pull out the kinks in this thing."

Presently they heard from a distance the sound of a shot, followed b
three wild yowls. It instantly removed a bond from the men in the darkene.
saloon. There was a shuffling of feet. They looked at each other. "Here h.
comes," they said.

III

A man in a maroon-colored flannel shirt, which had been purchased fo
purposes of decoration, and made principally by some Jewish women on th
East Side of New York, rounded a corner and walked into the middle o
the main street of Yellow Sky. In either hand the man held a long, heavy
blue-black revolver. Often he yelled, and these cries rang through a sem
blance of a deserted village, shrilly flying over the roofs in a volume tha
seemed to have no relation to the ordinary vocal strength of a man. It wa.
as if the surrounding stillness formed the arch of a tomb over him. Thes
cries of ferocious challenge rang against walls of silence. And his boots ha.
red tops with gilded imprints, of the kind beloved in winter by little sled.
ding boys on the hillsides of New England.

The man's face flamed in a rage begot of whisky. His eyes, rolling, an.
yet keen for ambush, hunted the still doorways and windows. He walke.
with the creeping movement of the midnight cat. As it occurred to him
he roared menacing information. The long revolvers in his hands were a.
easy as straws; they were moved with an electric swiftness. The little finger.

f each hand played sometimes in a musician's way. Plain from the low
ollar of the shirt, the cords of his neck straightened and sank, straightened
nd sank, as passion moved him. The only sounds were his terrible invi-
ations. The calm adobes preserved their demeanor at the passing of this
mall thing in the middle of the street.

There was no offer of fight—no offer of fight. The man called to the sky.
'here were no attractions. He bellowed and fumed and swayed his revolvers
ere and everywhere.

The dog of the barkeeper of the Weary Gentleman Saloon had not appre-
iated the advance of events. He yet lay dozing in front of his master's
oor. At sight of the dog, the man paused and raised his revolver humor-
usly. At sight of the man, the dog sprang up and walked diagonally away,
vith a sullen head, and growling. The man yelled, and the dog broke into a
allop. As it was about to enter an alley, there was a loud noise, a whistling,
nd something spat the ground directly before it. The dog screamed, and,
vheeling in terror, galloped head-long in a new direction. Again there was
 noise, a whistling, and sand was kicked viciously before it. Fear-stricken,
he dog turned and flurried like an animal in a pen. The man stood laughing,
is weapons at his hips.

Ultimately the man was attracted by the closed door of the Weary
Gentleman Saloon. He went to it, and, hammering with a revolver, de-
nanded drink.

The door remaining imperturbable, he picked a bit of paper from the
valk, and nailed it to the framework with a knife. He then turned his
•ack contemptuously upon this popular resort, and, walking to the op-
•osite side of the street, and spinning there on his heel quickly and
ithely, fired at the bit of paper. He missed it by a half-inch. He swore
•t himself, and went away. Later he comfortably fusilladed the windows of
is most intimate friend. The man was playing with this town; it was a toy
or him.

But still there was no offer of fight. The name of Jack Potter, his ancient
ntagonist, entered his mind, and he concluded that it would be a glad
hing if he should go to Potter's house, and by bombardment induce him to
ome out and fight. He moved in the direction of his desire, chanting
Apache scalp-music.

When he arrived at it, Potter's house presented the same still front as had
he other adobes. Taking up a strategic position, the man howled a chal-
enge. But this house regarded him as might a great stone god. It gave no
ign. After a decent wait, the man howled further challenges, mingling with
hem wonderful epithets.

Presently there came the spectacle of a man churning himself into
leepest rage over the immobility of a house. He fumed at it as the
vinter wind attacks a prairie cabin in the North. To the distance there

should have gone the sound of a tumult like the fighting of two hun¬
dred Mexicans. As necessity bade him, he paused for breath or to reload his
revolvers.

IV

Potter and his bride walked sheepishly and with speed. Sometimes they
laughed together shamefacedly and low.

"Next corner, dear," he said finally.

They put forth the efforts of a pair walking bowed against a strong wind.
Potter was about to raise a finger to point the first appearance of the new
home when, as they circled the corner, they came face to face with a man
in a maroon-colored shirt, who was feverishly pushing cartridges into a
large revolver. Upon the instant the man dropped his revolver to the ground
and, like lightning, whipped another from its holster. The second weapon
was aimed at the bridegroom's chest.

There was a silence. Potter's mouth seemed to be merely a grave for his
tongue. He exhibited an instinct to at once loosen his arm from the woman's
grip, and he dropped the bag to the sand. As for the bride, her face had
gone as yellow as old cloth. She was a slave to hideous rites, gazing at the
apparitional snake.

The two men faced each other at a distance of three paces. He of the
revolver smiled with a new and quiet ferocity.

"Tried to sneak up on me," he said. "Tried to sneak up on me!" His eyes
grew more baleful. As Potter made a slight movement, the man thrust his
revolver venomously forward. "No; don't you do it, Jack Potter. Don't you
move a finger toward a gun just yet. Don't you move an eyelash. The time
has come for me to settle with you, and I'm goin' to do it my own way, and
loaf along with no interferin'. So if you don't want a gun bent on you, just
mind what I tell you."

Potter looked at his enemy. "I ain't got a gun on me, Scratchy," he said.
"Honest, I ain't." He was stiffening and steadying, but yet somewhere at the
back of his mind a vision of the Pullman floated: the sea-green figured
velvet, the shining brass, silver, and glass, the wood that gleamed as darkly
brilliant as the surface of a pool of oil—all the glory of the marriage, the
environment of the new estate. "You know I fight when it comes to fighting,
Scratchy Wilson; but I ain't got a gun on me. You'll have to do all the
shootin' yourself."

His enemy's face went livid. He stepped forward, and lashed his weapon
to and fro before Potter's chest. "Don't you tell me you ain't got no gun
on you, you whelp. Don't tell me no lie like that. There ain't a man in

Texas ever seen you without no gun. Don't take me for no kid." His eyes blazed with light, and his throat worked like a pump.

"I ain't takin' you for no kid," answered Potter. His heels had not moved an inch backward. "I'm takin' you for a —— fool. I tell you I ain't got a gun, and I ain't. If you're goin' to shoot me up, you better begin now; you'll never get a chance like this again."

So much enforced reasoning had told on Wilson's rage; he was calmer. "If you ain't got a gun, why ain't you got a gun?" he sneered. "Been to Sunday-school?"

"I ain't got a gun because I've just come from San Anton' with my wife. I'm married," said Potter. "And if I'd thought there was going to be any galoots like you prowling around when I brought my wife home, I'd had a gun, and don't you forget it."

"Married!" said Scratchy, not at all comprehending.

"Yes, married. I'm married," said Potter, distinctly.

"Married?" said Scratchy. Seemingly for the first time, he saw the drooping, drowning woman at the other man's side. "No!" he said. He was like a creature allowed a glimpse of another world. He moved a pace backward, and his arm, with the revolver, dropped to his side. "Is this the lady?" he asked.

"Yes; this is the lady," answered Potter.

There was another period of silence.

"Well," said Wilson at last, slowly, "I s'pose it's all off now."

"It's all off if you say so, Scratchy. You know I did n't make the trouble." Potter lifted his valise.

"Well, I 'low it's off, Jack," said Wilson. He was looking at the ground. "Married!" He was not a student of chivalry; it was merely that in the presence of this foreign condition he was a simple child of the earlier plains. He picked up his starboard revolver, and, placing both weapons in their holsters, he went away. His feet made funnel-shaped tracks in the heavy sand.

Mann
Averchenko
Hesse
Móricz
Kafka
Čapek
Babel
Myriveles
Katayev
Sartre
Forster
Joyce
Woolf

The Later Accomplishment

Lawrence
Bowen
O'Faolain
Greene
O'Connor
James
O. Henry
Anderson
Porter
Fitzgerald
Hughes
Steinbeck
Boyle
Farrell
Bellow

Thomas Mann (1875–1955) was born in Lubeck,
Germany, but after the advent of Hitler he lived
mostly in the United States. A Nobel Prize winner,
Mann established his early reputation with Bud-
denbrooks (1901); his best-known novel is The
Magic Mountain (1924). For further reading: Stories
of Three Decades, translated by H. T. Lowe-Porter
(1936).

Gladius Dei

THOMAS MANN

Munich was radiant. Above the gay squares and white columned temples,
the classicistic monuments and the baroque churches, the leaping fountains,
the palaces and parks of the Residence there stretched a sky of luminous
blue silk. Well-arranged leafy vistas laced with sun and shade lay basking
in the sunshine of a beautiful day in early June.

There was a twittering of birds and a blithe holiday spirit in all the little
streets. And in the squares and past the rows of villas there swelled, rolled,
and hummed the leisurely, entertaining traffic of that easy-going, charming
town. Travellers of all nationalities drove about in the slow little droshkies,
looking right and left in aimless curiosity at the house-fronts; they mounted
and descended museum stairs. Many windows stood open and music was
heard from within: practising on piano, cello, or violin—earnest and well-
meant amateur efforts; while from the Odeon came the sound of serious
work on several grand pianos.

Young people, the kind that can whistle the Nothung motif, who fill the
pit of the Schauspielhaus every evening, wandered in and out of the University and Library with literary magazines in their coat pockets. A court
carriage stood before the Academy, the home of the plastic arts, which
spreads its white wings between the Türkenstrasse and the Siegestor. And
colourful groups of models, picturesque old men, women and children in
Albanian costume, stood or lounged at the top of the balustrade.

Indolent, unhurried sauntering was the mode in all the long streets of the
northern quarter. There life is lived for pleasanter ends than the driving
greed of gain. Young artists with little round hats on the backs of their
heads, flowing cravats and no canes—carefree bachelors who paid for their
lodgings with colour-sketches—were strolling up and down to let the clear

blue morning play upon their mood, also to look at the little girls, the pretty, rather plump type, with the brunette bandeaux, the too large feet, and the unobjectionable morals. Every fifth house had studio windows blinking in the sun. Sometimes a fine piece of architecture stood out from a middle-class row, the work of some imaginative young architect; a wide front with shallow bays and decorations in a bizarre style very expressive and full of invention. Or the door to some monotonous façade would be framed in a bold improvisation of flowing lines and sunny colours, with bacchantes, naiads, and rosy-skinned nudes.

It was always a joy to linger before the windows of the cabinet-makers and the shops for modern articles *de luxe*. What a sense for luxurious nothings and amusing, significant line was displayed in the shape of everything! Little shops that sold picture-frames, sculptures, and antiques there were in endless number; in their windows you might see those busts of Florentine women of the Renaissance, so full of noble poise and poignant charm. And the owners of the smallest and meanest of these shops spoke of Mino da Fiesole and Donatello as though he had received the rights of reproduction from them personally.

But on the Odeonsplatz, in view of the mighty loggia with the spacious mosaic pavement before it, diagonally opposite to the Regent's palace, people were crowding round the large windows and glass show-cases of the big art-shop owned by M. Blüthenzweig. What a glorious display! There were reproductions of the masterpieces of all the galleries in the world, in costly decorated and tinted frames, the good taste of which was precious in its very simplicity. There were copies of modern paintings, works of a joyously sensuous fantasy, in which the antiques seemed born again in humorous and realistic guise; bronze nudes and fragile ornamental glassware; tall, thin earthenware vases with an iridescent glaze produced by a bath in metal steam; *éditions de luxe* which were triumphs of modern binding and presswork, containing the works of the most modish poets, set out with every possible advantage of sumptuous elegance. Cheek by jowl with these, the portraits of artists, musicians, philosophers, actors, writers, displayed to gratify the public taste for personalities.—In the first window, next the book-shop, a large picture stood on an easel, with a crowd of people in front of it, a fine sepia photograph in a wide old-gold frame, a very striking reproduction of the sensation at this year's great international exhibition, to which public attention is always invited by means of effective and artistic posters stuck up everywhere on hoardings among concert programmes and clever advertisements of toilet preparations.

If you looked into the windows of the book-shop your eye met such titles as *Interior Decoration Since the Renaissance, The Renaissance in Modern Decorative Art, The Book as Work of Art, The Decorative Arts, Hunger for Art*, and many more. And you would remember that these thought-provoking pamphlets were sold and read by the thousand and that discussions on these subjects were the preoccupation of all the salons.

You might be lucky enough to meet in person one of the famous fair ones whom less fortunate folk know only through the medium of art; one of those rich and beautiful women whose Titian-blond colouring Nature's most sweet and cunning hand did *not* lay on, but whose diamond parures and beguiling charms had received immortality from the hand of some portrait-painter of genius and whose love-affairs were the talk of the town. These were the queens of the artist balls at carnival-time. They were a little painted, a little made up, full of haughty caprices, worthy of adoration, avid of praise. You might see a carriage rolling up the Ludwigstrasse, with such a great painter and his mistress inside. People would be pointing out the sight, standing still to gaze after the pair. Some of them would curtsy. A little more and the very policemen would stand at attention.

Art flourished, art swayed the destinies of the town, art stretched above it her rose-bound sceptre and smiled. On every hand obsequious interest was displayed in her prosperity, on every hand she was served with industry and devotion. There was a downright cult of line, decoration, form, significance, beauty. Munich was radiant.

A youth was coming down the Schellingstrasse. With the bells of cyclists ringing about him he strode across the wooden pavement towards the broad facade of the Ludwigskirche. Looking at him it was as though a shadow passed across the sky, or cast over the spirit some memory of melancholy hours. Did he not love the sun which bathed the lovely city in its festal light? Why did he walk wrapped in his own thoughts, his eyes directed on the ground?

No one in that tolerant and variety-loving town would have taken offence at his wearing no hat; but why need the hood of his ample black cloak have been drawn over his head, shadowing his low, prominent, and peaked forehead, covering his ears and framing his haggard cheeks? What pangs of conscience, what scruples and self-tortures had so availed to hollow out these cheeks? It is frightful, on such a sunny day, to see care sitting in the hollows of the human face. His dark brows thickened at the narrow base of his hooked and prominent nose. His lips were unpleasantly full, his eyes brown and close-lying. When he lifted them, diagonal folds appeared on the peaked brow. His gaze expressed knowledge, limitation, and suffering. Seen in profile his face was strikingly like an old painting preserved at Florence in a narrow cloister cell whence once a frightful and shattering protest issued against life and her triumphs.

Hieronymus walked along the Schellingstrasse with a slow, firm stride, holding his wide cloak together with both hands from inside. Two little girls, two of those pretty, plump little creatures with the bandeaux, the big feet, and the unobjectionable morals, strolled towards him arm in arm, on pleasure bent. They poked each other and laughed, they bent double with laughter, they even broke into a run and ran away still laughing, at his hood and his face. But he paid them no heed. With bent head, looking neither to the right nor to the left, he crossed the Ludwigstrasse and mounted the church steps.

The great wings of the middle portal stood wide open. From somewhere within the consecrated twilight, cool, dank, incense-laden, there came a pale red glow. An old woman with inflamed eyes rose from a prayer-stool and slipped on crutches through the columns. Otherwise the church was empty.

Hieronymus sprinkled brow and breast at the stoup, bent the knee before the high altar, and then paused in the centre nave. Here in the church his stature seemed to have grown. He stood upright and immovable; his head was flung up and his great hooked nose jutted domineeringly above the thick lips. His eyes no longer sought the ground, but looked straight and boldly into the distance, at the crucifix on the high altar. Thus he stood awhile, then retreating he bent the knee again and left the church.

He strode up the Ludwigstrasse, slowly, firmly, with bent head, in the centre of the wide unpaved road, towards the mighty loggia with its statues. But arrived at the Odeonsplatz, he looked up, so that the folds came out on his peaked forehead, and checked his step, his attention being called to the crowd at the windows of the big art-shop of M. Blüthenzweig.

People moved from window to window, pointing out to each other the treasures displayed and exchanging views as they looked over one another's shoulders. Hieronymus mingled among them and did as they did, taking in all these things with his eyes, one by one.

He saw the reproductions of masterpieces from all the galleries in the world, the priceless frames so precious in their simplicity, the Renaissance sculpture, the bronze nudes, the exquisitely bound volumes, the iridescent vases, the portraits of artists, musicians, philosophers, actors, writers; he looked at everything and turned a moment of his scrutiny upon each object. Holding his mantle closely together with both hands from inside, he moved his hood-covered head in short turns from one thing to the next, gazing at each awhile with a dull, inimical, and remotely surprised air, lifting the dark brows which grew so thick at the base of the nose. At length he stood in front of the last window, which contained the startling picture. For a while he looked over the shoulders of people before him and then in his turn reached a position directly in front of the window.

The large red-brown photograph in the choice old-gold frame stood on an easel in the centre. It was a Madonna, but an utterly unconventional one, a work of entirely modern feeling. The figure of the Holy Mother was revealed as enchantingly feminine and beautiful. Her great smouldering eyes were rimmed with darkness, and her delicate and strangely smiling lips were half-parted. Her slender fingers held in a somewhat nervous grasp the hips of the Child, a nude boy of pronounced, almost primitive leanness. He was playing with her breast and glancing aside at the beholder with a wise look in his eyes.

Two other youths stood near Hieronymus, talking about the picture. They were two young men with books under their arms, which they had fetched from the Library or were taking thither. Humanistically educated people, that is, equipped with science and with art.

"The little chap is in luck, devil take me!" said one.

"He seems to be trying to make one envious," replied the other. "A bewildering female!"

"A female to drive a man crazy! Gives you funny ideas about the Immaculate Conception."

"No, she doesn't look exactly immaculate. Have you seen the original?"

"Of course; I was quite bowled over. She makes an even more aphrodisiac impression in colour. Especially the eyes."

"The likeness is pretty plain."

"How so?"

"Don't you know the model? Of course he used his little dress-maker. It is almost a portrait, only with a lot more emphasis on the corruptible. The girl is more innocent."

"I hope so. Life would be altogether too much of a strain if there were many like this *mater amata*."

"The Pinakothek has bought it."

"Really? Well, well! They knew what they were about, anyhow. The treatment of the flesh and the flow of the linen garment are really first-class."

"Yes, an incredibly gifted chap."

"Do you know him?"

"A little. He will have a career, that is certain. He has been invited twice by the Prince Regent."

This last was said as they were taking leave of each other.

"Shall I see you this evening at the theatre?" asked the first. "The Dramatic Club is giving Machiavelli's *Mandragola*."

"Oh, bravo! That will be great, of course. I had meant to go to the Variété, but I shall probably choose our stout Niccolò after all. Good-bye."

They parted, going off to right and left. New people took their places and looked at the famous picture. But Hieronymus stood where he was, motionless, with his head thrust out; his hands clutched convulsively at the mantle as they held it together from inside. His brows were no longer lifted with that cool and unpleasantly surprised expression; they were drawn and darkened; his cheeks; half-shrouded in the black hood, seemed more sunken than ever and his thick lips had gone pale. Slowly his head dropped lower and lower, so that finally his eyes stared upwards at the work of art, while the nostrils of his great nose dilated.

Thus he remained for perhaps a quarter of an hour. The crowd about him melted away, but he did not stir from the spot. At last he turned slowly on the balls of his feet and went hence.

But the picture of the Madonna went with him. Always and ever, whether in his hard and narrow little room or kneeling in the cool church, it stood before his outraged soul, with its smouldering, dark-rimmed eyes, its riddlingly smiling lips—stark and beautiful. And no prayer availed to exorcize it.

But the third night it happened that a command and summons from on high came to Hieronymus, to intercede and lift his voice against the frivolity, blasphemy, and arrogance of beauty. In vain like Moses he protested that he had not the gift of tongues. God's will remained unshaken; in a loud voice He demanded that the faint-hearted Hieronymus go forth to sacrifice amid the jeers of the foe.

And since God would have it so, he set forth one morning and wended his way to the great art-shop of M. Blüthenzweig. He wore his hood over his head and held his mantle together in front from inside with both hands as he went.

The air had grown heavy, the sky was livid and thunder threatened. Once more crowds were besieging the show-cases at the art-shop and especially the window where the photograph of the Madonna stood. Hieronymus cast one brief glance thither; then he pushed up the latch of the glass door hung with placards and art magazines. "As God wills," said he, and entered the shop.

A young girl was somewhere at a desk writing in a big book. She was a pretty brunette thing with bandeaux of hair and big feet. She came up to him and asked pleasantly what he would like.

"Thank you," said Hieronymus in a low voice and looked her earnestly in the face, with diagonal wrinkles in his peaked brow. "I would speak not to you but to the owner of this shop, Herr Blüthenzweig."

She hesitated a little, turned away, and took up her work once more. He stood there in the middle of the shop.

Instead of the single specimens in the show-windows there was here a riot and a heaping-up of luxury, a fullness of colour, line, form, style, invention, good taste, and beauty. Hieronymus looked slowly round him, drawing his mantle close with both hands.

There were several people in the shop besides him. At one of the broad tables running across the room sat a man in a yellow suit, with a black goat's-beard, looking at a portfolio of French drawings, over which he now and then emitted a bleating laugh. He was being waited on by an undernourished and vegetarian young man, who kept on dragging up fresh port-folios. Diagonally opposite the bleating man sat an elegant old dame, ex-amining art embroideries with a pattern of fabulous flowers in pale tones standing together on tall perpendicular stalks. An attendant hovered about her too. A leisurely Englishman in a travelling-cap, with his pipe in his mouth, sat at another table. Cold and smooth-shaven, of indefinite age, in his good English clothes, he sat examining bronzes brought to him by M. Blüthenzweig in person. He was holding up by the head the dainty figure of a nude young girl, immature and delicately articulated, her hands crossed in coquettish innocence under her breast. He studied her thor-oughly, turning her slowly about. M. Blüthenzweig, a man with a short, heavy brown beard and bright brown eyes of exactly the same colour, moved in a semicircle round him, rubbing his hands, praising the statuette with all the terms his vocabulary possessed.

"A hundred and fifty marks, sir," he said in English. "Munich art—very charming, in fact. Simply full of charm, you know. Grace itself. Really ex-tremely pretty, good, admirable, in fact." Then he thought of some more and went on: "Highly attractive, fascinating." Then he began again from the beginning.

His nose lay a little flat on his upper lip, so that he breathed constantly with a slight sniff into his moustache. Sometimes he did this as he ap-proached a customer, stooping over as though he were smelling at him. When Hieronymus entered, M. Blüthenzweig had examined him cursorily in this way, then devoted himself again to his Englishman.

The elegant old dame made her selection and left the shop. A man en-tered. M. Blüthenzweig sniffed briefly at him as though to scent out his capacity to buy and left him to the young bookkeeper. The man purchased a faience bust of young Piero de' Medici, son of Lorenzo, and went out again. The Englishman began to depart. He had acquired the statuette of the young girl and left amid bowings from M. Blüthenzweig. Then the art-dealer turned to Hieronymus and came forward.

"You wanted something?" he said, without any particular courtesy.

Hieronymus held his cloak together with both hands and looked the other in the face almost without winking an eyelash. He parted his big lips slowly and said:

"I have come to you on account of the picture in the window there, the big photograph, the Madonna." His voice was thick and without modulation.

"Yes, quite right," said M. Blüthenzweig briskly and began rubbing his hands. "Seventy marks in the frame. It is unfadable—a first-class reproduc-tion. Highly attractive and full of charm."

Hieronymus was silent. He nodded his head in the hood and shrank a little into himself as the dealer spoke. Then he drew himself up again and said:

"I would remark to you first of all that I am not in the position to purchase anything, nor have I the desire. I am sorry to have to disappoint your expectations. I regret if it upsets you. But in the first place I am poor and in the second I do not love the things you sell. No, I cannot buy anything."

"No? Well, then?" asked M. Blüthenzweig, sniffing a good deal. "Then may I ask—"

"I suppose," Hieronymus went on, "that being what you are you look down on me because I am not in a position to buy."

"Oh—er—not at all," said M. Blüthenzweig. "Not at all. Only—"

"And yet I beg you to hear me and give some consideration to my words."

"Consideration to your words. H'm—may I ask—"

"You may ask," said Hieronymus, "and I will answer you. I have come to beg you to remove that picture, the big photograph, the Madonna, out of your window and never display it again."

M. Blüthenzweig looked awhile dumbly into Hieronymus's face—as though he expected him to be abashed at the words he had just uttered. But as this did not happen he gave a violent sniff and spoke himself:

"Will you be so good as to tell me whether you are here in any official capacity which authorizes you to dictate to me, or what does bring you here?"

"Oh, no," replied Hieronymus, "I have neither office nor dignity from the state. I have no power on my side, sir. What brings me hither is my conscience alone."

M. Blüthenzweig, searching for words, snorted violently into his moustache. At length he said:

"Your conscience . . . well, you will kindly understand that I take not the faintest interest in your conscience." With which he turned round and moved quickly to his desk at the back of the shop, where he began to write. Both attendants laughed heartily. The pretty Fräulein giggled over her account-book. As for the yellow gentleman with the goat's beard, he was evidently a foreigner, for he gave no sign of comprehension but went on studying the French drawings and emitting from time to time his bleating laugh.

"Just get rid of the man for me," said M. Blüthenzweig shortly over his shoulder to his assistant. He went on writing. The poorly paid young vegetarian approached Hieronymus, smothering his laughter, and the other salesman came up too.

"May we be of service to you in any other way?" the first asked mildly. Hieronymus fixed him with his glazed and suffering eyes.

"No," he said, "you cannot. I beg you to take the Madonna picture out of the window, at once and forever."

"But—why?"

"It is the Holy Mother of God," said Hieronymus in a subdued voice.

"Quite. But you have heard that Herr Blüthenzweig is not inclined to accede to your request."

"We must bear in mind that it is the Holy Mother of God," said Hieronymus again and his head trembled on his neck.

"So we must. But should we not be allowed to exhibit any Madonnas— or paint any?"

"It is not that," said Hieronymus, almost whispering. He drew himself up and shook his head energetically several times. His peaked brow under the hood was entirely furrowed with long, deep cross-folds. "You know very well that it is vice itself that is painted there—naked sensuality. I was standing near two simple young people and overhead with my own ears that it led them astray upon the doctrine of the Immaculate Conception."

"Oh, permit me—that it not the point," said the young salesman, smiling. In his leisure hours he was writing a brochure on the modern movement in art and was well qualified to conduct a cultured conversation. "The picture is a work of art," he went on, "and one must measure it by the appropriate standards as such. It has been very highly praised on all hands. The state has purchased it."

"I know that the state has purchased it," said Hieronymus. "I also know that the artist has twice dined with the Prince Regent. It is common talk— and God knows how people interpret the fact that a man can become famous by such work as this. What does such a fact bear witness to? To the blindness of the world, a blindness inconceivable, if not indeed shamelessly hypocritical. This picture has its origin in sensual lust and is enjoyed in the same—is that true or not? Answer me! And you too answer me, Herr Blüthenzweig!"

A pause ensued. Hieronymus seemed in all seriousness to demand an answer to his question, looking by turns at the staring attendants and the round back M. Blüthenzweig turned upon him, with his own piercing and anguishing brown eyes. Silence reigned. Only the yellow man with the goat's beard bending over the French drawings, broke it with his bleating laugh.

"It is true," Hieronymus went on in a hoarse voice that shook with his profound indignation. "You do not dare deny it. How then can honour be done to its creator, as though he had endowed mankind with a new ideal possession? How can one stand before it and surrender unthinkingly to the base enjoyment which it purveys, persuading onself in all seriousness that one is yielding to a noble and elevated sentiment, highly creditable to the human race? Is this reckless ignorance or abandoned hypocrisy? My understanding falters, it is completely at a loss when confronted by the absurd fact that a man can achieve renown on this earth by the stupid and shameless exploitation of the animal instincts. Beauty? What is beauty? What forces are they which use beauty as their tool today—and upon what does it work? No one can fail to know this, Herr Blüthenzweig. But who, understanding it clearly, can fail to feel disgust and pain? It is criminal to play upon the ignorance of the immature, the lewd, the brazen, and the unscrupulous by elevating beauty into an idol to be worshipped, to give it even more power over those who know not affliction and have no knowledge of redemption. You are unknown to me, and you look at me with black looks—yet answer me! Knowledge, I tell you, is the profoundest torture in the world; but it is the purgatory without whose purifying pangs no soul can reach salvation. It is not infantile, blasphemous shallowness that can save us, Herr Blüthenzweig; only knowledge can avail, knowledge in which the passions of our loathsome flesh die away and are quenched."

Silence.—The yellow man with the goat's beard gave a sudden little bleat.

"I think you really must go now," said the underpaid assistant mildly.

But Hieronymus made no move to do so. Drawn up in his hooded cape, he stood with blazing eyes in the centre of the shop and his thick lips poured out condemnation in a voice that was harsh and rusty and clanking.

"Art, you cry; enjoyment, beauty! Enfold the world in beauty and endow all things with the noble grace of style!—Profligate, away! Do you think to wash over with lurid colours the misery of the world? Do you think with the sounds of feasting and music to drown out the voice of the tortured earth? Shameless one, you err! God lets not Himself be mocked, and your impudent deification of the glistering surface of things is an abomination in His eyes. You tell me that I blaspheme art. I say to you that you lie. I do not blaspheme art. Art is no conscienceless delusion, lending itself to reinforce the allurements of the fleshly. Art is the holy torch which turns its light upon all the frightful depths, all the shameful and woeful abysses of life; art is the godly fire laid to the world that, being redeemed by pity, it may flame up and dissolve altogether with its shames and torments.—Take it out, Herr Blüthenzweig, take away the work of that famous painter out of your window—you would do well to burn it with a hot fire and strew its ashes to the four winds—yes, to all the four winds—"

His harsh voice broke off. He had taken a violent backwards step, snatched one arm from his black wrappings, and stretched it passionately forth, gesturing towards the window with a hand that shook as though palsied. And in this commanding attitude he paused. His great hooked nose seemed to jut more than ever, his dark brows were gathered so thick and high that folds crowded upon the peaked forehead shaded by the hood; a hectic flush mantled his hollow cheeks.

But at this point M. Blüthenzweig turned round. Perhaps he was outraged by the idea of burning his seventy-mark reproduction; perhaps Hieronymus's speech had completely exhausted his patience. In any case he was a picture of stern and righteous anger. He pointed with his pen to the door of the shop, gave several short, excited snorts into his moustache, struggled for words, and uttered with the maximum of energy those which he found:

"My fine fellow, if you don't get out at once I will have my packer help you—do you understand?"

"Oh, you cannot intimidate me, you cannot drive me away, you cannot silence my voice!" cried Hieronymus as he clutched his cloak over his chest with his fists and shook his head doughtily. "I know that I am single-handed and powerless, but yet I will not cease until you hear me, Herr Blüthenzweig! Take the picture out of your window and burn it even today! Ah, burn not it alone! Burn all these statues and busts, the sight of which plunges the beholder into sin! Burn these vases and ornaments, these shameless revivals of paganism, these elegantly bound volumes of erotic verse! Burn everything in your shop, Herr Blüthenzweig, for it is a filthiness in God's sight. Burn it, burn it!" he shrieked, beside himself, describing a wild, all-embracing circle with his arm. "The harvest is ripe for the reaper, the measure of the age's shamelessness is full—but I say unto you—"

"Krauthuber!" Herr Blüthenzweig raised his voice and shouted towards a door at the back of the shop. "Come in here at once!"

And in answer to the summons there appeared upon the scene a massive overpowering presence, a vast and awe-inspiring, swollen human bulk, whose limbs merged into each other like links of sausage—a gigantic son of the people, malt-nourished and immoderate, who weighed in, with puffings, bursting with energy, from the packing-room. His appearance in the upper reaches of his form was notable for a fringe of walrus beard; a hide apron fouled with paste covered his body from the waist down, and his yellow shirt-sleeves were rolled back from his heroic arms.

"Will you open the door for this gentleman, Krauthuber?" said M. Blüthenzweig; "and if he should not find the way to it, just help him into the street."

"Huh," said the man, looking from his enraged employer to Hieronymus and back with his little elephant eyes. It was a heavy monosyllable, suggesting reserve force restrained with difficulty. The floor shook with his tread as he went to the door and opened it.

Hieronymus had grown very pale. "Burn—" he shouted once more. He was about to go on when he felt himself turned round by an irresistible power, by a physical preponderance to which no resistance was even thinkable. Slowly and inexorably he was propelled towards the door.

"I am weak," he managed to ejaculate. "My flesh cannot bear the force . . . it cannot hold its ground, no . . . but what does that prove? Burn—"

He stopped. He found himself outside the art-shop. M. Blüthenzweig's giant packer had let him go with one final shove, which set him down on the stone threshold of the shop, supporting himself with one hand. Behind him the door closed with a rattle of glass.

He picked himself up. He stood erect, breathing heavily, and pulled his cloak together with one fist over his breast, letting the other hang down inside. His hollow cheeks had a grey pallor; the nostrils of his great hooked nose opened and closed; his ugly lips were writhen in an expression of hatred and despair and his red-rimmed eyes wandered over the beautiful square like those of a man in a frenzy.

He did not see that people were looking at him with amusement and curiosity. For what he beheld upon the mosaic pavement before the great loggia were all the vanities of this world: the masked costumes of the artist balls, the decorations, vases and art objects, the nude statues, the female busts, the picturesque rebirths of the pagan age, the portraits of famous beauties by the hands of masters, the elegantly bound erotic verse, the art brochures—all these he saw heaped in a pyramid and going up in crackling flames amid loud exultations from the people enthralled by his own frightful words. A yellow background of cloud had drawn up over the Theatinerstrasse, and from it issued wild rumblings; but what he saw was a burning fiery sword, towering in sulphurous light above the joyous city.

"Gladius Dei super terram . . ." his thick lips whispered; and drawing himself still higher in his hooded cloak while the hand hanging down inside it twitched convulsively, he murmured, quaking: *"cito et velociter!"*

Arcadii Timotheich Averchenko (1881–1925) was a skit writer, a dramatist, and a humorist. His fantastic skits were played in such theater-cabarets as the Crooked Mirror in St. Petersburg. He left Russia in 1917 and died in Constantinople. Few of his stories are available in English.

The Young Man Who Flew Past

ARCADII AVERCHENKO

This sad and tragic occurrence began thus:

Three persons, in three different poses, were carrying on an animated conversation on the sixth floor of a large apartment building.

The woman, with plump beautiful arms, was clutching a bed sheet to her breast, forgetting that a bed sheet could not do double duty and cover her shapely bare knees at the same time. The woman was crying, and in the intervals between sobs she was saying:

"Oh, John! I swear to you I'm not guilty! He set my head in a whirl, he seduced me—and, I assure you, all against my will, I resisted—"

One of the men, still in his hat and overcoat, was gesticulating wildly and upbraiding the third person in the room:

"Scoundrel! I'm going to show you right now that you will perish like a cur and the law will be on my side! You shall pay for this meek victim! You reptile! You base seducer!"

The third in this room was a young man who, although not dressed with the greatest meticulousness at the present moment, bore himself, nevertheless, with great dignity.

"I? Why, I haven't done anything! I——" he protested, gazing sadly into an empty corner of the room.

"You haven't? Take this, then, you scoundrel!"

The powerful man in the overcoat flung open the window giving out upon the street, gathered the young man who was none too meticulously dressed in his arms, and heaved him out.

Finding himself flying through the air the young man bashfully buttoned his vest, and whispered to himself in consolation:

"Never mind! Our failures merely serve to harden us!"

And he kept on flying downward.

He had not yet had time to reach the next floor (the fifth) in his flight, when a deep sigh issued from his breast.

A recollection of the woman whom he had just left poisoned with its bitterness all the delight in the sensation of flying.

"My God!" thought the young man. "Why, I loved her! And she could not find the courage even to confess everything to her husband! God be with her! Now I can feel that she is distant, and indifferent to me."

With this last thought he had already reached the fifth floor and, as he flew past a window he peeked in, prompted by curiosity.

A young student was sitting reading a book at a lopsided table, his head propped up in his hands.

Seeing him, the young man who was flying past recalled his life; recalled that heretofore he had passed all his days in worldly distractions, forgetful of learning and books; and he felt drawn to the light of knowledge, to the discovery of nature's mysteries with a searching mind, drawn to admiration before the genius of the great masters of words.

"Dear, beloved student!" he wanted to cry out to the man reading, "you have awakened within me all my dormant aspirations and cured me of the empty infatuation with the vanities of life, which have led me to such grievous disenchantment on the sixth floor—"

But, not wishing to distract the student from his studies, the young man refrained from calling out, flying down to the fourth floor instead, and here his thoughts took a different turn.

His heart contracted with a strange sweet pain, while his head grew dizzy —from delight and admiration.

A young woman was sitting at the window of the fourth floor and, with a sewing machine before her, was at work upon something.

But her beautiful white hands had forgotten about work at that moment, and her eyes—blue as cornflowers—were looking into the distance, pensive and dreamy.

The young man could not take his eyes off this vision, and some new feeling, great and mighty, spread and grew within his heart.

And he understood that all his former encounters with women had been no more than empty infatuations, and that only now he understood that strange mysterious word—Love.

And he was attracted to the quiet domestic life; to the endearments of a being beloved beyond words; to a smiling existence, joyous and peaceful.

The next story, past which he was flying just then, confirmed him still more in his inclination.

In the window of the third floor he saw a mother who, singing a soft lullaby and laughing, was bouncing a plump smiling baby; love, and a kind maternal pride were sparkling in her eyes.

"I, too, want to marry the girl on the fourth floor, and have just such rosy plump children as the one on the third floor," mused the young man, "and I would devote myself entirely to my family and find my happiness in this self-sacrifice."

But the second floor was now approaching. And the picture which the young man saw in a window of this floor forced his heart to contract again.

A man with disheveled hair and wandering gaze was seated at a luxurious writing table. He was gazing at a framed photograph before him; at the same time he was writing with his right hand and, holding a revolver in his left, was pressing its muzzle to his temple.

"Stop, madman!" the young man wanted to call out. "Life is so beautiful!" But some instinctive feeling restrained him.

The luxurious appointments of the room, its richness and comfort, led the young man to reflect that there was something else in life which could disrupt even all this comfort and contentment, as well as a whole family; something of the utmost force—mighty, terrific. . . .

"What can it be?" he wondered with a heavy heart. And, as if on purpose, Life gave him a harsh unceremonious answer in a window of the first floor, which he had reached by now.

Nearly concealed by the draperies, a young man was sitting at the window, sans coat and vest; a half-dressed woman was sitting on his knees, lovingly entwining the head of her beloved with her round rosy arms and passionately hugging him to her magnificent bosom. . . .

The young man who was flying past recalled that he had seen this woman (well-dressed) out walking with her husband—but this man was decidedly not her husband. Her husband was older, with curly black hair, half-gray, while this man had beautiful fair hair.

And the young man recalled his former plans: of studying, after the student's example; of marrying the girl on the fourth floor; of a peaceful, domestic life, à la the third—and once more his heart was heavily oppressed.

He perceived all the ~~ephemerality~~ possibilities, all the uncertainty of the happiness of which he had dreamed; beheld, in the near future, a whole procession of young men with beautiful fair hair about his wife and himself; remembered the torments of the man on the second floor and the measures which that man was taking to free himself from these torments—and he understood.

"After all I have witnessed living is not worth while! It is both foolish and tormenting," thought the young man, with a sickly, sardonic smile; and, contracting his eyebrows, he determinedly finished his flight to the very sidewalk.

Nor did his heart tremble when he touched the flagstones of the pavement with his hands and, breaking those now useless members, he dashed out his brains against the hard indifferent stone.

And, when the curious gathered around his motionless body, it never occurred to any of them what a complex drama the young man had lived through just a few moments before.

Hermann Hesse (1877–1962) was born in Wuttem-
berg, and after several jobs—none satisfactory—
he began to publish novels after the turn of the
century. A major theme in his work is the quest
for peace in a world that somewhat resembles a
jungle. His most celebrated novel is Magister Ludi
(1943); he was awarded the Nobel Prize in 1946.

The Poet

HERMANN HESSE

There is a story told that the Chinese poet, Han Fook, while yet a young
man had a strange and compelling wish to learn all there was to learn about
the art of poetry, and to strive for perfection in the writing of it. In those
days, he was still living in his home on the Yellow River, and with the help
of his family who loved him dearly, he had just become engaged to a young
lady of good family. The marriage was to be set for a day which promised
good fortune. Han Fook was then twenty years old, a handsome youth,
modest, well mannered, schooled in the sciences, and despite his youth, was
already recognized among men of letters of his homeland for some excellent
verse. Without being exactly rich, he had the prospect of an adequate
fortune which would be augmented by the dowry of his bride. Since this
bride was, moreover, very beautiful and virtuous, nothing seemed to be
lacking for the young man's happiness. Nevertheless, he was not satisfied,
for his heart was filled with the ambition to become a perfect poet.

One evening, as a festival of lanterns was being celebrated on the river, it
so happened that Han Fook was wandering alone on the far bank of the
river. He leaned against the trunk of a tree which grew over the water, and
saw reflected in the river thousands of lights swimming and shimmering.
He saw men and women and young girls greeting each other on the boats
and floats, all glowing like beautiful flowers in their festive dress. He heard
the soft murmur of the shining water, the songs of the girls, the humming
of the zithers, the sweet tones of the flutes, and over the whole scene the
blue night hovered like the vaulting of a temple. His heart beat faster as he
gave in to the mood rising within him. He was the only witness to all this
beauty! Even though he longed to cross the river and enjoy the festival in
the company of his bride and his friends, he wanted even more ardently to

remain an observer, to drink in his own impressions of the scene, and then to transform them into a perfect poem. The poem would reflect the deep blue of the night, the play of light on the water, the joy of the festival guests, and also the yearning of the silent onlooker who leans on the trunk of the tree over the river. He sensed that if even he were to experience all the festivals and all the pleasures of the earth, they would not make him completely happy, for he knew that he would remain an onlooker, a stranger, as it were, isolated in the midst of life. He sensed the unique quality of his soul, which at once compelled him to feel deeply the beauty of the earth, and also to know the secret longings of an outsider. The thought made him sad, but as he pursued it further, he realized that true happiness and satisfaction could only be his if he could once succeed in creating with his poetry a perfect mirror image of the world. In this way he would possess the world itself, refined and immortalized in reflected images.

Han Fook scarcely knew whether he was still awake or had fallen asleep when he heard a slight sound and saw a stranger standing next to the tree trunk. It was an old man with a venerable air, clad in violet-colored robes. Han Fook rose and spoke to the stranger with the usual words of greeting for old men and eminent people. The stranger, however, smiled, and spoke a few lines of poetry. The young man's heart stood still in wonder, for in these lines was all the beauty and perfection which he had just experienced, expressed according to all the rules of the great poets. "Oh, who are you," he asked, bowing deeply, "you who can see into my soul and who speak more beautiful verses than I have ever heard from my teachers?"

The stranger smiled the smile of one who has attained perfection, and said, "If you wish to become a poet, then come with me. You will find my hut by the source of the great river in the northwest mountains. I am called the Master of the Perfect Word."

With that the old man stepped into the narrow shadow cast by the tree and disappeared immediately. Han Fook, after searching for him in vain and finding not even a trace, now firmly believed that everything had been a dream brought on by fatigue. He hurried over to the boats across the river and took part in the festival, but between conversations and the sound of the flutes, he continued to hear the voice of the stranger. Han Fook's very soul seemed to have gone away with the man, for he sat apart with dreaming eyes among the merrymakers who teased him for his lovesickness.

A few days later, Han Fook's father wanted to call his friends and relatives together in order to set the day of the wedding. But the bridegroom opposed his father, saying: "Forgive me if I seem to violate the obedience which a son owes his father. But you know how great is my longing to distinguish myself in the art of poetry. Even though a few of my friends praise my poems, I well know that I am still a beginner and still have a long way to go. Therefore I ask you to let me go for awhile into isolation in order to pursue my studies of poetry, because once I have a wife and a house to take care of, I will be held back from those things. Now, while I am still young and free from other duties, I would like to live for some time for my poetry alone—and my poetry will, I hope, bring me joy and fame."

The father was amazed at this speech, and he said, "You must love this art above everything else, since you even want to postpone your wedding because of it. Or, if something has come between you and your bride, then tell me so that I can help you bring about a reconciliation or provide you with another bride."

But the son swore that he loved his bride no less than before, and that not even the shadow of a disagreement had fallen between them. At the same time he told his father that a great master had revealed himself to him in a dream on the day of the lantern festival, and that it was his greatest wish in the world to become the pupil of this master.

"Well and good," said the father, "then I will give you a year. In this time you may pursue this dream of yours which may have been sent to you by a god."

"It may be two years," said Han Fook hesitantly, "who can tell?"

The father let him go and was grieved. The young man wrote a letter to his bride, took leave of his family, and went his way.

When he had traveled for a very long time, he reached the source of the river and found a bamboo hut standing by itself in the wilderness. On a braided mat in front of the hut sat the old man whom Han Fook had seen on the bank by the tree trunk. The old man sat and played his lute, and when he saw the guest approach respectfully, he did not get up, nor did he greet him. He only smiled and let his sensitive fingers play over the strings. A magic music flowed like a silver cloud through the valley, so that the young man stood in wondering astonishment and forgot everything else until the Master of the Perfect Word put aside his small lute and stepped into his hut. So Han Fook followed him with awe and remained with him as his servant and pupil.

A month passed, and Han Fook had learned to despise all poems which he had written before. He erased them from his memory. And after a few more months he erased even those poems from his memory which he had learned from his teachers at home. The Master spoke hardly a word with him. Silently, he taught Han Fook the art of lute playing until the very being of the pupil was filled with music. Once Han Fook composed a small poem, in which he described the flight of two birds across the autumnal sky, a poem which pleased him quite well. He didn't dare show it to the Master, but one evening he sang it near the hut. The Master heard it well but said not a word. He only played softly on his lute. Immediately the air became cool and the darkness increased; a sharp wind arose even though it was the middle of summer. Across the sky, which had now become gray, flew two lines of birds in their mighty yearning for new lands. All of this was so much more beautiful and more perfect than the verses of the pupil, that Han Fook became sad and silent, and felt himself worthless. The old man made this come to pass each time. When a year had gone by, Han Fook had learned lute playing almost to perfection, but the art of poetry appeared ever more difficult and more sublime.

When two years had gone by, the young man became overwhelmingly homesick for his family, for his homeland, and for his bride. So he asked the Master to let him travel.

The Master smiled and nodded. "You are free," he said, "and may go wherever you want. You may come again, you may stay away, just as you like."

So the pupil started on his journey and travelled without stopping until one morning in the dawn he stood on his native shore and looked over the vaulted bridge to his home town. He crept furtively into his father's garden, and heard through the bedroom window the breathing of his father who was still asleep. Stealing among the trees next to the house of his bride, he climbed to the top of a pear tree and saw his bride standing in her room, combing her hair. When he compared the sight before his eyes with the vision that he had painted of it in his homesick imaginings, it became clear to him that he was indeed destined to be a poet: that in the dreams of poets there is a beauty and grace which one searches for in vain in everyday reality. So he climbed down from the tree, fled from the garden, fled over the bridge out of his native town, and returned to the high valley in the mountains. There as before sat the Master in front of his hut on his simple mat, plucking the lute with his fingers. Instead of a greeting, he spoke two verses about the blessings of art. Upon hearing these deep and harmonious sounds, Han Fook's eyes became filled with tears.

Again Han Fook remained with the Master of the Perfect Word, who now gave him lessons on the zither since he had mastered the lute. The months vanished like snow in the west wind. Twice more it happened that home-sickness overcame him. The first time he ran away secretly into the night, but before he had reached the last curve in the valley, the night wind blew over the zither which hung in the door of the hut and the sounds flowed after Han Fook and called him to return in such a way that he could not resist. The other time, however, he dreamed that he was planting a young tree in his garden and that his wife was standing by him and that his children were sprinkling the tree with wine and milk. When he awoke, the moon shone into his room. He got up, bewildered, and saw the Master lying asleep next to him, his gray beard trembling gently. Suddenly a feeling of bitter hatred towards this man came over him—this person who, it seemed to him, had destroyed his life and deceived him about his future. He wanted to fall upon him and murder him, when the old man opened his eyes and began immediately to smile with a fine, sad gentleness which disarmed the pupil. "Remember, Han Fook," and the old man quietly, "you are free to do whatever you wish. You may go into your home country and plant trees, you may hate me, or strike me dead,—it is of little importance."

"Oh, how could I hate you?" cried the poet deeply moved. "That would be like hating heaven itself."

So he remained, and learned to play the zither, and after that the flute. Later he began to write poems under the Master's direction. Slowly he learned the mysterious art of saying only that which is simple and straightforward, but in such a way as to stir up the listener's soul as the wind stirs up the surface of the water. He described the coming of the sun as it hesitates on the edge of the mountains, and the soundless slipping away of fish when they flee like shadows under the water, and the gentle rocking of a young willow in the spring winds. To hear it was not just to hear about the sun, the play of the fish, or the murmuring of the willow; rather it seemed that heaven and earth harmonized each time for a moment of perfect music. Each listener thought with joy or sorrow on whatever he loved or hated: a boy's thoughts would turn to games, a young man's to his beloved, and the old man's to death.

Han Fook no longer knew how many years he spent with the Master at the source of the great river. Often it seemed to him that he had entered the valley only yesterday and been welcomed by the old man's string music. Often he felt as if all the ages of Man and Time itself had fallen away and become insubstantial.

One morning he awoke alone in the hut and though he looked and called everywhere, the Master had disappeared. Overnight fall seemed to have come. A raw wind shook the old hut and large flocks of migrating birds flew over the ridge of the mountain range, although it was not yet time for them to do so.

Then Han Fook took his little lute and descended into his native country. Wherever he encountered people, they greeted him with the sign of greeting which is due old men and eminent people. When he came to his native town, his father, his bride, and his relatives had died. Other people lived in their houses. That evening, a lantern festival was celebrated on the river. The poet Han Fook stood on the far side of the river, on the darker side of the river, leaning against the trunk of an old tree. When he began to play his little lute, then the women sighed and glanced, delighted and disturbed, into the night. The young men called to the lute player, but they could not find him. They called loudly, because not one of them had ever heard such sounds from a lute before. But Han Fook smiled. He looked into the river, where the reflected images of a thousand lanterns were swimming. Just as he no longer knew how to distinguish the reflected images from the real ones, so he found no difference in his soul between this festival and the first one, when he had stood here as a young man and heard the words of the strange Master.

Zsigmond Móricz (1879–1942), one of Hungary's most celebrated authors, came to prominence in 1908 through contributions to Nyugat (West), a pioneering journal of modern Hungarian literature. Early novels include At the Back of Beyond (1911); The Torch (1917); Be Faithful unto Death (1920); and Transylvania (1922–1939), a three-volume historical novel. With the advant of fascism, Móricz's political views became more and more radical and are depicted in Little Orphan (1941) and Sándor Róza (1940–1942).

Everything is Good at the End of the World

ZSIGMOND MŐRICZ

The farm was at the centre of the world, the house was at the centre of the farm, mother dear was at the centre of the house and around her were her ten children.

But four-year-old little Rozi was only a state-supported orphan. She wasn't in the house, nor was she on the farm, she wasn't even in the world, she was just nowhere at all. She wormed her way in amongst the other children, but they knew she didn't belong among them.

Of course, little Rozi did not know what the words state-supported child meant. She had the same mother as the others and she even said 'mother dear' to the big and stocky dark-haired woman who was now ordering her numerous children to undress.

It was bath time and everyone had to be clean for the day after tomorrow, which was Easter.

They were all swarming about like bees in a hive, chirping away like birds in a nest, and bickering like old wives at the market. Every one of them was a girl. Ten girls in all. That was why they had taken in a state-supported child. If they had to provide for ten girls, there might as well be one more who paid.

Father dear was not at home just then and they were all glad of it. Uncle Tülkös was so dreadfully angry that his wife tricked him every year by coming up with daughter after daughter that he had taken to drink, and when he came home, he came with a whip and beat every last one of his clan.

Rozi could also have been getting undressed, but she just stood there pouting and watching how mother dear paid no attention to her whatever. Nobody paid any attention to her, for getting undressed caused so much commotion that every child was all taken up with herself. The oldest girl was fourteen and the youngest was still in the cradle. There were two other four-year-olds like Rozi, the twins. Who could eve⁻ have learned all their names? Even their mother got them mixed up all the time, never knowing which was Mari, Juli, Sári, Klári, or Cica-Maca (those were the twins). The three small ones did not even have names. Anyway, what would have been the use of calling to a six-month-old baby?

But there was one most unusual thing, and that was how inexpressibly grand Rozi felt among her sisters—much, much better than they felt among themselves. This little child even had a past of her own. It was not the first time she had got acquainted with a family, for this was the third place she had come to in her short life to bask in parental love. And it was just for this reason that she was the sole person hurt by the fact that nobody was paying the slightest attention to her—neither mother dear nor the children, neither Mari nor Juli, neither Sári nor Klári. She just stood to one side, moping and wondering what was to be done with her.

Mother dear emptied the hot water out of the cauldron into a large tub which was brought in from outside, and the girls piled in one after the other. The tub looked like a butt during the wine harvest, filled with bunches of grapes.

But Rozi was still standing there all by herself, not knowing what was to become of her. She stuck her thumb in her mouth and stood watching and watching.

The noise in the raftered room was shattering and nearly burst it apart, and all the time mother dear kept shouting:

"Stop that racket, you're driving me crazy!"

And this made them yell all the more, they just giggled in the tub and yelled.

So many naked girls. Mari already had thighs as big as bread loaves. Little Rozi was sulking, but dared not say a word. This was the way it was at mealtime also, it was the way of the world, and she had become quite used to it. She only got bread last, after everyone else had got it, provided there was any left. If there was none, then she got none. And she did not cry or yell or make demands. There was really something very mysterious about how a state-supported child learned that she was not supposed to cry or yell or ask, but only to wait. . . . And Rozi really would wait like a little beggar before the door for someone to give her alms. There was a fully developed sense of a have-not's rights in that tiny four-year-old girl. She had the right to stand there and wait until all ten children had bathed. She recalled that she had bathed with them during the winter and mother dear had even had to smack her hand to make her wait her turn. This was no longer necessary. It was very long ago, but she had not forgotten that her mission was to wait. So she waited. But watching was allowed.

"Go and have some milk!" mother dear cried out to her. "There's milk."

Yes, but for some incredible reason Rozi did not like milk. She didn't want any.

"No," she said stubbornly.

Mother dear always forgot which child liked what. There was always somebody who ate her portion before she even noticed.

"You don't want any milk?"

"No. Drink it yourself."

"The devil take your belly!" mother dear snapped at Rozi, and she began scrubbing the neck of one of her daughters with a rag and then with sand, for it was as black as the heifer's.

"Get out!" she yelled at Rozi.

The child had to be punished. The child always had to be punished or she would become unruly.

Rozi did not budge. She was so incorrigible, that state-supported child, that it was useless to order her about.

"Are you going to get out of here this minute?" And she gave her such a push that the little girl hurried out through the open door into the cool kitchen without knowing where she would stop.

Now she was standing out on the porch. The door was closed. She could have reached the door handle but she was so well trained that she just stared at it. For a long time she just stood there and stared and stared, but did not touch it. At the thought of the milk, however, she became hungry.

Without further ado she started out that very minute, leaving the door of the room and entering the pantry. It had a string for a handle, which she pulled, and this funny trick of simply pulling at a string made the door open. Rozi went in, and there was the bread right in front of her nose, half a loaf. She went to it, grabbed hold of it with her two dirty little hands, and broke off the tip. There was the bread in her hand. She turned around with a little skip and toddled along unconcerned. She passed the door of the room, heard the row, the giggling and yelling in there, and just kept on going, going, towards home. She headed for the hay, where they had slept the night before. . . .

Uncle Tülkös had come home reeking last night, so drunk he could barely walk. He kept taking big steps and banging his head against the wall, which little Rozi thought the most natural thing in the world. And Uncle Tülkös fished out a funny-looking thing that they had used to thresh the wheat at the end of summer—a thing with a small stick hanging from the end of a big one—and with that long thing he began to beat and thwack mother dear. And then the children who were now giggling so much began screaming. The ten girls shrieked like ten trumpets. Only little Rozi did not scream. Little Rozi did not have the right to scream.

She was asleep by then anyway, but mother dear snatched Rozi from her nook and ran into the yard with her even though it was really cold, and they all ran barefoot into the barn at the end of the yard and hid in the straw and hay. Oh, such big houses there were made of hay in that yard, even bigger than the one they lived in. And then the girls all made nests in the stack and hid one another inside, and it was dark and Uncle Tülkös did not go there after all and did not find them, and she was there, too, hidden in a hole with Sári. She was lucky she had fallen asleep without having undressed, and even her little shoes were still on, so she just slept and nothing else happened to her. Thus she was not even so very cold, and now she ran and ran, to her home in the straw house, trying to find the nest they had hidden in yesterday. She could not find it, but she did not search, for she felt protected by now and began to eat the bread she had brought, the heel of the loaf.

And the little state-supported orphan, like a dog when it steals or a little mouse when it finds something to nibble at, just stood there with her head stuck into the hay and munched away. She always loved bread and was very happy that she had some and ate it as if it were hers. She was smart in her own little clever way even though she was very young. She knew how the bread was baked and she knew how to get a piece off for herself even when she had no knife. And if she had had one, she would not have cut the bread anyway, for she did not know how. . . .

Her snack lasted until loud noises began coming from the direction of the house. This did not happen for quite a while. The baths were over and somehow mother dear thought of little Rozi. She yelled out for her to come in from the porch, but no answer came from there. She had to go out herself, and immediately she saw that the door to the pantry was ajar, because the little girl was not yet smart enough to hide her tracks. Of course, mother dear also saw that something sinful had happened to the bread and from this she knew right away where to look for little Rozi. And in less than one minute she was at the haystack, where she grabbed the little girl by the neck, lifting her up like a frog, shaking her, and giving the state-supported child powerful slaps wherever she could.

"You won't have a bath, you thieving pig!" she cried. "Now you can just stink at Easter and drop dead!"

But Rozi, the little ward of the state, had become used to this. Nor could it be any other way. How could she not get beaten? Why, she was always being beaten. And it didn't hurt so much that she had to scream. It hurt, but she was used to it; she was prepared to suffer a beating for every bite of food she got, so if they beat her she just kept silent. Why bother to cry?

Nobody would comfort her, nobody would save her from the beating, and there was nobody to dry her tears. A state-supported child gets beaten and that's all. She knew nothing yet about her being a state-supported child, she only knew that this was the procedure with these things. If she was beaten, she did not cry. If she found food, she ate it. If they hit her, she kept silent.

But this time a miracle happened.

The state appeared on the scene.

The Lady came, the superintendent Lady who was in charge of seeing to the care this foundling received after she was placed. And now she came out to the farmstead to see how little Rozi was doing and what Easter would bring, and she just happened to catch mother dear whipping the state-supported child.

Something very strange happened because of this. The gentle and quiet Lady began to yell, and stocky, dark-haired mother dear became very quiet.

"You think there's nobody else I can give this child to?" the Lady said. "You'll see that there certainly is. . . . Look at this little girl. Where are her clothes? Where are your clothes?"

With the inspiration of the innocent, Rozi said:

"Mother dear always gives them to Cica and Maca."

"What? You dress your cats in the child's clothes?"

And mother dear said ne'er a word.

The little wonder child understood that something was very wrong here. The Lady was stupid and thought her sisters were cats.

"Not cats, girls."

"Is that so?!" the Lady understood at last. "You dress your own children in the state's clothes? It's a good thing I found this out. Gather all of her clothes together immediately, I'm taking her away from here. I have just the place for her in the village."

There was no choice. Mother dear had to gather her clothes together and the Lady put the little girl up on the wagon and took her away just like that. And little Rozi did not utter a sound but prudently stuck to her policy of saying nothing when they dealt with her.

At last the wagon reached the village and came to a halt in front of a lovely house, out of which came a plump and pleasant lady with red cheeks who took Rozi in her arms and thanked the Lady very profusely for bringing her such a pretty Easter present.

Once again little Rozi felt as if she were not in the world, and she just kept quiet and stared sullenly out of her tiny dark eyes.

"I want to go to mother dear," she said, and wiped the kisses off her face.

But the plump woman just laughed and took her into the room, where she showed her a big doll and said:

"Look around. Everything you see will be yours if you stay here."

But Rozi just grew more and more suspicious, and she wouldn't have even believed Jesus himself if he had told her that her mother dear was not her mother dear. In vain did they tell her the woman hadn't given birth to her and she had no mother.

And she became more frightened and angry than ever that these strangers wanted to steal away her mother dear.

The Lady had already gone, saying reassuringly to the fat woman as she left:

"Just treat her well and you'll see that little Rozi will soon love you."

Little Rozi was on the verge of tears. Everything that had happened today, the baths, the beating, the Lady, the wagon, it was all too much for one Good Friday.

"I'm going to put you to bed, my little one. I have so very much work to do," said the plump woman, and she laid little Rozi down on the big couch just as she was and covered her with warm shawls.

Little Rozi just let her, for she thought slyly to herself in her cunning little head:

"Just you go out of here."

The very minute the plump woman left she jumped up and without any hesitation ran right out of the lovely room, past the big doll with long hair, out into the yard and on to the street. And she was so very lucky that nobody even noticed her. Everybody in the whole village was busy getting ready for Easter. There was nobody on the street and little Rozi could go wherever her feet would carry her.

She ran down the street on to the dusty highway and went wherever the road led her until she reached the end of the village. Then she kept on going and just walked and walked and walked, and she saw how the sky touched the earth, and thought to herself in her wee little head that that was the end of the world and everything would be good there.

And soon she even thought that she might grasp the end of the world with her little hand, but then a tree would suddenly appear on the road, and then a well, and the end of the world just did not want to come. She kept on going until she finally reached a village she had never seen before.

But she just continued walking and walking, although she was so very tired that she kept stopping and shivering with cold. Her lips were purple and her whole body was covered with gooseflesh, but she didn't know what that meant. She didn't even know that two and two made four.

All of a sudden a woman called out to her:

"Where are you going, little girl?"

There were big shaggy dogs all around and little Rozi was scared to death and just stared at the woman.

Suddenly, however, the woman clapped her hands together in recognition.

"I know this child, she's one of Mrs. Tülkös' daughters. However did you get here?"

Only now did Rozi come to her crafty little senses. She did not dare say that she had run away, so she said:

"I came with my mother dear to the market and mother dear lost me. I want to go to mother dear."

And for the first time that day she burst into tears. This time she felt that only crying would help her, for if she cried she would not have to talk, and if she cried they would feel sorry for her and do whatever she asked. And if she cried everything would be all right because everybody was afraid of tears, that is, of course, only strangers, for at home nobody was afraid if she cried, it was not worth the bother to cry at home.

And the crying did help her, after all. The woman took her hand, and when she felt how cold little Rozi's tiny hand was, she took her in her arms, covered her with her apron and brought her into the house. There they put her to bed and asked her all sorts of questions and felt sorry for her.

And sly little Rozi accepted all their sympathy and would only tell them: "Everything is good at the end of the world."

Nobody understood her. She slept there that night, and the next morning, the morning of Easter Saturday, the man of the house harnessed the horses to his wagon—because these people were rich and had horses and a wagon and a big house—and took her home to mother dear.

Oh, what an uproar there was as the children ran to her, and even mother dear winked at her, laughing in the strangest way!

"Well, you no-good dog, are you going to break off the heel of the bread again? You know," she explained to the woman, "she gets as much as she can eat, and still the little pig ran away from her bath into the haystack to eat bread. . . . The best thing to do would be to stamp out the insides of a state-supported brat like her!"

With that she bent down to little Rozi and wiped her face. But she could not resist giving her a resounding slap on the behind.

Little Rozi looked up and in the distance past the gate she saw the bottom of the sky. She felt very surprised that the end of the world was here, too. She had never noticed it before. . . .

"Well, is it good here at home, you brat?"

"There," she pointed far away with her tiny finger.

"What's there?"

"There . . . there. . . ."

She did not dare say that it is better there, at the end of the world. . . . It would be good there.

Franz Kafka (1883–1924) studied law and was later
employed in the workmen's compensation bureau
of the Austrian government. His work presents
dreamlike situations which are at once realistic in
detail and symbolic by implication. Most of his
books were published posthumously, including his
three novels: The Trial (1925); The Castle (1926)
Amerika (1927). For further reading: The Penal
Colony, translated by Willa and Edwin Muir (1948)

Jackals and Arabs

FRANZ KAFKA

We were camping in the oasis. My companions were asleep. The tall
white figure of an Arab passed by; he had been seeing to the camels and
was on his way to his own sleeping place.

I threw myself on my back in the grass; I tried to fall asleep; I could not,
a jackal howled in the distance; I sat up again. And what had been so far
away was all at once quite near. Jackals were swarming round me, eyes
gleaming dull gold and vanishing again, lithe bodies moving nimbly and
rhythmically, as if at the crack of a whip.

One jackal came from behind me, nudging right under my arm, pressing
against me, as if he needed my warmth, and then stood before me and
spoke to me almost eye to eye.

"I am the oldest jackal far and wide. I am delighted to have met you
here at last. I had almost given up hope, since we have been waiting endless
years for you; my mother waited for you, and her mother, and all our fore-
mothers right back to the first mother of all the jackals. It is true, believe
me!"

"That is surprising," said I, forgetting to kindle the pile of firewood
which lay ready to smoke away jackals, "that is very surprising for me to
hear. It is by pure chance that I have come here from the far North, and I
am making only a short tour of your country. What do you jackals want
then?"

As if emboldened by this perhaps too friendly inquiry the ring of jackals
closed in on me; all were panting and openmouthed.

"We know," began the eldest, "that you have come from the North; that
is just what we base our hopes on. You Northerners have the kind of intelli-

208

gence that is not to be found among Arabs. Not a spark of intelligence, let me tell you, can be struck from their cold arrogance. They kill animals for food, and carrion they despise."

"Not so loud," said I, "there are Arabs sleeping near by."

"You are indeed a stranger here," said the jackal, "or you would know that never in the history of the world has any jackal been afraid of an Arab. Why should we fear them? Is it not misfortune enough for us to be exiled among such creatures?"

"Maybe, maybe," said I, "matters so far outside my province I am not competent to judge; it seems to me a very old quarrel; I suppose it's in the blood, and perhaps will only end with it."

"You are very clever," said the old jackal; and they all began to pant more quickly; the air pumped out of their lungs although they were standing still; a rank smell which at times I had to set my teeth to endure streamed from their open jaws, "you are very clever; what you have just said agrees with our old tradition. So we shall draw blood from them and the quarrel will be over."

"Oh!" said I, more vehemently than I intended, "they'll defend themselves; they'll shoot you down in dozens with their muskets."

"You misunderstand us," said he, "a human failing which persists apparently even in the far North. We're not proposing to kill them. All the water in the Nile couldn't cleanse us of that. Why, the mere sight of their living flesh makes us turn tail and flee into cleaner air, into the desert, which for that very reason is our home."

And all the jackals around, including many new-comers from farther away, dropped their muzzles between their forelegs and wiped them with their paws; it was as if they were trying to conceal a disgust so overpowering that I felt like leaping over their heads to get away.

"Then what are you proposing to do?" I asked, trying to rise to my feet; but I could not get up; two young beasts behind me had locked their teeth through my coat and shirt; I had to go on sitting. "These are your train-bearers," explained the old jackal, quite seriously, "a mark of honor." "They must let go!" I cried, turning now to the old jackal, now to the youngsters. "They will, of course," said the old one, "if that is your wish. But it will take a little time, for they have got their teeth well in, as is our custom, and must first loosen their jaws bit by bit. Meanwhile, give ear to our petition." "Your conduct hasn't exactly inclined me to grant it," said I. "Don't hold it against us that we are clumsy," said he, and now for the first time had recourse to the natural plaintiveness of his voice, "we are poor creatures, we have nothing but our teeth; whatever we want to do, good or bad, we can tackle it only with our teeth." "Well, what do you want?" I asked, not much mollified.

"Sir," he cried, and all the jackals howled together; very remotely it seemed to resemble a melody. "Sir, we want you to end this quarrel that divides the world. You are exactly the man whom our ancestors foretold as born to do it. We want to be troubled no more by Arabs; room to breathe; a skyline cleansed of them; no more bleating of sheep knifed by an Arab; every beast to die a natural death; no interference till we have drained the carcass empty and picked its bones clean. Cleanliness, nothing but cleanliness is what we want"—and now they were all lamenting and sobbing—"how can you bear to live in such a world, O noble heart and kindly bowels? Filth is their white; filth is their black; their beards are a horror; the very sight of their eye sockets makes one want to spit; and when they lift an arm, the murk of hell yawns in the armpit. And so, sir, and so, dear sir, by means of your all-powerful hands slit their throats through with these scissors!" And in answer to a jerk of his head a jackal came trotting up with a small pair of sewing scissors, covered with ancient rust, dangling from an eyetooth.

"Well, here's the scissors at last, and high time to stop!" cried the Arab leader of our caravan who had crept upwind towards us and now cracked his great whip.

The jackals fled in haste, but at some distance rallied in a close huddle, all the brutes so tightly packed and rigid that they looked as if penned in a small fold girt by flickering will-o'-the-wisps.

"So you've been treated to their entertainment too, sir," said the Arab, laughing as gaily as the reserve of his race permitted. "You know, then, what the brutes are after?" I asked. "Of course," said he, "it's common knowledge; so long as Arabs exist, that pair of scissors goes wandering through the desert and will wander with us to the end of our days. Every European is offered it for the great work; every European is just the man that Fate has chosen for them. They have the most lunatic hopes, these beasts; they're just fools, utter fools. That's why we like them; they are our dogs; finer dogs than any of yours. Watch this, now, a camel died last night and I have had it brought here."

Four men came up with the heavy carcass and threw it down before us. It had hardly touched the ground before the jackals lifted up their voices. As if irresistibly drawn by cords each of them began to waver forward, crawling on his belly. They had forgotten the Arabs, forgotten their hatred, the all-obliterating immediate presence of the stinking carrion bewitched them. One was already at the camel's throat, sinking his teeth straight into an artery. Like a vehement small pump endeavoring with as much determination as hopefulness to extinguish some raging fire, every muscle in his body twitched and labored at the task. In a trice they were all on top of the carcass, laboring in common, piled mountain-high.

And now the caravan leader lashed his cutting whip crisscross over their backs. They lifted their heads, half swooning in ectasy; saw the Arabs standing before them; felt the sting of the whip on their muzzles; leaped and ran backwards a stretch. But the camel's blood was already lying in pools, reeking to heaven, the carcass was torn wide open in many places. They could not resist it; they were back again; once more the leader lifted his whip; I stayed his arm.

"You are right, sir," said he, "we'll leave them to their business; besides, it's time to break camp. Well, you've seen them. Marvelous creatures, aren't they? And how they hate us!"

Karel Čapek (1890–1938) was a Czech novelist, playwright, and short-story writer of great genius. His best novel, The War with the Newts, anticipates the fascist domination of Europe; his plays are "futuristic" and often comic. He invented the word "robot." Čapek supposedly died of a heart attack as parts of the German army entered Prague during World War II. For further reading: Tales from Two Pockets (1943).

The Last Judgment
KAREL ČAPEK

The notorious multiple-killer Kugler, pursued by several warrants and a whole army of policemen and detectives, swore that he'd never be taken. He wasn't either—at least not alive. The last of his nine murderous deeds was shooting a policeman who tried to arrest him. The policeman indeed died, but not before putting a total of seven bullets into Kugler. Of these seven, three were fatal. Kugler's death came so quickly that he felt no pain. And so it seemed Kugler had escaped earthly justice.

When his soul left his body, it should have been surprised at the sight of the next world—a world beyond space, grey, and infinitely desolate—but it wasn't. A man who has been jailed on two continents looks upon the next life merely as new surroundings. Kugler expected to struggle through, equipped only with a bit of courage, as he had in the last world.

At length the inevitable Last Judgment got around to Kugler.

Heaven being eternally in a state of emergency, Kugler was brought before a special court of three judges and not, as his previous conduct would ordinarily merit, before a jury. The courtroom was furnished simply, almost like courtrooms on earth, with this one exception: there was no provision for swearing in witnesses. In time, however, the reason for this will become apparent.

The judges were old and worthy councillors with austere, bored faces. Kugler complied with the usual tedious formalities: Ferdinand Kugler, unemployed, born on such and such a date, died . . . at this point it was shown Kugler didn't know the date of his own death. Immediately he realized this was a damaging omission in the eyes of the judges; his spirit of helpfulness faded.

"Do you plead guilty or not guilty?" asked the presiding judge.

"Not guilty," said Kugler obdurately.

"Bring in the first witness," the judge sighed.

Opposite Kugler appeared an extraordinary gentleman, stately, bearded, and clothed in a blue robe strewn with golden stars.

At his entrance the judges arose. Even Kugler stoop up, reluctant but fascinated. Only when the old gentleman took a seat did the judges again sit down.

"Witness," began the presiding judge, "Omniscient God, this court has summoned You in order to hear Your testimony in the case against Kugler, Ferdinand. As You are the Supreme Truth, You need not take the oath. In the interest of the proceedings, however, we ask You to keep to the subject at hand rather than branch out into particulars—unless they have a bearing on this case.

"And you, Kugler, don't interrupt the Witness. He knows everything, so there's no use denying anything.

"And now, Witness, if You would please begin."

That said, the presiding judge took off his spectacles and leaned comfortably on the bench before him, evidently in preparation for a long speech by the Witness. The oldest of the three judges nestled down in sleep. The recording angel opened the Book of Life.

God, the Witness, coughed lightly and began:

"Yes. Kugler, Ferdinand. Ferdinand Kugler, son of a factory worker, was a bad, unmanageable child from his earliest days. He loved his mother dearly, but was unable to show it; this made him unruly and defiant. Young man, you irked everyone! Do you remember how you bit your father on the thumb when he tried to spank you? You had stolen a rose from the notary's garden."

"The rose was for Irma, the tax collector's daughter," Kugler said.

"I know," said God. "Irma was seven years old at that time. Did you ever hear what happened to her?"

"No, I didn't."

"She married Oscar, the son of the factory owner. But she contracted a venereal disease from him and died of a miscarriage. You remember Rudy Zaruba?"

"What happened to him?"

"Why, he joined the navy and died accidentally in Bombay. You two were the worst boys in the whole town. Kugler, Ferdinand, was a thief before his tenth year and an inveterate liar. He kept bad company, too: old Gribble, for instance, a drunkard and an idler, living on handouts. Nevertheless, Kugler shared many of his own meals with Gribble."

The presiding judge motioned with his hand, as if much of this was perhaps unnecessary, but Kugler himself asked hesitantly, "And . . . what happened to his daughter?"

"Mary?" asked God. "She lowered herself considerably. In her fourteenth year she married. In her twentieth year she died, remembering you in the agony of her death. By your fourteenth year you were nearly a drunkard yourself, and you often ran away from home. Your father's death came about from grief and worry; your mother's eyes faded from crying. You brought dishonor to your home, and your sister, your pretty sister Martha, never married. No young man would come calling at the home of a thief. She's still living alone and in poverty, sewing until late each night. Scrimping has exhausted her, and patronizing customers hurt her pride."

"What's she doing right now?"

"This very minute she's buying thread at Wolfe's. Do you remember that shop? Once, when you were six years old, you bought a colored glass marble there. On that very same day you lost it and never, never found it. Do you remember how you cried with rage?"

"Whatever happened to it?" Kugler asked eagerly.

"Well, it rolled into the drain and under the gutterspout. As a matter of fact, it's still there, after thirty years. Right now it's raining on earth and your marble is shivering in the gush of cold water."

Kugler bent his head, overcome by this revelation.

But the presiding judge fitted his spectacles back on his nose and said mildly, "Witness, we are obliged to get on with the case. Has the accused committed murder?"

Here the Witness nodded his head.

"He murdered nine people. The first one he killed in a brawl, and it was during his prison term for this crime that he became completely corrupted. The second victim was his unfaithful sweetheart. For that he was sentenced to death, but he escaped. The third was an old man whom he robbed. The fourth was a night watchman."

"Then he died?" Kugler asked.

"He died after three days in terrible pain," God said. "And he left six children behind him. The fifth and sixth victims were an old married couple. He killed them with an axe and found only sixteen dollars, although they had twenty thousand hidden away."

Kugler jumped up.

"Where?"

"In the straw mattress," God said. "In a linen sack inside the mattress. That's where they hid all the money they acquired from greed and penny-pinching. The seventh man he killed in America; a countryman of his, a bewildered, friendless immigrant."

"So it was in the mattress," whispered Kugler in amazement.

"Yes," continued God. "The eighth man was merely a passerby who happened to be in Kugler's way when Kugler was trying to outrun the police. At that time Kugler had periostitis and was delirious from the pain. Young man, you were suffering terribly. The ninth and last was the policeman who killed Kugler exactly when Kugler shot him."

"And why did the accused commit murder?" asked the presiding judge.

"For the same reasons others have," answered God. "Out of anger or desire for money; both deliberately and accidentally—some with pleasure, others from necessity. However, he was generous and often helpful. He was kind to women, gentle with animals, and he kept his word. Am I to mention his good deeds?"

"Thank You," said the presiding judge, "but it isn't necessary. Does the accused have anything to say in his own defense?"

"No," Kugler replied with honest indifference.

"The judges of this court will now take this matter under advisement," declared the presiding judge, and the three of them withdrew.

Only God and Kugler remained in the courtroom.

"Who are they?" asked Kugler, indicating with his head the men who had just left.

"People like you," answered God. "They were judges on earth, so they're judges here as well."

Kugler nibbled his fingertips. "I expected . . . I mean, I never really thought about it. But I figured You would judge, since—"

"Since I'm God," finished the Stately Gentleman. "But that's just it, don't you see? Because I know everything, I can't possibly judge. That wouldn't do at all. By the way, do you know who turned you in this time?"

"No, I don't," said Kugler, surprised.

"Lucky, the waitress. She did it out of jealousy."

"Excuse me," Kugler ventured, "but You forgot about that good-for-nothing Teddy I shot in Chicago."

"Not at all," God said. "He recovered and is alive this very minute. I know he's an informer, but otherwise he's a very good man and terribly fond of children. You shouldn't think of any person as being completely worthless."

"But I still don't understand why You aren't the judge," Kugler said thoughtfully.

"Because my knowledge is infinite. If judges knew everything, absolutely everything, then they would also understand everything. Their hearts would ache. They couldn't sit in judgment—and neither can I. As it is, they know only about your crimes. I know all about you. The entire Kugler. And that's why I cannot judge."

"But why are they judging . . . the same people who were judges on earth?"

"Because man belongs to man. As you see, I'm only the witness. But the verdict is determined by man, even in heaven. Believe me, Kugler, this is the way it should be. Man isn't worthy of divine judgment. He deserves to be judged only by other men."

At that moment the three returned from their deliberation.

In heavy tones the presiding judge announced, "For repeated crimes of first degree murder, manslaughter, robbery, disrespect for the law, illegally carrying weapons, and for the theft of a rose: Kugler, Ferdinand, is sentenced to lifelong punishment in hell. The sentence is to begin immediately.

"Next case, please: Torrance, Frank.

"Is the accused present in court?"

Isaac Babel (1894–1941), the son of a Jewish shop-keeper, was born in Odessa. He graduated from Nicholas I Commercial School and at fifteen began to write stories in French; in the civil war, Babel was assigned to Budyonny's cavalry as a correspondent for ROSTA (later TASS). He was arrested in 1939, and his certificate of death is dated 1941. Fifteen years later the sentence was "revoked." For further reading: Red Cavalry (1926), Odessa Stories (1923), Collected Stories (1955).

The Awakening

ISAAC BABEL

All the people in our circle—small-time middlemen, shop-keepers, clerks in banks and steamship offices—were teaching their children music. Our fathers, seeing no way out for themselves, had struck on the notion of a lottery. This lottery they founded on the bones of the little ones. Odessa was possessed by this madness more than other towns were and, true enough, for several decades running our town supplied the Wunderkinder for the concert platforms of the world. Mischa Elman, Zimbalist, Gabrilovitch—they all came from Odessa! Jascha Heifetz got his start among us.

When a boy turned four or five his mother would lead the tiny and puny creature to Mr. Zagursky. Zagursky ran a factory of Wunderkinder, a factory that turned out Jewish dwarfs in little lace collars and little pumps of patent leather. He sought them out in the lairs of Moldavanka, in the malodorous courtyards of the Old Market. Zagursky gave them the first impetus; later on the children were sent off to Professor Auer in St. Petersburg. Mighty harmony dwelt within the souls of these starvelings with their bloated livid heads. They became celebrated virtuosi. And so my father decided to catch up with them, even though I was overage for a Wunderkind—I was going on fourteen; in height and puniness, however, I might have passed for an eight-year-old. Which constituted the last hope.

I was led off to Zagursky. Because of his high regard for my grandfather he consented to take only one rouble for each lesson—a cheap enough rate. My grandfather, Leivi Itzok, was the laughingstock of the town and, at the same time, its ornament. He walked about the streets in an opera hat and foot clouts and resolved points of doubt in the most obscure matters. They would ask him what a Gobelin was, why the Jacobins had betrayed Robespierre, how synthetic silk was prepared, what the Caesarian section was. My grandfather was able to answer all these questions. So, out of high regard for his learning and madness Zagursky took only one rouble a lesson from us. And it was also because he was afraid of Grandfather that he went to a lot of bother with me, since there was really nothing to bother with. The sounds slithered off my violin like metal shavings. These sounds grated on my own heart, yet my father would not give up. The talk at home was about nothing but Mischa Elman, who had been exempted from military service by the Czar himself. Zimbalist, according to information gathered by my father, had been presented to the King of England and had played at Buckingham Palace; the parents of Gabrilovitch had bought two mansions in St. Petersburg. These Wunderkinder had brought riches to their parents. My father might have reconciled himself to poverty, but fame was something he had to have.

"It is impossible," people who dined at his expense used to murmur in his ear, "it is impossible that the grandson of such a grandfather should fail—" However, my mind was on other things. During my violin exercises I would put the books of Turgenev or Dumas on the music stand and, as I scraped away, kept devouring page after page. In the daytime I told all sorts of cock-and-bull stories to the little boys in the neighborhood; at night I transferred these stories to paper. Writing was a hereditary compulsion in the family. Leivi Itzok, who had become touched in his old age, had been writing a novel all his life under the title of *The Man Without a Head*. I took after him.

Three times a week, loaded down with violin case and music, I used to plod to Witte Street (at one time called Gentry Street), to Zagursky's studio. There, lined along the wall awaiting their turns, hysterically fervent Jewish women sat hugging against their weak knees violins the dimensions of which exceeded those of the beings who were slated to play them in Buckingham Palace.

The door to the sanctum would open. Big-headed, freckled children with necks as slender as flower stalks and a hectic flush on their cheeks would come staggering out of Zagursky's study. The door would slam to after swallowing up the next dwarf. On the other side of the wall the teacher, sporting a Windsor tie, and curly red hair and legs more fluid than solid, was straining himself, chanting the notes and conducting. The director of this monstrous lottery was populating Moldavanka and the stygian dead ends of the Old Market with the specters of pizzicato and cantilena. Later on Professor Auer brought this sing-song to a diabolical brilliance.

I had no business among these sectarians. Much the same sort of dwarf as all of them, I nevertheless discerned a different admonition in the voice of my ancestors.

The first step came hard to me. One day I left the house laden like a beast of burden with violin case, violin, notes and twelve roubles—payment for a month's tuition. I was walking along Nezhinskaya Street and should have turned into Gentry Street to get to Zagursky's house; instead I went up Tiraspolskaya and found myself in the port. The hours supposed to be spent in learning the violin flew by in Practical Harbor. Thus did my liberation begin. Zagursky's reception room never saw me again. Matters of greater importance took up all my thoughts. Together with Nemanov, a classmate of mine, I took to haunting the steamer *Kensington*, visiting a certain old sailor by the name of Mr. Trottybairn. Nemanov was a year younger than I, but from the age of eight he had been carrying on the most intricate trading in the world. He was a genius in business and carried out whatever he promised to do. He is now a millionaire in New York, a director of the General Motors company, a firm which is just as tremendous as Ford. Nemanov dragged me along everywhere because I submitted to him in all things without offering a word of objection. He used to buy tobacco pipes from Mr. Trottybairn which were smuggled in. These pipes were turned out at Lincoln by a brother of the old sailor.

"Gentlemen," Mr. Trottybairn used to say to us, "mark my word: children must be made with one's own hands. Smoking a factory-made pipe is the same as putting an enema tube into your mouth. Do you know who Benvenuto Cellini was? There was a master! My brother in Lincoln could tell you about him. My brother doesn't stand in anybody's way. He is simply convinced that children must be made with one's own hands and not the hands of others. We cannot do otherwise than agree with him, gentlemen."

Nemanov sold Trottybairn's pipes to bank directors, foreign consuls, wealthy Greeks. He made 100 percent profit on them.

The pipes of the Lincoln master breathed poesy. A thought, a drop of eternity had been set within each one of them. A small yellow eye glinted in the mouthpiece of each; their cases were lined with satin. I tried to picture to myself how Matthew Trottybairn, the last of the master pipe makers, was living in old England as he resisted the course of things.

"We cannot do otherwise than agree, gentlemen, that children must be made with one's own hands."

The heavy waves near the sea wall removed me further and further from our house, permeated with the smell of onions and Jewish destiny. From Practical Harbor I migrated to the other side of the breakwater, where a small patch of sandy shoal was inhabited by urchins from Seafront Street. They did not bother putting on their pants from morning till night, diving under the wherries, stealing coconuts for their dinner, and biding their time till the watermelon-laden barges would come trailing one another from

Kherson and Kamenka and they would have a chance to split some of these watermelons against the stanchions in the port.

To be able to swim became a dream of mine. It was shameful to confess to these bronzed urchins that I, who had been born in Odessa, had not seen the sea until I was ten and that at fourteen I still did not know how to swim.

How late it befell me to learn the things one had to know! In my childhood, nailed down to the Gemara, I had led the life of a sage; when I grew up I took to climbing trees.

The ability to swim proved beyond me. The hydrophobia of all my ancestors—Spanish rabbis and Frankford money-changers—kept dragging me to the bottom. The water would not bear me up. Covered with welts, bloated with briny water, I would return to shore, to my violin and notes. I was bound to the instruments of my crime and was dragging them with me. The struggle of the rabbis against the sea continued until such time as the water god of those places—Ephim Nikitich Smolich, a proofreader on the Odessa *News*—took pity on me. Pity for little Jewish boys dwelt within the athletic bosom of this man. He was supreme ruler over hordes of rachitic starvelings. Nikitich used to collect them from the bedbug-ridden hovels of Moldavanka, lead them to the sea, bury them in the sand, do gymnastics with them, dive with them, teach them songs and, as he broiled himself under the direct rays of the sun, would tell them stories about fishermen and animals. To grownups Nikitich explained that he was a natural philosopher. The Jewish children laughed so hard at Nikitich's stories that they rolled on the ground; they fawned and squealed like puppies. The sun spattered them with crawling freckles that were the color of lizards.

This old man watched my monomachy against the sea as a silent bystander. Perceiving that the fight was hopeless and that I would never learn how to swim, he included me among the number of the lodgers in his heart. All of it was here with us, that gay heart of his; it never put on airs, it was not tainted with greed and was not disquieted. With his coppery shoulders, the head of an aged gladiator and bronzed legs that were just the least bit bandy, he would lie in our midst beyond the breakwater as if he were the sovereign of those waters abounding in watermelon rinds and reeking of kerosene. I came to love this man as only a boy afflicted with hysteria and headaches can come to love an athlete. I would not leave his side and tried to be of service to him.

"Don't go at it so hard," he told me. "Strengthen your nerves. Swimming will come of itself. How can it be that the water won't bear you up—why shouldn't it?"

Noticing how I was drawn to him, Nikitich made an exception of me among all his disciples, inviting me to visit him in his clean, roomy garret carpeted with matting, showed me his dogs, his hedgehog, turtle and pigeons. In exchange for his largess I brought him a tragedy I had written recently.

"I just knew that you wrote a bit," said Nikitich. "You even have that look about you. More and more often your eyes don't watch anything in particular—"

He read my writings, shrugged, passed his hand over his short gray curls, paced about his garret a little.

"I would guess," he pronounced drawlingly, pausing after each word, "that the divine spark is in you—"

We went out into the street. The old man stopped, tapped his stick hard against the sidewalk and fixed me with his eyes.

"What do you lack? The fact that you're young is no calamity—that will pass with the years. . . . What you lack is a feeling for nature."

With his stick he pointed out a tree to me; it had a brownish trunk and a low crown.

"What tree is that?"

I did not know.

"What's growing on that bush?"

I did not know that either. We were walking through a small square on the Alexandrovsky Prospect. The old man kept pointing his stick at all the trees; he clutched my shoulder whenever birds happened to fly past and compelled me to listen to the individual voice of each.

"What bird is singing now?"

I could not tell him anything in answer. The names of trees and birds, their division into genera, where the birds were flying to, what direction the sun rose in, when the dew was heaviest—all these things were beyond my ken.

"And you have the audacity to write? A man who does not live in the midst of nature the way a stone or an animal lives won't write two worthwhile lines in his whole lifetime. Your landscapes resemble descriptions of stage sets. What were your parents thinking about for fourteen years, may the Devil take me?"

What had my parents been thinking about? About protested promissory notes, about Mischa Elman's mansions. I did not say anything about this to Nikitich; I kept my mouth shut.

At home, during dinner, I did not touch my food. It stuck in my throat.

"A feeling for nature!" I kept thinking. "My God, why had no conception of that ever entered my head? Where can I find a man who will explain everything to me about the ways of birds and the names of trees? What do I know about them? I might be able to recognize lilacs—and even then only when they're in bloom. Lilacs—and acacias. De Ribas and Greek streets are lined with acacias—"

At dinner Father told a new story about Jascha Heifetz. Just before reaching Robinat's, Father had run into Mendelson, Jascha's uncle. The boy, it turned out, was getting eight hundred roubles for each appearance. Count that up—see how much that comes to if one gives fifteen concerts a month!

I did count it up: the result was twelve thousand a month. As I was doing the multiplication and carrying four, I happened to look out the window. In a gently billowing cape, with his tightly coiled, rusty-colored curls struggling out from under his soft hat, leaning upon a cane, Mr. Zagursky, my music teacher, was making stately progress through our small, concrete-paved courtyard. One could hardly say that he had been very prompt in discovering my truancy. By now more than three months had passed since my violin had foundered on the sands near the breakwater.

Zagursky was approaching our front door. I made a dash for the back entrance—and remembered it had been nailed up the evening before to keep burglars out. Whereupon I locked myself in the washroom. Within half an hour the whole family had gathered around my door. The women were weeping. One of my grandmothers was rubbing her fat shoulder against the door and going off into hysterical peals of sobbing. My father was silent. When he did break into speech he was quieter and more articulate than he had ever been in his whole life.

"I am an officer in the army," said my father. "I have an estate. I go hunting. The mouzhiks pay me rent. I have placed my son in the Cadet Corps. There is no need for me to worry about my son—"

He fell silent. The women were breathing hard. Then a terrific blow crashed against the washroom door. My father was pounding against it with his whole body; he persisted in running full tilt against it.

"I am an officer in the army!" he was screaming. "I go hunting! I'll kill him—this is the end!"

The hook flew off the door; there was a bolt on the door—it was still holding by a single nail. The women were rolling on the floor, they were catching my father's legs; out of his mind by now, he was struggling to get free. An old woman—my father's mother—came hurrying to find out what the hubbub was about.

"My child," she said to her son in Yiddish, "great is our grief. It has no bounds. The only thing lacking in our house is bloodshed. I do not want to see bloodshed in our house—"

My father broke into moans. I heard his steps receding. The bolt was hanging by its single nail.

I sat in my fortress till nightfall. When everybody had gone to bed my Aunt Bobka led me off to my grandmother's. The way there was a long one.

The moonlight lay in a catalepsy upon unknown bushes, upon trees for which there were no names. . . . Some unseen bird in the distance emitted a whistle and became extinguished: it may have gone to sleep. . . . What bird was it? What did they call it? Is there any dewfall of evenings? Where is the constellation of Ursa Major located? Where does the sun rise? . . .

We were walking along Post Office Street. Aunt Bobka had a firm hold of my hand, so that I would not run away. She was right. Flight was what I had in mind.

Strates Myriveles (1892–   ) is one of the foremost men of letters in modern Greece. A novelist and short-story writer, his work is notable for its emotional tone and its exploitation of materials which are "patriotic" by implication or by overt statement. The short fiction of Myriveles is far too little known in the English-speaking world.

The Chronicle of an Old Rose-Tree

STRATES MYRIVELES

I want to write the story of a rose-tree. We lived together for sixteen long years, sixteen of the most significant years of my life, replete with harrowing events. I loved that rose-tree, for she was an old rose-tree with many branches and many roses. I feel she was fond of me, too. Such a feeling can blossom between a man and a tree.

I know a true, strange story, told to me at Mytilini, a long time ago by some old convicts who were serving life-sentences at Castro. One of them had committed an appalling murder. He set fire to his house and burned up his wife and children—thinking the children weren't his. He was the one who told me what happened, his eyes scalding in tears. Such a mystery is man.

During his long years behind bars, he was once acquainted with another convict, a lad who had come to prison fresh as a daisy, and had left as a man with gray hair. In the prison yard, the lad planted a walnut; it sprouted. All his thoughts and cares from that time on were for tending this plant. For fear that it might get hurt before it became strong he surrounded it with wire; he watered it with his ration of drinking water. Years passed, and the lad became a man; the walnut tree grew up, sturdy and joyful.

One day the warden called the man into his office. He had been granted a pardon, and he could get his stuff and go. The prisoner stood speechless, amazed.

"And the walnut tree?" he stammered.

"What do you mean, the walnut tree?"

"I have no one in the world but that walnut tree," said the stunned prisoner.

The warden laughed.

"Well, what can we do? The walnut tree has to stay in its place."

The prisoner lowered his head; he could speak no more. He made a bundle of his rags. He sat on the horse-block facing the tree, and looked at it and shed bitter tears. Then a miracle happened, witnessed by all the prisoners who still tell of it. In the spring time of its life, all green with fresh, cool foliage, the tree began to wither. The leaves turned ragged and yellow; they crumpled completely, and fell. The trunk too, dried down to its roots.

The old man's eyes were big with burning tears while he told me this story.

But my rose-tree did not commit suicide because of grief. A knife cut off her life.

But let me tell her story from the beginning.

When the Germans entered Athens, I received a telegram from my uncle who owned a house there. He was stranded on Lesbos, where he died a year later, at eighty-five. His telegram told me to move my wife and children immediately into his vacant home—before the Germans requisitioned it.

It was an old Athenian mansion, two stories, with eight large rooms, and a small garden in front. A beautiful trellis overarched the garden gate; each spring the fragrance of leaves and flowers filled all of Eresso Street. In the middle of the yard, in the middle of a white and gray marble patio, there stood the rose-tree: a grand rose-tree. How old was she? I seem to remember her from my student years when I went sometimes to visit my uncle. Three trunks grew upward for more than six feet, each trunk big as my arm. Higher, a multitude of branches were always loaded with roses, and gave off a strong scent, winter and summer, for the blossoms appeared the year round. Around the courtyard was an iron fence, and the rose-tree hung over the spiked top, enticing the passers-by with her roses.

My uncle, the owner, was a strange old bachelor who spent most of his life in this house. As a student he came from the island, and he had rented one of its rooms from the first owner, an old French countess. Finally he bought the house and let her stay until she died of old age. She was a childless woman, alone, without anyone in the world. Alone, she idled her time reading old Parisian magazines, or she sometimes hummed Parisian songs of times past. She hummed them softly and heard them all alone. My uncle was like a parched reed; he lived alone there during and after his student years, an engineer by profession. He was slender, tall, austere, and always an elegant, meticulous dresser. He wore a fuzzed gray top hat, dangled a slim cane, and wrote in an impeccable *katharevousa*. He lived all alone beneath the gilded ceilings in those eight large rooms.

My uncle, it seemed, was also in love with the rose-tree; and she must have been the one and only love in his life, a life never adorned by a woman's grace. I say he must have been in love, for when the rose-tree grew tall above the iron spikes, the street urchins climbed the fence to gather the flowers. One day my uncle seized his pistol and chased them away—like a jealous lover. That day he called in workers to double the height of the iron fence so that no young rival could molest his tree.

In the sixteen years I lived there the rose-tree grew taller and taller, and put new branches over the second iron spikes.

My study was on the ground floor. It looked out a large window and into the yard. There the flowers of the rose-tree were abundant and rich in fragrance, for they were mayroses. To be sure the tree bloomed best in spring, but miraculously there were also blossoms in winter, in the fall, and all the year round. Even when Athens was covered with snow, she kept giving roses. If I opened my window, she spilled her branches into my room, soothing the bitter years of the occupation and the Communist reign of terror. She gave me great comfort. She was a symbol of hope. We were cold and hungry. We listened to the bullets ricochetting off the iron fence, but the rose-tree moved her blooming branches near us. No matter, we used to say. The sun will rise again, the grapes and peaches will bear fruit again, and love will come again to men who have become wild beasts, driven by a stupid, incomprehensible hate.

The streets had become deserted; no one dared show his face. One day a young woman passed by Exarcheia, hugging the walls. She held a bottle of milk. A rascal, on a rooftop, saw her, took aim and fired, killing her. Two or three neighbors rushed out to the rescue. Holding the bottle tight to her chest, she lived long enough to say:

"Give the milk to my child, neighbors. . . ."

Then she died.

I cut a rose, put it in a vase on my desk, in memory of the unknown mother. Later, peace gradually came and Greek ceased to fear Greek. Spring came, and our rose-tree reddened from top to bottom. It was so old, and yet so brimming with youth. Passers-by walked outside and stopped on the sidewalk to look at it, as one looks at a beautiful woman. They smiled at her and inhaled her strong fragrance. Couples in love stopped and asked for a rose. My jealous uncle was no longer alive, and those of us in the courtyard offered the blossoms. When we were not at home, a young gallant clambered up the fence, and holding to an iron spike, reached out to steal a rose for his young, fair Juliana.

Once I watched him from my desk, scampering down, jumping back red of face, redder than his rose, looking all round for fear that he might have been seen. The man behind the window saw him and smiled, for he too had stolen roses and even now, on occasion, cannot leave them alone. But the lad was not aware of that. The young man was of heroic countenance, as if he had plucked an edelweiss from the steepest peak of the Alps. For that, the man inside smiles at the rose-tree whose pillaged branch is still moving. The two exchange an understanding glance, so intended.

Then the good old days returned. Holy week came, churches opened their doors, and the Athenians swallowed their tears and waited for Easter. Then the maidens of the neighborhood came—and Neapolis has many lovely maidens—knocked at our door and asked that the rose-tree contribute to the decoration of the Epitaph. The young myrrh-bearers left with their baskets full.

All this, and much more, belongs to the Annals of the Rose-tree. I wonder how much more interesting the old rose-tree's own diary would be, starting with the time when the hands of the young French aristocrat first planted and watered the bush every evening from the well of the yard. Those hands which aged year by year within the eight empty rooms, withered, disfigured, died, and disintegrated many years ago.

And so did that young islander, the student of the Polytechnic, for forty years the only occupant of the house, who lived, grew, and grayed near the rose-tree. That jealous lover of hers who once when he saw a flock of urchins plundering its roses, chased them, waving his pistol. At that time he was a high state official, with a white mustache and a thin cane with a silver handle. He remained faithful to our rose-tree till he died.

Our old rose-tree also had its heroic and tragic days. Every March 25 of our four-year occupation by the Germans, every October 28 of our cruel occupation, my children and all young school children, cut all the roses to take to the tomb of the Unknown Soldier. Schoolboys and girls marched in procession with bouquets held high, and with the National Anthem on their lips. All around, bullets from the machine guns hissed; the armored car tracks chewed Athen's asphalt. But our children advanced in formation,

still singing. They looked hungry and gaunt, their legs emaciated, the bloom
of youth gone from their faces.

But high in their hands, above their heads, the roses shone red. The
conquerors grabbed the flowers, trampled them furiously. The children returned dusty, dirty, ragged, bruised, beaten by rifle butts. But their great
eyes shone with the Greek flame that burned inside them day and night.

Then came the blackest December that ever hovered over Athens. For
forty days mortars boomed and burst, shattering the branches of the rose-
tree. Neapolis was stunned, silent in fear and horror. One day the old rose-
tree stooped: below her branches the sidewalk by our gate was red. It was
not the red paint with which the maniacs splashed walls with their slogans
of fratricide. It was blood. Real, warm, oozing blood gushing from large
wounds from a street that had known only the joyful shouts of children.
Now the street echoed the moans of murdered men, six or seven innocent
persons dying there.

After their homes had been blown up by the maniacs, these men had
started from a corner of Athens, roving the streets, seeking shelter. A little
bell hung from the top of our yard gate. My wife heard the bell ringing,
ringing furiously. Germans, she thought, and was afraid to open the gate.
When the row ceased, she found in front of our gate a heap of wretched,
bloody corpses. These men had been ringing the little bell, seeking refuge.

But our old rose-tree was still there. Her roses spread and heartened us.
Roses are everywhere, she said to us. It is enough to push aside the leaves
and thorns, she kept telling us. Always there is a cool spring, delicate and
pure, waiting, its hands filled with flowers. Even in the heartaches of men
there is green in the heart of winter. Heave open your soul's windows, and
they will find a way of placing their bouquets inside. Deep inside.

When I first occupied the house, the rose-tree filled the whole square
of the yard, in the plot of ground at the center of the flagstone patio. Then
two significant events occurred in that space. First, a new little plant sprung
from the soil; no one knew what it was. Partaking of the water we gave
the rose-tree, it kept growing under the rose's shade. When the new plant
was about knee-high, a friend who knew about trees told us that by its
leaves it looked like a plum-tree. Each year it grew fast, taking its water
and nourishment from the same soil that fed the thick roots of the rose-
tree. With the years, its slender trunk made its way through the branches
that shaded it and popped out in full view of the sun it had been reaching
for. It had become a grown tree, a strong, powerful tree that selfishly overwhelmed our rose-tree.

One spring, for the first time, its foliage filled with white blossoms, and
then its branches bowed with red plums. It was bedecked with fruit like a
Christmas tree. It covered the rose-tree, spread its branches triumphantly
above the yard, and hung its plums invitingly over the iron fence. The

street urchins no longer climbed the fence for roses. Suspended from the fence, they reached the tips of the plum branches and filled their pockets with unripe plums. The shady branches of the plum had shrouded the rose-tree which had accorded it hospitality for so many years, and the rose-tree began to wither. The other was a new life, rampant, straining for light and juices; under the earth its roots swelled strong and avid, clutched the roots of the rose-tree, hugging them, twining around them, and sucking their soil. I watched this drama day after day. Now the plum tree soared in full beauty and untrammeled youth, spread its branches everywhere, conquered air, and light, and also conquered the soil.

Our rose-tree began to wither. Most of the trunks began to rot, and I cut them to rid the space of dried up branches. Each spring a few new shoots sprang from the roots, but they made little progress. They were sickly and feeble. They grew a little, then they wilted and withered. The remaining stalk produced only a few flowers. There was no longer the abundance of past years. But the rose-tree persisted in giving forth some flowers, in revealing her presence even in this desperate battle. Finally she made the great decision. She imitated her adversary. From a large, thick bush, she became a climbing rose. She gathered all her remaining forces into upward growth and began to climb the plum tree, in two twining tresses, like two green snakes that twirled upward in search of the sun. To succeed in this, she used as support the very stout trunk of the plum tree. She clung to it and began to climb among its limbs. It was a relentless struggle to the end. Each time the two stalks gained growth, they stopped to rest at that step, on some node of the tree, and then sprang upward again.

We saw this metamorphosis and thought that that was the end, that we would no longer see roses. Then we stopped paying attention to what was happening. By now the rose was so entwined with the plum tree that we could no longer tell them apart.

Meanwhile, the plum tree grew taller, as high as our two-story house. On the second floor, above my study, was my son's study. I rarely went up there because I did not want to intrude while he worked. But one day, when he was away in the country, I entered the room and stood at the window. When I opened the outside shutters, suddenly a branch whisked in and a fragrance caressed my face. It was a large cluster of roses. They had bloomed in the crown of the plum tree, in the splendid sun, a trophy, and a shout of victory.

It was something thrilling.

From then on, high up in the branches of the plum tree, we saw more roses. The last roses kept blooming.

The plum tree was the first, most significant event in the life of the old rose-tree. The second event was something more modest, but quite pleasing.

In the enclosed square where the two trees stood, from the year that we moved into the house, there grew two night-blooming plants. They sprang up each year, on opposite sides of the square, one to the left, one to the right. Who knows where the seeds came from? Each year the two stems emerged. They were fragile, succulent, full of sap and vigor. When fall came, they put out red buds which opened at dusk and gave forth a strong aroma all through the night. It was a sweet aroma that one could almost taste. In bloom they stood on each side of the rose and the plum tree like two large lighted candlesticks. They withered with winter, and we raked them away with the leaves. In time the soil was trampled on, and the earth became hard as concrete. The plants poked up again, nevertheless, each late spring, all freshness anew, growing within a few days and becoming loaded with buds. We had these annuals all sixteen years that we had the house.

Now the old mansion has been torn down in order to raise a new building. Down came the double iron fence that protected the rose-tree from her passing lovers. And down came the plum tree, chopped down, falling with the rose-tree in its embrace. So were the two luminous night-blooming plants extinguished forever. And with them died the romantic memory of the old French countess, whose spirit till then only the flowers of the rose-tree evoked. And so remembrance of the tall, slender old bachelor died, too, he who guarded the roses with his loaded revolver.

In this short story I wanted to save some vestiges from the life of sixteen years, a life filled with fears and griefs, and with the joys and anguish of children and trees.

Valentin Petrovich Katayev (1897–   ) volunteered for military service in World War I, was wounded, and gassed. In the 1920s he wrote satiric stories and plays; by the 1930s his fiction-criticism supported the Soviet regime. Katayev's works (in five volumes) appeared in Russia in 1956.

"Our Father Who Art in Heaven"

VALENTIN KATAYEV

"**I** want to sleep. I'm cold."

"Lord! I want to sleep too. Get dressed. And that's enough nonsense. Put on your scarf. Put on your cap. Put on your boots. Where are your mittens? Stand still. Stop squirming."

When the little boy was dressed, she took him by the hand and they left the house. The boy was not yet fully awake. He was four years old. He shivered from the cold and stumbled along. It was just beginning to get light. There was a frosty blue fog outside. The mother tightened the scarf on the boy's neck, straightened his collar, and kissed his sleepy, mischievous face.

The dry wild grape vines, hanging from the broken-down wooden arcades, seemed sugary from the hoarfrost. It was twenty-five degrees below zero. Thick steam poured out of their mouths. The courtyard was littered with ice-covered garbage.

"Mama, where are we going?"

"I told you—for a walk."

"Then why did you take a suitcase?"

"Just because. Now be quiet. Don't chatter. Keep your mouth closed or you'll catch cold. You see how cold it is. Better look where you're going or you'll slip."

A doorman dressed in a sheepskin coat and a white apron with a name-plate on his chest stood at the gate. She walked past him without looking. He closed the door silently behind them and fastened it with a great iron hook. They set out along the street. There was no snow—everything was covered with ice and frost. And wherever there was neither ice nor frost

229

there was smooth stone or earth as smooth and hard as stone. They walked under the bare, black acacia trees which were shaking resiliently in the cold.

The mother and son were dressed almost identically. They wore quite good coats made of artificial monkey-fur, soft leather boots and gaily colored wool mittens. The mother wore a checked kerchief on her head and the son wore a round monkey-fur cap with ear-flaps. The street was deserted. When they reached the crossing, the loudspeaker of the public address system gave such a loud crackle that the woman started. But she realized at once that the morning broadcast was beginning. As usual, it began with the crowing of a rooster. The exceedingly loud voice of the rooster shouted musically along the length of the street, heralding the beginning of a new day. The boy looked up at the loudspeaker.

"Mama, is that a rooster?"

"Yes darling."

"Isn't he cold up there?"

"No, he's not cold up there. Now don't squirm. And watch where you're going."

Then the loudspeaker crackled again, and a gentle, childish voice repeated with angelic tones:

"Good morning! Good morning! Good morning!"

Then the same voice, slowly, with great feeling, recited the prayer:

"Our Father Who art in heaven, hallowed be Thy name, Thy kingdom come, Thy will be done. . . ."

On the corner the woman turned away from the wind and almost ran up the alley, dragging the boy behind her, as if this too loud and too gentle voice were pursuing her. Soon the voice stopped. The prayer was finished. The wind blew from the sea across the icy passages of the streets. Ahead of them a bonfire was blazing, surrounded by a crimson fog, with a German guard warming himself beside it. The woman turned and crossed to the other side. The boy ran beside her, stamping his little leather boots. His cheeks were as red as cranberries. A frozen drop hung beneath his nose.

"Mama, are we taking a walk now?" the little boy asked.

"Yes, we are."

"I don't like to walk so fast."

"Be patient."

They walked through a courtyard and came out on another street. It was already light. The pink dawn shone brittlely through light and dark blue clouds of steam and hoarfrost. It was so cold that one's jaws shut and puckered just from its rosy color as from something sour. Several people appeared on the street. They walked in one direction. Almost all of them carried bundles. Some pushed their bundles before them on carts, or dragged along loaded sleds that scratched the bare pavement with their runners.

From all ends of the city, on this morning, people with heavy loads trudged slowly in one direction, like ants. These were Jews on their way to the ghetto. The ghetto was set up in the Peresip district, in that dull, depressed part of the city where scorched oil tanks stood at sea level, looking like traveling circus tents. The Fascists had surrounded a few dirty blocks with two rows of rusty barbed wire and left only one entrance, as in a mousetrap. The Jews made their way under the railroad bridges. They slipped on the icy sidewalks. There were old people among them who couldn't walk and some people sick with typhus. These were carried on stretchers. Some would fall down and remain lying there, leaning back against a lamp post or hugging an iron hitching post. Nobody was escorting them to the ghetto. They were going there by themselves, without any convoy. They knew that whoever stayed home would be shot. Therefore they were going by themselves. Anyone who gave shelter to a Jew would also be shot. For one hidden Jew everyone living in the apartment would be shot, without exception. From all parts of the city, along steep slopes, under railroad bridges, the Jews made their way to the ghetto, pushing their wheelbarrows before them, leading their bundled children by the hand. They walked one behind the other, like ants, passing houses and frost-covered trees. They walked past locked doors and gates, past smoky bonfires where German and Rumanian soldiers warmed themselves. The soldiers paid no attention to the Jews and went on warming themselves, stamping their boots and rubbing their ears with their mittens.

It was horribly cold. It was unusually cold even for a northern city. But for Odessa it was simply monstrous. Such cold hits Odessa once in thirty years. A tiny circle of sun shone weakly through clouds of thick blue and green steam. Hardened sparrows lay on the highways, killed in mid-flight by the cold. The sea was frozen to the very horizon. It was white. The wind blew in from it.

The woman looked like a Russian. The boy also looked Russian. The boy's father was a Russian. But this meant nothing: the mother was a Jew. They were required to go to the ghetto. The boy's father was an officer in the Red Army. The woman had torn up her passport and had thrown it into the ice-covered toilet that morning. She had gone out of the house with her son, counting on walking about the city until everything calmed down. She thought she'd manage it somehow. It was insane to go to the ghetto. That meant certain death. And so she had begun to walk about the city with her son, trying to avoid the most crowded streets. At first, thinking that they were taking a walk, the boy was quiet. But soon he began to misbehave.

"Mama, why are we walking all the time?"

"We're taking a walk."

"We never walk so fast. I'm tired."

"Be patient, darling. I'm also tired. But you see I'm not misbehaving."

She noticed that she really was walking too fast, almost running, as if someone were chasing her. She made herself slow down. The boy looked up at her and hardly recognized her. He saw with horror her swollen, bitten lips, the lock of hair, gray with frost, hanging untidily out of her kerchief, and her fixed, harsh, glassy eyes. That kind of eyes he had seen before only on his toy animals. She was looking at her watch and didn't see him. Squeezing his little hand, she dragged the boy behind her. He grew frightened. He began to cry.

"I want to go home. I want to go peepee."

Hastily she led him behind a billboard covered with German notices. While she unbuttoned and then buttoned him, shielding him from the wind, the boy continued to cry and shake from the cold. When they began to walk again he cried that he was hungry. She took him to a milk-bar, but two Rumanian policemen in heavy fur coats and dog-skin collars were eating there; because she had no documents and was afraid they'd be arrested and sent to the ghetto, she pretended she had walked into the wrong store by mistake. She excused herself and quickly slammed the door. The boy ran after her, understanding nothing and crying. The next milk-bar was empty. Relieved, they crossed the doorstep with a horseshoe nailed to it. There the woman bought a bottle of fermented milk and a thick roll for the boy. The bundled little boy, sitting on a tall chair, drank the fermented milk, which he loved, and chewed on the roll and she thought feverishly about what to do next. She could think of nothing. But there was an iron stove burning in the milk-bar and at least they could warm up. It seemed to the woman that the proprietress of the milk-bar was looking at her too carefully. She quickly began to pay the bill. The proprietress looked out of the window uneasily and invited the woman to sit by the stove a while longer. The stove was red-hot. It was almost cherry-colored, a little darker. Sparks flew about from it. The heat made the boy sleepy. He could hardly keep his eyes open. But the woman began to fidget. She thanked the proprietress and told her she was in a hurry. But still they sat there for nearly an hour. The sleepy, full little boy could hardly stand on his feet. She shook him by the shoulders, straightened his collar and pushed him lightly toward the door. He stumbled over the horseshoe. The woman took the boy's hand and again led him along the street. The street was lined with old plane trees. They walked by the dappled plane trees with their soft, frost-covered bark.

"I want to go to sleep," said the little boy, screwing up his face from the icy wind.

She pretended she didn't hear him. She knew that their situation was desperate. She had almost no friends in the city. She had come here two months before the war began and then found herself stranded. She was completely alone.

"My knees are frozen," the little boy whimpered.

She took him to one side and rubbed his knees. He quieted down. Suddenly she remembered that there was, after all, one family in the city whom she knew. They had met on the steamer *Georgia* on the way from Novorossiisk to Odessa and then several times afterward. This was the young Pavlovskys: he was an instructor at the University, and she had just finished the building trades' school. Her name was Vera. The women had taken a liking to each other and had managed to become friends while the steamer was going from Novorossiisk to Odessa. They had visited each other a few times afterward. The men too had become friends—once they had even gotten drunk together. Another time they had all gone together to a soccer game—Kharkov vs. Odessa. The Pavlovskys had rooted for Odessa; she and her husband had rooted for Kharkov. Odessa won. God, what went on then in that huge new stadium overlooking the sea! Screams, howls, columns of dust. . . . They almost came to blows. But now it was only pleasant to think about. Pavlovsky was out of town, in the Red Army. But Vera was stranded too, hadn't managed to get evacuated. Recently she had seen Vera in the Alexandrovsky market, and they had even chatted for a while. But it wasn't safe to stop too long at the market place. The Germans started round-ups almost every day. The women spoke for hardly five minutes. They hadn't met since then. But probably Vera was in the city. Where else could she go? The Pavlovskys were Russians. She might try to sit it out at Vera's. In any case, she could leave the boy there. The Pavlovskys lived quite far away, on Pirogovskaya and the corner of Frantsuzky Boulevard. The woman turned around.

"Where are we going, Mama? Home?"

"No darling, we're going visiting."

"Where?"

"Do you remember Aunt Vera Pavlovsky? We're going to visit Aunt Vera Pavlovsky."

"Good," said the boy, reassured. He loved to go visiting. He became more cheerful.

They walked across the Stroganovsky Bridge over the street leading to the harbor. The street was called Karantinny Hill. Below stood a group of rectangular sandstone houses. Some of them had been reduced to piles of rubble. Some had been burned down. The round arches of another bridge could be made out at the bottom of the hill and beyond the arches the angular ruins of the harbor came into view. Farther still, above the burned-out, fallen roof-tops lay the white sea, frozen to the horizon. On the horizon itself a band of unfrozen water shone deep blue. Several Rumanian troop-ships painted lead gray stood in the ice near the ruins of the famous Odessa lighthouse. Above the city on the mountain, far off to the left, the dome of the municipal theater shone like a sea shell through clouds of pink and delicate light-blue steam. The fencing of the Stroganovsky Bridge was made up of a long row of high, iron spikes. The spikes were a severe black. Below, people were climbing up Karantinny Hill with buckets. The water splashed out of the buckets and froze on the pavement, glistening like glass in the opaque light of the pink sun. All this was very beautiful. If worse came to worse, they could stay for a while at the Pavlovskys' and figure out what to do next.

They walked a very long time. The boy was tired but did not misbehave. He tramped on quickly in his little leather boots, just managing to keep up with his mother. He wanted to get to Aunt Vera's as fast as possible. He loved to go visiting. His mother wiped his whitened cheeks several times on the way. A bonfire was burning on the sidewalk next to the house where the Pavlovskys lived and some soldiers were warming themselves around it. The house was large, divided into several sections. The gate was locked with a chain. A round-up was going on. The documents of everyone going in and out were being checked. Pretending she was in a hurry, the woman walked past the gate. No one paid any attention to her. The boy began to misbehave again. Then she took him in her arms and began to run, stamping her feet on the dark-blue lavastone sidewalk. The boy calmed down. Again she began to roam about the city. It seemed to her that she was appearing in the same places too often and that people were beginning to notice her. Then she had the idea of spending a few hours at the movies. The showing started early since to be on the street after eight was forbidden on pain of death.

She felt nauseated and dizzy in the close, smelly hall, packed with soldiers and prostitutes driven in there, like herself, by the cold. But at least it was warm and they could sit down. She undid the scarf on the boy's neck and he fell right asleep, clutching her arm with both hands. She sat through two shows without leaving the hall, barely following what was happening on the screen. It seemed to be a war newsreel and then a comedy or something like that: she couldn't catch the thread of it. Everything was muddled. Sometimes the screen was filled with the head of a pretty girl and blond ringlets snuggling her cheek against the flat chest of a tall headless man, then they would sing a duet, then the girl would get into a sleek sports car, then sometimes there were black fountains of explosions, one, two, three, four in a row—with a tinny roar as if someone were tearing roofing iron into long strips—one, two, three, four strips in one stroke while black hunks of earth came down like hail, striking the tin drum, and tanks crawled along the shell-scarred earth with funeral crosses, grinding and plunging and shooting still longer tongues of flame and whirling streams of white smoke.

A German soldier wearing embroidered felt boots and a Russian fur cap with ear-flaps was leaning heavily against the woman's shoulder and tickling the boy's cheek with a big, dirty finger, trying to wake him up. He smelled strongly of garlic and raw alcohol. He laughed good-naturedly all the while, repeating idiotically, "Don't sleep, bube. Don't sleep, bube."

"Bube" means "little boy" in German. The boy didn't wake up, but only moved his head slightly and whimpered in his sleep. Then the German dropped his heavy head on the woman's shoulder, putting one arm around her, and began to knead the little boy's face with the other hand. The woman kept quiet, afraid of making the soldier angry. She was afraid he'd ask to see her documents. The German smelled of smoked fish. She was nauseated but made a terrific effort not to flare up. She kept persuading herself to stay calm. After all, the German wasn't doing anything especially awful. He was simply a boor. An altogether decent Fritz. Bearable. Moreover, the German soon fell asleep on her shoulder. She sat without moving. The German was very heavy. But she was glad he was asleep.

The girl with the blond ringlets moved across the screen again, and long shafts of black and white rays moved through the whole theater with her. And with an iron roar the black fountains flew up, and tanks crawled on, and German battalions marched across the desert sands, and an enormous German flag was mounted on the top of the Eiffel Tower, and Hitler with a little sharp nose and a lady's chin barked out from the screen, sticking out his womanish rear end, rolling his eyes and opening and closing his mouth very quickly. He opened and closed his mouth so quickly that the sound came a little behind: arf, arf, arf, arf. . . .

Soldiers were pinching girls in the dark and the girls were squealing. The hall was terribly hot and stuffy and smelled of garlic, smoked fish, raw alcohol, aspirin and the Rumanian perfume "Chat-Noir." Still and all, it was better here than out in the cold. The woman had rested a bit. The boy had had enough sleep. But the last show was over and they had to go out again. She took the boy by the hand and they set out. The city was completely dark. Only the dense, frosty steam curled in among the darkened houses. It made one's eyelashes stick together. Smoking bonfires, almost smothered by the cold, were burning in the streets. Somewhere, from time to time, solitary shots rang out. Patrols walked up and down the streets. It was after eight. She picked up the sleepy child and began to run, almost out of her mind from the one thought that a patrol might stop them. She chose the most deserted alleys. Plane trees and acacias, covered with frost, lined the streets like ghosts. The city was empty and dark. From time to time a door

would open in that blackness, and along with the bright band of light sud
denly lighting up the frozen cars by the entrance, the passionate, piercing
squeak of a violin rushed out for a moment. The woman ran safely to the
Shevchenko Park of Culture and Rest. The enormous park lay along the sea
Here all was quiet, forsaken. It was especially quiet down below, at the
bottom of the precipice by the sea frozen to the horizon. Silence as thick as
a wall lay over the sea. A few big stars twinkled above the white branches
of the trees. The light blue beam of a searchlight slid among the stars.

She walked along the broad asphalt pathway. On the left was the very
same stadium where they had all gone together for the Odessa-Kharkov
match. Beyond the wreckage of the stadium was the sea. It wasn't visible
in the dark, but one could sense it right away from the silence. The park
stretched out to the right. The broad asphalt pathway glittered like emery
paper in the starlight. As the woman walked along she noted the different
species of trees. Here were catalpas with their long pods hanging almost to
the ground like strings. And here were pyramidal acacias, plane trees
thuyas, vinegar trees. Covered with heavy frost, they melted together and
bent down to the ground like clouds. She took a deep breath and walked
more slowly along the endlessly long row of empty benches. But on one of
the benches someone was sitting! She walked by with a pounding heart
The black figure, its head leaning on the back of the bench, didn't move
The woman noticed then that the person was half covered with frost, like a
tree. Above the black cupola of the observatory which rose up among the
white clouds of the park twinkled the cut-glass stars of the Big Dipper. It
was very quiet and not at all frightening here. Maybe it wasn't frightening
because the woman was so tired.

And the next morning, before it was completely light, trucks drove
through the city picking up the bodies of people who had frozen during the
night. One truck drove slowly along the broad asphalt pathway in the
Shevchenko Park of Culture and Rest.

The truck stopped twice. It stopped first at the bench where a frozen old
man was sitting. It stopped a second time by the bench where a woman and
a little boy were sitting. She was holding the boy by the hand. They were
sitting side by side. They were dressed almost identically. They wore quite
good coats made of artificial monkey-fur, soft leather boots and gaily
colored wool mittens. They were sitting as if alive, only their faces, covered
with frost during the night, were completely white and fluffy, and a fringe
of ice hung from the eyelashes. When the soldiers picked them up they
didn't straighten out. The soldiers swung around and threw the woman, her
legs still in a sitting position, into the truck. She knocked against the old
man like a piece of wood. Then the soldiers swung around and lightly threw
in the boy, his legs still in a sitting position. He knocked against the woman
like a piece of wood and bounced back a little.

As the truck was rolling away, a rooster began to crow from the loud-speaker of the public address system, heralding the beginning of a new day. Then a gentle childish voice repeated with angelic tones:

"Good morning! Good morning! Good morning!"

Then the same voice, slowly, with great feeling, recited the Lord's Prayer:

"Our Father, Who art in heaven, hallowed be Thy name, Thy kingdom come. . . ."

Jean-Paul Sartre (1905–   ), novelist, short-story writer, critic, and literary theorist, is a professor of philosophy in Paris. Nausea (1938) is considered his most interesting novel. Sartre's contribution to the intellectual history of the age is in the area of existential thought. For further reading: Intimacy, translated by Lloyd Alexander (1949).

The Wall

JEAN-PAUL SARTRE

They pushed us into a big white room and I began to blink because the light hurt my eyes. Then I saw a table and four men behind the table, civilians, looking over the papers. They had bunched another group of prisoners in the back and we had to cross the whole room to join them. There were several I knew and some others who must have been foreigners. The two in front of me were blond with round skulls; they looked alike. I suppose they were French. The smaller one kept hitching up his pants; nerves.

It lasted about three hours; I was dizzy and my head was empty; but the room was well heated and I found that pleasant enough: for the past 24 hours we hadn't stopped shivering. The guards brought the prisoners up to the table, one after the other. The four men asked each one his name and occupation. Most of the time they didn't go any further—or they would simply ask a question here and there: "Did you have anything to do with the sabotage of munitions?" Or "Where were you the morning of the 9th and what were you doing?" They didn't listen to the answers or at least didn't seem to. They were quiet for a moment and then looking straight in front of them began to write. They asked Tom if it were true he was in the International Brigade; Tom couldn't tell them otherwise because of the papers they found in his coat. They didn't ask Juan anything but they wrote for a long time after he told them his name.

"My brother José is the anarchist," Juan said, "you know he isn't here any more. I don't belong to any party, I never had anything to do with politics."

They didn't answer. Juan went on, "I haven't done anything. I don't want to pay for somebody else."

His lips trembled. A guard shut him up and took him away. It was my turn.

"Your name is Pablo Ibbieta?"

"Yes."

The man looked at the papers and asked me, "Where's Ramon Gris?"

"I don't know."

"You hid him in your house from the 6th to the 19th."

"No."

The wrote for a minute and then the guards took me out. In the corridor Tom and Juan were waiting between two guards. We started walking. Tom asked one of the guards, "So?"

"So what?" the guard said.

"Was that the cross-examination or the sentence?"

"Sentence," the guard said.

"What are they going to do with us?"

The guard answered dryly, "Sentence will be read in your cell."

As a matter of fact, our cell was one of the hospital cellars. It was terrifically cold there because of the drafts. We shivered all night and it wasn't much better during the day. I had spent the previous five days in a cell in a monastery, a sort of hole in the wall that must have dated from the middle ages: since there were a lot of prisoners and not much room, they locked us up anywhere. I didn't miss my cell; I hadn't suffered too much from the cold but I was alone; after a long time it gets irritating. In the cellar I had company. Juan hardly ever spoke: he was afraid and he was too young to have anything to say. But Tom was a good talker and he knew Spanish well.

There was a bench in the cellar and four mats. When they took us back we sat and waited in silence. After a long moment, Tom said, "We're screwed."

"I think so too," I said, "but I don't think they'll do anything to the kid."

"They don't have a thing against him," said Tom. "He's the brother of a militiaman and that's all."

I looked at Juan: he didn't seem to hear. Tom went on, "You know what they do in Saragossa? They lay the men down on the road and run over them with trucks. A Moroccan deserter told us that. They said it was to save ammunition."

"It doesn't save gas," I said.

I was annoyed at Tom: he shouldn't have said that.

"Then there's officers walking along the road," he went on, "supervising it all. They stick their hands in their pockets and smoke cigarettes. You think they finish off the guys? Hell no. They let them scream. Sometimes for an hour. The Moroccan said he damned near puked the first time."

"I don't believe they'll do that here," I said. "Unless they're really short on ammunition."

Day was coming in through four airholes and a round opening they had made in the ceiling on the left, and you could see the sky through it. Through this hole, usually closed by a trap, they unloaded coal into the cellar. Just below the hole there was a big pile of coal dust; it had been used to heat the hospital but since the beginning of the war the patients were evacuated and the coal stayed there, unused; sometimes it even got rained on because they had forgotten to close the trap.

Tom began to shiver. "Good Jesus Christ I'm cold," he said. "Here it goes again."

He got up and began to do exercises. At each movement his shirt opened on his chest, white and hairy. He lay on his back, raised his legs in the air and bicycled. I saw his great rump trembling. Tom was husky but he had too much fat. I thought how rifle bullets or the sharp points of bayonets would soon be sunk into this mass of tender flesh as in a lump of butter. It wouldn't have made me feel like that if he'd been thin.

I wasn't exactly cold, but I couldn't feel my arms and shoulders any more. Sometimes I had the impression I was missing something and began to look around for my coat and then suddenly remembered they hadn't given me a coat. It was rather uncomfortable. They took our clothes and gave them to their soldiers, leaving us only our shirts—and those canvas pants that hospital patients wear in the middle of summer. After a while Tom got up and sat next to me, breathing heavily.

"Warmer?"

"Good Christ, no. But I'm out of wind."

Around eight o'clock in the evening a major came in with two *falangistas*. He had a sheet of paper in his hand. He asked the guard, "What are the names of those three?"

"Steinbock, Ibbieta and Mirbal," the guard said.

The major put on his eyeglasses and scanned the list: "Steinbock . . .

Steinbock . . . Oh yes . . . You are sentenced to death. You will be sho
tomorrow morning." He went on looking. "The other two as well."

"That's not possible," Juan said. "Not me."

The major looked at him amazed. "What's your name?"

"Juan Mirbal," he said.

"Well, your name is there," said the major. "You're sentenced."

"I didn't do anything," Juan said.

The major shrugged his shoulders and turned to Tom and me.

"You're Basque?"

"Nobody is Basque."

He looked annoyed. "They told me there were three Basques. I'm no
going to waste my time running after them. Then naturally you don't wan
a priest?"

We didn't even answer.

He said, "A Belgian doctor is coming shortly. He is authorized to spenc
the night with you." He made a military salute and left.

"What did I tell you," Tom said. "We get it."

"Yes," I said, "it's a rotten deal for the kid."

I said that to be decent but I didn't like the kid. His face was too thir
and fear and suffering had disfigured it, twisting all his features. Three
days before he was a smart sort of kid, not too bad; but now he lookec
like an old fairy and I thought how he'd never be young again, even if they
were to let him go. It wouldn't have been too hard to have a little pity fo:
him but pity disgusts me, or rather it horrifies me. He hadn't said anything
more but he had turned grey; his face and hands were both grey. He sa
down again and looked at the ground with round eyes. Tom was goo
hearted, he wanted to take his arm, but the kid tore himself away violently
and made a face.

"Let him alone," I said in a low voice, "you can see he's going tc
blubber."

Tom obeyed regretfully; he would have liked to comfort the kid, it woulc
have passed his time and he wouldn't have been tempted to think abou
himself. But it annoyed me: I'd never thought about death because I neve
had any reason to, but now the reason was here and there was nothing tc
do but think about it.

Tom began to talk. "So you think you've knocked guys off, do you?" he
asked me. I didn't answer. He began explaining to me that he had knockec
off six since the beginning of August; he didn't realize the situation anc
I could tell he didn't *want* to realize it. I hadn't quite realized it myself,
wondered if it hurt much, I thought of bullets, I imagined their burning
hail through my body. All that was beside the real question; but I wa:
calm: we had all night to understand. After a while Tom stopped talking
and I watched him out of the corner of my eye; I saw he too had turnec

grey and he looked rotten; I told myself "Now it starts." It was almost dark, a dim glow filtered through the airholes and the pile of coal and made a big stain beneath the spot of sky; I could already see a star through the hole in the ceiling: the night would be pure and icy.

The door opened and two guards came in, followed by a blonde man in a tan uniform. He saluted us. "I am the doctor," he said. " I have authorization to help you in these trying hours."

He had an agreeable and distinguished voice. I said, "What do you want here?"

"I am at your disposal. I shall do all I can to make your last moments less difficult."

"What did you come here for? There are others, the hospital's full of them."

"I was sent here," he answered with a vague look. "Ah! Would you like to smoke?" he added hurriedly, "I have cigarettes and even cigars."

He offered us English cigarettes and *puros*, but we refused. I looked him in the eyes and he seemed irritated. I said to him, "You aren't here on an errand of mercy. Besides, I know you. I saw you with the fascists in the barracks yard the day I was arrested."

I was going to continue, but something surprising suddenly happened to me; the presence of this doctor no longer interested me. Generally when I'm on somebody I don't let go. But the desire to talk left me completely; I shrugged and turned my eyes away. A little later I raised my head; he was watching me curiously. The guards were sitting on a mat. Pedro, the tall thin one, was twiddling his thumbs, the other shook his head from time to time to keep from falling asleep.

"Do you want a light?" Pedro suddenly asked the doctor. The other nodded "Yes": I think he was about as smart as a log, but he surely wasn't bad. Looking in his cold blue eyes it seemed to me that his only sin was lack of imagination. Pedro went out and came back with an oil lamp which he set on the corner of the bench. It gave a bad light but it was better than nothing: they had left us in the dark the night before. For a long time I watched the circle of light the lamp made on the ceiling. I was fascinated. Then suddenly I woke up, the circle of light disappeared and I felt myself crushed under an enormous weight. It was not the thought of death or fear; it was nameless. My cheeks burned and my head ached.

I shook myself and looked at my two friends. Tom had hidden his face in his hands. I could only see the fat white nape of his neck. Little Juan was the worst; his mouth was open and his nostrils trembled. The doctor went to him and put his hand on his shoulder to comfort him, but his eyes stayed cold. Then I saw the Belgian's hand drop stealthily along Juan's arm, down to the wrist. Juan paid no attention. The Belgian took his wrist between three fingers, distractedly, the same time drawing back a little and turning his back to me. But I leaned backward and saw him take a watch from his pocket and look at it for a moment, never letting go of the wrist. After a minute he let the hand fall inert and went and leaned his back against the wall, then, as if he suddenly remembered something very important which had to be jotted down on the spot, he took a notebook from his pocket and wrote a few lines. "Bastard," I thought angrily, "let him come and take my pulse. I'll shove my fist in his rotten face."

He didn't come but I felt him watching me. I raised my head and returned his look. Impersonally, he said to me, "Doesn't it seem cold to you here?" He looked cold, he was blue.

"I'm not cold," I told him.

He never took his hard eyes off me. Suddenly I understood and my hands went to my face: I was drenched in sweat. In this cellar, in the midst of winter, in the midst of drafts, I was sweating. I ran my hands through my hair, gummed together with perspiration; at the same time I saw my shirt was damp and sticking to my skin: I had been dripping for an hour and hadn't felt it. But that swine of a Belgian hadn't missed a thing; he had seen the drops rolling down my cheeks and thought: this is the manifestation of an almost pathological state of terror; and he had felt normal and proud of being alive because he was cold. I wanted to stand up and smash his face but no sooner had I made the slightest gesture than my rage and shame were wiped out; I fell back on the bench with indifference.

I satisfied myself by rubbing my neck with my handkerchief because now I felt the sweat dropping from my hair onto my neck and it was unpleasant. I soon gave up rubbing, it was useless; my handkerchief was already soaked and I was still sweating. My buttocks were sweating too and my damp trousers were glued to the bench.

Suddenly Juan spoke. "You're a doctor?"

"Yes," the Belgian said.

"Does it hurt . . . very long?"

"Huh? When . . . ? Oh, no," the Belgian said paternally. "Not at all. It's over quickly." He acted as though he were calming a cash customer.

"But I . . . they told me . . . sometimes they have to fire twice."

"Sometimes," the Belgian said, nodding. "It may happen that the first volley reaches no vital organs."

"Then they have to reload their rifles and aim all over again?" He thought for a moment and then added hoarsely, "That takes time!"

He had a terrible fear of suffering, it was all he thought about: it was his age. I never thought much about it and it wasn't fear of suffering that made me sweat.

I got up and walked to the pile of coal dust. Tom jumped up and threw me a hateful look: I had annoyed him because my shoes squeaked. I wondered if my face looked as frightened as his: I saw he was sweating too. The sky was superb, no light filtered into the dark corner and I had only to raise my head to see the Big Dipper. But it wasn't like it had been: the night before I could see a great piece of sky from my monastery cell and each hour of the day brought me a different memory. Morning, when the sky was a hard, light blue, I thought of beaches on the Atlantic; at noon I saw the sun and I remembered a bar in Seville where I drank *manzanilla* and ate olives and anchovies; afternoons I was in the shade and I thought of the deep shadow which spreads over half a bull-ring leaving the other half shimmering in sunlight; it was really hard to see the whole world reflected in the sky like that. But now I could watch the sky as much as I pleased, it no longer evoked anything in me. I liked that better. I came back and sat near Tom. A long moment passed.

Tom began speaking in a low voice. He had to talk, without that he wouldn't have been able to recognize himself in his own mind. I thought he was talking to me but he wasn't looking at me. He was undoubtedly afraid to see me as I was, grey and sweating: we were alike and worse than mirrors of each other. He watched the Belgian, the living.

"Do you understand?" he said. "I don't understand."

I began to speak in a low voice too. I watched the Belgian.

"Why? What's the matter?"

"Something is going to happen to us that I can't understand."

There was a strange smell about Tom. It seemed to me I was more sensitive than usual to odors. I grinned. "You'll understand in a while."

"It isn't clear," he said obstinately. "I want to be brave but first I have to know . . . Listen, they're going to take us into the courtyard. Good. They're going to stand up in front of us. How many?"

"I don't know. Five or eight. Not more."

"All right. There'll be eight. Someone'll holler 'aim!' and I'll see eight rifles looking at me. I'll think how I'd like to get inside the wall, I'll push against it with my back . . . with every ounce of strength I have, but the wall will stay, like in a nightmare. I can imagine all that. If you only knew how well I can imagine it."

"All right, all right!" I said, "I can imagine it too."

"It must hurt like hell. You know, they aim at the eyes and the mouth to disfigure you," he added mechanically. "I can feel the wounds already; I've had pains in my head and in my neck for the past hour. Not real pains. Worse. This is what I'm going to feel tomorrow morning. And then what?"

I well understood what he meant but I didn't want to act as if I did. I had pains too, pains in my body like a crowd of tiny scars. I couldn't get used to it. But I was like him, I attached no importance to it. "After," I said, "you'll be pushing up daisies."

He began to talk to himself: he never stopped watching the Belgian. The

Belgian didn't seem to be listening. I knew what he had come to do; he wasn't interested in what we thought; he came to watch our bodies, bodies dying in agony while yet alive.

"It's like a nightmare," Tom was saying. "You want to think of something, you always have the impression that it's all right, that you're going to understand and then it slips, it escapes you and fades away. I tell myself there will be nothing afterwards. But I don't understand what it means. Sometimes I almost can . . . and then it fades away and I start thinking about the pains again, bullets, explosions. I'm a materialist, I swear it to you; I'm not going crazy. But something's the matter. I see my corpse; that's not hard but I'm the one who sees it, with my eyes. I've got to think . . . think that I won't see anything anymore and the world will go on for the others. We aren't made to think that, Pablo. Believe me: I've already stayed up a whole night waiting for something. But this isn't the same: this will creep up behind us, Pablo, and we won't be able to prepare for it."

"Shut up," I said, "Do you want me to call a priest?"

He didn't answer. I had already noticed he had the tendency to act like a prophet and call me Pablo, speaking in a toneless voice. I didn't like that: but it seems all the Irish are that way. I had the vague impression he smelled of urine. Fundamentally, I hadn't much sympathy for Tom and I didn't see why, under the pretext of dying together, I should have any more. It would have been different with some others. With Ramon Gris, for example. But I felt alone between Tom and Juan. I liked that better, anyhow with Ramon I might have been more deeply moved. But I was terribly hard just then and I wanted to stay hard.

He kept on chewing his words, with something like distraction. He certainly talked to keep himself from thinking. He smelled of urine like an old prostate case. Naturally, I agreed with him, I could have said everything he said: it isn't *natural* to die. And since I was going to die, nothing seemed natural to me, not this pile of coal dust, or the bench, or Pedro's ugly face. Only it didn't please me to think the same things as Tom. And I knew that, all through the night, every five minutes, we would keep on thinking things at the same time. I looked at him sideways and for the first time he seemed strange to me: he wore death on his face. My pride was wounded: for the past twenty-four hours I had lived next to Tom, I had listened to him, I had spoken to him and I knew we had nothing in common. And now we looked as much alike as twin brothers, simply because we were going to die together. Tom took my hand without looking at me.

"Pablo, I wonder . . . I wonder if it's really true that everything ends."

I took my hand away and said, "Look between your feet, you pig."

There was a big puddle between his feet and drops fell from his pants-leg.

"What is it?" he asked frightened.

"You're pissing in your pants," I told him.

"It isn't true," he said furiously. "I'm not pissing. I don't feel anything."

The Belgian approached us. He asked with false solicitude, "Do you feel ill?"

Tom did not answer. The Belgian looked at the puddle and said nothing.

"I don't know what it is," Tom said ferociously. "But I'm not afraid. I swear I'm not afraid."

The Belgian did not answer. Tom got up and went to piss in a corner. He came back buttoning his fly, and sat down without a word. The Belgian was taking notes.

All three of us watched him because he was alive. He had the motions of a living human being, the cares of a living human being; he shivered in the cellar the way the living are supposed to shiver; he had an obedient, well-fed body. The rest of us hardly felt ours—not in the same way any-how. I wanted to feel my pants between my legs but I didn't dare; I watched the Belgian, balancing on his legs, master of his muscles, someone who could think about tomorrow. There we were, three bloodless shadows; we watched him and we sucked his life like vampires.

Finally he went over to little Juan. Did he want to feel his neck for some professional motive or was he obeying an impulse of charity? If he was act-ing by charity it was the only time during the whole night.

He caressed Juan's head and neck. The kid let himself be handled, his eyes never leaving him, then suddenly, he seized the hand and looked at it strangely. He held the Belgian's hand between his own two hands and there was nothing pleasant about them, two grey pincers gripping his fat and reddish hand. I suspected what was going to happen and Tom must have suspected it too: but the Belgian didn't see a thing, he smiled patern-ally. After a moment the kid brought the fat red hand to his mouth and tried to bite it. The Belgian pulled away quickly and stumbled back against the wall. For a second he looked at us with horror, he must have suddenly understood that we were not men like him. I began to laugh and one of the guards jumped up. The other was asleep, his wide open eyes were blank.

I felt relaxed and over-excited at the same time. I didn't want to think any more about what would happen at dawn, at death. It made no sense. I only found words or emptiness. But as soon as I tried to think of anything else I saw rifle barrels pointing at me. Perhaps I lived through my execution twenty times; once I even thought it was for good: I must have slept a minute. They were dragging me to the wall and I was struggling; I was asking for mercy. I woke up with a start and looked at the Belgian: I was afraid I might have cried out in my sleep. But he was stroking his mous-tache, he hadn't noticed anything. If I had wanted to, I think I could have slept a while; I had been awake for forty-eight hours. I was at the end of my rope. But I didn't want to lose two hours of life: they would come to wake me up at dawn, I would follow them, stupefied with sleep and I would have croaked without so much as an "Oof!"; I didn't want that, I didn't want to die like an animal, I wanted to understand. Then I was afraid of having nightmares. I got up, walked back and forth, and, to change my ideas, I began to think about my past life. A crowd of memories came back to me pellmell. There were good and bad ones—or at least I called them that *before*. There were faces and incidents. I saw the face of a little *novillero* who was gored in Valencia during the *Feria*, the face of one of my uncles, the face of Ramon Gris. I remembered my whole life: how I was out of work for three months in 1926, how I almost starved to death. I remembered a night I spent on a bench in Granada: I hadn't eaten for three days. I was angry, I didn't want to die. That made me smile. How madly I ran after happiness, after women, after liberty. Why? I wanted to free Spain, I admired Pi y Margall, I joined the anarchist movement, I spoke in public meetings: I took everything as seriously as if I were immortal.

At that moment I felt that I had my whole life in front of me, and I thought, "It's a damned lie." It was worth nothing because it was finished. I wondered how I'd been able to walk, to laugh with the girls: I wouldn't have moved so much as my little finger if I had only imagined I would die like this. My life was in front of me, shut, closed, like a bag and yet everything inside of it was unfinished. For an instant I tried to judge it. I wanted to tell myself, this is a beautiful life. But I couldn't pass judgment on it; it was only a sketch; I had spent my time counterfeiting eternity, I had understood nothing. I missed nothing: there were so many things I could have missed, the taste of *manzanilla* or the baths I took in summer in a little creek near Cadiz; but death had disenchanted everything.

The Belgian suddenly had a bright idea. "My friends," he told us, "I will undertake—if the military administration will allow it—to send a message for you, a souvenir to those who love you . . ."

Tom mumbled, "I don't have anybody."

I said nothing. Tom waited an instant then looked at me with curiosity. "You don't have anything to say to Concha?"

"No."

I hated this tender complicity: it was my own fault, I had talked about Concha the night before, I should have controlled myself. I was with her for a year. Last night I would have given an arm to see her again for five minutes. That was why I talked about her, it was stronger than I was. Now I had no more desire to see her, I had nothing more to say to her. I would not even have wanted to hold her in my arms: my body filled me with horror because it was grey and sweating—and I wasn't sure that her body didn't fill me with horror. Concha would cry when she found out I was dead, she would have no taste for life for months afterwards. But I was still the one who was going to die. I thought of her soft, beautiful eyes. When she looked at me something passed from her to me. But I knew it was over: if she looked at me *now* the look would stay in her eyes, it wouldn't reach me. I was alone.

Tom was alone too but not in the same way. Sitting cross-legged, he had begun to stare at the bench with a sort of smile, he looked amazed. He put out his hand and touched the wood cautiously as if he were afraid of breaking something, then drew back his hand quickly and shuddered. If I had been Tom I wouldn't have amused myself by touching the bench; this was some more Irish nonsense, but I too found that objects had a funny look: they were more obliterated, less dense than usual. It was enough for me to look at the bench, the lamp, the pile of coal dust, to feel that I was going to die. Naturally I couldn't think clearly about my death but I saw it everywhere, on things, in the way things fell back and kept their distance, discreetly, as people who speak quietly at the bedside of a dying man. It was *his* death which Tom had just touched on the bench.

In the state I was in, if someone had come and told me I could go home quietly, that they would leave me my life whole, it would have left me cold: several hours or several years of waiting is all the same when you have lost the illusion of being eternal. I clung to nothing, in a way I was calm. But it was a horrible calm—because of my body; my body, I saw with its eyes, I heard with its ears, but it was no longer me; it sweated and trembled by itself and I didn't recognize it any more. I had to touch it and look at it to find out what was happening, as if it were the body of some-one else. At times I could still feel it, I felt sinkings, and fallings, as when you're in a plane taking a nosedive, or I felt my heart beating. But that didn't reassure me. Everything that came from my body was all cock-eyed. Most of the time it was quiet and I felt no more than a sort of weight, a filthy presence against me; I had the impression of being tied to an enorm-ous vermin. Once I felt my pants and I felt they were damp; I didn't know whether it was sweat or urine, but I went to piss on the coal pile as a precaution.

The Belgian took out his watch, looked at it. He said, "It's three-thirty."

Bastard! He must have done it on purpose. Tom jumped; we hadn't noticed time was running out; night surrounded us like a shapeless, somber mass, I couldn't even remember that it had begun.

Little Juan began to cry. He wrung his hands, pleaded, "I don't want to die. I don't want to die."

He ran across the whole cellar waving his arms in the air, then fell sob-bing on one of the mats. Tom watched him with mournful eyes, without the slightest desire to console him. Because it wasn't worth the trouble: the kid made more noise than we did, but he was less touched: he was like a sick man who defends himself against his illness by fever. It's much more serious when there isn't any fever.

He wept: I could clearly see he was pitying himself; he wasn't thinking about death. For one second, one single second, I wanted to weep myself, to weep with pity for myself. But the opposite happened: I glanced at the kid, I saw his thin sobbing shoulders and I felt inhuman: I could pity neither the others nor myself. I said to myself, "I want to die cleanly."

Tom had gotten up, he placed himself just under the round opening and began to watch for daylight. I was determined to die cleanly and I only thought of that. But ever since the doctor told us the time, I felt time flying, flowing away drop by drop.

It was still dark when I heard Tom's voice: "Do you hear them?"

Men were marching in the courtyard.

"Yes."

"What the hell are they doing? They can't shoot in the dark."

After a while we heard no more. I said to Tom, "It's day."

Pedro got up, yawning, and came to blow out the lamp. He said to his buddy, "Cold as hell."

The cellar was all grey. We heard shots in the distance.

"It's starting," I told Tom. "They must do it in the court in the rear."

Tom asked the doctor for a cigarette. I didn't want one; I didn't want cigarettes or alcohol. From that moment on they didn't stop firing.

"Do you realize what's happening?" Tom said.

He wanted to add something but kept quiet, watching the door. The door opened and a lieutenant came in with four soldiers. Tom dropped his cigarette.

"Steinbock?"

Tom didn't answer Pedro pointed him out.

"Juan Mirbal?"

"On the mat."

"Get up," the lieutenant said.

Juan did not move. Two soldiers took him under the arms and set him on his feet. But he fell as soon as they released him.

The soldiers hesitated.

"He's not the first sick one," said the lieutenant. "You two carry him; they'll fix it up down there."

He turned to Tom. "Let's go."

Tom went out between two soldiers. Two others followed, carrying the kid by the armpits. He hadn't fainted; his eyes were wide open and tears ran down his cheeks. When I wanted to go out the lieutenant stopped me.

"You Ibbieta?"

"Yes."

"You wait here; they'll come for you later."

They left. The Belgian and the two jailers left too, I was alone. I did not understand what was happening to me but I would have liked it better if they had gotten it over with right away. I heard shots at almost regular intervals; I shook with each one of them. I wanted to scream and tear out my hair. But I gritted my teeth and pushed my hands in my pockets because I wanted to stay clean.

After an hour they came to get me and led me to the first floor, to a small room that smelt of cigars and where the heat was stifling. There were two officers sitting smoking in the armchairs, papers on their knees.

"You're Ibbieta?"

"Yes."

"Where is Ramon Gris?"

"I don't know."

The one questioning me was short and fat. His eyes were hard behind his glasses. He said to me, "Come here."

I went to him. He got up and took my arms, staring at me with a look that should have pushed me into the earth. At the same time he pinched my biceps with all his might. It wasn't to hurt me, it was only a game: he wanted to dominate me. He also thought he had to blow his stinking breath square in my face. We stayed for a moment like that, and I almost felt like laughing. It takes a lot to intimidate a man who is going to die; it didn't work. He pushed me back violently and sat down again. He said, "It's his life against yours. You can have yours if you tell us where he is."

These men dolled up with their riding crops and boots were still going to die. A little later than I, but not too much. They busied themselves looking for names in their crumpled papers, they ran after other men to imprison or suppress them; they had opinions on the future of Spain and on other subjects. Their little activities seemed shocking and burlesqued to me; I couldn't put myself in their place, I thought they were insane. The little man was still looking at me, whipping his boots with the riding crop. All his gestures were calculated to give him the look of a live and ferocious beast.

"So? You understand?"

"I don't know where Gris is," I answered. "I thought he was in Madrid."

The other officer raised his pale hand indolently. This indolence was also calculated. I saw through all their little schemes and I was stupefied to find there were men who amused themselves that way.

"You have a quarter of an hour to think it over," he said slowly. "Take him to the laundry, bring him back in fifteen minutes. If he still refuses he will be executed on the spot."

They knew what they were doing: I had passed the night in waiting; then they had made me wait an hour in the cellar while they shot Tom and Juan and now they were locking me up in the laundry; they must have prepared their game the night before. They told themselves that nerves eventually wear out and they hoped to get me that way.

They were badly mistaken. In the laundry I sat on a stool because I felt very weak and I began to think. But not about their proposition. Of course I knew where Gris was; he was hiding with his cousins, four kilometers from the city. I also knew that I would not reveal his hiding place unless they tortured me (but they didn't seem to be thinking about that). All that was perfectly regulated, definite and in no way interested me. Only I would have liked to understand the reasons for my conduct. I would rather die than give up Gris. Why? I didn't like Ramon Gris any more. My friendship for him had died a little while before dawn at the same time as my love for Concha, at the same time as my desire to live. Undoubtedly I thought highly of him: he was tough. But it was not for this reason that I consented to die in his place; his life had no more value than mine; no life had value. They were going to slap a man up against a wall and shoot at him until he died, whether it was I or Gris or somebody else made no difference. I knew he was more useful than I to the cause of Spain but I thought to hell with Spain and anarchy; nothing was important. Yet I was there, I could save my skin and give up Gris and I refused to do it. I found that somehow comic; it was obstinacy. I thought, "I must be stubborn!" And a droll sort of gaiety spread over me.

They came for me and brought me back to the two officers. A rat ran out from under my feet and that amused me. I turned to one of the *falangistas* and said, "Did you see the rat?"

He didn't answer. He was very sober, he took himself seriously. I wanted to laugh but I held myself back because I was afraid that once I got started I wouldn't be able to stop. The *falangista* had a moustache. I said to him again, "You ought to shave off your moustache, idiot." I thought it funny that he would let the hairs of his living being invade his face. He kicked me without great conviction and I kept quiet.

"Well," said the fat officer, "have you thought about it?"

I looked at them with curiosity, as insects of a very rare species. I told them, "I know where he is. He is hidden in the cemetery. In a vault or in the gravediggers' shack."

It was a farce. I wanted to see them stand up, buckle their belts and give orders busily.

They jumped to their feet. "Let's go. Molés, go get fifteen men from Lieutenant Lopez. You," the fat man said, "I'll let you off if you're telling the truth, but it'll cost you plenty if you're making monkeys out of us."

They left in a great clatter and I waited peacefully under the guard of *falangistas*. From time to time I smiled, thinking about the spectacle they would make. I felt stunned and malicious. I imagined them lifting up tombstones, opening the doors of the vaults one by one. I represented this situation to myself as if I had been someone else: this prisoner obstinately playing the hero, these grim *falangistas* with their moustaches and their men in uniform running among the graves; it was irresistibly funny. After half an hour the little fat man came back alone. I thought he had come to give the orders to execute me. The others must have stayed in the cemetery.

The officer looked at me. He didn't look at all sheepish. "Take him into the big courtyard with the others," he said. "After the military operations a regular court will decide what happens to him."

"Then they're not . . . not going to shoot me? . . ."

"Not now, anyway. What happens afterwards is none of my business."

I still didn't understand. I asked, "But why?"

He shrugged his shoulders without answering and the soldiers took me away. In the big courtyard there were about a hundred prisoners, women, children and a few old men. I began walking around the central grass-plot, I was stupefied. At noon they let us eat in the mess hall. Two or three people questioned me. I must have known them, but I didn't answer: I didn't even know where I was.

Around evening they pushed about ten new prisoners into the court. I recognized Garcia, the baker. He said, "What damned luck you have! I didn't think I'd see you alive."

"They sentenced me to death," I said, "and then they changed their minds, I don't know why."

"They arrested me at two o'clock," Garcia said.

"Why?" Garcia had nothing to do with politics.

"I don't know," he said. "They arrest everybody who doesn't think the way they do." He lowered his voice. "They got Gris."

I began to tremble. "When?"

"This morning. He messed it up. He left his cousin's on Tuesday because they had an argument. There were plenty of people to hide him but he didn't want to owe anything to anybody. He said, 'I'd go hide in Ibbieta's place, but they got him, so I'll go hide in the cemetery.' "

"In the cemetery?"

"Yes. What a fool. Of course they went by there this morning, that was sure to happen. They found him in the gravediggers' shack. He shot at them and they got him."

"In the cemetery!"

Everything began to spin and I found myself sitting on the ground: I laughed so hard I cried.

The Other Side of the Hedge

E. M. FORSTER

My pedometer told me that I was twenty-five; and, though it is a shocking thing to stop walking, I was so tired that I sat down on a milestone to rest. People outstripped me, jeering as they did so, but I was too apathetic to feel resentful, and even when Miss Eliza Dimbleby, the great educationist, swept past, exhorting me to persevere, I only smiled and raised my hat.

At first I thought I was going to be like my brother, whom I had had to leave by the roadside a year or two round the corner. He had wasted his breath on singing, and his strength on helping others. But I had travelled more wisely, and now it was only the monotony of the highway that oppressed me—dust under foot and brown crackling hedges on either side, ever since I could remember.

And I had already dropped several things—indeed, the road behind was strewn with the things we all had dropped; and the white dust was settling down on them, so that already they looked no better than stones. My muscles were so weary that I could not even bear the weight of those things I still carried. I slid off the milestone into the road, and lay there prostrate, with my face to the great parched hedge, praying that I might give up.

A little puff of air revived me. It seemed to come from the hedge; and, when I opened my eyes, there was a glint of light through the tangle of boughs and dead leaves. The hedge could not be as thick as usual. In my weak, morbid state, I longed to force my way in, and see what was on the other side. No one was in sight, or I should not have dared to try. For we of the road do not admit in conversation that there is another side at all.

I yielded to the temptation, saying to myself that I would come back in a minute. The thorns scratched my face, and I had to use my arms as a shield, depending on my feet alone to push me forward. Halfway through I would have gone back, for in the passage all the things I was carrying were scraped off me, and my clothes were torn. But I was so wedged that return was impossible, and I had to wriggle blindly forward, expecting every moment that my strength would fail me, and that I should perish in the undergrowth.

Suddenly cold water closed round my head, and I seemed sinking down for ever. I had fallen out of the hedge into a deep pool. I rose to the surface at last, crying for help, and I heard someone on the opposite bank laugh and say: "Another!" And then I was twitched out and laid panting on the dry ground.

Even when the water was out of my eyes, I was still dazed, for I had never been in so large a space, nor seen such grass and sunshine. The blue sky was no longer a strip, and beneath it the earth had risen grandly into hills—clean, bare buttresses, with beech trees in their folds, and meadows and clear pools at their feet. But the hills were not high, and there was in the landscape a sense of human occupation—so that one might have called it a park, or garden, if the words did not imply a certain triviality and constraint.

As soon as I got my breath, I turned to my rescuer and said:

"Where does this place lead to?"

"Nowhere, thank the Lord!" said he, and laughed. He was a man of fifty or sixty—just the kind of age we mistrust on the road—but there was no anxiety in his manner, and his voice was that of a boy of eighteen.

"But it must lead somewhere!" I cried, too much surprised at his answer to thank him for saving my life.

"He wants to know where it leads!" he shouted to some men on the hill side, and they laughed back, and waved their caps.

I noticed then that the pool into which I had fallen was really a moat which bent round to the left and to the right, and that the hedge followed it continually. The hedge was green on this side—its roots showed through the clear water, and fish swam about in them—and it was wreathed over with dog-roses and Traveller's Joy. But it was a barrier, and in a moment I lost all pleasure in the grass, the sky, the trees, the happy men and women, and realized that the place was but a prison, for all its beauty and extent.

We moved away from the boundary, and then followed a path almost parallel to it, across the meadows. I found it difficult walking, for I was always trying to out-distance my companion, and there was no advantage in doing this if the place led nowhere. I had never kept step with anyone since I left my brother.

I amused him by stopping suddenly and saying disconsolately, "This is perfectly terrible. One cannot advance: one cannot progress. Now we of the road——"

"Yes. I know."

"I was going to say, we advance continually."

"I know."

"We are always learning, expanding, developing. Why, even in my short life I have seen a great deal of advance—the Transvaal War, the Fiscal Question, Christian Science, Radium. Here for example—"

I took out my pedometer, but it still marked twenty-five, not a degree more.

"Oh, it's stopped! I meant to show you. It should have registered all the time I was walking with you. But it makes me only twenty-five."

"Many things don't work in here," he said. "One day a man brought in a Lee-Metford, and that wouldn't work."

"The laws of science are universal in their application. It must be the water in the moat that has injured the machinery. In normal conditions everything works. Science and the spirit of emulation—those are the forces that have made us what we are."

I had to break off and acknowledge the pleasant greetings of people whom we passed. Some of them were singing, some talking, some engaged in gardening, hay-making, or other rudimentary industries. They all seemed happy; and I might have been happy too, if I could have forgotten that the place led nowhere.

I was startled by a young man who came sprinting across our path, took a little fence in fine style, and went tearing over a ploughed field till he plunged into a lake, across which he began to swim. Here was true energy, and I exclaimed: "A cross-country race! Where are the others?"

"There are no others," my companion replied; and, later on, when we passed some long grass from which came the voice of a girl singing exquisitely to herself, he said again: "There are no others." I was bewildered at the waste in production, and murmured to myself, "What does it all mean?"

He said: "It means nothing but itself"—and he repeated the words slowly, as if I were a child.

"I understand," I said quietly, "but I do not agree. Every achievement is worthless unless it is a link in the chain of development. And I must not trespass on your kindness any longer. I must get back somehow to the road, and have my pedometer mended."

"First, you must see the gates," he replied, "for we have gates, though we never use them."

I yielded politely, and before long we reached the moat again, at a point where it was spanned by a bridge. Over the bridge was a big gate, as white as ivory, which was fitted into a gap in the boundary hedge. The gate opened outwards, and I exclaimed in amazement, for from it ran a road— just such a road as I had left—dusty under foot, with brown crackling hedges on either side as far as the eye could reach.

"That's my road!" I cried.

He shut the gate and said: "But not your part of the road. It is through this gate that humanity went out countless ages ago, when it was first seized with the desire to walk."

I denied this, observing that the part of the road I myself had left was not more than two miles off. But with the obstinacy of his years he repeated: "It is the same road. This is the beginning, and though it seems to run straight away from us, it doubles so often, that it is never far from our boundary and sometimes touches it." He stooped down by the moat, and traced on its moist margin an absurd figure like a maze. As we walked back through the meadows, I tried to convince him of his mistake.

"The road sometimes doubles, to be sure, but that is part of our discipline. Who can doubt that its general tendency is onward? To what goal we know not—it may be to some mountain where we shall touch the sky, it may be over precipices into the sea. But that it goes forward—who can doubt that? It is the thought of that that makes us strive to excel, each in his own way, and gives us an impetus which is lacking with you. Now that man who passed us—it's true that he ran well, and jumped well, and swam well; but we have men who can run better, and men who can jump better, and who can swim better. Specialization has produced results which would surprise you. Similarly, that girl——"

Here I interrupted myself to exclaim: "Good gracious me! I could have sworn it was Miss Eliza Dimbleby over there, with her feet in the fountain!"

He believed that it was.

"Impossible! I left her on the road, and she is due to lecture this evening at Tunbridge Wells. Why, her train leaves Cannon Street in—of course my watch has stopped like everything else. She is the last person to be here."

"People always are astonished at meeting each other. All kinds come through the hedge, and come at all times—when they are drawing ahead in the race, when they are lagging behind, when they are left for dead. I often stand near the boundary listening to the sounds of the road—you know what they are—and wonder if anyone will turn aside. It is my great happiness to help someone out of the moat, as I helped you. For our country fills up slowly, though it was meant for all mankind."

"Mankind have other aims," I said gently, for I thought him well-meaning; "and I must join them." I bade him good evening, for the sun was declining, and I wished to be on the road by nightfall. To my alarm, he caught hold of me, crying: "You are not to go yet!" I tried to shake him off, for we had no interests in common, and his civility was becoming irksome to me.

But for all my struggles the tiresome old man would not let go; and, as wrestling is not my specialty, I was obliged to follow him.

It was true that I could have never found alone the place where I came in, and I hoped that, when I had seen the other sights about which he was worrying, he would take me back to it. But I was determined not to sleep in the country, for I mistrusted it, and the people too, for all their friendliness. Hungry though I was, I would not join them in their evening meals of milk and fruit, and, when they gave me flowers, I flung them away as soon as I could do so unobserved. Already they were lying down for the night like cattle—some out on the bare hillside, others in groups under the beeches. In the light of an orange sunset I hurried on with my unwelcome guide, dead tired, faint for want of food, but murmuring indomitably: "Give me life, with its struggles and victories, with its failures and hatreds, with its deep moral meaning and its unknown goal!"

At last we came to a place where the encircling moat was spanned by another bridge, and where another gate interrupted the line of the boundary hedge. It was different from the first gate; for it was half transparent like horn, and opened inwards. But through it, in the waning light, I saw again just such a road as I had left—monotonous, dusty, with brown crackling hedges on either side, as far as the eye could reach.

I was strangely disquieted at the sight, which seemed to deprive me of all self-control. A man was passing us, returning for the night to the hills, with a scythe over his shoulder and a can of some liquid in his hand. I forgot the destiny of our race. I forgot the road that lay before my eyes, and I sprang at him, wrenched the can out of his hand, and began to drink.

It was nothing stronger than beer, but in my exhausted state it overcame me in a moment. As in a dream, I saw the old man shut the gate, and heard him say: "This is where your road ends, and through this gate humanity—all that is left of it— will come in to us."

Though my senses were sinking into oblivion, they seemed to expand ere they reached it. They perceived the magic song of nightingales, and the odour of invisible hay, and stars piercing the fading sky. The man whose beer I had stolen lowered me down gently to sleep off its effects, and, as he did so, I saw that he was my brother.

James Joyce (1882–1941), a poet, short-story writer, and novelist, was born in Ireland. However, for most of his adult life, Joyce lived in self-imposed exile, mostly in Italy and France. Partially blind, impoverished, his works banned by the censors and pirated by publishers, Joyce nevertheless forged one of the greatest literary careers in the twentieth century. His major novel Ulysses (1922), on which he worked seven years, was banned in Ireland and did not become legally available in the United States until 1933. For further reading: Dubliners (1914).

The Sisters

JAMES JOYCE

There was no hope for him this time: it was the third stroke. Night after night I had passed the house (it was vacation time) and studied the lighted square of window: and night after night I had found it lighted in the same way, faintly and evenly. If he was dead, I thought, I would see the reflection of candles on the darkened blind for I knew that two candles must be set at the head of a corpse. He had often said to me: "I am not long for this world," and I had thought his words idle. Now I knew they were true. Every night as I gazed up at the window I said softly to myself the word paralysis. It had always sounded strangely in my ears, like the word gnomon in the Euclid and the word simony in the Catechism. But now it sounded to me like the name of some maleficent and sinful being. It filled me with fear, and yet I longed to be nearer to it and to look upon its deadly work.

Old Cotter was sitting at the fire, smoking, when I came downstairs to supper. While my aunt was ladling out my stirabout he said, as if returning to some former remark of his:

"No, I wouldn't say he was exactly . . . but there was something queer . . . there was something uncanny about him. I'll tell you my opinion. . . ."

He began to puff at his pipe, no doubt arranging his opinion in his mind. Tiresome old fool! When we knew him first he used to be rather interesting, talking of faints and worms; but I soon grew tired of him and his endless stories about the distillery.

"I have my own theory about it," he said. "I think it was one of those . . . peculiar cases. . . . But it's hard to say. . . ."

He began to puff again at his pipe without giving us his theory. My uncle saw me staring and said to me:

"Well, so your old friend is gone, you'll be sorry to hear."

"Who?" said I.

"Father Flynn."

"Is he dead?"

"Mr. Cotter here has just told us. He was passing by the house."

I knew that I was under observation so I continued eating as if the news had not interested me. My uncle explained to old Cotter.

"The youngster and he were great friends. The old chap taught him a great deal, mind you; and they say he had a great wish for him."

"God have mercy on his soul," said my aunt piously.

Old Cotter looked at me for a while. I felt that his little beady black eyes were examining me but I would not satisfy him by looking up from my plate. He returned to his pipe and finally spat rudely into the grate.

"I wouldn't like children of mine," he said, "to have too much to say to a man like that."

"How do you mean, Mr. Cotter?" asked my aunt.

"What I mean is," said old Cotter, "it's bad for children. My idea is: let a young lad run about and play with young lads of his own age and not be . . . Am I right, Jack?"

"That's my principle, too," said my uncle. "Let him learn to box his corner. That's what I'm always saying to that Rosicrucian there: take exercise. Why, when I was a nipper every morning of my life I had a cold bath, winter and summer. And that's what stands to me now. Education is all very fine and large. . . . Mr. Cotter might take a pick of that leg of mutton," he added to my aunt.

"No, no, not for me," said old Cotter.

My aunt brought the dish from the safe and put it on the table.

"But why do you think it's not good for children, Mr. Cotter?" she asked.

"It's bad for children," said old Cotter, "because their minds are so impressionable. When children see things like that, you know, it has an effect. . . ."

I crammed my mouth with stirabout for fear I might give utterance to my anger. Tiresome old red-nosed imbecile!

It was late when I fell asleep. Though I was angry with old Cotter for alluding to me as a child, I puzzled my head to extract meaning from his unfinished sentences. In the dark of my room I imagined that I saw again the heavy grey face of the paralytic. I drew the blankets over my head and tried to think of Christmas. But the grey face still followed me. It murmured; and I understood that it desired to confess something. I felt my soul receding into some pleasant and vicious region; and there again I found it waiting for me. It began to confess to me in a murmuring voice and I wondered why it smiled continually and why the lips were so moist with spittle. But then I remembered that it had died of paralysis and I felt that I too was smiling feebly as if to absolve the simoniac of his sin.

The next morning after breakfast I went down to look at the little house in Great Britain Street. It was an unassuming shop, registered under the vague name of *Drapery*. The drapery consisted mainly of children's bootees and umbrellas; and on ordinary days a notice used to hang in the window, saying: *Umbrellas Re-covered*. No notice was visible now for the shutters were up. A crape bouquet was tied to the door-knocker with ribbon. Two poor women and a telegram boy were reading the card pinned on the crape. I also approached and read:

July 1st, 1895

The Rev. James Flynn (formerly of S. Catherine's Church, Meath Street), aged sixty-five years.

R. I. P.

The reading of the card persuaded me that he was dead and I was disturbed to find myself at check. Had he not been dead I would have gone into the little dark room behind the shop to find him sitting in his armchair by the fire, nearly smothered in his great-coat. Perhaps my aunt would have given me a packet of High Toast for him and this present would have roused him from his stupefied doze. It was always I who emptied the packet into his black snuff-box for his hands trembled too much to allow him to do this without spilling half the snuff about the floor. Even as he raised his large trembling hand to his nose little clouds of smoke dribbled through his fingers over the front of his coat. It may have been these constant showers of snuff which gave his ancient priestly garments their green faded look for the red handkerchief, blackened, as it always was, with the snuff-stains of a week, with which he tried to brush away the fallen grains, was quite inefficacious.

I wished to go in and look at him but I had not the courage to knock. I walked away slowly along the sunny side of the street, reading all the theatrical advertisements in the shop-windows as I went. I found it strange that neither I nor the day seemed in a mourning mood and I felt even annoyed at discovering in myself a sensation of freedom as if I had been freed from something by his death. I wondered at this for, as my uncle had said the night before, he had taught me a great deal. He had studied in the Irish college in Rome and he had taught me to pronounce Latin properly. He had told me stories about the catacombs and about Napoleon Bonaparte, and he had explained to me the meaning of the different ceremonies of the Mass and of the different vestments worn by the priest. Sometimes he had amused himself by putting difficult questions to me, asking me what one should do in certain circumstances or whether such and such sins were mortal or venial or only imperfections. His questions showed me how complex and mysterious were certain institutions of the Church which I had always regarded as the simplest acts. The duties of the priest towards the Eucharist and towards the secrecy of the confessional seemed so grave to me that I wondered how anybody had ever found in himself the courage to undertake them; and I was not surprised when he told me that the fathers of the Church had written books as thick as the *Post Office Directory* and as closely printed as the law notices in the newspaper, elucidating all these intricate questions. Often when I thought of this I could make no answer or only a very foolish and halting one upon which he used to smile and nod his head twice or thrice. Sometimes he used to put me through the responses of the Mass which he had made me learn by heart; and, as I pattered, he used to smile pensively and nod his head, now and then pushing huge pinches of snuff up each nostril alternately. When he smiled he used to uncover his big discoloured teeth and let his tongue lie upon his lower lip—a habit which had made me feel uneasy in the beginning of our acquaintance before I knew him well.

As I walked along in the sun I remembered old Cotter's words and tried to remember what had happened afterwards in the dream. I remembered that I had noticed long velvet curtains and a swinging lamp of antique fashion. I felt that I had been very far away, in some land where the customs were strange—in Persia, I thought. . . . But I could not remember the end of the dream.

In the evening my aunt took me with her to visit the house of mourning. It was after sunset; but the window-panes of the houses that looked to the west reflected the tawny gold of a great bank of clouds. Nannie received us in the hall; and, as it would have been unseemly to have shouted at her, my aunt shook hands with her for all. The old woman pointed upwards interrogatively and, on my aunt's nodding, proceeded to toil up the narrow staircase before us, her bowed head being scarcely above the level of the banister-rail. At the first landing she stopped and beckoned us forward encouragingly towards the open door of the dead-room. My aunt went in and the old woman, seeing that I hesitated to enter, began to beckon to me again repeatedly with her hand.

I went in on tiptoe. The room through the lace end of the blind was suffused with dusky golden light amid which the candles looked like pale thin flames. He had been coffined. Nannie gave the lead and we three knelt down at the foot of the bed. I pretended to pray but I could not gather my thoughts because the old woman's mutterings distracted me. I noticed how clumsily her skirt was hooked at the back and how the heels of her cloth boots were trodden down all to one side. The fancy came to me that the old priest was smiling as he lay there in his coffin.

But no. When we rose and went up to the head of the bed I saw that he was not smiling. There he lay, solemn and copious, vested as for the altar, his large hands loosely retaining a chalice. His face was very truculent, grey and massive, with black cavernous nostrils and circled by a scanty white fur. There was a heavy odour in the room—the flowers.

We crossed ourselves and came away. In the little room downstairs we found Eliza seated in his arm-chair in state. I groped my way towards my usual chair in the corner while Nannie went to the sideboard and brought out a decanter of sherry and some wine-glasses. She set these on the table and invited us to take a little glass of wine. Then, at her sister's bidding, she filled out the sherry into the glasses and passed them to us. She pressed me to take some cream crackers also but I declined because I thought I would make too much noise eating them. She seemed to be somewhat disappointed at my refusal and went over quietly to the sofa where she sat down behind her sister. No one spoke: we all gazed at the empty fireplace.

My aunt waited until Eliza sighed and then said:

"Ah, well, he's gone to a better world."

Eliza sighed again and bowed her head in assent. My aunt fingered the stem of her wine-glass before sipping a little.

"Did he . . . peacefully?" she asked.

"Oh, quite peacefully, ma'am," said Eliza. "You couldn't tell when the breath went out of him. He had a beautiful death, God be praised."

"And everything . . . ?"

"Father O'Rourke was in with him a Tuesday and anointed him and prepared him and all."

"He knew then?"

"He was quite resigned."

"He looks quite resigned," said my aunt.

"That's what the woman we had in to wash him said. She said he just looked as if he was asleep, he looked that peaceful and resigned. No one would think he'd make such a beautiful corpse."

"Yes, indeed," said my aunt.

She sipped a little more from her glass and said:

"Well, Miss Flynn, at any rate it must be a great comfort for you to know that you did all you could for him. You were both very kind to him, I must say."

Eliza smoothed her dress over her knees.

"Ah, poor James!" she said. "God knows we done all we could, as poor as we are—we wouldn't see him want anything while he was in it."

Nannie had leaned her head against the sofa-pillow and seemed about to fall asleep.

"There's poor Nannie," said Eliza, looking at her, "she's wore out. All the work we had, she and me, getting in the woman to wash him and then laying him out and then the coffin and then arranging about the Mass in the chapel. Only for Father O'Rourke I don't know what we'd done at all. It was him brought us all them flowers and them two candlesticks out of the chapel and wrote out the notice for the *Freeman's General* and took charge of all the papers for the cemetery and poor James's insurance."

"Wasn't that good of him?" said my aunt.

Eliza closed her eyes and shook her head slowly.

"Ah, there's no friends like the old friends," she said, "when all is said and done, no friends that a body can trust."

"Indeed, that's true," said my aunt. "And I'm sure now that he's gone to his eternal reward he won't forget you and all your kindness to him."

"Ah, poor James!" said Eliza. "He was no great trouble to us. You wouldn't hear him in the house any more than now. Still, I know he's gone and all to that. . . ."

"It's when it's all over that you'll miss him," said my aunt.

"I know that," said Eliza. "I won't be bringing him in his cup of beef-tea any more, nor you, ma'am, sending him his snuff. Ah, poor James!"

She stopped, as if she were communing with the past and then said shrewdly:

"Mind you, I noticed there was something queer coming over him latterly. Whenever I'd bring in his soup to him there I'd find him with his breviary fallen to the floor, lying back in the chair and his mouth open!"

She laid a finger against her nose and frowned: then she continued:

"But still and all he kept on saying that before the summer was over he'd go out for a drive one fine day just to see the old house again where we were all born down in Irishtown and take me and Nannie with him. If we could only get one of them new-fangled carriages that makes no noise that Father O'Rourke told him about, them with the rheumatic wheels, for the day cheap—he said, at Johnny Rush's over the way there and drive out the three of us together of a Sunday evening. He had his mind set on that. . . . Poor James!"

"The Lord have mercy on his soul!" said my aunt.

Eliza took out her handkerchief and wiped her eyes with it. Then she put it back again in her pocket and gazed into the empty grate for some time without speaking.

"He was too scrupulous always," she said. "The duties of the priesthood was too much for him. And then his life was, you might say, crossed."

"Yes," said my aunt. "He was a disappointed man. You could see that."

A silence took possession of the little room and, under cover of it, I approached the table and tasted my sherry and then returned quietly to my chair in the corner. Eliza seemed to have fallen into a deep revery. We waited respectfully for her to break the silence: and after a long pause she said slowly:

"It was that chalice he broke. . . . That was the beginning of it. Of course, they say it was all right, that it contained nothing, I mean. But still. . . . They say it was the boy's fault. But poor James was so nervous, God be merciful to him!"

"And was that it?" said my aunt. "I heard something. . . ."

Eliza nodded.

"That affected his mind," she said. "After that he began to mope by himself, talking to no one and wandering about by himself. So one night he was wanted for to go on a call and they couldn't find him anywhere. They looked high up and low down; and still they couldn't see a sight of him anywhere. So then the clerk suggested to try the chapel. So then they got the keys and opened the chapel and the clerk and Father O'Rourke and another priest that was there brought in a light for to look for him. . . . And what do you think but there he was, sitting up by himself in the dark in his confession-box, wide-awake and laughing-like softly to himself?"

She stopped suddenly as if to listen. I too listened; but there was no sound in the house; and I knew that the old priest was lying still in his coffin as we had seen him, solemn and truculent in death, an idle chalice on his breast.

Eliza resumed:

"Wide-awake and laughing-like to himself. . . . So then, of course, when they saw that, that made them think that there was something gone wrong with him. . . ."

The Duchess and the Jeweller

VIRGINIA WOOLF

Oliver Bacon lived at the top of a house overlooking the Green Park. He
had a flat; chairs jutted out at the right angles—chairs covered in hide.
Sofas filled the bays of the windows—sofas covered in tapestry. The windows, the three long windows, had the proper allowance of discreet net and
figured satin. The mahogany sideboard bulged discreetly with the right
brandies, whiskeys, and liqueurs. And from the middle window he looked
down upon the glossy roofs of fashionable cars packed in the narrow straits
of Piccadilly. A more central position could not be imagined. And at eight
in the morning he would have his breakfast brought in on a tray by a man-
servant: the man-servant would unfold his crimson dressing-gown; he
would rip his letters open with his long pointed nails and would extract
thick white cards of invitation upon which the engraving stood up roughly
from duchesses, countesses, viscountesses, and Honourable Ladies. Then he
would wash; then he would eat his toast; then he would read his paper by
the bright burning fire of electric coals.

"Behold Oliver," he would say, addressing himself. "You who began life
in a filthy little alley, you who . . ." and he would look down at his legs, so
shapely in their perfect trousers; at his boots; at his spats. They were all
shapely, shining; cut from the best cloth by the best scissors in Savile Row.
But he dismantled himself often and became again a little boy in a dark
alley. He had once thought *that* the height of his ambition—selling stolen

dogs to fashionable women in Whitechapel. And once he had been done. "Oh, Oliver," his mother had wailed. "Oh, Oliver! When will you have sense, my son?" ... Then he had gone behind a counter; had sold cheap watches; then he had taken a wallet to Amsterdam. ... At that memory he would chuckle—the old Oliver remembering the young. Yes, he had done well with the three diamonds; also there was the commission on the emerald. After that he went into the private room behind the shop in Hatton Garden; the room with the scales, the safe, the thick magnifying glasses. And then ... and then. ... He chuckled. When he passed through the knots of jewellers in the hot evening who were discussing prices, gold mines, diamonds, reports from South Africa, one of them would lay a finger to the side of his nose and murmur, "Hum-m-m," as he passed. It was no more than a murmur; no more than a nudge on the shoulder, a finger on the nose, a buzz that ran through the cluster of jewellers in Hatton Garden on a hot afternoon—oh, many years ago now! But still Oliver felt it purring down his spine, the nudge, the murmur that meant, "Look at him—young Oliver, the young jeweller—there he goes." Young he was then. And he dressed better and better; and had, first a hansom cab; then a car; and first he went up to the dress circle, then down into the stalls. And he had a villa at Richmond, overlooking the river, with trellises of red roses; and Mademoiselle used to pick one every morning and stick it in his button-hole.

"So," said Oliver Bacon, rising and stretching his legs. "So...."

And he stood beneath the picture of an old lady on the mantelpiece and raised his hands. "I have kept my word," he said, laying his hands together, palm to palm, as if he were doing homage to her. "I have won my bet." That was so; he was the richest jeweller in England; but his nose, which was long and flexible, like an elephant's trunk, seemed to say by its curious quiver at the nostrils (but it seemed as if the whole nose quivered, not only the nostrils) that he was not satisfied yet; still smelt something under the ground a little further off. Imagine a giant hog in a pasture rich with truffles; after unearthing this truffle and that, still it smells a bigger, a blacker truffle under the ground further off. So Oliver snuffed always in the rich earth of Mayfair another truffle, a blacker, a bigger further off.

Now then he straightened the pearl in his tie, cased himself in his smart blue overcoat; took his yellow gloves and his cane; and swayed as he descended the stairs and half snuffed, half sighed through his long sharp nose as he passed out into Piccadilly. For was he not still a sad man, a dissatisfied man, a man who seeks something that is hidden, though he had won his bet?

He swayed slightly as he walked, as the camel at the zoo sways from side to side when it walks along the asphalt paths laden with grocers and their wives eating from paper bags and throwing little bits of silver paper crumpled up on to the path. The camel despises the grocers; the camel is dissatisfied with its lot; the camel sees the blue lake and the fringe of palm trees in front of it. So the great jeweller, the greatest jeweller in the whole world, swung down Piccadilly, perfectly dressed, with his gloves, with his cane; but dissatisfied still, till he reached the dark little shop, that was famous in France, in Germany, in Austria, in Italy, and all over America—the dark little shop in the street off Bond Street.

As usual, he strode through the shop without speaking, though the four men, the two old men, Marshall and Spencer, and the two young men, Hammond and Wicks, stood straight and looked at him, envying him. It was only with one finger of the amber-coloured glove, waggling, that he acknowledged their presence. And he went in and shut the door of his private room behind him.

Then he unlocked the grating that barred the window. The cries of Bond Street came in; the purr of the distant traffic. The light from reflectors at the back of the shop struck upwards. One tree waved six green leaves, for it was June. But Mademoiselle had married Mr. Pedder of the local brewery—no one stuck roses in his buttonhole now.

"So," he half sighed, half snorted, "so—"

Then he touched a spring in the wall and slowly the panelling slid open, and behind it were the steel safes, five, no, six of them, all of burnished steel. He twisted a key; unlocked one; then another. Each was lined with a pad of deep crimson velvet; in each lay jewels—bracelets, necklaces, rings, tiaras, ducal coronets; loose stones in glass shells; rubies, emeralds, pearls, diamonds. All safe, shining, cool, yet burning, eternally, with their own compressed light.

"Tears!" said Oliver, looking at the pearls.

"Heart's blood!" he said, looking at the rubies.

"Gunpowder!" he continued, rattling the diamonds so that they flashed and blazed.

"Gunpowder enough to blow Mayfair—sky high, high, high!" He threw his head back and made a sound like a horse neighing as he said it.

The telephone buzzed obsequiously in a low muted voice on his table. He shut the safe.

"In ten minutes," he said. "Not before." And he sat down at his desk and looked at the heads of the Roman emperors that were graved on his sleeve links. And again he dismantled himself and became once more the little boy playing marbles in the alley where they sell stolen dogs on Sunday. He became that wily astute little boy, with lips like wet cherries. He dabbled his fingers in ropes of tripe; he dipped them in pans of frying fish; he dodged in and out among the crowds. He was slim, lissome, with eyes like licked stones. And now—now—the hands of the clock ticked on, one, two, three, four. . . . The Duchess of Lambourne waited his pleasure; the Duchess of Lambourne, daughter of a hundred Earls. She would wait for ten minutes on a chair at the counter. She would wait his pleasure. She would wait till he was ready to see her. He watched the clock in its shagreen case. The hand moved on. With each tick the clock handed him—so it seemed—pâté de foie gras, a glass of champagne, another of fine brandy, a cigar costing one guinea. The clock laid them on the table beside him as the ten minutes passed. Then he heard soft slow footsteps approaching; a rustle in the corridor. The door opened. Mr. Hammond flattened himself against the wall.

"Her Grace!" he announced.

And he waited there, flattened against the wall.

And Oliver, rising, could hear the rustle of the dress of the Duchess as she came down the passage. Then she loomed up, filling the door, filling the room with the aroma, the prestige, the arrogance, the pomp, the pride of all the Dukes and Duchesses swollen in one wave. And as a wave breaks, she broke, as she sat down, spreading and splashing and falling over Oliver Bacon, the great jeweller, covering him with sparkling bright colours, green, rose, violet; and odours; and iridescences; and rays shooting from fingers, nodding from plumes, flashing from silk; for she was very large, very fat, tightly girt in pink taffeta, and past her prime. As a parasol with many flounces, as a peacock with many feathers, shuts its flounces, folds its feathers, so she subsided and shut herself as she sank down in the leather armchair.

"Good morning, Mr. Bacon," said the Duchess. And she held out her hand which came through the slit of her white glove. And Oliver bent low as he shook it. And as their hands touched the link was forged between them once more. They were friends, yet enemies; he was master, she was mistress; each cheated the other, each needed the other, each feared the other, each felt this and knew this every time they touched hands thus in the little back room with the white light outside, and the tree with its six leaves, and the sound of the street in the distance and behind them the safes.

"And today, Duchess—what can I do for you today?" said Oliver, very softly.

The Duchess opened her heart, her private heart, gaped wide. And with a sigh but no word she took from her bag a long wash-leather pouch—it looked like a lean yellow ferret. And from a slit in the ferret's belly she dropped pearls—ten pearls. They rolled from the slit in the ferret's belly—one, two, three, four—like the eggs of some heavenly bird.

"All that's left me, dear Mr. Bacon," she moaned. Five, six, seven—down they rolled, down the slopes of the vast mountain sides that fell between her knees into one narrow valley—the eighth, the ninth, and the tenth. There they lay in the glow of the peach-blossom taffeta. Ten pearls.

"From the Appleby cincture," she mourned. "The last . . . the last of them all."

Oliver stretched out and took one of the pearls between finger and thumb.

It was round, it was lustrous. But real was it, or false? Was she lying again? Did she dare?

She laid her plump padded finger across her lips. "If the Duke knew . . ." she whispered. "Dear Mr. Bacon, a bit of bad luck. . . ."

Been gambling again, had she?

"That villain! That sharper!" she hissed.

The man with the chipped cheek bone? A bad 'un. And the Duke was straight as a poker; with side whiskers; would cut her off, shut her up down there if he knew—what I know, thought Oliver, and glanced at the safe.

"Araminta, Daphne, Diana," she moaned. "It's for *them*."

The ladies Araminta, Daphne, Diana—her daughters. He knew them; adored them. But it was Diana he loved.

"You have all my secrets," she leered. Tears slid; tears fell; tears, like diamonds, collecting powder in the ruts of her cherry blossom cheeks.

"Old friend," she murmured, "old friend."

"Old friend," he repeated, "old friend," as if he licked the words.

"How much?" he queried.

She covered the pearls with her hand.

"Twenty thousand," she whispered.

But was it real or false, the one he held in his hand? The Appleby cincture—hadn't she sold it already? He would ring for Spencer or Hammond. "Take it and test it," he would say. He stretched to the bell.

"You will come down tomorrow?" she urged, she interrupted. "The Prime Minister—His Royal Highness. . . ." She stopped. "And Diana . . ." she added.

Oliver took his hand off the bell.

He looked past her, at the backs of the houses in Bond Street. But he saw, not the houses in Bond Street, but a dimpling river; and trout rising and salmon; and the Prime Minister; and himself too, in white waistcoat; and then, Diana. He looked down at the pearl in his hand. But how could he test it, in the light of the river, in the light of the eyes of Diana? But the eyes of the Duchess were on him.

"Twenty thousand," she moaned. "My honour!"

The honour of the mother of Diana! He drew his cheque book towards him; he took out his pen.

"Twenty—" he wrote. Then he stopped writing. The eyes of the old woman in the picture were on him—of the old woman his mother.

"Oliver!" she warned him. "Have sense! Don't be a fool!"

"Oliver!" the Duchess entreated—it was "Oliver" now, not "Mr. Bacon." "You'll come for a long week-end?"

Alone in the woods with Diana! Riding alone in the woods with Diana!

"Thousand," he wrote, and signed it.

"Here you are," he said.

And there opened all the flounces of the parasol, all the plumes of the peacock, the radiance of the wave, the swords and spears of Agincourt, as she rose from her chair. And the two old men and the two young men, Spencer and Marshall, Wicks and Hammond, flattened themselves behind the counter envying him as he led her through the shop to the door. And he waggled his yellow glove in their faces, and she held her honour—a cheque for twenty thousand pounds with his signature—quite firmly in her hands.

"Are they false or are they real?" asked Oliver, shutting his private door. There they were, ten pearls on the blotting-paper on the table. He took them to the window. He held them under his lens to the light. . . . This, then, was the truffle he had routed out of the earth! Rotten at the centre—rotten at the core!

"Forgive me, oh, my mother!" he sighed, raising his hand as if he asked pardon of the old woman in the picture. And again he was a little boy in the alley where they sold dogs on Sunday.

"For," he murmured, laying the palms of his hands together, "it is to be a long week-end."

D. H. Lawrence (1885–1930), a short-story writer and novelist of genius, was the son of a coal miner in Nottinghamshire. After winning a high school scholarship, he went on to college and for a time taught school. Like Joyce, he struggled all his life against censors' attempts to suppress his work. His best-known novels are Sons and Lovers (1913) and Lady Chatterley's Lover (1928). For further reading: The Prussian Officer, and Other Stories (1914), The Captain's Doll, and Other Stories (1923).

The Blind Man

D. H. LAWRENCE

Isabel Pervin was listening for two sounds—for the sound of wheels on the drive outside and for the noise of her husband's footsteps in the hall. Her dearest and oldest friend, a man who seemed almost indispensable to her living, would drive up in the rainy dusk of the closing November day. The trap had gone to fetch him from the station. And her husband, who had been blinded in Flanders, and who had a disfiguring mark on his brow, would be coming in from the out-houses.

He had been home for a year now. He was totally blind. Yet they had been very happy. The Grange was Maurice's own place. The back was a farmstead, and the Wernhams, who occupied the rear premises, acted as farmers. Isabel lived with her husband in the handsome rooms in front. She and he had been almost entirely alone together since he was wounded. They talked and sang and read together in a wonderful and unspeakable intimacy. Then she reviewed books for a Scottish newspaper, carrying on her old interest, and he occupied himself a good deal with the farm. Sightless, he could still discuss everything with Wernham, and he could also do a good deal of work about the place—menial work, it is true, but it gave him satisfaction. He milked the cows, carried in the pails, turned the separator, attended to the pigs and horses. Life was still very full and strangely serene for the blind man, peaceful with the almost incomprehensible peace of immediate contact in darkness. With his wife he had a whole world, rich and real and invisible.

They were newly and remotely happy. He did not even regret the loss of his sight in these times of dark, palpable joy. A certain exultance swelled his soul.

270

But as time wore on, sometimes the rich glamour would leave them. Sometimes, after months of this intensity, a sense of burden overcame Isabel, a weariness, a terrible *ennui*, in that silent house approached between a colonnade of tall-shafted pines. Then she felt she would go mad, for she could not bear it. And sometimes he had devastating fits of depression, which seemed to lay waste his whole being. It was worse than depression—a black misery, when his own life was a torture to him, and when his presence was unbearable to his wife. The dread went down to the roots of her soul as these black days recurred. In a kind of panic she tried to wrap herself up still further in her husband. She forced the old spontaneous cheerfulness and joy to continue. But the effort it cost her was almost too much. She knew she could not keep it up. She felt she would scream with the strain, and would give anything, anything, to escape. She longed to possess her husband utterly; it gave her inordinate joy to have him entirely to herself. And yet, when again he was gone in a black and massive misery, she could not bear him, she could not bear herself; she wished she could be snatched away off the earth altogether, anything rather than live at this cost.

Dazed, she schemed for a way out. She invited friends, she tried to give him some further connection with the outer world. But it was no good. After all their joy and suffering, after their dark, great year of blindness and solitude and unspeakable nearness, other people seemed to them both shallow, rattling, rather impertinent. Shallow prattle seemed presumptuous. He became impatient and irritated, she was wearied. And so they lapsed into their solitude again. For they preferred it.

But now, in a few weeks' time, her second baby would be born. The first had died, an infant, when her husband first went out to France. She looked with joy and relief to the coming of the second. It would be her salvation. But also she felt some anxiety. She was thirty years old, her husband was a year younger. They both wanted the child very much. Yet she could not help feeling afraid. She had her husband on her hands, a terrible joy to her, and a terrifying burden. The child would occupy her love and attention. And then, what of Maurice? What would he do? If only she could feel that he, too, would be at peace and happy when the child came! She did so want to luxuriate in a rich, physical satisfaction of maternity. But the man, what would he do? How could she provide for him, how avert those shattering black moods of his, which destroyed them both?

She sighed with fear. But at this time Bertie Reid wrote to Isabel. He was her old friend, a second or third cousin, a Scotchman, as she was a Scotchwoman. They had been brought up near to one another, and all her life he had been her friend, like a brother, but better than her own brothers. She loved him—though not in the marrying sense. There was a sort of kinship between them, an affinity. They understood one another instinctively. But Isabel would never have thought of marrying Bertie. It would have seemed like marrying in her own family.

Bertie was a barrister and a man of letters, a Scotchman of the intellectual type, quick, ironical, sentimental, and on his knees before the woman he adored but did not want to marry. Maurice Pervin was different. He came of a good old country family—the Grange was not a very great distance from Oxford. He was passionate, sensitive, perhaps oversensitive, wincing— a big fellow with heavy limbs and a forehead that flushed painfully. For his mind was slow, as if drugged by the strong provincial blood that beat in his veins. He was very sensitive to his own mental slowness, his feelings being quick and acute. So that he was just the opposite to Bertie, whose mind was much quicker than his emotions, which were not so very fine.

From the first the two men did not like each other. Isabel felt that they *ought* to get on together. But they did not. She felt that if only each could have the clue to the other there would be such a rare understanding between them. It did not come off, however. Bertie adopted a slightly ironical attitude, very offensive to Maurice, who returned the Scotch irony with English resentment, a resentment which deepened sometimes into stupid hatred.

This was a little puzzling to Isabel. However, she accepted it in the course of things. Men were made freakish and unreasonable. Therefore, when Maurice was going out to France for the second time, she felt that, for her husband's sake, she must discontinue her friendship with Bertie. She wrote to the barrister to this effect. Bertram Reid simply replied that in this, as in all other matters, he must obey her wishes, if these were indeed her wishes.

For nearly two years nothing had passed between the two friends. Isabel rather gloried in the fact; she had no compunction. She had one great article of faith, which was, that husband and wife should be so important to one another, that the rest of the world simply did not count. She and Maurice were husband and wife. They loved one another. They would have children. Then let everybody and everything else fade into insignificance outside this connubial felicity. She professed herself quite happy and ready to receive Maurice's friends. She was happy and ready: the happy wife, the ready woman in possession. Without knowing why, the friends retired abashed, and came no more. Maurice, of course, took as much satisfaction in this connubial absorption as Isabel did.

He shared in Isabel's literary activities, she cultivated a real interest in agriculture and cattle-raising. For she, being at heart perhaps an emotional enthusiast, always cultivated the practical side of life and prided herself on her mastery of practical affairs. Thus the husband and wife had spent the five years of their married life. The last had been one of blindness and unspeakable intimacy. And now Isabel felt a great indifference coming over her, a sort of lethargy. She wanted to be allowed to bear her child in peace, to nod by the fire and drift vaguely, physically, from day to day. Maurice was like an ominous thunder-cloud. She had to keep waking up to remember him.

When a little note came from Bertie, asking if he were to put up a tombstone to their dead friendship, and speaking of the real pain he felt on account of her husband's loss of sight, she felt a pang, a fluttering agitation of re-awakening. And she read the letter to Maurice.

"Ask him to come down," he said.

"Ask Bertie to come here!" she re-echoed.

"Yes—if he wants to."

Isabel paused for a few moments.

"I know he wants to—he'd only be too glad," she replied. "But what about you, Maurice? How would you like it?"

"I should like it."

"Well—in that case—But I thought you didn't care for him——"

"Oh, I don't know. I might think differently of him now," the blind man replied. It was rather abstruse to Isabel.

"Well, dear," she said, "if you're quite sure——"

"I'm sure enough. Let him come," said Maurice.

So Bertie was coming, coming this evening, in the November rain and darkness. Isabel was agitated, racked with her old restlessness and indecision. She had always suffered from this pain of doubt, just an agonizing sense of uncertainty. It had begun to pass off, in the lethargy of maternity. Now it returned, and she resented it. She struggled as usual to maintain her calm, composed, friendly bearing, a sort of mask she wore over all her body.

A woman had lighted a tall lamp beside the table and spread the cloth. The long dining-room was dim, with its elegant but rather severe pieces of old furniture. Only the round table glowed softly under the light. It had a rich, beautiful effect. The white cloth glistened and dropped its heavy, pointed lace corners to the carpet, the china was old and handsome, creamy-yellow, with a blotched pattern of harsh red and deep blue, the cups large and bell-shaped, the teapot gallant. Isabel looked at it with superficial appreciation.

Her nerves were hurting her. She looked automatically again at the high, uncurtained windows. In the last dusk she could just perceive outside a huge fir-tree swaying its boughs: it was as if she thought it rather than saw it. The rain came flying on the window panes. Ah, why had she no peace? These two men, why did they tear at her? Why did they not come—why was there this suspense?

She sat in a lassitude that was really suspense and irritation. Maurice, at least, might come in—there was nothing to keep him out. She rose to her feet. Catching sight of her reflection in a mirror, she glanced at herself with a slight smile of recognition, as if she were an old friend to herself. Her face was oval and calm, her nose a little arched. Her neck made a beautiful line down to her shoulder. With hair knotted loosely behind, she had something of a warm, maternal look. Thinking this of herself, she arched her eyebrows and her rather heavy eyelids, with a little flicker of a smile, and for a moment her grey eyes looked amused and wicked, a little sardonic, out of her transfigured Madonna face.

Then, resuming her air of womanly patience—she was really fatally self-determined—she went with a little jerk towards the door. Her eyes were slightly reddened.

She passed down the wide hall and through a door at the end. Then she was in the farm premises. The scent of dairy, and of farm-kitchen, and of farm-yard and of leather almost overcame her: but particularly the scent of dairy. They had been scalding out the pans. The flagged passage in front of her was dark, puddled, and wet. Light came out from the open kitchen door. She went forward and stood in the doorway. The farm-people were at tea, seated at a little distance from her, round a long, narrow table, in the center of which stood a white lamp. Ruddy faces, ruddy hands holding food, red mouths working, heads bent over the tea-cups: men, land-girls, boys: it was tea-time, feeding-time. Some faces caught sight of her. Mrs. Wernham, going round behind the chairs with a large black teapot, halting slightly in her walk, was not aware of her for a moment. Then she turned suddenly.

"Oh, is it Madam!" she exclaimed. "Come in, then, come in! We're at tea." And she dragged forward a chair.

"No, I won't come in," said Isabel. "I'm afraid I interrupt your meal."

"No—no—not likely, Madam, not likely."

"Hasn't Mr. Pervin come in, do you know?"

"I'm sure I couldn't say! Missed him, have you, Madam?"

"No, I only wanted him to come in," laughed Isabel, as if shyly.

"Wanted him, did ye? Get up, boy—get up, now——"

Mrs. Wernham knocked one of the boys on the shoulder. He began to scrape to his feet, chewing largely.

"I believe he's in top stable," said another face from the table.

"Ah! No, don't get up. I'm going myself," said Isabel.

"Don't you go out of a dirty night like this. Let the lad go. Get along wi' ye, boy," said Mrs. Wernham.

"No, no," said Isabel, with a decision that was always obeyed. "Go on with your tea, Tom. I'd like to go across to the stable, Mrs. Wernham."

"Did ever you hear tell!" exclaimed the woman.

"Isn't the trap late?" asked Isabel.

"Why, no," said Mrs. Wernham, peering into the distance at the tall, dim clock. "No, Madam—we can give it another quarter or twenty minutes yet, good—yes, every bit of a quarter."

"Ah! It seems late when darkness falls so early," said Isabel.

"It do, that it do. Bother the days, that they draw in so," answered Mrs. Wernham. "Proper miserable!"

"They are," said Isabel, withdrawing.

She pulled on her overshoes, wrapped a large tartan shawl around her, put on a man's felt hat, and ventured out along the causeways of the first yard. It was very dark. The wind was roaring in the great elms behind the outhouses. When she came to the second yard the darkness seemed deeper. She was unsure of her footing. She wished she had brought a lantern. Rain blew against her. Half she liked it, half she felt unwilling to battle.

She reached at last the just visible door of the stable. There was no sign of a light anywhere. Opening the upper half, she looked in: into a simple well of darkness. The smell of horses, and ammonia, and of warmth was startling to her, in that full night. She listened with all her ears but could hear nothing save the night, and the stirring of a horse.

"Maurice!" she called softly and musically, though she was afraid. "Maurice—are you there?"

Nothing came from the darkness. She knew the rain and wind blew in upon the horses, the hot animal life. Feeling it wrong, she entered the stable and drew the lower half of the door shut, holding the upper part close. She did not stir, because she was aware of the presence of the dark hind-quarters of the horses, though she could not see them, and she was afraid. Something wild stirred in her heart.

She listened intensely. Then she heard a small noise in the distance— far away, it seemed—the chink of a pan, and a man's voice speaking a brief word. It would be Maurice, in the other part of the stable. She stood motionless, waiting for him to come through the partition door. The horses were so terrifyingly near to her, in the invisible.

The loud jarring of the inner door-latch made her start; the door was opened. She could hear and feel her husband entering and invisibly passing among the horses near to her, darkness as they were, actively intermingled. The rather low sound of his voice as he spoke to the horses came velvety to her nerves. How near he was, and how invisible! The darkness seemed to be in a strange swirl of violent life, just upon her. She turned giddy.

Her presence of mind made her call, quietly and musically:

"Maurice! Maurice—dea-ar!"

"Yes," he answered. "Isabel?"

She saw nothing, and the sound of his voice seemed to touch her.

"Hello!" she answered cheerfully, straining her eyes to see him. He was still busy, attending to the horses near her, but she saw only darkness. It made her almost desperate.

"Won't you come in, dear?" she said.

"Yes, I'm coming. Just half a minute. *Stand over—now!* Trap's not come, has it?"

"Not yet," said Isabel.

His voice was pleasant and ordinary, but it had a slight suggestion of the stable to her. She wished he would come away. Whilst he was so utterly invisible, she was afraid of him.

"How's the time?" he asked.

"Not yet six," she replied. She disliked to answer into the dark. Presently he came very near to her, and she retreated out of doors.

"The weather blows in here," he said, coming steadily forward, feeling for the doors. She shrank away. At last she could dimly see him.

"Bertie won't have much of a drive," he said, as he closed the doors.

"He won't indeed!" said Isabel calmly, watching the dark shape at the door.

"Give me your arm, dear," she said.

She pressed his arm close to her, as she went. But she longed to see him, to look at him. She was nervous. He walked erect, with face rather lifted, but with a curious tentative movement of his powerful, muscular legs. She could feel the clever, careful, strong contact of his feet with the earth, as she balanced against him. For a moment he was a tower of darkness to her, as if he rose out of the earth.

In the house-passage he wavered and went cautiously, with a curious look of silence about him as he felt for the bench. Then he sat down heavily. He was a man with rather sloping shoulders, but with heavy limbs, powerful legs that seemed to know the earth. His head was small, usually carried high and light. As he bent down to unfasten his gaiters and boots he did not look blind. His hair was brown and crisp, his hands were large, reddish, intelligent, the veins stood out in the wrists; and his thighs and knees seemed massive. When he stood up his face and neck were surcharged with blood, the veins stood out on his temples. She did not look at his blindness.

Isabel was always glad when they had passed through the dividing door into their own regions of repose and beauty. She was a little afraid of him, out there in the animal grossness of the back. His bearing also changed, as he smelt the familiar indefinable odour that pervaded his wife's surroundings, a delicate, refined scent, very faintly spicy. Perhaps it came from the potpourri bowls.

He stood at the foot of the stairs, arrested, listening. She watched him, and her heart sickened. He seemed to be listening to fate.

"He's not here yet," he said. "I'll go up and change."

"Maurice," she said, "you're not wishing he wouldn't come, are you?"

"I couldn't quite say," he answered. "I feel myself rather on the qui vive."

"I can see you are," she answered. And she reached up and kissed his cheek. She saw his mouth relax into a slow smile.

"What are you laughing at?" she said roguishly.

"You consoling me," he answered.

"Nay," she answered. "Why should I console you? You know we love each other—you know *how* married we are! What does anything else matter?"

"Nothing at all, my dear."

He felt for her face and touched it, smiling.

"*You're* all right, aren't you?" he asked anxiously.

"I'm wonderfully all right, love," she answered. "It's you I am a little troubled about, at times."

"Why me?" he said, touching her cheeks delicately with the tips of his fingers. The touch had an almost hypnotizing effect on her.

He went away upstairs. She saw him mount into the darkness, unseeing and unchanging. He did not know that the lamps on the upper corridor were unlighted. He went on into the darkness with unchanging step. She heard him in the bath-room.

Pervin moved about almost unconsciously in his familiar surroundings, dark though everything was. He seemed to know the presence of objects before he touched them. It was a pleasure to him to rock thus through a world of things, carried on the flood in a sort of blood-prescience. He did not think much or trouble much. So long as he kept this sheer immediacy of blood-contact with the substantial world he was happy, he wanted no intervention of visual consciousness. In this state there was a certain rich positivity, bordering sometimes on rapture. Life seemed to move in him like a tide lapping, lapping, and advancing, enveloping all things darkly. It was a pleasure to stretch forth the hand and meet the unseen object, clasp it, and possess it in pure contact. He did not try to remember, to visualize. He did not want to. The new way of consciousness substituted itself in him.

The rich suffusion of this state generally kept him happy, reaching its culmination in the consuming passion for his wife. But at times the flow would seem to be checked and thrown back. Then it would beat inside him like a tangled sea, and he was tortured in the shattered chaos of his own blood. He grew to dread this arrest, this throw-back, this chaos inside himself, when he seemed merely at the mercy of his own powerful and conflicting elements. How to get some measure of control or surety, this was the question. And when the question rose maddening in him, he would clench his fists as if he would *compel* the whole universe to submit to him. But it was in vain. He could not even compel himself.

Tonight, however, he was still serene, though little tremors of unreasonable exasperation ran through him. He had to handle the razor very carefully, as he shaved, for it was not at one with him, he was afraid of it. His hearing also was too much sharpened. He heard the woman lighting the lamps on the corridor, and attending to the fire in the visitors' room. And then, as he went to his room, he heard the trap arrive. Then came Isabel's voice, lifted and calling, like a bell ringing:

"Is it you, Bertie? Have you come?"

And a man's voice answered out of the wind:

"Hello, Isabel! There you are."

"Have you had a miserable drive? I'm so sorry we couldn't send a closed carriage. I can't see you at all, you know."

"I'm coming. No, I liked the drive—it was like Perthshire. Well, how are you? You're looking fit as ever, as far as I can see."

"Oh, yes," said Isabel. "I'm wonderfully well. How are you? Rather thin, I think——"

"Worked to death—everybody's old cry. But I'm all right, Ciss. How's Pervin?—isn't he here?"

"Oh, yes, he's upstairs changing. Yes, he's awfully well. Take off your wet things; I'll send them to be dried."

"And how are you both, in spirits? He doesn't fret?"

"No—no, not at all. No, on the contrary, really. We've been wonderfully happy, incredibly. It's more than I can understand—so wonderful: the nearness, and the peace——"

"Ah! Well, that's awfully good news——"

They moved away. Pervin heard no more. But a childish sense of desolation had come over him, as he heard their brisk voices. He seemed shut out—like a child that is left out. He was aimless and excluded, he did not know what to do with himself. The helpless desolation came over him. He fumbled nervously as he dressed himself, in a state almost of childishness. He disliked the Scotch accent in Bertie's speech, and the slight response it found on Isabel's tongue. He disliked the slight purr of complacency in the Scottish speech. He disliked intensely the glib way in which Isabel spoke of their happiness and nearness. It made him recoil. He was fretful and beside himself like a child, he had almost a childish nostalgia to be included in the life circle. And at the same time he was a man, dark and powerful and infuriated by his own weakness. By some fatal flaw, he could not be by himself, he had to depend on the support of another. And this very dependence enraged him. He hated Bertie Reid, and at the same time he knew the hatred was nonsense, he knew it was the outcome of his own weakness.

He went downstairs. Isabel was alone in the dining-room. She watched him enter, head erect, his feet tentative. He looked so strong-blooded and healthy and, at the same time, cancelled. Cancelled—that was the word that flew across her mind. Perhaps it was his scar suggested it.

"You heard Bertie come, Maurice?" she said.

"Yes—isn't he here?"

"He's in his room. He looks very thin and worn."

"I suppose he works himself to death."

A woman came in with a tray—and after a few minutes Bertie came down. He was a little dark man, with a very long forehead, thin, wispy hair, and sad, large eyes. His expression was inordinately sad—almost funny. He had odd, short legs.

Isabel watched him hesitate under the door, and glance nervously at her husband. Pervin heard him and turned.

"Here you are, now," said Isabel. "Come, let us eat."

Bertie went across to Maurice.

"How are you, Pervin?" he said, as he advanced.

The blind man stuck his hand out into space, and Bertie took it.

"Very fit. Glad you've come," said Maurice.

Isabel glanced at them, and glanced away, as if she could not bear to see them.

"Come," she said. "Come to table. Aren't you both awfully hungry? I am, tremendously."

"I'm afraid you waited for me," said Bertie, as they sat down.

Maurice had a curious monolithic way of sitting in a chair, erect and distant. Isabel's heart always beat when she caught sight of him thus.

"No," she replied to Bertie. "We're very little later than usual. We're having a sort of high tea, not dinner. Do you mind? It gives us such a nice long evening, uninterrupted."

"I like it," said Bertie.

Maurice was feeling, with curious little movements, almost like a cat kneading her bed, for his plate, his knife and fork, his napkin. He was getting the whole geography of his cover into his consciousness. He sat erect and inscrutable, remote-seeming. Bertie watched the static figure of the blind man, the delicate tactile discernment of the large, ruddy hands, and the curious mindless silence of the brow, above the scar. With difficulty he looked away, and without knowing what he did, picked up a little crystal bowl of violets from the table, and held them to his nose.

"They are sweet-scented," he said. "Where do they come from?"

"From the garden—under the windows," said Isabel.

"So late in the year—and so fragrant! Do you remember the violets under Aunt Bell's south wall?"

The two friends looked at each other and exchanged a smile, Isabel's eyes lighting up.

"Don't I?" she replied. "*Wasn't* she queer!"

"A curious old girl," laughed Bertie. "There's a streak of freakishness in the family, Isabel."

"Ah—but not in you and me, Bertie," said Isabel. "Give them to Maurice, will you?" she added, as Bertie was putting down the flowers. "Have you smelled the violets, dear? Do!—they are so scented."

Maurice held out his hand, and Bertie placed the tiny bowl against his large, warm-looking fingers. Maurice's hand closed over the thin white fingers of the barrister. Bertie carefully extricated himself. Then the two watched the blind man smelling the violets. He bent his head and seemed to be thinking. Isabel waited.

"Aren't they sweet, Maurice?" she said at last, anxiously.

"Very," he said. And he held out the bowl. Bertie took it. Both he and Isabel were a little afraid, and deeply disturbed.

The meal continued. Isabel and Bertie chatted spasmodically. The blind man was silent. He touched his food repeatedly, with quick, delicate touches of his knife-point, then cut irregular bits. He could not bear to be helped. Both Isabel and Bertie suffered: Isabel wondered why. She did not suffer when she was alone with Maurice. Bertie made her conscious of a strangeness.

After the meal the three drew their chairs to the fire, and sat down to talk. The decanters were put on a table near at hand. Isabel knocked the logs on the fire, and clouds of brilliant sparks went up the chimney. Bertie noticed a slight weariness in her bearing.

"You will be glad when your child comes now, Isabel?" he said.

She looked up to him with a quick wan smile.

"Yes, I shall be glad," she answered. "It begins to seem long. Yes, I shall be very glad. So will you, Maurice, won't you?" she added.

"Yes, I shall," replied her husband.

"We are both looking forward so much to having it," she said.

"Yes, of course," said Bertie.

He was a bachelor, three or four years older than Isabel. He lived in beautiful rooms overlooking the river, guarded by a faithful Scottish man-servant. And he had his friends among the fair sex—not lovers, friends. So long as he could avoid any danger of courtship or marriage, he adored a few good women with constant and unfailing homage, and he was chivalrously fond of quite a number. But if they seemed to encroach on him, he withdrew and detested them.

Isabel knew him very well, knew his beautiful constancy, and kindness, also his incurable weakness, which made him unable ever to enter into close contact of any sort. He was ashamed of himself because he could not marry, could not approach women physically. He wanted to do so. But he could not. At the centre of him he was afraid, helplessly and even brutally afraid. He had given up hope, had ceased to expect any more that he could escape his own weakness. Hence he was a brilliant and successful barrister, also a *littérateur* of high repute, a rich man, and a great social success. At the centre he felt himself neuter, nothing.

Isabel knew him well. She despised him even while she admired him. She looked at his sad face, his little short legs, and felt contempt of him. She looked at his dark grey eyes, with their uncanny, almost childlike, intuition, and she loved him. He understood amazingly—but she had no fear of his understanding. As a man she patronized him.

And she turned to the impassive, silent figure of her husband. He sat leaning back, with folded arms, and face a little uplifted. His knees were straight and massive. She sighed, picked up the poker, and again began to prod the fire, to rouse the clouds of soft brilliant sparks.

"Isabel tells me," Bertie began suddenly, "that you have not suffered unbearably from the loss of sight."

Maurice straightened himself to attend but kept his arms folded.

"No," he said, "not unbearably. Now and again one struggles against it, you know. But there are compensations."

"They say it is much worse to be stone deaf," said Isabel.

"I believe it is," said Bertie. "Are there compensations?" he added, to Maurice.

"Yes. You cease to bother about a great many things." Again Maurice stretched his figure, stretched the strong muscles of his back, and leaned backwards, with uplifted face.

"And that is a relief," said Bertie. "But what is there in place of the bothering? What replaces the activity?"

There was a pause. At length the blind man replied, as out of a negligent, unattentive thinking:

"Oh, I don't know. There's a good deal when you're not active."

"Is there?" said Bertie. "What, exactly? It always seems to me that when there is no thought and no action, there is nothing."

Again Maurice was slow in replying.

"There is something," he replied. "I couldn't tell you what it is."

And the talk lapsed once more, Isabel and Bertie chatting gossip and reminiscence, the blind man silent.

At length Maurice rose restlessly, a big obtrusive figure. He felt tight and hampered. He wanted to go away.

"Do you mind," he said, "if I go and speak to Wernham?"

"No—go along, dear," said Isabel.

And he went out. A silence came over the two friends. At length Bertie said:

"Nevertheless, it is a great deprivation, Cissie."

"It is, Bertie. I know it is."

"Something lacking all the time," said Bertie.

"Yes, I know. And yet—and yet—Maurice is right. There is something else, something *there*, which you never knew was there, and which you can't express."

"What is there?" asked Bertie.

"I don't know—it's awfully hard to define it—but something strong and immediate. There's something strange in Maurice's presence—indefinable —but I couldn't do without it. I agree that it seems to put one's mind to sleep. But when we're alone I miss nothing; it seems awfully rich, almost splendid, you know."

"I'm afraid I don't follow," said Bertie.

They talked desultorily. The wind blew loudly outside, rain chattered on the window-panes, making a sharp drum-sound because of the closed, mellow-golden shutters inside. The logs burned slowly, with hot, almost invisible small flames. Bertie seemed uneasy, there were dark circles round his eyes. Isabel, rich with her approaching maternity, leaned looking into the fire. Her hair curled in odd, loose strands, very pleasing to the man. But she had a curious feeling of old woe in her heart, old, timeless night-woe.

"I suppose we're all deficient somewhere," said Bertie.

"I suppose so," said Isabel wearily.

"Damned, sooner or later."

"I don't know," she said, rousing herself. "I feel quite all right, you know. The child coming seems to make me indifferent to everything, just placid. I can't feel that there's anything to trouble about, you know."

"A good thing, I should say," he replied slowly.

"Well, there it is. I suppose it's just Nature. If only I felt I needn't trouble about Maurice, I should be perfectly content——"

"But you feel you must trouble about him?"

"Well—I don't know——" She even resented this much effort.

The night passed slowly. Isabel looked at the clock. "I say," she said. "It's nearly ten o'clock. Where can Maurice be? I'm sure they're all in bed at the back. Excuse me a moment."

She went out, returning almost immediately.

"It's all shut up and in darkness," she said. "I wonder where he is. He must have gone out to the farm——"

Bertie looked at her.

"I suppose he'll come in," he said.

"I suppose so," she said. "But it's unusual for him to be out now."

"Would you like me to go out and see?"

"Well—if you wouldn't mind. I'd go, but——" She did not want to make the physical effort.

Bertie put on an old overcoat and took a lantern. He went out from the side door. He shrank from the wet and roaring night. Such weather had a nervous effect on him: too much moisture everywhere made him feel almost imbecile. Unwilling, he went through it all. A dog barked violently at him. He peered in all the buildings. At last, as he opened the upper door of a sort of intermediate barn, he heard a grinding noise, and looking in, holding up his lantern, saw Maurice in his shirt-sleeves, standing listening, holding the handle of a turnip-pulper. He had been pulping sweet roots, a pile of which lay dimly heaped in a corner behind him.

"That you, Wernham?" said Maurice, listening.

"No, it's me," said Bertie.

A large, half-wild grey cat was rubbing at Maurice's leg. The blind man stooped to rub its sides. Bertie watched the scene, then unconsciously entered and shut the door behind him. He was in a high sort of barn-place, from which, right and left, ran off the corridors in front of the stalled cattle. He watched the slow, stooping motion of the other man, as he caressed the great cat.

Maurice straightened himself.

"You came to look for me?" he said.

"Isabel was a little uneasy," said Bertie.

"I'll come in. I like messing about doing these jobs."

The cat had reared her sinister, feline length against his leg, clawing at his thigh affectionately. He lifted her claws out of his flesh.

"I hope I'm not in your way at all at the Grange here," said Bertie, rather shy and stiff.

"My way? No, not a bit. I'm glad Isabel has somebody to talk to. I'm afraid it's I who am in the way. I know I'm not very lively company. Isabel's all right, don't you think? She's not unhappy, is she?"

"I don't think so."

"What does she say?"

"She says she's very content—only a little troubled about you."

"Why me?"

"Perhaps afraid that you might brood," said Bertie, cautiously.

"She needn't be afraid of that." He continued to caress the flattened grey head of the cat with his fingers. "What I am a bit afraid of," he resumed, "is that she'll find me a dead weight, always alone with me down here."

"I don't think you need think that," said Bertie, though this was what he feared himself.

"I don't know," said Maurice. "Sometimes I feel it isn't fair that she's saddled with me." Then he dropped his voice curiously. "I say," he asked, secretly struggling, "is my face much disfigured? Do you mind telling me?"

"There is the scar," said Bertie, wondering. "Yes, it is a disfigurement. But more pitiable than shocking."

"A pretty bad scar, though," said Maurice.

"Oh, yes."

There was a pause.

"Sometimes I feel I am horrible," said Maurice, in a low voice, talking as if to himself. And Bertie actually felt a quiver of horror.

"That's nonsense," he said.

Maurice again straightened himself, leaving the cat.

"There's no telling," he said. Then again, in an odd tone, he added: "I don't really know you, do I?"

"Probably not," said Bertie.

"Do you mind if I touch you?"

The lawyer shrank away instinctively. And yet, out of very philanthropy, he said, in a small voice: "Not at all."

But he suffered as the blind man stretched out a strong, naked hand to him. Maurice accidentally knocked off Bertie's hat.

"I thought you were taller," he said, starting. Then he laid his hand on

Bertie Reid's head, closing the dome of the skull in a soft, firm grasp, gathering it, as it were; then, shifting his grasp and softly closing again, with a fine, close pressure, till he had covered the skull and the face of the smaller man, tracing the brows, and touching the full, closed eyes, touching the small nose and the nostrils, the rough, short moustache, the mouth, the rather strong chin. The hand of the blind man grasped the shoulder, the arm, the hand of the other man. He seemed to take him, in the soft, traveling grasp.

"You seem young," he said quietly, at last.

The lawyer stood almost annihilated, unable to answer.

"Your head seems tender, as if you were young," Maurice repeated. "So do your hands. Touch my eyes, will you?—touch my scar."

Now Bertie quivered with revulsion. Yet he was under the power of the blind man, as if hypnotized. He lifted his hand, and laid the fingers to the scar, on the scarred eyes. Maurice suddenly covered them with his own hand, pressed the fingers of the other man upon his disfigured eye-sockets, trembling in every fibre, and rocking slightly, slowly, from side to side. He remained thus for a minute or more, whilst Bertie stood as if in a swoon, unconscious, imprisoned.

Then suddenly Maurice removed the hand of the other man from his brow, and stood holding it in his own.

"Oh, my God," he said, "we shall know each other now, shan't we? We shall know each other now."

Bertie could not answer. He gazed mute and terror-struck, overcome by his own weakness. He knew he could not answer. He had an unreasonable fear, lest the other man should suddenly destroy him. Whereas Maurice was actually filled with hot, poignant love, the passion of friendship. Perhaps it was this very passion of friendship which Bertie shrank from most.

"We're all right together now, aren't we?" said Maurice. "It's all right now, as long as we live, so far as we're concerned?"

"Yes," said Bertie, trying by any means to escape.

Maurice stood with head lifted, as if listening. The new delicate fulfilment of mortal friendship had come as revelation and surprise to him, something exquisite and unhoped-for. He seemed to be listening to hear if it were real.

Then he turned for his coat.

"Come," he said, "we'll go to Isabel."

Bertie took the lantern and opened the door. The cat disappeared. The two men went in silence along the causeways. Isabel, as they came, thought their footsteps sounded strange. She looked up pathetically and anxiously for their entrance. There seemed a curious elation about Maurice. Bertie was haggard, with sunken eyes.

"What is it?" she asked.

"We've become friends," and Maurice, standing with his feet apart, like a strange colossus.

"Friends!" re-echoed Isabel. And she looked again at Bertie. He met her eyes with a furtive, haggard look; his eyes were as if glazed with misery.

"I'm so glad," she said, in sheer perplexity.

"Yes," said Maurice.

He was indeed so glad. Isabel took his hand with both hers, and held it fast.

"You'll be happier now, dear," she said.

But she was watching Bertie. She knew that he had one desire—to escape from this intimacy, this friendship, which had been thrust upon him. He could not bear it that he had been touched by the blind man, his insane reserve broken in. He was like a mollusc whose shell is broken.

Elizabeth Bowen (1899–   ) lives in Cork, Ireland. A prolific writer, she has published six collections of stories, nine novels, and three volumes of essays. Her best novels include The Death of the Heart (1939) and The Heat of the Day (1949). For further reading: Joining Charles (1929), Look at All Those Roses (1941), Stories by Elizabeth Bowen (1959).

Her Table Spread

ELIZABETH BOWEN

Alban had few opinions on the subject of marriage; his attitude to women was negative, but in particular he was not attracted to Miss Cuffe. Coming down early for dinner, red satin dress cut low, she attacked the silence with loud laughter before he had spoken. He recollected having heard that she was abnormal—at twenty-five, of statuesque development, still detained in childhood. The two other ladies, in beaded satins, made entrances of a surprising formality. It occurred to him, his presence must constitute an occasion: they certainly sparkled. Old Mr. Rossiter, uncle to Mrs. Treye, came last, more sourly. They sat for some time without the addition of lamplight. Dinner was not announced; the ladies, by remaining on guard, seemed to deprecate any question of its appearance. No sound came from other parts of the Castle.

Miss Cuffe was an heiress to whom the Castle belonged and whose guests they all were. But she carefully followed the movements of her aunt, Mrs. Treye; her ox-eyes moved from face to face in happy submission rather than expectancy. She was continually preoccupied with attempts at gravity, as though holding down her skirts in a high wind. Mrs. Treye and Miss Carbin combined to cover her excitement; still, their looks frequently stole from the company to the windows, of which there were too many. He received a strong impression someone outside was waiting to come in. At last, with a sigh, they got up: dinner had been announced.

The Castle was built on high ground, commanding the estuary; a steep hill, with trees, continued above it. On fine days the view was remarkable, of almost Italian brilliance, with that constant reflection up from the water that even now prolonged the too-long day. Now, in continuous evening rain, the winding wooded line of the further shore could be seen and, nearer the windows, a smothered island with the stump of a watch-tower. Where the Castle stood, a higher tower had answered the island's. Later a keep, then wings, had been added; now the fine peaceful residence had French windows opening on to the terrace. Invasions from the water would henceforth be social, perhaps amorous. On the slope down from the terrace, trees began again; almost, but not quite concealing the destroyer. Alban, who knew nothing, had not yet looked down.

It was Mr. Rossiter who first spoke of the destroyer—Alban meanwhile glancing along the table; the preparations had been stupendous. The destroyer had come to-day. The ladies all turned to Alban: the beads on their bosoms sparkled. So this was what they had here, under their trees. Engulfed by their pleasure, from now on he disappeared personally. Mr. Rossiter, rising a note, continued. The estuary, it appeared, was deep, with a channel buoyed up it. By a term of the Treaty, English ships were permitted to anchor in these waters.

"But they've been afraid of the rain!" chimed in Valeria Cuffe.

"Hush," said her aunt, "that's silly. Sailors would be accustomed to getting wet."

But, Miss Carbin reported, that spring there *had* already been one destroyer. Two of the officers had been seen dancing at the hotel at the head of the estuary.

"So," said Alban, "you are quite in the world." He adjusted his glasses in her direction.

Miss Carbin—blonde, not forty, and an attachment of Mrs. Treye's—shook her head despondently. "We were all away at Easter. Wasn't it curious they should have come then? The sailors walked in the demesne but never touched the daffodils."

"As though I should have cared!" exclaimed Valeria passionately.

"Morale too good," stated Mr. Rossiter.

"But next evening," continued Miss Carbin, "the officers did not go to the hotel. They climbed up here through the trees to the terrace—you see, they had no idea. Friends of ours were staying here at the Castle, and they apologised. Our friends invited them in to supper. . . ."

"Did they accept?"

The three ladies said in a breath: "Yes, they came."

Valeria added urgently, "So don't you *think*—?"

"So to-night we have a destroyer to greet you," Mrs. Treye said quickly to Alban. "It is quite an event; the country people are coming down from the mountains. These waters are very lonely; the steamers have given up since the bad times; there is hardly a pleasure-boat. The weather this year has driven visitors right away."

"You are beautifully remote."

"Yes," agreed Miss Carbin. "Do you know much about the Navy? Do you think, for instance, that this is likely to be the same destroyer?"

"Will they remember?" Valeria's bust was almost on the table. But with a rustle Mrs. Treye pressed Valeria's toe. For the dining-room also looked out across the estuary, and the great girl had not once taken her eyes from the window. Perhaps it was unfortunate that Mr. Alban should have coincided with the destroyer. Perhaps it was unfortunate for Mr. Alban too.

For he saw now he was less than half the feast; unappeased, the party sat looking through him, all grouped at an end of the table—to the other, chairs had been pulled up. Dinner was being served very slowly. Candles—possible to see from the water—were lit now; some wet peonies glistened. Outside, day still lingered hopefully. The bushes over the edge of the terrace were like heads—you could have sworn sometimes you saw them mounting, swaying in manly talk. Once, wound up in the rain, a bird whistled, seeming hardly a bird.

"Perhaps since then they have been to Greece, or Malta?"

"That would be the Mediterranean fleet," said Mr. Rossiter.

They were sorry to think of anything out in the rain to-night.

"The decks must be streaming," said Miss Carbin.

Then Valeria, exclaiming, "Please excuse me!" pushed her chair in and ran from the room.

"She is impulsive," explained Mrs. Treye. "Have *you* been to Malta, Mr. Alban?"

In the drawing-room, empty of Valeria, the standard lamps had been lit.

Through their ballet-skirt shades, rose and lemon, they gave out a deep, welcoming light. Alban, at the ladies' invitation, undraped the piano. He played, but they could see he was not pleased. It was obvious he had always been a civilian, and when he had taken his place on the piano-stool—which he twirled round three times, rather fussily—his dinner-jacket wrinkled across the shoulders. It was sad they should feel so indifferent, for he came from London. Mendelssohn was exasperating to them—they opened all four windows to let the music downhill. They preferred not to draw the curtains; the air, though damp, being pleasant to-night, they said.

The piano was damp, but Alban played almost all his heart out. He played out the indignation of years his mild manner concealed. He had failed to love; nobody did anything about this; partners at dinner gave him less than half their attention. He knew some spring had dried up at the root of the world. He was fixed in the dark rain, by an indifferent shore. He played badly, but they were unmusical. Old Mr. Rossiter, who was not what he seemed, went back to the dining-room to talk to the parlourmaid.

Valeria, glittering vastly, appeared in a window.

"Come *in!*" her aunt cried in indignation. She would die of a chill, childless, in fact unwedded; the Castle would have to be sold and where would they all be?

But—"Lights down there!" Valeria shouted above the music.

They had to run out for a moment, laughing and holding cushions over their bare shoulders. Alban left the piano: they looked boldly down from the terrace. Indeed, there they were: two lights like arc-lamps, blurred by rain and drawn down deep in reflection into the steady water. There were, too, ever so many portholes, all lit up.

"Perhaps they are playing bridge," said Miss Carbin.

"Now I wonder if Uncle Robert ought to have called," said Mrs. Treye. "Perhaps we have seemed remiss—one calls on a regiment."

"Patrick could row him out to-morrow."

"He hates the water." She sighed. "Perhaps they will be gone."

"Let's go for a row now—let's go for a row with a lantern," besought Valeria, jumping and pulling her aunt's elbow. They produced such indignation she disappeared again—wet satin skirts and all—into the bushes. The ladies could do no more: Alban suggested the rain might spot their dresses.

"They must lose a great deal, playing cards throughout an evening for high stakes," Miss Carbin said with concern as they all sat down again.

"Yes, if you come to think of it, somebody must win."

But the naval officers who so joyfully supped at Easter had been, Miss Carbin knew, a Mr. Graves and a Mr. Garrett: *they* would certainly lose. "At all events, it is better than dancing at the hotel; there would be nobody of their type."

"There is nobody there at all."

"I expect they are best where they are. . . . Mr. Alban, a Viennese waltz?"

He played while the ladies whispered, waving the waltz time a little distractedly. Mr. Rossiter, coming back, momentously stood: they turned in hope: even the waltz halted. But he brought no news. "You should call Valeria in. You can't tell who may be round the place. She's not fit to be out to-night."

"Perhaps she's not out."

"She is," said Mr. Rossiter crossly. "I just saw her racing past the window with a lantern."

Valeria's mind was made up: she was a princess. Not for nothing had she had the dining-room silver polished and all set out. She would pace around in red satin that swished behind, while Mr. Alban kept on playing a loud waltz. They would be dazed at all she had to offer—also her two new statues and the leopard-skin from the auction.

When he and she were married (she inclined a little to Mr. Garrett) they would invite all the Navy up the estuary and give them tea. Her estuary would be filled up, like a regatta, with loud excited battleships tooting to one another and flags flying. The terrace would be covered with grateful sailors, leaving room for the band. She would keep the peacocks her aunt did not allow. His friends would be surprised to notice that Mr. Garrett had meanwhile become an admiral, all gold. He would lead the other admirals into the castle and say, while they wiped their feet respectfully: "These are my wife's statues; she has given them to me. One is Mars, one is Mercury. We have a Venus, but she is not dressed. And wait till I show you our silver and gold plates . . ." The Navy would be unable to tear itself away.

She had been excited for some weeks at the idea of marrying Mr. Alban, but now the lovely appearance of the destroyer put him out of her mind. He would not have done; he was not handsome. But she could keep him to play the piano on quiet afternoons.

Her friends had told her Mr. Garrett was quite a Viking. She was so very familiar with his appearance that she felt sometimes they had already been married for years—though still, sometimes, he could not realise his good luck. She still had to remind him the island was hers too. . . . To-night, Aunt and darling Miss Carbin had so fallen in with her plans, putting on their satins and decorating the drawing-room, that the dinner became a betrothal feast. There was some little hitch about the arrival of Mr. Garrett—she had heard that gentlemen sometimes could not tie their ties. And now he was late and would be discouraged. So she must now go half-way down to the water and wave a lantern.

But she put her two hands over the lantern, then smothered it in her dress. She had a panic. Supposing she should prefer Mr. Graves?

She had heard Mr. Graves was stocky, but very merry; when he came to supper at Easter he slid in the gallery. He would teach her to dance, and

take her to Naples and Paris. . . . Oh, dear, oh, dear, then they must fight
for her; that was all there was to it. . . . She let the lantern out of her skirts
and waved. Her fine arm with bangles went up and down, up and down,
with the staggering light; the trees one by one jumped up from the dark,
like savages.

Inconceivably the destroyer took no notice.

Undisturbed by oars, the rain stood up from the waters; not a light rose
to peer, and the gramophone, though it remained very faint, did not cease
or alter.

In mackintoshes, Mr. Rossiter and Alban meanwhile made their way to
the boat-house, Alban did not know why. "If that goes on," said Mr. Rossiter, nodding towards Valeria's lantern, "they'll fire one of their guns at us."

"Oh, no. Why?" said Alban. He buttoned up, however, the collar of his
mackintosh.

"Nervous as cats. It's high time that girl was married. She's a nice girl in
many ways, too."

"Couldn't we get the lantern away from her?" They stepped on a paved
causeway and heard the water nibble the rocks.

"She'd scream the place down. She's of age now, you see."

"But if—"

"Oh, she won't do that; I was having a bit of fun with you." Chuckling
equably, Mrs. Treye's uncle unlocked and pulled open the boat-house door.
A bat whistled out.

"Why are we here?"

"She might come for the boat; she's a fine oar," said Mr. Rossiter wisely.
The place was familiar to him; he lit an oil-lamp and, sitting down on a
trestle with a staunch air of having done what he could, reached a bottle of
whisky out of the boat. He motioned the bottle to Alban. "It's a wild night,"
he said. "Ah, well, we don't have these destroyers every day."

"That seems fortunate."

"Well, it is and it isn't." Restoring the bottle to the vertical, Mr. Rossiter
continued: "It's a pity you don't want a wife. You'd be the better for a wife,
d'you see, a young fellow like you. She's got a nice character; she's a girl
you could shape. She's got a nice income." The bat returned from the rain
and knocked round the lamp. Lowering the bottle frequently, Mr. Rossiter
talked to Alban (whose attitude remained negative) of women in general
and the parlourmaid in particular. . . .

"*Bat!*" Alban squealed irrepressibly, and with his hand to his ear—where
he still felt it—fled from the boat-house. Mr. Rossiter's conversation continued. Alban's pumps squelched as he ran; he skidded along the causeway
and baulked at the upward steps. His soul squelched equally: he had been
warned; he had been warned. He had heard they were all mad; he had erred
out of headiness and curiosity. A degree of terror was agreeable to his van-

ity: by express wish he had occupied haunted rooms. Now he had no other pumps in this country, no idea where to buy them, and a ducal visit ahead. Also, wandering as it were among the apples and amphoras of an art school, he had blundered into the life room: woman revolved gravely.

"Hell," he said to the steps, mounting, his mind blank to the outcome.

He was nerved for the jumping lantern, but half-way up to the Castle darkness was once more absolute. Her lantern had gone out; he could orientate himself—in spite of himself—by her sobbing. Absolute desperation. He pulled up so short that, for balance, he had to cling to a creaking tree.

"Hi!" she croaked. Then: "You *are* there! I hear you!"

"Miss Cuffe—"

"How too bad you are! I never heard you rowing. I thought you were never coming—"

"Quietly, my dear girl."

"Come up quickly. I haven't even seen you. Come up to the windows—"

"Miss Cuffe—"

"Don't you remember the way?" As sure but not so noiseless as a cat in the dark, Valeria hurried to him.

"Mr. Garrett—" she panted. "I'm Miss Cuffe. Where have you been? I've destroyed my beautiful red dress and they've eaten up your dinner. But we're still waiting. Don't be afraid; you'll soon be there now. I'm Miss Cuffe; this is my Castle—"

"Listen, it's I, Mr. Alban—"

"Ssh, ssh, Mr. Alban: *Mr. Garrett has landed.*"

Her cry, his voice, some breath of the joyful intelligence, brought the others on to the terrace, blind with lamplight.

"Valeria?"

"Mr. Garrett has landed!"

Mrs. Treye said to Miss Carbin under her breath, "Mr. Garrett has come."

Miss Carbin, half weeping with agitation, replied, "We must go in." But uncertain who was to speak next, or how to speak, they remained leaning over the darkness. Behind, through the windows, lamps spread great skirts of light, and Mars and Mercury, unable to contain themselves, stooped from their pedestals. The dumb keyboard shone like a ballroom floor.

Alban, looking up, saw their arms and shoulders under the bright rain. Close by, Valeria's fingers creaked on her warm wet satin. She laughed like a princess, magnificently justified. Their unseen faces were all three lovely, and, in the silence after the laughter, such a strong tenderness reached him that, standing there in full manhood, he was for a moment not exiled. For the moment, without moving or speaking, he stood in the dark, in a flame, as though all three said: "My darling. . . ."

Perhaps it was best for them all that early, when next day first lightened the rain, the destroyer steamed out—below the extinguished Castle where Valeria lay with her arms wide, past the boat-house, where Mr. Rossiter lay insensible and the bat hung masked in its wings—down the estuary into the open sea.

Sean O'Faolain (1900–   ), one of the best-known interpreters of modern Irish life, lives in Killiney in County Dublin. His first novel, A Nest of Simple Folk (1933), is considered his best. Rich in poetic suggestion and evocative detail, the stories are collected in Midsummer Night Madness and Other Stories (1932), A Purse of Coppers (1937), Teresa and Other Stories (1947), and The Man Who Invented Sin (1948).

The Trout

SEAN O'FAOLAIN

One of the first places Julia always ran to when they arrived in G—— was The Dark Walk. It is a laurel walk, very old; almost gone wild, a lofty midnight tunnel of smooth, sinewy branches. Underfoot the tough brown leaves are never dry enough to crackle: there is always a suggestion of damp and cool trickle.

She raced right into it. For the first few yards she always had the memory of the sun behind her, then she felt the dusk closing swiftly down on her so that she screamed with pleasure and raced on to reach the light at the far end; and it was always just a little too long in coming so that she emerged gasping, clasping her hands, laughing, drinking in the sun. When she was filled with the heat and glare she would turn and consider the ordeal again.

This year she had the extra joy of showing it to her small brother, and of terrifying him as well as herself. And for him the fear lasted longer because his legs were so short and she had gone out at the far end while he was still screaming and racing.

When they had done this many times they came back to the house to tell everybody that they had done it. He boasted. She mocked. They squabbled.

"Cry babby!"

"You were afraid yourself, so there!"

"I won't take you any more."

"You're a big pig."

"I hate you."

Tears were threatening so somebody said, "Did you see the well?" She opened her eyes at that and held up her long lovely neck suspiciously and decided to be incredulous. She was twelve and at that age little girls are beginning to suspect most stories: they have already found out too many, from Santa Claus to the Stork. How could there be a well! In The Dark Walk? That she had visited year after year? Haughtily she said, "Nonsense."

But she went back, pretending to be going somewhere else, and she found a hole scooped in the rock at the side of the walk, choked with damp leaves, so shrouded by ferns that she only uncovered it after much searching. At the back of this little cavern there was about a quart of water. In the water she suddenly perceived a panting trout. She rushed for Stephen and dragged him to see, and they were both so excited that they were no longer afraid of the darkness as they hunched down and peered in at the fish panting in his tiny prison, his silver stomach going up and down like an engine.

Nobody knew how the trout got there. Even old Martin in the kitchen-garden laughed and refused to believe that it was there, or pretended not to believe, until she forced him to come down and see. Kneeling and pushing back his tattered old cap he peered in.

"Be cripes, you're right. How the divil in hell did that fella get there?"

She stared at him suspiciously.

"You knew?" she accused; but he said, "The divil a know"; and reached down to lift it out. Convinced she hauled him back. If she had found it then it was her trout.

Her mother suggested that a bird had carried the spawn. Her father thought that in the winter a small streamlet might have carried it down there as a baby, and it had been safe until the summer came and the water began to dry up. She said, "I see," and went back to look again and consider the matter in private. Her brother remained behind, wanting to hear the whole story of the trout, not really interested in the actual trout but much interested in the story which his mummy began to make up for him on the lines of, "So one day Daddy Trout and Mammy Trout. . . ." When he retailed it to her she said, "Pooh."

It troubled her that the trout was always in the same position; he had no room to turn; all the time the silver belly went up and down; otherwise he was motionless. She wondered what he ate and in between visits to Joey Pony, and the boat and a bathe to get cool, she thought of his hunger. She brought him down bits of dough; once she brought him a worm. He ignored the food. He just went on panting. Hunched over him she thought how, all the winter, while she was at school he had been in there. All the winter, in The Dark Walk, all day, all night, floating around alone. She drew the leaf of her hat down around her ears and chin and stared. She was still thinking of it as she lay in bed.

It was late June, the longest days of the year. The sun had sat still for a week, burning up the world. Although it was after ten o'clock it was still bright and still hot. She lay on her back under a single sheet, with her long legs spread, trying to keep cool. She could see the D of the moon through the fir-tree—they slept on the ground floor. Before they went to bed her mummy had told Stephen the story of the trout again, and she, in her bed, had resolutely presented her back to them and read her book. But she kept one ear cocked.

"And so, in the end, this naughty fish who would not stay at home got bigger and bigger and bigger, and the water got smaller and smaller. . . ."

Passionately she had whirled and cried, "Mummy, don't make it a horrible old moral story!" Her mummy had brought in a Fairy Godmother, then, who sent lots of rain, and filled the well, and a stream poured out and the trout floated away down to the river below. Staring at the moon she knew that there are no such things as Fairy Godmothers and that the trout, down in The Dark Walk, was panting like an engine. She heard somebody unwind a fishing-reel. Would the *beasts* fish him out!

She sat up. Stephen was a hot lump of sleep, lazy thing. The Dark Walk would be full of little scraps of moon. She leaped up and looked out the window, and somehow it was not so lightsome now that she saw the dim mountains far away and the black firs against the breathing land and heard a dog say, bark-bark. Quietly she lifted the ewer of water, and climbed out the window and scuttled along the cool but cruel gravel down to the maw of the tunnel. Her pyjamas were very short so that when she splashed water it wet her ankles. She peered into the tunnel. Something alive rustled inside there. She raced in, and up and down she raced, and flurried, and cried aloud, "Oh, Gosh, I can't find it," and then at last she did. Kneeling down in the damp she put her hand into the slimy hole. When the body lashed they were both mad with fright. But she gripped him and shoved him into the ewer and raced, with her teeth ground, out to the other end of the tunnel and down the steep paths to the river's edge.

All the time she could feel him lashing his tail against the side of the ewer. She was afraid he would jump right out. The gravel cut into her soles until she came to the cool ooze of the river's bank where the moon-mice on the water crept into her feet. She poured out watching until he plopped. For a second he was visible in the water. She hoped he was not dizzy. Then all she saw was the glimmer of the moon in the silent-flow-ing river, the dark firs, the dim mountains, and the radiant pointed face laughing down at her out of the empty sky.

She scuttled up the hill, in the window, plonked down the ewer and flew through the air like a bird into bed. The dog said bark-bark. She heard the fishing-reel whirring. She hugged herself and giggled. Like a river of joy her holiday spread before her.

In the morning Stephen rushed to her, shouting that "he" was gone, and asking "where" and "how." Lifting her nose in the air she said super-ciliously, "Fairy Godmother, I suppose?" and strolled away patting the palms of her hands.

Graham Greene (1904–   ) worked for the London Times after graduating from Oxford University. A poet, novelist, and essayist, he is known for his preoccupation with Roman Catholic problems. His early novels were "thrillers," or "entertainments" as he called them. Many of his later novels were hailed as artistic successes, for example, The Power and the Glory (1940). For further reading: Nineteen Stories (1949).

Brother

GRAHAM GREENE

The Communists were the first to appear. They walked quickly, a group of about a dozen, up the boulevard which runs from Combat to Ménilmon-tant; a young man and a girl lagged a little way behind because the man's leg was hurt and the girl was helping him along. They looked impatient, harassed, hopeless, as if they were trying to catch a train which they knew already in their hearts they were too late to catch.

The proprietor of the café saw them coming when they were still a long way off; the lamps at that time were still alight (it was later that the bullets broke the bulbs and dropped darkness all over that quarter of Paris), and the group showed up plainly in the wide barren boulevard. Since sunset only one customer had entered the café, and very soon after sunset firing could be heard from the direction of Combat; the Métro station had closed hours ago. And yet something obstinate and undefeatable in the proprietor's character prevented him from putting up the shutters; it might have been avarice; he could not himself have told what it was as he pressed his broad yellow forehead against the glass and stared this way and that, up the boulevard and down the boulevard.

But when he saw the group and their air of hurry he began immediately to close his café. First he went and warned his only customer, who was practising billiard shots, walking round and round the table, frowning and stroking a thin moustache between shots, a little green in the face under the low diffused lights.

"The Reds are coming," the proprietor said, "you'd better be off. I'm putting up the shutters."

"Don't interrupt. They won't harm me," the customer said. "This is a tricky shot. Red's in baulk. Off the cushion. Screw on spot." He shot his ball straight into a pocket.

"I knew you couldn't do anything with that," the proprietor said, nodding his bald head. "You might just as well go home. Give me a hand with the shutters first. I've sent my wife away." The customer turned on him maliciously, rattling the cue between his fingers. "It was your talking that spoilt the shot. You've cause to be frightened, I dare say. But I'm a poor man. I'm safe. I'm not going to stir." He went across to his coat and took out a dry cigar. "Bring me a bock." He walked round the table on his toes and the balls clicked and the proprietor padded back into the bar, elderly and irritated. He did not fetch the beer but began to close the shutters; every move he made was slow and clumsy. Long before he had finished the group of Communists was outside.

He stopped what he was doing and watched them with furtive dislike. He was afraid that the rattle of the shutters would attract their attention. If I am very quiet and still, he thought, they may go on, and he remembered with malicious pleasure the police barricade across the Place de la République. That will finish them. In the meanwhile I must be very quiet, very still, and he felt a kind of warm satisfaction at the idea that worldly wisdom dictated the very attitude most suited to his nature. So he stared through the edge of a shutter, yellow, plump, cautious, hearing the billiard balls crackle in the other room, seeing the young man come limping up the pavement on the girl's arm, watching them stand and stare with dubious faces up the boulevard towards Combat.

But when they came into the café he was already behind the bar, smiling and bowing and missing nothing, noticing how they had divided forces, how six of them had begun to run back the way they had come.

The young man sat down in a dark corner above the cellar stairs and the others stood round the door waiting for something to happen. It gave the proprietor an odd feeling that they should stand there in his café not asking for a drink, knowing what to expect, when he, the owner, knew nothing, understood nothing. At last the girl said "Cognac," leaving the others and coming to the bar, but when he had poured it out for her, very careful to give a fair and not a generous measure, she simply took it to the man sitting in the dark and held it to his mouth.

"Three francs," the proprietor said. She took the glass and sipped a little and turned it so that the man's lips might touch the same spot. Then she knelt down and rested her forehead against the man's forehead and so they stayed.

"Three francs," the proprietor said, but he could not make his voice bold. The man was no longer visible in his corner, only the girl's back, thin and shabby in a black cotton frock, as she knelt, leaning forward to find the man's face. The proprietor was daunted by the four men at the door, by the knowledge that they were Reds who had no respect for private property, who would drink his wine and go away without paying, who would rape his women (but there was only his wife, and she was not there), who would rob his bank, who would murder him as soon as look at him. So with fear in his heart he gave up the three francs as lost rather than attract any more attention.

Then the worst that he contemplated happened.

One of the men at the door came up to the bar and told him to pour out four glasses of cognac. "Yes, yes," the proprietor said, fumbling with the cork, praying secretly to the Virgin to send an angel, to send the police, to send the Gardes Mobiles, now, immediately, before the cork came out, "that will be twelve francs."

"Oh, no," the man said, "we are all comrades here. Share and share alike. Listen," he said, with earnest mockery, leaning across the bar, "all we have is yours just as much as it's ours, comrade," and stepping back a pace he presented himself to the proprietor, so that he might take his choice of stringy tie, of threadbare trousers, of starved features. "And it follows from that, comrade, that all you have is ours. So four cognacs. Share and share alike."

"Of course," the proprietor said, "I was only joking." Then he stood with bottle poised, and the four glasses tingled upon the counter. "A machine-gun," he said, "up by Combat," and smiled to see how for the moment the men forgot their brandy as they fidgeted near the door. Very soon now, he thought, and I shall be quit of them.

"A machine-gun," the Red said incredulously, "they're using machine-guns?"

"Well," the proprietor said, encouraged by this sign that the Gardes Mobiles were not very far away, "you can't pretend that you aren't armed yourselves." He leant across the bar in a way that was almost paternal. "After all, you know, your ideas—they wouldn't do in France. Free love."

"Who's talking of free love?" the Red said.

The proprietor shrugged and smiled and nodded at the corner. The girl knelt with her head on the man's shoulder, her back to the room. They were quite silent and the glass of brandy stood on the floor beside them. The girl's beret was pushed back on her head and one stocking was laddered and darned from knee to ankle.

"What, those two? They aren't lovers."

"I," the proprietor said, "with my bourgeois notions would have thought. . . ."

"He's her brother," the Red said.

The men came clustering round the bar and laughed at him, but softly as if a sleeper or a sick person were in the house. All the time they were listening for something. Between their shoulders the proprietor could look out across the boulevard; he could see the corner of the Faubourg du Temple.

"What are you waiting for?"

"For friends," the Red said. He made a gesture with open palm as if to say, You see, we share and share alike. We have no secrets.

Something moved at the corner of the Faubourg du Temple.

"Four more cognacs," the Red said.

"What about those two?" the proprietor asked.

"Leave them alone. They'll look after themselves. They're tired."

How tired they were. No walk up the boulevard from Ménilmontant could explain the tiredness. They seemed to have come farther and fared a great deal worse than their companions. They were more starved; they were infinitely more hopeless, sitting in their dark corner away from the friendly gossip, the amicable desperate voices which now confused the proprietor's brain, until for a moment he believed himself to be a host entertaining friends.

He laughed and made a broad joke directed at the two of them; but they made no sign of understanding. Perhaps they were to be pitied, cut off from the camaraderie round the counter; perhaps they were to be envied for their deeper comradeship. The proprietor thought for no reason at all of the bare grey trees of the Tuileries like a series of exclamation marks drawn against the winter sky. Puzzled, disintegrated, with all his bearings, lost, he stared out through the door towards the Faubourg.

It was as if they had not seen each other for a long while and would soon again be saying good-bye. Hardly aware of what he was doing he filled the four glasses with brandy. They stretched out worn blunted fingers for them.

"Wait," he said. "I've got something better than this"; then paused, conscious of what was happening across the boulevard. The lamplight splashed down on blue steel helmets; the Gardes Mobiles were lining out across the entrance to the Faubourg, and a machine-gun pointed directly at the café windows.

So, the proprietor thought, my prayers are answered. Now I must do my part not look, not warn them, save myself. Have they covered the side door? I will get the other bottle. Real Napoleon brandy. Share and share alike.

He felt a curious lack of triumph as he opened the trap of the bar and came out. He tried not to walk quickly back towards the billiard room. Nothing that he did must warn these men; he tried to spur himself with the thought that every slow casual step he took was a blow for France, for his café, for his savings. He had to step over the girl's feet to pass her; she was asleep. He noted the sharp shoulder blades thrusting through the cotton, and raised his eyes and met her brother's, filled with pain and despair.

He stopped. He found he could not pass without a word. It was as if he needed to explain something, as if he belonged to the wrong party. With false bonhomie he waved the corkscrew he carried in the other's face. "Another cognac, eh?"

"It's no good talking to them," the Red said. "They're German. They don't understand a word."

"German?"

"That's what's wrong with his leg. A concentration camp."

The proprietor told himself that he must be quick, that he must put a door between him and them, that the end was very close, but he was bewildered by the hopelessness in the man's gaze. "What's he doing here?" Nobody answered him. It was as if his question were too foolish to need a reply. With his head sunk upon his breast the proprietor went past, and the girl slept on. He was like a stranger leaving a room where all the rest are friends. A German. They don't understand a word; and up, up through the heavy darkness of his mind, through the avarice and the dubious triumph, a few German words remembered from very old days climbed like spies into the light: a line from the *Lorelei* learnt at school, *Kamerad* with its war-time suggestion of fear and surrender, and oddly from nowhere the phrase *mein Bruder*. He opened the door of the billiard room and closed it behind him and softly turned the key.

"Spot in baulk," the customer explained and leant across the great green table, but while he took aim, wrinkling his narrow peevish eyes, the firing started. It came in two bursts with a rip of glass between. The girl cried out something, but it was not one of the words he knew. Then feet ran across the floor, the trap of the bar slammed. The proprietor sat back against the table and listened and listened for any further sound; but silence came in under the door and silence through the keyhole.

"The cloth. My God, the cloth," the customer said, and the proprietor looked down at his own hand which was working the corkscrew into the table.

"Will this absurdity never end?" the customer said. "I shall go home."

"Wait," the proprietor said. "Wait." He was listening to voices and footsteps in the other room. These were voices he did not recognize. Then a car drove up and presently drove away again. Somebody rattled the handle of the door.

"Who is it?" the proprietor called.

"Who are you? Open that door."

"Ah," the customer said with relief, "the police. Where was I now? Spot in baulk." He began to chalk his cue. The proprietor opened the door. Yes, the Gardes Mobiles had arrived; he was safe again, though his windows were smashed. The Reds had vanished as if they had never been. He looked at the raised trap, at the smashed electric bulbs, at the broken bottle which dripped behind the bar. The café was full of men, and he remembered with odd relief that he had not had time to lock the side door.

"Are you the owner?" the officer asked. "A bock for each of these men and a cognac for myself. Be quick about it."

The proprietor calculated: "Nine francs fifty," and watched closely with bent head the coins rattle down upon the counter.

"You see," the officer said with significance, "we pay." He nodded towards the side door. "Those others: did they pay?"

No, the proprietor admitted, they had not paid, but as he counted the coins and slipped them into the till, he caught himself silently repeating the officer's order—"A bock for each of these men." Those others, he thought, one's got to say that for them, they weren't mean about the drink. It was four cognacs with them. But, of course, they did not pay. "And my windows," he complained aloud with sudden asperity, "what about my windows?"

"Never you mind," the officer said, "the government will pay. You have only to send in your bill. Hurry up now with my cognac. I have no time for gossip."

"You can see for yourself" the proprietor said, "how the bottles have been broken. Who will pay for that?"

"Everything will be paid for," the officer said.

"And now I must go to the cellar to fetch more."

He was angry at the reiteration of the word pay. They enter my café, he thought, they smash my windows, they order me about and think that all is well if they pay, pay, pay. It occurred to him that these men were intruders.

"Step to it," the officer said and turned and rebuked one of the men who had leant his rifle against the bar.

At the top of the cellar stairs the proprietor stopped. They were in darkness, but by the light from the bar he could just make out a body half-way down. He began to tremble violently, and it was some seconds before he could strike a match. The young German lay head downwards, and the blood from his head had dropped on to the step below. His eyes were open and stared back at the proprietor with the old despairing expression of life. The proprietor would not believe that he was dead. "Kamerad," he said bending down, while the match singed his fingers and went out, trying to recall some phrase in German, but he could only remember, as he bent lower still, "mein Bruder." Then suddenly he turned and ran up the steps, waved the match-box in the officer's face, and called out in a low hysterical voice to him and his men and to the customer stooping under the low green shade, "Cochons. Cochons."

"What was that? What was that?" the officer exclaimed. "Did you say that he was your brother? It's impossible," and he frowned incredulously at the proprietor and rattled the coins in his pocket.

Frank O'Connor (Michael Donovan) (1903–1966)
was educated at Cork and was a member of
the Irish Academy of Letters. He was the author of
about twenty-five volumes, largely short stories.
By profession he was once a librarian. For further
reading: The Stories of Frank O'Connor (1952),
More Stories of Frank O'Connor (1954).

Christmas Morning

FRANK O'CONNOR

I never really liked my brother, Sonny. From the time he was a baby he
was always the mother's pet and always chasing her to tell her what mischief I was up to. Mind you, I was usually up to something. Until I was
nine or ten I was never much good at school, and I really believe it was to
spite me that he was so smart at his books. He seemed to know by instinct
that this was what Mother had set her heart on, and you might almost say
he spelt himself into her favour.

"Mummy," he'd say, "will I call Larry in to his t-e-a?" or: "Mummy, the
k-e-t-e-l is boiling," and, of course, when he was wrong she'd correct him,
and next time he'd have it right and there would be no standing him.
"Mummy," he'd say, "aren't I a good speller?" Cripes, we could all be good
spellers if we went on like that!

Mind you, it wasn't that I was stupid. Far from it. I was just restless
and not able to fix my mind for long on any one thing. I'd do the lessons
for the year before, or the lessons for the year after: what I couldn't stand
were the lessons we were supposed to be doing at the time. In the evenings
I used to go out and play with the Doherty gang. Not, again, that I was
rough, but I liked the excitement, and for the life of me I couldn't see what
attracted Mother about education.

"Can't you do your lessons first and play after?" she'd say, getting white
with indignation. "You ought to be ashamed of yourself that your baby
brother can read better than you."

She didn't seem to understand that I wasn't, because there didn't seem
to me to be anything particularly praiseworthy about reading, and it struck
me as an occupation better suited to a sissy kid like Sonny.

"The dear knows what will become of you," she'd say. "If only you'd stick to your books you might be something good like a clerk or an engineer."

"I'll be a clerk, Mummy," Sonny would say smugly.

"Who wants to be an old clerk?" I'd say, just to annoy him. "I'm going to be a soldier."

"The dear knows, I'm afraid that's all you'll ever be fit for," she would add with a sigh.

I couldn't help feeling at times that she wasn't all there. As if there was anything better a fellow could be!

Coming on to Christmas, with the days getting shorter and the shopping crowds bigger, I began to think of all the things I might get from Santa Claus. The Dohertys said there was no Santa Claus, only what your father and mother gave you, but the Dohertys were a rough class of children you wouldn't expect Santa to come to anyway. I was rooting round for whatever information I could pick up about him, but there didn't seem to be much. I was no hand with a pen, but if a letter would do any good I was ready to chance writing to him. I had plenty of initiative and was always writing off for free samples and prospectuses.

"Ah, I don't know will he come at all this year," Mother said with a worried air. "He has enough to do looking after steady boys who mind their lessons without bothering about the rest."

"He only comes to good spellers, Mummy," said Sonny. "Isn't that right?"

"He comes to any little boy who does his best, whether he's a good speller or not," Mother said firmly.

Well, I did my best. God knows I did! It wasn't my fault if, four days before the holidays, Flogger Dawley gave us sums we couldn't do, and Peter Doherty and myself had to go on the lang. It wasn't for love of it, for, take it from me, December is no month for mitching, and we spent most of our time sheltering from the rain in a store on the quays. The only mistake we made was imagining we could keep it up till the holidays without being spotted. That showed real lack of foresight.

Of course, Flogger Dawley noticed and sent home word to know what was keeping me. When I came in on the third day the mother gave me a look I'll never forget, and said: "Your dinner is there." She was too full to talk. When I tried to explain to her about Flogger Dawley and the sums she brushed it aside and said: "You have no word." I saw then it wasn't the langing she minded but the lies, though I still didn't see how you could lang without lying. She didn't speak to me for days. And even then I couldn't make out what she saw in education, or why she wouldn't let me grow up naturally like anyone else.

To make things worse, it stuffed Sonny up more than ever. He had the air of one saying: "I don't know what they'd do without me in this blooming house." He stood at the front door, leaning against the jamb with his hands in his trouser pockets, trying to make himself look like Father, and shouted to the other kids so that he could be heard all over the road.

"Larry isn't left go out. He went on the lang with Peter Doherty and me mother isn't talking to him."

And at night, when we were in bed, he kept it up.

"Santa Claus won't bring you anything this year, aha!"

"Of course he will," I said.

"How do you know?"

"Why wouldn't he?"

"Because you went on the lang with Doherty. I wouldn't play with them Doherty fellows."

"You wouldn't be left."

"I wouldn't play with them. They're no class. They had the bobbies up to the house."

"And how would Santa know I was on the lang with Peter Doherty?" I growled, losing patience with the little prig.

"Of course he'd know. Mummy would tell him."

"And how could Mummy tell him and he up at the North Pole? Poor Ireland, she's rearing them yet! 'Tis easy seen you're only an old baby."

"I'm not a baby, and I can spell better than you, and Santa won't bring you anything."

"We'll see whether he will or not," I said sarcastically, doing the old man on him.

But, to tell the God's truth, the old man was only bluff. You could never tell what powers these superhuman chaps would have of knowing what you were up to. And I had a bad conscience about the langing because I'd never before seen the mother like that.

That was the night I decided that the only sensible thing to do was to see Santa myself and explain to him. Being a man, he'd probably understand. In those days I was a good-looking kid and had a way with me when I liked. I had only to smile nicely at one old gent on the North Mall to get a penny from him, and I felt if only I could get Santa by himself I could do the same with him and maybe get something worth while from him. I wanted a model railway: I was sick of Ludo and Snakes-and-Ladders.

I started to practise lying awake, counting five hundred and then a thousand, and trying to hear first eleven, then midnight, from Shandon. I felt sure Santa would be round by midnight, seeing that he'd be coming from the north, and would have the whole of the South Side to do afterwards. In some ways I was very farsighted. The only trouble was the things I was farsighted about.

I was so wrapped up in my own calculations that I had little attention to spare for Mother's difficulties. Sonny and I used to go to town with her, and while she was shopping we stood outside a toyshop in the North Main Street, arguing about what we'd like for Christmas.

On Christmas Eve when Father came home from work and gave her the housekeeping money, she stood looking at it doubtfully while her face grew white.

"Well?" he snapped, getting angry. "What's wrong with that?"

"What's wrong with it?" she muttered. "On Christmas Eve!"

"Well," he asked truculently, sticking his hands in his trouser pockets as though to guard what was left, "do you think I get more because it's Christmas?"

"Lord God," she muttered distractedly. "And not a bit of cake in the house, nor a candle, nor anything!"

"All right," he shouted, beginning to stamp. "How much will the candle be?"

"Ah, for pity's sake," she cried, "will you give me the money and not argue like that before the children? Do you think I'll leave them with nothing on the one day of the year?"

"Bad luck to you and your children!" he snarled. "Am I to be slaving from one year's end to another for you to be throwing it away on toys? Here," he added, tossing two half-crowns on the table, "that's all you're going to get, so make the most of it."

"I suppose the publicans will get the rest," she said bitterly.

Later she went into town, but did not bring us with her, and returned with a lot of parcels, including the Christmas candle. We waited for Father to come home to his tea, but he didn't, so we had our own tea and a slice of Christmas cake each, and then Mother put Sonny on a chair with the holy-water stoup to sprinkle the candle, and when he lit it she said: "The light of heaven to our souls." I could see she was upset because Father wasn't in—it should be the oldest and youngest. When we hung up our stockings at bedtime he was still out.

Then began the hardest couple of hours I ever put in. I was mad with sleep but afraid of losing the model railway, so I lay for a while, making up things to say to Santa when he came. They varied in tone from frivolous to grave, for some old gents like kids to be modest and well-spoken, while others prefer them with spirit. When I had rehearsed them all I tried to wake Sonny to keep me company, but that kid slept like the dead.

Eleven struck from Shandon, and soon after I heard the latch, but it was only Father coming home.

"Hello, little girl," he said, letting on to be surprised at finding Mother waiting up for him, and then broke into a self-conscious giggle. "What have you up so late?"

"Do you want your supper?" she asked shortly.

"Ah, no, no," he replied. "I had a bit of pig's cheek at Daneen's on my way up (Daneen was my uncle). I'm very fond of a bit of pig's cheek. . . . My goodness, is it that late?" he exclaimed, letting on to be astonished. "If I knew that I'd have gone to the North Chapel for midnight Mass. I'd like to hear the *Adeste* again. That's a hymn I'm very fond of—a most touching hymn."

Then he began to hum it falsetto.

> *Adeste fideles*
> *Solus domus dagus.*

Father was very fond of Latin hymns, particularly when he had a drop in, but as he had no notion of the words he made them up as he went along, and this always drove Mother mad.

"Ah, you disgust me!" she said in a scalded voice, and closed the room door behind her. Father laughed as if he thought it a great joke; and he struck a match to light his pipe and for a while puffed at it noisily. The light under the door dimmed and went out but he continued to sing emotionally.

> *Dixie medearo*
> *Tutum tonum tantum*
> *Venite adoremus.*

He had it all wrong but the effect was the same on me. To save my life I couldn't keep awake.

Coming on to dawn, I woke with the feeling that something dreadful had happened. The whole house was quiet, and the little bedroom that looked out on the foot and a half of back yard was pitch-dark. It was only when I glanced at the window that I saw how all the silver had drained out of the sky. I jumped out of bed to feel my stocking, well knowing that the worst had happened. Santa had come while I was asleep, and gone away with an entirely false impression of me, because all he had left me was some sort of book, folded up, a pen and pencil, and a tuppenny bag of sweets. Not even Snakes-and-Ladders! For a while I was too stunned even to think. A fellow who was able to drive over rooftops and climb down chimneys without getting stuck—God, wouldn't you think he'd know better?

Then I began to wonder what that foxy boy, Sonny, had. I went to his side of the bed and felt his stocking. For all his spelling and sucking-up he hadn't done so much better, because, apart from a bag of sweets like mine, all Santa had left him was a popgun, one that fired a cork on a piece of string and which you could get in any huxter's shop for sixpence.

All the same, the fact remained that it was a gun, and a gun was better than a book any day of the week. The Dohertys had a gang, and the gang fought the Strawberry Lane kids who tried to play football on our road. That gun would be very useful to me in many ways, while it would be lost on Sonny who wouldn't be let play with the gang, even if he wanted to.

Then I got the inspiration, as it seemed to me, direct from heaven. Suppose I took the gun and gave Sonny the book! Sonny would never be any good in the gang: he was fond of spelling and a studious child like him could learn a lot of spellings from a book like mine. As he hadn't seen Santa any more than I had, what he hadn't seen wouldn't grieve him. I was doing no harm to anyone; in fact, if Sonny only knew, I was doing him a good turn which he might have cause to thank me for later. That was one thing I was always keen on; doing good turns. Perhaps this was Santa's intention the whole time and he had merely become confused between us. It was a mistake that might happen to anyone. So I put the book, the pencil, and the pen into Sonny's stocking and the popgun into my own, and returned to bed and slept again. As I say, in those days I had plenty of initiative.

It was Sonny who woke me, shaking me to tell me that Santa had come and left me a gun. I let on to be surprised and rather disappointed in the gun, and to divert his mind from it made him show me his picture book, and cracked it up to the skies.

As I knew, that kid was prepared to believe anything, and nothing would do him then but to take the presents in to show Father and Mother. This was a bad moment for me. After the way she had behaved about the langing, I distrusted Mother, though I had the consolation of believing that the only person who could contradict me was now somewhere up by the North Pole. That gave me a certain confidence, so Sonny and I burst in with our presents, shouting: "Look what Santa Claus brought!"

Father and Mother woke, and Mother smiled, but only for an instant. As she looked at me her face changed. I knew that look; I knew it only too well. It was the same she had worn the day I came home from langing, when she said I had no word.

"Larry," she said in low voice, "where did you get that gun?"

"Santa left it in my stocking, Mummy," I said, trying to put on an injured air, though it baffled me how she guessed that he hadn't. "He did, honest."

"You stole it from that poor child's stocking while he was asleep," she said, her voice quivering with indignation. "Larry, Larry, how could you be so mean?"

"Now, now, now," Father said deprecatingly, " 'tis Christmas morning."

"Ah," she said with real passion, "it's easy it comes to you. Do you think I want my son to grow up a liar and a thief?"

"Ah, what thief, woman?" he said testily. "Have sense, can't you?" He was as cross if you interrupted him in his benevolent moods as if they were of the other sort, and this one was probably exacerbated by a feeling of guilt for his behaviour of the night before. "Here, Larry," he said, reaching out for the money on the bedside table, "here's sixpence for you and one for Sonny. Mind you don't lose it now!"

But I looked at Mother and saw what was in her eyes. I burst out crying, threw the popgun on the floor, and ran bawling out of the house before anyone on the road was awake. I rushed up the lane behind the house and threw myself on the wet grass.

I understood it all, and it was almost more than I could bear; that there was no Santa Claus, as the Dohertys said, only Mother trying to scrape together a few coppers from the housekeeping; that Father was mean and common and a drunkard, and that she had been relying on me to raise her out of the misery of the life she was leading. And I knew that the look in her eyes was the fear that, like my father, I should turn out to be mean and common and a drunkard.

Europe

HENRY JAMES

I

"**O**ur feeling is, you know, that Becky *should go*." That earnest little remark comes back to me, even after long years, as the first note of something that began, for my observation, the day I went with my sister-in-law to take leave of her good friends. It is a memory of the American time, which revives so at present—under some touch that doesn't signify—that it rounds itself off as an anecdote. That walk to say good-bye was the beginning; and the end, so far as I was concerned with it, was not till long after; yet even the end also appears to me now as of the old days. I went, in those days, on occasion, to see my sister-in-law, in whose affairs, on my brother's death, I had had to take a helpful hand. I continued to go, indeed, after these little matters were straightened out, for the pleasure, periodically, of the impression—the change to the almost pastoral sweetness of the good Boston suburb from the loud, longitudinal New York. It was another world, with other manners, a different tone, a different taste; a savour nowhere so mild, yet so distinct, as in the square white house—with the pair of elms, like gigantic wheat-sheaves in front, the rustic orchard not far behind, the old-fashioned doorlights, the big blue and white jars in the porch, the straight, bricked walk from the high-gate—that enshrined the extraordinary merit of Mrs. Rimmle and her three daughters.

These ladies were so much of the place and the place so much of themselves that, from the first of their being revealed to me, I felt that nothing else at Brookbridge much mattered. They were what, for me, at any rate, Brookbridge had most to give: I mean in the way of what it was naturally strongest in, the thing that we called in New York the New England expression, the air of Puritanism reclaimed and refined. The Rimmles had brought it down to a wonderful delicacy. They struck me even then—all four almost equally—as very ancient and very earnest, and I think theirs must have been the house, in all the world, in which 'culture' first came to the aid of morning calls. The head of the family was the widow of a great public character—as public characters were understood at Brookbridge— whose speeches on anniversaries formed a part of the body of national eloquence spouted in the New England schools by little boys covetous of the most marked, though perhaps the easiest, distinction. He was reported to have been celebrated, and in such fine declamatory connections that he seemed to gesticulate even from the tomb. He was understood to have made, in his wife's company, the tour of Europe at a date not immensely removed from that of the battle of Waterloo. What was the age, then, of the bland, firm, antique Mrs. Rimmle at the period of her being first revealed to me? That is a point I am not in a position to determine—I remember mainly that I was young enough to regard her as having reached the limit. And yet the limit for Mrs. Rimmle must have been prodigiously extended; the scale of its extension is, in fact, the very moral of this reminiscence. She was old, and her daughters were old, but I was destined to know them all as older. It was only by comparison and habit that—however much I recede—Rebecca, Maria, and Jane were the "young ladies."

I think it was felt that, though their mother's life, after thirty years of widowhood, had had a grand backward stretch, her blandness and firmness —and this in spite of her extreme physical frailty—would be proof against any surrender not overwhelmingly justified by time. It had appeared, years before, at a crisis of which the waves had not even yet quite subsided, a surrender not justified by anything, that she should go, with her daughters, to Europe for her health. Her health was supposed to require constant support; but when it had at that period tried conclusions with the idea of Europe, it was not the idea of Europe that had been insidious enough to prevail. She had not gone, and Becky, Maria, and Jane had not gone, and this was long ago. They still merely floated in the air of the visit achieved, with such introductions and such acclamations, in the early part of the century; they still, with fond glances at the sunny parlour-walls, only referred, in conversation, to divers pictoral and other reminders of it. The Miss Rimmles had quite been brought up on it, but Becky, as the most literary, had most mastered the subject. There were framed letters—tributes to their eminent father—suspended among the mementos, and of two or three of these, the most foreign and complimentary, Becky had executed translations that figured beside the text. She knew already, through this and other illumination, so much about Europe that it was hard to believe, for her, in that limit of adventure which consisted only of her having been twice to Philadelphia. The others had not been to Philadelphia, but there was a legend that Jane had been to Saratoga. Becky was a short, stout, fair person with round, serious eyes, a high forehead, the sweetest, neatest enunciation, and a miniature of her father—"done in Rome"—worn as a breastpin. She had written the life, she had edited the speeches, of the original of this ornament, and now at last, beyond the seas, she was really to tread in his footsteps.

Fine old Mrs. Rimmle, in the sunny parlour and with a certain austerity of cap and chair—though with a gay new "front" that looked like rusty brown plush—had had so unusually good a winter that the question of her sparing two members of her family for an absence had been threshed as fine, I could feel, as even under that Puritan roof any case of conscience had ever been threshed. They were to make their dash while the coast, as it were, was clear, and each of the daughters had tried—heroically, angelically, and for the sake of each of her sisters—not to be one of the two. What I encountered that first time was an opportunity to concur with enthusiasm in the general idea that Becky's wonderful preparation would be wasted if she were the one to stay with their mother. They talked of Becky's preparation—they had a sly, old-maidish humour that was as mild as milk—as if it were some mixture, for application somewhere, that she kept in a precious bottle. It had been settled, at all events, that, armed with this concoction and borne aloft by their introductions, she and Jane were to start. They were wonderful on their introductions, which proceeded naturally from their mother and were addressed to the charming families that, in vague generations, had so admired vague Mr. Rimmle. Jane, I found at Brookbridge, had to be described, for want of other description, as the pretty one, but it would not have served to identify her unless you had seen the others. *Her* preparation was only this figment of her prettiness —only, that is, unless one took into account something that, on the spot, I silently divined: the lifelong, secret, passionate ache of her little rebellious desire. They were all growing old in the yearning to go, but Jane's yearning was the sharpest. She struggled with it as people at Brookbridge mostly struggled with what they liked, but fate, by threatening to prevent what she *dis*liked, and what was therefore duty—which was to stay at home instead of Maria—had bewildered her, I judged, not a little. It was she who, in the words I have quoted, mentioned to me Becky's case and Becky's affinity as the clearest of all. Her mother, moreover, on the general subject, had still more to say.

"I positively desire, I really quite insist that they shall go," the old lady explained to us from her stiff chair. "We've talked about it so often, and they've had from me so clear an account—I've amused them again and again with it—of what is to be seen and enjoyed. If they've had hitherto too many duties to leave, the time seems to have come to recognize that there are also many duties to *seek*. Wherever we go we find them—I always remind the girls of that. There's a duty that calls them to those wonderful countries, just as it called, at the right time, their father and myself —if it be only that of laying up for the years to come the same store of remarkable impressions, the same wealth of knowledge and food for conversation as, since my return, I have found myself so happy to possess." Mrs. Rimmle spoke of her return as of something of the year before last, but the future of her daughters was, somehow, by a different law, to be on the scale of great vistas, of endless aftertastes. I think that, without my being quite ready to say it, even this first impression of her was somewhat upsetting; there was a large, placid perversity, a grim secrecy of intention, in her estimate of the ages.

"Well, I'm so glad you don't delay it longer," I said to Miss Becky before we withdrew. "And whoever should go," I continued in the spirit of the sympathy with which the good sisters had already inspired me, "I quite feel, with your family, you know, that *you* should. But of course I hold that every one should." I suppose I wished to attenuate my solemnity; there was something in it, however, that I couldn't help. It must have been a faint foreknowledge.

"Have you been a great deal yourself?" Miss Jane, I remember, inquired.

"Not so much but that I hope to go a good deal more. So perhaps we shall meet," encouragingly suggested.

I recall something—something in the nature of susceptibility to encouragement—that this brought into the more expressive brown eyes to which Miss Jane mainly owed it that she was the pretty one. "Where, do you think?"

I tried to think. "Well, on the Italian lakes—Como, Bellagio, Lugano." I liked to say the names to them.

" 'Sublime, but neither bleak nor bare—nor misty are the mountains there!' " Miss Jane softly breathed, while her sister looked at her as if her familiarity with the poetry of the subject made her the most interesting feature of the scene she evoked.

But Miss Becky presently turned to me. "Do you know everything——?"

"Everything?"

"In Europe."

"Oh, yes," I laughed, "and one or two things even in America."

The sisters seemed to me furtively to look at each other. "Well, you'll have to be quick—to meet *us*," Miss Jane resumed.

"But surely when you're once there you'll stay on."

"Stay on?"—they murmured it simultaneously and with the oddest vibration of dread as well as of desire. It was as if they had been in the presence of a danger and yet wished me, who "knew everything," to torment them with still more of it.

Well, I did my best. "I mean it will never do to cut it short."

"No, that's just what I keep saying," said brilliant Jane. "It would be better, in that case, not to go."

"Oh, don't talk about not going—at this time!" It was none of my business, but I felt shocked and impatient.

"No, not at *this* time!" broke in Miss Maria, who, very red in the face, had joined us. Poor Miss Maria was known as the flushed one; but she was not flushed—she only had an unfortunate surface. The third day after this was to see them embark.

Miss Becky, however, desired as little as any one to be in any way extravagant. "It's only the thought of our mother," she explained.

I looked a moment at the old lady, with whom my sister-in-law was engaged. "Well—your mother's magnificent."

"*Isn't* she magnificent?"—they eagerly took it up.

She *was*—I could reiterate it with sincerity, though I perhaps mentally drew the line when Miss Maria again risked, as a fresh ejaculation: "I think she's better than Europe!"

"Maria!" they both, at this, exclaimed with a strange emphasis; it was as if they feared she had suddenly turned cynical over the deep domestic drama of their casting of lots. The innocent laugh with which she answered them gave the measure of her cynicism.

We separated at last, and my eyes met Mrs. Rimmle's as I held for an instant her aged hand. It was doubtless only my fancy that her calm, cold look quietly accused me of something. Of what *could* it accuse me? Only, I thought, of thinking.

II

I left Brookbridge the next day, and for some time after that had no occasion to hear from my kinswoman; but when she finally wrote there was a passage in her letter that affected me more than all the rest. "Do you know the poor Rimmles never, after all, 'went'? The old lady, at the eleventh hour, broke down; everything broke down, and all of *them* on top of it, so that the dear things are with us still. Mrs. Rimmle, the night after our call, had, in the most unexpected manner, a turn for the worse— something in the nature (though they're rather mysterious about it) of a seizure; Becky and Jane felt it—dear, devoted, stupid angels that they are— heartless to leave her at such a moment, and Europe's indefinitely postponed. However, they think they're still going—or *think* they think it— when she's better. They also think—or think they think—that she *will* be better. I certainly pray she may." So did I—quite fervently. I was conscious of a real pang—I didn't know how much they had made me care.

Late that winter my sister-in-law spent a week in New York; when almost my first inquiry on meeting her was about the health of Mrs. Rimmle.

"Oh, she's rather bad—she really is, you know. It's not surprising that at her age she should be infirm."

"Then what the deuce *is* her age?"

"I can't tell you to a year—but she's immensely old."

"That of course I saw," I replied—"unless you literally mean so old that the records have been lost."

My sister-in-law thought. "Well, I believe she wasn't positively young when she married. She lost three or four children before these women were born."

We surveyed together a little, on this, the "dark backward." "And they were born, I gather, *after* the famous tour? Well, then, as the famous tour was in a manner to celebrate—wasn't it?—the restoration of the Bourbons —" I considered, I gasped. "My dear child, what on earth do you make her out?"

My relative, with her Brookbridge habit, transferred her share of the question to the moral plane—turned it forth to wander, by implication at least, in the sandy desert of responsibility. "Well, you know, we all immensely admire her."

"You can't admire her more than I do. She's awful."

My interlocutress looked at me with a certain fear. "She's *really* ill."

"Too ill to get better?"

"Oh, no—we hope not. Because then they'll be able to go."

"And *will* they go, if she should?"

"Oh, the moment they should be quite satisfied. I mean *really*," she added.

I'm afraid I laughed at her—the Brookbridge "really" was a thing so by itself. "But if she shouldn't get better?" I went on.

"Oh, don't speak of it! They want so to go."

"It's a pity they're so infernally good," I mused.

"No—don't say that. It's what keeps them up."

"Yes, but isn't it what keeps *her* up too?"

My visitor looked grave. "Would you like them to kill her?"

I don't know that I was then prepared to say I should—though I believe I came very near it. But later on I burst all bounds, for the subject grew and grew. I went again before the good sisters ever did—I mean I went to Europe. I think I went twice, with a brief interval, before my fate again brought round for me a couple of days at Brookbridge. I had been there repeatedly, in the previous time, without making the acquaintance of the Rimmles; but now that I had had the revelation I couldn't have it too much, and the first request I preferred was to be taken again to see them. I remember well indeed the scruple I felt—the real delicacy—about betraying that *I* had, in the pride of my power, since our other meeting, stood, as their phrase went, among romantic scenes; but they were themselves the first to speak of it, and what, moreover, came home to me was that the coming and going of their friends in general—Brookbridge itself having even at that period one foot in Europe—was such as to place constantly before them the pleasure that was only postponed. They were thrown back, after all, on what the situation, under a final analysis, had most to give— the sense that, as every one kindly said to them and they kindly said to every one, Europe would keep. Every one felt for them so deeply that their own kindness in alleviating every one's feeling was really what came out most. Mrs. Rimmle was still in her stiff chair and in the sunny parlour, but if *she* made no scruple of introducing the Italian lakes my heart sank to observe that she dealt with them, as a topic, not in the least in the leave-taking manner in which Falstaff babbled of green fields.

I am not sure that, after this, my pretexts for a day or two with my sister-in-law were not apt to be a mere cover for another glimpse of these particulars: I at any rate never went to Brookbridge without an irrepressible eagerness for our customary call. A long time seems to me thus to have passed, with glimpses and lapses, considerable impatience and still more pity. Our visits indeed grew shorter, for, as my companion said, they were more and more of a strain. It finally struck me that the good sisters even shrank from me a little, as from one who penetrated their circumstances in spite of himself. It was as if they knew where I thought they ought to be, and were moved to deprecate at last, by a systematic silence on the subject of that hemisphere, the criminality I fain would fix on them. They were full instead—as with the instinct of throwing dust in my eyes— of little pathetic hypocrisies about Brookbridge interests and delights. I dare say that as time went on my deeper sense of their situation came practically to rest on my companion's report of it. I think I recollect, at all events, every word we ever exchanged about them, even if I have lost the thread of the special occasions. The impression they made on me after each interval always broke out with extravagance as I walked away with her.

"*She* may be as old as she likes—I don't care. It's the fearful age the 'girls' are reaching that constitutes the scandal. One shouldn't pry into such matters, I know; but the years and the chances are really going. They're all growing old together—it will presently be too late; and their mother meanwhile perches over them like a vulture—what shall I call it? —calculating. Is she waiting for them successively to drop off? She'll survive them each and all. There's something too remorseless in it."

"Yes; but what do you want her to do? If the poor thing *can't* die, she can't. Do you want her to take poison or to open a blood-vessel? I dare say she would prefer to go."

"I beg your pardon," I must have replied; "you daren't say anything of the sort. If she would prefer to go she *would* go. She would feel the propriety, the decency, the necessity of going. She just prefers *not* to go. She prefers to stay and keep up the tension, and her calling them 'girls' and talking of the good time they'll still have is the mere conscious mischief of a subtle old witch. They won't have *any* time—there isn't any time to have! I mean there's, on her own part, no real loss of measure or of perspective in it. She *knows* she's a hundred and ten, and takes a cruel pride in it."

My sister-in-law differed with me about this; she held that the old woman's attitude was an honest one and that her magnificent vitality, so great in spite of her infirmities, made it inevitable she should attribute youth to persons who had come into the world so much later. "Then suppose she should die?"—so my fellow-student of the case always put it to me.

"Do you mean while her daughters are away? There's not the least fear of that—not even if at the very moment of their departure she should be *in extremis*. They would find her all right on their return."

"But think how they would feel not to have been with her!"

"That's only, I repeat, on the unsound assumption. If they would only go to-morrow—literally make a good rush for it—they'll be with her when they come back. That will give them plenty of time." I'm afraid I even heartlessly added that if she *should*, against every probability, pass away in their absence, they wouldn't have to come back at all—which would be just the compensation proper to their long privation. And then Maria would come out to join the two others, and they would be—though but for the too scanty remnant of their career—as merry as the day is long.

I remained ready, somehow, pending the fulfilment of that vision, to sacrifice Maria; it was only over the urgency of the case for the others respectively that I found myself balancing. Sometimes it was for Becky I thought the tragedy deepest—sometimes, and in quite a different manner, I thought it most dire for Jane. It was Jane, after all, who had most sense of life. I seemed in fact dimly to descry in Jane a sense—as yet undescried by herself or by any one—of all sorts of queer things. Why didn't *she* go? I used desperately to ask; why didn't she make a bold personal dash for it, strike up a partnership with some one or other of the traveling spinsters in whom Brookbridge more and more abounded? Well, there came a flash for me at a particular point of the grey middle desert: my correspondent was able to let me know that poor Jane at last *had* sailed. She had gone of a sudden—I like my sister-in-law's view of suddenness—with the kind Hathaways, who had made an irresistible grab at her and lifted her off her feet. They were going for the summer and for Mr. Hathaway's health, so that the opportunity was perfect, and it was impossible not to be glad that something very like physical force had finally prevailed. This was the general feeling at Brookbridge, and I might imagine what Brookbridge had been brought to from the fact that, at the very moment she was hustled off, the doctor called to her mother at the peep of dawn, had considered that *he* at least must stay. There had been real alarm—greater than ever before; it actually did seem as if this time the end had come. But it was Becky, strange to say, who, though fully recognising the nature of the crisis, had kept the situation in hand and insisted upon action. This, I remember, brought back to me a discomfort with which I had been familiar from the first. One of the two had sailed, and I was sorry it was not the other. But if it had been the other I should have been equally sorry.

I saw with my eyes, that very autumn, what a fool Jane would have been if she had again backed out. Her mother had of course survived the peril of which I had heard, profiting by it indeed as she had profited by every other; she was sufficiently better again to have come down stairs. It was there that, as usual, I found her, but with a difference of effect produced somehow by the absence of one of the girls. It was as if, for the others, though they had not gone to Europe, Europe had come to them: Jane's letters had been so frequent and so beyond even what could have been hoped. It was the first time, however, that I perceived on the old woman's part a certain failure of lucidity. Jane's flight was, clearly, the great fact with her, but she spoke of it as if the fruit had now been plucked and the parenthesis closed. I don't know what sinking sense of still further physical duration I gathered, as a menace, from this first hint of her confusion of mind.

"My daughter has been; my daughter has been——" She kept saying it, but didn't say where; that seemed unnecessary, and she only repeated the words to her visitors with a face that was all puckers and yet now, save in so far as it expressed an ineffaceable complacency, all blankness. I think she wanted us a little to know that she had not stood in the way. It added to something—I scarce knew what—that I found myself desiring to extract privately from Becky. As our visit was to be of the shortest my opportunity —for one of the young ladies always came to the door with us—was at hand. Mrs. Rimmle, as we took leave, again sounded her phrase, but she added this time: "I'm so glad she's going to have always——"

I knew so well what she meant that, as she again dropped, looking at me queerly and becoming momentarily dim, I could help her out. "Going to have what *you* have?"

"Yes, yes—my privilege. Wonderful experience," she mumbled. She bowed to me a little as if I would understand. "She has things to tell."

I turned, slightly at a loss, to Becky. "She has then already arrived?"

Becky was at that moment looking a little strangely at her mother, who answered my questions. "She reached New York this morning—she comes on to-day."

"Oh, then——!" But I let the matter pass as I met Becky's eye—I saw there was a hitch somewhere. It was not she but Maria who came out with us; on which I cleared up the question of their sister's reappearance.

"Oh, no, not to-night," Maria smiled; "that's only the way mother puts it. We shall see her about the end of November—the Hathaways are so indulgent. They kindly extended their tour."

"For *her* sake? How sweet of them!" my sister-in-law exclaimed.

I can see our friend's plain, mild old face take on a deeper mildness, even though a higher colour, in the light of the open door. "Yes, it's for Jane they prolong it. And do you know what they write?" She gave us time, but it was too great a responsibility to guess. "Why, that it has brought her out."

"Oh, I knew it *would!*" my companion sympathetically sighed.

Maria put it more strongly still. "They say we wouldn't know her."

This sounded a little awful, but it was, after all, what I had expected.

III

My correspondent in Brookbridge came to me that Christmas, with my niece, to spend a week; and the arrangement had of course been prefaced by an exchange of letters, the first of which from my sister-in-law scarce took space for acceptance of my invitation before going on to say: "The Hathaways are back—but without Miss Jane!" She presented in a few words the situation thus created at Brookbridge, but was not yet, I gathered, fully in possession of the other one—the situation created in "Europe" by the presence there of that lady. The two together, at any rate, demanded, I quickly felt, all my attention, and perhaps my impatience to receive my relative was a little sharpened by my desire for the whole story. I had it at last, by the Christmas fire, and I may say without reserve that it gave me all I could have hoped for. I listened eagerly, after which I produced the comment: "Then she simply refused——"

"To budge from Florence? Simply. She had it out there with the poor Hathaways, who felt responsible for her safety, pledged to restore her to her mother's, to her sisters' hands, and showed herself in a light, they mention under their breath, that made their dear old hair stand on end. Do you know what, when they first got back, they said of her—at least it was *his* phrase—to two or three people?"

I thought a moment. "That she had 'tasted blood'?"

My visitor fairly admired me. "How clever of you to guess! It's exactly what he did say. She appeared—she continues to appear, it seems—in a new character."

I wondered a little. "But that's exactly—don't you remember?—what Miss Maria reported to us from them; that we 'wouldn't know her.' "

My sister-in-law perfectly remembered. "Oh, yes—she broke out from the first. But when they left her she was worse."

"Worse?"

"Well, different—different from anything she ever *had* been, or—for that matter—had had a chance to be." My interlocutress hung fire a moment, but presently faced me. "Rather strange and free and obstreperous."

"Obstreperous?" I wondered again.

"Peculiarly so, I inferred, on the question of not coming away. She wouldn't hear of it, and, when they spoke of her mother, said she had given her mother up. She had thought she should like Europe, but didn't know she should like it so much. They had been fools to bring her if they expected to take her away. She was going to see what she could—she hadn't yet seen half. The end of it was, at any rate, that they had to leave her alone."

I seemed to see it all—to see even the scared Hathaways. "So she is alone?"

"She told them, poor thing, it appears, and in a tone they'll never forget, that she was, at all events, quite old enough to be. She cried—she quite went on—over not having come sooner. That's why the only way for her." my companion mused, "*is*, I suppose, to stay. They wanted to put her with some people or other—to find some American family. But she says she's on her own feet."

"And she's still in Florence?"

"No—I believe she was to travel. She's bent on the East."

I burst out laughing. "Magnificient Jane! It's most interesting. Only I feel that I distinctly *should* 'know' her. To my sense, always, I must tell you, she had it in her."

My relative was silent a little. "So it now appears Becky always felt."

"And yet pushed her off? Magnificient Becky!"

My companion met my eyes a moment. "You don't know the queerest part. I mean the way it has *most* brought her out."

I turned it over; I felt I should like to know—to that degree indeed that, oddly enough, I jocosely disguised my eagerness. "You don't mean she has taken to drink?"

My visitor hesitated ."She has taken to flirting."

I expressed dissapointment. "Oh, she took to *that* long ago. Yes," I declared at my kinswoman's stare, "she positively flirted—with *me!*"

The stare perhaps sharpened. "Then you flirted with *her?*"

"How else could I have been as sure as I wanted to be? But has she means?"

"Means to flirt?"—my friend looked an instant as if she spoke literally. "I don't understand about the means—though of course they have something. But I have my impression," she went on. "I think that Becky——" It seemed almost too grave to say.

But *I* had no doubts. "That Becky's backing her?"

She brought it out. "Financing her."

"Stupendous Becky! So that morally then———"

"Becky's quite in sympathy. But isn't it too odd?" my sister-in-law asked.

"Not in the least. Didn't we know, as regards Jane, that Europe was to bring her out? Well, it has also brought out Rebecca."

"It has indeed!" my companion indulgently sighed. "So what would it do if she were there?"

"I should like immensely to see. And we *shall* see."

"Why, do you believe she'll still go?"

"Certainly. She *must*."

But my friend shook it off. "She won't."

"She shall!" I retorted with a laugh. But the next moment I said: "And what does the old woman say?"

"To Jane's behavior? Not a word—never speaks of it. She talks now much less than she used—only seems to wait. But it's my belief she thinks."

"And—do you mean—knows?"

"Yes, knows that she's abandoned. In her silence there she takes it in."

"It's her way of making Jane pay?" At this, somehow, I felt more serious. "Oh, dear, dear—she'll disinherit her!"

When, in the following June, I went on to return my sister-in-law's visit the first object that met my eyes in her little white parlour was a figure that, to my stupefaction, presented itself for the moment as that of Mrs. Rimmle. I had gone to my room after arriving, and, on dressing, had come down: the apparition I speak of had arisen in the interval. Its ambiguous character lasted, however, but a second or two—I had taken Becky for her mother because I knew no one but her mother of that extreme age. Becky's age was quite startling; it had made a great stride, though, strangely enough, irrecoverably seated as she now was in it, she had a wizened brightness that I had scarcely yet seen in her. I remember indulging on this occasion in two silent observations: one to the effect that I had not hitherto been conscious of her full resemblance to the old lady, and the other to the effect that, as I had said to my sister-in-law at Christmas, "Europe," even as reaching her only through Jane's sensibilities, had really at last brought her out. She was in fact "out" in a manner of which this encounter offered to my eyes a unique example: it was the single hour, often as I had been at Brookbridge, of my meeting her elsewhere than in her mother's drawing-room. I surmise that, besides being adjusted to her more marked time of life, the garments she wore abroad, and in particular her little plain bonnet, presented points of resemblance to the close sable sheath and the quaint old headgear that, in the white house behind the elms, I had from far back associated with the external image in the stiff chair. Of course I immediately spoke of Jane, showing an interest and

asking for news; on which she answered me with a smile, but not at all as
I had expected.

"*Those* are not really the things you want to know—where she is, whom
she's with, how she manages and where she's going next—oh, no!" And
the admirable woman gave a laugh that was somehow both light and sad—
sad, in particular, with a strange, long weariness. "What you do want to
know is when she's coming back."

I shook my head very kindly, but out of a wealth of experience that, I
flattered myself, was equal to Miss Becky's. "I do know it. Never."

Miss Becky, at this, exchanged with me a long, deep look. "Never."

We had, in silence, a little luminous talk about it, in the course of which
she seemed to tell me the most interesting things. "And how's your
mother?" I then inquired.

She hesitated, but finally spoke with the same serenity. "My mother's all
right. You see, she's not alive."

"Oh, Becky!" my sister-in-law pleadingly interjected.

But Becky only addressed herself to me. "Come and see if she is. *I* think
she isn't—but Maria perhaps isn't so clear. Come, at all events, and judge
and tell me."

It was a new note, and I was a little bewildered. "Ah, but I'm not a
doctor!"

"No, thank God—you're not. That's why I ask you." And now she said
good-bye.

I kept her hand a moment. "*You're* more alive than ever!"

"I'm very tired." She took it with the same smile, but for Becky it was
much to say.

IV

"Not alive," the next day, was certainly what Mrs. Rimmle looked when,
coming in according to my promise, I found her, with Miss Maria, in her
usual place. Though shrunken and diminished she still occupied her high-
backed chair with a visible theory of erectness, and her intensely aged face
—combined with something dauntless that belonged to her very presence
and that was effective even in this extremity—might have been that of
some centenarian sovereign, of indistinguishable sex, brought forth to be
shown to the people as a disproof of the rumor of extinction. Mummified
and open-eyed she looked at me, but I had no impression that she made
me out. I had come this time without my sister-in-law, who had frankly
pleaded to me—which also, for a daughter of Brookbridge, was saying
much—that the house had grown too painful. Poor Miss Maria excused

Miss Becky on the score of her not being well—and that, it struck me, was saying most of all. The absence of the others gave the occasion a different note; but I talked with Miss Maria for five minutes and perceived that—save for her saying, of her own movement, anything about Jane—she now spoke as if her mother had lost hearing or sense, or both, alluding freely and distinctly, though indeed favourably, to her condition. "She has expected your visit and she much enjoys it," my interlocutress said, while the old woman, soundless and motionless, simply fixed me without expression. Of course there was little to keep me; but I became aware, as I rose to go, that there was more than I had supposed. On my approaching her to take leave Mrs. Rimmle gave signs of consciousness.

"Have you heard about Jane?"

I hesitated, feeling a responsibility, and appealed for direction to Maria's face. But Maria's face was troubled, was turned altogether to her mother's. "About her life in Europe?" I then rather helplessly asked.

The old woman fronted me, on this, in a manner that made me feel silly. "Her life?"—and her voice, with this second effort, came out stronger. "Her death, if you please."

"Her death?" I echoed, before I could stop myself, with the accent of deprecation.

Miss Maria uttered a vague sound of pain, and I felt her turn away, but the marvel of her mother's little unquenched spark still held me. "Jane's dead. We've heard," said Mrs. Rimmle. "We've heard from—where is it we've heard from?" She had quite revived—she appealed to her daughter.

The poor old girl, crimson, rallied to her duty. "From Europe."

Mrs. Rimmle made at us both a little grim inclination of the head. "From Europe." I responded, in silence, with a deflection from every rigour, and, still holding me, she went on. "And now Rebecca's going."

She had gathered by this time such emphasis to say it that again, before I could help myself, I vibrated in reply. "To Europe—now?" It was as if for an instant she had made me believe it.

She only stared at me, however, from her wizened mask; then her eyes followed my companion. "Has she gone?"

"Not yet, mother." Maria tried to treat it as a joke, but her smile was embarrassed and dim.

"Then where is she?"

"She's lying down."

The old woman kept up her hard, queer gaze, but directing it, after a minute, to me. "She's going."

"Oh, some day!" I foolishly laughed; and on this I got to the door, where I separated from my younger hostess, who came no further. Only, as I held the door open, she said to me under cover of it and very quietly:

"It's poor mother's idea."

I saw—it was her idea. Mine was—for some time after this, even after I had returned to New York and to my usual occupations—that I should never again see Becky. I had seen her for the last time, I believed, under my sister-in-law's roof, and in the autumn it was given to me to hear from that fellow-admirer that she had succumbed at last to the situation. The day of the call I have just described had been a date in the process of her slow shrinkage—it was literally the first time she had, as they said at Brookbridge, given up. She had been ill for years, but the other state of health in the contemplation of which she had spent so much of her life had left her, till too late, no margin for meeting it. The encounter, at last, came simply in the form of the discovery that it *was* too late; on which, naturally, she had given up more and more. I had heard indeed, all summer, by letter, how Brookbridge had watched her do so; whereby the end found me in a manner prepared. Yet in spite of my preparation there remained with me a soreness, and when I was next—it was some six months later—on the scene of her martyrdom I replied, I fear, with an almost rabid negative to the question put to me in due course by my kinswoman. "Call on them? Never again!"

I went, none the less, the very next day. Everything was the same in the sunny parlour—everything that most mattered, I mean: the immemorial mummy in the high chair and the tributes, in the little frames on the walls, to the celebrity of its late husband. Only Maria Rimmle was different: if Becky, on my last seeing her, had looked as old as her mother, Maria—save that she moved about—looked older. I remember that she moved about, but I scarce remember what she said; and indeed what was there to say? When I risked a question, however, she had a reply.

"But *now* at least—?" I tried to put it to her suggestively.

At first she was vague. " 'Now?' "

"Won't Miss Jane come back?"

Oh, the headshake she gave me! "Never." It positively pictured to me, for the instant, a well-preserved woman, a sort of rich, ripe *seconde jeunesse* by the Arno.

"Then that's only to make more sure of your finally joining her."

Maria Rimmle repeated her headshake. "Never."

We stood so, a moment, bleakly face to face; I could think of no attenuation that would be particularly happy. But while I tried I heard a hoarse gasp that, fortunately, relieved me—a signal strange and at first formless from the occupant of the high-backed chair. "Mother wants to speak to you," Maria then said.

So it appeared from the drop of the old woman's jaw, the expression of her mouth opened as if for the emission of sound. It was difficult to me, somehow, to seem to sympathise without hypocrisy, but, so far as a step nearer could do so, I invited communication. "Have you heard where Becky's gone?" the wonderful witch's white lips then extraordinarily asked.

It drew from Maria, as on my previous visit, an uncontrollable groan, and this, in turn, made me take time to consider. As I considered, however, I had an inspiration. "To Europe?"

I must have adorned it with a strange grimace, but my inspiration had been right. "To Europe," said Mrs. Rimmle.

O. Henry (William Sydney Porter) (1862–1910) was born in Greensboro, N.C. He began to write—tradition has it—while he was the night druggist at the Ohio State Prison, having been convicted of embezzling from the bank where he was employed. During his lifetime he wrote more than six hundred short stories and at one point was producing them at the rate of one a week for the New York World. **For further reading:** The Complete Works of O. Henry **(1953).**

While the Auto Waits

O. HENRY

Promptly at the beginning of twilight, came again to that quiet corner of that quiet, small park the girl in gray. She sat upon a bench and read a book, for there was yet to come a half hour in which print could be accomplished.

To repeat: Her dress was gray, and plain enough to mask its impeccancy of style and fit. A large-meshed veil imprisoned her turban hat and a face that shone through it with a calm and unconscious beauty. She had come there at the same hour on the day previous, and on the day before that; and there was one who knew it.

The young man who knew it hovered near, relying upon burnt sacrifices to the great joss, Luck. His piety was rewarded, for, in turning a page, her book slipped from her fingers and bounded from the bench a full yard away.

The young man pounced upon it with instant avidity, returning it to its owner with that air that seems to flourish in parks and public places—a compound of gallantry and hope, tempered with respect for the policeman on the beat. In a pleasant voice, he risked an inconsequent remark upon the weather—that introductory topic responsible for so much of the world's unhappiness—and stood poised for a moment, awaiting his fate.

The girl looked him over leisurely; at his ordinary, neat dress and his features distinguished by nothing particular in the way of expression.

"You may sit down, if you like," she said, in a full, deliberate contralto. "Really, I would like to have you do so. The light is too bad for reading. I would prefer to talk."

The vassal of Luck slid upon the seat by her side with complaisance.

"Do you know," he said, speaking the formula with which park chair-men open their meetings, "that you are quite the stunningest girl I have seen in a long time? I had my eye on you yesterday. Didn't know somebody was bowled over by those pretty lamps of yours, did you, honeysuckle?"

"Whoever you are," said the girl, in icy tones, "you must remember that I am a lady. I will excuse the remark you have just made because the mistake was, doubtless, not an unnatural one—in your circle. I asked you to sit down; if the invitation must constitute me your honeysuckle, consider it withdrawn."

"I earnestly beg your pardon," pleaded the young man. His expression of satisfaction had changed to one of penitence and humility. "It was my fault, you know—I mean, there are girls in parks, you know—that is, of course, you don't know, but——"

"Abandon the subject, if you please. Of course I know. Now, tell me about these people passing and crowding, each way, along these paths. Where are they going? Why do they hurry so? Are they happy?"

The young man had promptly abandoned his air of coquetry. His cue was now for a waiting part; he could not guess the rôle he would be expected to play.

"It *is* interesting to watch them," he replied, postulating her mood. "It is the wonderful drama of life. Some are going to supper and some to—er—other places. One wonders what their histories are."

"I do not," said the girl; "I am not so inquisitive. I come here to sit because here, only, can I be near the great, common, throbbing heart of humanity. My part in life is cast where its beats are never felt. Can you surmise why I spoke to you, Mr.——?"

"Parkenstacker," supplied the young man. Then he looked eager and hopeful.

"No," said the girl, holding up a slender finger, and smiling slightly. "You would recognize it immediately. It is impossible to keep one's name out of print. Or even one's portrait. This veil and this hat of my maid furnish me with an *incog.* You should have seen the chauffeur stare at it when he thought I did not see. Candidly, there are five or six names that belong in the holy of holies, and mine, by the accident of birth, is one of them. I spoke to you, Mr. Stackenpot——"

"Parkenstacker," corrected the young man, modestly.

"—Mr. Parkenstacker, because I wanted to talk, for once, with a natural man—one unspoiled by the despicable gloss of wealth and supposed social superiority. Oh! you do not know how weary I am of it—money, money, money! And of the men who surround me, dancing like little marionettes all cut by the same pattern. I am sick of pleasure, of jewels, of travel, of society, of luxuries of all kinds."

"I always had an idea," ventured the young man, hesitatingly, "that money must be a pretty good thing."

"A competence is to be desired. But when you have so many millions that——!" She concluded the sentence with a gesture of despair. "It is the monotony of it," she continued, "that palls. Drives, dinners, theatres, balls, suppers, with the gilding of superfluous wealth over it all. Sometimes the very tinkle of the ice in my champagne glass nearly drives me mad."

Mr. Parkenstacker looked ingenuously interested.

"I have always liked," he said, "to read and hear about the ways of wealthy and fashionable folks. I suppose I am a bit of a snob. But I like to have my information accurate. Now, I had formed the opinion that champagne is cooled in the bottle and not by placing ice in the glass."

The girl gave a musical laugh of genuine amusement.

"You should know," she explained, in an indulgent tone, "that we of the non-useful class depend for our amusement upon departure from precedent. Just now it is a fad to put ice in champagne. The idea was originated by a visiting Prince of Tartary while dining at the Waldorf. It will soon give way to some other whim. Just as at a dinner party this week on Madison Avenue a green kid glove was laid by the plate of each guest to be put on and used while eating olives."

"I see," admitted the young man, humbly. "These special diversions of the inner circle do not become familiar to the common public."

"Sometimes," continued the girl, acknowledging his confession of error by a slight bow, "I have thought that if I ever should love a man it would be one of lowly station. One who is a worker and not a drone. But, doubtless, the claims of caste and wealth will prove stronger than my inclination. Just now I am besieged by two. One is a Grand Duke of a German principality. I think he has, or has had, a wife, somewhere, driven mad by his intemperance and cruelty. The other is an English Marquis, so cold and mercenary that I even prefer the diabolism of the Duke. What is it that impels me to tell you these things, Mr. Packenstacker?"

"Parkenstacker," breathed the young man. "Indeed, you cannot know how much I appreciate your confidences."

The girl contemplated him with the calm, impersonal regard that befitted the difference in their stations.

"What is your line of business, Mr. Parkenstacker?" she asked.

"A very humble one. But I hope to rise in the world. Were you really in earnest when you said that you could love a man of lowly position?"

"Indeed I was. But I said 'might.' There is the Grand Duke and the Marquis, you know. Yes; no calling could be too humble were man what I would wish him to be."

"I work," declared Mr. Parkenstacker, "in a restaurant."

The girl shrank slightly.

"Not as a waiter?" she said, a little imploringly. "Labor is noble, but— personal attendance, you know—valets and——"

"I am not a waiter. I am cashier in"—on the street they faced that bounded the opposite side of the park was the brilliant electric sign "RES-TAURANT"—"I am cashier in that restaurant you see there."

The girl consulted a tiny watch set in a bracelet of rich design upon her left wrist, and rose, hurriedly. She thrust her book into a glittering reticule suspended from her waist, for which, however, the book was too large.

"Why are you not at work?" she asked.

"I am on the night turn," said the young man; "it is yet an hour before my period begins. May I not hope to see you again?"

"I do not know. Perhaps—but the whim may not seize me again. I must go quickly now. There is a dinner, and a box at the play—and, oh! the same old round. Perhaps you noticed an automobile at the upper corner of the park as you came. One with a white body."

"And red running gear?" asked the young man, knitting his brows re-flectively.

"Yes. I always come in that. Pierre waits for me there. He supposes me to be shopping in the department store across the square. Conceive of the bondage of the life wherein we must deceive even our chauffeurs. Good-night."

"But it is dark now," said Mr. Parkenstacker, "and the park is full of rude men. May I not walk——?"

"If you have the slightest regard for my wishes," said the girl firmly, "you will remain at this bench for ten minutes after I have left. I do not mean to accuse you, but you are probably aware that autos generally bear the monogram of their owner. Again, good-night."

Swift and stately she moved away through the dusk. The young man watched her graceful form as she reached the pavement at the park's edge, and turned up along it toward the corner where stood the automobile. Then he treacherously and unhesitatingly began to dodge and skim among the park trees and shrubbery in a course parallel to her route, keeping her well in sight.

When she reached the corner she turned her head to glance at the motor car, and then passed it, continuing on across the street. Sheltered behind a convenient standing cab, the young man followed her movements closely with his eyes. Passing down the sidewalk of the street opposite the park, she entered the restaurant with the blazing sign. The place was one of those frankly glaring establishments, all white paint and glass, where one may dine cheaply and conspicuously. The girl penetrated the restaurant to some retreat at its rear, whence she quickly emerged without her hat and veil.

The cashier's desk was well to the front. A red-haired girl on the stool climbed down, glancing pointedly at the clock as she did so. The girl in gray mounted in her place.

The young man thrust his hands into his pockets and walked slowly back along the sidewalk. At the corner his foot struck a small, paper-covered volume lying there, sending it sliding to the edge of the turf. By its picturesque cover he recognized it as the book the girl had been reading. He picked it up carelessly, and saw that its title was "New Arabian Nights," the author being of the name of Stevenson. He dropped it again upon the grass, and lounged, irresolute, for a minute. Then he stepped into the automobile, reclined upon the cushions, and said two words to the chauffeur:

"Club, Henri."

Sherwood Anderson (1876–1941) left the paint manu-
facturing business to become an author and an
editor. Although his own work is irregular, his
influence has been very great on a whole generation of younger American writers. For further
reading: Winesburg, Ohio (1919), Death in the
Woods (1933).

The Egg

SHERWOOD ANDERSON

My father was, I am sure, intended by nature to be a cheerful, kindly
man. Until he was thirty-four years old he worked as a farm-hand for a
man named Thomas Butterworth whose place lay near the town of Bidwell,
Ohio. He had then a horse of his own and on Saturday evenings drove into
town to spend a few hours in social intercourse with other farm-hands. In
town he drank several glasses of beer and stood about in Ben Head's
saloon—crowded on Saturday evenings with visiting farm-hands. Songs
were sung and glasses thumped on the bar. At ten o'clock father drove
home along a lonely country road, made his horse comfortable for the night
and himself went to bed, quite happy in his position in life. He had at that
time no notion of trying to rise in the world.

It was in the spring of his thirty-fifth year that father married my
mother, then a country school-teacher, and in the following spring I came
wriggling and crying into the world. Something happened to the two people.
They became ambitious. The American passion for getting up in the world
took possession of them.

It may have been that mother was responsible. Being a school-teacher
she had no doubt read books and magazines. She had, I presume, read of
how Garfield, Lincoln, and other Americans rose from poverty to fame and
greatness and as I lay beside her—in the days of her lying-in—she may
have dreamed that I would some day rule men and cities. At any rate she
induced father to give up his place as a farm-hand, sell his horse and embark on an independent enterprise of his own. She was a tall silent woman
with a long nose and troubled grey eyes. For herself she wanted nothing.
For father and myself she was incurably ambitious.

The first venture into which the two people went turned out badly. They
rented ten acres of poor stony land on Griggs's Road, eight miles from

Bidwell, and launched into chicken raising. I grew into boyhood on the place and got my first impressions of life there. From the beginning they were impressions of disaster and if, in my turn, I am a gloomy man inclined to see the darker side of life, I attribute it to the fact that what should have been for me the happy joyous days of childhood were spent on a chicken farm.

One unversed in such matters can have no notion of the many and tragic things that can happen to a chicken. It is born out of an egg, lives for a few weeks as a tiny fluffy thing such as you will see pictured on Easter cards, then becomes hideously naked, eats quantities of corn and meal bought by the sweat of you father's brow, gets diseases called pip, cholera, and other names, stands looking with stupid eyes at the sun, becomes sick and dies. A few hens and now and then a rooster, intended to serve God's mysterious ends, struggle through to maturity. The hens lay eggs out of which come other chickens and the dreadful cycle is thus made complete. It is all unbelievably complex. Most philosophers must have been raised on chicken farms. One hopes for so much from a chicken and is so dreadfully disillusioned. Small chickens, just setting out on the journey of life, look so bright and alert and they are in fact so dreadfully stupid. They are so much like people they mix one up in one's judgments of life. If disease does not kill them they wait until your expectations are thoroughly aroused and then walk under the wheels of a wagon—to go squashed and dead back to their maker. Vermin infest their youth, and fortunes must be spent for curative powders. In later life I have seen how a literature has been built up on the subject of fortunes to be made out of the raising of chickens. It is intended to be read by the gods who have just eaten of the tree of the knowledge of good and evil. It is a hopeful literature and declares that much may be done by simple ambitious people who own a few hens. Do not be led astray by it. It was not written for you. Go hunt for gold on the frozen hills of Alaska, put your faith in the honesty of a politician, believe if you will that the world is daily growing better and that good will triumph over evil, but do not read and believe the literature that is written concerning the hen. It was not written for you.

I, however, digress. My tale does not primarily concern itself with the hen. If correctly told it will centre on the egg. For ten years my father and mother struggled to make our chicken farm pay and then they gave up that struggle and began another. They moved into the town of Bidwell, Ohio and embarked in the restaurant business. After ten years of worry with incubators that did not hatch, and with tiny—and in their own way lovely —balls of fluff that passed on into semi-naked pullethood and from that into dead henhood, we threw all aside and packing our belongings on a wagon drove down Griggs's Road toward Bidwell, a tiny caravan of hope looking for a new place from which to start on our upward journey through life.

We must have been a sad looking lot, not, I fancy, unlike refugees fleeing from a battlefield. Mother and I walked in the road. The wagon that contained our goods had been borrowed for the day from Mr. Albert Griggs, a neighbor. Out of its sides stuck the legs of cheap chairs and at the back of the pile of beds, tables, and boxes filled with kitchen utensils was a crate of live chickens, and on top of that the baby carriage in which I had been wheeled about in my infancy. Why we stuck to the baby carriage I don't know. It was unlikely other children would be born and the wheels were broken. People who have few possessions cling tightly to those they have. That is one of the facts that make life so discouraging.

Father rode on top of the wagon. He was then a bald-headed man of forty-five, a little fat and from long association with mother and the chickens he had become habitually silent and discouraged. All during our ten years on the chicken farm he had worked as a laborer on neighboring farms and most of the money he had earned had been spent for remedies to cure chicken diseases, on Wilmer's White Wonder Cholera Cure or Professor Bidlow's Egg Producer or some other preparations that mother found advertised in the poultry papers. There were two little patches of hair on father's head just above his ears. I remember that as a child I used to sit looking at him when he had gone to sleep in a chair before the stove on Sunday afternoons in the winter. I had at that time already begun to read books and have notions of my own and the bald path that led over the top of his head was, I fancied, something like a broad road, such a road as Caesar might have made on which to lead his legions out of Rome and into the wonders of an unknown world. The tufts of hair that grew above father's ears were, I thought, like forests. I fell into a half-sleeping, half-waking state and dreamed I was a tiny thing going along the road into a far beautiful place where there were no chicken farms and where life was a happy eggless affair.

One might write a book concerning our flight from the chicken farm into town. Mother and I walked the entire eight miles—she to be sure that nothing fell from the wagon and I to see the wonder of the world. On the seat of the wagon beside father was his greatest treasure. I will tell you of that.

On a chicken farm where hundreds and even thousands of chickens come out of eggs surprising things sometimes happen. Grotesques are born out of eggs as out of people. The accident does not often occur—perhaps once in a thousand births. A chicken is, you see, born that has four legs, two pairs of wings, two heads or what not. The things do not live. They go quickly back to the hand of their maker that has for a moment trembled.

The fact that the poor little things could not live was one of the tragedies of life to father. He had some sort of notion that if he could but bring into henhood or roosterhood a five-legged hen or a two-headed rooster his fortune would be made. He dreamed of taking the wonder about to county fairs and of growing rich by exhibiting it to other farm-hands.

At any rate he saved all the little monstrous things that had been born on our chicken farm. They were preserved in alcohol and put each in its own glass bottle. These he had carefully put into a box and on our journey into town it was carried on the wagon seat beside him. He drove the horses with one hand and with the other clung to the box. When we got to our destination the box was taken down at once and the bottles removed. All during our days as keepers of a restaurant in the town of Bidwell, Ohio, the grotesques in their little glass bottles sat on a shelf back of the counter. Mother sometimes protested but father was a rock on the subject of his treasure. The grotesques were, he declared, valuable. People, he said, liked to look at strange and wonderful things.

Did I say that we embarked in the restaurant business in the town of Bidwell, Ohio? I exaggerated a little. The town itself lay at the foot of a low hill and on the shore of a small river. The railroad did not run through the town and the station was a mile away to the north at a place called Pickleville. There had been a cider mill and pickle factory at the station, but before the time of our coming they had both gone out of business. In the morning and in the evening busses came down to the station along a road called Turner's Pike from the hotel on the main street of Bidwell. Our going to the out of the way place to embark in the restaurant business was mother's idea. She talked of it for a year and then one day went off and rented an empty store building opposite the railroad station. It was her idea that the restaurant would be profitable. Travelling men, she said, would be always waiting around to take trains out of town and town people would come to the station to await incoming trains. They would come to the restaurant to buy pieces of pie and drink coffee. Now that I am older I know that she had another motive in going. She was ambitious for me. She wanted me to rise in the world, to get into a town school and become a man of the towns.

At Pickleville father and mother worked hard as they always had done. At first there was the necessity of putting our place into shape to be a restaurant. That took a month. Father built a shelf on which he put tins of vegetables. He painted a sign on which he put his name in large red letters. Below his name was the sharp command—"EAT HERE"—that was so seldom obeyed. A show case was bought and filled with cigars and tobacco. Mother scrubbed the floor and the walls of the room. I went to school in the town and was glad to be away from the farm and from the presence of the discouraged, sad-looking chickens. Still I was not very joyous. In the evening I walked home from school along Turner's Pike and remembered the children I had seen playing in the town school yard. A troop of little girls had gone hopping about and singing. I tried that. Down along the frozen road I went hopping solemnly on one leg. "Hippity Hop To The Barber Shop," I sang shrilly. Then I stopped and looked doubtfully about. I was afraid of being seen in my gay mood. It must have seemed to me that I was doing a thing that should not be done by one who, like myself, had been raised on a chicken farm where death was a daily visitor.

Mother decided that our restaurant should remain open at night. At ten in the evening a passenger train went north past our door followed by a local freight. The freight crew had switching to do in Pickleville and when the work was done they came to our restaurant for hot coffee and food. Sometimes one of them ordered a fried egg. In the morning at four they returned north-bound and again visited us. A little trade began to grow up. Mother slept at night and during the day tended the restaurant and fed our boarders while father slept. He slept in the same bed mother had occupied during the night and I went off to the town of Bidwell and to school. During the long nights, while mother and I slept, father cooked meats that were to go into sandwiches for the lunch baskets of our boarders. Then an idea in regard to getting up in the world came into his head. The American spirit took hold of him. He also became ambitious.

In the long nights when there was little to do father had time to think. That was his undoing. He decided that he had in the past been an unsuccessful man because he had not been cheerful enough and that in the future he would adopt a cheerful outlook on life. In the early morning he came upstairs and got into bed with mother. She woke and the two talked. From my bed in the corner I listened.

It was father's idea that both he and mother should try to entertain the people who came to eat at our restaurant. I cannot now remember his words, but he gave the impression of one about to become in some obscure way a kind of public entertainer. When people, particularly young people from the town of Bidwell, came into our place, as on very rare occasions they did, bright entertaining conversation was to be made. From father's words I gathered that something of the jolly inn-keeper effect was to be sought. Mother must have been doubtful from the first, but she said nothing discouraging. It was father's notion that a passion for the company of himself and mother would spring up in the breasts of the younger people of the town of Bidwell. In the evening bright happy groups would come singing down Turner's Pike. They would troop shouting with joy and laughter into our place. There would be song and festivity. I do not mean to give the impression that father spoke so elaborately of the matter. He was as I have said an uncommunicative man. "They want some place to go. I tell you they want some place to go," he said over and over. That was as far as he got. My own imagination has filled in the blanks.

For two or three weeks this notion of father's invaded our house. We did not talk much, but in our daily lives tried earnestly to make smiles take the place of glum looks. Mother smiled at the boarders and I, catching the infection, smiled at our cat. Father became a little feverish in his anxiety to please. There was no doubt, lurking somewhere in him, a touch of the spirit of the showman. He did not waste much of his ammunition on the railroad men he served at night but seemed to be waiting for a young man or woman from Bidwell to come in to show what he could do. On the counter in the restaurant there was a wire basket kept always filled with eggs, and it must have been before his eyes when the idea of being entertaining was born in his brain. There was something pre-natal about the way eggs kept themselves connected with the development of his idea. At any rate an egg ruined his new impulse in life. Late one night I was awakened by a roar of anger coming from father's throat. Both mother and I sat upright in our beds. With trembling hands she lighted a lamp that stood on a table by her head. Downstairs the front door of our restaurant went shut with a bang and in a few minutes father tramped up the stairs. He held an egg in his hand and his hand trembled as though he were having a chill. There was a half insane light in his eyes. As he stood glaring at us I was sure he intended throwing the egg at either mother or me. Then he laid it gently on the table beside the lamp and dropped on his knees beside mother's bed. He began to cry like a boy and I, carried away by his grief, cried with him. The two of us filled the little upstairs room with our wailing voices. It is ridiculous, but of the picture we made I can remember only the fact that mother's hand continually stroked the bald path that ran across the top of his head. I have forgotten what mother said to him and how she induced him to tell her of what had happened downstairs. His explanation also has gone out of my mind. I remember only my own grief and fright and the shiny path over father's head glowing in the lamp light as he knelt by the bed.

As to what happened downstairs. For some unexplainable reason I know the story as well as though I had been a witness to my father's discomfiture. One in time gets to know many unexplainable things. On that evening young Joe Kane, son of a merchant of Bidwell, came to Pickleville to meet his father, who was expected on the ten o'clock evening train from the South. The train was three hours late and Joe came into our place to loaf about and to wait for its arrival. The local freight train came in and the freight crew were fed. Joe was left alone in the restaurant with father.

From the moment he came into our place the Bidwell young man must have been puzzled by my father's actions. It was his notion that father was angry at him for hanging around. He noticed that the restaurant keeper was apparently disturbed by his presence and he thought of going out. However, it began to rain and he did not fancy the long walk to town and back. He bought a five-cent cigar and ordered a cup of coffee. He had a newspaper in his pocket and took it out and began to read. "I'm waiting for the evening train. It's late," he said apologetically.

For a long time father, whom Joe Kane had never seen before, remained silently gazing at his visitor. He was no doubt suffering from an attack of stage fright. As so often happens in life he had thought so much and so often of the situation that now confronted him that he was somewhat nervous in its presence.

For one thing, he did not know what to do with his hands. He thrust one of them nervously over the counter and shook hands with Joe Kane. "How-de-do," he said. Joe Kane put his newspaper down and stared at him. Father's eye lighted on the basket of eggs that sat on the counter and he began to talk. "Well," he began hesitatingly, "well, you have heard of Christopher Columbus, eh?" He seemed to be angry. "That Christopher Columbus was a cheat," he declared emphatically. "He talked of making an egg stand on its end. He talked, he did, and then he went and broke the end of the egg."

My father seemed to his visitor to be beside himself at the duplicity of Christopher Columbus. He muttered and swore. He declared it was wrong to teach children that Christopher Columbus was a great man when, after all, he cheated at the critical moment. He had declared he would make an egg stand on end and then when his bluff had been called he had done a trick. Still grumbling at Columbus, father took an egg from the basket on the counter and began to walk up and down. He rolled the egg between the palms of his hands. He smiled genially. He began to mumble words regarding the effect to be produced on an egg by the electricity that comes out of the human body. He declared that without breaking its shell and by virtue of rolling it back and forth in his hands he could stand the egg on its end. He explained that the warmth of his hands and the gentle rolling movement he gave the egg created a new centre of gravity, and Joe Kane was mildly interested. "I have handled thousands of eggs," father said. "No one knows more about eggs than I do."

He stood the egg on the counter and it fell on its side. He tried the trick again and again, each time rolling the egg between the palms of his hands and saying the words regarding the wonders of electricity and the laws of gravity. When after a half hour's effort he did succeed in making the egg stand for a moment he looked up to find that his visitor was no longer watching. By the time he had succeeded in calling Joe Kane's attention to the success of his effort the egg had again rolled over and lay on its side.

Afire with the showman's passion and at the same time a good deal disconcerted by the failure of his first effort, father now took the bottles containing the poultry monstrosities down from their place on the shelf and began to show them to his visitor. "How would you like to have seven legs and two heads like this fellow?" he asked, exhibiting the most remarkable of his treasures. A cheerful smile played over his face. He reached over the counter and tried to slap Joe Kane on the shoulder as he had seen men do in Ben Head's saloon when he was a young farmhand and drove to town on Saturday evenings. His visitor was made a little ill by the sight of the body of the terribly deformed bird floating in the alcohol in the bottle and got up to go. Coming from behind the counter father took hold of the young man's arm and led him back to his seat. He grew a little angry and for a moment had to turn his face away and force himself to smile. Then he put the bottles back on the shelf. In an outburst of generosity he fairly compelled Joe Kane to have a fresh cup of coffee and another cigar at his expense. Then he took a pan and filling it with vinegar, taken from a jug that sat beneath the counter, he declared himself about to do a new trick. "I will heat this egg in this pan of vinegar," he said. "Then I will put it through the neck of a bottle without breaking the shell. When the egg is inside the bottle it will resume its normal shape and the shell will become hard again. Then I will give the bottle with the egg in it to you. You can take it about with you wherever you go. People will want to know how you got the egg in the bottle. Don't tell them. Keep them guessing. That is the way to have fun with this trick."

Father grinned and winked at his visitor. Joe Kane decided that the man who confronted him was mildly insane but harmless. He drank the cup of coffee that had been given him and began to read his paper again. When the egg had been heated in vinegar father carried it on a spoon to the counter and going into a back room got an empty bottle. He was angry because his visitor did not watch him as he began to do his trick, but nevertheless went cheerfully to work. For a long time he struggled, trying to get the egg to go through the neck of the bottle. He put the pan of vinegar back on the stove, intending to reheat the egg, then picked it up and burned his fingers. After a second bath in the hot vinegar the shell of the egg had been softened a little but not enough for his purpose. He worked and worked and a spirit of desperate determination took possession of him. When he thought that at last the trick was about to be consummated the delayed train came in at the station and Joe Kane started to go nonchalantly out at the door. Father made a last desperate effort to conquer the egg and make it do the things that would establish his reputation as one who knew how to entertain guests who came into his restaurant. He worried the egg. He attempted to be somewhat rough with it. He swore and the sweat stood out on his forehead. The egg broke under his hand.

When the contents spurted over his clothes, Joe Kane, who had stopped at the door, turned and laughed.

A roar of anger rose from my father's throat. He danced and shouted a string of inarticulate words. Grabbing another egg from the basket on the counter, he threw it, just missing the head of the young man as he dodged through the door and escaped.

Father came upstairs to mother and me with an egg in his hand. I do not know what he intended to do. I imagine he had some idea of destroying it, of destroying all eggs, and that he intended to let mother and me see him begin. When, however, he got into the presence of mother something happened to him. He laid the egg gently on the table and dropped on his knees by the bed as I have already explained. He later decided to close the restaurant for the night and to come upstairs and get into bed. When he did so he blew out the light and after much muttered conversation both he and mother went to sleep. I suppose I went to sleep also, but my sleep was troubled. I awoke at dawn and for a long time looked at the egg that lay on the table. I wondered why eggs had to be and why from the egg came the hen who again laid the egg. The question got into my blood. It has stayed there, I imagine, because I am the son of my father. At any rate, the problem remains unsolved in my mind. And that, I conclude, is but another evidence of the complete and final triumph of the egg—at least as far as my family is concerned.

Rope

KATHERINE ANNE PORTER

On the third day after they moved to the country he came walking back
from the village carrying a basket of groceries and a twenty-four-yard coil
of rope. She came out to meet him, wiping her hands on her green smock
Her hair was tumbled, her nose was scarlet with sunburn; he told her that
already she looked like a born country woman. His gray flannel shirt stuck
to him, his heavy shoes were dusty. She assured him he looked like a rural
character in a play.

Had he brought the coffee? She had been waiting all day long for coffee
They had forgot it when they ordered at the store the first day.

Gosh, no, he hadn't. Lord, now he'd have to go back. Yes, he would if it
killed him. He thought, though, he had everything else. She reminded him it
was only because he didn't drink coffee himself. If he did he would re
member it quick enough. Suppose they ran out of cigarettes? Then she saw
the rope. What was that for? Well, he thought it might do to hang clothes
on, or something. Naturally she asked him if he thought they were going to
run a laundry? They already had a fifty-foot line hanging right before his
eyes? Why, hadn't he noticed it, really? It was a blot on the landscape to
her.

He thought there were a lot of things a rope might come in handy for
She wanted to know what, for instance. He thought a few seconds, but
nothing occurred. They could wait and see, couldn't they? You need all
sorts of strange odds and ends around a place in the country. She said, yes
that was so; but she thought just at that time when every penny counted, it
seemed funny to buy more rope. That was all. She hadn't meant anything
else. She hadn't just seen, not at first, why he felt it was necessary.

Well, thunder, he had bought it because he wanted to, and that was all there was to it. She thought that was reason enough, and couldn't understand why he hadn't said so, at first. Undoubtedly it would be useful, twenty-four yards of rope, there were hundreds of things, she couldn't think of any at the moment, but it would come in. Of course. As he had said, things always did in the country.

But she was a little disappointed about the coffee, and oh, look, look, look at the eggs! Oh, my, they're all running! What had he put on top of them? Hadn't he known eggs mustn't be squeezed? Squeezed, who had squeezed them, he wanted to know. What a silly thing to say. He had simply brought them along in the basket with the other things. If they got broke it was the grocer's fault. He should know better than to put heavy things on top of eggs.

She believed it was the rope. That was the heaviest thing in the pack, she saw him plainly when he came in from the road, the rope was a big package on top of everything. He desired the whole wide world to witness that this was not a fact. He had carried the rope in one hand and the basket in the other, and what was the use of her having eyes if that was the best they could do for her?

Well, anyhow, she could see one thing plain: no eggs for breakfast. They'd have to scramble them now, for supper. It was too damned bad. She had planned to have steak for supper. No ice, meat wouldn't keep. He wanted to know why she couldn't finish breaking the eggs in a bowl and set them in a cool place.

Cool place! If he could find one for her, she'd be glad to set them there. Well, then, it seemed to him they might very well cook the meat at the same time they cooked the eggs and then warm up the meat for tomorrow. The idea simply choked her. Warmed-over meat, when they might as well have had it fresh. Second best and scraps and makeshifts, even to the meat! He rubbed her shoulder a little. It doesn't really matter so much, does it, darling? Sometimes when they were playful, he would rub her shoulder and she would arch and purr. This time she hissed and almost clawed. He was getting ready to say that they could surely manage somehow when she turned on him and said, if he told her they could manage somehow she would certainly slap his face.

He swallowed the words red hot, his face burned. He picked up the rope and started to put it on the top shelf. She would not have it on the top shelf, the jars and tins belonged there; positively she would not have the top shelf cluttered up with a lot of rope. She had borne all the clutter she meant to bear in the flat in town, there was space here at least and she meant to keep things in order.

Well, in that case, he wanted to know what the hammer and nails were doing up there? And why had she put them there when she knew very well he needed that hammer and those nails upstairs to fix the window sashes She simply slowed down everything and made double work on the place with her insane habit of changing things around and hiding them.

She was sure she begged his pardon, and if she had had any reason to believe he was going to fix the sashes this summer she would have left the hammer and nails right where he put them; in the middle of the bedroom floor where they could step on them in the dark. And now if he didn't clear the whole mess out of there she would throw them down the well.

Oh, all right, all right—could he put them in the closet? Naturally not there were brooms and mops and dustpans in the closet, and why couldn't he find a place for his rope outside her kitchen? Had he stopped to consider there were seven God-forsaken rooms in the house, and only one kitchen.

He wanted to know what of it? And did she realize she was making a complete fool of herself? And what did she take him for, a three-year-old idiot? The whole trouble with her was she needed something weaker than she was to heckle and tyrannize over. He wished to God now they had a couple of children she could take it out on. Maybe he'd get some rest.

Her face changed at this, she reminded him he had forgot the coffee and had bought a worthless piece of rope. And when she thought of all the things they actually needed to make the place even decently fit to live in well, she could cry, that was all. She looked so forlorn, so lost and despairing he couldn't believe it was only a piece of rope that was causing all the racket. What *was* the matter, for God's sake?

Oh, would he please hush and go away, and *stay* away, if he could, for five minutes? By all means, yes, he would. He'd stay away indefinitely if she wished. Lord, yes, there was nothing he'd like better than to clear out and never come back. She couldn't for the life of her see what was holding him then. It was a swell time. Here she was, stuck, miles from a railroad, with a half-empty house on her hands, and not a penny in her pocket, and everything on earth to do; it seemed the God-sent moment for him to get out from under. She was surprised he hadn't stayed in town as it was until she had come out and done the work and got things straightened out. It was his usual trick.

It appeared to him that this was going a little far. Just a touch out of bounds, if she didn't mind his saying so. Why the hell had he stayed in town the summer before? To do a half-dozen extra jobs to get the money he had sent her. That was it. She knew perfectly well they couldn't have done it otherwise. She had agreed with him at the time. And that was the only time so help him he had ever left her to do anything by herself.

Oh, he could tell that to his great-grandmother. She had her notion of what had kept him in town. Considerably more than a notion, if he wanted to know. So, she was going to bring all that up again, was she? Well, she could just think what she pleased. He was tired of explaining. It may have

looked funny but he had simply got hooked in, and what could he do? It
was impossible to believe that she was going to take it seriously. Yes, yes,
she knew how it was with a man: if he was left by himself a minute, some
woman was certain to kidnap him. And naturally he couldn't hurt her feelings by refusing!

Well, what was she raving about? Did she forget she had told him those
two weeks alone in the country were the happiest she had known for four
years? And how long had they been married when she said that? All right,
shut up! If she thought that hadn't stuck in his craw.

She hadn't meant she was happy because she was away from him. She
meant she was happy getting the devilish house nice and ready for him.
That was what she had meant, and now look! Bringing up something she
had said a year ago simply to justify himself for forgetting her coffee and
breaking the eggs and buying a wretched piece of rope they couldn't afford.
She really thought it was time to drop the subject, and now she wanted
only two things in the world. She wanted him to get that rope from underfoot, and go back to the village and get her coffee, and if he could remember
it, he might bring a metal mitt for the skillets, and two more curtain rods,
and if there were any rubber gloves in the village, her hands were simply
raw, and a bottle of milk of magnesia from the drugstore.

He looked out at the dark blue afternoon sweltering on the slopes, and
mopped his forehead and sighed heavily and said, if only she could wait a
minute for *anything*, he was going back. He had said so, hadn't he, the very
instant they found he had overlooked it?

Oh, yes, well . . . run along. She was going to wash windows. The country
was so beautiful! She doubted they'd have a moment to enjoy it. He meant
to go, but he could not until he had said that if she wasn't such a hopeless
melancholiac she might see that this was only for a few days. Couldn't she
remember anything pleasant about the other summers? Hadn't they ever
had any fun? She hadn't time to talk about it, and now would he please not
leave that rope lying around for her to trip on? He picked it up, somehow it
had toppled off the table, and walked out with it under his arm.

Was he going this minute? He certainly was. She thought so. Sometimes
it seemed to her he had second sight about the precisely perfect moment to
leave her ditched. She had meant to put the mattresses out to sun, if they
put them out this minute they would get at least three hours, he must have
heard her say that morning she meant to put them out. So of course he
would walk off and leave her to it. She supposed he thought the exercise
would do her good.

Well, he was merely going to get her coffee. A four-mile walk for two
pounds of coffee was ridiculous, but he was perfectly willing to do it. The
habit was making a wreck of her, but if she wanted to wreck herself there
was nothing he could do about it. If he thought it was coffee that was mak-

ing a wreck of her, she congratulated him: he must have a damned easy conscience.

Conscience or no conscience, he didn't see why the mattresses couldn't very well wait until tomorrow. And anyhow, for God's sake, were they living *in* the house, or were they going to let the house ride them to death? She paled at this, her face grew livid about the mouth, she looked quite dangerous, and reminded him that housekeeping was no more her work than it was his: she had other work to do as well, and when did he think she was going to find time to do it at this rate?

Was she going to start on that again? She knew as well as he did that his work brought in the regular money, hers was only occasional, if they depended on what *she* made—and she might as well get straight on this question once for all!

That was positively not the point. The question was, when both of them were working on their own time, was there going to be a division of the housework, or wasn't there? She merely wanted to know, she had to make her plans. Why, he thought that was all arranged. It was understood that he was to help. Hadn't he always, in summers?

Hadn't he, though? Oh, just hadn't he? And when, and where, and doing what? Lord, what an uproarious joke!

It was such a very uproarious joke that her face turned slightly purple, and she screamed with laughter. She laughed so hard she had to sit down, and finally a rush of tears spurted from her eyes and poured down into the lifted corners of her mouth. He dashed towards her and dragged her up to her feet and tried to pour water on her head. The dipper hung by a string on a nail and he broke it loose. Then he tried to pump water with one hand while she struggled in the other. So he gave it up and shook her instead.

She wrenched away, crying out for him to take his rope and go to hell, she had simply given him up: and ran. He heard her high-heeled bedroom slippers clattering and stumbling on the stairs.

He went out around the house and into the lane; he suddenly realized he had a blister on his heel and his shirt felt as if it were on fire. Things broke so suddenly you didn't know where you were. She could work herself into a fury about simply nothing. She was terrible, damn it: not an ounce of reason. You might as well talk to a sieve as that woman when she got going. Damned if he'd spend his life humoring her. Well, what to do now? He would take back the rope and exchange it for something else. Things accumulated, things were mountainous, you couldn't move them or sort them out or get rid of them. They just lay and rotted around. He'd take it back. Hell, why should he? He wanted it. What was it anyhow? A piece of rope. Imagine anybody caring more about a piece of rope than about a man's feelings. What earthly right had she to say a word about it? He re-membered all the useless, meaningless things she bought for herself: Why?

because I wanted it, that's why! He stopped and selected a large stone by the road. He would put the rope behind it. We would put it in the tool-box when he got back. He'd heard enough about it to last him a life-time.

When he came back she was leaning against the post box beside the road waiting. It was pretty late, the smell of broiled steak floated nose high in the cooling air. Her face was young and smooth and freshlooking. Her unmanageable funny black hair was all on end. She waved to him from a distance, and he speeded up. She called out that supper was ready and waiting, was he starved?

You bet he was starved. Here was the coffee. He waved it at her. She looked at his other hand. What was that he had there?

Well, it was the rope again. He stopped short. He had meant to exchange it but forgot. She wanted to know why he should exchange it, if it was something he really wanted. Wasn't the air sweet now, and wasn't it fine to be here?

She walked beside him with one hand hooked into his leather belt. She pulled and jostled him a little as he walked, and leaned against him. He put his arm clear around her and patted her stomach. They exchanged wary smiles. Coffee, coffee for the Ootsum-Wootsums! He felt as if he were bringing her a beautiful present.

He was a love, she firmly believed, and if she had had her coffee in the morning, she wouldn't have behaved so funny. . . . There was a whippoorwill still coming back, imagine, clear out of season, sitting in the crab-apple tree calling all by himself. Maybe his girl stood him up. Maybe she did. She hoped to hear him once more, she loved whippoorwills. . . . He knew how she was, didn't he?

Sure, he knew how she was.

F. Scott Fitzgerald (1896–1940) attended Princeton, but did not graduate; in World War I he served as a lieutenant in the army. In the 1920s he was a spokesman for the postwar "lost generation." The Great Gatsby (1925) and Tender Is the Night (1934) are his best-known novels. For further reading: Flappers and Philosophers, Tales of the Jazz Age (1922), All the Sad Young Men (1926).

The Long Way Out

F. SCOTT FITZGERALD

We were talking about some of the older castles in Touraine and we touched upon the iron cage in which Louis XI imprisoned Cardinal Balue for six years, then upon oubliettes and such horrors. I had seen several of the latter, simply dry wells thirty or forty feet deep where a man was thrown to wait for nothing; since I have such a tendency to claustrophobia that a Pullman berth is a certain nightmare, they had made a lasting impression. So it was rather a relief when a doctor told this story—that is, it was a relief when he began it, for it seemed to have nothing to do with the tortures long ago.

There was a young woman named Mrs. King who was very happy with her husband. They were well-to-do and deeply in love, but at the birth of her second child she went into a long coma and emerged with a clear case of schizophrenia or "split personality." Her delusion, which had something to do with the Declaration of Independence, had little bearing on the case and as she regained her health it began to disappear. At the end of ten months she was a convalescent patient scarcely marked by what had happened to her and very eager to go back into the world.

She was only twenty-one, rather girlish in an appealing way and a favorite with the staff of the sanitarium. When she became well enough so that she could take an experimental trip with her husband there was a general interest in the venture. One nurse had gone into Philadelphia with her to get a dress, another knew the story of her rather romantic courtship in Mexico and everyone had seen her two babies on visits to the hospital. The trip was to Virginia Beach for five days.

It was a joy to watch her make ready, dressing and packing meticulously and living in the gay trivialities of hair waves and such things. She was ready half an hour before the time of departure and she paid some visits on the floor in her powder-blue gown and her hat that looked like one minute after an April shower. Her frail lovely face, with just that touch of startled sadness that often lingers after an illness, was alight with anticipation.

"We'll just do nothing," she said. "That's my ambition. To get up when I want to for three straight mornings and stay up late for three straight nights. To buy a bathing suit by myself and order a meal."

When the time approached Mrs. King decided to wait downstairs instead of in her room and as she passed along the corridors, with an orderly carrying her suitcase, she waved to the other patients, sorry that they too were not going on a gorgeous holiday. The superintendent wished her well, two nurses found excuses to linger and share her infectious joy.

"What a beautiful tan you'll get, Mrs. King."

"Be sure and send a postcard."

About the time she left her room her husband's car was hit by a truck on his way from the city—he was hurt internally and was not expected to live more than a few hours. The information was received at the hospital in a glassed-in office adjoining the hall where Mrs. King waited. The operator, seeing Mrs. King and knowing that the glass was not sound proof, asked the head nurse to come immediately. The head nurse hurried aghast to a doctor and he decided what to do. So long as the husband was still alive it was best to tell her nothing, but of course she must know that he was not coming today.

Mrs. King was greatly disappointed.

"I suppose it's silly to feel that way," she said. "After all these months what's one more day? He said he'd come tomorrow, didn't he?" The nurse was having a difficult time but she managed to pass it off until the patient was back in her room. Then they assigned a very experienced and phlegmatic nurse to keep Mrs. King away from other patients and from newspapers. By the next day the matter would be decided one way or another.

But her husband lingered on and they continued to prevaricate. A little before noon next day one of the nurses was passing along the corridor when she met Mrs. King, dressed as she had been the day before but this time carrying her own suitcase.

"I'm going to meet my husband," she explained. "He couldn't come yesterday but he's coming today at the same time."

The nurse walked along with her. Mrs. King had the freedom of the building and it was difficult to simply steer her back to her room, and the nurse did not want to tell a story that would contradict what the authorities were telling her. When they reached the front hall she signaled to the operator, who fortunately understood. Mrs. King gave herself a last inspection in the mirror and said:

"I'd like to have a dozen hats just like this to remind me to be this happy always."

When the head nurse came in frowning a minute later she demanded: "Don't tell me George is delayed?"

"I'm afraid he is. There is nothing much to do but be patient."

Mrs. King laughed ruefully. "I wanted him to see my costume when it was absolutely new."

"Why, there isn't a wrinkle in it."

"I guess it'll last till tomorrow. I oughtn't to be blue about waiting one more day when I'm so utterly happy."

"Certainly not."

That night her husband died and at a conference of doctors next morning there was some discussion about what to do—it was a risk to tell her and a risk to keep it from her. It was decided finally to say that Mr. King had been called away and thus destroy her hope of an immediate meeting; when she was reconciled to this they could tell her the truth.

As the doctors came out of the conference one of them stopped and pointed. Down the corridor toward the outer hall walked Mrs. King carrying her suitcase.

Dr. Pirie, who had been in special charge of Mrs. King, caught his breath.

"This is awful," he said. "I think perhaps I'd better tell her now. There's no use saying he's away when she usually hears from him twice a week, and if we say he's sick she'll want to go to him. Anybody else like the job?"

II

One of the doctors in the conference went on a fortnight's vacation that afternoon. On the day of his return in the same corridor at the same hour, he stopped at the sight of a little procession coming toward him—an orderly carrying a suitcase, a nurse and Mrs. King dressed in the powder-blue suit and wearing the spring hat.

"Good morning, Doctor," she said. "I'm going to meet my husband and we're going to Virginia Beach. I'm going to the hall because I don't want to keep him waiting."

He looked into her face, clear and happy as a child's. The nurse signaled to him that it was as ordered, so he merely bowed and spoke of the pleasant weather.

"It's a beautiful day," said Mrs. King, "but of course even if it was raining it would be a beautiful day for me."

The doctor looked after her, puzzled and annoyed—why are they letting this go on, he thought. What possible good can it do?

Meeting Dr. Pirie, he put the question to him.

"We tried to tell her," Dr. Pirie said. "She laughed and said we were trying to see whether she's still sick. You could use the word unthinkable in an exact sense here—his death is unthinkable to her."

"But you can't just go on like this."

"Theoretically no," said Dr. Pirie. "A few days ago when she packed up as usual the nurse tried to keep her from going. From out in the hall I could see her face, see her begin to go to pieces—for the first time, mind you. Her muscles were tense and her eyes glazed and her voice was thick and shrill when she very politely called the nurse a liar. It was touch and go there for a minute whether we had a tractable patient or a restraint case—and I stepped in and told the nurse to take her down to the reception room."

He broke off as the procession that had just passed appeared again, headed back to the ward. Mrs. King stopped and spoke to Dr. Pirie.

"My husband's been delayed," she said. "Of course I'm disappointed but they tell me he's coming tomorrow and after waiting so long one more day doesn't seem to matter. Don't you agree with me, Doctor?"

"I certainly do, Mrs. King."

She took off her hat.

"I've got to put aside these clothes—I want them to be as fresh tomorrow as they are today." She looked closely at the hat. "There's a speck of dust on it, but I think I can get it off. Perhaps he won't notice."

"I'm sure he won't."

"Really I don't mind waiting another day. It'll be this time tomorrow before I know it, won't it?"

When she had gone along the younger doctor said:

"There are still the two children."

"I don't think the children are going to matter. When she 'went under,' she tied up this trip with the idea of getting well. If we took it away she'd have to go to the bottom and start over."

"Could she?"

"There's no prognosis," said Dr. Pirie. "I was simply explaining why she was allowed to go to the hall this morning."

"But there's tomorrow morning and the next morning."

"There's always the chance," said Dr. Pirie, "that some day he will be there."

The doctor ended his story here, rather abruptly. When we pressed him to tell what happened he protested that the rest was anticlimax—that all sympathy eventually wears out and that finally the staff of the sanitarium had simply accepted the fact.

"But does she still go to meet her husband?"

"Oh yes, it's always the same—but the other patients, except new ones, hardly look up when she passes along the hall. The nurses manage to substitute a new hat every year or so but she still wears the same suit. She's always a little disappointed but she makes the best of it, very sweetly too. It's not an unhappy life as far as we know, and in some funny way it seems to set an example of tranquillity to the other patients. For God's sake let's talk about something else—let's go back to oubliettes."

Langston Hughes (1902–1967), poet, novelist, and short-story writer, has stated that his "writing has been largely concerned with the depicting of Negro life in America." His first book of poetry, The Weary Blues (1926), started him on a distinguished career as professional writer and lecturer. For the short stories see Laughing to Keep From Crying (1951), The Best of Simple (1961), and Something in Common (1963).

Poor Little Black Fellow

LANGSTON HUGHES

Amanda Lee had been a perfect servant. And her husband Arnold likewise. That the Lord had taken them both so soon was a little beyond understanding. But then, of course, the Lord was just. And He had left the Pembertons poor little black Arnie as their Christian duty. There was no other way to consider the little colored boy whom they were raising as their own, *their very own*, except as a Christian duty. After all, they were white. It was no easy thing to raise a white child, even when it belonged to one, whereas this child was black, and had belonged to their servants, Amanda and Arnold.

But the Pembertons were never known to shirk a duty. They were one of New England's oldest families, one of the finest. They were wealthy. They had a family tree. They had a house in a charming maple-shaded town a few hours from Boston, a cottage at the beach, and four servants.

On Tuesdays and Fridays Mr. Pemberton went to town. He had an office of some sort there. But the ladies, Grace Pemberton and her sister, sat on the wide porch at home and crocheted. Or maybe they let James take them for a drive in the car. One of them sang in the choir.

Sometimes they spoke about the two beautiful Negro servants they once had, Amanda and Arnold. They liked to tell poor little Arnie how faithful and lovely his parents had been in life. It would encourage the boy. At present, of course, all their servants were white. Negroes were getting so unsteady. You couldn't keep them in the villages any more. In fact, there were none in Mapleton now. They all went running off to Boston or New York, sporting their money away in the towns. Well, Amanda and Arnold were never like that. They had been simple, true, honest, hard-working. Their qualities had caused the Pembertons to give, over a space of time, more than ten thousand dollars to a school for Negroes at Hampton, Va. Because they thought they saw in Amanda and Arnold the real qualities of an humble and gentle race. That, too, was why they had decided to keep Arnie, poor little black fellow.

The Pembertons had lost nobody in the·war except Arnold, their black stable man, but it had been almost like a personal loss. Indeed, after his death, they had kept horses no longer. And the stable had been turned into a garage.

Amanda, his wife, had grieved terribly, too. She had been all wrapped up in Arnold, and in her work with the Pembertons (she was their house-keeper) and in her little dark baby, Arnold, Junior. The child was five when his father went to war; and six when Amanda died of pneumonia a few weeks after they learned Arnold had been killed in the Argonne. The Pembertons were proud of him. A Negro who died for his country. But when that awful Winter of 1919 ended (the Pembertons judged it must have been awful from what they read), when that Winter ended the family was minus two perfect servants who could never come back. And they had on their hands an orphan.

"Poor little black fellow," said Grace Pemberton to her husband and her sister. "In memory of Arnold and Amanda, I think it is our Christian duty to keep it, and raise it up in the way it should go." Somehow, for a long time she called Arnie "it".

"We can raise it, without keeping it," said her husband. "Why not send it to Hampton?"

"Too young for that," said Emily, Mrs. Pemberton's sister. "I have been to Hampton, and they don't take them under twelve there."

So it was decided to keep the little black boy right in Mapleton, to send him to the village school, and to raise him up a good Christian and a good worker. And, it must be admitted, things went pretty well for some years. The white servants were kind to Arnie. The new housekeeper, a big-bosomed Irish woman who came after Amanda's death, treated him as though he were her very own, washed him and fed him. Indeed, they all treated him as if he were their very own.

II

Mr. Pemberton took Arnie to Boston once a season and bought him clothes. On his birthday, they gave him a party—on the lawn—because, after all, his birthday came in the Spring, and there was no need of filling the living-room with children. There was much more room on the lawn. In Summer Arnie went to the sea-shore with the rest of the family.

And Arnie, dark as he was, thrived. He grew up. He did well in his classes. He did well at home, helped with the chores about the house, raked the yard in the Fall, and shoveled snow when the long Winters set in. On Sundays he went to church with the family, listened to a dry and intelligent sermon, chanted the long hymns, and loved the anthems in which Miss Emily sang the solo parts.

Arnie, in church, a little black spot in a forest of white heads above stiff pews. Arnie, out of church, a symbol of how Christian charity should really be administered in the true spirit of the human brotherhood.

The church and the Pembertons were really a little proud of Arnie. Did they not all accept him as their own? And did they not go out of their way to be nice to him—a poor little black fellow whom they, through Christ, had taken in? Throughout the years the whole of Mapleton began to preen itself on its charity and kindness to Arnie. One would think that nobody in the town need ever again do a good deed: that this acceptance of a black boy was quite enough.

Arnie realized how they felt, but he didn't know what to do about it. He kept himself quiet and inconspicuous, and studied hard. He was very grateful, and very lonely. There were no other colored children in the town. But all the grown-up white people made their children be very nice to him, always very nice. "Poor little black boy," they said. "An orphan, and colored. And the Pembertons are so good to him. You be nice to him, too, do you hear? Share your lunch with him. And don't fight him. Or hurt his feelings. He's only a poor little Negro who has no parents." So even the children were over-kind to Arnie.

Everything might have been all right forever had not Arnie begun to grow up. The other children began to grow up, too. Adolescence. The boys had girls. They played kissing games, and learned to dance. There were parties to which Arnie was not invited—really couldn't be invited—with the girls and all. And after generations of peace the village of Mapleton, and the Pembertons, found themselves beset with a Negro problem. Everyone was a little baffled and a little ashamed.

To tell the truth, everybody had got so used to Arnie that nobody really thought of him as a Negro—until he put on long trousers and went to high-school. Now they noticed that he was truly very black. And his voice suddenly became deep and mannish, even before the white boys in Arnie's class talked in the cracks and squeaks of coming manhood.

Then there had arisen that problem of the Boy Scouts. When Arnie was sixteen the Pembertons applied for him to be admitted to a Summer camp for the Scouts at Barrow Beach, and the camp had refused. In a personal letter to Mr. Pemberton, they said they simply could not admit Negroes. Too many parents would object. So several of Arnie's friends and classmates went off to camp in June, and Arnie could not go. The village of Mapleton and the Pembertons felt awfully apologetic for American democracy's attitude to Arnie, whose father had died in the War. But, after all, they couldn't control the Boy Scout Camp. It was a semi-private institution. They were extra nice to Arnie, though—everybody.

That Summer, the Pembertons bought him a bicycle. And toward the end of the Summer (because they thought it was dull for him at the bungalow) they sent him to a Negro charity camp near Boston. It would be nice for him to come to know some of his own people. But Arnie hated it. He stayed a week and came home. The charity camp was full of black kids from the slums of Boston who cussed and fought and made fun of him because he didn't know how to play the dozens. So Arnie, to whom Negroes were a new nation, even if he was black, was amazed and bewildered, and came home. The Pembertons were embarrassed to find him alone in his attic room in the big empty house when they and the servants returned from the beach.

But they wanted so to be nice to him. They asked him if he'd met any friends he'd like to ask down for a week-end. They thought they would give him the whole top floor of the garage that year for a little apartment of his own and he could have his colored friends there. But Arnie hadn't met anyone he wanted to have. He had no colored friends.

The Pembertons knew that he couldn't move in the social world of Mapleton much longer. He was too big. But, really, what could they do? Grace Pemberton prayed. Emily talked it over with the mission board at church, and Mr. Pemberton spoke to the Urban League in Boston. Why not send him to Hampton now?

Arnie had only one more year in the high-school. Then, of course, he would go to college. But to one of the nicer Negro colleges like Fisk, they decided, where those dear Jubilee singers sang so beautifully, and where he would be with his own people, and wouldn't be embarrassed. No, Fisk wasn't as good as Harvard, they knew, but then Arnie had to find his own world after all. They'd have to let him go, poor black fellow! Certainly, he was their very own! But in Mapleton, what could he do, how could he live, whom could he marry? The Pembertons were a bit worried, even, about this one more year. So they decided to be extra nice to him. Indeed, everybody in Mapleton decided to be extra nice to him.

The two rooms over the garage made a fine apartment for a growing boy. His pennants and books and skis were there. Sometimes the white boys came in the evenings and played checkers and smoked forbidden cigarettes. Sometimes they walked out and met the girls at the soda-fountain in Dr. Jourdain's drug-store, and Arnie had a soda with the group. But he always came away alone, while the others went off in pairs. When the Christmas parties were being given, many of the girls were lovely in dresses that looked almost like real evening gowns, but Arnie wasn't invited anywhere but to the Allens'. (And they really didn't count in Mapleton—they were very poor white folks.)

The Pembertons were awfully sorry, of course. They were one of New England's oldest families, and they were raising Arnie as their son. But he was an African, a nice Christian African, and he ought to move among his own people. There he could be a good influence and have a place. The Pembertons couldn't help it that there were no Negroes in Mapleton. Once there had been some, but now they had all moved away. It was more fashionable to have white help. And even as a servant in Mapleton, Arnie would have been a little out of place. But he was smart in school, and a good clean boy. He sang well. (All Negroes were musical.) He skated and swam and played ball. He loved and obeyed the Pembertons. They wanted him to find his place in the world, poor fine little black fellow. Poor dear Arnie.

So it was decided that he would go to Fisk next year. When Arnie agreed, the Pembertons breathed a sort of sigh of joy. They thought he might remember the camp at Boston, and not want to go to a Negro college.

III

And now the Summer presented itself, the last Summer before they let Arnie go away—the boy whom they'd raised as their own. They didn't want that last Summer spoiled for him. Or for them. They wanted no such incidents as the Boy Scout business. The Pembertons were kind people. They wanted Arnie to remember with pleasure his life with them.

Maybe it would be nice to take him to Europe. They themselves had not been abroad for a long time. Arnie could see Paris and his father's grave and the Tower of London. The Pembertons would enjoy the trip, too. And on their return, Arnie could go directly to Fisk, where his life at college, and in the grown-up world, would begin. Maybe he'd marry one of those lovely brown girls who sang spirituals so beautifully, and live a good Christian man—occasionally visiting the Pembertons, and telling them about his influence on the poor black people of the South.

Graduation came. Arnie took high honors in the class, and spoke on the program. He went to the senior prom, but he didn't dance with any of the girls. He just sort of stood around the punch-bowl, and joked with the fellows. So nobody was embarrassed, and everyone was glad to see him there. The one dark spot in a world of whiteness. It was too bad he didn't have a partner to stand with him when they sang the Alma Mater after the final dance. But he was a lucky chap to be going to Europe. Not many youngsters from Mapleton had been. The Pembertons were doing well by him, everybody said aloud, and the church board had got him into Fisk.

But with all their careful planning, things weren't going so well about the European trip. When the steamship company saw the passports, they cancelled the cabin that had been engaged for Arnie. Servants always went second class, they wrote. That Arnie wasn't a servant, it was revealed ultimately, made no difference. He was a Negro, wasn't he?

So it ended with the Pembertons going first, and Arnie second class on the same boat. They would have all gone second, out of sympathy for Arnie, except that accommodations in that class had been completely booked for months ahead. Only as a great favor to first-class passengers had the steamship company managed to find a place for Arnie at all. The Pembertons and their boy had a cross to bear, but they bore it like Christians. At Cherbourg they met the little black fellow again on an equal footing. The evening found them in Paris.

Paris, loveliest of cities, where at dusk the lights are a great necklace among the trees of the Champs Elysées. Paris, song-city of the world. Paris, with the lips of a lovely woman kissing without fear. June, in Paris.

The Pembertons stopped at one of the best hotels. They had a suite which included a room for Arnie. Everything was very nice. The Louvre and the Eiffel Tower and the Café de la Paix were very nice. All with Arnie. Very nice. Everything would have gone on perfectly, surely; and there would have been no story, and Arnie and the Pembertons would have continued in Christian love forever—Arnie at Fisk, of course, and the Pembertons at Mapleton, then Arnie married and the Pembertons growing old, and so on and on—had not Claudina Lawrence moved into the very hotel where the Pembertons were staying. Claudina Lawrence! My God!

True, they had all seen dark faces on the boulevards, and a Negro quartet at the Olympia, but only very good Americans and very high English people were staying at this hotel with the Pembertons. Then Claudina Lawrence moved in—the Claudina who had come from Atlanta, Georgia, to startle the Old World with the new beauty of brown flesh behind footlights. That Claudina who sang divinely and danced like a dryad and had amassed a terrible amount of fame and money in five years. Even the Pembertons had heard of Claudina Lawrence in the quiet and sedate village of Mapleton. Even Arnie had heard of her. And Arnie had been a little bit proud. She was a Negro.

But why did she have to move next door to the Pembertons in this hotel? "Why, Lord, oh, why?" said Grace Pemberton. "For the sake of Arnie, why?" But here the tale begins.

IV

A lot of young Negroes, men and women, shiny and well-dressed, with good and sophisticated manners, came at all hours to see Claudina. Arnie and the Pembertons would meet them in the hall. They were a little too well dressed to suit the Pembertons. They came with white people among them, too—very pretty French girls. And they were terribly lively and gay and didn't seem dependent on anybody. Their music floated out of the windows on the Summer night. The Pembertons hoped they wouldn't get hold of Arnie. They would be a bad influence.

But they did get hold of Arnie.

One morning, as he came out to descend to the lobby to buy post-cards, Claudina herself stepped into the hall at the same time. They met at the elevator. She was the loveliest creature Arnie had ever seen. In pink, all tan and glowing. And she was colored.

"Hello," she said to the young black boy who looked old enough to be less shy. "You look like a home-towner."

"I'm from Mapleton," Arnie stuttered.

"You sound like you're from London," said Claudina, noting his New England accent and confusing it with Mayfair. "But your face says Alabama."

"Oh, I'm colored all right," said Arnie, happy to be recognized by one of his own. "And I'm glad to know you."

"Having a good time?" asked Claudina, as the elevator came.

"No," Arnie said, suddenly truthful. "I don't know anybody."

"Jesus!" said Claudina, sincerely. "That's a shame. A lot of boys and girls are always gathering in my place. Knock on the door some time. I can't see one of my down-home boys getting the blues in Paris. Some of the fellows in my band'll take you around a bit, maybe. They know all the holes and corners. Come in later."

"Thanks awfully," said Arnie.

Claudina left him half-dazed in the lobby. He saw her get into her car at the curb, saw the chauffeur tip his hat, and then drive away. For the first time in his life Arnie was really happy. Somebody had offered him something without charity, without condescension, without prayer, without distance, and without being nice.

All the pictures in the Luxembourg blurred before his eyes that afternoon, and Miss Emily's explanations went in one ear and out the other. He was thinking about Claudina and the friends he might meet in her rooms, the gay and well-dressed Negroes he had seen in the hall, the Paris they could show him, the girls they would be sure to know.

That night he went to see Claudina. He told the Pembertons he didn't care about going to the Odéon, so they went without him, a little reluctantly—because they didn't care about going either, really. They had been sticking rather strenuously to their program of cultural Paris. They were tired. Still, the Pembertons went to the Odéon—it was a play they really should see—and Arnie went next door to Claudina's. But only after he was sure the Pembertons were sitting in the theatre.

Claudina was playing whist. A young Englishman was her partner. Two sleek young colored men were their opponents. "Sit down, honey," Claudina said as if she had known Arnie for years. "You can take a hand in a minute, if you'd like to play. Meet Mr. So and so and so. . . ." She introduced him to the group. "It's kinda early yet. Most of our gang are at work. The theatres aren't out. . . . Marie, bring him a drink." And the French maid poured a cocktail.

A knock, and a rather portly brown-skinned woman, beautifully dressed, entered. "Hello! Who's holding all the trump cards? Glad to meet you, Mr. Arnie. From Boston, you say? My old stamping-ground. Do you know the Roundtrees there?"

"No'm," Arnie said.

"Well, I used to study at the Conservatory and knew all the big shots," the brown-skin woman went on. "Did you just come over? Tourist, heh? Well, what's new in the States now? I haven't been home for three years. Don't intend to go soon. The color-line's a little too much for me. What are they dancing now-a-days? You must've brought a few of the latest steps with you. Can you do the Lindy Hop?"

"No'm," said Arnie.

"Well, I'm gonna see," said the brown-skin lady. She put a record on the victrola, and took Arnie in her arms. Even if he couldn't do the Lindy Hop, he enjoyed dancing with her and they got along famously. Several more people came in, a swell-looking yellow girl, some rather elderly musicians, in spats, and a young colored art student named Harry Jones. Cocktails went around.

"I'm from Chicago," Harry said eventually. "Been over here about a year and like it a hell of a lot. You will, too, soon as you get to know a few folks."

Gradually the room took on the life and gaiety of a party. Somebody sat down at a piano in the alcove, and started a liquid ripple of jazz. Three or four couples began to dance. Arnie and the lovely yellow girl got together. They danced a long time, and then they drank cocktails. Arnie forgot about the clock. It was long after midnight.

Somebody suggested that they all go to the opening of a new Martinique ballroom where a native orchestra would play rattles and drums.

"Come on, Arnie," Harry Jones said. "You might as well make a night of it. Tomorrow's Sunday."

"I start rehearsals tomorrow," Claudina said. "so I can't go. But listen here," she warned. "Don't you-all take Arnie out of here and lose him. Some of these little French girls are liable to put him in their pockets, crazy as they are about chocolate."

Arnie hoped he wouldn't meet the Pembertons in the hall. He didn't. They were long since in bed. And when Arnie came in at dawn, his head was swimming with the grandest night he'd ever known.

At the Martinique ball he'd met dozens of nice girls: white girls and brown girls, and yellow girls, artists and students and dancers and models and tourists. Harry knew everybody. And everybody was gay and friendly. Paris and music and cocktails made you forget what color people were—and what color you were yourself. Here it didn't matter—color.

Arnie went to sleep dreaming about a little Rumanian girl named Vivi. Harry said she was a music student. But Arnie didn't care what she was, she had such soft black hair and bright grey eyes. How she could dance! And she knew quite a little English. He'd taken her address. Tomorrow he would go to see her. Aw, hell, tomorrow the Pembertons wanted to go to Versailles!

V

When Arnie woke up it was three o'clock. This time Grace Pemberton had actually banged on the door. Arnie was frightened. He'd never slept so late before. What would the Pembertons think?

"What ever is the matter, Arnold?" Mrs. Pemberton called. Only when she was put out did she call him Arnold.

"Up late reading," Arnie muttered through the closed door. "I was up late reading." And then was promptly ashamed of himself for having lied.

"Well, hurry up," Mrs. Pemberton said. "We're about to start for Versailles."

"I don't want to go," said Arnie.

"What ever is the matter with you, boy?" gasped Grace Pemberton.

Arnie had slipped on a bathrobe, so he opened the door.

"Good morning," he said. "I've met some friends. I want to go out with them."

The contrariness of late adolescence was asserting itself. He felt stubborn and mean.

"Friends?" said Grace Pemberton. "What friends, may I ask?"

"A colored student and some others."

"Where did you meet them?"

"Next door, at Miss Lawrence's."

Grace Pemberton stiffened like a bolt. "Get ready, young man," she said, "and come with us to Versailles." She left the room. The young man got ready.

Arnie pouted, but he went with the Pembertons. The sun gave him a headache, and he didn't give a damn about Versailles. That evening, after a private lecture by Mr. Pemberton on the evils of Paris (Grace and Emily had spoken about the beauty of the city), he went to bed feeling very black and sick.

For several days, he wasn't himself at all, what with constant excursions to museums and villages and chateaux, when he wanted to be with Vivi and Harry and Claudina. (Once he did sneak away with Harry to meet Vivi.) Meanwhile, the Pembertons lectured him on his surliness. They were inclined to be dignified and distant to the poor little black fellow now. After all, it had cost them quite a lot to bring him to Paris. Didn't he appreciate what they were doing for him? They had raised him. Had they then no right to forbid him going about with a crowd of Negroes from the theatres?

"He's a black devil," said Mr. Pemberton.

"Poor little fellow," said Grace. She was a little sorry for him.

"After all, he doesn't know. He's young. Let us just try loving him, and being very nice to him."

So once again the Pembertons turned loose on Arnie their niceness. They took him to the races, and they bought him half a dozen French ties from a good shop, and they treated him better than if he were their own.

But Arnie was worse than ever. He stayed out all night one night. Grace knew, because she knocked on his door at two o'clock. And the Negroes next door, how they laughed! How they danced! How the music drifted through the windows. It seemed as if the actual Devil had got into Arnie. Was he going to the dogs before their very eyes? Grace Pemberton was worried. After all, he *was* the nearest thing she'd ever had to a son. She was really fond of him.

As for Arnie, it wasn't the Devil at all that had got him. It wasn't even

Claudina. It was Vivi, the little girl he'd met through Harry at the Martinique ball. The girl who played Chopin on the piano, and had grey eyes and black hair and came from Rumania. By himself, Arnie had managed to find, from the address she had given him, the tall house near the Parc Monceau where she lived in an attic room. Up six flights of stairs he walked. He found her with big books on theory in front of her and blank music pages, working out some sort of exercise in harmony. Her little face was very white, her grey eyes very big, and her black hair all fluffy around her head. Arnie didn't know why he had come to see her except that he liked her very much.

They talked all afternoon and Arnie told her about his life at home, how white people had raised him, and how hard it was to be black in America. Vivi said it didn't make any difference in Rumania, or in Paris either, about being black.

"Here it's only hard to be poor," Vivi said.

But Arnie thought he wouldn't mind being poor in a land where it didn't matter what color you were.

"Yes, you would mind," Vivi said.

"Being poor's not easy anywhere. But then," and her eyes grew bigger, "by and by the Revolution will come. In Rumania the Revolution will come. In France, too. Everywhere poor people are tired of being poor."

"What Revolution?" Arnie asked, for he hadn't heard about it in Mapleton.

Vivi told him.

"Where we live, it's quiet," he said. "My folks come from Massachusetts."

VI

And then the devil whispered to Arnie. Maybe Vivi would like to meet some real Americans. Anyway, he would like the Pembertons to meet her. He'd like to show them that there actually was a young white girl in the world who didn't care about color. They were always educating him. He would educate them a bit. So Arnie invited Vivi to dinner at the hotel that very night.

The Pembertons had finished their soup when he entered the sparkling dining-room of the hotel. He made straight for their table. The orchestra was playing Strauss. Gentlemen in evening clothes and ladies in diamonds scanned a long and expensive menu. The Pembertons looked up and saw Arnie coming, guiding Vivi by the hand. Grace Pemberton gasped and put her spoon back in the soup. Emily went pale. Mr. Pemberton's mouth opened. All the Americans stared. Such a white, white girl and such a black, black boy coming across the dining-room floor! The girl had a red mouth and grey eyes.

The Pembertons had been waiting for Arnie since four o'clock. Today a charming Indian mystic, Nadjuti, had come to tea with them, especially to see the young Negro student they had raised in America. The Pembertons were not pleased that Arnie had not been there.

"This is my friend," Arnie said. "I've brought her to dinner."

Vivi smiled and held out her hand, but the Pembertons bowed in their stiffest fashion. Nobody noticed her hand.

"I'm sorry," said Grace Pemberton, "but there's room for only four at our table."

"Oh," said Arnie. He hadn't thought they'd be rude. Polite and formal, maybe, but not rude. "Oh! Don't mind us then. Come on, Vivi." His eyes were red as he led her away to a vacant table by the fountain. A waiter came and took their orders with the same deference he showed everyone else. The Pembertons looked and could not eat.

"Where ever did he get her?" whispered Emily in her thin New England voice, as her cheeks burned. "Is she a woman from the streets?" The Pembertons couldn't imagine that so lovely a white girl would go out with a strange Negro unless she were a prostitute. They were terribly mortified. What would he do next?

"But maybe he doesn't know. Did you warn him, John?" Grace Pemberton addressed her husband.

"I did," replied Mr. Pemberton shortly.

"A scarlet woman," said Emily faintly. "A scarlet. . . . I think I shall go to my room. All the Americans in the dining-room must have seen." She was white as she rose. "We've been talked about enough as it is—travelling with a colored boy. For our sakes, he might have been careful."

The Pembertons left the dining-room. But Grace Pemberton was afraid for Arnie. Near the door, she turned and came over to the table by the fountain. "Please, Arnold, come to my room before you go."

"Yes, Miss Grace, I'll come," he said.

"You mustn't mind." Vivi patted his arm. The orchestra was playing "The Song of India." "All old people are the same."

As they ate, Vivi and Arnie talked about parents. Vivi told him how her folks hadn't allowed her to come away to study music, how they'd even tried to stop her at the station. "Most elderly people are terrible," she said, "especially parents."

"But they're not my parents," Arnie said. "They are white people."

When he took Vivi home, he kissed her. Then he came back and knocked on the living-room door.

VII

"Come in," Grace Pemberton said. "Come in, Arnie, I want to talk to you." She was sitting there alone, very straight with her iron-grey hair low on her neck. "Poor little black fellow," she said, as though Arnie had done a great and careless wrong. "Come here."

When Arnie saw her pale white face from the door, he was a little sad and ashamed that he might have done something to hurt her. But when she began to pity him, "poor little black fellow", a sudden anger shook him from head to foot. His eyes grew sultry and red, his spirit stubborn.

"Arnold," she said, "I think we'd better go home, back to America."

"I don't want to go," he replied.

"But you don't seem to appreciate what we are doing for you here," she said, "at all."

"I don't," Arnie answered.

"You don't!" Grace Pemberton's throat went dry. "You don't? We're showing you the best of Paris, and you don't? Why, we've done all we could for you always, Arnie boy. We've raised you as our own. And we want to do more. We're going to send you to college, of course, to Fisk this Fall."

"I don't want to go to Fisk," Arnie said.

"What?"

"No," said Arnie. "I don't want to go. It'll be like that camp in Boston. Everything in America's like that camp in Boston." His eyes grew redder. "Separate, segregated, shut-off! Black people kept away from everybody else. I go to Fisk; my classmates, Harvard and Amherst and Yale. . . . I sleep in the garage, you sleep in the house."

"Oh," Grace Pemberton said. "We didn't mean it like that!"

Arnie was being cruel, just cruel. She began, in spite of herself, to cry.

"I don't want to go back home," Arnie went on. "I hate America."

"But your father *died* for America," Grace Pemberton cried.

"I guess he was a fool," said Arnie.

The hall door opened. Mr. Pemberton and his sister-in-law came in from a walk through the park. They saw Mrs. Pemberton's eyes wet, and Arnie's sultry face. Mrs. Pemberton told them what he'd said.

"So you want to stay here," said Mr. Pemberton, trying to hold his temper. "Well, stay. Take your things and stay. Stay now. Get out! Go!"

Anger possessed him, fury against this ungrateful black boy who made his wife cry. Grace Pemberton never cried over anything Mr. Pemberton did. And now, she was crying over this . . . this. . . . In the back of his mind was the word *nigger*. Arnold felt it.

"I want to go," said Arnie. "I've always wanted to go."

"You little black fool!" said Emily.

"Where will you go?" Grace Pemberton asked. Why, oh why, didn't Arnie say he was sorry, beg their pardon, and stay? He knew he could if he wanted to.

"I'll go to Vivi," Arnie said.

"Vivi?" a weak voice gasped.

"Yes, marry Vivi!"

"Marry white, eh?" said Mr. Pemberton. Emily laughed drily. But Grace Pemberton fainted.

Next door, just then, the piano was louder than ever. Somebody was doing a tap dance. The dancing and the music floated through the windows on the soft Paris air. Outside, the lights were a necklace of gold over the Champs Elysées. Autos honked. Trees rustled. People passed.

Arnie went out.

John Steinbeck (1902–1968) supported himself for many years as ranch hand, carpenter, fruit picker, and reporter. After several unsuccessful novels, Tortilla Flat (1935) brought him critical acclaim. In Dubious Battle (1936), Of Mice and Men (1937), and The Grapes of Wrath (1939)—for which he received the Pulitzer Prize in 1940—established his reputation. In 1962 he received the Nobel Prize. His collection of short stories is titled The Long Valley (1938).

The Leader of the People

JOHN STEINBECK

On Saturday afternoon Billy Buck, the ranch-hand, raked together the last of the old year's haystack and pitched small forkfuls over the wire fence to a few mildly interested cattle. High in the air small clouds like puffs of cannon smoke were driven eastward by the March wind. The wind could be heard whishing in the brush on the ridge crests, but no breath of it penetrated down into the ranch-cup.

The little boy, Jody, emerged from the house eating a thick piece of buttered bread. He saw Billy working on the last of the haystack. Jody tramped down scuffing his shoes in a way he had been told was destructive to good shoe-leather. A flock of white pigeons flew out of the black cypress tree as Jody passed, and circled the tree and landed again. A half-grown tortoise-shell cat leaped from the bunkhouse porch, galloped on stiff legs across the road, whirled and galloped back again. Jody picked up a stone to help the game along, but he was too late, for the cat was under the porch before the stone could be discharged. He threw the stone into the cypress tree and started the white pigeons on another whirling flight.

Arriving at the used-up haystack, the boy leaned against the barbed wire fence. "Will that be all of it, do you think?" he asked.

The middle-aged ranch-hand stopped his careful raking and stuck his fork into the ground. He took off his black hat and smoothed down his hair. "Nothing left of it that isn't soggy from ground moisture," he said. He replaced his hat and rubbed his dry leathery hands together.

"Ought to be plenty mice," Jody suggested.

"Lousy with them," said Billy. "Just crawling with mice."

"Well, maybe, when you get all through, I could call the dogs and hunt the mice."

"Sure, I guess you could," said Billy Buck. He lifted a forkful of the damp ground-hay and threw it into the air. Instantly three mice leaped out and burrowed frantically under the hay again.

Jody sighed with satisfaction. Those plump, sleek, arrogant mice were doomed. For eight months they had lived and multiplied in the haystack. They had been immune from cats, from traps, from poison and from Jody. They had grown smug in their security, overbearing and fat. Now the time of disaster had come; they would not survive another day.

Billy looked up at the top of the hills that surrounded the ranch. "Maybe you better ask your father before you do it," he suggested.

"Well, where is he? I'll ask him now."

"He rode up to the ridge ranch after dinner. He'll be back pretty soon."

Jody slumped against the fence post. "I don't think he'd care."

As Billy went back to his work he said ominously, "You'd better ask him anyway. You know how he is."

Jody did know. His father, Carl Tiflin, insisted upon giving permission for anything that was done on the ranch, whether it was important or not. Jody sagged farther against the post until he was sitting on the ground. He looked up at the little puffs of wind-driven cloud. "It is like to rain, Billy?"

"It might. The wind's good for it, but not strong enough."

"Well, I hope it don't rain until after I kill those damn mice." He looked over his shoulder to see whether Billy had noticed the mature profanity. Billy worked on without comment.

Jody turned back and looked at the side-hill where the road from the outside world came down. The hill was washed with lean March sunshine. Silver thistles, blue lupins and a few poppies bloomed among the sage bushes. Halfway up the hill Jody could see Doubletree Mutt, the black dog, digging in a squirrel hole. He paddled for a while and then paused to kick bursts of dirt out between his hind legs, and he dug with an earnestness which belied the knowledge he must have had that no dog had ever caught a squirrel by digging in a hole.

Suddenly, while Jody watched, the black dog stiffened, and backed out of the hole and looked up the hill toward the cleft in the ridge where the road came through. Jody looked up too. For a moment Carl Tiflin on horseback stood out against the pale sky and then he moved down the road toward the house. He carried something white in his hand.

The boy started to his feet. "He's got a letter," Jody cried. He trotted away toward the ranch house, for the letter would probably be read aloud and he wanted to be there. He reached the house before his father did, and ran in. He heard Carl dismount from his creaking saddle and slap the horse on the side to send it to the barn where Billy would unsaddle it and turn it out.

Jody ran into the kitchen. "We got a letter!" he cried.

His mother looked up from a pan of beans. "Who has?"

"Father has. I saw it in his hand."

Carl strode into the kitchen then, and Jody's mother asked, "Who's the letter from, Carl?"

He frowned quickly. "How did you know there was a letter?"

She nodded her head in the boy's direction. "Big-Britches Jody told me."

Jody was embarrassed.

His father looked down at him contemptuously. "He *is* getting to be a Big-Britches," Carl said. "He's minding everybody's business but his own. Got his big nose into everything."

Mrs. Tiflin relented a little. "Well, he hasn't enough to keep him busy. Who's the letter from?"

Carl still frowned on Jody. "I'll keep him busy if he isn't careful." He held out a sealed letter. "I guess it's from your father."

Mrs. Tiflin took a hairpin from her head and slit open the flap. Her lips pursed judiciously. Jody saw her eyes snap back and forth over the lines. "He says," she translated, "he says he's going to drive out Saturday to stay for a little while. Why, this is Saturday. The letter must have been delayed." She looked at the postmark. "This was mailed day before yesterday.

It should have been here yesterday." She looked up questioningly at her husband, and then her face darkened angrily. "Now what have you got that look on you for? He doesn't come often."

Carl turned his eyes away from her anger. He could be stern with her most of the time, but when occasionally her temper arose, he could not combat it.

"What's the matter with you?" she demanded again.

In his explanation there was a tone of apology Jody himself might have used. "It's just that he talks," Carl said lamely. "Just talks."

"Well, what of it? You talk yourself."

"Sure I do. But your father only talks about one thing."

"Indians!" Jody broke in excitedly. "Indians and crossing the plains!"

Carl turned fiercely on him. "You get out, Mr. Big-Britches! Go on, now! Get out!"

Jody went miserably out the back door and closed the screen with elaborate quietness. Under the kitchen window his shamed, downcast eyes fell upon a curiously shaped stone, a stone of such fascination that he squatted down and picked it up and turned it over in his hands.

The voices came clearly to him through the open kitchen window. "Jody's damn well right," he heard his father say. "Just Indians and crossing the plains. I've heard that story about how the horses got driven off about a thousand times. He just goes on and on, and he never changes a word in the things he tells."

When Mrs. Tiflin answered her tone was so changed that Jody, outside the window, looked up from his study of the stone. Her voice had become soft and explanatory. Jody knew how her face would have changed to match the tone. She said quietly, "Look at it this way, Carl. That was the big thing in my father's life. He led a wagon train clear across the plains to the coast, and when it was finished, his life was done. It was a big thing to do, but it didn't last long enough. Look!" she continued, "it's as though he was born to do that, and after he finished it, there wasn't anything more for him to do but think about it and talk about it. If there'd been any farther west to go, he'd have gone. He's told me so himself. But at last there was the ocean. He lives right by the ocean where he had to stop."

She had caught Carl, caught him and entangled him in her soft tone.

"I've seen him," he agreed quietly. "He goes down and stares off west over the ocean." His voice sharpened a little. "And then he goes up to the Horseshoe Club in Pacific Grove, and he tells people how the Indians drove off the horses."

She tried to catch him again. "Well, it's everything to him. You might be patient with him and pretend to listen."

Carl turned impatiently away. "Well, if it gets too bad, I can always go down to the bunkhouse and sit with Billy," he said irritably. He walked through the house and slammed the front door after him.

Jody ran to his chores. He dumped the grain to the chickens without chasing any of them. He gathered the eggs from the nests. He trotted into the house with the wood and interlaced it so carefully in the wood-box that two armloads seemed to fill it to overflowing.

His mother had finished the beans by now. She stirred up the fire and brushed off the stove-top with a turkey wing. Jody peered cautiously at her to see whether any rancor toward him remained. "Is he coming today?" Jody asked.

"That's what his letter said."

"Maybe I better walk up the road to meet him."

Mrs. Tiflin clanged the stove-lid shut. "That would be nice," she said. "He'd probably like to be met."

"I guess I'll just do it then."

Outside, Jody whistled shrilly to the dogs. "Come on up the hill," he commanded. The two dogs waved their tails and ran ahead. Along the roadside the sage had tender new tips. Jody tore off some pieces and rubbed them on his hands until the air was filled with the sharp wild smell. With a rush the dogs leaped from the road and yapped into the brush after a rabbit. That was the last Jody saw of them, for when they failed to catch the rabbit, they went back home.

Jody plodded on up the hill toward the ridge top. When he reached the little cleft where the road came through, the afternoon wind struck him and blew up his hair and ruffled his shirt. He looked down on the little hills and ridges below and then out at the huge green Salinas Valley. He could see the white town of Salinas far out in the flat and the flash of its windows under the waning sun. Directly below him, in an oak tree, a crow congress had convened. The tree was black with crows all cawing at once.

Then Jody's eyes followed the wagon road down from the ridge where he stood, and lost it behind a hill, and picked it up again on the other side. On that distant stretch he saw a cart slowly pulled by a bay horse. It disappeared behind the hill. Jody sat down on the ground and watched the place where the cart would reappear again. The wind sang on the hilltops and the puff-ball clouds hurried eastward.

Then the cart came into sight and stopped. A man dressed in black dismounted from the seat and walked to the horse's head. Although it was so far away, Jody knew he had unhooked the check-rein, for the horse's head dropped forward. The horse moved on, and the man walked slowly up the hill beside it. Jody gave a glad cry and ran down the road toward them. The squirrels bumped along off the road, and a road-runner flirted its tail and raced over the edge of the hill and sailed out like a glider.

Jody tried to leap into the middle of his shadow at every step. A stone rolled under his foot and he went down. Around a little bend he raced, and there, a short distance ahead, were his grandfather and the cart. The boy dropped from his unseemly running and approached at a dignified walk.

The horse plodded stumble-footedly up the hill and the old man walked beside it. In the lowering sun their giant shadows flickered darkly behind them. The grandfather was dressed in a black broadcloth suit and he wore kid congress gaiters and a black tie on a short, hard collar. He carried his black slouch hat in his hand. His white beard was cropped close and his white eyebrows overhung his eyes like moustaches. The blue eyes were sternly merry. About the whole face and figure there was a granite dignity, so that every motion seemed an impossible thing. Once at rest, it seemed the old man would be stone, would never move again. His steps were slow and certain. Once made, no step could ever be retraced; once headed in a direction, the path would never bend nor the pace increase nor slow.

When Jody appeared around the bend, Grandfather waved his hat slowly in welcome, and he called, "Why, Jody! Come down to meet me, have you?"

Jody sidled near and turned and matched his step to the old man's step and stiffened his body and dragged his heels a little. "Yes, sir," he said. "We got your letter only today."

"Should have been here yesterday," said Grandfather. "It certainly should. How are all the folks?"

"They're fine, sir." He hesitated and then suggested shyly, "Would you like to come on a mouse hunt tomorrow, sir?"

"Mouse hunt, Jody?" Grandfather chuckled. "Have the people of this generation come down to hunting mice? They aren't very strong, the new people, but I hardly thought mice would be game for them."

"No, sir. It's just play. The haystack's gone. I'm going to drive out the mice to the dogs. And you can watch, or even beat the hay a little."

The stern, merry eyes turned down on him. "I see. You don't eat them, then. You haven't come to that yet."

Jody explained, "The dogs eat them, sir. It wouldn't be much like hunting Indians, I guess."

"No, not much—but then later, when the troops were hunting Indians and shooting children and burning teepees, it wasn't much different from your mouse hunt."

They topped the rise and started down into the ranch cup, and they lost the sun from their shoulders. "You've grown," Grandfather said. "Nearly an inch, I should say."

"More," Jody boasted. "Where they mark me on the door, I'm up more than an inch since Thanksgiving even."

Grandfather's rich throaty voice said, "Maybe you're getting too much water and turning to pith and stalk. Wait until you head out, and then we'll see."

Jody looked quickly into the old man's face to see whether his feelings should be hurt, but there was no will to injure, no punishing nor putting-in-your-place light in the keen blue eyes. "We might kill a pig," Jody suggested.

"Oh, no! I couldn't let you do that. You're just humoring me. It isn't the time and you know it."

"You know Riley, the big boar, sir?"

"Yes. I remember Riley well."

"Well, Riley ate a hole into that same haystack, and it fell down on him and smothered him."

"Pigs do that when they can," said Grandfather.

"Riley was a nice pig, for a boar, sir. I rode him sometimes, and he didn't mind."

A door slammed at the house below them, and they saw Jody's mother standing on the porch waving her apron in welcome. And they saw Carl Tiflin walking up from the barn to be at the house for the arrival.

The sun had disappeared from the hills by now. The blue smoke from the house chimney hung in flat layers in the purpling ranch-cup. The puff-ball clouds, dropped by the falling wind, hung listlessly in the sky.

Billy Buck came out of the bunkhouse and flung a wash basin of soapy water on the ground. He had been shaving in mid-week, for Billy held Grandfather in reverence, and Grandfather said that Billy was one of the few men of the new generation who had not gone soft. Although Billy was in middle age, Grandfather considered him a boy. Now Billy was hurrying toward the house too.

When Jody and Grandfather arrived, the three were waiting for them in front of the yard gate.

Carl said, "Hello, sir. We've been looking for you."

Mrs. Tiflin kissed Grandfather on the side of his beard, and stood still while his big hand patted her shoulder. Billy shook hands solemnly, grinning under his straw moustache. "I'll put up your horse," said Billy, and he led the rig away.

Grandfather watched him go, and then, turning back to the group, he said as he had said a hundred times before, "There's a good boy. I knew his father, old Mule-tail Buck. I never knew why they called him Mule-tail except he packed mules."

Mrs. Tiflin turned and led the way into the house. "How long are you going to stay, Father? Your letter didn't say."

"Well, I don't know. I thought I'd stay about two weeks. But I never stay as long as I think I'm going to."

In a short while they were sitting at the white oilcloth table eating their supper. The lamp with the tin reflector hung over the table. Outside the dining-room windows the big moths battered softly against the glass.

Grandfather cut his steak into tiny pieces and chewed slowly. "I'm hungry," he said. "Driving out here got my appetite up. It's like when we were crossing. We all got so hungry every night we could hardly wait to let the meat get done. I could eat about five pounds of buffalo meat every night."

"It's moving around does it," said Billy. "My father was a government packer. I helped him when I was a kid. Just the two of us could about clean up a deer's ham."

"I knew your father, Billy," said Grandfather. "A fine man he was. They called him Mule-tail Buck. I don't know why except he packed mules."

"That was it," Billy agreed. "He packed mules."

Grandfather put down his knife and fork and looked around the table. "I remember one time we ran out of meat—" His voice dropped to a curious low sing-song, dropped into a tonal groove the story had worn for itself. "There was no buffalo, no antelope, not even rabbits. The hunters couldn't even shoot a coyote. That was the time for the leader to be on the watch. I was the leader, and I kept my eyes open. Know why? Well, just the minute the people began to get hungry they'd start slaughtering the team oxen. Do you believe that? I've heard of parties that just ate up their draft cattle. Started from the middle and worked toward the ends. Finally they'd eat the lead pair, and then the wheelers. The leader of a party had to keep them from doing that."

In some manner a big moth got into the room and circled the hanging kerosene lamp. Billy got up and tried to clap it between his hands. Carl struck with a cupped palm and caught the moth and broke it. He walked to the window and dropped it out.

"As I was saying," Grandfather began again, but Carl interrupted him. "You'd better eat some more meat. All the rest of us are ready for our pudding."

Jody saw a flash of anger in his mother's eyes. Grandfather picked up his knife and fork. "I'm pretty hungry, all right," he said. "I'll tell you about that later."

When supper was over, when the family and Billy Buck sat in front of the fireplace in the other room, Jody anxiously watched Grandfather. He saw the signs he knew. The bearded head leaned forward; the eyes lost their sternness and looked wonderingly into the fire; the big lean fingers laced themselves on the black knees. "I wonder," he began, "I just wonder whether I ever told you how those thieving Piutes drove off thirty-five of our horses."

"I think you did," Carl interrupted. "Wasn't it just before you went up into the Tahoe country?"

Grandfather turned quickly toward his son-in-law. "That's right. I guess I must have told you that story."

"Lots of times," Carl said cruelly, and he avoided his wife's eyes. But he felt the angry eyes on him, and he said, " 'Course I'd like to hear it again."

Grandfather looked back at the fire. His fingers unlaced and laced again. Jody knew how he felt, how his insides were collapsed and empty. Hadn't Jody been called a Big-Britches that very afternoon? He arose to heroism and opened himself to the term Big-Britches again. "Tell about Indians," he said softly.

Grandfather's eyes grew stern again. "Boys always want to hear about Indians. It was a job for men, but boys want to hear about it. Well, let's see. Did I ever tell you how I wanted each wagon to carry a long iron plate?"

Everyone but Jody remained silent. Jody said, "No. You didn't."

"Well, when the Indians attacked, we always put the wagons in a circle and fought from between the wheels. I thought that if every wagon carried a long plate with rifle holes, the men could stand the plates on the outside of the wheels when the wagons were in the circle and they would be protected. It would save lives and that would make up for the extra weight of the iron. But of course the party wouldn't do it. No party had done it before and they couldn't see why they should go to the expense. They lived to regret it, too."

Jody looked at his mother, and knew from her expression that she was not listening at all. Carl picked at a callus on his thumb and Billy Buck watched a spider crawling up the wall.

Grandfather's tone dropped into its narrative groove again. Jody knew in advance exactly what words would fall. The story droned on, speeded up for the attack, grew sad over the wounds, struck a dirge at the burials on the great plains. Jody sat quietly watching Grandfather. The stern blue eyes were detached. He looked as though he were not very interested in the story himself.

When it was finished, when the pause had been politely respected as the frontier of the story, Billy Buck stood up and stretched and hitched his trousers. "I guess I'll turn in," he said. Then he faced Grandfather. "I've got an old powder horn and a cap and ball pistol down to the bunkhouse. Did I ever show them to you?"

Grandfather nodded slowly. "Yes, I think you did, Billy. Reminds me of a pistol I had when I was leading the people across." Billy stood politely until the little story was done, and then he said, "Good night," and went out of the house.

Carl Tiflin tried to turn the conversation then. "How's the country between here and Monterey? I've heard it's pretty dry."

"It is dry," said Grandfather. "There's not a drop of water in the Laguna Seca. But it's a long pull from '87. The whole country was powder then, and in '61 I believe all the coyotes starved to death. We had fifteen inches of rain this year."

"Yes, but it all came too early. We could do with some now." Carl's eye fell on Jody. "Hadn't you better be getting to bed?"

Jody stood up obediently. "Can I kill the mice in the old haystack, sir?"

"Mice? Oh! Sure, kill them all off. Billy said there isn't any good hay left."

Jody exchanged a secret and satisfying look with Grandfather. "I'll kill every one tomorrow," he promised.

Jody lay in his bed and thought of the impossible world of Indians and buffaloes, a world that had ceased to be forever. He wished he could have been living in the heroic time, but he knew he was not of heroic timber. No one living now, save possibly Billy Buck, was worthy to do the things that had been done. A race of giants had lived then, fearless men, men of a staunchness unknown in this day. Jody thought of the wide plains and of the wagons moving across like centipedes. He thought of Grandfather on a huge white horse, marshaling the people. Across his mind marched the great phantoms, and they marched off the earth and they were gone.

He came back to the ranch for a moment, then. He heard the dull rushing sound that space and silence make. He heard one of the dogs, out in the doghouse, scratching a flea and bumping his elbow against the floor with every stroke. Then the wind arose again and the black cypress groaned and Jody went to sleep.

He was up half an hour before the triangle sounded for breakfast. His mother was rattling the stove to make the flames roar when Jody went through the kitchen. "You're up early," she said. "Where are you going?"

"Out to get a good stick. We're going to kill the mice today."

"Who is 'we'?"

"Why, Grandfather and I."

"So you've got him in it. You always like to have someone in with you in case there's blame to share."

"I'll be right back," said Jody. "I just want to have a good stick ready for after breakfast."

He closed the screen door after him and went out into the cool blue morning. The birds were noisy in the dawn and the ranch cats came down from the hill like blunt snakes. They had been hunting gophers in the dark, and although the four cats were full of gopher meat, they sat in a semicircle at the back door and mewed piteously for milk. Doubletree Mutt and Smasher moved sniffing along the edge of the brush, performing the duty with rigid ceremony, but when Jody whistled, their heads jerked up and their tails waved. They plunged down to him, wriggling their skins and yawning. Jody patted their heads seriously, and moved on to the weathered scrap pile. He selected an old broom handle and a short piece of inch-square scrap wood. From his pocket he took a shoelace and tied the ends of the sticks loosely together to make a flail. He whistled his new weapon through the air and struck the ground experimentally, while the dogs leaped aside and whined with apprehension.

Jody turned and started down past the house toward the old haystack ground to look over the field of slaughter, but Billy Buck, sitting patiently on the back steps, called to him, "You better come back. It's only a couple of minutes till breakfast."

Jody changed his course and moved toward the house. He leaned his flail against the steps. "That's to drive the mice out," he said. "I'll bet they're fat. I'll bet they don't know what's going to happen to them today."

"No, nor you either," Billy remarked philosophically, "nor me, nor anyone."

Jody was staggered by this thought. He knew it was true. His imagination twitched away from the mouse hunt. Then his mother came out on the back porch and struck the triangle, and all thoughts fell in a heap.

Grandfather hadn't appeared at the table when they sat down. Billy nodded at his empty chair. "He's all right? He isn't sick?"

"He takes a long time to dress," said Mrs. Tiflin. "He combs his whiskers and rubs up his shoes and brushes his clothes."

Carl scattered sugar on his mush. "A man that's led a wagon train across the plains has got to be pretty careful how he dresses."

Mrs. Tiflin turned to him. "Don't do that, Carl! Please don't!" There was more of threat than of request in her tone. And the threat irritated Carl.

"Well, how many times do I have to listen to the story of the iron plates, and the thirty-five horses? That time's done. Why can't he forget it, now it's done?" He grew angrier while he talked, and his voice rose. "Why does he have to tell them over and over? He came across the plains. All right! Now it's finished. Nobody wants to hear about it over and over."

The door into the kitchen closed softly. The four at the table sat frozen. Carl laid his mush spoon on the table and touched his chin with his fingers.

Then the kitchen door opened and Grandfather walked in. His mouth smiled tightly and his eyes were squinted. "Good morning," he said, and he sat down and looked at his mush dish.

Carl could not leave it there. "Did—did you hear what I said?"

Grandfather jerked a little nod.

"I don't know what got into me, sir. I didn't mean it. I was just being funny."

Jody glanced in shame at his mother, and he saw that she was looking at

Carl, and that she wasn't breathing. It was an awful thing that he was doing. He was tearing himself to pieces to talk like that. It was a terrible thing to him to retract a word, but to retract it in shame was infinitely worse.

Grandfather looked sidewise. "I'm trying to get right side up," he said gently. "I'm not being mad. I don't mind what you said, but it might be true, and I would mind that."

"It isn't true," said Carl. "I'm not feeling well this morning. I'm sorry I said it."

"Don't be sorry, Carl. An old man doesn't see things sometimes. Maybe you're right. The crossing is finished. Maybe it should be forgotten, now it's done."

Carl got up from the table. "I've had enough to eat. I'm going to work. Take your time, Billy!" He walked quickly out of the dining-room. Billy gulped the rest of his food and followed soon after. But Jody could not leave his chair.

"Won't you tell any more stories?" Jody asked.

"Why, sure I'll tell them, but only when—I'm sure people want to hear them."

"I like to hear them, sir."

"Oh! Of course you do, but you're a little boy. It was a job for men, but only little boys like to hear about it."

Jody got up from his place. "I'll wait outside for you, sir. I've got a good stick for those mice."

He waited by the gate until the old man came out on the porch. "Let's go down and kill the mice now," Jody called.

"I think I'll just sit in the sun, Jody. You go kill the mice."

"You can use my stick if you like."

"No, I'll just sit here a while."

Jody turned disconsolately away, and walked down toward the old haystack. He tried to whip up his enthusiasm with thoughts of the fat juicy mice. He beat the ground with his flail. The dogs coaxed and whined about him, but he could not go. Back at the house he could see Grandfather sitting on the porch, looking small and thin and black.

Jody gave up and went to sit on the steps at the old man's feet.

"Back already? Did you kill the mice?"

"No, sir. I'll kill them some other day."

The morning flies buzzed close to the ground and the ants dashed about in front of the steps. The heavy smell of sage slipped down the hill. The porch boards grew warm in the sunshine.

Jody hardly knew when Grandfather started to talk. "I shouldn't stay here, feeling the way I do." He examined his strong old hands. "I feel as though the crossing wasn't worth doing." His eyes moved up the side-hill and stopped on a motionless hawk perched on a dead limb. "I tell those old stories, but they're not what I want to tell. I only know how I want people to feel when I tell them.

"It wasn't Indians that were important, nor adventures, nor even getting out here. It was a whole bunch of people made into one big crawling beast. And I was the head. It was westering and westering. Every man wanted something for himself, but the big beast that was all of them wanted only westering. I was the leader, but if I hadn't been there, someone else would have been the head. The thing had to have a head.

"Under the little bushes the shadows were black at white noonday. When we saw the mountains at last, we cried—all of us. But it wasn't getting here that mattered, it was movement and westering.

"We carried life out here and set it down the way those ants carry eggs. And I was the leader. The westering was as big as God, and the slow steps that made the movement piled up and piled up until the continent was crossed.

"Then we came down to the sea, and it was done." He stopped and wiped his eyes until the rims were red. "That's what I should be telling instead of stories."

When Jody spoke, Grandfather started and looked down at him. "Maybe I could lead the people some day," Jody said.

The old man smiled. "There's no place to go. There's the ocean to stop you. There's a line of old men along the shore hating the ocean because it stopped them."

"In boats I might, sir."

"No place to go, Jody. Every place is taken. But that's not the worst—no, not the worst. Westering has died out of the people. Westering isn't a hunger any more. It's all done. Your father is right. It is finished." He laced his fingers on his knee and looked at them.

Jody felt very sad. "If you'd like a glass of lemonade I could make it for you."

Grandfather was about to refuse, and then he saw Jody's face. "That would be nice," he said. "Yes, it would be nice to drink a lemonade."

Jody ran into the kitchen where his mother was wiping the last of the breakfast dishes. "Can I have a lemon to make a lemonade for Grandfather?"

His mother mimicked—"And another lemon to make a lemonade for you."

"No, ma'am. I don't want one."

"Jody! You're sick!" Then she stopped suddenly. "Take a lemon out of the cooler," she said softly. "Here, I'll reach the squeezer down to you."

Kay Boyle (1903–   ) was born in Minnesota, but married young and spent most of her adult life in Europe. A novelist and short-story writer, she has had her stories widely reprinted, especially in the O. Henry Memorial Award anthologies. Presently she is a writer-in-residence in California. For further reading: The White Horses of Vienna, and Other Stories (1936).

Black Boy

KAY BOYLE

A t that time, it was the forsaken part, it was the other end of the city, and on early spring mornings there was no one about. By soft words, you could woo the horse into the foam, and ride her with the sea knee-deep around her. The waves came in and out there, as indolent as ladies, gathered up their skirts in their hands and, with a murmur, came tiptoeing in across the velvet sand.

The wooden promenade was high there, and when the wind was up the water came running under it like wild. On such days, you had to content yourself with riding the horse over the deep white drifts of dry sand on the other side of the walks; the horse's hoofs here made no sound and the sparks of sand stung your face in fury. It had no body to it, like the mile or two of sand packed hard that you could open out on once the tide was down.

My little grandfather, Puss, was alive then, with his delicate gait and ankles, and his belly pouting in his dove-gray clothes. When he saw from the window that the tide was sidling out, he put on his pearl fedora and came stepping down the street. For a minute, he put one foot on the sand, but he was not at ease there. On the boardwalk over our heads was some other kind of life in progress. If you looked up, you could see it in motion through the cracks in the timber: rolling chairs, and women in high heels proceeding, if the weather were fair.

"You know," my grandfather said, "I think I might like to have a look at a shop or two along the boardwalk." Or: "I suppose you don't feel like leaving the beach for a minute," or: "If you would go with me, we might take a chair together, and look at the hats and the dresses and roll along in the sun."

He was alive then, taking his pick of the broad easy chairs and the black boys.

"There's a nice skinny boy," he'd say. "He looks as though he might put some action into it. Here you are, sonny. Push me and the little girl down to the Million Dollar Pier and back."

The cushions were red velvet with a sheen of dew over them. And Puss settled back on them and took my hand in his. In his mind there was no hesitation about whether he would look at the shops on one side, or out on the vacant side where there was nothing shining but the sea.

"What's your name, Charlie?" Puss would say without turning his head to the black boy pushing the chair behind our shoulders.

"Charlie's my name, sir," he'd answer with his face dripping down like tar in the sun.

"What's your name, sonny?" Puss would say another time, and the black boy answered:

"Sonny's my name, sir."

"What's your name, Big Boy?"

"Big Boy's my name."

He never wore a smile on his face, the black boy. He was thin as a shadow but darker, and he was pushing and sweating, getting the chair down to the Million Dollar Pier and back again, in and out through the people. If you turned toward the sea for a minute, you could see his face out of the corner of your eye, hanging black as a bat's wing, nodding and nodding like a dark heavy flower.

But in the early morning, he was the only one who came down onto the sand and sat under the beams of the boardwalk, sitting idle there with a languor fallen on every limb. He had long bones. He sat idle there, with his clothes shrunk up from his wrists and his ankles, with his legs drawn up, looking out at the sea.

"I might be a king if I wanted to be," was what he said to me.

Maybe I was twelve years old, or maybe I was ten when we used to sit eating dog biscuits together. Sometimes when you broke them in two, a worm fell out and the black boy lifted his sharp finger and flecked it carelessly from off his knee.

"I seen kings," he said, "with a kind of cloth over they heads, and kind of jewels-like around here and there. They weren't any blacker than me, if as black," he said. "I could be almost anything I made up my mind to be."

"King Nebuchadnezzar," I said. "He wasn't a white man."

The wind was off the ocean and was filled with alien smells. It was early in the day, and no human sign was given. Overhead were the green beams of the boardwalk and no wheel or step to sound it.

"If I was a king," said the black boy with his biscuit in his fingers, "I wouldn't put much stock in hanging around here."

Great crystal jelly beasts were quivering in a hundred different colors on the wastes of sand around us. The dogs came, jumping them, and when they saw me still sitting still, they wheeled like gulls and sped back to the sea.

"I'd be traveling around," he said, "here and there. Now here, now there. I'd change most of my habits."

His hair grew all over the top of his head in tight dry rosettes. His neck was longer and more shapely than a white man's neck, and his fingers ran in and out of the sand like the blue feet of a bird.

"I wouldn't have much to do with pushing chairs around under them circumstances," he said. "I might even give up sleeping out here on the sand."

Or if you came out when it was starlight, you could see him sitting there in the clear white darkness. I could go and come as I liked, for whenever I went out the door, I had the dogs shouldering behind me. At night, they shook the taste of the house out of their coats and came down across the sand. There he was, with his knees up, sitting idle.

"They used to be all kinds of animals come down here to drink in the dark," he said. "They was a kind of a mirage came along and gave that impression. I seen tigers, lions, lambs, deer; I seen ostriches drinking down there side by side with each other. They's the Northern Lights gets crossed some way and switches the wrong picture down."

It may be that the coast has changed there, for even then it was changing. The lighthouse that had once stood far out on the white rocks near the outlet was standing then like a lighted torch in the heart of the town. And the deep currents of the sea may have altered so that the clearest water runs in another direction, and houses may have been built down as far as where the brink used to be. But the brink was so perilous then that every word the black boy spoke seemed to fall into a cavern of beauty.

"I seen camels; I seen zebras," he said. "I might have caught any of one of them if I'd felt inclined."

The street was so still and wide then that when Puss stepped out of the house, I could hear him clearing his throat of the sharp salty air. He had no intention of soiling the soles of his boots, but he came down the street to find me.

"If you feel like going with me," he said, "we'll take a chair and see the fifty-seven varieties changing on the electric sign."

And then he saw the black boy sitting quiet. His voice drew up short on his tongue and he touched his white mustache.

"I shouldn't think it a good idea," he said, and he put his arm through my arm. "I saw another little oak not three inches high in the Jap's window yesterday. We might roll down the boardwalk and have a look at it. You know," said Puss, and he put his kind gloves carefully on his fingers, "that black boy might do you some kind of harm."

"What kind of harm could he do me?" I said.

"Well," said Puss with the garlands of lights hanging around him, "he might steal some money from you. He might knock you down and take your money away."

"How could he do that?" I said. "We just sit and talk there." Puss looked at me sharply.

"What do you find to sit and talk about?" he said.

"I don't know," I said. "I don't remember. It doesn't sound like much to tell it."

The burden of his words was lying there on my heart when I woke up in the morning. I went out by myself to the stable and led the horse to the door and put the saddle on her. If Puss were ill at ease for a day or two, he could look out the window in peace and see me riding high and mighty away. The day after tomorrow, I thought, or the next day, I'll sit down on the beach again and talk to the black boy. But when I rode out, I saw him seated idle there, under the boardwalk, heedless, looking away to the cool wide sea. He had been eating peanuts and the shells lay all around him. The dogs came running at the horse's heels, nipping the foam that lay along the tide.

The horse was as shy as a bird that morning, and when I drew her up beside the black boy, she tossed her head on high. Her mane went back and forth, from one side to the other, and a flight of joy in her limbs sent her forelegs like rockets into the air. The black boy stood up from the cold smooth sand, unsmiling, but a spark of wonder shone in his marble eyes. He put out his arm in the short tight sleeve of his coat and stroked her shivering shoulder.

"I was going to be a jockey once," he said, "but I changed my mind."

I slid down on one side while he climbed up the other.

"I don't know as I can ride him right," he said as I held her head. "The kind of saddle you have, it gives you nothing to grip your heels around. I ride them with their bare skin."

The black boy settled himself on the leather and put his feet in the stirrups. He was quiet and quick with delight, but he had no thought of smiling as he took the reins in his hands.

I stood on the beach with the dogs beside me, looking after the horse as she ambled down to the water. The black boy rode easily and straight, letting the horse stretch out and sneeze and canter. When they reached the jetty, he turned her casually and brought her loping back.

"Some folks licks hell out of their horses," he said. "I'd never raise a hand to one, unless he was to bite me or do something I didn't care for."

He sat in the saddle at ease, as though in a rocker, stroking her shoulder with his hand spread open, and turning in the stirrups to smooth her shining flank.

"Jockeys make a pile of money," I said.

"I wouldn't care for the life they have," said the black boy. "They have to watch their diet so careful."

His fingers ran delicately through her hair and laid her mane back on her neck.

When I was up on the horse again, I turned her toward the boardwalk.

"I'm going to take her over the jetty," I said. "You'll see how she clears it. I'll take her up under the boardwalk to give her a good start."

I struck her shoulder with the end of my crop, and she started toward the tough black beams. She was under it, galloping, when the dogs came down the beach like mad. They had chased a cat out of cover and were after it, screaming as they ran, with a wing of sand blowing wide behind them, and when the horse saw them under her legs, she jumped sidewise in sprightliness and terror and flung herself against an iron arch.

For a long time I heard nothing at all in my head except the melody of someone crying, whether it was my dead mother holding me in comfort, or the soft wind grieving over me where I had fallen. I lay on the sand asleep; I could feel it running with my tears through my fingers. I was rocked in a cradle of love, cradled and rocked in sorrow.

"Oh, my little lamb, my little lamb pie!" Oh, sorrow, sorrow, wailed the wind, or the tide, or my own kin about me. "Oh, lamb, oh, lamb!"

I could feel the long swift fingers of love untying the terrible knot of pain that bound my head. And I put my arms around him and lay close to his heart in comfort.

Puss was alive then, and when he met the black boy carrying me up to the house, he struck him square across the mouth.

James T. Farrell (1904–   ), a native of Chicago, established his reputation as a novelist with the Studs Lonigan trilogy (1935). Noted for his focus on social inequities among the lower middle class, he is generally regarded as a representative figure of contemporary "naturalistic" fiction. For further reading: $1,000 a Week, and Other Stories (1942), To Whom It May Concern (1944).

The Benefits of American Life

JAMES T. FARRELL

Takiss Tillios was a strong shepherd boy whose home land was located just at the hollow valley of two mountains in Arcadia, Greece, in the central section of the Peloponnesus. He grew up on goat's milk and on pitch black bread whose cinders were not separated so as to produce more bread per pound. His hard-working mother sold a piece of land, which produced enough wheat to pull the family through the whole year, in order to pay his steerage fare to America. For in America the streets were paved with gold; the buildings were taller than mountains; the women all dressed like princesses and the men had their pockets lined with money; every boy had a bicycle; and every man and woman owned an automobile. At the age of thirteen, Takiss, large for his age, arrived in a paradise known as Chicago.

He was met at the railroad station, a scared and bewildered boy, by a relative who took him to a home on South Halsted Street. With voluable beneficence, the relative immediately employed Takiss, offering him a salary of fifteen dollars a month and the privilege of sleeping on marble slabs in his candy kitchen. He told Takiss that all successful Greek men started that way, and he showed the boy Greek newspapers with pictures of stern, mustachioed Greek restaurant owners and candy-store proprietors who recounted the story of their rise to fame and offered themselves as favorable candidates for marriage. And as a final word of advice, the relative told Takiss that his mother was getting old now, and that he should send her some of his wages to help her out.

Takiss quickly discovered what it meant to live in paradise. It meant working from six in the morning until six in the evening, and until even later on week-ends. It meant sweeping out the store, washing dishes and windows, polishing, arranging, mopping, running errands. It meant attending night school to learn English when he could scarcely keep his eyes open and where he was frequently laughed at for his blundering efforts. It meant walking along, living in the midst of dirty streets where coal dust, soot, smoke, and poisonous fumes of automobiles choked his nostrils and made him cough. It meant lonesome memories. For a long period, Takiss was a lonely boy remembering his homeland and his Grecian mountain, remembering the long, slow days with the sheep, remembering the smile and kiss of his old mother, remembering always.

And he was afraid of America, and of that tremendous paradise known as Chicago. He worked doggedly day after day, earning fifteen dollars a month, catching a cough from sleeping on marble slabs. He worked doggedly, and from his wages he saved a pittance which he deposited in an immigrant's savings bank. But he looked ahead to the day when he would be famous, with his picture in the Greek newspapers, a pride and an honor to his native Greece and to the great tradition of the great Socrates about whom his relative so frequently boasted. He dreamed of the time when he would become like Americans, talk like them, wear their clothes, ride in automobiles just as they did, walk along the streets with pretty American girls.

In time, Takiss learned things. He learned American words, but never how to speak them like an American. He learned that he was considered a dirty Greek greenhorn, and that many Americans would have been just as pleased if he and many of his countrymen had never come to their land. And he learned that American girls laughed sardonically at a young Greek greenhorn. Also, he learned of a place owned by a cousin of his, where for a little money he could go and find American girls who did not laugh at a Greek greenhorn, at least for five or ten minutes. He learned how to buy American clothes on installments, to wear a purple silk shirt, purple socks, and an orange tie. And he learned, also, that in the store he could put some of the money received for sales into his pocket instead of into the cash register.

Eventually, the cousin employing him discharged him in anger, branding him a crook, a robber, a traitor. In the heated quarrel, Takiss asked him why, if he wanted honesty, he paid only six dollars a week wages, when he made so much money himself selling bad products and got his picture in the Greek newspapers as a successful pioneer in America.

Takiss was employed by other of his countrymen, in fruit stores, soda parlors, at hot-dog stands, and in restaurants. He acquired additional American knowledge, and more American words. And sometimes when he was dressed up, wearing his purple silk shirt, with socks to match, and the orange tie, he would walk in the parks or along Halsted Street, seeing American girls, wishing that he had one of his own, a blonde girl with a beautiful pink-white complexion.

Time slid from under Takiss, and he was a young man in his early twenties, with his first citizenship papers. He had worked like a dog, and he was still slaving at the same jobs, performing the same tasks and chores as he had always done since he had come to America. He earned eight dollars a week and was busy twelve hours a day in a candy store. He cleaned and mopped; he scrubbed; he polished; he washed; he waited on trade. And often when he was alone in the store he pocketed money from the cash register. Every week he deposited money in the bank, and almost nightly he looked in his bank book, proud of his savings, thinking of how he was going to achieve fame in America. But he was never able to save money, because he was always quitting or losing jobs and having to use savings to support himself between jobs, as well as to send money to his mother.

And he learned another thing . . . he learned how to dance like Americans. A Greek-American friend told him of a dancing school called a taxi-dance hall on West Madison Street, and showed him an advertisement from the Greek-American owner, Professor Christopolos, who stated in the ad that anyone could be as graceful as he if they learned dancing from his beautiful girls at only ten cents a dance. He paid a dollar and was given ten tickets and entered the dimly lighted dancing school of Professor Christopolos on the fourth floor of a dingy and decrepit building. Each ticket was good for one dance which lasted from a minute to a minute and a half. Any girl in the place would dance with him, because she received five cents for each dance. Takiss' tickets were quickly used up, and he bought more. It did not matter if he danced woodenly and clumsily, and the girls acted delighted to teach him. He went to this taxi-dance hall regularly, spending three, four, and five dollars every visit, and once in a while a girl would ask him if he wanted to take her home, and for a few more dollars he could get other favors, too. After he started going to the taxi-dance hall regularly he was able to save less money, and he sent little to his mother.

Takiss then spent some of his savings for a suit with bell-bottom trousers. He cultivated a mustache and long sideburns, greased his hair and parted it in the middle with meticulous attention. He began to look like a sheik, and listened to pick up all the words which the American-born sheiks used. He went to public dance halls where there was only an admission fee and longer dances. At these places, there were always swarms of girls, pretty American girls, some of them tall and beautiful blondes with milky skins and red lips like cherries. He would ask them to dance. Often they would dance with him, once. He would talk, and they would catch his accent, and when he asked them for a second dance they would thank him with great regret and exclaim that all their other dances were taken. So he would quickly be driven to dancing with the homely and ugly girls who were called wall-flowers. And then he would go back to Professor Christopolos' dancing school, where all the girls would dance with him for ten cents a dance.

One day, Takiss was twenty-five. His native Grecian mountains seemed to have receded in time and he saw them only in painful mists of memory, recalling their details and contours with lessening concreteness. Greece to him was a memory. He had been in America for twelve years, and he was working ten hours a day in a hot-dog stand for ten dollars a week, and able to graft from three to five dollars a week extra. He wanted to make money and to become famous like some of his Americanized countrymen. And when he was a rich man with a hot-dog stand or a restaurant of his own, he would return to Greece with an American wife and act like a millionaire. And he had thirty-five dollars in the bank as a start toward these riches. He wanted to get more money, but not by running a brothel as his fourth cousin George did, and not bootlegging as did George's friend, Mike. He remembered the things his mother, now dead, had told him, and he wanted to make his money and his fame in a way that his mother would have approved of. And then he would have his picture in a Greek-American newspaper.

And hard times came to America. Takiss was out of work in the winter, and again his savings melted. He was employed for ten dollars a week in a candy store, still working twelve hours a day, and in four months that job was gone. He worked for seven dollars a week washing dishes in a large restaurant, and then his pay was cut to five dollars, and he went home every night tired, with chafed hands and an aching back. He had less money, also, for taxi dances. And he lost that job.

He walked the streets looking for other work, and always he learned the same story . . . hard times. He ate very frugally, lived in a chilly, rat-infested room, and wished that he was back home again in his native Grecian mountains, or else that he was a rich and famous American-Greek. Every day he went out looking for a job, and sometimes he found work for a few days or a few weeks and was able to skim along while he tried again to find work.

One day he saw an advertisement with large letters at the top . . . DANCE MARATHON. The word Marathon struck him. Greek. He would win it and win another victory for his country as it had been done in ancient times. He would become a famous Greek athlete. He investigated, and learned that it was a contest in which everybody tried to dance longer than the others, and the winner received a five-hundred-dollar prize. And maybe if he won it, he would get a job in the moving pictures and become the idol of American girls, or go on the vaudeville stage, or be hired to dance in a cabaret. And while he was in the contest, he would be cared for, fed, and there would be no room rent to pay. He was strong and husky, even if he had been getting coughs in his chest for years ever since he had slept on those marble slabs. And he could dance. He was used to standing on his feet all day at work. And this was his chance to become rich. He would no longer have to tramp all over town to be told that there were no jobs because it was hard times. This was much better than saving up to own a candy store and grow fat like the American-Greeks for whom he had worked. And after he won this contest, and became famous, he would go back to Greece with a trunk full of clothes and money, and maybe a rich American girl whose skin was like milk.

Takiss entered the dance marathon, and when the rules were explained to him, he only understood that he was to stay out on the floor and dance, and if he was able to do that longer than anyone else, he would get five hundred dollars. A number was pinned on his back, and he was assigned a partner named Marie Glenn, a beautiful blonde American girl of the type he had always dreamed of as a possible wife. At first, when she met him, she shuddered, and her face broke into an expression of disgust. But then she saw that he was strong and husky with broad shoulders, and she smiled, offering him a limp hand and sweetly telling him that she knew they were sure going to be the winners.

The dance marathon was conducted in a public dance hall on the south side of Chicago. A ring was placed in the center with an orchestra dais at one end. Around the ring there were box seats, and behind them, rising rows of bleacher benches. The opening was described, in advertisements, as gala. An announcer talked through a microphone, and the promoters and judges wearing tuxedos also addressed a full house. The contestants were introduced and some of them, but not Takiss, spoke to the crowd and the large radio audience all over America. It was all a new and promising, if confusing, world to Takiss, and he walked around the floor, feeling as lost and as out of place as he had on those first days in America. But it was leading at last to paradise.

The contest swung into action. They danced for three minutes out of every ten, and walked around and around the floor for the remaining time; and they were given fifteen minutes rest out of every hour. There was glamor in being watched by so many people, in eating sandwiches and drinking coffee before them, in receiving attention from doctors and nurses, and meeting all the others who, like himself, saw at the end of this contest five hundred dollars and fame. As the contestants got to talking to each other, Takiss heard them using one word over and over again . . . celebrity. A celebrity was somebody who was important, like Jack Dempsey and movie stars and Mr. Delphos, the famous American-Greek who was wealthy and owned a large dance hall known as the Bourbon Palace. They all wanted to be celebrities. And Takiss, too, he determined that he was going to be a celebrity.

Takiss had not imagined that anyone could dance for more than a week like this, and that maybe after a sleepless and tiring week he would be the winner. In less than twenty-four hours he learned that it was a grind more gruelling than he had calculated, and while he doggedly gritted his teeth, he determined that he would not let himself drop out. Still, he wished that he had not entered it. He wished he were back working in fruit stores and ice cream parlors the way he had been before hard times had come. He wished that he were a shepherd back in the Grecian mountains.

When his partner was tired, she put her arms around his neck or hips, laid her head against him, and fell asleep while he dragged her heavily around the floor, and when he fell asleep she did the same thing with him. Again and again their bodies were jolted, shoved, pushed against each other, and he began wanting her so that her very nearness became excruciating. And he noticed that she, particularly in the early dog hours of the mornings when there were scarcely any spectators in the hall, began brushing herself against him at every opportunity, looking feverishly into his eyes and telling him smutty jokes. And the other dancers became the same way, and the fellows used to tell him how much they wanted one of these girls, any girl.

Day after day the marathon went on. His eyes grew heavy. His back ached. His feet became sore and raw, so that each step was pain and he felt often as if he were walking on fire. The hall was almost continuously stale with cigarette smoke and foul with body odors. He felt constantly dirty, sweaty, itchy. Dust got into his nostrils and his eyes. He began to cough again. His muscles knotted. He became like a person who was always only half awake, and everything took on the semblance of being a semi-dream. Marie, also, changed. She began to swell around the buttocks. Deep circles grew under her eyes. She became haggard and blowsy and looked like a worn-out prostitute. She used more and more cosmetics, and her face became like a ghastly caricature of the pretty girl who had entered the contest.

In the beginning, particularly because of his accent and Greek heritage, Takiss became the butt of many jokes. Constantly, he would be asked why he wasn't running a restaurant, and he would be given orders for a piece zapple pie kid. He was nicknamed Restaurant, Fruit Store, Socrates, and Zapple Pie Kid. In time, this wore down and failed to anger or disturb him. The grind settled into habitual misery and torture. He, like the other contestants, would long for fresh air, and during rest periods, when they were not so tired that they would be dragged like walking somnambulists to the rest cots, they would enter the vile and filthy dressing rooms or the equally unsavory lavatory and jam their heads out of the windows to breathe fresh air and to look yearningly down at the street where people walked free to do what they wished, not tired, able to breathe fresh air, even the fresh air of a city street that was saturated with carbon monoxide fumes and sootiness.

Day after day dragged on. Sometimes Takiss, Marie, or the other contestants would live in stupors of six, twelve hours a day, even longer. As

the time passed, the contestants would switch from affected and over-stimu-
lated good spirits to nasty, fighting nervousness, and then into that glaze-
eyed stupor. Particularly in those dog hours of the early morning, they
would be raw, if awake, and fight and curse. Sex, too, became a growing
obsession, and in time was almost madness. Living so near to one another,
their bodies touching so frequently, they told smuttier and smuttier jokes.
Perversities and desires or propositions for perversities sprang up among
them. It became a relentless process of both physical and mental torture.
Constipation, diarrhea, sudden inabilities to control their kidneys so that
now and then a contestant would be walking around the floor, drugged in
sleep, with wet lines down his trousers, or if a girl, down her beach pyjamas
which most of them wore regularly. Broken blood vessels and swollen veins
in the legs. Headaches, eye troubles, sore throats, fevers, colds. Periods of
sweatiness, followed by shivers and chills. And always that returning stupor,
caused by sleeplessness and fatigue, and by the dreams and fantasies which
they entertained as relief from that endless procession around and around
the floor. And at the end of it all, money, the chance to become a celebrity,
sex, and clean white bed sheets and a soft, fresh bed.

Ways of making money from day to day quickly developed and were
used to the utmost so that all of the contestants started bank accounts.
Every one of them developed some trick or act, a song, a dance, a stunt
of some kind, and after putting it on, they would be showered with money
from the crowd. One of the contestants, a raw country youth of Lithuanian
origin with a nasal twang to his voice, chewed razor blades as his stunt.
Takiss learned a dance. Stores, theatres, and politicians also paid them fees
to wear signs or sweaters and jerseys with advertising printed on the front
or back. Money was sent to them, mash notes, written in as ignorant and
as bad English as that which Takiss used and wrote in. The various spectators picked favorites, cheered for them, shouted encouragement.

And still the days stretched out, past the first month, with contestant
after contestant dropping out, and the field narrowing down. One day there
would be a birthday party. Another day there was a floor wedding between
two of the contestants who had been on the floor, and the wedding provided
endless hours of raw jokes and humor about when they would have their
wedding night, until, sex-crazed, both of the newlyweds went temporarily
out of their heads and the girl screamed until she was dragged off the floor.
Disqualified, they were out of the marathon, and a new note was introduced
in the humor. Another day, a girl had an abscessed tooth extracted on the
floor, and immediately afterward she rejoined the endless walking procession that tramped around in this ever dullening stupor. Another day, an
Italian boy, who with his wife had entered the marathon because they were
both unemployed and had been evicted, required crutches and ran a high
fever. With his eyes intense from the fever, with suffering imprinted on his

haggard face, he hobbled around and around. After twelve such hours he was forced out by the judges on the advice of a doctor.

Again and again Takiss wanted to quit and satisfy himself with the incidental money he had taken in, and as repeatedly he would go patiently on. Like the others, he would fall into that lumbrous sleep, and external means would be necessary to awaken him so that he might continue. The male nurses would slap him in the face with wet towels, put his shoes on the wrong feet, strap him into an electric vibrator machine, poke their fingers down his throat, tickle his calloused soles. During one period, his cough developed into a severe cold in the chest. For another period, he was not out of his stupor for three days. And Marie, his partner, experienced the same tortures. They went on. Days and nights, and days and nights, with the field narrowing to thirteen, ten, eight, five, finally two couples. Then Marie collapsed and was carried off the floor and shipped to a hospital, and Takiss was disqualified. They each collected the two hundred and fifty dollars second place money.

After recuperation, Takiss entered other dance marathons, and became a professional. He secured a copy of *Yes, We Have No Bananas* with a Greek translation, and this, with his dance stunt, became very popular. He was able, with both attractions and with a growing audience of fans, to earn from ten to fifteen dollars a day in extra money. Even when he was forced to retire from marathons or was disqualified, he departed with added money. Again the desire to return to his homeland like a rich American grew upon him, and now his bank account, with foreign exchange rates, would make him very rich in Greece. He was something of a celebrity in this new world of his. His biography and picture appeared in Greek newspapers. A Greek merchant who sold a raisin beverage paid him and Marie each a hundred dollars to be photographed for a newspaper advertisement in which there was their signed testimony that they drank this beverage. He had a run of a week at a small theatre on South Halsted Street where there were many Greeks. Takiss became a famous American-Greek.

In all, Takiss participated in sixteen dance marathons. In eight of them, he collected money and was the winner of a thousand-dollar super-marathon in which only finalists from other marathons were permitted to enter and in which there were no rest periods. He had money now, five thousand dollars. He returned to Greece. But the strain of the marathons had ruined his lungs and he had tuberculosis. Resorts for tuberculosis had been developed in his native mountains, and when he returned it was necessary for him to become a patient in one of them, and the money he had earned was paid out while he lived there with his lungs rotting away on him.

Saul Bellow (1915–   ) was born in Quebec, Canada, but grew up in Chicago where he still teaches on occasion at the University of Chicago. His first novel was The Dangling Man (1944), followed by The Adventures of Augie March (1953), Henderson the Rain King (1959), and Herzog (1964). For his selected stories, read Seize the Day (1957).

Looking for Mr. Green

SAUL BELLOW

Whatsoever thy hand findeth to do, do it with thy might. . . .

Hard work? No, it wasn't really so hard. He wasn't used to walking and stair-climbing, but the physical difficulty of his new job was not what George Grebe felt most. He was delivering relief checks in the Negro district, and although he was a native Chicagoan this was not a part of the city he knew much about—it needed a depression to introduce him to it. No, it wasn't literally hard work, not as reckoned in foot-pounds, but yet he was beginning to feel the strain of it, to grow aware of its peculiar difficulty. He could find the streets and numbers, but the clients were not where they were supposed to be, and he felt like a hunter inexperienced in the camouflage of his game. It was an unfavorable day, too—fall, and cold, dark weather, windy. But, any way, instead of shells in his deep trenchcoat pocket he had the cardboard of checks, punctured for the spindles of the file, the holes reminding him of the holes in player-piano paper. And he didn't look much like a hunter, either; his was a city figure entirely, belted up in this Irish conspirator's coat. He was slender without being tall, stiff in the back, his legs looking shabby in a pair of old tweed pants gone through and fringy at the cuffs. With this stiffness, he kept his head forward, so that his face was red from the sharpness of the weather; and it was an indoors sort of face with gray eyes that persisted in some kind of thought and yet seemed to avoid definiteness of conclusion. He wore sideburns that surprised you somewhat by the tough curl of the blond hair and the effect of assertion in their length. He was not so mild as he looked, nor so youthful; and nevertheless there was no effort on his part to seem what he was not. He was an educated man; he was a bachelor; he was in some ways simple; without lushing, he liked a drink; his luck had not been good. Nothing was deliberately hidden.

He felt that his luck was better than usual today. When he had reported for work that morning he had expected to be shut up in the relief office at a clerk's job, for he had been hired downtown as a clerk, and he was glad to have, instead, the freedom of the streets and welcomed, at least at first, the vigor of the cold and even the blowing of the hard wind. But on the other hand he was not getting on with the distribution of the checks. It was true that it was a city job; nobody expected you to push too hard at a city job. His supervisor, that young Mr. Raynor, had practically told him that. Still, he wanted to do well at it. For one thing, when he knew how quickly he could deliver a batch of checks, he would know also how much time he could expect to clip for himself. And then, too, the clients would be waiting for their money. That was not the most important consideration, though it certainly mattered to him. No, but he wanted to do well, simply for doing-well's sake, to acquit himself decently of a job because he so rarely had a job to do that required just this sort of energy. Of the peculiar energy he now had a superabundance; once it had started to flow, it flowed all too heavily. And, for the time being anyway, he was balked. He could not find Mr. Green.

So he stood in his big-skirted trenchcoat with a large envelope in his hand and papers showing from his pocket, wondering why people should be so hard to locate who were too feeble or sick to come to the station to collect their own checks. But Raynor had told him that tracking them down was not easy at first and had offered him some advice on how to proceed. "If you can see the postman, he's your first man to ask, and your best bet. If you can't connect with him, try the stores and tradespeople around. Then the janitor and the neighbors. But you'll find the closer you come to your man the less people will tell you. They don't want to tell you anything."

"Because I'm a stranger."

"Because you're white. We ought to have a Negro doing this, but we don't at the moment, and of course you've got to eat, too, and this is public employment. Jobs have to be made. Oh, that holds for me too. Mind you, I'm not letting myself out. I've got three years of seniority on you, that's all. And a law degree. Otherwise, you might be back of the desk and I might be going out into the field this cold day. The same dough pays us both and for the same, exact, identical reason. What's my law degree got to do with it? But you have to pass out these checks, Mr. Grebe, and it'll help if you're stubborn, so I hope you are."

"Yes, I'm fairly stubborn."

Raynor sketched hard with an eraser in the old dirt of his desk, left-handed, and said, "Sure, what else can you answer to such a question. Anyhow, the trouble you're going to have is that they don't like to give information about anybody. They think you're a plain-clothes dick or an installment collector, or summons-server or something like that. Till you've been seen around the neighborhood for a few months and people know you're only from the relief."

It was dark, ground-freezing, pre-Thanksgiving weather; the wind played hob with the smoke, rushing it down, and Grebe missed his gloves, which he had left in Raynor's office. And no one would admit knowing Green. It was past three o'clock and the postman had made his last delivery. The nearest grocer, himself a Negro, had never heard the name Tulliver Green, or said he hadn't. Grebe was inclined to think that it was true, that he had in the end convinced the man that he wanted only to deliver a check. But he wasn't sure. He needed experience in interpreting looks and signs and, even more, the will not to be put off or denied and even the force to bully if need be. If the grocer did know, he had got rid of him easily. But since most of his trade was with reliefers, why should he prevent the delivery of a check? Maybe Green, or Mrs. Green, if there was a Mrs. Green, patronized another grocer. And was there a Mrs. Green? It was one of Grebe's great handicaps that he hadn't looked at any of the case records. Raynor should have let him read files for a few hours. But he apparently saw no need for that, probably considering the job unimportant. Why prepare systematically to deliver a few checks?

But now it was time to look for the janitor. Grebe took in the building in the wind and gloom of the late November day—trampled, frost-hardened lots on one side; on the other, an automobile junk yard and then the infinite work of Elevated frames, weak-looking, gaping with rubbish fires; two sets of leaning brick porches three stories high and a flight of cement stairs to the cellar. Descending, he entered the underground passage, where he tried the doors until one opened and he found himself in the furnace room. There someone rose toward him and approached, scraping on the coal grit and bending under the canvas-jacketed pipes.

"Are you the janitor?"

"What do you want?"

"I'm looking for a man who's supposed to be living here. Green."

"What Green?"

"Oh, you maybe have more than one Green?" said Grebe with new, pleasant hope. "This is Tulliver Green."

"I don't think I c'n help you, mister. I don't know any."

"A crippled man."

The janitor stood bent before him. Could it be that he was crippled? Oh, God! what if he was. Grebe's gray eyes sought with excited difficulty to see. But no, he was only very short and stooped. A head awakened from meditation, a strong-haired beard, low, wide shoulders. A staleness of sweat and coal rose from his black shirt and the burlap sack he wore as an apron.

"Crippled how?"

Grebe thought and then answered with the light voice of unmixed candor, "I don't know. I've never seen him." This was damaging, but his only other choice was to make a lying guess, and he was not up to it. "I'm delivering checks for the relief to shut-in cases. If he weren't crippled he'd come to collect himself. That's why I said crippled. Bedridden, chair-ridden—is there anybody like that?"

This sort of frankness was one of Grebe's oldest talents, going back to childhood. But it gained him nothing here.

"No suh. I've got four buildin's same as this that I take care of. I don' know all the tenants, leave alone the tenants' tenants. The rooms turn over so fast, people movin' in and out every day. I can't tell you."

The janitor opened his grimy lips but Grebe did not hear him in the piping of the valves and the consuming pull of air to flame in the body of the furnace. He knew, however, what he had said.

"Well, all the same, thanks. Sorry I bothered you. I'll prowl around upstairs again and see if I can turn up someone who knows him."

Once more in the cold air and early darkness he made the short circle from the cellarway to the entrance crowded between the brickwork pillars and began to climb to the third floor. Pieces of plaster ground under his feet; strips of brass tape from which the carpeting had been torn away marked old boundaries at the sides. In the passage, the cold reached him worse than in the street; it touched him to the bone. The hall toilets ran like springs. He thought grimly as he heard the wind burning around the building with a sound like that of the furnace, that this was a great piece of constructed shelter. Then he struck a match in the gloom and searched for names and numbers among the writings and scribbles on the walls. He saw WHOODY-DOODY GO TO JESUS, and zigzags, caricatures, sexual scrawls, and curses. So the sealed rooms of pyramids were also decorated, and the caves of human dawn.

The information on his card was, TULLIVER GREEN—APT 3D. There were no names, however, and no numbers. His shoulders drawn up, tears of cold in his eyes, breathing vapor, he went the length of the corridor and told himself that if he had been lucky enough to have the temperament for it he would bang on one of the doors and bawl out "Tulliver Green!" until he got results. But it wasn't in him to make an uproar and he continued to burn matches, passing the light over the walls. At the rear, in a corner off the hall, he discovered a door he had not seen before and he thought it best to investigate. It sounded empty when he knocked, but a young Negress answered, hardly more than a girl. She opened only a bit, to guard the warmth of the room.

"Yes suh?"

"I'm from the district station on Prairie Avenue. I'm looking for a man named Tulliver Green to give him his check. Do you know him?"

No, she didn't; but he thought she had not understood anything of what he had said. She had a dream-bound, dream-blind face, very soft and black, shut off. She wore a man's jacket and pulled the ends together at her throat. Her hair was parted in three directions, at the sides and transversely, standing up at the front in a dull puff.

"Is there somebody around here who might know?"

"I jus' taken this room las' week."

He observed that she shivered, but even her shiver was somnambulistic and there was no sharp consciousness of cold in the big smooth eyes of her handsome face.

"All right, miss, thank you. Thanks," he said, and went to try another place.

Here he was admitted. He was grateful, for the room was warm. It was full of people, and they were silent as he entered—ten people, or a dozen, perhaps more, sitting on benches like a parliament. There was no light, properly speaking, but a tempered darkness that the window gave, and everyone seemed to him enormous, the men padded out in heavy work clothes and winter coats, and the women huge, too, in their sweaters, hats, and old furs. And, besides, bed and bedding, a black cooking range, a piano piled towering to the ceiling with papers, a dining-room table of the old style of prosperous Chicago. Among these people Grebe, with his cold-heightened fresh color and his smaller stature, entered like a schoolboy. Even though he was met with smiles and good will, he knew, before a single word was spoken, that all the currents ran against him and that he would make no headway. Nevertheless he began. "Does anybody here know how I can deliver a check to Mr. Tulliver Green?"

"Green?" It was the man that had let him in who answered. He was in short sleeves, in a checkered shirt, and had a queer, high head, profusely overgrown and long as a shako; the veins entered it strongly from his forehead. "I never heard mention of him. Is this where he live?"

"This is the address they gave me at the station. He's a sick man, and he'll need his check. Can't anybody tell me where to find him?"

He stood his ground and waited for a reply, his crimson wool scarf wound about his neck and drooping outside his trenchcoat, pockets weighted with the block of checks and official forms. They must have realized that he was not a college boy employed afternoons by a bill collector, trying foxily to pass for a relief clerk, recognized that he was an older man who knew himself what need was, who had had more than an average seasoning in hardship. It was evident enough if you looked at the marks under his eyes and at the sides of his mouth.

"Anybody know this sick man?"

"No suh." On all sides he saw heads shaken and smiles of denial. No one knew. And maybe it was true, he considered, standing silent in the earthen, musky human gloom of the place as the rumble continued. But he could never really be sure.

"What's the matter with this man?" said shako-head.

"I've never seen him. All I can tell you is that he can't come in person for his money. It's my first day in this district."

"Maybe they given you the wrong number?"

"I don't believe so. But where else can I ask about him?" He felt that this persistence amused them deeply, and in a way he shared their amusement that he should stand up so tenaciously to them. Though smaller, though slight, he was his own man, he retracted nothing about himself, and he looked back at them, gray-eyed, with amusement and also with a sort of courage. On the bench some man spoke in his throat, the words impossible to catch, and a woman answered with a wild, shrieking laugh, which was quickly cut off.

"Well, so nobody will tell me?"

"Ain't nobody who knows."

"At least, if he lives here, he pays rent to someone. Who manages the building?"

"Greatham Company. That's on Thirty-ninth Street."

Grebe wrote it in his pad. But, in the street again, a sheet of wind-driven paper clinging to his leg while he deliberated what direction to take next, it seemed a feeble lead to follow. Probably this Green didn't rent a flat, but a room. Sometimes there were as many as twenty people in an apartment; the real-estate agent would know only the lessee. And not even the agent could tell who the renters were. In some places the beds were even used in shifts, watchmen or jitney drivers or short-order cooks in night joints turning out after a day's sleep and surrendering their beds to a sister, a nephew, or perhaps a stranger, just off the bus. There were large numbers of newcomers in this terrific, blight-bitten portion of the city between Cottage Grove and Ashland, wandering from house to house and room to room. When you saw them, how could you know them? They didn't carry bundles on their backs or look picturesque. You only saw a man, a Negro, walking in the street or riding in the car, like everyone else, with his thumb closed on a transfer. And therefore how were you supposed to tell? Grebe thought the Greatham agent would only laugh at his question.

But how much it would have simplified the job to be able to say that Green was old, or blind, or consumptive. An hour in the files, taking a few notes, and he needn't have been at such a disadvantage. When Raynor gave him the block of checks he asked, "How much should I know about these people?" Then Raynor had looked as though he were preparing to accuse him of trying to make the job more important than it was. He smiled, because by then they were on fine terms, but nevertheless he had been getting ready to say something like that when the confusion began in the station over Staika and her children.

Grebe had waited a long time for this job. It came to him through the pull of an old schoolmate in the Corporation Counsel's office, never a close friend, but suddenly sympathetic and interested—pleased to show, moreover, how well he had done, how strongly he was coming on even in these miserable times. Well, he was coming through strongly, along with the Democratic administration itself. Grebe had gone to see him in City Hall, and they had had a counter lunch or beers at least once a month for a year, and finally it had been possible to swing the job. He didn't mind being assigned the lowest clerical grade, nor even being a messenger, though Raynor thought he did.

This Raynor was an original sort of guy and Grebe had taken to him immediately. As was proper on the first day, Grebe had come early, but he waited long, for Raynor was late. At last he darted into his cubicle of an office as though he had just jumped from one of those hurtling huge red Indian Avenue cars. His thin, rough face was wind-stung and he was grinning and saying something breathlessly to himself. In his hat, a small fedora, and his coat, the velvet collar a neat fit about his neck, and his silk muffler that set off the nervous twist of his chin, he swayed and turned himself in his swivel chair, feet leaving the ground; so that he pranced a little as he sat. Meanwhile he took Grebe's measure out of his eyes, eyes of an unusual vertical length and slightly sardonic. So the two men sat for a while, saying nothing, while the supervisor raised his hat from his miscombed hair and put it in his lap. His cold-darkened hands were not clean. A steel beam passed through the little makeshift room, from which machine belts once had hung. The building was an old factory.

"I'm younger than you; I hope you won't find it hard taking orders from me," said Raynor. "But I don't make them up, either. You're how old, about?"

"Thirty-five."

"And you thought you'd be inside doing paper work. But it so happens I have to send you out."

"I don't mind."

"And it's mostly a Negro load we have in this district."

"So I thought it would be."

"Fine. You'll get along. *C'est un bon boulot.* Do you know French?"

"Some."

"I thought you'd be a university man."

"Have you been in France?" said Grebe.

"No, that's the French of the Berlitz School. I've been at it for more than a year, just as I'm sure people have been, all over the world, office boys in China and braves in Tanganyika. In fact, I damn well know it. Such is the attractive power of civilization. It's overrated, but what do you want? *Que voulez-vous?* I get *Le Rire* and all the spicy papers, just like in Tanganyika. It must be mystifying, out there. But my reason is that I'm aiming at the diplomatic service. I have a cousin who's a courier, and the way he describes it is awfully attractive. He rides in the *wagon-lits* and reads books. While we—What did you do before?"

"I sold."

"Where?"

"Canned meat at Stop and Shop. In the basement."

"And before that?"

"Window shades at Goldblatt's."

"Steady work?"

"No, Thursdays and Saturdays. I also sold shoes."

"You've been a shoe-dog too. Well. And prior to that? Here it is in your folder." He opened the record. "Saint Olaf's College, instructor in classical languages. Fellow, University of Chicago, 1926–27. I've had Latin, too. Let's trade quotations—'*Dum spiro spero.*' "

" '*Da dextram misero.*' "

" '*Alea jacta est.*' "

" '*Excelsior.*' "

Raynor shouted with laughter, and other workers came to look at him over the partition. Grebe also laughed, feeling pleased and easy. The luxury of fun on a nervous morning.

When they were done and no one was watching or listening, Raynor said rather seriously, "What made you study Latin in the first place? Was it for the priesthood?"

"No."

"Just for the hell of it? For the culture? Oh, the things people think they can pull!" He made his cry hilarious and tragic. "I ran my pants off so I could study for the bar, and I've passed the bar, so I get twelve dollars a week more than you as a bonus for having seen life straight and whole. I'll tell you, as a man of culture, that even though nothing looks to be real, and everything stands for something else, and that thing for another thing, and that thing for a still another one—there ain't any comparison between twenty-five and thirty-seven dollars a week, regardless of the last reality. Don't you think that was clear to your Greeks? They were a thoughtful people, but they didn't part with their slaves."

This was a great deal more than Grebe had looked for in his first interview with his supervisor. He was too shy to show all the astonishment he felt. He laughed a little, aroused, and brushed at the sunbeam that covered his head with its dust. "Do you think my mistake was so terrible?"

"Damn right it was terrible, and you know it now that you've had the whip of hard times laid on your back. You should have been preparing yourself for trouble. Your people must have been well off to send you to the university. Stop me, if I'm stepping on your toes. Did your mother pamper you? Did your father give in to you? Were you brought up tenderly,

with permission to go and find out what were the last things that everything else stands for while everybody else labored in the fallen world of
appearances?"

"Well, no, it wasn't exactly like that." Grebe smiled. *The fallen world of
appearances!* no less. But now it was his turn to deliver a surprise. "We
weren't rich. My father was the last genuine English butler in Chicago—"

"Are you kidding?"

"Why should I be?"

"In a livery?"

"In livery. Up on the Gold Coast."

"And he wanted you to be educated like a gentleman?"

"He did not. He sent me to the Armour Institute to study chemical engineering. But when he died I changed schools."

He stopped himself and considered how quickly Raynor had reached
him. In no time he had your valise on the table and all your stuff unpacked.
And afterward, in the streets, he was still reviewing how far he might have
gone, and how much he might have been led to tell if they had not been
interrupted by Mrs. Staika's great noise.

But just then a young woman, one of Raynor's workers, ran into the
cubicle exclaiming, "Haven't you heard all the fuss?"

"We haven't heard anything."

"It's Staika, giving out with all her might. The reporters are coming. She
said she phoned the papers, and you know she did."

"But what is she up to?" said Raynor.

"She brought her wash and she's ironing it here, with our current, because the relief won't pay her electric bill. She has her ironing board set up
by the admitting desk, and her kids are with her, all six. They never are in
school more than once a week. She's always dragging them around with her
because of her reputation."

"I don't want to miss any of this," said Raynor, jumping up. Grebe, as he
followed with the secretary, said, "Who is this Staika?"

"They call her the 'Blood Mother of Federal Street.' She's a professional
donor at the hospitals. I think they pay ten dollars a pint. Of course it's no
joke, but she makes a very big thing out of it and she and the kids are in
the papers all the time."

A small crowd, staff and clients divided by a plywood barrier, stood in
the narrow space of the entrance, and Staika was shouting in a gruff, mannish voice, plunging the iron on the board and slamming it on the metal
rest.

"My father and mother came in a steerage, and I was born in our house,
Robey by Huron. I'm no dirty immigrant. I'm a U.S. citizen. My husband
is a gassed veteran from France with lungs weaker'n paper, that hardly can
he go to the toilet by himself. These six children of mine, I have to buy the

shoes for their feet with my own blood. Even a lousy little white Communion necktie, that's a couple of drops of blood; a little piece of mosquito veil for my Vadja so she won't be ashamed in church for the other girls, they take my blood for it by Goldblatt. That's how I keep goin'. A fine thing if I had to depend on the relief. And there's plenty of people on the rolls—fakes! There's nothin' *they* can't get, that can go and wrap bacon at Swift and Armour any time. They're lookin' for them by the Yards. They never have to be out of work. Only they rather lay in their lousy beds and eat the public's money." She was not afraid, in a predominantly Negro station, to shout this way about Negroes.

Grebe and Raynor worked themselves forward to get a closer view of the woman. She was flaming with anger and with pleasure at herself, broad and huge, a golden-headed woman who wore a cotton cap laced with pink ribbon. She was barelegged and had on black gym shoes, her Hoover apron was open and her great breasts, not much restrained by a man's undershirt, hampered her arms as she worked at the kid's dress on the ironing board. And the children, silent and white, with a kind of locked obstinacy, in sheepskins and lumberjackets, stood behind her. She had captured the station, and the pleasure this gave her was enormous. Yet her grievances were true grievances. She was telling the truth. But she behaved like a liar. The look of her small eyes was hidden, and while she raged she also seemed to be spinning and planning.

"They send me out college case workers in silk pants to talk me out of what I got comin'. Are they better'n me? Who told them? Fire them. Let 'em go and get married, and then you won't have to cut electric from people's budget."

The chief supervisor, Mr. Ewing, couldn't silence her and he stood with folded arms at the head of his staff, bald, bald-headed, saying to his subordinates like the ex-school principal he was, "Pretty soon she'll be tired and go."

"No she wont," said Raynor to Grebe. "She'll get what she wants. She knows more about the relief than Ewing. She's been on the rolls for years, and she always gets what she wants because she puts on a noisy show. Ewing knows it. He'll give in soon. He's only saving face. If he gets bad publicity, the Commissioner'll have him on the carpet, downtown. She's got him submerged; she'll submerge everybody in time, and that includes nations and governments."

Grebe replied with his characteristic smile, disagreeing completely. Who would take Staika's orders, and what changes could her yelling ever bring about?

No, what Grebe saw in her, the power that made people listen, was that her cry expressed the war of flesh and blood, perhaps turned a little crazy and certainly ugly, on this place and this condition. And at first, when he went out, the spirit of Staika somehow presided over the whole district for him, and it took color from her; he saw her color, in the spotty curb fires, and the fires under the El, the straight alley of flamy gloom. Later, too, when he went into a tavern for a shot of rye, the sweat of beer, association with West Side Polish streets, made him think of her again.

He wiped the corners of his mouth with his muffler, his handkerchief being inconvenient to reach for, and went out again to get on with the delivery of his checks. The air bit cold and hard and a few flakes of snow formed near him. A train struck by and left a quiver in the frames and a bristling icy hiss over the rails.

Crossing the street, he descended a flight of board steps into a basement grocery, setting off a little bell. It was a dark, long store and it caught you with its stinks of smoked meat, soap, dried peaches, and fish. There was a fire wrinkling and flapping in the little stove, and the proprietor was waiting, an Italian with a long, hollow face and stubborn bristles. He kept his hands warm under his apron.

No, he didn't know Green. You knew people but not names. The same man might not have the same name twice. The police didn't know, either, and mostly didn't care. When somebody was shot or knifed they took the body away and didn't look for the murderer. In the first place, nobody would tell them anything. So they made up a name for the coroner and called it quits. And in the second place, they didn't give a goddamn anyhow. But they couldn't get to the bottom of a thing even if they wanted to. Nobody would get to know even a tenth of what went on among these people. They stabbed and stole, they did every crime and abomination you ever heard of, men and men, women and women, parents and children, worse than the animals. They carried on their own way, and the horrors passed off like a smoke. There was never anything like it in the history of the whole world.

It was a long speech, deepening with every word in its fantasy and passion and becoming increasingly senseless and terrible: a swarm amassed by suggestion and invention, a huge, hugging, despairing knot, a human wheel of heads, legs, bellies, arms, rolling through his shop.

Grebe felt that he must interrupt him. He said sharply, "What are you talking about! All I asked was whether you knew this man."

"That isn't even the half of it. I been here six years. You probably don't want to believe this. But suppose it's true?"

"All the same," said Grebe, "there must be a way to find a person."

The Italian's close-spaced eyes had been queerly concentrated, as were his muscles, while he leaned across the counter trying to convince Grebe. Now he gave up the effort and sat down on his stool. "Oh—I suppose. Once in a while. But I been telling you, even the cops don't get anywhere."

"They're always after somebody. It's not the same thing."

"Well, keep trying if you want. I can't help you."

But he didn't keep trying. He had no more time to spend on Green. He slipped Green's check to the back of the block. The next name on the list was FIELD, WINSTON.

He found the back-yard bungalow without the least trouble; it shared a lot with another house, a few feet of yard between. Grebe knew these two-shack arrangements. They had been built in vast numbers in the days before the swamps were filled and the streets raised, and they were all the same—a boardwalk along the fence, well under street level, three or four ball-headed posts for clotheslines, greening wood, dead shingles, and a long, long flight of stairs to the rear door.

A twelve-year-old boy let him into the kitchen, and there the old man was, sitting by the table in a wheel chair.

"Oh, it's d' Government man," he said to the boy when Grebe drew out his checks. "Go bring me my box of papers." He cleared a space on the table.

"Oh, you don't have to go to all that trouble," said Grebe. But Field laid out his papers: Social Security card, relief certification, letters from the state hospital in Manteno, and a naval discharge dated San Diego, 1920.

"That's plenty," Grebe said. "Just sign."

"You got to know who I am," the old man said. "You're from the Government. It's not your check, it's a Government check and you got no business to hand it over till everything is proved."

He loved the ceremony of it, and Grebe made no more objections. Field emptied his box and finished out the circle of cards and letters.

"There's everything I done and been. Just the death certificate and they can close book on me." He said this with a certain happy pride and magnificence. Still he did not sign; he merely held the little pen upright on the golden-green corduroy of his thigh. Grebe did not hurry him. He felt the old man's hunger for conversation.

"I got to get better coal," he said. "I send my little gran'son to the yard with my order and they fill his wagon with screening. The stove ain't made for it. It fall through the grate. The order says Franklin County egg-size coal."

"I'll report it and see what can be done."

"Nothing can be done, I expect. You know and I know. There ain't no little ways to make things better, and the only big thing is money. That's the only sunbeams, money. Nothing is black where it shines, and the only place you see black is where it ain't shining. What we colored have to have is our own rich. There ain't no other way."

Grebe sat, his reddened forehead bridged levelly by his close-cut hair and his cheeks lowered in the wings of his collar—the caked fire shone hard within the isinglass-and-iron frames but the room was not comfortable—

sat and listened while the old man unfolded his scheme. This was to create one Negro millionaire a month by subscription. One clever, good-hearted young fellow elected every month would sign a contract to use the money to start a business employing Negroes. This would be advertised by chain letters and word of mouth, and every Negro wage earner would contribute a dollar a month. Within five years there would be sixty millionaires.

"That'll fetch respect," he said with a throat-stopped sound that came out like a foreign syllable. "You got to take and organize all the money that gets thrown away on the policy wheel and horse race. As long as they can take it away from you, they got no respect for you. Money, that's d' sun of human kind!" Field was a Negro of mixed blood, perhaps Cherokee, or Natchez; his skin was reddish. And he sounded, speaking about a golden sun in this dark room, and looked, shaggy and slab-headed, with the mingled blood of his face and broad lips, the little pen still upright in his hand, like one of the underground kings of mythology, old judge Minos himself.

And now he accepted the check and signed. Not to soil the slip, he held it down with his knuckles. The table budged and creaked, the center of the gloomy, heathen midden of the kitchen covered with bread, meat, and cans, and the scramble of papers.

"Don't you think my scheme'd work?"

"It's worth thinking about. Something ought to be done, I agree."

"It'll work if people will do it. That's all. That's the only thing, any time. When they understand it in the same way, all of them."

"That's true," said Grebe, rising. His glance met the old man's.

"I know you got to go," he said. "Well, God bless you, boy you ain't been sly with me. I can tell it in a minute."

He went back through the buried yard. Someone nursed a candle in a shed, where a man unloaded kindling wood from a sprawl-wheeled baby buggy and two voices carried on a high conversation. As he came up the sheltered passage he heard the hard boost of the wind in the branches and against the house fronts, and then, reaching the sidewalk, he saw the needle-eye red of cable towers in the open icy height hundreds of feet above the river and the factories—those keen points. From here, his view was obstructed all the way to the South Branch and its timber banks, and the cranes beside the water. Rebuilt after the Great Fire, this part of the city was, not fifty years later, in ruins again, factories boarded up, buildings deserted or fallen, gaps of prairie between. But it wasn't desolation that this made you feel, but rather a faltering of organization that set free a huge energy, an escaped, unattached, unregulated power from the giant raw place. Not only must people feel it but, it seemed to Grebe, they were compelled to match it. In their very bodies. He no less than others, he realized. Say that his parents had been servants in their time, whereas he was not supposed to be one. He thought that they had never done any service like this, which no one visible asked for, and probably flesh and blood could not even perform. Nor could anyone show why it should be performed; or see where the performance would lead. That did not mean that he wanted to be released from it, he realized with a grimly pensive face. On the contrary. He had something to do. To be compelled to feel this energy and yet have no task to do—that was horrible; that was suffering; he knew what that was. It was now quitting time. Six o'clock. He could go home if he liked, to his room, that is, to wash in hot water, to pour a drink, lie down on his quilt, read the paper, eat some liver paste on crackers before going out to dinner. But to think of this actually made him feel a little sick, as though he had swallowed hard air. He had six checks left, and he was determined to deliver at least one of these: Mr. Green's check.

So he started again. He had four or five dark blocks to go, past open lots, condemned houses, old foundations, closed schools, black churches, mounds, and he reflected that there must be many people alive who had once seen the neighborhood rebuilt and new. Now there was a second layer of ruins; centuries of history accomplished through human massing. Numbers had given the place forced growth; enormous numbers had also broken it down. Objects once so new, so concrete that it could have occurred to anyone they stood for other things, had crumbled. Therefore, reflected Grebe, the secret of them was out. It was that they stood for themselves by agreement, and were natural and not unnatural by agreement, and when the things themselves collapsed the agreement became visible. What was it, otherwise, that kept cities from looking peculiar? Rome, that was almost permanent, did not give rise to thoughts like these. And was it abidingly real? But in Chicago, where the cycles were so fast and the familiar died out, and again rose, changed, and died again in thirty years, you saw the common agreement or covenant, and you were forced to think about appearances and realities. (He remembered Raynor and he smiled. Raynor was a clever boy.) Once you had grasped this, a great many things became intelligible. For instance, why Mr. Field should conceive such a scheme. Of course, if people were to agree to create a millionaire, a real millionaire would come into existence. And if you wanted to know how Mr. Field was inspired to think of this, why, he had within sight of his kitchen window the chart, the very bones of a successful scheme—the El with its blue and green confetti of signals. People consented to pay dimes and ride the crash-box cars, and so it was a success. Yet how absurd it looked; how little reality there was to start with. And yet Yerkes, the great financier who built it, had known that he could get people to agree to do it. Viewed as itself, what a scheme of a scheme it seemed, how close to an appearance. Then why wonder at Mr. Field's idea? He had grasped a principle. And then Grebe remembered, too, that Mr. Yerkes had established the Yerkes Observatory and endowed it with millions. Now how did the notion come to him in his New York museum of a palace or his Aegean-bound yacht to give money to astronomers? Was he awed by the success of his bizarre enterprise and therefore ready to spend money to find out where in the universe being and seeming were identical? Yes, he wanted to know what abides; and whether flesh is Bible grass; and he offered money to be burned in the fire of suns. Okay, then, Grebe thought further, these things exist because people consent to exist with them—we have got so far—and also there is a reality which doesn't depend on consent but within which consent is a game. But what about need, the need that keeps so many vast thousands in position? You tell me that, you *private* little gentleman and *decent* soul—he used these words against himself scornfully. Why is the consent given to misery? And why so painfully ugly? Because there is *something* that is dismal and permanently ugly? Here he sighed and gave it up, and thought it was enough for the present moment that he had a real check in his pocket for a Mr. Green who must be real beyond question. If only his neighbors didn't think they had to conceal him.

This time he stopped at the second floor. He struck a match and found a door. Presently a man answered his knock and Grebe had the check ready and showed it even before he began. "Does Tulliver Green live here? I'm from the relief."

The man narrowed the opening and spoke to someone at his back.

"Does he live here?"

"Uh-uh. No."

"Or anywhere in this building? He's a sick man and he can't come for his dough." He exhibited the check in the light, which was smoky—the air smelled of charred lard—and the man held off the brim of his cap to study it.

"Uh-uh. Never seen the name."

"There's no body around here that uses crutches?"

He seemed to think, but it was Grebe's impression that he was simply waiting for a decent interval to pass.

"No, suh. Nobody I ever see."

"I've been looking for this man all afternoon"—Grebe spoke out with sudden force—"and I'm going to have to carry this check back to the station. It seems strange not to be able to find a person to *give* him something when you're looking for him for a good reason. I suppose if I had bad news for him I'd find him quick enough."

There was a responsive motion in the other man's face. "That's right, I reckon."

"It almost doesn't do any good to have a name if you can't be found by it. It doesn't stand for anything. He might as well not have any," he went on, smiling. It was as much of a concession as he could make to his desire to laugh.

"Well, now, there's a little old knot-back man I see once in a while. He might be the one you lookin' for. Downstairs."

"Where? Right side or left? Which door?"

"I don't know which. Thin-face little knot-back with a stick."

But no one answered to any of the doors on the first floor. He went to the end of the corridor, searching by matchlight, and found only a stairless exit to the yard, a drop of about six feet. But there was a bungalow near the alley, an old house like Mr. Field's. To jump was unsafe. He ran from the front door, through the underground passage and into the yard. The place was occupied. There was a light through the curtains, upstairs. The name on the ticket under the broken, scoop-shaped mailbox was Green! He exultantly rang the bell and pressed against the locked door. Then the lock clicked faintly and a long staircase opened before him. Someone was slowly coming down—a woman. He had the impression in the weak light that she was shaping her hair as she came, making herself presentable, for he saw her arms raised. But it was for support that they were raised, she was feeling her way downward, down the wall, stumbling. Next he wondered about the pressure of her feet on the treads; she did not seem to be wearing shoes. And it was a freezing stairway. His ring had got her out of bed, perhaps, and she had forgotten to put them on. And then he saw that she was not only shoeless but naked; she was entirely naked, climbing down while she talked to herself, a heavy woman, naked and drunk. She blundered into him. The contact of her breasts, though they touched only his coat, made him go back against the door with a blind shock. See what he had tracked down, in his hunting game!

The woman was saying to herself, furious with insult, "So I cain't ——k, huh? I'll show that son-of-a-bitch kin I, cain't I."

What should he do now? Grebe asked himself. Why, he should go. He should turn away and go. He couldn't talk to this woman. He couldn't keep her standing naked in the cold. But when he tried he found himself unable to turn away.

He said, "Is this where Mr. Green lives?"

But she was still talking to herself and did not hear him.

"Is this Mr. Green's house?"

At last she turned her furious drunken glance on him. "What do you want?"

Again her eyes wandered from him; there was a dot of blood in their enraged brilliance. He wondered why she didn't feel the cold.

"I'm from the relief."

"Awright, what?"

"I've got a check for Tulliver Green."

This time she heard him and put out her hand.

"No, no, for *Mr.* Green. He's got to sign," he said. How was he going to get Green's signature tonight!

"I'll take it. He can't."

He desperately shook his head, thinking of Mr. Field's precautions about identification. "I can't let you have it. It's for him. Are you Mrs. Green?"

"Maybe I is, and maybe I ain't. Who want to know?"

"Is he upstairs?"

"Awright. Take it up yourself, you gaddamn fool."

Sure, he was a goddamn fool. Of course he could not go up because Green would probably be drunk and naked, too. And perhaps he would appear on the landing soon. He looked eagerly upward. Under the light was a high narrow brown wall. Empty! It remained empty!

"Hell with you, then!" he heard her cry. To deliver a check for coal and clothes, he was keeping her in the cold. She did not feel it, but his face was burning with frost and self-ridicule. He backed away from her.

"I'll come tomorrow, tell him."

"Ah, hell with you. Don' never come. What you doin' here in the night-time? Don' come back." She yelled so that he saw the breadth of her tongue. She stood astride in the long cold box of the hall and held on to the banister and the wall. The bungalow itself was shaped something like a box, a clumsy, high box pointing into the freezing air with its sharp, wintry lights.

"If you are Mrs. Green, I'll give you the check," he said, changing his mind.

"Give here, then." She took it, took the pen offered with it in her left hand, and tried to sign the receipt on the wall. He looked around, almost as though to see whether his madness was being observed, and came near believing that someone was standing on a mountain of used tires in the auto-junking shop next door.

"But are you Mrs. Green?" he now thought to ask. But she was already climbing the stairs with the check, and it was too late, if he had made an error, if he was now in trouble, to undo the thing. But he wasn't going to worry about it. Though she might not be Mrs. Green, he was convinced that Mr. Green was upstairs. Whoever she was, the woman stood for Green, whom he was not to see this time. Well, you silly bastard, he said to himself, so you think you found him. So what? Maybe you really did find him—what of it? But it was important that there was a real Mr. Green whom they could not keep him from reaching because he seemed to come as an emissary from hostile appearances. And though the self-ridicule was slow to diminish, and his face still blazed with it, he had, nevertheless, a feeling of elation, too. "For after all," he said, "he *could* be found!"

Vasconcelos
Borges
Malamud
Jackson
Mrozek
Landolfi
Cassill

New Dimensions

Hughes
Robbe-Grillet
Beckett
Rosenfeld
Hall
Hildesheimer
Mishima
McPherson
Böll
O'Connor

José Vasconcelos (1882–1959) is one of Mexico's foremost masters of prose fiction. Working in the grand tradition of writer–teacher–statesman, he served as head of the National University of Mexico (1920–1924) and as Minister of Education under the regime of Alvaro Obregón. In 1929 he was an unsuccessful candidate for the Mexican presidency. Few of his stories are available in English at the present time.

The Boar Hunt

JOSÉ VASCONCELOS

We were four companions, and we went by the names of our respective nationalities: the Colombian, the Peruvian, the Mexican; the fourth, a native of Ecuador, was called Quito for short. Unforeseen chance had joined us together a few years ago on a large sugar plantation on the Peruvian coast. We worked at different occupations during the day and met during the evening in our off time. Not being Englishmen, we did not play cards. Instead, our constant discussions led to disputes. These didn't stop us from wanting to see each other the next night, however, to continue the interrupted debates and support them with new arguments. Nor did the rough sentences of the preceding wrangles indicate a lessening of our affection, of which we assured ourselves reciprocally with the clasping of hands and a look. On Sundays we used to go on hunting parties. We roamed the fertile glens, stalking, generally with poor results, the game of the warm region around the coast, or we entertained ourselves killing birds that flew in the sunlight during the siesta hour.

We came to be tireless wanderers and excellent marksmen. Whenever we climbed a hill and gazed at the imposing range of mountains in the interior, its attractiveness stirred us and we wanted to climb it. What attracted us more was the trans-Andean region: fertile plateaus extending on the other side of the range in the direction of the Atlantic toward the immense land of Brazil. It was as if primitive nature called us to her breast. The vigor of the fertile, untouched jungles promised to rejuvenate our minds, the same vigor which rejuvenates the strength and the thickness of the trees each year. At times we devised crazy plans. As with all things that are given a lot of thought, these schemes generally materialized. Ultimately nature and

407

events are largely what our imaginations make them out to be. And so we went ahead planning and acting. At the end of the year, with arranged vacations, accumulated money, good rifles, abundant munitions, stone- and mudproof boots, four hammocks, and a half dozen faithful Indians, our caravan descended the Andean slopes, leading to the endless green ocean.

At last we came upon a village at the edge of the Marañón River. Here we changed our safari. The region we were going to penetrate had no roads. It was the unexplored underbrush into which we could enter only by going down the river in a canoe. In time we came to the area where we proposed to carry out the purpose of our journey, the hunting of wild boars.

We had been informed that boars travel in herds of several thousands, occupying a region, eating grass and staying together, exploiting the grazing areas, organized just like an army. They are very easy to kill if one attacks them when they are scattered out satisfying their appetites—an army given over to the delights of victory. When they march about hungry, on the other hand, they are usually vicious. In our search we glided down river between imposing jungles with our provisions and the company of three faithful Indian oarsmen.

One morning we stopped at some huts near the river. Thanks to the information gathered there, we decided to disembark a little farther on in order to spend the night on land and continue the hunt for the boars in the thicket the following day.

Sheltered in a backwater, we came ashore, and after a short exploration found a clearing in which to make camp. We unloaded the provisions and the rifles, tied the boat securely, then with the help of the Indians set up our camp one half kilometer from the river bank. In marking the path to the landing, we were careful not to lose ourselves in the thicket. The Indians withdrew toward their huts, promising to return two days later. At dawn we would set out in search of the prey.

Though night had scarcely come and the heat was great, we gathered at the fire to see each other's faces, to look instinctively for protection. We talked a little, smoked, confessed to being tired, and decided to go to bed. Each hammock had been tied by one end to a single tree, firm though not very thick in the trunk. Stretching out from this axis in different directions, the hammocks were supported by the other end on other trunks. Each of us carried his rifle, cartridges, and some provisions which couldn't remain exposed on the ground. The sight of the weapons made us consider the place where we were, surrounded by the unknown. A slight feeling of terror made us laugh, cough, and talk. But fatigue overcame us, that heavy fatigue which compels the soldier to scorn danger, to put down his rifle, and to fall asleep though the most persistent enemy pursues him. We scarcely noticed the supreme grandeur of that remote tropical night.

I don't know whether it was the light of the magnificent dawn or the strange noises which awakened me and made me sit up in my hammock and look carefully at my surroundings. I saw nothing but the awakening of that life which at night falls into the lethargy of the jungle. I called my sleeping companions and, alert and seated in our hanging beds, we dressed ourselves. We were preparing to jump to the ground when we clearly heard a somewhat distant, sudden sound of rustling branches. Since it did not continue, however, we descended confidently, washed our faces with water from our canteens, and slowly prepared and enjoyed breakfast. By about 11:00 in the morning we were armed and bold and preparing to make our way through the jungle.

But then the sound again. Its persistence and proximity in the thicket made us change our minds. An instinct made us take refuge in our hammocks. We cautiously moved our cartridges and rifles into them again, and without consulting each other we agreed on the idea of putting our provisions safely away. We passed them up into the hammocks, and we ourselves finally climbed in. Stretched out face down, comfortably suspended with rifles in hand, we did not have to wait long. Black, agile boars quickly appeared from all directions. We welcomed them with shouts of joy and well-aimed shots. Some fell immediately, giving comical snorts, but many more came out of the jungle. We shot again, spending all the cartridges in the magazine. Then we stopped to reload. Finding ourselves safe in the height of our hammocks, we continued after a pause.

We counted dozens of them. At a glance we made rapid calculations of the magnitude of the destruction, while the boars continued to come out of the jungle in uncountable numbers. Instead of going on their way or fleeing, they seemed confused. All of them emerged from the jungle where it was easy for us to shoot them. Occasionally we had to stop firing because the frequent shooting heated the barrels of our rifles. While they were cooling we smoked and were able to joke, celebrating our good fortune. The impotent anger of the boars amazed us. They raised their tusks in our direction, uselessly threatening us. We laughed at their snorts, quietly aimed at those who were near, and Bang! a dead boar. We carefully studied the angle of the shoulder blade so that the bullet would cross the heart. The slaughter lasted for hours.

At 4:30 P.M. we noticed an alarming shortage of our ammunition. We had been well supplied and had shot at will. Though the slaughter was gratifying, the boars must have numbered, as we had been informed previously, several thousands, because their hordes didn't diminish. On the contrary, they gathered directly beneath our hammocks in increasing groups. They slashed furiously at the trunk of the tree which held the four points of the hammocks. The marks of the tusks remained on the hard bark. Not without a certain fear we watched them gather compactly, tenaciously, in tight masses against the resisting trunk. We wondered what would happen to a man who fell within their reach. Our shots were now sporadic, well aimed, carefully husbanded. They did not drive away the aggressive beasts, but only redoubled their fury. One of us ironically noted that from being the attackers we had gone on the defensive. We did not laugh very long at the joke. Now we hardly shot at all. We needed to save our cartridges.

The afternoon waned and evening came upon us. After consulting each other, we decided to eat in our hammocks. We applauded ourselves for taking the food up—meat, bread, and bottles of water. Stretching ourselves on our hammocks, we passed things to each other, sharing what we needed. The boars deafened us with their angry snorts.

After eating, we began to feel calm. We lit cigars. Surely the boars would go. Their numbers were great, but they would finally leave peacefully. As we said so, however, we looked with greedy eyes at the few unused cartridges that remained. Our enemies, like enormous angry ants, stirred beneath us, encouraged by the ceasing of our fire. From time to time we carefully aimed and killed one or two of them, driving off the huge group of uselessly enraged boars at the base of the trunk which served as a prop for our hammocks.

Night enveloped us almost without our noticing the change from twilight. Anxiety also overtook us. When would the cursed boars leave? Already there were enough dead to serve as trophies to several dozen hunters. Our feat would be talked about; we had to show ourselves worthy of such fame. Since there was nothing else to do, it was necessary to sleep. Even if we had had enough bullets it would have been impossible to continue the fight in the darkness. It occurred to us to start a fire to drive the herd off with flames, but apart from the fact that we couldn't leave the place in which we were suspended, there were no dry branches in the lush forest. Finally, we slept.

We woke up a little after midnight. The darkness was profound, but the well-known noise made us aware that our enemies were still there. We imagined they must be the last ones which were leaving, however. If a good army needs several hours to break camp and march off, what can be expected of a vile army of boars but disorder and delay? The following morning we would fire upon the stragglers, but this painful thought bothered us: they were in large and apparently active numbers. What were they up to? Why didn't they leave? We thus spent long hours of worry. Dawn finally came, splendid in the sky but noisy in the jungle still enveloped inwardly in shadows. We eagerly waited for the sun to penetrate the foliage in order to survey the appearance of the field of battle of the day before.

What we finally saw made us gasp. It terrified us. The boars were painstakingly continuing the work which they had engaged in throughout the entire night. Guided by some extraordinary instinct, with their tusks they were digging out the ground underneath the tree from which our hammocks hung; they gnawed the roots and continued to undermine them like large, industrious rats. Presently the tree was bound to fall and we with it, among the beasts. From that moment we neither thought nor talked. In desperation we used up our last shots, killing more ferocious beasts. Still the rest renewed their activity. They seemed to be endowed with intelligence. However much we concentrated our fire against them, they did not stop their attack against the tree.

Soon our shots stopped. We emptied our pistols, and then silently listened to the tusks gnawing beneath the soft, wet, pleasant-smelling earth. From time to time the boars pressed against the tree, pushing it and making it creak, eager to smash it quickly. We looked on hypnotized by their devilish activity. It was impossible to flee because the black monsters covered every inch in sight. It seemed to us that, by a sudden inspiration, they were preparing to take revenge on us for the ruthless nature of man, the unpunished destroyer of animals since the beginning of time. Our imagination, distorted by fear, showed us our fate as an atonement for the unpardonable crimes implicit in the struggle of biological selection. Before my eyes passed the vision of sacred India, where the believer refuses to eat meat in order to prevent the methodical killing of beasts and in order to atone for man's evil, bloody, treacherous slaughter, such as ours, for mere vicious pleasure. I felt that the multitude of boars was raising its accusing voice against me. I now understood the infamy of the hunter, but what was repentance worth if I was going to die with my companions, hopelessly devoured by that horde of brutes with demonlike eyes?

Stirred by terror and without realizing what I was doing, I hung from the upper end of my hammock, I balanced myself in the air, I swung in a long leap, I grasped a branch of a tree facing the one on which the boars were digging. From there I leaped to other branches and to others, reviving in myself habits which the species had forgotten.

The next moment a terrifying sound and unforgettable cries told me of the fall of the tree and the end of my companions. I clung to a trunk, trembling and listening to the chattering of my jaws. Later, the desire to flee gave me back my strength. Leaning out over the foliage, I looked for a path, and I saw the boars in the distance, marching in compressed ranks and holding their insolent snouts in the air. I knew that they were now withdrawing, and I got down from the tree. Horror overwhelmed me as I approached the site of our encampment, but some idea of duty made me return there. Perhaps one of my friends had managed to save himself. I approached hesitantly. Each dead boar made me tremble with fear.

But what I saw next was so frightful that I could not fix it clearly in my mind: remains of clothing—and footwear. There was no doubt; the boars

had devoured them. Then I ran toward the river, following the tracks we
had made two days before. I fled with great haste, limbs stiff from panic.

Running with long strides, I came upon the boat. With a great effort, I
managed to row to the huts. There I went to bed with a high fever which
lasted many days.

I will participate in no more hunts. I will contribute, if I have to, to the
extermination of harmful beasts. But I will not kill for pleasure. I will not
amuse myself with the ignoble pleasure of the hunt.

Jorge Luis Borges (1899–   ) was born in Buenos
Aires and educated in Geneva and Spain. Widely
read abroad, his work suggests Poe, Baudelaire, and
Valéry. He is a poet, essayist, and short-story
writer and has also written detective narratives and
two movie scripts. Unquestionably, Borges is a short-
story writer of worldwide stature. For further reading: Labyrinths, Selected Stories and Other Writings
(1962).

The Secret Miracle

JORGE LUIS BORGES

And God had him die for a hundred years and
then revived him and said:
"How long have you been here?"
"A day or a part of a day," he answered.
Koran, II, 261

The night of March 14, 1943, in an apartment in the Zeltnergasse of
Prague, Jaromir Hladik, the author of the unfinished drama entitled *The
Enemies*, of *Vindication of Eternity* and of a study of the indirect Jewish

sources of Jakob Böhme, had a dream of a long game of chess. The players were not two persons, but two illustrious families; the game had been going on for centuries. Nobody could remember what the stakes were, but it was rumored that they were enormous, perhaps infinite; the chessmen and the board were in a secret tower. Jaromir (in his dream) was the first-born of one of the contending families. The clock struck the hour for the game, which could not be postponed. The dreamer raced over the sands of a rainy desert, and was unable to recall either the pieces or the rules of chess. At that moment he awoke. The clangor of the rain and of the terrible clocks ceased. A rhythmic, unanimous noise, punctuated by shouts of command, arose from the Zeltnergasse. It was dawn, and the armored vanguard of the Third Reich was entering Prague.

On the nineteenth the authorities received a denunciation; that same nineteenth, toward evening, Jaromir Hladik was arrested. He was taken to an aseptic, white barracks on the opposite bank of the Moldau. He was unable to refute a single one of the Gestapo's charges; his mother's family name was Jaroslavski, he was of Jewish blood, his study on Böhme had a marked Jewish emphasis, his signature had been one more on the protest against the *Anschluss*. In 1928 he had translated the *Sepher Yezirah* for the publishing house of Hermann Barsdorf. The fulsome catalogue of the firm had exaggerated, for publicity purposes, the translator's reputation, and the catalogue had been examined by Julius Rothe, one of the officials who held Hladik's fate in his hands. There is not a person who, except in the field of his own specialization, is not credulous; two or three adjectives in Gothic type were enough to persuade Julius Rothe of Hladik's importance, and he ordered him sentenced to death *pour encourager les autres*. The execution was set for March 29th, at 9:00 A.M. This delay (whose importance the reader will grasp later) was owing to the desire on the authorities' part to proceed impersonally and slowly, after the manner of vegetables and plants.

Hladik's first reaction was mere terror. He felt he would not have shrunk from the gallows, the block, or the knife, but that death by a firing squad was unbearable. In vain he tried to convince himself that the plain, unvarnished fact of dying was the fearsome thing, not the attendant circumstances. He never wearied of conjuring up these circumstances, senselessly trying to exhaust all their possible variations. He infinitely anticipated the process of his dying, from the sleepless dawn to the mysterious volley. Before the day set by Julius Rothe he died hundreds of deaths in courtyards whose forms and angles strained geometrical probabilities, machine-gunned by variable soldiers in changing numbers, who at times killed him from a distance, at others from close by. He faced these imaginary executions with real terror (perhaps with real bravery); each simulacrum lasted a few seconds. When the circle was closed, Jaromir returned once more and interminably to the tremulous vespers of his death. Then he reflected that reality does not usually coincide with our anticipation of it; with a logic of his own he inferred that to foresee a circumstantial detail is to prevent its happening. Trusting in this weak magic, he invented, *so that they would not happen*, the most gruesome details. Finally, as was natural, he came to fear that they were prophetic. Miserable in the night, he endeavored to find some way to hold fast to the fleeting substance of time. He knew that it was rushing headlong toward the dawn of the twenty-ninth. He reasoned aloud: "I am now in the night of the twenty-second; while this night lasts (and for six nights more), I am invulnerable, immortal." The nights of sleep seemed to him deep, dark pools in which he could submerge himself. There were moments when he longed impatiently for the final burst of fire that would free him, for better or for worse, from the vain compulsion of his imaginings. On the twenty-eighth, as the last sunset was reverberating from the high barred windows, the thought of his drama, *The Enemies*, deflected him from these abject considerations.

Hladik had rounded forty. Aside from a few friendships and many habits, the problematic exercise of literature constituted his life. Like all writers, he measured the achievements of others by what they had accomplished, asking of them that they measure him by what he envisaged or planned. All the books he had published had left him with a complex feeling of repentance. His studies of the work of Böhme, of Ibn Ezra, and of Fludd had been characterized essentially by mere application; his translation of the *Sepher Yezirah*, by carelessness, fatigue, and conjecture. *Vindication of Eternity* perhaps had fewer shortcomings. The first volume gave a history of man's various concepts of eternity, from the immutable Being of Parmenides to the modifiable Past of Hinton. The second denied (with Francis Bradley) that all the events of the universe make up a temporal series, arguing that the number of man's possible experiences is not infinite, and that a single "repetition" suffices to prove that time is a fallacy ...Unfortunately, the arguments that demonstrate this fallacy are equally fallacious. Hladik was in the habit of going over them with a kind of contemptuous perplexity. He had also composed a series of Expressionist poems; to the poet's chagrin they had been included in an anthology published in 1924, and no subsequent anthology but inherited them. From all this equivocal, uninspired past Hladik had hoped to redeem himself with his drama in verse, *The Enemies*. (Hladik felt the verse form to be essential because it makes it impossible for the spectators to lose sight of irreality, one of art's requisites.)

The drama observed the unities of time, place, and action. The scene was laid in Hradčany, in the library of Baron von Roemerstadt, on one of the last afternoons of the nineteenth century. In the first scene of the first act a strange man visits Roemerstadt. (A clock was striking seven, the vehemence of the setting sun's rays glorified the windows, a passionate, familiar Hungarian music floated in the air.) This visit is followed by others; Roemerstadt does not know the people who are importuning him, but he has the uncomfortable feeling that he has seen them somewhere, perhaps in a dream. They all fawn upon him, but it is apparent—first to the audience and then to the Baron—that they are secret enemies, in league to ruin him. Roemerstadt succeeds in checking or evading their involved schemings. In the dialogue mention is made of his sweetheart, Julia von Wiedenau, and a certain Jaroslav Kubin, who at one time pressed his attentions on her. Kubin has now lost his mind, and believes himself to be Roemerstadt. The dangers increase; Roemerstadt, at the end of the second act, is forced to kill one of the conspirators. The third and final act opens. The incoherencies gradually increase; actors who had seemed out of the play reappear; the man Roemerstadt killed returns for a moment. Someone points out that evening has not fallen; the clock strikes seven, the high windows reverberate in the western sun, the air carries an impassioned Hungarian melody. The first actor comes on and repeats the lines he had spoken in the first scene of the first act. Roemerstadt speaks to him without surprise; the audience understands that Roemerstadt is the miserable Jaroslav Kubin. The drama has never taken place; it is the circular delirium that Kubin lives and relives endlessly.

Hladik had never asked himself whether this tragicomedy of errors was preposterous or admirable, well thought out or slipshod. He felt that the plot I have just sketched was best contrived to cover up his defects and point up his abilities and held the possibility of allowing him to redeem (symbolically) the meaning of his life. He had finished the first act and one or two scenes of the third; the metrical nature of the work made it possible for him to keep working it over, changing the hexameters, without the manuscript in front of him. He thought how he still had two acts to do, and that he was going to die very soon. He spoke with God in the darkness: "If in some fashion I exist, if I am not one of Your repetitions and mistakes, I exist as the author of *The Enemies*. To finish this drama, which can justify You, I need another year. Grant me these days, You to whom the centuries and time belong." This was the last night, the most dreadful of all, but ten minutes later sleep flooded over him like a dark water.

Toward dawn he dreamed that he had concealed himself in one of the naves of the Clementine Library. A librarian wearing dark glasses asked him: "What are you looking for?" Hladik answered: "I am looking for God." The librarian said to him: "God is in one of the letters on one of the pages of one of the four hundred thousand volumes of the Clementine. My fathers and the fathers of my fathers have searched for this letter; I have grown blind seeking it." He removed his glasses, and Hladik saw his eyes, which were dead. A reader came in to return an atlas. "This atlas is worthless," he said, and handed it to Hladik, who opened it at random. He saw a map of India as in a daze. Suddenly sure of himself, he touched one of the tiniest letters. A ubiquitous voice said to him: "The time of your labor has been granted." At this point Hladik awoke.

He remembered that men's dreams belong to God, and that Maimonides had written that the words heard in a dream are divine when they are distinct and clear and the person uttering them cannot be seen. He dressed: two soldiers came into the cell and ordered him to follow them.

From behind the door, Hladik had envisaged a labyrinth of passageways, stairs, and separate buildings. The reality was less spectacular: they descended to an inner court by a narrow iron stairway. Several soldiers—some with uniform unbuttoned—were examining a motorcycle and discussing it. The sergeant looked at the clock; it was 8:44. They had to wait until it struck nine. Hladik, more insignificant than pitiable, sat down on a pile of wood. He noticed that the soldiers' eyes avoided his. To ease his wait, the sergeant handed him a cigarette. Hladik did not smoke; he accepted it out of politeness or humility. As he lighted it, he noticed that his hands were shaking. The day was clouding over; the soldiers spoke in a low voice as though he were already dead. Vainly he tried to recall the woman of whom Julia von Weidenau was the symbol.

The squad formed and stood at attention. Hladik, standing against the barracks wall, waited for the volley. Someone pointed out that the wall was going to be stained with blood; the victim was ordered to step forward a few paces. Incongruously, this reminded Hladik of the fumbling preparations of photographers. A big drop of rain struck one of Hladik's temples and rolled slowly down his cheek; the sergeant shouted the final order.

The physical universe came to a halt.

The guns converged on Hladik, but the men who were to kill him stood motionless. The sergeant's arm eternized an unfinished gesture. On a paving stone of the courtyard a bee cast an unchanging shadow. The wind had ceased, as in a picture. Hladik attempted a cry, a word, a movement of the hand. He realized that he was paralyzed. Not a sound reached him from the halted world. He thought: "I am in hell, I am dead." He thought: "I am mad." He thought: "Time has stopped." Then he reflected that if that was the case, his mind would have stopped too. He wanted to test this; he repeated (without moving his lips) Vergil's mysterious fourth Eclogue. He imagined that the now remote soldiers must be sharing his anxiety; he longed to be able to communicate with them. It astonished him not to feel the least fatigue, not even the numbness of his protracted immobility. After an indeterminate time he fell asleep. When he awoke the world continued motionless and mute. The drop of water still clung to his cheek, the shadow of the bee to the stone. The smoke from the cigarette he had thrown away had not dispersed. Another "day" went by before Hladik understood.

He had asked God for a whole year to finish his work; His omnipotence had granted it. God had worked a secret miracle for him; German lead would kill him at the set hour, but in his mind a year would go by between the order and its execution. From perplexity he passed to stupor, from stupor to resignation, from resignation to sudden gratitude.

He had no document but his memory; the training he had acquired with each added hexameter gave him a discipline unsuspected by those who set down and forget temporary, incomplete paragraphs. He was not working for posterity or even for God, whose literary tastes were unknown to him. Meticulously, motionlessly, secretly, he wrought in time his lofty, invisible labyrinth. He worked the third act over twice. He eliminated certain symbols as over-obvious, such as the repeated striking of the clock, the music. Nothing hurried him. He omitted, he condensed, he amplified. In certain instances he came back to the original version. He came to feel an affection for the courtyard, the barracks; one of the faces before him modified his conception of Roemerstadt's character. He discovered that the wearying cacophonies that bothered Flaubert so much are mere visual superstitions, weakness and limitation of the written word, not the spoken . . . He concluded his drama. He had only the problem of a single phrase. He found it. The drop of water slid down his cheek. He opened his mouth in a maddened cry, moved his face, dropped under the quadruple blast.

Jaromir Hladik died on March 29, at 9:02 A.M.

Bernard Malamud (1914–   ) was born in Brooklyn
and attended both the College of the City of New
York and Columbia University. He has taught in
New York City high schools and at Oregon State
University. Currently he lives with his wife and
children in Vermont. For further reading: The Magic
Barrel (1958), Idiots First (1964).

The Jewbird

BERNARD MALAMUD

The window was open so the skinny bird flew in. Flippity-flap with its
frazzled black wings. That's how it goes. It's open, you're in. Closed, you're
out and that's your fate. The bird wearily flapped through the open kitchen
window by Harry Cohen's top-floor apartment on First Avenue near the
lower East River. On a rod on the wall hung an escaped canary cage, its
door wide open, but this blacktype longbeaked bird—its ruffled head and
small dull eyes, crossed a little, making it look like a dissipated crow—
landed if not smack on Cohen's thick lamb chop, at least on the table, close
by. The frozen foods salesman was sitting at supper with his wife and
young son on a hot August evening a year ago. Cohen, a heavy man with
hairy chest and beefy shorts; Edie, in skinny yellow shorts and red halter;
and their ten-year-old Morris (after her father)—Maurie, they called him, a
nice kid though not overly bright—were all in the city after two weeks out,
because Cohen's mother was dying. They had been enjoying Kingston,
New York, but drove back when Mama got sick in her flat in the Bronx.

"Right on the table," said Cohen, putting down his beer glass and
swatting at the bird. "Son of a bitch."

"Harry, take care with your language," Edie said, looking at Maurie,
who watched every move.

The bird cawed hoarsely and with a flap of its bedraggled wings—
feathers tufted this way and that—rose heavily to the top of the open
kitchen door, where it perched staring down.

"Gevalt, a pogrom!"

"It's a talking bird," said Edie in astonishment.

"In Jewish," said Maurie.

"Wise guy," muttered Cohen. He gnawed on his chop, then put down the bone. "So if you can talk, say what's your business. What do you want here?"

"If you can't spare a lamb chop," said the bird, "I'll settle for a piece of herring with a crust of bread. You can't live on your nerve forever."

"This ain't a restaurant," Cohen replied. "All I'm asking is what brings you to this address?"

"The window was open," the bird sighed; adding after a moment, "I'm running. I'm flying but I'm also running."

"From whom?" asked Edie with interest.

"Anti-Semeets."

"Anti-Semites?" they all said.

"That's from who."

"What kind of anti-Semites bother a bird?" Edie asked.

"Any kind," said the bird, "also including eagles, vultures, and hawks. And once in a while some crows will take your eyes out."

"But aren't you a crow?"

"Me? I'm a Jewbird."

Cohen laughed heartily. "What do you mean by that?"

The bird began dovening. He prayed without Book or tallith, but with passion. Edie bowed her head though not Cohen. And Maurie rocked back and forth with the prayer, looking up with one wide-open eye.

When the prayer was done Cohen remarked, "No hat, no phylacteries?"

"I'm an old radical."

"You're sure you're not some kind of a ghost or dybbuk?"

"Not a dybbuk," answered the bird, "though one of my relatives had such an experience once. It's all over now, thanks God. They freed her from a former lover, a crazy jealous man. She's now the mother of two wonderful children."

"Birds?" Cohen asked slyly.

"Why not?"

"What kind of birds?"

"Like me. Jewbirds."

Cohen tipped back in his chair and guffawed. "That's a big laugh. I've heard of a Jewfish but not a Jewbird."

"We're once removed." The bird rested on one skinny leg, then on the other. "Please, could you spare maybe a piece of herring with a small crust of bread?"

Edie got up from the table.

"What are you doing?" Cohen asked her.

"I'll clear the dishes."

Cohen turned to the bird. "So what's your name, if you don't mind saying?"

"Call me Schwartz."

"He might be an old Jew changed into a bird by somebody," said Edie, removing a plate.

"Are you?" asked Harry, lighting a cigar.

"Who knows?" answered Schwartz. "Does God tell us everything?"

Maurie got up on his chair. "What kind of herring?" he asked the bird in excitement.

"Get down, Maurie, or you'll fall," ordered Cohen.

"If you haven't got matjes, I'll take schmaltz," said Schwartz.

"All we have is marinated, with slices of onion—in a jar," said Edie.

"If you'll open for me the jar I'll eat marinated. Do you have also, if you don't mind, a piece of rye bread—the spitz?"

Edie thought she had.

"Feed him out on the balcony," Cohen said. He spoke to the bird. "After that take off."

Schwartz closed both bird eyes. "I'm tired and it's a long way."

"Which direction are you headed, north or south?"

Schwartz, barely lifting his wings, shrugged.

"You don't know where you're going?"

"Where there's charity I'll go."

"Let him stay, papa," said Maurie. "He's only a bird."

"So stay the night," Cohen said, "but no longer."

In the morning Cohen ordered the bird out of the house but Maurie cried, so Schwartz stayed for a while. Maurie was still on vacation from school and his friends were away. He was lonely and Edie enjoyed the fun he had, playing with the bird.

"He's no trouble at all," she told Cohen, "and besides his appetite is very small."

"What'll you do when he makes dirty?"

"He flies across the street in a tree when he makes dirty, and if nobody passes below, who notices?"

"So all right," said Cohen, "but I'm dead set against it. I warn you he ain't gonna stay here long."

"What have you got against the poor bird?"

"Poor bird, my ass. He's a foxy bastard. He thinks he's a Jew."

"What difference does it make what he thinks?"

"A Jewbird, what a chuzpah. One false move and he's out on his drumsticks."

At Cohen's insistence Schwartz lived out on the balcony in a new wooden birdhouse Edie had bought him.

"With many thanks," said Schwartz, "though I would rather have a human roof over my head. You know how it is at my age. I like the warm, the windows, the smell of cooking. I would also be glad to see once in a while the *Jewish Morning Journal* and have now and then a schnapps because it helps my breathing, thanks God. But whatever you give me, you won't hear complaints."

However, when Cohen brought home a bird feeder full of dried corn, Schwartz said, "Impossible."

Cohen was annoyed. "What's the matter, crosseyes, is your life getting too good for you? Are you forgetting what it means to be migratory? I'll bet a helluva lot of crows you happen to be acquainted with, Jews or otherwise, would give their eyeteeth to eat this corn."

Schwartz did not answer. What can you say to a grubber yung?

"Not for my digestion," he later explained to Edie. "Cramps. Herring is better even if it makes you thirsty. At least rainwater don't cost anything." He laughed sadly in breathy caws.

And herring, thanks to Edie, who knew where to shop, was what Schwartz got, with an occasional piece of potato pancake, and even a bit of soupmeat when Cohen wasn't looking.

When school began in September, before Cohen would once again suggest giving the bird the boot, Edie prevailed on him to wait a little while until Maurie adjusted.

"To deprive him right now might hurt his school work, and you know what trouble we had last year."

"So okay, but sooner or later the bird goes. That I promise you."

Schwartz, though nobody had asked him, took on full responsibility for Maurie's performance in school. In return for favors granted, when he was let in for an hour or two at night, he spent most of his time overseeing the boy's lessons. He sat on top of the dresser near Maurie's desk as he laboriously wrote out his homework. Maurie was a restless type and Schwartz gently kept him to his studies. He also listened to him practice his screechy violin, taking a few minutes off now and then to rest his ears in the bathroom. And they afterwards played dominoes. The boy was an indifferent checker player and it was impossible to teach him chess. When he was sick, Schwartz read him comic books though he personally disliked them. But Maurie's work improved in school and even his violin teacher admitted his playing was better. Edie gave Schwartz credit for these improvements though the bird pooh-poohed them.

Yet he was proud there was nothing lower than C minuses on Maurie's report card, and on Edie's insistence celebrated with a little schnapps.

"If he keeps up like this," Cohen said, "I'll get him in an Ivy League college for sure."

"Oh I hope so," sighed Edie.

But Schwartz shook his head. "He's a good boy—you don't have to worry. He won't be a shicker or a wifebeater, God forbid, but a scholar he'll never be, if you know what I mean, although maybe a good mechanic. It's no disgrace in these times."

"If I were you," Cohen said, angered, "I'd keep my big snoot out of other people's private business."

"Harry, please," said Edie.

"My goddamn patience is wearing out. That crosseyes butts into everything."

Though he wasn't exactly a welcome guest in the house, Schwartz gained a few ounces although he did not improve in appearance. He looked bedraggled as ever, his feathers unkempt, as though he had just flown out of a snowstorm. He spent, he admitted, little time taking care of himself. Too much to think about. "Also outside plumbing," he told Edie. Still there was more glow to his eyes so that though Cohen went on calling him crosseyes he said it less emphatically.

Liking his situation, Schwartz tried tactfully to stay out of Cohen's way, but one night when Edie was at the movies and Maurie was taking a hot shower, the frozen foods salesman began a quarrel with the bird.

"For Christ sake, why don't you wash yourself sometimes? Why must you always stink like a dead fish?"

"Mr. Cohen, if you'll pardon me, if somebody eats garlic he will smell from garlic. I eat herring three times a day. Feed me flowers and I will smell like flowers."

"Who's obligated to feed you anything at all? You're lucky to get herring."

"Excuse me, I'm not complaining," said the bird. "You're complaining."

"What's more," said Cohen, "even from out on the balcony I can hear you snoring away like a pig. It keeps me awake at night."

"Snoring," said Schwartz, "isn't a crime, thanks God."

"All in all you are a goddamn pest and free loader. Next thing you'll want to sleep in bed next to my wife."

"Mr. Cohen," said Schwartz, "on this rest assured. A bird is a bird."

"So you say, but how do I know you're a bird and not some kind of a goddamn devil?"

"If I was a devil you would know already. And I don't mean because your son's good marks."

"Shut up, you bastard bird," shouted Cohen.

"Grubber yung," cawed Schwartz, rising to the tips of his talons, his long wings outstretched.

Cohen was about to lunge for the bird's scrawny neck but Maurie came out of the bathroom, and for the rest of the evening until Schwartz's bedtime on the balcony, there was pretended peace.

But the quarrel had deeply disturbed Schwartz and he slept badly. His snoring woke him, and awake, he was fearful of what would become of him. Wanting to stay out of Cohen's way, he kept to the birdhouse as much as possible. Cramped by it, he paced back and forth on the balcony ledge, or sat on the birdhouse roof, staring into space. In the evenings, while overseeing Maurie's lessons, he often fell asleep. Awakening, he nervously hopped around exploring the four corners of the room. He spent much time in Maurie's closet, and carefully examined his bureau drawers when they were left open. And once when he found a large paper bag on the floor, Schwartz poked his way into it to investigate what possibilities were. The boy was amused to see the bird in the paper bag.

"He wants to build a nest," he said to his mother.

Edie, sensing Schwartz's unhappiness, spoke to him quietly.

"Maybe if you did some of the things my husband wants you, you would get along better with him."

"Give me a for instance," Schwartz said.

"Like take a bath, for instance."

"I'm too old for baths," said the bird. "My feathers fall out without baths."

"He says you have a bad smell."

"Everybody smells. Some people smell because of their thoughts or because who they are. My bad smell comes from the food I eat. What does his come from?"

"I better not ask him or it might make him mad," said Edie.

In late November Schwartz froze on the balcony in the fog and cold, and especially on rainy days he woke with stiff joints and could barely move his wings. Already he felt twinges of rheumatism. He would have liked to spend more time in the warm house, particularly when Maurie was in school and Cohen at work. But though Edie was good-hearted and might have sneaked him in in the morning, just to thaw out, he was afraid to ask her. In the meantime Cohen, who had been reading articles about the migration of birds, came out on the balcony one night after work when Edie was in the kitchen preparing pot roast, and peeking into the birdhouse, warned Schwartz to be on his way soon if he knew what was good for him. "Time to hit the flyways."

"Mr. Cohen, why do you hate me so much?" asked the bird. "What did I do to you?"

"Because you're an A-number-one trouble maker, that's why. What's more, whoever heard of a Jewbird? Now scat or it's open war."

But Schwartz stubbornly refused to depart so Cohen embarked on a campaign of harassing him, meanwhile hiding it from Edie and Maurie. Maurie hated violence and Cohen didn't want to leave a bad impression. He thought maybe if he played dirty tricks on the bird he would fly off without being physically kicked out. The vacation was over, let him make his easy living off the fat of somebody else's land. Cohen worried about the effect of the bird's departure on Maurie's schooling but decided to take the chance, first, because the boy now seemed to have the knack of studying—give the black bird-bastard credit—and second, because Schwartz was driving him bats by being there always, even in his dreams.

The frozen foods salesman began his campaign against the bird by mixing watery cat food with the herring slices in Schwartz's dish. He also blew up and popped numerous paper bags outside the birdhouse as the bird slept, and when he had got Schwartz good and nervous, though not enough to leave, he brought a full-grown cat into the house, supposedly a gift for little Maurie, who had always wanted a pussy. The cat never stopped springing up at Schwartz whenever he saw him, one day managing to claw out several of his tailfeathers. And even at lesson time, when the cat was usually excluded from Maurie's room, though somehow or other he quickly found his way in at the end of the lesson, Schwartz was desperately fearful of his life and flew from pinnacle to pinnacle—light fixture to clothestree to door-top—in order to elude the beast's wet jaws.

Once when the bird complained to Edie how hazardous his existence was, she said, "Be patient, Mr. Schwartz. When the cat gets to know you better he won't try to catch you any more."

"When he stops trying we will both be in Paradise," Schwartz answered. "Do me a favor and get rid of him. He makes my whole life worry. I'm losing feathers like a tree loses leaves."

"I'm awfully sorry but Maurie likes the pussy and sleeps with it."

What could Schwartz do? He worried but came to no decision, being afraid to leave. So he ate the herring garnished with cat food, tried hard not to hear the paper bags bursting like fire crackers outside the birdhouse at night, and lived terror-stricken closer to the ceiling than the floor, as the cat, his tail flicking, endlessly watched him.

Weeks went by. Then on the day after Cohen's mother had died in her flat in the Bronx, when Maurie came home with a zero on an arithmetic test, Cohen, enraged, waited until Edie had taken the boy to his violin lesson, then openly attacked the bird. He chased him with a broom on the balcony and Schwartz frantically flew back and forth, finally escaping into his birdhouse. Cohen triumphantly reached in and grabbing both skinny legs, dragged the bird out, cawing loudly, his wings wildly beating. He whirled the bird around and around his head. But Schwartz, as he moved in circles, managed to sweep down and catch Cohen's nose in his beak, and hung on for dear life. Cohen cried out in great pain, punched the bird with his fist, and tugged at its legs with all his might, pulled his nose free. Again he swung the yawking Schwartz around till the bird grew dizzy, then with a furious heave, flung him into the night. Schwartz sank like stone into the street. Cohen then tossed the birdhouse and feeder after him, listening at the ledge until they crashed on the sidewalk below. For a full hour, broom in hand, his heart palpitating and nose throbbing with pain, Cohen waited for Schwartz to return but the broken-hearted bird didn't.

That's the end of that dirty bastard, the salesman thought and went in. Edie and Maurie had come home.

"Look," said Cohen, pointing to his bloody nose swollen three times its normal size, "what that sonofabitchy bird did. It's a permanent scar."

"Where is he now?" Edie asked, frightened.

"I threw him out and he flew away. Good riddance."

Nobody said no, though Edie touched a handkerchief to her eyes and Maurie rapidly tried the nine times table and found he knew approximately half.

In the spring when the winter's snow had melted, the boy, moved by a memory, wandered in the neighborhood, looking for Schwartz. He found a dead black bird in a small lot near the river, his two wings broken, neck twisted, and both bird-eyes plucked clean.

"Who did it to you, Mr. Schwartz?" Maurie wept.

"Anti-Semeets," Edie said later.

Shirley Jackson (1916–1965) was born in San Francisco and was a novelist, essayist, and short-story writer. Her work was strongly influenced by the discipline of anthropology. For further reading: The Lottery, or The Adventures of James Harris (1949), We have Always Lived in the Castle (1962).

The Lottery

SHIRLEY JACKSON

The morning of June 27th was clear and sunny, with the fresh warmth of a full-summer day; the flowers were blossoming profusely and the grass was richly green. The people of the village began to gather in the square, between the post office and the bank, around ten o'clock; in some towns there were so many people that the lottery took two days and had to be started on June 26th, but in this village, where there were only about three hundred people, the whole lottery took less than two hours, so it could begin at ten o'clock in the morning and still be through in time to allow the villagers to get home for noon dinner.

The children assembled first, of course. School was recently over for the summer, and the feeling of liberty sat uneasily on most of them; they tended to gather together quietly for a while before they broke into boisterous play, and their talk was still of the classroom and the teacher, of books and reprimands. Bobby Martin had already stuffed his pockets full of stones, and the other boys soon followed his example, selecting the smoothest and roundest stones; Bobby and Harry Jones and Dickie Delacroix—the villagers pronounced this name "Dellacroy"—eventually made a great pile of stones in one corner of the square and guarded it against the raids of the other boys. The girls stood aside, talking among themselves, looking over their shoulders at the boys, and the very small children rolled in the dust or clung to the hands of their older brothers or sisters.

Soon the men began to gather, surveying their own children, speaking of planting and rain, tractors and taxes. They stood together, away from the pile of stones in the corner, and their jokes were quiet and they smiled rather than laughed. The women, wearing faded house dresses and sweaters, came shortly after their menfolk. They greeted one another and exchanged bits of gossip as they went to join their husbands. Soon the women, standing by their husbands, began to call to their children, and the children came reluctantly, having to be called four or five times. Bobby Martin ducked under his mother's grasping hand and ran, laughing, back to the pile of stones. His father spoke up sharply, and Bobby came quickly and took his place between his father and his oldest brother.

The lottery was conducted—as were the square dances, the teen-age club, the Halloween program—by Mr. Summers, who had time and energy to devote to civic activities. He was a round-faced, jovial man and he ran the coal business, and people were sorry for him, because he had no children and his wife was a scold. When he arrived in the square, carrying the black wooden box, there was a murmur of conversation among the villagers, and he waved and called, "Little late today, folks." The postmaster, Mr. Graves, followed him, carrying a three-legged stool, and the stool was put in the center of the square and Mr. Summers set the black box down on it. The villagers kept their distance, leaving a space between themselves and the stool, and when Mr. Summers said, "Some of you fellows want to give me a hand?" there was a hesitation before two men, Mr. Martin and his oldest son, Baxter, came forward to hold the box steady on the stool while Mr. Summers stirred up the papers inside it.

The original paraphernalia for the lottery had been lost long ago, and the black box now resting on the stool had been put into use even before Old Man Warner, the oldest man in town, was born. Mr. Summers spoke frequently to the villagers about making a new box, but no one liked to upset even as much tradition as was represented by the black box. There was a story that the present box had been made with some pieces of the box that had preceded it, the one that had been constructed when the first people settled down to make a village here. Every year, after the lottery, Mr. Summers began talking again about a new box, but every year the subject was allowed to fade off without anything's being done. The black box grew shabbier each year; by now it was no longer completely black but splintered badly along one side to show the original wood color, and in some places faded or stained.

Mr. Martin and his oldest son, Baxter, held the black box securely on the stool until Mr. Summers had stirred the papers thoroughly with his hand. Because so much of the ritual had been forgotten or discarded, Mr. Summers had been successful in having slips of paper substituted for the chips of wood that had been used for generations. Chips of wood, Mr. Summers had argued, had been all very well when the village was tiny, but now that the population was more than three hundred and likely to keep on growing, it was necessary to use something that would fit more easily into the black box. The night before the lottery, Mr. Summers and Mr. Graves made up the slips of paper and put them in the box, and it was then taken to the safe of Mr. Summers' coal company and locked up until Mr. Summers was ready to take it to the square next morning. The rest of the year, the box was put away, sometimes one place, sometimes another; it had spent one year in Mr. Graves's barn and another year under foot in the post office, and sometimes it was set on a shelf in the Martin grocery and left there.

There was a great deal of fussing to be done before Mr. Summers declared the lottery open. There were the lists to make up—of heads of families, heads of households in each family, members of each household in each family. There was the proper swearing-in of Mr. Summers by the postmaster, as the official of the lottery; at one time, some people remembered, there had been a recital of some sort; performed by the official of the lottery, a perfunctory, tuneless chant that had been rattled off duly each year; some people believed that the official of the lottery used to stand just so when he said or sang it, others believed that he was supposed to walk among the people, but years and years ago this part of the ritual had been allowed to lapse. There had been, also, a ritual salute, which the official of the lottery had had to use in addressing each person who came up to draw from the box, but this also had changed with time, until now it was felt necessary only for the official to speak to each person approaching. Mr. Summers was very good at all this; in his clean white shirt and blue jeans, with one hand resting carelessly on the black box, he seemed very proper and important as he talked interminably to Mr. Graves and the Martins.

Just as Mr. Summers finally left off talking and turned to the assembled villagers, Mrs. Hutchinson came hurriedly along the path to the square, her sweater thrown over her shoulders, and slid into place in the back of the crowd. "Clean forgot what day it was," she said to Mrs. Delacroix, who stood next to her, and they both laughed softly. "Thought my old man was out back stacking wood," Mrs. Hutchinson went on, "and then I looked out the window and the kids was gone, and then I remembered it was the twenty-seventh and came a-running." She dried her hands on her apron, and Mrs. Delacroix said, "You're in time, though. They're still talking away up there."

Mrs. Hutchinson craned her neck to see through the crowd and found her husband and children standing near the front. She tapped Mrs. Delacroix on the arm as a farewell and began to make her way through the crowd. The people separated good-humoredly to let her through; two or three people said, in voices just loud enough to be heard across the crowd, "Here comes your Missus, Hutchinson," and "Bill, she made it after all." Mrs. Hutchinson reached her husband, and Mr. Summers, who had been waiting, said cheerfully, "Thought we were going to have to get on without you, Tessie." Mrs. Hutchinson said, grinning, "Wouldn't have me leave m'dishes in the sink, now, would you, Joe?," and soft laughter ran through the crowd as the people stirred back into position after Mrs. Hutchinson's arrival.

"Well, now," Mr. Summers said soberly, "guess we better get started, get this over with, so's we can go back to work. Anybody ain't here?"

"Dunbar," several people said. "Dunbar, Dunbar."

Mr. Summers consulted his list. "Clyde Dunbar," he said. "That's right. He's broke his leg, hasn't he? Who's drawing for him?"

"Me, I guess," a woman said, and Mr. Summers turned to look at her. "Wife draws for her husband," Mr. Summers said. "Don't you have a grown boy to do it for you, Janey?" Although Mr. Summers and everyone else in the village knew the answer perfectly well, it was the business of the official of the lottery to ask such questions formally. Mr. Summers waited with an expression of polite interest while Mrs. Dunbar answered.

"Horace's not but sixteen yet," Mrs. Dunbar said regretfully. "Guess I gotta fill in for the old man this year."

"Right," Mr. Summers said. He made a note on the list he was holding. Then he asked, "Watson boy drawing this year?"

A tall boy in the crowd raised his hand. "Here," he said. "I'm drawing for m'mother and me." He blinked his eyes nervously and ducked his head as several voices in the crowd said things like "Good fellow, Jack," and "Glad to see your mother's got a man to do it."

"Well," Mr. Summers said, "guess that's everyone. Old Man Warner make it?"

"Here," a voice said, and Mr. Summers nodded.

A sudden hush fell on the crowd as Mr. Summers cleared his throat and looked at the list. "All ready?" he called. "Now, I'll read the names—heads of families first—and the men come up and take a paper out of the box. Keep the paper folded in your hand without looking at it until everyone has had a turn. Everything clear?"

The people had done it so many times that they only half listened to the directions; most of them were quiet, wetting their lips, not looking around. Then Mr. Summers raised one hand high and said, "Adams." A man disengaged himself from the crowd and came forward. "Hi, Steve," Mr. Summers said, and Mr. Adams said, "Hi, Joe." They grinned at one another humorlessly and nervously. Then Mr. Adams reached into the black box and took out a folded paper. He held it firmly by one corner as he turned and went hastily back to his place in the crowd, where he stood a little apart from his family not looking down at his hand.

"Allen," Mr. Summers said. "Anderson. . . . Bentham."

"Seems like there's no time at all between lotteries any more," Mrs. Delacroix said to Mrs. Graves in the back row. "Seems like we got through with the last one only last week."

"Time sure goes fast," Mrs. Graves said.

"Clark. . . . Delacroix."

"There goes my old man," Mrs. Delacroix said. She held her breath while her husband went forward.

"Dunbar," Mr. Summers said, and Mrs. Dunbar went steadily to the box while one of the women said, "Go on, Janey," and another said, "There she goes."

"We're next," Mrs. Graves said. She watched while Mr. Graves came around from the side of the box, greeted Mr. Summers gravely, and selected a slip of paper from the box. By now, all through the crowd there were men holding the small folded papers in their large hands, turning them over and over nervously. Mrs. Dunbar and her two sons stood together, Mrs. Dunbar holding the slip of paper.

"Harburt. . . . Hutchinson."

"Get up there, Bill," Mrs. Hutchinson said, and the people near her laughed.

"Jones."

"They do say," Mr. Adams said to Old Man Warner, who stood next to him, "that over in the north village they're talking of giving up the lottery."

Old Man Warner snorted. "Pack of crazy fools," he said. "Listening to the young folks, nothing's good enough for *them*. Next thing you know, they'll be wanting to go back to living in caves, nobody work any more, live *that* way for a while. Used to be a saying about 'Lottery in June, corn be heavy soon.' First thing you know, we'd all be eating stewed chickweed and acorns. There's *always* been a lottery," he added petulantly. "Bad enough to see young Joe Summers up there joking with everybody."

"Some places have already quit lotteries," Mrs. Adams said.

"Nothing but trouble in *that*," Old Man Warner said stoutly. "Pack of young fools."

"Martin." And Bobby Martin watched his father go forward. "Over-dyke. . . . Percy."

"I wish they'd hurry," Mrs. Dunbar said to her older son. "I wish they'd hurry."

"They're almost through," her son said.

"You get ready to run tell Dad," Mrs. Dunbar said.

Mr. Summers called his own name and then stepped forward precisely and selected a slip from the box. Then he called, "Warner."

"Seventy-seventh year I been in the lottery," Old Man Warner said as he went through the crowd. "Seventy-seventh time."

"Watson." The tall boy came awkwardly through the crowd. Someone said, "Don't be nervous, Jack," and Mr. Summers said, "Take your time, son."

"Zanini."

After that, there was a long pause, a breathless pause, until Mr. Summers, holding his slip of paper in the air, said, "All right, fellows." For a minute, no one moved, and then all the slips of paper were opened. Suddenly, all the women began to speak at once, saying, "Who is it?," "Who's got it?," "Is it the Dunbars?," "Is it the Watsons?" Then the voices began to say, "It's Hutchinson. It's Bill," "Bill Hutchinson's got it."

"Go tell your father," Mrs. Dunbar said to her older son.

People began to look around to see the Hutchinsons. Bill Hutchinson was standing quiet, staring down at the paper in his hand. Suddenly, Tessie Hutchinson shouted to Mr. Summers, "You didn't give him time enough to take any paper he wanted. I saw you. It wasn't fair!"

"Be a good sport, Tessie," Mrs. Delacroix called, and Mrs. Graves said, "All of us took the same chance."

"Shut up, Tessie," Bill Hutchinson said.

"Well, everyone," Mr. Summers said, "that was done pretty fast, and now we've got to be hurrying a little more to get done in time." He consulted his next list. "Bill," he said, "you draw for the Hutchinson family. You got any other households in the Hutchinsons?"

"There's Don and Eva," Mrs. Hutchinson yelled. "Make *them* take their chance!"

"Daughters draw with their husbands' families, Tessie," Mr. Summers said gently. "You know that as well as anyone else."

"It wasn't *fair*," Tessie said.

"I guess not, Joe," Bill Hutchinson said regretfully. "My daughter draws with her husband's family, that's only fair. And I've got no other family except the kids."

"Then, as far as drawing for families is concerned, it's you," Mr. Summers said in explanation, "and as far as drawing for households is concerned, that's you, too. Right?"

"Right," Bill Hutchinson said.

"How many kids, Bill?" Mr. Summers asked formally.

"Three," Bill Hutchinson said. "There's Bill, Jr., and Nancy, and little Dave. And Tessie and me."

"All right, then," Mr. Summers said. "Harry, you got their tickets back?"

Mr. Graves nodded and held up the slips of paper. "Put them in the box, then," Mr. Summers directed. "Take Bill's and put it in."

"I think we ought to start over," Mrs. Hutchinson said, as quietly as she could. "I tell you it wasn't *fair*. You didn't give him time enough to choose. *Everybody* saw that."

Mr. Graves had selected the five slips and put them in the box, and he dropped all the papers but those onto the ground, where the breeze caught them and lifted them off.

"Listen, everybody," Mrs. Hutchinson was saying to the people around her.

"Ready, Bill?" Mr. Summers asked, and Bill Hutchinson, with one quick glance around at his wife and children, nodded.

"Remember," Mr. Summers said, "take the slips and keep them folded until each person has taken one. Harry, you help little Dave." Mr. Graves took the hand of the little boy, who came willingly with him up to the box. "Take a paper out of the box, Davy," Mr. Summers said. Davy put his hand into the box and laughed. "Take just *one* paper," Mr. Summers said. "Harry, you hold it for him." Mr. Graves took the child's hand and removed the folded paper from the tight fist and held it while little Dave stood next to him and looked up at him wonderingly.

"Nancy next," Mr. Summers said. Nancy was twelve, and her school friends breathed heavily as she went forward, switching her skirt, and took a slip daintily from the box. "Bill, Jr.," Mr. Summers said, and Billy, his face red and his feet over-large, nearly knocked the box over as he got a paper out. "Tessie," Mr. Summers said. She hesitated for a minute, looking around defiantly, and then set her lips and went up to the box. She snatched a paper out and held it behind her.

"Bill," Mr. Summers said, and Bill Hutchinson reached into the box and felt around, bringing his hand out at last with the slip of paper in it.

The crowd was quiet. A girl whispered, "I hope it's not Nancy," and the sound of the whisper reached the edges of the crowd.

"It's not the way it used to be," Old Man Warner said clearly. "People ain't the way they used to be."

"All right," Mr. Summers said. "Open the papers. Harry, you open little Dave's."

Mr. Graves opened the slip of paper and there was a general sigh through the crowd as he held it up and everyone could see that it was blank. Nancy and Bill, Jr., opened theirs at the same time, and both beamed and laughed, turning around to the crowd and holding their slips of paper above their heads.

"Tessie," Mr. Summers said. There was a pause, and then Mr. Summers looked at Bill Hutchinson, and Bill unfolded his paper and showed it. It was blank.

"It's Tessie," Mr. Summers said, and his voice was hushed. "Show us her paper, Bill."

Bill Hutchinson went over to his wife and forced the slip of paper out of her hand. It had a black spot on it, the black spot Mr. Summers had made the night before with the heavy pencil in the coal-company office. Bill Hutchinson held it up, and there was a stir in the crowd.

"All right, folks," Mr. Summers said. "Let's finish quickly."

Although the villagers had forgotten the ritual and lost the original black box, they still remembered to use stones. The pile of stones the boys had made earlier was ready; there were stones on the ground with the blowing scraps of paper that had come out of the box. Mrs. Delacroix selected a stone so large she had to pick it up with both hands and turned to Mrs. Dunbar. "Come on," she said. "Hurry up."

Mrs. Dunbar had small stones in both hands, and she said, gasping for breath, "I can't run at all. You'll have to go ahead and I'll catch up with you."

The children had stones already, and someone gave little Davy Hutchinson a few pebbles.

Tessie Hutchinson was in the center of a cleared space by now, and she held her hands out desperately as the villagers moved in on her. "It isn't fair," she said. A stone hit her on the side of the head.

Old Man Warner was saying, "Come on, come on, everyone." Steve Adams was in the front of the crowd of villagers, with Mrs. Graves beside him.

"It isn't fair, it isn't right," Mrs. Hutchinson screamed, and then they were upon her.

Check!

SLAWOMIR MROZEK

The day was cloudy. I do not mind the weather myself, but I met a friend
who seemed to be very worried about it.

"I'm developing rheumatism. Can't be helped. I wouldn't pay much attention to it, but what's worse, I caught a cold a few days ago. But all I
need now is to get soaked through. I already have the beginnings of a 'flu.
My bones are aching. And what next? Nobody can be sure that there will
be no serious complications."

I pointed out that after all he did not have to get soaked through; all he
had to do was to stay under cover when it rained. And thank God we were
not short of roofs.

"It's easy for you to talk, you've no outdoor duties. But I have to work
in the open day in day out. One has got to live."

I asked about his work. We had known each other for a long time.
Together we had worked as extras in the theatre. We had had a succession
of temporary jobs, always at the mercy of changing circumstances: delivery
men, part-time caretakers, fourth men at bridge or fourteenth at dinner,
temporary comforters, birds of passage, bodyguards, baby-sitters and professional guests.

He explained that he had found relatively light work, which would have
been entirely satisfactory if it were not for his inborn sensitivity to changes
of temperature.

"Do you know what living chess is? It's exactly the same as normal
chess, except that instead of a chessboard on a table one uses a much
larger board marked out on the pavement of a square; instead of inani-
mate chessmen real men suitably dressed up take part in the game. The
players themselves must, of course, be in raised positions at the opposite
sides of the board so that they can see it all at a glance. Because of its

value as a spectacle, live chess is organized as a part of celebrations and open-air festivals. The public likes it very much. After all, how many people can watch a game on a normal board? Three, five at the most, and they disturb the players. Now, any number can watch live chess, while the players, separated from the multitude, are able to concentrate on the problem of winning. Add to that the attraction of colourful costumes and you'll see why live chess is a popular spectacle. You will find it also in clubs which have a suitable courtyard or other space at their disposal.

"Apart from space you need, of course, the personnel. Sixteen men for the white and sixteen for the black, and a few reserve (men are only human), and also a wardrobe. The volunteers don't have to pass any exams. After the first few minutes of enjoyment the attractions of the game, which had made them offer their services, tend to evaporate. Soon they get tired and impatient and then withdraw under the slightest pretext (death in the family, an electric iron left on at home, an alleged headache) thus spoiling an interesting game. What's needed are regulars, men who having had no interest in the game don't stand the risk of losing it and can be relied upon to stick it to the end without any ups or downs. They get a regular salary, and as professionals they give the required standard of service.

"The work is relatively light. I say, relatively, because this depends on a number of variable factors. In the summer, when the sun shines, it can be quite pleasant, as long as you don't suffer from sunstroke. In the autumn, during protracted foul weather, it can give you a cold and induce melancholia. The winter is worst. There are games played in a snow storm, when you can't see more than two squares ahead and one has got to be careful not to take one of one's own pieces.

"At the moment it's still summer, but a rainy one. I wouldn't complain," ended my friend, "if it were not for the clouds and my tonsils. If I don't go to work to-day, they can give me notice. I'm playing a Bishop. I reached that position with a great deal of effort and to the envy of my colleagues. Will you take over for one day only? Please! Perhaps to-morrow the weather will improve. You'll get full day's pay. It's not too bad; Bishops get more because there is so much running to do. Anyway all the figures get more. One day I might become King."

"I can't," I replied. "I can't stand people looking at me. Don't you remember how this caused difficulties at the theatre? A staring crowd embarrasses me and this leads to a counter-reaction, forcing me into excessively open and frank behaviour. It seems to me that since they come to look at me, it would be less than honest not to show them everything. I was thrown out of the theatre because during a first night, under the influence of so many pairs of eyes, I showed the spectators my boil. And you have said yourself that living chess is a spectacle."

"You needn't worry about that," my friend reassured me. "On this occasion there is no question of a spectacle. I'm working for two old men who have been advised by their doctor to seek outdoor exercise. That's why they gave up ordinary and took up living chess. It's a private game. Apart from the participants you won't see a soul, there won't be a single spectator."

I reflected that I had nothing else to do that day. There was no reason to refuse a favour to a friend, while earning some money at the same time.

"All right," I said, "but will I know how to do it?"

"It is quite simple and the Knight will give you the few essential bits of advice. I'm in the white team and we stand next to each other on the left. At the beginning of each game, before developments separate us, we always manage to exchange a few words."

"Fine. I'll go."

"Go. I'll retire to bed."

We parted.

The game took place in the courtyard of an old palace, enclosed on four sides by two-storied cloisters. I entered through a tunnel-like gateway. A grey square of sky covered the enormous box of the courtyard, so vast that the huge chessboard marked out on its floor did not look large at all. Here and there on the walls vertical pools of Russian vine screened the cloisters. Perhaps because of them the whole courtyard was swathed in an emerald gloom, the intensity of which varied with the passage of mists and clouds high above. A few human figures moving about looked strangely small because we are accustomed to seeing people indoors in restricted spaces, which make them appear large. Here however I found myself under an open sky and yet indoors, as if clever architecture had joined space to enclosure.

As I approached some of the figures acquired a super-natural size. It was because of their costumes. While the pawns were not much larger than normal human beings, the Bishops, Rooks and Knights looked enormous. Only their feet, protruding from under the fantastic dress, remained normal, shod in a variety of old shoes. Above them necks and heads of horses, their teeth bared, each tooth the size of a tile, the severe-looking, geometric and crenellated Rooks, the saucer-like ruffs of the Bishops.

Daunted by all this I involuntarily stopped on the edge of the courtyard. The cavernous gateway, unpleasantly ready to reflect and magnify the slightest noise, suddenly seemed friendly and snug. I did not notice that a black Rook had appeared behind me.

"You are not allowed in here," said a voice from within the castle. I looked at the Rook and noticed painted horizontal and vertical white lines imitating the pointing between bricks. Automatically I looked up to the battlements, though I knew that the head of the speaker must be level with mine.

I explained politely that I was not a casual gaper, but had come to stand in for a sick colleague. The Rook towered over me silently for a while and then from within came the sound as of spitting and he moved away, his heavy shoes creaking on the stones. I entered the courtyard.

On the left wing of the whites I noticed the Knight to whose care my friend had recommended me. I spoke to him and he turned his massive *papier maché* chest and his mane frozen in a picturesque disarray, until his nostrils were right above my head.

"All right," he said. "I'll help you to change. Got a cigarette? We are not allowed to smoke during work, but we could have one now. Mind you, one has to make sure that the smoke doesn't go up, because this can be seen and a supervisor might pick on you. But if you blow the smoke into your trousers, it comes out at the bottom and all's well. You must learn these little tricks."

Under the Knight's guidance I put on the Bishop's involucre. It was dark and stuffy inside it. Through the eye-holes I could see the edge of my frill and a part of the courtyard plunged in a green dusk.

"Yes, my friend," said the Knight, "you've got to know the ins and outs here. Now, for instance, we can have a smoke, but we've got to be careful. We can also eat our sandwiches, but you must remember not to drop the wrapping paper on the ground. Later it is more difficult."

The Queen took her place on my right. Instinctively I looked at her feet and saw frayed trouser turn-ups and shoes with cracked uppers. A bit farther along towered the majestic silhouette of the King with tennis shoes sticking out from under it.

"The King gets the highest salary," explained the Knight, "because he is the heaviest of the lot. In spite of it he is played by an elderly man; though the piece is heavy there's not much walking to be done, and that's important when you are past sixty. Also in old age the few extra pennies come very handy indeed. Should you notice that it is his turn and he's not moving, you'll do him a service if you knock on his side, that's if you are near enough. Sometimes he falls asleep inside still standing on his feet."

The ranks of the white and black pieces were filling in. Beyond them I could see the cloisters. The air, saturated with damp, was far from clear, the clouds in the sky cast their shadows over everything, and the overhanging roof made the walls darker still. Because of all this the columns, arches and balustrades, here and there obliterated by patches of vine, looked like a flat and misty drawing.

"Oho," said the pawn in front of me, "the black Bishop has again been at the bottle."

"He really shouldn't drink," commented the Knight. "Bishops have to run in straight lines. It's different when you're a Knight. Nobody notices if you stray from your course a little bit because as it is you've got to move sideways. . . ."

"Attention," warned the pawn. "It's beginning."

I used to play chess in my time, not badly either, but one did not have to be a master to notice the low level of the game in which I had to take part. First of all the pauses between moves were of such duration that one could not help wondering if the players had fallen asleep or, perhaps, gone away altogether, forgetting to tell us that they had given up. Hidden in the cloisters they kept on falling into endless contemplation, while our legs were getting numb. Eventually their mental efforts led to hopeless and chaotic moves, which betrayed a complete lack of skill on both sides.

Like all the pieces I was moved about a few times without rhyme or reason and this began to worry me.

"What's the matter?" I whispered to the Knight when at last I found myself again at his side.

"Sclerosis," he whispered back. "A short while ago they could still get through a game in five or six hours, but it seems they've got worse."

"Which of the two plays a better game?"

"Neither. That's why it's such hard work. Sometimes they can't finish before it gets too dark and then they leave us where we stand overnight and finish the game the following day. I'm afraid this is going to happen to-night. The game is going badly and the weather is uncertain."

We walked about the chessboard hither and thither, from one square to another. A few pawns got captured. We looked at them with envy as they walked away.

It started raining. A fine rain, the sort that lasts a long time; it starts with deliberation, knowing that it has a few days in hand and need not hurry, and then gradually gathers momentum. My cardboard costume protected me at first, but I was worried about my feet shod only in light shoes.

"See that Rook in boots?" The Knight pointed at a black figure. "Watch out. He likes to give your ankle a kick when capturing you. He'll also tell on you if you squat for a moment to give your tired feet a rest. A proper patriot he is, too. God forbid that black should start losing. He's at his worst then. Sometimes he gets so excited that he starts crying."

"Is it his game, or what?"

"He's just passionate."

Something started dripping under my collar. The dome-like carboard structure over my head had parted in one place and was letting through the rain, its drops unpleasantly cold.

The intervals between moves became incredibly long as the players seemed to have increasing difficulty in taking in the state of the game. As the rain thickened, the gargoyles, through which the rain gutters were discharging, began to sing, shyly at first, but with increasing confidence. From all sides came the individual whisper of drops falling against the general background of a noisy downpour. The black Bishop, his alcoholic euphoria gone, had obviously lost heart and swayed sadly two squares away from me. My friend, the Knight, had been shifted to the other end of the board.

Anger swelled inside me. It was all very well for all those old professionals, used to this kind of discomfort. But my feet were getting wet and I could not reconcile myself to it. And there was no prospect whatsoever of the game ever coming to an end.

"Perhaps someone will capture me," I thought hopefully for a moment. "Then I shall be able to go home. But one cannot rely on a happy accident. What else? Wait. And if they leave us overnight? The Knight said that this could happen."

I could see so many openings, which if exploited could help to bring about a decision. . . . But the most obvious, the most glittering chances were being systematically wasted by both sides. The thought that because of this incompetence I might get pneumonia gave another spur to my anger. Not able to bear it all any longer I decided off my own bat to bring the game to a conclusion.

I was sure that I could get away with a little cheating, with moving one or two squares without any orders. Around me I could see only general apathy. The sclerotic players immersed in their thoughts would not notice anything. Slowly, unobtrusively, I started to shift my position and move into the next square. One had to be careful not to overdo it and brazenly move from a black into a white square, because everyone knows that a Bishop has to stick to one colour throughout the game. But if I avoided such glaring mistakes I was bound to succeed.

Now I had to make my decisive move. Having found myself on the same diagonal as the black Bishop was I had to take my courage in both hands and capture him? But there was a chance that the player directing the black side, seeing his Bishop opposite me, might decide to have me captured. I had to wait. Anyhow I did not want to move about too much. Minutes passed and nothing happened. I counted up to a hundred and decided to take the risk. Moving with purpose I walked up to the black Bishop.

"You're captured, my friend," I said. "You can go home."

In choosing him as my first victim I counted on the fact that in his drunken stupor he was paying even less attention to the game than the others. When I spoke to him he swayed, cleared his throat and did not disguise his joy.

"Splendid. I'm on my way," he cried. "What? Can't a man have a drink?" He spoke with sudden billigerence and fled without waiting for an answer I occupied his square as if it was mine of right.

My calculations proved right. The general boredom and indifference were such that nobody knew or cared if it was white's move or black's. The players themselves must have had one of their mental blackouts and I was also helped by the rain and the gathering dusk.

Just in case, however, I waited a few moments before polishing off two black pawns. Neither of them uttered a word, and with obvious relief they left the chessboard. In this way acting in my own interest I was helping my colleagues.

I could not have cared less about white's victory for which I was working. All I wanted was to bring the game to a conclusion. I expected that once I had captured all the black pieces, even the dimmest idiot would be able to checkmate the lonely King. Gradually I grew insolent and captured any handy piece without stopping in between. I was, however, on guard as far the black Rook in heavy boots was concerned. Not only did I leave him alone, but I also tried to operate as far from him as possible, so that he should not notice what I was doing.

I was just preparing to have a go at one of the black Knights when I noticed that something was wrong.

In spite of all my efforts, the numerical balance of the opposing forces remained unchanged. True that there were fewer pieces on the board, but both sides had been equally depleted. Could it be that the man playing black has suddenly woken up and shown unexpected enterprise? I started to observe closely what was happening around me and discovered that the black Rook in heavy boots was cheating.

Now I understood why, even if he suspected something, he did not expose me. His own hands were far from clean. He was doing the same as I, but from quite different motives—he was the only jingoist in the game. All my efforts were being wasted. The balance between the sides remained unchanged and the chances of the game coming to an end had not increased.

The black Rook was becoming insolent. I saw him jump at our poor Queen, kicking brutally with his heavy boots at the miserable old shoes of my colleague. The enemy had given up all pretence and I could not remain idle. Without wasting a moment I removed the black Queen. It was clear that the black Rook knew what I was doing, but he also knew that I was aware of his activities. He was avoiding me and I could see that he hated me.

On my side, apart from the King of course, only my friend the Knight and a few pawns were left in the game. On the other side the position was similar.

"I don't want to interfere," said the Knight, "but do be careful. I would like to help you, but I'm regular here. If they notice, they'll throw me out, and I want to keep the job. With you it's different. There's nothing they can do to you, because you are here only for the day. Ow!..." He cried out with pain as the black Rook, who had approached stealthily, gave him the usual vicious kick. "Farewell," he called to me walking off the field. He was the only one who understood what was happening. But I could not stop to say good-bye, because I had to run and polish off the black Knight. Then came the turn of the remaining pawns. We finished with them in no time, without even trying to keep up appearances. Only the two Kings, the black Rook and myself were left on the board. No further cheating was possible in the now wide open space.

It was now raining cats and dogs. My cardboard costume was sodden and heavy, my shoes full of water. The rain had softened the battlements of the Rook and paint was running off the Kings. The ingenious orchestration of drops and rivulets disappeared under the steady noise now filling the courtyard.

The players made a few primitive moves, putting each other's Kings in check, but it was all pointless and could bring no solution. Then came an endless pause and one really did not know if the players were still there or had gone home. The four of us were standing there, soaking in the rain, and with despair I could see no end to it. Worse still was the possibility, mentioned by the Knight, that we should be left there till the morning, the players hoping in vain to finish the game the following day. The light was failing and the rain splashed with increasing force.

I watched the black Rook, determined to be the first to kick should he approach me. He must have guessed and kept his distance. For a while we stood still, watching each other. At last he gave up and, turning to the white King, said: "Check!"

I decided to put an end to it.

"Listen," I said to the Rook, "let's not delude ourselves. It's dark and pouring with rain. I know you are a patriot and want your side to win, but you can see that the game is inconclusive. It's a draw. Let's go home."

"If I say check," he declared gloomily, "it is check!"

I could see that there was no point in arguing with him. My King had not budged, he must have fallen asleep in spite of the rain. I could not be sure that enraged by this the black Rook would not cause him some bodily harm. I knocked at the King's side.

"Eh? What is it?" The old man woke up.

"You are in check, granpa. Didn't you hear?"

"All right, all right." He shuffled to the adjoining square. The Rook immediately checked him again. Making sure that I was not exposing myself to the Rook, I gently propelled the King to the edge of the board. The stillness of the courtyard, woven out of the murmur and gurgling of the rain, was interrupted by a succession of hoarse cries of "check!"

"We are going home," I managed to whisper to the black King as we passed him. He yawned, said "Good-night" and walked off. It was already so dark that the enraged black Rook did not even notice.

When we reached the edge of the chessboard I made a dash for the cloisters, pulling the King with me. Panting we hid behind a column. I ordered the King to keep quiet and started listening.

It was now coming down in buckets and the invisible courtyard was splashing and drumming. I expected to hear the heavy boots on the pavement. We waited for a time but the sound did not come.

"Finished," I said. "We are going."

"Check!" roared a voice right behind us.

We fled across the courtyard in the direction of the gate. While running as fast as I could I figured out how he managed to surprise us. He must have taken off his boots and in stockinged feet walked stealthily along the cloisters.

I was already under the archway leading to freedom when I noticed that the old man, burdened with age and the costume made doubly heavy by the rain, had fallen behind. His heavy breathing and the squelching of his tennis shoes echoed under the vaulted ceiling. I realized that we could not escape. It was probaly fear that suggested a way out. I peeled off my costume, turned back and feverishly started to remove the King's superstructure. Then I threw it as far as I could. The huge, stiff scarecrow settled on the floor with a dull thud. We jumped behind the pillars.

The black Rook was right behind us. He found what he wanted and stopped. Then in the echoing darkness we heard repeated dull blows of a knife piercing a dummy—the empty royal shell of wet cardboard and *papier maché*.

We walked away slowly. There was no more any need to hurry.

Tommaso Landolfi (1908–   ) has been called the
Italian Kafka. His work is often linked with the
surrealists, and his feeling for fantasy suggests
Borges. In general his work presents a combination
of humor, prodigious imagination, and controlled
irony. For further reading: Gogol's Wife and Other
Stories, translated by Rosenthal, Longrigg, and
Young. (1963).

Wedding Night

TOMMASO LANDOLFI

At the end of the wedding banquet the chimney sweep was announced.
The father, out of joviality, and because it seemed proper to him that a
ceremony such as the cleaning of the chimney should be celebrated on just
that day, gave the order to let him come in. But the man did not appear;
he preferred to remain in the kitchen, where the great hearth was. Not all
the toasts had yet been given, and this was why some of the guests, in their
heart of hearts, criticized the interruption; nonetheless, due to the uproar
made by the children, everyone rose from the table.

The bride had never seen a chimney sweep: she had been in boarding
school when he used to come. Going into the kitchen she saw a tall, rather
corpulent man, with a serious gray beard and bent shoulders; he was
dressed in a corduroy suit the color of linseed oil. His stoop was counter-
balanced by the weight of two huge mountain boots which seemed to hold
his entire body erect. Although he had just washed very carefully, the skin
of his face was deeply tinted with black, as though many black-heads of
varying dimensions had taken root there; a black deposit, gathered between
the lines of his forehead and cheeks, conferred a quality of meditative wisdom on that physiognomy. But this impression quickly dissolved, and the
man's great timidity became quite obvious, especially when his features
broke into a sort of smile.

He nearly frightened the young bride, because he was standing behind
the door, though he acted frightened himself; and, as if he had been caught
doing something reprehensible and had to justify his presence in that place,
he began to repeat, speaking directly to the young bride, some sentences
which she did not hear or did not understand. He stammered insistently and
behaved as if he thought that what he said concerned her greatly and, all

the while, he looked at her with the eyes of a beaten dog and yet significantly. From the very first moment the young bride was aware of his caterpillar nature.

He took off his jacket and began to unbutton his vest. She slipped out through the other door, but continued to follow what was going on in the kitchen; she had the feeling that something improper was about to happen and that her presence might make him uneasy in the performance of his rites. Somehow she almost felt ashamed for him. But there was no noise to feed her imagination and so she went back in again. The children had been sent away and he was alone. At that moment he was climbing a ladder set up inside the hood of the fireplace; his feet were bare and he was in his shirtsleeves, a brown shirt. Across his chest, fastened with leather straps, he had a tool which resembled the scraper for a kneading trough but whose use remained forever unknown to the young bride. And he had a kind of black gag, tied up behind his ears, which fitted over his mouth and nose. But she did not see him enter the flue of the chimney, because she ran away again.

When she came back the second time, the kitchen was empty and a strange smell, a terrible smell, had spread through it. Looking around her, the young bride connected it first with the man's large shoes set in a corner next to a bundle of clothes; it was, however, the death smell of the soot which was piling up on the hearthstone, falling in intermittent showers to the rhythm of a dull scraping which gnawed at the marrow of the house and which she felt echoing in her own entrails. In the intervals, a muffled rubbing revealed the man's laborious ascent.

An instant of absolute silence fell, an instant of lacerating suspense for the young bride. She continued to stare at the mouth of the flue, there under the hood at the end of the fireplace's black funnel; this mouth was not square but narrow, a dark slit.

Then a very high, guttural, inhuman cry sounded from some mysterious place, from the well, from the stones of the house, from the soul of the kitchen's pots and pans, from the very breast of the young bride, who was shaken by it through and through. That bestial howl of agony soon proved to be a kind of joyous call: the man had burst through onto the roof. The muffled rubbings resumed more rapidly now; finally a black foot came down out of the slit searching for support—the foot of a hanged man. The foot found the first rung of the ladder and the young bride ran away.

In the courtyard, as the bride sat on a millstone, the old housekeeper, one of those women for whom everything is new, assumed the task of keeping her informed; she walked back and forth bringing her the news with a mysterious air. "Now he is doing his cleaning under the hood," and the young bride pictured him as he shook off the soot, standing upright on the pile like a gravedigger on a mound of earth. "But what does he put on his feet to claw into the wall?" And then she ran after him to ask him: "My good man, what do you put on your feet to claw into the wall?" A gay reply followed which could not be heard clearly. "Now he is eating breakfast," and the housekeeper remained inside. Then she reappeared with a few small edelweiss; she said that the man had taken them out of a very clean little box and had offered them for the young bride.

After some time he himself came out, dressed again and with a pack on his back. He crossed the countyard to leave, but the father stopped him and began to question him benevolently about his life. The young bride approached, too. Here the man, in the weak sun of winter, his face darker, his beard flecked with black and his eyes puckered by the light, looked like a big moth, a nocturnal bird surprised by the day. Or rather he looked like a spider or crab louse; the fact is that the hood of the hearth, when seen from below and if there is enough light outside, is not completely black but leaks a gray and slimy sheen.

He said that for thirty-five years he had been traveling through those towns cleaning the chimneys, that next year he would take his young son along to teach him the trade, that picking edelweiss was now forbidden and he had been able to gather those few flowers on the sly, and other such inconsequential things. Yet, whether astute or halting, it was quite clear that he only wished to hide himself behind those words, that he let the curtain of words fall in the same way that the cuttlefish beclouds the water.

He knew about all the deaths in the family, yet none of them had ever seen him!

By now the young bride felt that she was no longer ashamed for him, but was actually ashamed of herself.

After the chimney sweep had gone, she placed the few edelweiss beneath the portraits of the dead.

R. V. Cassill (1919–   ) was born in Iowa and
began his artistic career as a painter. He is the
author of more than a dozen novels; his short
stories are widely anthologized. For further reading:
15 × 3 (1957), The Father and Other Stories (1965).

Happy Marriage

R. V. CASSILL

The skinny was always:

You married specifically against death. Young enough I had said "Better
marry" and "I will not die here," when *here* was the attic in Chesterfield
where I found the arrowheads in the trunk under dust-smelling calico, the
letters of Genevieve Wren to Morton Wren, and the old book with angel
pictures (really cupids, their bare butts square in my face when I opened
the pages). I knew at once that love's chemistry burned such fat.

Outside, the grass was browning in the degeneration of August, the sore-
pocked shepherd dog chased chickens, the fishpool scummed, and the wind
turned high and blue on a wheel's paradigm, turning on the dear axle of my
body. I shouldn't die here, I thought. I love this dark attic too well and
myself bare like these angels.

Once I found a pine cone in the dark woods. Put it in a milk bottle filled
with water and hid it way. Later the water had turned purple. Thus God
instructed me.

And once we went to the cabin on Crow Island in May when the river
was low enough to ford. Behind Clayton on his pony the rest of the troop
rode bikes or went scout's pace. The ranked cottonwoods of the island
were to be our fort against the Nebraska sky. The undersides of logs
drifted on the island were still wet from the floods in April, and we found
mushrooms warm as our hands in the sticky shadows. Rhubarb and dutch-
man's britches lined the path to the abandoned Scout Cabin. The path was
velvet with fine grass like the fuzz that grows on a burn scar. The insignia
of the Eagle troop hung on a rusting nail beside the door.

In the afternoon we stripped and lay belly down on the sandbar and
talked about Clayton's cousin—who was eleven and that was the sweetest
age for girls—and how she ought to be there with us. I looked up and saw
her coming in over the cottonwoods like a highjumper or a monoplane,

naked as a cloud and about eighty feet tall. Judas, I yelled. I had to run and throw myself in the cold water while the sports laughed at my trouble and flung sand.

At night all the girls we knew were among us when we jabbered and tight-closed our eyes. I saw them all parade hot white and featureless as mushrooms. Reasoning toward midnight, I knew clearly that never in this world of dark in the trees and wind and river sweeping our island was Clayton's cousin going to wrap me with her candy arms. I turned my face to the logs and in loneliness asserted the possibility realized on the mainland of June, in a more sober year, in an apartment we were lucky to find for $22 a month. We had two rooms and the kitchen window looked out on a slate roof, more sky, and more noon than God bargained for when he made my world. Pure luck.

Mr. Nixon, when I told him I would marry without it if I had to, gave me a raise to $105 and fixed things so I'd have time at noon to walk home to her and that great window. Who do you love? she said in jealousy of my staring out. You, I said.

One of our first days there she was cleaning the apartment and found in the cupboard under the sink a mouse's skull. Our insects had eaten it clean. It was so fresh it still looked pink and white as a flower, or the fresh bone on a butcher's table. She shivered and tried loyally to hide it from me. Put it back and leave it, I said. It's the totem to bless this house. She laughed and that afternoon while I was at work took it out with the trash.

When I knew it was lost I was afraid. Where do I have to go to find it? I said.

Then there was the war and I came back from it to a different apartment. The first winter home I was sick, and one night in a fever dream I told her where the skull had gone.

You found it there, she said. Cheat.

I said, That's right. In the amphitheater of water fear I crushed it. It was more fragile than I had thought.

You won't die out there, she said. Look, I've put yellow curtains at the window, as I wrote you. Come home and cry.

I woke crying all right, and there she was in the kitchenette as big and pretty as life, breaking an egg into water and saying, Do you want it on toast, my lad? You'll feel better if you eat.

Not yet, I said. Wait a while. Come listen.

To what?

To me.

II

I have a twin named Lynch, I said. His soles walk on the soles of my feet.
That's chummy, she said.

He is in death. He braces against me on the edge between life and death. You have no business knowing him, since you threw the skull away, but I know him. I was down there with him.

I thought you were in the Army.

Listen, I said. I *went to* that island. I know what it's like. You don't.

Is his name really Lynch? Or is that a joke?

Lynch by name, Lynch by character. He was absolutely no good. Liar, crazy, cheat, half-wit, Regular Army chicken and the Captain's suck. Face like an old man's except no calm in it. Simultaneously sleepy and tormented. Didn't know a soul in the outfit except by name and didn't want to. Wanted to "get up North" and get him a Jap's ears. Wrote no letters, got no mail. Never played softball in the evenings with the rest of us. Played poker only to win. So he was in my work crew for two weeks while we were building the airstrip at Pallikula. I had trouble with him every day. So one day we were blasting coral. I had lit all the fuses and started to run. He was there beside me, grabbing my arm, saying, What's the matter, Sergeant, you scared? I hadn't been, but he scared me. What's the use of running? he said and showed his teeth. I jerked away like an animal that pulls its leg off to get out of a trap, and sprinted to flop behind a coconut log. Real flat on my belly, real flat, like I was holding onto you. Waited. I wouldn't look up to see if the bastard had taken cover. Then all three of the charges I set went at once, and it seems he hadn't.

Dead? she asked. I could feel the jerk go through her when I answered and then the terrible unstiffening of her arm. We were sitting among pillows in our Dearborn Street apartment, God's safest children, but something hit us. Flying coral.

It wasn't your fault, she said.

No; my death, I said. I had it in my hand to save but I squeezed too hard. When I looked over the log and saw the black blood coming from his mouth I knew I had nothing to hang onto but love. I think I let him go for your sake.

That's enough, she said.

No. I'll tip. You don't understand, I said.

If I don't, help me, she said. Help me.

When the finger touches the hollow in the elbow and the wiggle of the ordinarily hidden vein, touches skin running from oil smooth to dusty rough on the circumference of the thigh, the stubble in the armpit, the loaded velvet of the lip, the humorous wobble of the kneecap, the hard curve of rib, the rebounding curve of the breast and the frantic nipple—there is no understanding.

Or when the body settles like a rigid numeral paired with a nubile zero, what understands us is not ourselves.

Understanding is afterward, the long afterward and the falling apart. As decay is a vegetable.

What *doth* man of woman require?

The spangled lineaments which represent desire? Or only the seabrine reminiscent harbor of the sea's disaster?

Within the shell of happiness the kernel of repudiation. In the timbre of the sex-cry, wailing. In the after-fondness (counterfeited) the true coin of innocence. In promise, denial. In wholeness the explanatory shape of division.

Is all that possible, darling, my darling?

No.

III

Whom do you love? some others said, conventionally.

"Qu'est-ce-que tu aime?" the whore said. What do you love?

Thee, when I came in from the snow-bewildered street, moist snow dripping from my hat brim; when I ordered a cognac from fat Margot, the barmaid with the biggest radio—six bands and enough dials to tune in clear any station in Europe.

"Une femme cruelle? Les garçons?"

Thou—when you bumped plumply against my knee without taking your eyes from the red-headed soldier in the corner; when you said—as if the pity of it might brim over the cup and anoint me with its excess—"Lousy night. It's always slow the week before you pay your GI's." Then did I wish to make the house, to lay down in a joke the aspiration with its strange device, the image of man, instructed and moralized. I offered her the watching skull. I said to her, As Pascal cried in anguish, *Who watched with Lynch?*

"You have fear?" she said, who knew I had.

I bought that out, I said. Am buying.

"It costs dearly."

Dearly.

In lieu of action, for 1500 francs I recounted my triumphs in the erotic field, the time I went down on a nightingale at Dover Beach, frolicked with the blue china poor Rupert loved, made out with a sonnet, got to the Hegelian dialectic, exposed myself to bullfights, Mahler, and the sea.

I love plain living and high thinking.

Excellence.

Airplanes.

Samson Agonistes.

I will not let you go until you bless me, I said.

The loathing and contempt of her eyes made me think of a mongoose examining a garter snake. "Qu'est-ce-que tu aime?" she said.

Everything.

She grunted. "Some other night, then, cheri?"

In the springtime.

But in the springtime, the season sweet and colored in lofty blossoms like the skulls of mice, what was there to do but act out the mysteries with two Danish girls? Their eyes were all four blue as that original window opening North. They were sixteen and seventeen and hitchhiking around Europe. For culture.

"My name is meaning the night," the sixteen-year-old explained. I had bought her peppermint candy and her tongue was red as macaw feathers. She bobbed like an earnest daisy when she insisted, "I is always loving dezz."

I laughed and lightly told her what Rimbaud, dying, said to his sister, "Tomorrow you will be in the sun and I will be in the dark."

She licked her candy and seemed pleased, as though I had paid her a personal compliment. But the next morning, lying in her friend's arms, she called across the hotel room to me, "No, *you* will be in the sun and I will be in Hell wiz my sisser here."

Their Danish wrists were laced delicately with the scars of old razor cuts. I had never pondered that Gillette had undone so many.

"We has found somezing beyond the ee roh teek," she called. From her tone that something could have been faith, wisdom, or charity. Turned out to be ether.

We lay in the Parisian spring, three cotton pads to our faces, dreaming that outside the room bells rang a chivalry of disaster. Under chestnut trees the dead girls paraded, those whom Paris loved, and in spacious evenings they rumored the infidelity of life as if they might be gossiping the anxieties of fashionable love.

The spike of her bird-feather tongue was bitter with the taste of ether. We lay two days conversing in our respective languages. She told me how the razors tickled her wrists like shy schoolboys, driven to horror that so much beauty was abroad in the uncertainty of a temporal world, unsaved among war, lechery, or the fluctuations of paper currency. Like a painter's brushes the razors had stroked to fix that beauty—a fresco in a lightless corridor. Her father, she said once, in the children's hour when we had all three sobered enough to use common words, when we looked down together from the hotel windows into the damning illusion of the street—her father was literally a painter, had known Munch and Ensor many years ago. Her mother was younger and danced the Charleston. She must send them a postcard so they would not worry about her.

They must not worry, she said, slopping the virgin handful of cotton from a newly opened liter. There was nothing to worry about. In the gently downward planes of these dimensions neither she nor her sisterfriend and I must worry that sometime in a Marseilles canal her dancer's body would float headless, with an illiterate love note stuffed into her brassiere.

I should not worry, the ether and the razors said, that I had been unfaithful to living friends and wives. You never wanted any more, they whispered to me, than just to eat your cake and have the eating of it, than praise for the bashfulness with which you sinned, than immortality, than to bury the dead in another chance and time to come.

There were no razors but I felt them crawl like instructive maggots on the wrists to which I held a claim. Little brothers beyond the ee roh teek. By the second night I had learned everything from them.

I can tell you that Ee Roh Teek is a mountain in Central Africa and not everyone knows why there should be leopards on it. It is the yellow sugar gate to Hell and beyond it are all the eyes. Beyond it everyone may call for Lynch and anyone may answer. He will approach you like a child and whisper, "Lead me back."

Come on, I said.

"Is it far?"

Not very *far*, but there isn't any *way*.

IV

Out of sheer habit I came back.

With the damnedest hangover, an oceanic, sloshing void in which floated everything. A hangover as big and hollow as a cosmos in which a filament suspended me at the center of appearances.

I was in my room behind the Sorbonne and had no idea how I'd come there, except that my ragged pulse suggested I might have galloped on all fours. I closed my eyes and tried to imagine what a fish would do if it wanted to evolve into a man. There must be something it could take, I thought. I expected to die unless I could damn soon discover why to live. I tried to remember back to Crow Island. If I could lie by the muddy edge of the water in a growing season and count new pubic hairs, if I could climb to a blue window or the attic in August to feel the sweat pour out of me like evil going home, if I could remember why Morton Wren loved Genevieve then I could instruct my body how it must endure.

Looking at my unmarked wrists I could not even remember for a while whose were scarred. Who is in the sun and who is in the dark? It seemed to me I had left her, too, beyond the mountain, but the her I left had no identity. Something I had done, as with a razor, had fragmented the person with whom I had talked and lain. I knew I wasn't winning and then my only chance was trying to make it to a bar.

In the blue morning the tower of Ste. Chapelle trembled like a flower stem. Now I'm all right, I thought: since it was real I could put my hand to steady it. But then I passed a newsstand and saw the headlines about an English murderer. He had slashed the wrists of innumerable girls and they, poor things, those moorings cut, had gone drifting down the streams of summer. The killer, I read, was still at large.

Still at large. I took a deep breath. The medium I breathed was horror, and all its aspects were fair to the eye. The shade that fingered the sunny pavements was horrible and lovely and I was still, horribly, at large.

I sat outside *Old Navy* Bar-Tabac fingering a glass of wine the color of the Danish girls' hair. They were my guides, I thought. I needed the right girls to lead me past the meridian, where I could admit in the presence of judges that I had renounced my rebellion against death. Through the luxury of their doomed flesh I had come to where the ideal Lynch had meant that I must. Now I would leave him where he was nothing. The negative twin no longer had to exist. I had bought out the title of my fear.

Now, in the noonward tending light, and a hangover imitation of the Passion, it seemed permissible to remember Lynch and the other dead. Now, I could fix the place in time—far back, far back—when I had seen the naked bone like a flagstaff in the gutted foxhole, when I had tried to swear *I will come back one more time to give you a decent burial, O denied.* Now, like an animal of the afternoon which does not remember the morning in which the bones lived, I could enter in the body of the abstract woman and hive in the moisture of time to come. That spot of blood was a ruptured capillary. Only from drunkenness.

In my jacket pocket was a card with the names of the girls. *De votre malheur il ne reste que les noms.* Goodbye, I said. O, Goodbye.

Then it was the sun's noon, and under every morsel and scrap on the pavement the shape of shadows changed. The jerk of my healing finger tapped the wine glass on the table top. In the yellow-white ripples I saw all timeless constancy twitch and quiver to the disturbance of my inconstant caress. I believed this city was mine.

Ted Hughes (1930–   ) was born in England and still resides in Great Britain, where he is known as a poet, a short-story writer, and a critic. He is one of the few new writers in England, at the present time, who seeks new directions for the short-story form.

Snow

TED HUGHES

And let me repeat this over and over again: beneath my feet is the earth, some part of the surface of the earth. Beneath the snow beneath my feet, that is. What else could it be? It is firm, I presume, and level. If it is not actually soil and rock, it must be ice. It is very probably ice. Whichever it may be, it is proof—the most substantial proof possible—that I am somewhere on the earth, the known earth. It would be absurd to dig down through the snow, just to determine exactly what is underneath, earth or ice. This bedded snow may well be dozens of feet deep. Besides, the snow filling all the air and rivering along the ground would pour into the hole as fast as I could dig, and cover me too—very quickly.

This could be no other planet: the air is perfectly natural, perfectly good.

Our aircraft was forced down by this unusual storm. The pilot tried to make a landing, but misjudged the extraordinary power of the wind and the whereabouts of the ground. The crash was violent. The fuselage buckled and gaped, and I was flung clear. Unconscious of everything save the need to get away from the disaster, I walked farther off into the blizzard and collapsed, which explains why when I came to full consciousness and stood up out of the snow that was burying me I could see nothing of either the aircraft or my fellow passengers. All round me was what I have been looking at ever since. The bottomless dense motion of snow. I started to walk.

Of course, everything previous to that first waking may have been entirely different since I don't remember a thing about it. Whatever chance dropped me here in the snow evidently destroyed my memory. That's one thing of which there is no doubt whatsoever. It is, so to speak, one of my facts. The aircraft crash is a working hypothesis, that merely.

There's no reason why I should not last quite a long time yet. I seem to have an uncommon reserve of energy. To keep my mind firm, that is the essential thing, to fix it firmly in my reasonable hopes, and lull it there, encourage it. Mesmerise it slightly with a sort of continuous prayer. Because when my mind is firm, my energy is firm. And that's the main thing here—energy. No matter how circumspect I may be, or how lucid, without energy I am lost on the spot. Useless to think about it. Where my energy ends I end, and all circumspection and all lucidity end with me. As long as I have energy I can correct my mistakes, outlast them, outwalk them—for instance the unimaginable error that as far as I know I am making at this very moment. This step, this, the next five hundred, or five thousand—all mistaken, all absolute waste, back to where I was ten hours ago. But we recognise that thought. My mind is not my friend. My support, my defence, but my enemy too—not perfectly intent on getting me out of this. If I were mindless perhaps there would be no difficulty whatsoever. I would simply go on aware of nothing but my step by step success in getting over the ground. The thing to do is to keep alert, keep my mind fixed in alertness, recognise these treacherous paralysing, yes, lethal thoughts the second they enter, catch them before they can make that burrowing plunge down the spinal cord.

Then gently and without any other acknowledgment push them back—out into the snow where they belong. And that *is* where they belong. They are the infiltrations of the snow, encroachments of this immensity of lifelessness. But they enter so slyly! We are true, they say, or at least very probably true, and on that account you must entertain us and even give us the run of your life, since above all things you are dedicated to the truth. That is the air they have, that's how they come in. What do I know about the truth? As if simple-minded dedication to truth were the final law of existence! I only know more and more clearly what is good for me. It's my mind that has this contemptible awe for the probably true, and my mind, I know, I prove it every minute, is not me and is by no means sworn to help me. Am I a lie? I must survive—that's a truth sacred as any, and as the hungry truths devour the sleepy truths I shall digest every other possible truth to the substance and health and energy of my own, and the ones I can't digest I shall spit out, since in this situation my intention to survive is the one mouth, the one digestive tract, so to speak, by which I live. But those others! I relax for a moment, I leave my mind to itself for a moment—and they are in complete possession. They plunge into me, exultantly, mercilessly. There is no question of their intention or their power. Five seconds of carelessness, and they have struck. The strength melts from me, my bowels turn to water, my consciousness darkens and shrinks, I have to stop.

What are my facts? I do have some definite facts.

Taking six steps every five seconds, I calculate—allowing for my brief regular sleeps—that I have been walking through this blizzard for five months and during that time have covered something equal to the breadth of the Atlantic between Southampton and New York. Two facts, and a third: throughout those five months this twilight of snow has not grown either darker or brighter.

So.

There seems no reason to doubt that I am somewhere within either the Arctic or the Antarctic Circle. That's a comfort. It means my chances of survival are not uniquely bad. Men have walked the length of Asia simply to amuse themselves.

Obviously I am not travelling in a straight line. But that needn't give me any anxiety. Perhaps I made a mistake when I first started walking, setting my face against the wind instead of downwind. Coming against the wind I waste precious energy and there is always this wearisome snow blocking my eyes and mouth. But I had to trust the wind. This resignation to the wind's guidance is the very foundation of my firmness of mind. The wind is not simply my compass. In fact, I must not think of it as a compass at all. The wind is my law. As a compass nothing could be more useless. No need to dwell on that. It's extremely probable indeed and something I need not hide from myself that this wind is leading me to and fro in quite a tight maze—always shifting too stealthily for me to notice the change. Or, if the sun is circling the horizon, it seems likely that the wind is swinging with it through the three hundred and sixty degrees once in every twenty-four hours, turning me as I keep my face against it in a perfect circle not more than seven miles across. This would explain the otherwise strange fact that in spite of the vast distance I have covered the terrain is still dead level, exactly as when I started. A frozen lake, no doubt. This is a strong possibility and I must get used to it without letting it overwhelm me, and without losing sight of its real advantages.

The temptation to trust to luck and instinct and cut out across wind is to be restricted. The effect on my system of confidence would be disastrous. My own judgment would naturally lead me in a circle. I would have to make deliberate changes of direction to break out of that circle—only to go in a larger circle or a circle in the opposite direction. So more changes. Wilder and more sudden changes, changes of my changes—all to evade an enemy that showed so little sign of itself it might as well not have existed. It's clear where all that would end. Shouting and running and so on. Staggering round like a man beset by a mob. Falling, grovelling. So on. The snow.

No. All I have to do is endure: that is, keep my face to the wind. My face to the wind, a firm grip on my mind, and everything else follows naturally. There is not the slightest need to be anxious. Any time now the Polar night will arrive, bringing a drastic change of climate—inevitable. Clearing the sky and revealing the faultless compass of the stars.

The facts are overwhelmingly on my side. I could almost believe in
Providence. After all, if one single circumstance were slightly—only
slightly—other than it is! If, for instance, instead of waking in a blizzard on
a firm level place I had come to consciousness falling endlessly through
snow-cloud. Then I might have wondered very seriously whether I were in
the gulf or not. Or if the atmosphere happened to consist of, say, ammonia. I could not have existed. And in the moment before death by
asphyxiation I would certainly have been convinced I was out on some
lifeless planet. Or if I had no body but simply arms and legs growing out
of a head, my whole system of confidence would have been disoriented
from the start. My dreams, for instance, would have been meaningless to
me, or rather an argument of my own meaninglessness. I would have died
almost immediately, out of sheer bewilderment. I wouldn't need nearly such
extreme differences either. If I had been without these excellent pigskin
boots, trousers, jacket, gloves and hood, the cold would have extinguished
me at once.

And even if I had double the clothing that I have, where would I be
without my chair? My chair is quite as important as one of my lungs. As
both my lungs, indeed, for without it I should be dead. Where would I
have slept? Lying in the snow. But lying flat, as I have discovered, I am
buried by the snow in just under a minute, and the cold begins to take
over my hands and my feet and my face. Sleep would be impossible. In
other words, I would very soon collapse of exhaustion and be buried. As it
is, I unsnap my chair harness, plant the chair in the snow, sit on it, set my
feet on the rung between the front legs, my arms folded over my knees
and my head resting on my arms, and am able in this way to take a sleep
of fully ten minutes before the snow piles over me.

The chain of providential coincidences is endless. Or rather, like a chain
mail, it is complete without one missing link to betray and annul the rest.
Even my dreams are part of it. They are as tough and essential a link as
any, since there can no longer be any doubt that they are an accurate
reproduction of my whole previous life, of the world as it is and as I
knew it—all without one contradictory detail. Yet if my amnesia had been
only a little bit stronger!—it needed only that. Because without this evidence of the world and my identity I could have known no purpose in continuing the ordeal. I could only have looked, breathed and died, like a
nestling fallen from the nest.

Everything fits together. And the result—my survival, and my determination to survive. I should rejoice.

The chair is of conventional type: nothing in the least mystifying about
it. A farmhouse sort of chair: perfectly of a piece with my dreams, as indeed are my clothes, my body and all the inclinations of my mind. It is of
wood, painted black, though in places showing a coat of brown beneath

the black. One of the nine struts in the back is missing and some child—I suppose it was a child—has stuck a dab of chewing-gum into the empty socket. Obviously the chair has been well used, and not too carefully. The right foreleg has been badly chewed, evidently by a puppy, and on the seat both black and brown paints are wearing through showing the dark grain of the pale wood. If all this is not final evidence of a reality beyond my own, of the reality of the world it comes from, the world I re-dream in my sleeps—I might as well lie down in the snow and be done with.

The curious harness needn't worry me. The world, so far as I've dreamed it at this point, contains no such harness, true. But since I've not yet dreamed anything from after my twenty-sixth birthday, the harness might well have been invented between that time and the time of my disaster. Probably it's now in general use. Or it may be the paraphernalia of some fashionable game that came in during my twenty-seventh or later year, and to which I got addicted. Sitting on snow peaks in nineteenth-century chairs. Or perhaps I developed a passion for painting polar scenery and along with that a passion for this particular chair as my painting seat, and had the harness designed specially. A lucky eccentricity! It is perfectly adapted to my present need. But all that's in the dark still. There's a lot I haven't dreamed yet. From my twenty-third and twenty-fourth years I have almost nothing—a few insignificant episodes. Nothing at all after my twenty-sixth birthday. The rest, though, is about complete, which suggests that any time now I ought to be getting my twenty-third and twenty-fourth years in full and, more important, my twenty-seventh year, or as much of it as there is, along with the accurate account of my disaster and the origin of my chair.

There seems little doubt of my age. Had I been dreaming my life chronologically there would have been real cause for worry. I could have had no idea how much was still to come. Of course, if I were suddenly to dream something from the middle of my sixtieth year I would have to reorganise all my ideas. What really convinces me of my youth is my energy. The appearance of my body tells me nothing. Indeed, from my hands and feet—which are all I have dared to uncover—one could believe I was several hundred years old, or even dead, they are so black and shrunken on the bone. But the emaciation is understandable, considering that for five months I have been living exclusively on will-power, without the slightest desire for food.

I have my job to get back to, and my mother and father will be in despair. And God knows what will have happened to Helen. Did I marry her? I have no wedding ring. But we were engaged. And it is another confirmation of my youth that my feelings for her are as they were then—stronger, in fact, yes a good deal stronger, though speaking impartially these feelings that seem to be for her might easily be nothing but my desperate longing to get back to the world in general—a longing that is using my onetime affection for Helen as a sort of form or model. It's possible, very possible, that I have in reality forgotten her, even that I am sixty years old, that she has been dead for thirty-four years. Certain things may be very difficult from what I imagine. If I were to take this drift of thoughts to the logical extreme there is no absolute proof that my job, my parents, Helen and the whole world are not simply my own invention, fantasies my imagination has improvised on the simple themes of my own form, of clothes, my chair, and the properties of my present environment. I am in no position to be sure about anything.

But there is more to existence, fortunately, than consideration of possibilities. There is conviction, faith. If there were not, where would I be? The moment I allow one of these "possibilities" the slightest intimacy—a huge futility grips me, as it were physically, by the heart, as if the organ itself were despairing of this life and ready to give up.

Courageous and calm. That should be my prayer. I should repeat that, repeat it like the Buddhists with their "O jewel of the lotus". Repeat it till it repeats itself in my very heart, till every heartbeat drives it through my whole body. Courageous and calm. This is the world, think no more about it.

My chair will keep me sane. My chair, my chair, my chair—I might almost repeat that. I know every mark on it, every grain. So near and true! It alone predicates a Universe, the entire Universe, with its tough carpentering, its sprightly, shapely design—so delicate, so strong. And while I have the game I need be afraid of nothing. Though it is dangerous. Tempting, dangerous, but—it is enough to know that the joy is mine. I set the chair down in the snow, letting myself think I am going to sleep, but instead of sitting I step back a few paces into the snow. How did I think of that? The first time, I did not dare look away from it. I had never before let it out of my hand, never let it go for a fraction between unbuckling it and sitting down on it. But then I let it go and stepped back into the snow. I had never heard my voice before. I was astonished at the sound that struggled up out of me. Well, I need the compensations. And this game does rouse my energies, so it is, in a sense, quite practical. After the game, I could run. That's the moment of danger, though, the moment of overpowering impatience when I could easily lose control and break out, follow my instinct, throw myself on luck, run out across the wind.

But there is a worse danger. If I ran out across the wind I would pretty soon come to my senses, turn my face back into the wind. It is the game itself, the stage of development it has reached, that is dangerous now. I no longer simply step back. I set the chair down, turn my face away and walk off into the blizzard, counting my steps carefully. At fourteen paces I stop. Fifteen is the limit of vision in this dense flow of snow, so at fourteen I stop, and turn. Let those be the rules. Let me fix the game at that. Because at first I see nothing. That should be enough for me. Everywhere, pouring silent grey, a silence like a pressure, like the slow coming to bear of some incalculable pressure, too gradual to detect. If I were simply to stand there my mind would crack in a few moments. But I concentrate, I withdraw my awe from the emptiness and look pointedly into it. At first, everything is as usual—as I have seen it for five months. Then my heart begins to thump unnaturally, because I seem to make out a dimness, a shadow that wavers deep in the grey turmoil, vanishes and darkens, rises and falls. I step one pace forward and using all my will-power stop again. The shadow is as it was. Another step. The shadow seems to be a little darker. Then it vanishes and I lunge two steps forward but immediately stop because there it is, quite definite, no longer moving. Slowly I walk towards it. The rules are that I keep myself under control, that I restrain all sobs or shouts though of course it is impossible to keep the breathing regular—at this stage at least, and right up to the point where the shadow resolves into a chair. In that vast grey dissolution—my chair! The snowflakes are drifting against the legs and gliding between the struts, bumping against them, clinging and crawling over the seat. To control myself then it not within human power. Indeed I seem to more or less lose consciousness at that point. I'm certainly not responsible for the weeping, shouting thing that falls on my chair, embracing it, kissing it, bruising his cheeks against it. As the snowflakes tap and run over my gloves and over the chair I begin to call them names. I peer into each one as if it were a living face, full of speechless recognition, and I call to them—Willy, Joanna, Peter, Jesus, Ferdinand, anything that comes into my head, and shout to them and nod and laugh. Well, it's harmless enough madness.

The temptation to go beyond the fourteen paces is now becoming painful. To go deep into the blizzard. Forty paces. Then come back, peering. Fifteen paces, twenty paces. Stop. A shadow.

That would not be harmless madness. If I were to leave my chair like that the chances are I would never find it again. My footprints do not exist in this undertow of snow. Weeks later, I would still be searching, casting in great circles, straining at every moment to pry a shadow out of the grey sameness. My chair meanwhile a hundred miles away in the blizzard, motionless—neat legs and elegant back, sometimes buried, sometimes uncovering again. And for centuries, long after I'm finished, still sitting there, intact with its tooth-marks and missing strut, waiting for a darkening shape to come up out of the nothingness and shout to it and fall on it and possess it.

But my chair is here, on my back, here. There's no danger of my ever losing it. Never so long as I keep control, keep my mind firm. All the facts are on my side. I have nothing to do but endure.

Alain Robbe-Grillet (1922–   ) was born in Brest and subsequently graduated from the Institut National Agronomique. He has done research in Morocco, Equatorial Africa, and the French Antilles. He is a French "new novelist" whose Les Gommes (The Erasers) (1962) and Le Voyeur (1959) became centers of controversy. His work pays minute attention to objective details. Much of his short fiction has not yet been translated into English.

The Secret Room

ALAIN ROBBE-GRILLET

First there is a red spot, bright, red, shiny but dark, shading to almost black. It forms an irregular, clearly outlined rosette, extended on several sides by wide streaks of varying lengths which then divide and dwindle until they are no more than meandering threads. The entire area stands out against the pallor of a smooth, rounded, dull and yet pearly surface, a half-sphere gently curving to an expanse of the same pale hue—a whiteness attenuated by the gloom of the place: dungeon, crypt or cathedral—gleaming with a diffused luster in the darkness.

Beyond, the space is occupied by the cylindrical shafts of columns that grow more numerous and blurred in the distance, where the beginning of a huge stone staircase can be made out, gradually turning and narrowing as it rises toward the high vaulting into which it vanishes.

The whole of this scene is empty, staircase and colonnades. Alone in the foreground, glimmers the prone body, on which the red spot is spreading— a white body suggesting the luminous, supple, doubtless fragile and vulnerable flesh. Beside the bloodstained half-sphere, another identical though intact globe can be seen from almost the same angle; but the darker ringed tip crowning it is here quite recognizable, whereas the first is almost completely destroyed, or at least concealed, by the wound.

In the background, toward the bend of the stairs, a black figure is vanishing from sight, a man wrapped in a long, loose cape, who mounts the last steps without turning around, his crime committed. A faint vapor rises in intertwining spirals from a kind of incense burner set on a high, silvery-metal stand. Quite near lies the milky body where wide rivulets of blood are flowing from the left breast, down the side and over the hip.

It is a woman's body, its forms opulent but not heavy, completely naked, lying on its back, the bust half-raised by thick cushions laid on the floor, which is covered by rugs of Oriental design. The waist is very narrow, the neck long and slender, curved to one side, the head thrown back into a darker area where the features of the face can still be discerned, the mouth half open, the large eyes wide, gleaming with a fixed luster, and the mass of the long black hair spread out in waves of formal disorder on the heavy folds of some fabric, velvet perhaps, on which the arm and shoulder also rest.

It is a smooth, dark-violet velvet, or seems to be in this light. But violet, brown and blue also seem to prevail in the colors of the cushions—of which only a small part is concealed by the velvet material and which extend farther down under the bust and the waist—as well as in the Oriental patterns of the rugs on the floor. Beyond, these same colors recur in the stone of the slabs and columns, the arches of the vaulting, the staircase, the vaguer surfaces where the limits of the room are lost to view.

It is difficult to specify the latter's dimensions; the slaughtered young woman seems at first glance to occupy a considerable place in it, but the vast proportions of the staircase descending toward her would suggest, on the contrary, that she does not take up the whole room, for a noticeable area must actually extend to the right and the left, as well as toward those distant browns and blues in the various rows of columns, perhaps toward other sofas, heavy rugs, piles of cushions and fabrics, other tortured bodies, other incenseburners.

It is also difficult to say where the light is coming from. Nothing, on the columns or on the floor, suggests the direction of its source. Moreover, there is no window in sight, and no torch. It is the milky body itself that seems to illuminate the scene, the neck and the swelling breasts, the curve of the hips, the belly, the full thighs, the legs stretched out, wide apart, and the black fleece, of the sex exposed—provocative, proffered, henceforth useless.

The man has already moved several strides away. Now he is already on the first steps of the staircase which he is about to mount. The lower steps are long and deep, like the shallow stairs leading to some public edifice, temple or theatre; they then gradually diminish in size as they rise, and at the same time begin a broad spiral movement, so gradual that the staircase has not yet effected a half-turn when, reduced to an awkward narrow passageway without a railing, even vaguer in the deepening darkness, it disappears toward the top of the vaulting.

But the man is not looking in this direction, where his steps will nonetheless carry him; his left foot on the second step and his right already set on the third, knee bent, he has turned around to take a look at the scene. The long loose cape which he has hastily thrown over his shoulders, and which he holds at his waist with one hand, has been swept by the rotation which has just brought his head and upper body around to face away from the direction he is going, a flap of material raised in the air as though by the effect of a gust of wind; the corner, which folds back on itself in a loose S, reveals the gold-embroidered, red-stain lining.

The man's features are impassive, but strained, as though in anticipation—fear perhaps—of some sudden event, or rather reassuring himself as to the total immobility of the scene. Although he looks back in this way, his whole body has remained leaning slightly forward, as though he were still continuing his ascent. His right arm—the one not holding the edge of the cape—is half extended to the left, toward a point in space where the railing would be if there were one on this staircase, an interrupted, almost incomprehensible gesture, unless it is an instinctive impulse to catch hold of the missing support?

As for the direction of his gaze, it is unquestionably toward the body of the victim lying exposed on the cushions, the limbs extended in a cross, the bust raised slightly, the head thrown back. But perhaps the face is hidden from the man's eyes by one of the columns which rises at the foot of the stairs. The young woman's right hand touches the floor just at this column's base. A thick iron fetter encircles the delicate wrist. The arm is almost in shadow, the hand alone receiving enough light for the slender, spread fingers to be clearly visible against the circular rim that forms a base for the stone shaft. A black-metal chain is fastened around the shaft and passes through a ring on the fetter, closely attaching the wrist to the column.

At the arm's other end, a round shoulder, raised by the cushions, is also plainly lighted, as are the neck, the throat and the other shoulder, the armpit and its down, the left arm stretched behind the body too and its wrist attached in the same way to the base of another column, quite close to the foreground; here the iron ring and the chain are clearly seen, drawn with great distinctness down to the smallest detail.

Seen in the same way, still in the foreground but on the other side, is a similar though somewhat lighter chain which twice encircles the ankle directly, attaching it to a heavy ring set in the floor. About a yard or so behind it, the right foot is chained in the same manner. But it is the left foot and its chain that are represented with the most precision.

The foot is small, delicate, finely modeled. The chain has bruised the flesh in places, making noticeable though small depressions. Its links are oval, thick and about the size of an eye. The ring is like those used for hitching horses; it is lying almost flat on the stone slab, in which it is held by a massive spike. The edge of a rug begins an inch or so away; it is raised by a fold produced, no doubt, by the victim's convulsive though necessarily limited movements when she attempted to struggle.

The man is still half leaning over her, standing about a yard away. He examines her face tilted back, the dark eyes enlarged by cosmetics, the mouth wide as if in a scream. The man's position reveals only one-quarter of his face, but he is evidently in the grip of violent excitement, despite his rigid position, silence, and immobility. His back is bent slightly. His left hand, the only one that can be seen, holds away from his body a piece of fabric, some dark garment which trails on the rug and which must be the long cape with its gold-embroidered lining.

This massive figure greatly conceals the naked flesh where the red spot, which has spread over the bulge of the breast, flows in long rivulets which branch out as they grow thinner, against the pale background of the torso and the whole side. One of them has reached the armpit and traces a fine, almost straight line the length of the arm; others have run down toward the waist and drawn a more arbitrary network, which is already congealing over the belly, the hip and the top of the thigh. Three or four veinules have reached as far as the hollow of the groin and formed a meandering line which joins the point of the V formed by the parted legs and vanishes in the black fleece.

There, now the flesh is still intact, the black fleece and the white belly, the gentle curve of the hips, the slender waist and, above, the pearly breasts which rise in time to the rapid breathing, whose rhythm grows faster. The man, close beside her, one knee on the ground, bends farther forward. The head with the long wavy hair, which alone has kept some freedom of movement, stirs, struggles; finally the girl's mouth opens and twists, while the flesh yields, the blood spurts out over the tender smooth skin, the skillfully painted black eyes widen enormously, the mouth opens still further, the head is flung from right to left, violently, one last time, then more gently, finally falling back motionless in the mass of black hair spread out on the velvet.

At the very top of the stone staircase, the little door is open, releasing a yellow, sustained light, against which the dark figure of the man wrapped in his long cape is silhouetted. He has no more than a few steps to climb in order to reach the threshold.

Then the whole scene is empty, the enormous violet-shadowed room with its stone columns extending on all sides, the monumental staircase with no railing that turns as it rises, growing narrower and vaguer as it mounts into the darkness toward the top of the vaulting, where it vanishes.

Near the prone body whose wound has congealed, whose luster is already fading, the faint vapor from the incense burner forms complicated volutes in the calm air: at first it is a strand inclined to the left, then rises and increases slightly in height, then returns toward the axis of its point of departure, exceeds it on the right, again starts in the other direction, only to return once more, thus tracing an irregular, gradually fading sinusoid, which rises vertically toward the top of the canvas.

Samuel Beckett (1906–   ) was born in Dublin and was a lecteur d'anglais in the late twenties in Paris. He now prefers French as a medium for his novels, plays, and short stories. Since 1938 he has resided outside of Paris and leads a life of austerity and isolation. He is a follower of Joyce (whom he knew personally), but came to fame in his own right with the play Waiting for Godot (1952). He received the Nobel Prize for literature in 1969. For further reading: Novels and Texts for Nothing (1955).

Stories and Texts for Nothing, III

SAMUEL BECKETT

Leave, I was going to say leave all that. What matter who's speaking, someone said what matter who's speaking. There's going to be a departure, I'll be there, it won't be me, I'll be here, I'll say I'm far, it won't be me, I won't say anything, there's going to be a story, someone's going to try and tell a story. Yes, enough denials, all is false, there's no one, it's agreed, there's nothing, enough phrases, let's be dupes, dupes of time, all time, until it's over, all over, and the voices are stilled, they're only voices, only lies. Here, leave here and go elsewhere, or stay here, but coming and going. Move first, there must be a body, as of old, I don't say no, I won't say no any more, I'll say I have a body, a body that moves, forward, backward, up and down, as required. With a clutter of limbs and organs, all that's needed to live once again, to hold out, a short spell, I'll call that living, I'll say it's me, I'll stand up, I'll think no more, I'll be too taken up, standing up, keeping standing up, moving about, holding out, getting to the next day, the next week, that will be enough, a week will be enough, a week in spring, that will be bracing. It's enough to will, I'm going to will, will myself a body, will myself a head, a little strength, a little courage, I'm going to start, a week is soon over, then back here, this inextricable place, far from the days, the days are far, it's not going to be easy. And why, after all, no no, leave it, don't start that again, don't listen to everything, don't say everything, all is old, all one, that's settled. There you are up, I give you my word, I swear it's mine, work your hands, palp your skull, seat of the understanding, without it nothing doing, then the rest, the lower parts, can't do without them, and say what you are, what kind of man, have a guess, there must be a man, or a woman, feel between your legs, no need of beauty, or strength, a week is soon over, no one's going to love you, don't worry. No, not like that, too sudden, I gave myself a fright. And to start with stop panting, no one's going to kill you, oh no, no one's going to love you and no one's going to kill you. You may emerge in the high depression of Gobi, there you'll feel at home. I'll wait for you here, my mind at rest, at rest for you, no, I'm alone, I alone am, it's I must go, this time it's I. I know what I'll do, I'll be a man, I must, a kind of man, a kind of old infant, I'll have a nurse, she'll be fond of me, she'll give me her hand, to cross over, she'll let me loose in gardens, I'll be good, I'll sit in a corner and comb my beard, smooth it down, to be nicer looking, a little nicer, if it could be like that. She'll say to me, Come, lamb, it's time for home. I won't have any responsibility, she'll have all the responsibility, her name will be Nanny, I'll call her Nanny, if it could only be like that. Come, pet, it's time for bottle. Who taught me all I know, I alone, when I was still a wanderer, I deduced it all, from nature, with the aid of an all-in-one, I know it's not true, but it's too late now, too late to deny it, the knowledge is there, items of knowledge, gleaming in turn, far and near, flickering over the abyss, allies. Leave it and go, I must go, I must say so anyway, the moment is come, one doesn't know why. What does it matter where you say you are, here or elsewhere, fixed or movable, shapeless or oblong like man, without light or in the light of heaven, I don't know, it seems to matter, it's not going to be easy. If I went back to where all went out and then on from there, no, that wouldn't lead anywhere, that never led anywhere, the memory of it has gone out too, a great flame and then blackness, a great spasm and then no more bulk or traversable space, I don't know. I tried to have me fall, off the cliff, in the street in the midst of mortals, that led nowhere, I gave up. Travel the road again that cast me up here, before going back the way I came, or on, wise advice. That's so that I'll never stir again, dribble on here till time is done, murmuring every ten centuries, it's not me, it's not true, it's not me, I'm far. No no, I'll speak now of the future, I'll speak in the future, as in the days when I said to myself, in the night, Tomorrow I'll put on my blue tie, the one with the stars, and put it on, when the night was past. Quick quick before I weep. I'll have a friend, my own age, my own bog, an old warrior, we'll fight our battles over again and compare our scratches. Quick quick. He had served in the navy, perhaps under Jellicoe, while I was potting at the invader from behind a barrel of Guinness, with my arquebus. We have not long, that's right, in the present, not long to live, it's our last winter of all, halleluiah. We wonder what will carry us off finally. He's gone in the wind, I in the bladder rather. We envy each other, he envies me, I envy him, on and off. I catheterize myself unaided, with trembling hand, standing in the public pisshouse, bent double, under cover of my cape,

people take me for a dirty old man. Meanwhile he waits for me on a bench,
coughing up his guts, spitting into a snuff-box which no sooner overflows
than he empties it into the canal, out of public-spiritedness. We have de-
served well of our motherland, she'll get us into hospital before we die. We
spend our life, it's ours, trying to unite in the same instant a ray of sunshine and a free bench, in an oasis of public greenery, we have taken to a
love of nature, in our sere and yellow, it belongs to one and all, in places.
He reads to me in choking murmur from the paper of the day before, he had
better been the blind one. Our passion is horse-racing, dog-racing too, we
have no political opinions, just limply republican. But we also have a warm
spot for the Windsors, the Hanoverians, I forget, the Hohenzollerns is it.
Nothing human is foreign to us, once we have digested the dogs and horses.
No, alone, I'd be better off alone, it would be quicker. He'd feed me, he had
a friend, a pork-butcher, he'd ram my soul back down my gullet with black
pudding. With his consolations, allusions to cancer, recollections of im-
perishable raptures, he'd prevent discouragement from sapping my foundations. And I, instead of concentrating on my own horizons, which might
have enabled me to throw them under a lorry, would have my mind distracted by his. I'd say to him, Come on, son, leave all that, think no more
about it, and it's I would think no more about it, besotted with brotherli-
ness. And the obligations, I have in mind particularly the appointments at
ten o'clock in the morning, rain, hail or shine, in front of Duggan's, throng-
ing already with sporting men in a hurry to get their bets out of harm's
way before the bars opened. We were, there we are past and gone again,
so much the better, so much the better, most punctual, I must say. To see
the remains of Vincent arriving in sheets of rain, with the brave involuntary
swagger of the old tar, his head swathed in a bloody clout and a gleam in
his eye, was for the acute observer an example of what man is capable of,
in his thirst for enjoyment. With one hand he sustained his sternum, with
the heel of the other his spinal column, no, that's all memories, last shifts
more ancient than the flood. To see what's happening here, where there's no
one, where nothing happens, to get something to happen here, someone to
be here, then put an end to it, make silence, enter silence, or another noise,
a noise of other voices than those of life and death, of lives and deaths that
never will be mine, enter my story, in order to leave it, no, that's all fiddle-
faddle. Is it possible I'll sprout a head in the end, all my own, in which to
brew some poisons worthy of me, and legs to kick my heels, I'd be there at
last, I could go, it's all I ask, no, I can't ask anything. Nothing but the head
and the two legs, or just one, in the middle, I'd go hopping. Or nothing
but the head, nice and round, nice and smooth, no need of features, I'd
roll, downhill, almost a pure spirit, no, that wouldn't work, all's uphill from
here, there'd have to be a leg, or the equivalent, an annular joint or so,
contractile, with them you go a long way. To set forth from Duggan's door,

on a spring morning of rain and shine, not knowing if you'll ever come to evening, what's wrong there? It would be so easy. To be buried in that flesh or in another, in that arm held by a friendly hand, and in that hand, without arms, without hands, and without soul in those trembling souls, through the crowd, the hoops, the toy balloons, what's wrong there? I don't know, I'm here, that's all I know, and that it's still not me, that's what you have to make the best of. There's no flesh anywhere, nor any means of dying, leave all that, to want to leave all that, without knowing what that means, all that, it's soon said, soon done, in vain, nothing has stirred, no one spoken. Here nothing will happen, there will be no one here, for many a long day. Departures, stories, they're not for tomorrow. And the voices, wherever they come from, are stone dead.

Isaac Rosenfeld (1918–1956) died young and thus cut short a promising literary career. Although he left a relatively small body of work in the short story, the quality of his vision and his themes shows that Rosenfeld was distinctly a man of his time. For further reading: Passage From Home (1961), An Age of Enormity . . . (1962).

The Brigadier

ISAAC ROSENFELD

We have been fighting the enemy a very long time. So long that I, who entered the war a foot soldier, have had time to receive more than the usual number of decorations and promotions and to become a brigadier, attached to staff headquarters. I forget how many times I have been wounded and the names of all the battles and campaigns in which I have participated. The greater number of them, however, are not to be forgotten: Striplitz, Bougaumères, Trèle, Bzelokhorets, Kovinitsa, Laud Ingaume, El Khabhar, Woozi-Fassam, and so on. I am the oldest man in our field office, though not in the brigade itself. Lately, the newcomers have not been rising from the ranks, but from the Academy. They are young men who have not proved themselves in any way; some have not even fought.

I am settled into my work, which for many years, I am pleased to say, has been of an absorbing nature. It is difficult to recall the time when I fretted with impatience to return to what I considered my natural life as a citizen. I am happy that I am no longer impatient. I have developed, instead, a great eagerness—an eagerness, however, which is thoroughly disciplined and in every way related to our military enterprise. I do not hesitate to call our enterprise the most glorious and far-reaching that has ever been undertaken.

Far-reaching is not quite the word—though it is only in an unofficial capacity that I admit as much. Let me say that it is not the word for me to use. As a matter, simply, of objective fact, what we are engaged in is, of course, that—I mean far-reaching—and much else besides. But for myself it is not enough, and the work I do must be otherwise defined. I have been studying the ends of our warfare while pursuing them; I have tried to make them a part of myself. I should not want it to be said that the Objective is one thing, and the brigadier's effort in its behalf is quite another, not related to it as the word one and the number one are related. My work is the war itself.

The office in which I do my work was once a schoolhouse; it stands in what used to be enemy country. A section of blackboard, cracked down the middle, is still affixed to the wall near my desk and on it you can read a lesson in the enemy's language, written by one of his children; when the chalk began to fade, I had it carefully restored and covered with a coat of shellac. I can read the enemy's hand—which is sometimes difficult even for scholars, as the script is spidery and irregular and varies not only with the dialect but with the very temperament of the writer. The broken lines read: ". . . of the cat and the dog? What will she . . . ;" here the first line ends, broken off at the jagged edge of the board. "We," runs the second line, "know that the . . . [several words are obliterated] while the bird was singing. . . ." The third and last line: ". . . is what we all love. It makes us very happy." I like to imagine, although I know this is nothing but a child's exercise, that these broken lines, could I only complete them, would tell me more about the enemy than all the work of our specialists combined. As for my subordinates, I have led them to believe that these scraps of writing have something to do with logistics—which is all they care about.

The benches, the charts, the books and other blackboards of the schoolhouse have long since been removed. The rooms are now occupied by sturdy desks of our own design, developed during the war, and the walls are lined with filing cabinets and hung with maps of the region. The sides of the house have been reinforced against blast with sandbags, and the windows have been covered with interesting strips of wire and tape which, when the sun is right, cast patterns of shadow upon our papers. If there were nothing else to do, it would be a pleasure to trace some of these patterns. The glass—these are the enemy's original panes—is very bright and clear. The enemy is known for the quality of his glass works. A strange people.

Our office is a relay station among the various fronts. The position of the fronts has grown so complicated through the years, that I never attempt to give our location with reference to the lines of battle. We are well in the center of one circle of fighting, on the periphery of a second, and connected by a long tangent with a third. From time to time our position appears enveloped, and we pack our papers, dismantle our immobile equipment, and prepare to retreat. Subsequent intelligence, however, informs us that the first reports, owing to the complexity of the warfare, were erroneous in many respects and that, far from being encircled, our position may be described as part of an arc thrown round the enemy's flank. The lines of battle, the longer I study them, seem to me more and more like the arms of many embracing bodies.

It is our general purpose, but not my specific task, to supply logistical information to headquarters in the front and in the rear. We are one of a number of stations that co-ordinate the numerous reports both of the enemy's movements and of our own, and relay these back and forth. These reports never fail to conflict with one another, and no matter how well trained our spies, pilots, observers, and scouts may be, we must keep a large staff working round the clock to prevent mistakes, repetitions, and inconsistencies from appearing in our dispatches. Even so we have blundered many times, and our only consolation, and at the same time the reason that reprimands from headquarters have not been more severe, is the fact that the enemy must work under the same disadvantages. Very often a report so complicated and contradictory that it seems impossible to submit, is nevertheless a true picture of the fighting. You can see what we are up against. And then there are the many spontaneous breakdowns of routine for which no one is to blame, the impatience of my superiors which is always interfering with the work, the orders handed down from above, countermanding orders that have already been carried out, and so many other difficulties that are part of the day's normal detail. To make matters worse a training class for scouts is held in the basement of our schoolhouse and we often hear them laughing or crying out in pain as they tumble about on the mats. I have been trying to get this class removed, thus far without success.

My own work developed as a subsidiary of the main logistical operation. My superiors are not yet convinced of the importance of my task (I have been at it for eleven years!), but some of them are interested, and all my equals and subordinates support me in it, so I am not required to give up my investigations. I work in a semiofficial capacity, filling in and sending out my own reports and as much corroborative material as I can lay my hands on—all this in addition to my regular duties. I am kept very busy indeed, seldom working less than sixteen hours at a stretch. I sometimes think, sitting as I do in an old schoolhouse, that I am both schoolmaster and pupil: a teacher to those who are beneath me in rank and an idiot child to my superiors.

I work on the enemy proper. I am trying to discover what he is, what motivates him, what his nature is. And if you say, as so many of my superiors do, that this is known, I reply that I am attacking his very essence. This is not known. In spite of the many long years that we have been at war with him, and the periods of time, in the past, when we lived at his side in restless peace, we know nothing of him that is really worth knowing and that must be known. I myself am convinced that victory will be impossible until we gain this knowledge—and it is precisely to this knowledge that I am devoting my life.

What do we know? The enemy is darker than we, and shorter in stature. His language, as I have indicated, has nothing in common with our own; his religion is an obscenity to all of us who have not made a specialty of studying it. Well then, as I say, he is shorter and darker, two positive facts. His language, though it would be too much trouble to go into it here, is of such and such a kind—a third fact—and his religion is this, that and the other thing, which gives us still another fact. So much we know. Still, what is he?

I have gone many times to the camps and hospitals in the rear to interview the prisoners we have taken. It teaches me nothing, but I nevertheless make my regular visits, and just the other week I returned from one of our hospitals. There was the usual sight in the wards; I am hardened to it. (And yet, almost as if to test myself, I try to recall what I have seen. Am I absolutely hardened?) There were the lightly wounded, their personalities not distorted by pain, and the natural qualities of these men could be observed: their churlishness, stupidity, sullenness, or good nature. They are much like our own soldiers, especially in their boredom. I spoke with them, I took my usual sampling—so many boys (as with our own troops, eleven-year-olds are not uncommon), so many youths, so many of the middle-aged, so many old men, old campaigners. The usual questions, the usual answers—home, parents, occupation, the government, women, disease, God, the purpose of the war, of life, of history, etc. There is nothing to be learned here that we don't already know. Then the wards of the severely wounded—the amputations, the blinded, the infected. The stench is the same as our own stench (the hospital orderlies deny this, maintaining that the enemy's is worse!). The ones with fever have fever, though their skins and eyes show it differently from ours. The delirious rave, the chilled shiver, the poisoned vomit and groan. There are outcries, the usual hysteria, weeping, coughing, and hemorrhage. One lies in a coma, the stump of his leg is gangrenous, it is too late, he cannot be saved. Another soldier has nearly every bone in his body broken: he has both his thighs in traction, a broken back, a broken arm, his skull wound in bandages. Can he be said to suffer either more or less than one of our own men in similar circumstances, or in any way differently from him? I attend an operation—it is the same thing over and over again. The mental casualties in their guarded ward are no different from ours. Some in straightjackets, strapped to their beds, some screaming, some colorless, lifeless, forever immobile. Here and there a dead body, not yet removed. I lift the sheet; the face is already puffed up. The shock of it is gone, and I can no longer remember what it actually used to be like. I poke a finger into a puffy cheek, leaving a depression which takes a long time to fill up again. It is the same death as our own.

I go to the hospitals, though I learn nothing there, and I go to the prison camps, also in vain. Once I had myself incarcerated, disguised as an enemy soldier. I slept with the men in their barracks, ate with them, studied them, was soon infested with the same lice. I was involved in a plan to escape, of which I informed our guards. No one saw through my disguise, and I, in turn, failed to see through the undisguised men and learned nothing. In fact, the few weeks I spent in prison camp were extremely discouraging, for if the gap between the enemy and ourselves is so small that I can pose, undetected, as one of his men, why is it that I can't cross over to him?

I have even suspected my project of a subtle treason. By "cross over to him," I mean of course, "cross the gulf that separates us from knowledge of his true nature." Now I know where I stand in this regard and it no longer troubles me; but at one time I feared that the second expression really meant nothing more than the first and I thought surely that my whole ambition was only to desert to the enemy. Perhaps he fascinated me in the precise sense of attraction, drawing me, through my desire to know, closer and closer to his side. My conscience drove me to my superior, Major General Box. He believes in my project and follows my reports with interest. The General reassured me; it is his opinion that we are all drawn to the enemy, particularly in such a long war, and that the enemy is drawn to us. In certain respects we even begin to resemble each other. But this is only natural, and has nothing to do with my project, which, far from being treason, remains the most important of the war.

I was reassured, but was soon taken with a fresh disquietude. A suggestion that the General had made, without meaning to do so, set me on a new course of activity. The General had said that in certain respects we come to resemble the enemy. What are these respects? Perhaps the knowledge that I was seeking really lay in myself? The resemblance to the enemy might have grown so strong in my case, that it was my own nature I would have to know in order to know his. I took a leave from the service, the only one I have had in the entire campaign, and spent a month in one of the enemy's mountain villages that had been captured by our troops. I lived away from the men, attended only by goats which forage high up among the rocks in this region. I had a hut to myself, and all the mountains necessary to a great introspection. But I learned nothing, nothing that I did not already know.

It was when I returned to active service that I began the most desperate work that I have as yet undertaken. I selected a group of twenty prisoners, all young, sturdy, healthy men. I lived with them until I grew to know them well; some were like my own sons, and one in particular, a peasant boy named Reri, I will say that I loved. I spent long hours out of doors with my companions, joined them in races and various sports, their own as well as ours. We went on long camping and fishing trips about the country, and I developed so great a trust in them that I even provided them with firearms and let them hunt with me. Evenings, when we were not camping under the open sky, we entertained ourselves in my lodge, drinking, playing cards or chess, listening to music, or holding the most intimate conversations—conversations and confidences that verged on love. We became very intimate; there has never been a group of men whom I have known or loved so well, never a youth as my Reri for whom I have had such a close and tender feeling. It was above all with Reri that I carried on my desperate yet gentle work; I strove to know him as completely as one man can ever hope to know another, and something in his response to me, perhaps an intuitive comprehension of my motive, promised that my effort would be rewarded. He was a handsome boy, taller than the average among the enemy, and fairer in color and complexion. Certainly one such as he could be known, a face as open as his could not long conceal the secrets of the inner nature. Often when I was not with him I would picture his face to myself, trusting that a chance moment of insight might reveal him, and therefore his whole people, to me. And I studied his image, sketching him and taking many photographs while he sat patiently before me. (I have kept these sketches and photographs, and look at them from time to time as I once looked at the living Reri. His image still saddens and preplexes me.) So, with all my companions, I engaged in an unceasing search after friendship and understanding, hoping that love would teach me what I was determined to know.

But my ultimate means were not to be gentle, and when I failed again I had to resort, with great reluctance, in shame and disgust, to the final means I had selected to attain my objective. As I had been their friend and lover and father, their teacher in the ways of our people and their pupil in the ways of theirs, so, at last, I became their torturer, hoping now to break them down and force them to yield what they had not been able to give freely. One day I ordered them whipped, the next, beaten; all of them, incuding Reri. I stood by, directing their tortures and noting their surprise, their hatred of me, their screams and their pleas for mercy. I could not help feeling that I had betrayed them; but my guilt only excited me the more and made me inflict always greater agony and humiliation upon them. It must have been guilt that was responsible for my extreme excitement, in the grip of which, while supervising the tortures, I would feel an overwhelming hatred of the enemy, and become convinced that my hatred had brought me so much farther than love, to the very brink of knowledge. When my companions died, I trained, in much the same manner, a new group, in which I included some of the enemy's women. The experiment was repeated. This time I did not spare myself, but submitted in their company to some of the same tortures, as if there might still be lurking in me an essential particle of their enemy's nature which was itself either capable of yielding the truth, or of preventing me from finding it. The experiment failed again. Again I learned nothing, nothing at all.

I still go to the wards and the camps, and from time to time I still conduct tortures. I have devised many other means of coping with my problem, some of them not yet tested. Over the years, I have grown hardened to failure: I more or less expect it now as an essential element of my work. But though I am hardened and toughened and experienced, I find that my work grows more and more difficult. Because of my interest in prisoners, new duties have been assigned to me. Recently negotiations for the exchange of prisoners broke down between the enemy and ourselves, and their number keeps piling up, as ours does in their camps; it is now my duty to arrange for their transportation to the interior. And then there are still the many administrative details of my department, to which I must somehow find time to attend; there are still the hazards and ever. greater complications of our old war, which we have not yet won, and which, I have become absolutely certain, we will never win unless I succeed in my task. To know the enemy! It is the whole purpose and nature of our war, its ultimate meaning, its glory and its greatness. Already I have succeeded in my own character, for I have become my task in my whole being. Nothing comes between me and the work I do. I have triumphed in my character and in my person, but I must still triumph over the enemy. Sometimes I see his armies standing before me, clearly revealed in their dark, powerful mass, and I rush out of the schoolhouse, out of our office, and I feel that in a moment, but one moment more, I will know the truth. And when I hear our gunfire from the front that winds around us in all directions, I know that if my faith is only great enough, the knowledge will come to me and I will win.

James B. Hall (1918–   ), novelist and poet, was
born in rural Ohio. Before becoming a professor of
English he was a merchant sailor. Many of his short
stories have been anthologized. For further reading:
15 × 3 (1957), Us He Devours (1964).

Us He Devours

JAMES B. HALL

The goat coughed in the tree outside her window.

Oh she had waited so long to see the hoofs firm upon the lowest
branches, the flanks slender, stretched upward among the catalpa leaves,
the head half concealed, the backward curving horns erect, glistening in the
moist light of the moon.

Miss Festner had thought all these times were past, forever, but now her
branches rustled louder, and she stiffened in her bed. Stringy and coarse
and rancid as a chicken house floor, the odor afloat in the catalpa tree came
to her. She lay in her bed and she felt her back and her thighs harden. This
time she was determined to wait.

From experience Miss Festner knew that to leap from her bed, to rush to
the casement, to cry out, was useless. When younger she had cried out, in
fear; later she knew she must wait without emotion. Not always did the
goat leap with a terrible cracking of small branches, and scramble pawing
across her window sill.

Sometimes it came—perhaps silently—then deserted her. Sometimes the
cry of reed pipes swelled inside her room until her ears and heart and her
hard breasts ached: sometimes, after the cry of the loon and after the last
crackling noise of great weight among branches, it went away. If it
awakened her, and then deserted her, she would go to her window and stare
out across the town, which fell away below her windows toward the river.
Therefore she did not now dare look toward the window when the odor of
stalls and rabbit hutches and stables came to her like smoke from the leaves
of the shimmering tree.

For this it seemed she had been waiting a very long time. She had almost
given up hope, but now she did what she could. Her quick money-counting
fingers dug deeper into the little holes in the farthest edges of her mattress.
The sheet across her knees and thighs and her dry belly made spasms of
motion.

Some things she could not control, but some things she could do: always she left her window open, she used only the lightest of sheets, and always she was *clean, clean.* If she looked now the eyes she might see would flee into the kingdom of her dreams. But oh tonight she could not wait.

With her eyes still closed she threw the small sheet from her body. Exposed. Yes and on display and naked as the first day her quick money-counting fingers worked inside her Teller's cage. From Escrows in the bank, she had gone behind a Teller's window. Since then she had her window at the bank, with bars, and the businessmen of the town came to her with money and she handled each day the hard, hand-fitting, phallic rolls of dimes, nickels, and quarters. That night in spring, for the first time, the goat coughed in the catalpa tree in the yard of her small house and in her inexperience and her fear she had run too quickly to her bedroom window and the musk-scented thing had fled somewhere across the roiled shadows of her yard.

Finally she learned to wait motionless in her bed, for only then would the wool-soft yarn and the perfume and the polished mother-of-pearl horns and the soft resilient body—only then would it stay lovely as flowers unfolding beside and over her until the dawn humming awoke in her arms. Those mornings she telephoned Mr. Nelscot at the bank. She did not go down the hill to sit behind the window of her Teller's cage until after her lunch.

Louder now outside her bedroom window the small branches scattered. Was now the time, this night?

In the catalpa tree outside she heard it whet the saber of its horns against the topmost branches. Were the hoarse violent eyes staring at her now?

She resisted a moment, and then she no longer cared. To see, to glimpse it among branches seemed enough. She opened wide her eyes.

No. Not there. Gone.

The cry of the loon in the frozen trees chilled her. She felt more deserted, and more forlorn, than ever before. Yet she was not and never could be sinfully passive, for urgency even in her waking hours grew like a fuse somewhere inside her. She recognized, she even welcomed, the desperation that came galloping to her. She knew she must go out, must seek, must search once more.

Of late when the goat coughed in the branches outside her window and then deserted her, she had followed. Once she had been astonished at her own headlong urgency, but she had gone on because she believed that in frenzy was the hot little kernel of satisfaction. Now that restraint was somewhere far behind her she could think of nothing at all except a highway, twisting somewhere ahead.

II

Furiously she drove the country, limestone roads. Ahead on a curve the guardrails writhed in her headlight beams. At a crossroad she saw the shadow of a country mailbox lie black beside some farmer's lane, and as she passed the black check mark shadow seemed to fade, and then to become a check mark of flame in the corner of her headlong eye.

The constant search, it was, that vexed her. At one time the first place she stopped was always the right place. But as the years fled her, she found the right place was now always farther away, until now she was resigned to the longest drive of all: this night she knew without caring that she would go far beyond a familiar tilt-roofed, ramshackle barn that roosted in a pasture, reviled even by the shoat's moist farming nose.

One spring she had first gone outside. She had gone directly to a certain creek that divided two meadows, where a sand bar of supine luminous tissues of gravel lay exposed between rocks and the water. Later she found her sand bar was not the right place and she had to drive on to a field freshly harrowed, and then on still farther, in the fall, to a place of stubbles, of wheat lately under the sickle bars of harvest. From habit, or from some terrible wish, she still drove first to the sand bar and then to the fields, in order of their discovery. Finally she came to a familiar bridge. Across this bridge was a grove of oaks that was lovely and dark and deep, a mat of green between two hills.

The planks of the bridge seemed to say this was the place that she must find. But she could accept no comfort from the mutter of planks. Always, until the final moment, there was uncertainty. Suppose the place now had to be still more remote, a place where she could never travel, a place so cleverly concealed in a shaggy-thighed wood that no one could ever find it. She could not think upon that ultimate possibility. As always, at this time, she knew with the Bible-black certainty of prayer that here was the place. Here nothing would be denied her.

The boxes and packages she kept locked in the car trunk. These were things she bought on impulse during her lunch hour or on Saturday, as though each purchase were for herself. She had not thought there were so many, but the oblong, white boxes and the largest flat box—all of them— seemed to leap into her arms. Without pausing she ran across a culvert and across a flat small meadow and into the first sentinel trees at the oak grove's edge.

Too late she realized the briers also guarded the grove. They had grown and had become heavy as barbed wire since the last time.

With the white boxes held high above her head, and with her robe open, flapping behind her, she leaped high and for a moment seemed to float above the caress of briers. She landed running. Her legs burned. But Miss Festner did not cry out.

Ahead she saw the smooth arena, in the center of her secret grove of oaks.

"Here, oh here," she said to the briers, which seemed to roll away in unbroken humps of light toward a creek beyond.

"Here. I am here, now," she said to the crossed branches of the trees overhead. "Here. . . ."

She took off her robe.

She spread the robe near the boxes, at the edge of the clearing. Carefully in the moonlight she searched the clay ground, inch by inch; there was no dung, and no hair of cattle wedged in the bark of the oak trees. As she had imagined as she drove those limestone roads, the grove was clean, clean.

In the middle of the hoof-packed clay in the center of the grove of oaks, Miss Festner lay herself down upon the ground, which now seemed warm under the muscles of her flesh.

Nothing did come to her.

She was alone.

She listened but she heard only the mockery of silence among the trunks of trees. The intricate thunder of possibility shook her: was this the end, was she to be deserted like this at the final meeting place between two hills.

Then she heard it cough.

Nearby in the encircling brier she heard its jaws nibble the harsh vegetation. A small branch ripped under the plunge of a hoof. Then she heard it above her, high in the canopy of branches overhead; perhaps it was now looking down at the raised, white supplication of her arms.

She heard once more the cry of the loon: near, then far away. She heard something hoarse, and very close, in the ring of the briers. Held fast in the bondage of her desire, she lay with eyes closed in the moonlight, and still nothing came to her.

Over, she thought. Oh over and gone and never again to return to me. She realized a truth about herself: since the first time when the hair was sweet as a cloud of wool above her she had given more and more of herself. She had walked much, had driven farther and farther into strange woods. Then, like a reprieve, the coarse odor came to her. The lust of its eye rustled the briers.

The gifts. Yes, the boxes piled near her robe. Each time, with gifts, she also gave more and more. At first it was only a flower tossed lightly upon the sand bar. Then her gifts were only the green enticement, but finally she had to give the silks of reward, everything.

In a frenzy she opened her gifts.

Against rocks she broke the expensive, sullen perfumes. Each vial shattered and split and this enticement by odor overwhelmed even the trunks of the black trees.

Oh, come to me?

She paused, listened.

Somewhere beyond the shadows, somewhere in the forest of that night she felt something advance. She felt something come closer to her.

Her quick money-counting fingers clawed at the smaller boxes. She ripped tissue paper from all the jewels she had purchased at all the big jewelry stores all across the city. Tiaras and small rings and pearls in white strands, all these she tore into shreds of diamonds and single rubies and broken pearls, and these she threw into the encircling briers.

Oh, come to me?

The odor—so lurid, no near—seemed to stroke her thighs, and then in the old way it seemed to retreat beyond her farthest gifts.

Without her seeming to touch the hoof-packed clay she ran to the largest, final package. This she had saved, for the habit of frugality could also be with her, even in moments of extravagance.

She opened the box. The white, intense fleece of a lamb was what she held aloft. She waved the fleece in the light of the clearing. She held the fleece above her lowing mouth. She allowed the fleece to fall like a shower of myrrh and spice, to fall like the color of flowers around her, to cover her shoulders and her back with the incense of new wool.

Oh, come to me?

When nothing came to her, Miss Festner ran toward the thing she heard, toward a harsh plunging noise, in those final briers.

But she stopped. She knew it had deceived her, and therefore she stood weeping and ruined, fanned by the hot cry of the loon, in the center of briers and all her nights.

III

Escrow, Checking, Loans, and finally a Teller's cage: she had worked through each department, and now as the green floodgate doors of the bank opened, promptly at ten, she watched people swim into the bright hard marble pool of light, the interior of First National, Main.

In the hard security of a Teller's cage, she began this day by loosening the green drawstrings of green moneybags. Rolls of coins were what she found in each puffy little sack, rolls of dimes, and quarters, and half dollars, each roll made especially for her hand. In even rows the packets of bills, the twenties and fifties, fit precisely into each slot of her tray, and she felt the first smile of the morning hazard its first trial with the flesh of her own lips and cheeks as a customer snuffled just beyond the bars of her window.

From up the line, from Window Number One, Miss Festner heard the money-counting sound of laughter. The sound of the laughter made her see the two derby hats and the two false beards of the two men who were shaking hands with a Vice-President in the officers' enclosure, across the room. When she also saw the two beards rise and fall with the handshakes of the two men, she felt her own mouth pick up the laughter and pass it on to the next Teller in the long, money-counting line.

The State's Centennial Year, it was. The State Banking Inspectors were making believe. Across the room, in the officers' marble enclosure, two short men in make-believe beards began to laugh and laugh.

While her fingers counted out sixty-nine-sixty of the pensioner's check, which had snuffled under the bars of her window, she knew the ledgers and the adding machine tapes folded and held with paper clips and the dormant accounts and the Escrows were writhing, somewhere in the vaults or the storage rooms of First National, Main Branch.

Though the bills and the coins flowed through and around and over her fingers as water flows over and around a sand bar in some moonlit creek, the two derby hats and the beards of false gray hair seemed to float, seemed to become an echo, in the high corners of the main floor.

The edges of marble, the parallel shadows on the foot-trampled floor, the parallel lines of the brass-barred window before her, were the squares and the bars of a place she clearly remembered.

Across the bridge, beyond the village edge, was where the pens were. There in Ohio, beyond the edge of a limestone road, she had awakened from the sleepless dawns of girlhood to hear the cruel roosters cry *blood, blood, bloooood* across the sties and pens and across the hen yard's dusty wallows. Often she lay in her bed, listening to the sounds of animals already awake; the snigger of boars or somewhere in the corner of a pasture the dry dirt-pawing hoof of her father's bull. The dirt, the droppings of turkeys and pea fowl, and the dung of sparrows on a beam under the barn's eave were always there, or were seen in memory only as a brown composite of wind and random dust flapping across barnyards.

In that house the women swept floors, brushed crumbs from tables, rocked toward evening, waited for the odor of farm boots and the odor of work clothes, denim jackets, and old felt hats to walk through kitchen doors; waited until the warm odor of milk drifted into the fried heat of a kitchen in March.

In summer a tomcat lolled on the tendrils and the matted leaves of a grape arbor, and stared all day at the martin's box high on a curved, white pole.

Mostly she remembered the things maimed: a rabbit leaping from stubble into the light of her father's sickle bar; the cut-shoat's lyric scream; the pullet, headless toward noon, butting a post of her mother's clothesline. Or the hired men, their fingers aligned at the thresher's dinner table, each man with something clipped off, missing: a finger gone to the nibbling belt of a corn sheller, a toe left at a chopping block, a hand or a forearm shucked by the whirling, frost-wet picker rolls.

All of that was past. She had gone to school, though she had visited her old home out of sentiment at the change of each season. For three years she taught at a consolidated high school. Though she tried to beat them with a yardstick the hulking baseball and football and basketball players refused to obey her. Finally the principal said why after all the First National, Main, paid twice as much, and then she could really have a place of her own. Therefore she had gone to live at the edge of this town, where sometimes a goat coughed in the catalpa leaves, and the backward curve of horn was mother-of-pearl in the moist light of the moon.

The two Inspectors came back toward noon.

Finally they began to work. Because it really was the Centennial Year, they wore derby hats and gray, false whiskers while they walked in and out of the officers' marble enclosure, or in and out of the vaults. She heard them laughing as they worked, and from her window it seemed they walked through the glass partitions. Toward three o'clock they walked past, together, nibbling a candy bar with their white goat teeth; and then they were behind the row of Tellers, nibbling stacks and stacks of twenties and fifties with their money-counting fingers.

At four o'clock doors were locked and the blinds were drawn, and only the feet and the knees of people walked past in the disembodied street. When she saw the legs walking past, Miss Festner thought, Why yes, tomorrow or the next day some one of the officers will walk up behind me and will stare and will then walk away as though he had seen something different. Then she would say what she knew all the others like her always said to the press: For my friends, for my friends, I did it, because I wanted them to be as happy as I have always been. You see, I gave it all to my friends. . . .

At check-out, in the steel-lined vault, she saw the other money trays, all in a row. She knew this might be her last night at home in her own bed, in the room where the catalpa leaves were sometimes perfume in the night.

For the last time, tonight, she knew she might hear the hoofs firm upon the lowest branches, might see the flanks slender, stretched upward among the leaves, and might see also that final, unwinking eye stare at her from the tenderness of leaves.

Without hesitation she opened her massive, over-the-shoulder purse. Into the wide unlatched maw she stuffed all the singles and bundles of twenties and bundles of fifty dollar bills that her country hands could gather. In case, oh, in case it was money that was wanted, after all.

As always, Mr. Nelscot was standing at the bank door.

He smiled and he bowed very slightly as he let Miss Festner and her valise of a purse out of the door.

All over again she heard the click of the door of First National, Main, behind her. She knew he would never do more than smile, would never do more than bow ever so slightly as he opened the door for her to leave. Or had that been his voice, after all; had he said as she left, as the door shut and clicked somewhere in the past and also in the future of her days, had he said too late, "See you. Same time tomorrow?"

Wolfgang Hildesheimer (1916–) is one of a group of new German writers, including Heinrich Böll and Gerd Gaiser, who define the remarkable growth of the short story in Germany since World War II. At present, only a few short stories by Hildesheimer are available in English. For further reading: Great German Short Stories, **edited by Stephen Spender (1960).**

A World Ends

WOLFGANG HILDESHEIMER

The Marchesa Montetristo's last evening party has impressed itself indelibly on my memory. This is partly due, of course, to its extraordinary conclusion but in other ways as well the evening was unforgettable.

My acquaintance with the Marchesa—a Waterman by birth, of Little Gidding, Ohio—came about by a coincidence. I had sold her, through the intermediary of my friend, Herr von Perlhuhn (I mean of course the Abraham-a-Santa Clara expert, not the neo-mystic), the bathtub in which Marat was murdered. It is perhaps not generally known that it had been until then in my possession. Gambling debts obliged me to offer it for sale. So it was that I came to the Marchesa who had long wanted this appliance for her collection of eighteenth-century washing utensils. This was the occasion of my getting to know her. From the bathtub our conversation soon passed to more general esthetic topics. I noticed that the possession of this collector's piece had given me a certain prestige in her eyes. And I was not surprised when one day I was invited to one of her famous parties in her palazzo on the artificial island of San Amerigo. The Marchesa had had the island thrown up a few miles southeast of Murano on a sudden whim, for she detested the mainland—she said it was hurtful to her spiritual equilibrium, and she could find nothing to suit her in the existing stock of islands. So here she resided, devoting her life to the cult of the antique and forgotten, or, as she liked to put it, of the "true and eternal."

The invitation card gave the time of the party as eight o'clock, which meant that the guests were expected at ten. So custom ordered it. Further it ordered that the guests should come in gondolas. In this fashion, it is true, the crossing lasted nearly two hours and was moreover uncomfortable when the sea was rough, but these were unwritten rules of behavior at which no one but a barbarian would cavil—and barbarians were not invited. Besides, many of the younger guests, not yet fully sensible of the dignity of the occasion, would hire a *vaporetto* to take them within a hundred yards of the island whence they were ferried over one by one in a gondola which had been brought in tow.

The splendor of the building needs no description from me. For outside it was an exact replica of the Palazzo Vendramin, and inside every period, from the Gothic onward, was represented. But of course they were not intermingled. Each one had its own room. The Marchesa could really not be accused of breaches of style. Nor need the opulence of the catering be referred to her. Anyone who has ever attended a state banquet in a monarchy—and it is to such that I principally addressed myself—knows what it was like. Moreover it would hardly be true to the spirit of the Marchesa and her circle to mention the pleasures of the table, especially here, where I have to describe the last hours on earth of some of the most eminent figures of the age, which I as sole survivor had the privilege to witness.

After exchanging a few civilities with my hostess and stroking the long-haired Pekinese which never stirred from her side, I was introduced to the Dombrowska, a woman doubly famous, first for her contributions to the rhythmic-expressionist dance, a vanishing art form, and secondly as the author of the book *Back to Youth*, which, as the title indicates, argued in favor of a return to youthfulness of style and which, I need hardly remind the reader, has won adherents far and wide. While we were chatting together, an elderly gentleman of upright bearing came up to us. It was Golch. The Golch. (Unnecessary to give further particulars of a man whose share in the enrichment of our intellectual life is so widely known.) The Dombrowska introduced me: "Herr Sebald, the late owner of Marat's bathtub." My fame had spread.

"Aha," said Golch. I inferred, from the inflection he gave to these syllables, that he was weighing my potentialities as a candidate for the cultural élite. I asked him how he had liked the exhibition of contemporary painting in Luxemburg. For one might, indeed one must, assume that those here assembled had seen, read, and heard everything of any real importance. That was why they were here. Golch raised his eyes as if looking for a word in space and said, "Passé." (He used the English accentuation of the word which was then in fashion. The words "cliché" and "pastiche" too were pronounced à l'anglaise. I don't know what the current usage is. I am now too much taken up with everyday affairs to concern myself with such matters.) I noticed in any case that I had blundered in thus mentioning the contemporary. I had gone down a step, but I had learnt my lesson.

A move was made to the buffet. Here I encountered Signora Sgambati, the astrologer, who had recently made a considerable stir by her theory that not only the fate of individuals but whole trends in the history of ideas could be read in the stars. She was no ordinary phenomenon, this Sgambati, as was at once clear from her appearance. Yet I find it incomprehensible in the circumstances that she did not see in the constellation of the heavens the imminent engulfment of so many substantial members of the intellectual world. She was deep in conversation with Professor Kuntz-Satori, the politician and royalist, who had been trying for decades to introduce a monarchy in Switzerland. Another notable figure.

After taking some refreshment the company moved to the Silver Room for what was to be the climax of the evening's entertainment, a performance of a special kind—the world première of two flute sonatas by Antonio Giambattista Bloch, a contemporary and friend of Rameau, who had been discovered by the musicologist Weltli. He too of course was there. They were played by the flautist Beranger (yes, a descendant) and accompanied by the Marchesa herself, on the self-same harpsichord on which Celestine Rameau had initiated her son into the fundamental principles of counterpoint, and which had been sent for from Paris. The flute too had a history, but I have forgotten it. The two performers had put on rococo costume for the occasion, and the little ensemble looked—they had purposely so arranged themselves—like a picture by Watteau. The performance of course took place by the dimmest of candlelight. There was not a person there who would have found electric light for such an occasion anything but intolerable. By a further sensitive whim of the Marchesa the guests were required after the first sonata (D major) to move over from the Silver Room (Baroque) to the Golden Room (early Rococo), there to enjoy the second sonata. For the Silver Room had a major resonance, the Golden, it could not be disputed, a minor.

At this point I must remark that the tedious elegance which clings to the flute sonatas of second-rank, and more particularly of newly discovered,

masters of this period, was in the present case to be explained by the fact
that no such person as Giambattista Bloch had ever lived. The works here
performed had in reality been composed by the musicologist Weltli. Although this circumstance did not become known till later, I cannot, in retro-
spect, help feeling it a humiliation for the Marchesa that she should have
employed her last moments in the interpretation, however masterly, of a
forgery.

During the second movement of the F minor sonata I saw a rat creeping
along the wall. I was astonished. At first I thought it might have been lured
from its hole by the sound of the flute—such things do happen, they say—
but it was creeping in the opposite direction. It was followed by another rat.
I looked at the guests. They had not noticed anything, and indeed most of
them were keeping their eyes closed in order to be able to abandon themselves to the harmonies of Weltli's forgery. I now heard a dull reverberation, like very distant thunder. The floor began to vibrate. Again I looked
at the guests. If they had heard anything—and something they must be
hearing—it was at any rate not discernible from their hunched-up postures.
I however was made uneasy by these strange symptoms.

A manservant entered. This is barely the place to remark that in the
unusual costume worn by the Marchesa's domestic staff he looked like a
character out of *Tosca*. He went up to the performers and whispered something in the Marchesa's ear. I saw her turn pale. How well it suited her in
the dim candlelight! But she controlled herself and without interruption
played the *andante* calmly to the end. Then she nodded to the flautist,
stood up, and addressed the company.

"Ladies and gentlemen," she said, "I have just learnt that the foundations
of the island and those of the palace with them are breaking up. The Office
of Submarine Works has been informed. The right thing, I think we shall
all agree, is to go on with the music."

She sat down again, gave the sign to Monsieur Beranger, and they played
the *allegro con brio*, the last movement, which did seem to me at the time,
though I had yet no inkling that it was a forgery, little suited to the
uniqueness of the situation.

On the polished floor small puddles were forming. The reverberation had
grown louder and sounded nearer. Most of the guests were now sitting
upright, their faces ashen in the candlelight, and looking as if they were
long dead already. I stood up and said, "I'm going," not so loud as to give
offense to the musicians, but loud enough to intimate to the other guests
that I had the courage to admit my fear. The floor was now almost evenly
covered with water. Although I walked on tiptoe, I could not help splashing
an evening dress or two as I passed. But, in view of what was soon to come,
the damage I did must be reckoned inconsiderable. Few of the guests
thought me worthy of a glance, but I did not care. As I opened the door to

the passage a wave of water poured into the room and caused Lady Fitz-jones (the preserver of Celtic customs) to draw her fur wrap more closely about her—no doubt a reflex movement, for it could not be of any use. Before shutting the door behind me I saw Herr von Perlhuln (the neo-mystic, not the Abraham-a-Santa Clara expert) casting a half-contemptuous, half-melancholy glance in my direction. He too was now sitting in water almost to his knees. So was the Marchesa, who could no longer use the pedals. I do not as a matter of fact know how essential they are on the harpsichord. I remember thinking that if the piece had been a cello sonata, they would perforce have had to break it off here since the instrument would not sound in water. Strange what irrelevant thoughts occur to one in such moments.

In the entrance hall it was suddenly as quiet as in a grotto, only in the distance a sound of rushing water was to be heard. I divested myself of my tail coat and was soon swimming through the sinking palace toward the portals. My splashes echoed mysteriously from the walls and columns. Not a soul was to be seen. Evidently the servants had all fled. And why should they not? They had no obligation to the true and eternal culture, and those assembled here had no further need of their services.

Outside the moon shone as if nothing were amiss, and yet a world, no less, was here sinking beneath the ocean. As if at a great distance I could still hear the high notes of Monsieur Beranger's flute. He had a wonderful *embouchure*, that one must allow him.

I unhitched the last gondola which the escaping servants had left behind and pushed out to sea. Through the windows past which I paddled the water was now flooding into the palace. I saw that the guests had risen from their seats. The sonata must be at an end, for they were clapping, their hands held high over their heads, since the water was now up to their chins. With dignity the Marchesa and Monsieur Beranger were acknowledging the applause, though in the circumstances they could not bow.

The water had now reached the candles. Slowly they were extinguished, and as the darkness grew, it became quiet; the applause was silenced. Suddenly I heard the crash and roar of a building in collapse. The Palazzo was falling. I steered the gondola seaward so as not to be hit by plaster fragments.

After paddling some hundreds of yards across the lagoon in the direction of the island of San Giorgio, I turned round once more. The sea lay dead calm in the moonlight as if no island had ever stood there. A pity about the bathtub, I thought, for that was a loss which could never be made good. The thought was perhaps rather heartless but experience teaches us that we need a certain distance from such events in order to appreciate their full scope.

Yukio Mishima (1925–   ) is the pseudonym of
Kimitake Hiraoka. Born in Tokyo, he is the most
distinguished and prolific of contemporary Japanese writers. He has published thirteen novels,
thirty-three plays, seventy-four short stories, and
many articles. Translation of his works have appeared in many Western countries; his modern Nō
plays are performed in America and elsewhere.
Among his works in English are The Sound of Waves
(1956), The Temple of the Golden Pavilion (1959),
After the Banquet (1963), The Sailor Who Fell from
Grace with the Sea (1965), and Forbidden Colors
(1968).

Three Million Yen

YUKIO MISHIMA

"We're to meet her at nine?" asked Kenzō.

"At nine, she said, in the toy department on the ground floor," replied
Kiyoko. "But it's too noisy to talk there, and I told her about the coffee
shop on the third floor instead."

"That was a good idea."

The young husband and wife looked up at the neon pagoda atop the
New World Building, which they were approaching from the rear.

It was a cloudy, muggy night, of a sort common in the early-summer
rainy season. Neon lights painted the low sky in rich colors. The delicate
pagoda, flashing on and off in the softer of neon tones, was very beautiful
indeed. It was particularly beautiful when, after all the flashing neon tubes
had gone out together, they suddenly flashed on again, so soon that the
after-image had scarcely disappeared. To be seen from all over Asakusa,
the pagoda had replaced Gourd Pond, now filled in, as the main landmark of
the Asakusa night.

To Kenzō and Kiyoko the pagoda seemed to encompass in all its purity
some grand, inaccessible dream of life. Leaning against the rail of the parking lot, they looked absently up at it for a time.

Kenzō was in an undershirt, cheap trousers, and wooden clogs. His skin
was fair but the lines of the shoulders and chest were powerful, and bushes

of black hair showed between the mounds of muscle at the armpits. Kiyoko, in a sleeveless dress, always had her own armpits carefully shaved. Kenzō was very fussy. Because they hurt when the hair began to grow again, she had become almost obsessive about keeping them shaved, and there was a faint flush on the white skin.

She had a round little face, the pretty features as though woven of cloth. It reminded one of some earnest, unsmiling little animal. It was a face which a person trusted immediately, but not one on which to read thoughts. On her arm she had a large pink plastic handbag and Kenzō's pale blue sports shirt. Kenzō liked to be empty-handed.

From her modest coiffure and make-up one sensed the frugality of their life. Her eyes were clear and had no time for other men.

They crossed the dark road in front of the parking lot and went into the New World. The big market on the ground floor was filled with myriad-colored mountains of splendid, gleaming, cheap wares, and salesgirls peeped from crevices in the mountains. Cool fluorescent lighting poured over the scene. Behind a grove of antimony models of the Tokyo Tower was a row of mirrors painted with Tokyo scenes, and in them, as the two passed, were rippling, waving images of the mountain of ties and summer shirts opposite.

"I couldn't stand living in a place with so many mirrors," said Kiyoko. "I'd be embarrassed."

"Nothing to be embarrassed about." Though his manner was gruff, Kenzō was not one to ignore what his wife said, and his answers were generally perceptive. The two had come to the toy department.

"She knows how you love the toy department. That's why she said to meet her here."

Kenzō laughed. He was fond of the trains and automobiles and space missiles, and he always embarrassed Kiyoko, getting an explanation for each one and trying each one out, but never buying. She took his arm and steered him some distance from the counter.

"It's easy to see that you want a boy. Look at the toys you pick."

"I don't care whether it's a boy or a girl. I just wish it would come soon."

"Another two years, that's all."

"Everything according to plan."

They had divided the savings account they were so assiduously building up into several parts, labeled Plan X and Plan Y and Plan Z and the like. Children must come strictly according to plan. However much they might want a child now, it would have to wait until sufficient money for Plan X had accumulated. Seeing the inadvisability, for numerous reasons, of installment buying, they waited until the money for Plan A or Plan B or

Plan C had accumulated, and then paid cash for an electric washing machine or refrigerator or a television set. Plan A and Plan B had already been carried out. Plan D required little money, but, since it had as its object a low-priority clothes cupboard, it was always being pushed back. Neither of them was much interested in clothes. What they had they could hang in the closet, and all they really needed was enough to keep them warm in the winter.

They were very cautious when making a large purchase. They collected catalogues and looked at various possibilities and asked the advice of people who had already made the purchase, and, when the time for buying finally came, went off to a wholesaler in Okachimachi.

A child was still more serious. First there had to be a secure livelihood and enough money, more than enough money, to see that the child had surroundings of which a parent need not be ashamed, if not, perhaps, enough to see it all the way to adulthood. Kenzō had already made thorough inquiries with friends who had children, and knew what expenditures for powdered milk could be considered reasonable.

With their own plans so nicely formed, the two had nothing but contempt for the thoughtless, floundering ways of the poor. Children were to be produced according to plan in surroundings ideal for rearing them, and the best days were waiting after a child had arrived. Yet they were sensible enough not to pursue their dreams too far. They kept their eyes on the light immediately before them.

There was nothing that enraged Kenzō more than the view of the young that life in contemporary Japan was without hope. He was not a person given to deep thinking, but he had an almost religious faith that if a man respected nature and was obedient to it, and if he but made an effort for himself, the way would somehow open. The first thing was reverence for nature, founded on connubial affection. The greatest antidote for despair was the faith of a man and woman in each other.

Fortunately, he was in love with Kiyoko. To face the future hopefully, therefore, he had only to follow the conditions laid down by nature. Now and then some other woman made a motion in his direction, but he sensed something unnatural in pleasure for the sake of pleasure. It was better to listen to Kiyoko complaining about the dreadful price these days of vegetables and fish.

The two had made a round of the market and were back at the toy department.

Kenzō's eyes were riveted to the toy before him, a station for flying saucers. On the sheet-metal base the complicated mechanism was painted as if viewed through a window, and a revolving light flashed on and off inside the control tower. The flying saucer, of deep-blue plastic, worked on the old principle of the flying top. The station was apparently suspended in space, for the background of the metal base was covered with stars and clouds, among the former the familiar rings of Saturn.

The bright stars of the summer night were splendid. The painted metal surface was indescribably cool, and it was as if all the discomfort of the muggy night would go if a person but gave himself up to that sky.

Before Kiyoko could stop him, Kenzō had resolutely snapped a spring at one corner of the station.

The saucer went spinning toward the ceiling.

The salesgirl reached out and gave a little cry.

The saucer described a gentle arc toward the pastry counter across the aisle and settled square on the million yen crackers.

"We're in!" Kenzō ran over to it.

"What do you mean, we're in?" Embarrassed, Kiyoko turned quickly away from the salesgirl and started after him.

"Look. look where it landed. This means good luck. Not a doubt about it."

The oblong crackers were in the shape of decidedly large banknotes, and the baked-in design, again like a banknote, carried the words "One Million Yen." On the printed label of the cellophane wrapper, the figure of a bald shopkeeper took the place of Prince Shotoku, who decorates most banknotes. There were three large crackers in each package.

Over the objections of Kiyoko, who thought fifty yen for three crackers ridiculous, Kenzō bought a package to make doubly sure of the good luck. He immediately broke the wrapping, gave a cracker to Kiyoko, and took one himself. The third went into her handbag.

As his strong teeth bit into the cracker, a sweet, slightly bitter taste flowed into his mouth. Kiyoko took a little mouse-like bite from her own cracker, almost too large for her grasp.

Kenzō brought the flying saucer back to the toy counter. The salesgirl, out of sorts, looked away as she reached to take it.

Kiyoko had high, arched breasts, and, though she was small, her figure was good. When she walked with Kenzō she seemed to be hiding in his shadow. At street crossings he would take her arm firmly, look to the right and the left, and help her across, pleased at the feel of the rich flesh.

Kenzō liked the pliant strength in a woman who, although she could perfectly well do things for herself, always deferred to her husband. Kiyoko had never read a newspaper, but she had an astonishingly accurate knowledge of her surroundings. When she took a comb in her hand or turned over the leaf of a calendar or folded a summer kimono, it was not as if she were engaged in housework, but rather as if, fresh and alert, she were keeping company with the "things" known as comb and calendar and kimono. She soaked in her world of things as she might soak in a bath.

"There's an indoor amusement park on the fourth floor. We can kill time there," said Kenzō. Kiyoko followed silently into a waiting elevator, but when they reached the fourth floor she tugged at his belt.

"It's a waste of money. Everything seems so cheap, but it's all arranged so that you spend more money than you intend to."

"That's no way to talk. This is our good night, and if you tell yourself it's like a first-run movie it doesn't seem so expensive."

"What's the sense in a first-run movie? If you wait a little while you can see it for half as much."

Her earnestness was most engaging. A brown smudge from the cracker clung to her puckered lips.

"Wipe your mouth," said Kenzō. "You're making a mess of yourself."

Kiyoko looked into a mirror on a near-by pillar and removed the smear with the nail of her little finger. She still had two thirds of a cracker in her hand.

They were at the entrance to "Twenty Thousand Leagues Under the Sea." Jagged rocks reached to the ceiling, and the porthole of a submarine on the sea floor served as the ticket window: forty yen for adults, twenty yen for children.

"But forty yen is too high," said Kiyoko, turning away from the mirror. "You aren't any less hungry after you look at all those cardboard fish, and for forty yen you can get a hundred grams of the best kind of real fish."

"Yesterday they wanted forty for a cut of black snapper. Oh, well. When you're chewing on a million yen you don't talk like a beggar."

The brief debate finished, Kenzō bought the tickets.

"You've let that cracker go to your head."

"But it isn't bad at all. Just right when you're hungry."

"You just ate."

At a landing like a railway platform five or six little boxcars, each large enough for two people, stood at intervals along a track. Three or four other couples were waiting, but the two climbed unabashedly into a car. It was in fact a little tight for two, and Kenzō had to put his arm around his wife's shoulders.

The operator was whistling somewhat disdainfully. Kenzō's powerful arm, on which the sweat had dried, was solid against Kiyoko's naked shoulders and back. Naked skin clung to naked skin like the layers of some intricately folded insect's wing. The car began to shake.

"I'm afraid," said Kiyoko, with the expression of one not in the least afraid.

The cars, each some distance from the rest, plunged into a dark tunnel of rock. Immediately inside there was a sharp curve, and the reverberations were deafening.

A huge shark with shining green scales passed, almost brushing their heads, and Kiyoko ducked away. As she clung to her young husband he gave her a kiss. After the shark had passed, the car ground around a curve in pitch darkness again, but his lips landed unerringly on hers, little fish speared in the dark. The little fish jumped and were still.

The darkness made Kiyoko strangely shy. Only the violent shaking and grinding sustained her. As she slipped deep into the tunnel, her husband's arms around her, she felt naked and flushed crimson. The darkness, dense and impenetrable, had a strength that seemed to render clothes useless. She thought of a dark shed she had secretly played in as a child.

Like a flower springing from the darkness, a red beam of light flashed at them, and Kiyoko cried out once more. It was the wide, gaping mouth of a big angler fish on the ocean floor. Around it, coral fought with the poisonous dark green of seaweed.

Kenzō put his cheek to his wife's—she was still clinging to him—and with the fingers of the arm around her shoulders played with her hair. Compared to the motion of the car the motion of the fingers was slow and deliberate. She knew that he was enjoying the show and enjoying her fright at it as well.

"Will it be over soon? I'm afraid." But her voice was drowned out in the roar.

Once again they were in darkness. Though frightened, Kiyoko had her store of courage. Kenzō's arms were around her, and there was no fight and no shame she could not bear. Because hope had never left them, the state of happiness was for the two of them just such a state of tension.

A big, muddy octopus appeared before them. Once again Kiyoko cried out. Kenzō promptly kissed the nape of her neck. The great tentacles of the octopus filled the cave, and a fierce lightning darted from its eyes.

At the next curve a drowned corpse was standing disconsolately in a seaweed forest.

Finally the light at the far end began to show, the car slowed down, and they were liberated from the unpleasant noise. At the bright platform the uniformed attendant waited to catch the forward handle of the car.

"Is that all?" asked Kenzō.

The man said that it was.

Arching her back, Kiyoko climbed to the platform and whispered in Kenzō's ear: "It makes you feel like a fool, paying forty yen for that."

At the door they compared their crackers. Kiyoko had two thirds left, and Kenzō more than half.

"Just as big as when we came in," said Kenzo. "It was so full of thrills that we didn't have time to eat."

"If you think about it that way, it doesn't seem so bad after all."

Kenzō's eyes were already on the gaudy sign by another door. Electric decorations danced around the word "Magicland," and green and red lights flashed on and off in the startled eyes of a cluster of dwarfs, their domino costumes shining in gold and silver dust. A bit shy about suggesting immediately that they go in, Kenzō leaned against the wall and munched away at his cracker.

"Remember how we crossed the parking lot? The light brought out our shadows on the ground, maybe two feet apart, and a funny idea came to me. I thought to myself how it would be if a little boy's shadow bobbed up and we took it by the hand. And just then a shadow really did break away from ours and come between them."

"No!"

"Then I looked around, and it was someone behind us. A couple of drivers were playing catch, and one of them had dropped the ball and run after it."

"One of these days we really will be out walking, three of us."

"And we'll bring it here." Kenzō motioned toward the sign. "And so we ought to go in and have a look at it first."

Kiyoko said nothing this time as he started for the ticket window.

Possibly because it was a bad time of the day, Magicland was not popular. On both sides of the path as they entered there were flashing banks of artificial flowers. A music box was playing.

"When we build our house this is the way we'll have the path."

"But it's in very bad taste," objected Kiyoko.

How would it feel to go into a house of your own? A building fund had not yet appeared in the plans of the two, but in due course it would. Things they scarcely dreamed of would one day appear in the most natural way imaginable. Usually so prudent, they let their dreams run on this evening, perhaps, as Kiyoko said, because the million-yen crackers had gone to their heads.

Great artificial butterflies were taking honey from the artificial flowers. Some were as big as brief cases, and there were yellow and black spots on their translucent red wings. Tiny bulbs flashed on and off in their protuberant eyes. In the light from below, a soft aura as of sunset in a mist bathed the plastic flowers and grasses. It may have been dust rising from the floor.

The first room they came to, following the arrow, was the leaning room. The floor and all the furnishings leaned so that when one entered upright there was a grating, discordant note to the room.

"Not the sort of house I'd want to live in," said Kenzō, bracing himself against a table on which there were yellow wooden tulips. The words were like a command. He was not himself aware of it, but his decisiveness was that of the privileged one whose hope and well-being refuse to admit outsiders. It was not strange that in the hope there was a scorn for the hopes of others and that no one was allowed to lay a finger on the well-being.

Braced against the leaning table, the determined figure in the undershirt made Kiyoko smile. It was a very domestic scene. Kenzō was like an outraged young man who, having built an extra room on his Sunday holidays, had made a mistake somewhere and ended up with the windows and floors all askew.

"You *could* live in a place like this, though," said Kiyoko. Spreading her arms like a mechanical doll, she leaned forward as the room leaned, and her face approached Kenzō's broad left shoulder at the same angle as the wooden tulips.

His brow wrinkled in a serious young frown, Kenzō smiled. He kissed the cheek that leaned toward him and bit roughly into his million-yen cracker.

By the time they had emerged from the wobbly staircases, the shaking passageways, the log bridges from the railings of which monster heads protruded, and numerous other curious places as well, the heat was too much for them. Kenzo finished his own cracker, took what was left of his wife's between his teeth, and set out in search of a cool evening breeze. Beyond a row of rocking horses a door led out to a balcony.

"What time is it?" asked Kiyoko.

"A quarter to nine. Let's go out and cool off till nine."

"I'm thirsty. The cracker was so dry." She fanned at her perspiring white throat with Kenzō's sports shirt.

"In a minute you can have something to drink."

The night breeze was cool on the wide balcony. Kenzō yawned a wide yawn and leaned against the railing beside his wife. Bare young arms caressed the black railing, wet with the night dew.

"It's much cooler than when we came in."

"Don't be silly," said Kenzō. "It's just higher."

Far below, the black machines of the outdoor amusement park seemed to slumber. The bare seats of the merry-go-round, slightly inclined, were exposed to the dew. Between the iron bars of the aerial observation car, suspended chairs swayed gently in the breeze.

The liveliness of the restaurant to the left was in complete contrast. They had a bird's-eye view into all the corners of the wide expanse inside its walls. Everything was there to look at, as if on a stage: the roofs of the separate cottages, the passages joining them, the ponds and brooks in the garden, the stone lanterns, the interiors of the Japanese rooms, some with serving maids whose kimono sleeves were held up by red cords, others with dancing geisha. The strings of lanterns at the eaves were beautiful, and their white lettering was beautiful too.

The wind carried away the noises of the place, and there was something almost mystically beautiful about it, congealed in delicate detail there at the bottom of the murky summer night.

"I'll bet it's expensive." Kiyoko was once more at her favorite romantic topic.

"Naturally. Only a fool would go there."

"I'll bet they say that cucumbers are a great delicacy, and they charge some fantastic price. How much?"

"Two hundred, maybe." Kenzō took his sports shirt and started to put it on.

Buttoning it for him, Kiyoko continued: "They must think their customers are fools. Why, that's ten times what cucumbers are worth. You can get three of the very best for twenty yen."

"Oh? They're getting cheap."

"The price started going down a week or so ago."

It was five to nine. They went out to look for a stairway to the coffee shop on the third floor. Two of the crackers had disappeared. The other was too large for Kiyoko's very large handbag, and protruded from the unfastened clasp.

The old lady, an impatient person, had arrived early and was waiting. The seats from which the loud jazz orchestra could best be seen were all taken, but there were vacant places where the bandstand was out of sight, beside the potted palm probably rented from some gardener. Sitting alone in a summer kimono, the old lady seemed wholly out of place.

She was a small woman not far past middle age, and she had the clean, well-tended face of the plebian lowlands. She spoke briskly with many delicate gestures. She was proud of the fact that she got along so nicely with young people.

"You'll be treating me, of course, so I ordered something expensive while I was waiting." Even as she spoke the tall glass arrived, pieces of fruit atop a parfait.

"Now that was generous of you. All we needed was soda water."

Her outstretched little finger taut, the old lady plunged in with her spoon and skillfully brought out the cream beneath. Meanwhile she was talking along at her usual brisk pace.

"It's nice that this place is so noisy and no one can hear us. Tonight we go to Nakano—I think I mentioned it over the phone. An ordinary private house and—can you imagine it?—the customers are housewives having a class reunion. There's not much that the rich ladies don't know about these days. And I imagine they walk around pretending the idea never entered their heads. Anyway, I told them about you, and they said they had to have you and no one else. They don't want someone who's all beaten up by the years, you know. And I must say that I can't blame them. So I asked a good stiff price and she said it was low and if they were pleased they'd give you a good tip. They haven't any idea what the market rate is, of course. But I want you to do your best, now. I'm sure I don't need to tell you, but if they're pleased we'll get all sorts of rich customers. There aren't many that go as well together as you two do, of course, and I'm not worried, but don't do anything to make me ashamed of you. Well, anyhow, the woman of the house is the wife of some important person or other, and she'll be waiting for us at the coffee shop in front of Nakano station. You know what will happen next. She'll send the taxi through all sorts of back alleys to get us mixed up. I don't imagine she'll blindfold us, but she'll pull us through the back door so we don't have a chance to read the sign on the gate. I won't like it any better than you will, but she has herself to consider, after all. Don't let it bother you. Me? Oh, I'll be doing the usual thing, keeping watch in the hall. I can bluff my way through, I don't care who comes in. Well, maybe we ought to get started. And let me say it again, I want a good performance from you."

It was late in the night, and Kiyoko and Kenzō had left the old lady and were back in Asakusa. They were even more exhausted than usual. Kenzō's wooden clogs dragged along the street. The billboards in the park were a poisonous black under the cloudy sky.

Simultaneously, they looked up at the New World. The neon pagoda was dark.

"What a rotten bunch. I don't think I've ever seen such a rotten, stuck-up bunch," said Kenzō.

Her eyes on the ground, Kiyoko did not answer.

"Well? Did you ever see a worse bunch of affected old women?"

"No. But what can you do? The pay was good."

"Playing around with money they pry from their husbands. Don't get to be that way when you have money."

"Silly." Kiyoko's smiling face was sharply white in the darkness.

"A really nasty bunch." Kenzō spat in a strong white arc. "How much?"

"This." Kiyoko reached artlessly into her handbag and pulled out some bills.

"Five thousand? We've never made that much before. And the old woman took three thousand. Damn! I'd like to tear it up, that's what I'd like to do. That would really feel good."

Kiyoko took the money back in some consternation. Her finger touched the last of the million-yen crackers.

"Tear this up in its place," she said softly.

Kenzō took the cracker, wadded the cellophane wrapper, and threw it to the ground. It crackled sharply on the silent, deserted street. Too large for one hand, he took the cracker in both hands and tried to break it. It was damp and soggy, and the sweet surface stuck to his hands. The more it bent the more it resisted. He was in the end unable to break it.

James Alan McPherson (1943–   ) grew up in Savannah, Georgia, and after schooling at Morgan State College in Baltimore and Morris Brown College in Atlanta, graduated in 1968 from Harvard Law School. He has been a reporter for the Bay State Banner and presently is a contributing editor of Atlantic Monthly and a Fellow of College V, University of California, Santa Cruz. His first collection of short stories is Hue and Cry (1969).

Of Cabbages and Kings

JAMES ALAN McPHERSON

Claude Sheats had been in the Brotherhood all his life, and then he had tried to get out. Some of his people and most of his friends were still in the Brotherhood and were still very good members, but Claude was no longer a good member because he had tried to get out after over twenty years. To get away from the Brotherhood and all his friends who were still active in it, he moved to Washington Square and took to reading about being militant. But, living there, he developed a craving for whiteness the way a nicely broke-in virgin craves sex. In spite of this, he maintained a steady black girl, whom he saw at least twice a month to keep up appearances, and once he took both of us with him when he visited his uncle in Harlem who was still in the Brotherhood.

"She's a nice girl, Claude," his uncle's wife had told him that night, because the girl, besides being attractive, had some very positive ideas about the Brotherhood. Her name was Marie, she worked as a secretary in my office, and it was on her suggestion that I had moved in with Claude Sheats.

"I'm glad to see you don't waste your time on hippies," the uncle had said. "All our young men are selling out these days."

The uncle was the kind of fellow who had played his cards right. He was much older than his wife, and I had the impression that night that he must have given her time to experience enough and to become bored enough before he overwhelmed her with his success. He wore glasses and combed his hair back and had that oily composure that made me think of a

495

waiter waiting to be tipped. He was very proud of his English, I observed, and how he always ended his words with just the right sound. He must have felt superior to people who didn't. He must have felt superior to Claude because he was still with the Brotherhood and Claude had tried to get out.

Claude did not like him and always seemed to feel guilty whenever we visited his uncle's house. "Don't mention any of my girls to him," he told me after our first visit.

"Why would I do that?" I said.

"He'll try to psych you into telling him."

"Why should he suspect you? He never comes over to the apartment."

"He just likes to know what I'm doing. I don't want him to know about my girls."

"I won't say anything," I promised.

He was almost twenty-three and had no steady girls except Marie. He was well built so that he had no trouble in the Village area. It was like going to the market for him. During my first days in the apartment the process had seemed like a game. And once, when he was going out, I said: "Bring back two."

Half an hour later he came back with two girls. He got their drinks, and then he called me into his room to meet them.

"This is Doris," he said, pointing to the smaller one, "and I forgot your name," he said to the big blonde.

"Jane," she said.

"This is Howard," he told her.

"Hi," I said. Neither one of them smiled. The big blonde in white pants sat on the big bed, and the little one sat on a chair near the window. He had given them his worst bourbon.

"Excuse me a minute," Claude said to the girls. "I want to talk to Howard for a minute." He put on a record before we went outside into the hall between our rooms. He was always extremely polite and gentle, and he was very soft-spoken in spite of his size.

"Listen," he said to me outside, "you can have the blonde."

"What can I do with that amazon?"

"I don't care. Just get her out of the room."

"She's dirty," I said.

"So you can give her a bath."

"It wouldn't help much."

"Well, just take her out and talk to her," he told me. "Remember, you asked for her."

We went in. "Where you from?" I said to the amazon.

"Brighton."

"What school?"

"No. I just got here."

"From where?"

"*Brighton!*"

"Where's that?" I said.

"*England,*" she said. Claude Sheats looked at me.

"How did you find Washington Square so fast?"

"I got friends."

She was very superior about it all and showed the same slight irritation of a professional theater critic waiting for a late performance to begin. The little one sat on the chair, her legs crossed, staring at the ceiling. Her white pants were dirty too. Both girls looked as though they would have been relieved if we had taken off our clothes and danced for them around the room and across the bed, and made hungry sounds in our throats with our mouths slightly opened.

I said that I had to go out to the drugstore and would be back very soon; but once outside, I walked a whole hour in one direction, and then I walked back. I passed them a block away from our apartment. They were walking fast and did not slow down or speak when I passed them.

Claude Sheats was drinking heavily when I came into the apartment.

"What the hell are you trying to pull?" he said.

"I couldn't find a drugstore open."

He got up from the living room table and walked toward me. "You should have asked me," he said. "I got more than enough."

"I wanted some mouthwash too," I said.

He fumed a while longer, and then told me how I had ruined his evening because the amazon would not leave the room to wait for me and the little one would not do anything with the amazon around. He suddenly thought of going down and bringing them back, and he went out for a while. But he came back without them, saying that they had been picked up again.

"When a man looks out for you, you got to look out for him," he warned me.

"I'm sorry."

"A hell of a lot of good *that* does. And that's the last time I look out for *you*, baby," he said. "From now on it's *me* all the way."

"Thanks," I said.

"If she was too much for you I could of taken the amazon."

"It didn't matter that much," I said.

"You could of had Doris if you couldn't handle the amazon."

"They were both too much," I told him.

But Claude Sheats did not answer. He just looked at me.

After two months of living with him I concluded that Claude hated whites as much as he loved them. And he hated himself with the very same passion. He hated the country and his place in it, and he loved the country and his place in it. He loved the Brotherhood and all that being in it had taught him, and he still believed in what he had been taught, even after he had left it and did not have to believe in anything.

"This Man is going *down*, Howard," he would announce with conviction.

"Why?" I would ask.

"Because it's the Black Man's time to rule again. They had five thousand years, now we get five thousand years."

"What if I don't *want* to rule?" I asked. "What happens if I don't want to take over?"

He looked at me with pity in his face. "You go down with the rest of the country."

"I guess I wouldn't mind much anyway," I said. "It would be a hell of a place with nobody to hate."

But I could never get him to smile about it the way I tried to smile about it. He was always serious. And once, when I questioned the mysticism in the teachings of the Brotherhood, Claude almost attacked me. "Another man might kill you for saying that," he had said. "Another man might not let you get away with saying something like that." He was quite deadly, and he stood over me with an air of patient superiority. And because he could afford to be generous and forgiving, being one of the saved, he sat down at the table with me under the single light bulb and began to teach me. He told me the stories about how it was in the beginning before the whites took over, and about all the little secret significances of black, and about the subtle infiltration of white superiority into everyday objects.

"You've never seen me eat white bread or white sugar, have you?"

"No," I said. He used brown bread and brown sugar.

"Or use bleached flour or white rice?"

"No."

"You know why, don't you?" He waited expectantly.

"No," I finally said. "I don't know why."

He was visibly shocked, so much so that he dropped that line of instruction and began to draw on a pad before him on the living room table. He moved his big shoulders over the yellow pad to conceal his drawings and looked across the table at me. "Now I'm going to tell you something that white men have paid thousands of dollars to learn," he said. "Men have been killed for telling this, but I'm telling you for nothing. I'm warning you not to repeat it because if the whites find out, you know, you could be killed too."

"You know me," I said. "I wouldn't repeat any secrets."

He gave me a long, thoughtful look.

I gave him back a long, eager, honest look.

Then he leaned across the table, and whispered: "Kennedy isn't buried in this country. He was the only President who never had his coffin opened during the funeral. The body was in state all that time, and they never opened the coffin once. You know why?"

"No."

"Because he's not *in it!* They buried an empty coffin. Kennedy was a Thirty-third Degree Mason. His body is in Jerusalem right now."

"How do you know?" I asked.

"If I told you, it would put your life in danger."

"Did his family know about it?"

"No. His lodge kept it secret."

"No one knew?"

"I'm telling you, *no!*"

"Then how did you find out?"

He sighed, more from tolerance than from boredom with my inability to comprehend the mysticism of pure reality in its most unadulterated form. Of course I could not believe him, and we argued about it, back and forth; but to cap all my uncertainties he drew the thirty-three-degree circle, showed me the secret signs that men had died to learn, and spoke about the time when our black ancestors chased an evil genius out of their kingdom and across a desert and onto an island somewhere in the sea; from which, hundreds of years later, this same evil genius sent forth a perfected breed of white-skinned and evil creatures who, through trickery, managed to enslave for five thousand years the onetime Black Masters of the world. He further explained the significance of the East and why all the saved must go there once during their lifetime, and possibly be buried there, as Kennedy had been.

It was dark and late at night, and the glaring bulb cast his great shadow into the corners so that there was the sense of some outraged spirit, fuming in the halls and dark places of our closets, waiting to extract some terrible and justifiable revenge from him for disclosing to me, an unbeliever, the closest-kept of secrets. But I was aware of them only for an instant, and then I did not believe him again.

The most convincing thing about it all was that he was very intelligent and had an orderly, well-regimented life-style, and yet *he* had no trouble with believing. He believed in the certainty of statistical surveys, which was his work; the nutritional value of wheat germ sprinkled on eggs; the sensuality of gin; and the dangers inherent in smoking. He was stylish in that he did not believe in God, but he was extremely moral and warm and kind; and I wanted sometimes to embrace him for his kindness and bigness and gentle manners. He lived his life so carefully that no matter what he said, I could not help believing him sometimes. But I did not want to, because I knew that once I started I could not stop; and then there would be no purpose to my own beliefs and no real conviction or direction in my own efforts to achieve when always, in the back of my regular thoughts, there would be a sense of futility and a fear of the unknown all about me. So, for the sake of necessity, I chose not to believe him.

He felt that the country was doomed and that the safe thing to do was to make enough money as soon as possible and escape to the Far East. He forecast summer riots in certain Northern cities and warned me, religiously, to avoid all implicating ties with whites so that I might have a chance to be saved when that time came. And I asked him about *his* ties, and the girls, and how it was never a movie date with coffee afterward but always his room and the cover-all blanket of Motown sounds late into the night.

"A man has different reasons for doing certain things," he had said.

He never seemed to be comfortable with any of the girls. He never seemed to be in control. And after my third month in the apartment I had concluded that he used his virility as a tool and forged, for however long it lasted, a little area of superiority which could never, it seemed, extend itself beyond the certain confines of his room, no matter how late into the night the records played. I could see him fighting to extend the area, as if an increase in the number of girls he saw could compensate for what he had lost in duration. He saw many girls: curious students, unexpected bus-stop pickups, and assorted other one-nighters. And his rationalizations allowed him to believe that each one was an actual conquest, a physical affirmation of a psychological victory over all he hated and loved and hated in the little world of his room.

But then he seemed to have no happiness, even in this. Even here I sensed some intimations of defeat. After each girl, Claude would almost immediately come out of his room, as if there were no need for aftertalk; as if, after it was over, he felt a brooding, silent emptiness that quickly intensified into nervousness and instantaneous shyness and embarrassment, so that the cold which sets in after that kind of emotional drain came in very sharp against his skin, and he could not bear to have her there any longer. And when the girl had gone, he would come into my room to talk. These were the times when he was most like a little boy; and these were the times when he really began to trust me.

"That bitch called me everything but the son of God," he would chuckle. And I would put aside my papers brought home from the office, smile at him, and listen.

He would always eat or drink afterward, and in those early days I was glad for his companionship and the return of his trust, and sometimes we drank and talked until dawn. During these times he would tell me more subtleties about the Man and would repredict the fall of the country. Once he warned me, in a fatherly way, about reading life from books before experiencing it; and another night he advised me on how to schedule girls so that one could run them without being run in return. These were usually good times of good-natured arguments and predictions; but as we drank more often he tended to grow excited and quick-tempered, especially after he had just entertained. Sometimes he would seethe with hate, and every drink he took gave life to increasingly bitter condemnations of the present system and our place in it. There were actually flying saucers, he told me once, piloted by things from other places in the universe, which would eventually destroy the country for what it had done to the black man. He had run into his room on that occasion, and had brought out a book by a man who maintained that the government was deliberately withholding from the public overwhelming evidence of flying saucers and strange creatures from other galaxies that walked among us every day. Claude emphasized the fact that the writer was a Ph.D. who must know what he was talking about, and insisted that the politicians withheld the information because they knew that their time was almost up and if they made it public, the black man would know that he had outside friends who would help him take over the world again. Nothing I said could make him reconsider the slightest bit of his information.

"What are we going to use for weapons when we take over?" I asked him once.

"We've got atomic bombs stockpiled and waiting for the day."

"How can you believe that crap?"

He did not answer, but said instead: "You are the living example of what the Man has done to my people."

"I just try to think things out for myself," I said.

"You can't think. The handkerchief over your head is too big."

I smiled.

"I know," he continued. "I know all there is to know about whites because I've been studying them all my life."

I smiled some more.

"I ought to know," he said slowly. "I have supernatural powers."

"I'm tired," I told him. "I want to go to sleep now."

Claude started to leave the room, then he turned. "Listen," he said at the door. He pointed his finger at me to emphasize the gravity of his pronouncement. "I predict that within the next week something is going to happen to this country that will hurt it even more than Kennedy's assassination."

"Good-night," I said as he closed the door.

He opened it again. "Remember that I predicted it when it happens," he said. For the first time I noticed that he had been deadly serious all along.

Two days later several astronauts burned to death in Florida. He raced into my room hot with the news.

"Do you believe in me *now?*" he said. "Just two days and look what happened."

I tried to explain, as much to myself as to him, that in any week of the year something unfortunate was bound to occur. But he insisted that this was only part of a divine plan to bring the country to its knees. He said that he intended to send a letter off right away to Jeane Dixon in D.C. to let her know that she was not alone because he also had the same power. Then he thought that he had better not because the FBI knew that he had been active in the Brotherhood before he got out.

At first it was good fun believing that someone important cared enough to watch us. And sometimes when the telephone was dead a long time before the dial tone sounded, I would knock on his door and together we would run through our telephone conversations for that day to see if either of us had said anything implicating or suspect, just in case they were listening. This feeling of persecution brought us closer together, and soon the instruction sessions began to go on almost every night. At this point I could not help believing him a little. And he began to trust me again, like a tolerable little brother, and even confided that the summer riots would break out simultaneously in Harlem and Watts during the second week in August. For some reason, something very difficult to put into words, I spent three hot August nights on the streets of Harlem, waiting for the riot to start.

In the seventh month of our living together, he began to introduce me to his girls again when they came in. Most of them came only once, but all of them received the same mechanical treatment. He discriminated only with liquor, the quality of which improved with the attractiveness or reluctance of the girl: gin for slow starters, bourbon for momentary strangers, and the scotch he reserved for those he hoped would come again. There was first the trek into his room, his own trip out for the ice and glasses while classical music was played within; then after a while the classical piece would be replaced by several Motowns. Finally, there was her trip to the bathroom, his calling a cab in the hall, and the sound of both their feet on the stairs as he walked her down to the cab. Then he would come to my room in his red bathrobe, glass in hand, for the aftertalk.

Then in the ninth month the trouble started. It would be very easy to pick out one incident, one day, one area of misundertsanding in that month and say: "That was where it began." It would be easy, but not accurate. It might have been one instance or a combination of many. It might have been the girl who came into the living room when I was going over the proposed blueprints for a new settlement house, and who lingered too long outside his room in conversation because her father was a builder somewhere. Or it might have been nothing at all. But after that time he warned me about being too friendly with his company.

Another night, when I was leaving the bathroom in my shorts, he came out of his room with a girl who smiled. "Hi," she said to me.

I nodded hello as I ducked back into the bathroom.

When he had walked her down to the door he came to my room and knocked. He did not have a drink. "Why didn't you speak to my company?" he demanded.

"I was in my shorts."

"She felt bad about it. She asked what the hell was wrong with you. What could I tell her—'He got problems'?"

"I'm sorry," I said. "But I didn't want to stop in my shorts."

"I see through you, Howard," he said. "You're just jealous of me and try to insult my girls to get to me."

"Why should I be jealous of you?"

"Because I'm a man and you're not."

"What makes a man anyway?" I said. "Your fried eggs and wheat germ? Why should I be jealous of you *or* what you bring in?"

"Some people don't need a reason. You're a black devil and you'll get yours. I predict that you'll get yours."

"Look," I told him, "I'm sorry about the girl. Tell her I'm sorry when you see her again."

"You treated her so bad she probably won't come back."

I said nothing more, and he stood there silently for a long time before he . turned to leave the room. But at the door he turned again, and said: "I see through you, Howard. You're a black devil."

It should have ended there, and it might have with anyone else. I took great pains to speak to his girls after that, even though he tried to get them into the room as quickly as possible. But a week later he accused me of walking about in his room after he had gone out some two weeks before.

"I swear I wasn't in your room," I protested.

"I saw your shadow on the blinds from across the street at the bus stop," he insisted.

"I've *never* been in your room when you weren't there," I told him.

"I *saw* you!"

We went into his room, and I tried to explain how, even if he could see the window from the bus stop, the big lamp next to the window prevented any shadow from being cast on the blinds. But he was convinced in his mind that at every opportunity I plundered his closets and drawers. He had no respect for simple logic in these matters, no sense of the absurdity of his accusations, and the affair finally ended with my confessing that I might have done it without actually knowing, and if I had, I would not do it again.

But what had been a gesture for peace on my part became a vindication for him, proof that I *was* a black devil, capable of lying and lying until he confronted me with the inescapable truth of the situation. And so he persisted in creating situations from which, if he insisted on a point long enough and with enough self-righteousness, he could draw my inevitable confession.

And I confessed eagerly, goaded on by the necessity of maintaining peace. I confessed to mixing white sugar crystals in with his own brown crystals so that he could use it and violate the teachings of the Brotherhood; I confessed to cleaning the bathroom all the time merely because I wanted to make him feel guilty for not having ever cleaned it. I confessed to telling the faithful Marie, who brought a surprise dinner over for him, that he was working late at his office in order to implicate him with the girls who worked there. I confessed to leaving my papers about the house so that his company could ask about them and develop an interest in me. And I pleaded guilty to a record of other little infamies, which multiplied into countless others, and again subdivided into hundreds of little subtleties until my every movement was a threat to him. If I had a girlfriend to dinner, we should eat in my room instead of at the table because he had to use the bathroom a lot, and he was embarrassed to be seen going to the bathroom.

If I protested, he would fly into a tantrum and shake his big finger at me vigorously. And so I retreated, step by step, into my room, from which I emerged only to go to the bathroom or kitchen or out of the house. I tried to stay out on nights when he had company. But he had company so often that I could not always help being in my room after he had walked her to the door. Then he would knock on my door for his talk. He might offer me a drink, and if I refused, he would go to his room for a while and then come back. He would pace about for a while, like a big little boy who wants to ask for money over his allowance. At these times my mind would move feverishly over all our contacts for as far back as I could make it reach, searching and attempting to pull out that one incident which would surely be the point of his attack. But it was never any use.

"Howard, I got something on my chest, and I might as well get it off."

"What is it?" I asked from my bed.

"You been acting strange lately. Haven't been talking to me. If you got something on your chest, get it off now."

"I have nothing on my chest," I said.

"Then why don't you talk?"

I did not answer.

"You hardly speak to me in the kitchen. If you have something against me, tell me now."

"I have nothing against you."

"Why don't you talk, then?" He looked directly at me. "If a man doesn't talk, you think *something's* wrong!"

"I've been nervous lately, that's all. I got problems, and I don't want to talk."

"Everybody's got problems. That's no reason for going around making a man feel guilty."

"For God's sake, I don't want to talk."

"I know what's wrong with you. Your conscience is bothering you. You're so evil that your conscience is giving you trouble. You got everybody fooled but *me*. I know you're a black devil."

"I'm a black devil," I said. "Now will you let me sleep?"

He went to the door. "You dish it out, but you can't take it," he said. "That's *your* trouble."

"I'm a black devil," I said.

I lay there, after he left, hating myself but thankful that he hadn't called me into his room for the fatherly talk as he had done another time. That was the worst. He had come to the door and said: "Come out of there, I want to talk to you." He had walked ahead of me into his room and had sat down in his big leather chair next to the lamp with his legs spread wide and his big hands in his lap. He had said: "Don't be afraid. I'm not going to hurt you. Sit down. I'm not going to argue. What are you so nervous about? Have a drink," in his kindest, most fatherly way, and that had been the worst of all. That was the time he had told me to eat in my room. Now I could hear him pacing about in the hall, and I knew that it was not over for the night. I began to pray that I could sleep before he came. I did not care what he did as long as I did not have to face him. I resolved to confess to anything he accused me of if it would make him leave sooner. I was about to go out into the hall for my confession when the door was kicked open and he charged into the room.

"You black son of a bitch!" he said. "I ought to *kill* you." He stood over the bed in the dark room and shook his big fist over me. And I lay there hating the overpowering cowardice in me, which kept my body still and my eyes closed, and hoping that he would kill all of it when his heavy fist landed.

"First you insult a man's company, then you ignore him. I been *good* to you. I let you live here, I let you eat my uncle's food, and I taught you things. But you're a ungrateful m-f. I ought to *kill* you right now!"

And I still lay there, as he went on, not hearing him, with nothing in me but a loud throbbing which pulsed through the length of my body and made the sheets move with its pounding. I lay there secure and safe in cowardice for as long as I looked up at him with my eyes big and my body twitching and my mind screaming out to him that it was all right, and I thanked him, because now I truly believed in the new five thousand years of Black Rule.

It is night again. I am in bed again, and I can hear the new blond girl closing the bathroom door. I know that in a minute he will come out in his red robe and call a cab. His muffled voice through my closed door will seem very tired, but just as kind and patient to the dispatcher as it is to everyone, and as it was to me in those old times. I am afraid, because when they came up the stairs earlier they caught me working at the living room table with my back to them. I had not expected him back so soon; but then I should have known that he would not go out. I had turned around in the chair, and she smiled and said hello, and I said "Hi" before he hurried her into the room. I *did* speak, and I know that she heard. But I also know that I must have done something wrong; if not to her, then to him earlier today or yesterday or last week, because he glared at me before following her into the room, and he almost paused to say something when he came out to get the glasses and ice. I wish that I could remember just what it was. But it does not matter. I *am* guilty, and he knows it.

Now that he knows about me I am afraid. I could move away from the apartment and hide my guilt from him, but I know that he would find me. The brainwashed part of my mind tells me to call the police while he is still busy with her, but what could I charge him with when I know that he is only trying to help me? I could move the big ragged yellow chair in front of the door, but that would not stop him, and it might make him impatient with me. Even if I pretended to be asleep and ignored him, it would not help when he comes. He has not bothered to knock for weeks.

In the black shadows over my bed and in the corners I can sense the outraged spirits who help him when they hover about his arms as he gestures, with his lessons, above my bed. I am determined now to lie here and take it. It is the price I must pay for all the black secrets I have learned, and all the evil I have learned about myself. I *am* jealous of him, of his learning, of his girls. I am not the same handkerchief-head I was nine months ago. I have Marie to thank for that, and Claude, and the spirits. They know about me, and perhaps it is they who make him do it and he cannot help himself. I believe in the spirits now, just as I believe most of the time that I am a black devil.

They are going down to the cab now.

I will not ever blame him for it. He is helping me. But I blame the girls. I blame them for not staying on afterward, and for letting all the good nice happy love talk cut off automatically after it is over. *I* need to have them there, after it is over. And he needs it; he needs it much more and much longer than they could ever need what he does for them. He should be able to teach them, as he has taught me. And he should have their appreciation, as he has mine. I blame them. I blame them for letting him try and try and never get just a little of the love there is left in the world.

I can hear him coming back from the cab.

Heinrich Böll (1917–   ) is a postwar German novelist and short-story writer. His general rejection of the senselessness of war and the duplicity of modern life has made him one of the vital voices on the European literary scene. His works include Billiards at Half-past Nine (1962), The Clown (1965), 18 Stories (1966), and End of a Mission (1968).

Like a Bad Dream

HEINRICH BÖLL

That evening we had invited the Zumpens over for dinner, nice people; it was through my father-in-law that we had got to know them: ever since we have been married he has helped me to meet people who can be useful to me in business, and Zumpen can be useful: he is chairman of a committee which places contracts for large housing projects, and I have married into the excavating business.

I was tense that evening, but Bertha, my wife, reassured me. "The fact," she said, "that he's coming at all is promising. Just try and get the conversation round to the contract. You know it's tomorrow they're going to be awarded."

I stood looking through the net curtains of the glass front door, waiting for Zumpen. I smoked, ground the cigarette butts under my foot, and shoved them under the mat. Next I took up a position at the bathroom window and stood there wondering why Zumpen had accepted the invitation; he couldn't be that interested in having dinner with us, and the fact that the big contract I was involved in was going to be awarded tomorrow must have made the whole thing as embarrassing to him as it was to me.

I thought about the contract too: it was a big one, I would make 20,000 marks on the deal, and I wanted the money.

Bertha had decided what I was to wear: a dark jacket, trousers a shade lighter and a conservative tie. That's the kind of thing she learned at home, and at boarding school from the nuns. Also what to offer guests: when to pass the cognac, and when the vermouth, how to arrange dessert. It is comforting to have a wife who knows all about such things.

But Bertha was tense too: as she put her hands on my shoulders, they touched my neck, and I felt her thumbs damp and cold against it.

"It's going to be all right," she said, "You'll get the contract."

"Christ," I said, "it means 20,000 marks to me, and you know how we need the money."

"One should never," she said gently, "mention Christ's name in connection with money!"

A dark car drew up in front of our house, a make I didn't recognize, but it looked Italian. "Take it easy," Bertha whispered, "wait till they've rung, let them stand there for a couple of seconds, then walk slowly to the door and open it."

I watched Mr. and Mrs. Zumpen come up the steps: he is slender and tall, with graying temples, the kind of man who fifty years ago would have been known as a "ladies' man"; Mrs. Zumpen is one of those thin dark women who always make me think of lemons. I could tell from Zumpen's face that it was a frightful bore for him to have dinner with us.

Then the doorbell rang, and I waited one second, two seconds, walked slowly to the door and opened it.

"Well," I said, "how nice of you to come!"

Cognac glasses in hand, we went from room to room in our apartment, which the Zumpens wanted to see. Bertha stayed in the kitchen to squeeze some mayonnaise out of a tube onto the appetizers; she does this very nicely: hearts, loops, little houses. The Zumpens complimented us on our apartment; they exchanged smiles when they saw the big desk in my study, at that moment it seemed a bit too big even to me.

Zumpen admired a small rococo cabinet, a wedding present from my grandmother, and a baroque Madonna in our bedroom.

By the time we got back to the dining room, Bertha had dinner on the table; she had done this very nicely too, it was all so attractive yet so natural, and dinner was pleasant and relaxed. We talked about movies and books, about the recent elections, and Zumpen praised the assortment of cheeses, and Mrs. Zumpen praised the coffee and the pastries. Then we showed the Zumpens our honeymoon pictures: photographs of the Breton coast, Spanish donkeys, and street scenes from Casablanca.

After that we had some more cognac, and when I stood up to get the box with the photos of the time when we were engaged, Bertha gave me a sign, and I didn't get the box. For two minutes there was absolute silence, because we had nothing more to talk about, and we all thought about the contract; I thought of the 20,000 marks, and it struck me that I could deduct the bottle of cognac from my income tax. Zumpen looked at his watch and said. "Too bad, it's ten o'clock; we have to go. It's been such a pleasant evening!" And Mrs. Zumpen said: "It was really delightful, and I hope you'll come to us one evening."

"We would love to," Bertha said, and we stood around for another half-minute all thinking again about the contract, and I felt Zumpen was waiting for me to take him aside and bring up the subject. But I didn't. Zumpen kissed Bertha's hand, and I went ahead, opened the doors, and held the car door open for Mrs. Zumpen down below.

"Why," said Bertha gently, "didn't you mention the contract to him? You know it's going to be awarded tomorrow."

"Well," I said, "I didn't know how to bring the conversation round to it."

"Now look," she said in a quiet voice, "you could have used any excuse to ask him into your study, that's where you should have talked to him. You must have noticed how interested he is in art. You ought to have said: I have an eighteenth-century crucifix in there you might like to have a look at, and then . . ."

I said nothing, and she sighed and tied on her apron. I followed her into the kitchen; we put the rest of the appetizers back in the refrigerator, and I crawled about on the floor looking for the top of the mayonnaise tube. I put away the remains of the cognac, counted the cigars: Zumpen had smoked only one. I emptied the ashtrays, ate another pastry, and looked to see if there was any coffee left in the pot. When I went back to the kitchen, Bertha was standing there with the car key in her hand.

"What's up?" I asked.

"We have to go over there, of course," she said.

"Over where?"

"To the Zumpens," she said, "where do you think?"

"It's nearly half past ten."

"I don't care if it's midnight," Bertha said, "all I know is, there's 20,000 marks involved. Don't imagine they're squeamish."

She went into the bathroom to get ready, and I stood behind her watching her wipe her mouth and draw in new outlines, and for the first time I noticed how wide and primitive that mouth is. When she tightened the knot of my tie I could have kissed her, the way I always used to when she fixed my tie, but I didn't.

Downtown the cafés and restaurants were brightly lit. People were sitting outside on the terraces, and the light from the street lamps was caught in the silver ice-cream dishes and ice buckets. Bertha gave me an encouraging look; but she stayed in the car when we stopped in front of the Zumpens' house, and I pressed the bell at once and was surprised how quickly the door was opened. Mrs. Zumpen did not seem surprised to see me; she had on some black lounging pajamas with loose full trousers embroidered with yellow flowers, and this made me think more than ever of lemons.

"I beg your pardon," I said, "I would like to speak to your husband."

"He's gone out again," she said, "he'll be back in half an hour."

In the hall I saw a lot of Madonnas, gothic and baroque, even rococo Madonnas, if there is such a thing.

"I see," I said, "well then, if you don't mind, I'll come back in half an hour."

Bertha had bought an evening paper; she was reading it and smoking, and when I sat down beside her she said: "I think you could have talked about it to her too."

"But how do you know he wasn't there?"

"Because I know he is at the Gaffel Club playing chess, as he does every Wednesday evening at this time."

"You might have told me that earlier."

"Please try and understand," said Bertha, folding the newspaper. "I am trying to help you, I want you to find out for yourself how to deal with such things. All we had to do was call up Father and he would have settled the whole thing for you with one phone call, but I want you to get the contract on your own."

"All right," I said, "then what'll we do: wait here half an hour, or go up right away and have a talk with her?"

"We'd better go up right away," said Bertha.

We got out of the car and went up in the elevator together. "Life," said Bertha, "consists of making compromises and concessions."

Mrs. Zumpen was no more surprised now than she had been earlier, when I had come alone. She greeted us, and we followed her into her husband's study. Mrs. Zumpen brought some cognac, poured it out, and before I could say anything about the contract she pushed a yellow folder toward me: "Housing Project Fir Tree Haven," I read, and looked up in alarm at Mrs. Zumpen, at Bertha, but they both smiled, and Mrs. Zumpen said: "Open the folder," and I opened it; inside was another one, pink, and on this I read: "Housing Project Fir Tree Haven—Excavation Work." I opened this too, saw my estimate lying there on top of the pile; along the upper edge someone had written in red: "Lowest bid."

I could feel myself flushing with pleasure, my heart thumping, and I thought of the 20,000 marks.

"Christ," I said softly, and closed the file, and this time Bertha forgot to rebuke me.

"*Prost*," said Mrs. Zumpen with a smile, "let's drink to it then."

We drank, and I stood up and said: "It may seem rude of me, but perhaps you'll understand that I would like to go home now."

"I understand perfectly," said Mrs. Zumpen, "there's just one small item to be taken care of." She took the file, leafed through it, and said: "Your price per square meter is thirty pfennigs below that of the next-lowest bidder. I suggest you raise your price by fifteen pfennigs: that way you'll still be the lowest and you'll have made an extra four thousand five hundred marks. Come on, do it now!" Bertha took her pen out of her purse and offered it to me, but I was in too much of a turmoil to write; I gave the file to Bertha and watched her alter the price with a steady hand, rewrite the total, and hand the file back to Mrs. Zumpen.

"And now," said Mrs. Zumpen, "just one more little thing. Get out your check book and write a check for three thousand marks: it must be a cash check and endorsed by you."

She had said this to me, but it was Bertha who pulled our check book out of her purse and made out the check.

"It won't be covered," I said in a low voice.

"When the contract is awarded, there will be an advance, and then it will be covered," said Mrs. Zumpen.

Perhaps I failed to grasp what was happening at the time. As we went down in the elevator, Bertha said she was happy, but I said nothing.

Bertha chose a different way home, we drove through quiet residential districts, I saw lights in open windows, people sitting on balconies drinking wine; it was a clear, warm night.

"I suppose the check was for Zumpen?" was all I said, softly, and Bertha replied, just as softly: "Of course."

I looked at Bertha's small, brown hands on the steering wheel, so confident and quiet. Hands, I thought, that sign checks and squeeze mayonnaise tubes, and I looked higher—at her mouth, and still felt no desire to kiss it.

That evening I did not help Bertha put the car away in the garage, nor did I help her with the dishes. I poured myself a large cognac, went up to my study, and sat down at my desk, which was much too big for me. I was wondering about something. I got up, went into the bedroom and looked at the baroque Madonna, but even there I couldn't put my finger on the thing I was wondering about.

The ringing of the phone interrupted my thoughts; I lifted the receiver and was not surprised to hear Zumpen's voice.

"Your wife," he said, "made a slight mistake. She raised the price by twenty-five pfennigs instead of fifteen."

I thought for a moment and then said: "That wasn't a mistake, she did it with my consent."

He was silent for a second or two, then said with a laugh: "So you had already discussed the various possibilities?"

"Yes," I said.

"All right, then make out another check for a thousand."

"Five hundred," I said, and I thought: It's like a bad dream—that's what it's like.

"Eight hundred," he said, and I said with a laugh: "Six hundred," and I knew, although I had no experience to go on, that he would now say seven hundred and fifty, and when he did I said "Yes" and hung up.

It was not yet midnight when I went downstairs and over to the car to give Zumpen the check; he was alone and laughed as I reached in to hand him the folded check. When I walked slowly back into the house, there was no sign of Bertha; she didn't appear when I went back into my study; she didn't appear when I went downstairs again for a glass of milk from the refrigerator, and I knew what she was thinking; she was thinking: he has to get over it, and I have to leave him alone; this is something he has to understand.

But I never did understand. It is beyond understanding.

Flannery O'Connor (1925–1964) was born and raised in Georgia, where she spent most of her adult life. Her first novel, Wise Blood (1952), received wide critical acclaim, although it was her short stories that established her reputation as a writer. Flannery O'Connor's early death brought to an end one of the strongest talents in modern Southern fiction. For further reading: A Good Man Is Hard to Find (1955).

The Life You Save May Be Your Own

FLANNERY O'CONNOR

The old woman and her daughter were sitting on their porch when Mr. Shiftlet came up their road for the first time. The old woman slid to the edge of her chair and leaned forward, shading her eyes from the piercing sunset with her hand. The daughter could not see far in front of her and continued to play with her fingers. Although the old woman lived in this desolate spot with only her daughter and she had never seen Mr. Shiftlet before, she could tell, even from a distance, that he was a tramp and no one to be afraid of. His left coat sleeve was folded up to show there was only half an arm in it and his gaunt figure listed slightly to the side as if the breeze were pushing him. He had on a black town suit and a brown felt hat that was turned up in the front and down in the back and he carried a tin tool box by a handle. He came on, at an amble, up her road, his face turned toward the sun which appeared to be balancing itself on the peak of a small mountain.

The old woman didn't change her position until he was almost into her yard; then she rose with one hand fisted on her hip. The daughter, a large girl in a short blue organdy dress, saw him all at once and jumped up and began to stamp and point and make excited speechless sounds.

Mr. Shiftlet stopped just inside the yard and set his box on the ground and tipped his hat to her as if she were not in the least afflicted; then he turned toward the old woman and swung the hat all the way off. He had long black slick hair that hung flat from a part in the middle to beyond the tips of his ears on either side. His face descended in forehead for more than half its length and ended suddenly with his features just balanced over a jutting steel-trap jaw. He seemed to be a young man but he had a look of composed dissatisfaction as if he understood life thoroughly.

"Good evening," the old woman said. She was about the size of a cedar fence post and she had a man's gray hat pulled down low over her head.

The tramp stood looking at her and didn't answer. He turned his back and faced the sunset. He swung both his whole and his short arm up slowly so that they indicated an expanse of sky and his figure formed a crooked cross. The old woman watched him with her arms folded across her chest as if she were the owner of the sun, and the daughter watched, her head thrust forward and her fat helpless hands hanging at the wrists. She had long pink-gold hair and eyes as blue as a peacock's neck.

He held the pose for almost fifty seconds and then he picked up his box and came on to the porch and dropped down on the bottom step. "Lady," he said in a firm nasal voice, "I'd give a fortune to live where I could see me a sun do that every evening."

"Does it every evening," the old woman said and set back down. The daughter sat down too and watched him with a cautious sly look as if he were a bird that had come up very close. He leaned to one side, rooting in his pants pocket, and in a second he brought out a package of chewing gum and offered her a piece. She took it and unpeeled it and began to chew without taking her eyes off him. He offered the old woman a piece but she only raised her upper lip to indicate she had no teeth.

Mr. Shiftlet's pale sharp glance had already passed over everything in the yard—the pump near the corner of the house and the big fig tree that three or four chickens were preparing to roost in—and had moved to a shed where he saw the square rusted back of an automobile. "You ladies drive?" he asked.

"That car ain't run in fifteen year," the old woman said. "The day my husband died, it quit running."

"Nothing is like it used to be, lady," he said. "The world is almost rotten."

"That's right," the old woman said. "You from around here?"

"Name Tom T. Shiftlet," he murmured, looking at the tires.

"I'm pleased to meet you," the old woman said. "Name Lucynell Crater and daughter Lucynell Crater. What you doing around here, Mr. Shiftlet?"

He judged the car to be about a 1928 or '29 Ford. "Lady," he said, and turned and gave her his full attention, "lemme tell you something. There's one of these doctors in Atlanta that's taken a knife and cut the human heart—the human heart," he repeated, leaning forward, "out of a man's chest and held it in his hand," and he held his hand out, palm up, as if it were slightly weighted with the human heart, "and studied it like it was a day-old chicken, and, lady," he said, allowing a long significant pause in which his head slid forward and his clay-colored eyes brightened, "he don't know no more about it than you or me."

"That's right," the old woman said.

"Why, if he was to take that knife and cut into every corner of it, he still wouldn't know no more than you or me. What you want to bet?"

"Nothing," the old woman said wisely. "Where you come from, Mr. Shiftlet?"

He didn't answer. He reached into his pocket and brought out a sack of tobacco and a package of cigarette papers and rolled himself a cigarette, expertly with one hand, and attached it in a hanging position to his upper lip. Then he took a box of wooden matches from his pocket and struck one on his shoe. He held the burning match as if he were studying the mystery of flame while it traveled dangerously toward his skin. The daughter began to make loud noises and to point to his hand and shake her finger at him, but when the flame was just before touching him, he leaned down with his hand cupped over it as if he were going to set fire to his nose and lit the cigarette.

He flipped away the dead match and blew a stream of gray into the evening. A sly look came over his face. "Lady," he said, "nowadays, people'll do anything anyways. I can tell you my name is Tom T. Shiftlet and I come from Tarwater, Tennessee, but you never have seen me before: how you know I ain't lying? How you know my name ain't Aaron Sparks, lady, and I come from Singleberry, Georgia, or how you know it's not George Speeds and I come from Lucy, Alabama, or how you know I ain't Thompson Bright from Toolafalls, Mississippi?"

"I don't know nothing about you," the old woman muttered, irked.

"Lady," he said, "people don't care how they lie. Maybe the best I can tell you is, I'm a man; but listen, lady," he said and paused and made his tone more ominous still, "what is a man?"

The old woman began to gum a seed. "What you carry in that tin box, Mr. Shiftlet?" she asked.

"Tools," he said, put back. "I'm a carpenter."

"Well, if you come out here to work, I'll be able to feed you and give you a place to sleep but I can't pay. I'll tell you that before you begin," she said.

There was no answer at once and no particular expression on his face. He leaned back against the two-by-four that helped support the porch roof. "Lady," he said slowly, "there's some men that some things mean more to them than money." The old woman rocked without comment and the daughter watched the trigger that moved up and down in his neck. He told the old woman then that all most people were interested in was money, but he asked what a man was made for. He asked her if a man was made for money, or what. He asked her what she thought she was made for but she didn't answer, she only sat rocking and wondered if a one-armed man could put a new roof on her garden house. He asked a lot of questions that she didn't answer. He told her that he was twenty-eight years old and had lived a varied life. He had been a gospel singer, a foreman on the railroad, an assistant in an undertaking parlor, and he had come over the radio for three months with Uncle Roy and his Red Creek Wranglers. He said he had fought and bled in the Arm Service of his country and visited every foreign land and that everywhere he had seen people that didn't care if they did a thing one way or another. He said he hadn't been raised thataway.

A fat yellow moon appeared in the branches of the fig tree as if it were going to roost there with the chickens. He said that a man had to escape to the country to see the world whole and that he wished he lived in a desolate place like this where he could see the sun go down every evening like God make it to do.

"Are you married or are you single?" the old woman asked.

There was a long silence. "Lady," he asked finally, "where would you find an innocent woman today? I wouldn't have any of this trash I could just pick up."

The daughter was leaning very far down, hanging her head almost between her knees, watching him through a triangular door she had made in her overturned hair; and she suddenly fell in a heap on the floor and began to whimper. Mr. Shiftlet straightened her out and helped her get back in the chair.

"Is she your baby girl?" he asked.

"My only," the old woman said, "and she's the sweetest girl in the world. I wouldn't give her up for nothing on earth. She's smart too. She can sweep the floor, cook, wash, feed the chickens, and hoe. I wouldn't give her up for a casket of jewels."

"No," he said kindly, "don't ever let any man take her away from you."

"Any man come after her," the old woman said, " 'll have to stay around the place."

Mr. Shiftlet's eye in the darkness was focused on a part of the automobile bumper that glittered in the distance. "Lady," he said, jerking his short arm up as if he could point with it to her house and yard and pump, "there ain't a broken thing on this plantation that I couldn't fix for you, one-arm jackleg or not. I'm a man," he said with a sullen dignity, "even if I ain't a whole one. I got," he said, tapping his knuckles on the floor to emphasize the immensity of what he was going to say, "a moral intelligence!" and his face pierced out of the darkness into a shaft of doorlight and he stared at her as if he were astonished himself at this impossible truth.

The old woman was not impressed with the phrase. "I told you you could hang around and work for food," she said, "if you don't mind sleeping in that car yonder."

"Why listen, Lady," he said with a grin of delight, "the monks of old slept in their coffins!"

"They wasn't as advanced as we are," the old woman said.

The next morning he began on the roof of the garden house while Lucynell, the daughter, sat on a rock and watched him work. He had not been around a week before the change he had made in the place was apparent. He had patched the front and back steps, built a new hog pen, restored a fence, and taught Lucynell, who was completely deaf and had never said a word in her life, to say the word "bird." The big rosy-faced girl followed him everywhere, saying "Burrttddt ddbirrrttdt," and clapping her hands. The old woman watched from a distance, secretly pleased. She was ravenous for a son-in-law.

Mr. Shiftlet slept on the hard narrow back seat of the car with his feet out the side window. He had his razor and a can of water on a crate that served him as a bedside table and he put up a piece of mirror against the back glass and kept his coat neatly on a hanger that he hung over one of the windows.

In the evenings he sat on the steps and talked while the old woman and Lucynell rocked violently in their chairs on either side of him. The old woman's three mountains were black against the dark blue sky and were visited off and on by various planets and by the moon after it had left the chickens. Mr. Shiftlet pointed out that the reason he had improved this plantation was because he had taken a personal interest in it. He said he was even going to make the automobile run.

He had raised the hood and studied the mechanism and he said he could tell that the car had been built in the days when cars were really built. You take now, he said, one man puts in one bolt and another man puts in another bolt and another man puts in another bolt so that it's a man for a bolt. That's why you have to pay so much for a car: you're paying all those men. Now if you didn't have to pay but one man, you could get you a cheaper car and one that had had a personal interest taken in it, and it would be a better car. The old woman agreed with him that this was so.

Mr. Shiftlet said that the trouble with the world was that nobody cared, or stopped and took any trouble. He said he never would have been able to teach Lucynell to say a word if he hadn't cared and stopped long enough.

"Teach her to say something else," the old woman said.

"What you want her to say next?" Mr. Shiftlet asked.

The old woman's smile was broad and toothless and suggestive. "Teach her to say, 'sugarpie,' " she said.

Mr. Shiftlet already knew what was on her mind.

The next day he began to tinker with the automobile and that evening he told her that if she would buy a fan belt, he would be able to make the car run.

The old woman said she would give him the money. "You see that girl yonder?" she asked, pointing to Lucynell who was sitting on the floor a foot away, watching him, her eyes blue even in the dark. "If it was ever a man wanted to take her away, I would say, 'No man on earth is going to take that sweet girl of mine away from me!' but if he was to say, 'Lady, I don't want to take her away, I want her right here,' I would say, 'Mister, I don't blame you none. I wouldn't pass up a chance to live in a permanent place and get the sweetest girl in the world myself. You ain't no fool,' I would say."

"How old is she?" Mr. Shiftlet asked casually.

"Fifteen, sixteen," the old woman said. The girl was nearly thirty but because of her innocence it was impossible to guess.

"It would be a good idea to paint it too," Mr. Shiftlet remarked. "You don't want it to rust out."

"We'll see about that later," the old woman said.

The next day he walked into town and returned with the parts he needed, and a can of gasoline. Late in the afternoon, terrible noises issued from the shed and the old woman rushed out of the house, thinking Lucynell was somewhere having a fit. Lucynell was sitting on a chicken crate, stamping her feet and screaming, "Burrddttt! bddurrddtttt!" but her fuss was drowned out by the car. With a volley of blasts it emerged from the shed, moving in a fierce and stately way. Mr. Shiftlet was in the driver's seat, sitting very erect. He had an expression of serious modesty on his face as if he had just raised the dead.

That night, rocking on the porch, the old woman began her business at once. "You want you an innocent woman, don't you?" she asked sympathetically. "You don't want none of this trash."

"No'm, I don't," Mr. Shiftlet said.

"One that can't talk," she continued, "can't sass you back or use foul language. That's the kind for you to have. Right there," and she pointed to Lucynell sitting cross-legged in her chair, holding both feet in her hands.

"That's right," he admitted. "She wouldn't give me any trouble."

"Saturday," the old woman said, "you and her and me can drive into town and get married."

Mr. Shiftlet eased his position on the steps.

"I can't get married right now," he said. "Everything you want to do takes money and I ain't got any."

"What you need with money?" she asked.

"It takes money," he said. "Some people'll do anything anyhow these days, but the way I think, I wouldn't marry no woman that I couldn't take on a trip like she was somebody. I mean take her to a hotel and treat her. I wouldn't marry the Duchesser Windsor," he said firmly, "unless I could take her to a hotel and give her something good to eat.

"I was raised thataway and there ain't a thing I can do about it. My old mother taught me how to do."

"Lucynell don't even know what a hotel is," the old woman muttered. "Listen here, Mr. Shiftlet," she said, sliding forward in her chair, "you'd be getting a permanent house and a deep well and the most innocent girl in the world. You don't need no money. Lemme tell you something: there ain't any place in the world for a poor disabled friendless drifting man."

The ugly words settled in Mr. Shiftlet's head like a group of buzzards in the top of a tree. He didn't answer at once. He rolled himself a cigarette and lit it and then he said in an even voice, "Lady, a man is divided into parts, body and spirit."

The old woman clamped her gums together.

"A body and a spirit," he repeated. "The body, lady, is like a house: it don't go anywhere; but the spirit, lady, is like a automobile: always on the move, always . . ."

"Listen, Mr. Shiftlet," she said, "my well never goes dry and my house is always warm in the winter and there's no mortgage on a thing about this place. You can go to the courthouse and see for yourself. And yonder under that shed is a fine automobile." She laid the bait carefully. "You can have it painted by Saturday. I'll pay for the paint."

In the darkness, Mr. Shiftlet's smile stretched like a weary snake waking up by a fire. "Yes'm," he said softly.

After a second he recalled himself and said, "I'm only saying a man's spirit means more to him than anything else. I would have to take my wife off for the weekend without no regards at all for cost. I got to follow where my spirit says to go."

"I'll give you fifteen dollars for a weekend trip," the old woman said in a crabbed voice. "That's the best I can do."

"That wouldn't hardly pay for more than the gas and the hotel," he said. "It wouldn't feed her."

"Seventeen-fifty," the old woman said. "That's all I got so it isn't any use you trying to milk me. You can take a lunch."

Mr. Shiftlet was deeply hurt by the word "milk." He didn't doubt that she had more money sewed up in her mattress but he had already told her he was not interested in her money. "I'll make that do," he said, and rose and walked off without treating with her further.

On Saturday the three of them drove into town in the car that the paint had barely dried on and Mr. Shiftlet and Lucynell were married in the Ordinary's office while the old woman witnessed. As they came out of the courthouse, Mr. Shiftlet began twisting his neck in his collar. He looked morose and bitter as if he had been insulted while someone held him. "That didn't satisfy me none," he said. "That was just something a woman in an office did, nothing but paper work and blood tests. What do they know about my blood? If they was to take my heart and cut it out," he said, "they wouldn't know a thing about me. It didn't satisfy me at all."

"It satisfied the law," the old woman said sharply.

"The law," Mr. Shiftlet said, and spit. "It's the law that don't satisfy me."

He had painted the car dark green with a yellow band around it just under the windows. The three of them climbed in the front seat and the old woman said, "Don't Lucynell look pretty? Looks like a baby doll." Lucynell was dressed up in a white dress that her mother had uprooted from a trunk and there was a Panama hat on her head with a bunch of red wooden cherries on the brim. Every now and then her placid expression was changed by a sly isolated little thought like a shoot of green in the desert. "You got a prize!" the old woman said.

Mr. Shiftlet didn't even look at her.

They drove back to the house to let the old woman off and pick up the lunch. When they were ready to leave, she stood staring in the window of the car, with her fingers clenched around the glass. Tears began to seep sideways out of her eyes and run along the dirty creases in her face. "I ain't ever been parted with her for two days before," she said.

Mr. Shiftlet started the motor.

"And I wouldn't let no man have her but you because I seen you would do right. Goodbye, Sugarbaby," she said, clutching at the sleeve of the white dress. Lucynell looked straight at her and didn't seem to see her there at all. Mr. Shiftlet eased the car forward so that she had to move her hands.

The early afternoon was clear and open and surrounded by pale blue sky. The hills flattened under the car one after another and the climb and dip and swerve went entirely to Mr. Shiftlet's head so that he forgot his morning bitterness. He had always wanted an automobile but he had never been able to afford one before. He drove very fast because he wanted to make Mobile by nightfall.

Occasionally he stopped his thoughts long enough to look at Lucynell in the seat beside him. She had eaten the lunch as soon as they were out of the yard and now she was pulling the cherries off the hat one by one and throwing them out the window. He became depressed in spite of the car. He had driven about a hundred miles when he decided that she must be hungry again and at the next small town they came to, he stopped in front of an aluminum-painted eating place called The Hot Spot and took her in and ordered her a plate of ham and grits. The ride had made her sleepy and as soon as she got up on the stool, she rested her head on the counter and shut her eyes. There was no one in The Hot Spot but Mr. Shiftlet and the boy behind the counter, a pale youth with a greasy rag hung over his shoulder. Before he could dish up the food, she was snoring gently.

"Give it to her when she wakes up," Mr. Shiftlet said. "I'll pay for it now."

The boy bent over her and stared at the long pink-gold hair and the half-shut sleeping eyes. Then he looked up and stared at Mr. Shiftlet. "She looks like an angel of Gawd," he murmured.

"Hitch-hiker," Mr. Shiftlet explained. "I can't wait. I got to make Tuscaloosa."

The boy bent over again and very carefully touched his fingers to a strand of the golden hair and Mr. Shiftlet left.

He was more depressed than ever as he drove on by himself. The late afternoon had grown hot and sultry and the country had flattened out. Deep in the sky a storm was preparing very slowly and without thunder as if it meant to drain every drop of air from the earth before it broke. There were times when Mr. Shiftlet preferred not to be alone. He felt too that a man with a car had a responsibility to others and he kept his eye out for a hitch-hiker. Occasionally he saw a sign that warned: "Drive carefully. The life you save may be your own."

The narrow road dropped off on either side into dry fields and here and there a shack or a filling station stood in a clearing. The sun began to set directly in front of the automobile. It was a reddening ball that through his windshield was slightly flat on the bottom and top. He saw a boy in overalls and a gray hat standing on the edge of the road and he slowed the car down and stopped in front of him. The boy didn't have his hand raised to thumb the ride, he was only standing there, but he had a small cardboard suitcase and his hat was set on his head in a way to indicate that he had left somewhere for good. "Son," Mr. Shiftlet said, "I see you want a ride."

The boy didn't say he did or he didn't but he opened the door of the car and got in, and Mr. Shiftlet started driving again. The child held the suitcase on his lap and folded his arms on top of it. He turned his head and looked out the window away from Mr. Shiftlet. Mr. Shiftlet felt oppressed. "Son," he said after a minute, "I got the best old mother in the world so I reckon you only got the second best."

The boy gave him a quick dark glance and then turned his face back out the window.

"It's nothing so sweet," Mr. Shiftlet continued, "as a boy's mother. She taught him his first prayers at her knee, she give him love when no other would, she told him what was right and what wasn't, and she seen that he done the right thing. Son," he said, "I never rued a day in my life like the one I rued when I left that old mother of mine."

The boy shifted in his seat but he didn't look at Mr. Shiftlet. He unfolded his arms and put one hand on the door handle.

"My mother was a angel of Gawd," Mr. Shiftlet said in a very strained voice. "He took her from heaven and giver to me and I left her." His eyes were instantly clouded over with a mist of tears. The car was barely moving.

The boy turned angrily in the seat. "You go to the devil!" he cried. "My old woman is a flea bag and yours is a stinking pole cat!" and with that he flung the door open and jumped out with his suitcase into the ditch.

Mr. Shiftlet was so shocked that for about a hundred feet he drove along slowly with the door still open. A cloud, the exact color of the boy's hat and shaped like a turnip, had descended over the sun, and another, worse looking, crouched behind the car. Mr. Shitflet felt that the rottenness of the world was about to engulf him. He raised his arm and let it fall again to his breast. "Oh, Lord!" he prayed. "Break forth and wash the slime from this earth!"

The turnip continued slowly to descend. After a few minutes there was a guffawing peal of thunder from behind and fantastic raindrops, like tin-can tops, crashed over the rear of Mr. Shiftlet's car. Very quickly he stepped on the gas and with his stump sticking out the window he raced the galloping shower into Mobile.

Chronology of Authors

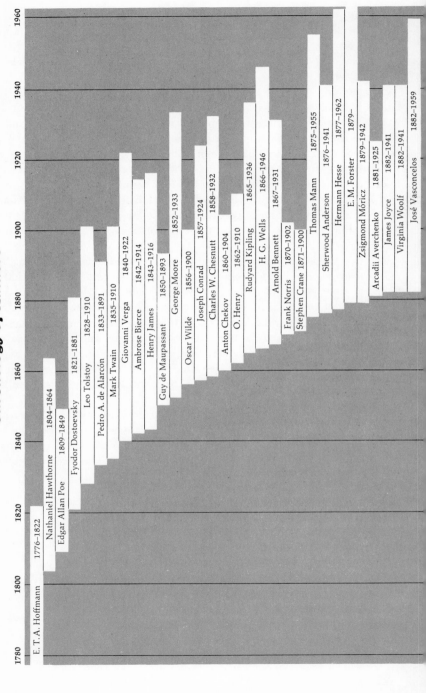

E. T. A. Hoffmann 1776–1822

Nathaniel Hawthorne 1804–1864

Edgar Allan Poe 1809–1849

Fyodor Dostoevsky 1821–1881

Leo Tolstoy 1828–1910

Pedro A. de Alarcón 1833–1891

Mark Twain 1835–1910

Giovanni Verga 1840–1922

Ambrose Bierce 1842–1914

Henry James 1843–1916

Guy de Maupassant 1850–1893

George Moore 1852–1933

Oscar Wilde 1856–1900

Joseph Conrad 1857–1924

Charles W. Chesnutt 1858–1932

Anton Chekov 1860–1904

O. Henry 1862–1910

Rudyard Kipling 1865–1936

H. G. Wells 1866–1946

Arnold Bennett 1867–1931

Frank Norris 1870–1902

Stephen Crane 1871–1900

Thomas Mann 1875–1955

Sherwood Anderson 1876–1941

Hermann Hesse 1877–1962

E. M. Forster 1879–

Zsigmond Móricz 1879–1942

Arcadii Averchenko 1881–1925

James Joyce 1882–1941

Virginia Woolf 1882–1941

José Vasconcelos 1882–1959

Franz Kafka 1883–1924
D. H. Lawrence 1885–1930
Karel Čapek 1890–1938
Strates Myriveles 1892–
Isaac Babel 1894–1941
Katherine Anne Porter 1894–
F. Scott Fitzgerald 1896–1940
Valentin Katayev 1897–
Jorge Luis Borges 1899–
Elizabeth Bowen 1899–
Sean O'Faolain 1900–
Langston Hughes 1902–1967
John Steinbeck 1902–1968
Kay Boyle 1903–
Frank O'Connor 1903—1966
James T. Farrell 1904–
Graham Greene 1904–
Jean-Paul Sartre 1905–
Samuel Beckett 1906–
Tommaso Landolfi 1908–
Bernard Malamud 1914–
Saul Bellow 1915–
Wolfgang Hildesheimer 1916–
Heinrich Böll 1917–
James B. Hall 1918–
Isaac Rosenfeld 1918–1956
R. V. Cassill 1919–
Shirley Jackson 1919–1965
Alain Robbe-Grillet 1922–
Flannery O'Connor 1924–1964
Yukio Mishima 1925–
Ted Hughes 1930–
Slawomir Mrozek 1930–
James Alan McPherson 1943–

Acknowledgments

Sherwood Anderson, "The Egg" from *The Triumph of the Egg* by Sherwood Anderson, published by B. W. Huebsch. Copyright 1921 by B. W. Huebsch, Inc. Renewed 1948 by Eleanor C. Anderson. Reprinted by permission of Harold Ober Associates Incorporated.

Arcadii Averchenko, "The Young Man Who Flew Past" from *A Treasury of Russian Literature,* published by Vanguard Press, Inc. Translated by Bernard Guilbert Guerney. Copyright 1943 by Bernard Guilbert Guerney. Copyright © 1965 by Bernard Guilbert Guerney. By permission of Bernard Guilbert Guerney.

Isaac Babel, "The Awakening" from *An Anthology of Russian Literature in the Soviet Period from Gorki to Pasternak,* translated and edited by Bernard Guilbert. Copyright © 1960 by Bernard Guilbert Guerney. Reprinted by permission of Random House, Inc.

Samuel Beckett, "Stories and Texts for Nothing, III." Copyright © Editions de Minuit 1955, English translation by Anthony Bonner and Samuel Beckett. First published in *Great French Short Stories* selected and introduced by Germaine Brée, © 1960 by Germaine Brée, Dell Publishing Co., Inc.

Saul Bellow, "Looking for Mr. Green" from *Mosby's Memoirs and Other Stories* by Saul Bellow. Copyright 1951 by Saul Bellow. Reprinted by permission of The Viking Press, Inc.

Arnold Bennett, "The Sisters Qita" from *Tales of Five Towns.* Published by Chatto & Windus Ltd. By permission of A. P. Watt & Son and Mrs. Dorothy Cheston Bennett.

Ambrose Bierce, "One Kind of Officer" from *In the Midst of Life: Tales of Soldiers and Civilians.* Published in 1899.

Heinrich Böll, "Like a Bad Dream" from *18 Stories* by Heinrich Böll. Copyright © 1966 by Heinrich Böll (translated by Leila Vennewitz). Used with permission of McGraw-Hill Book Company.

Jorge Luis Borges, "The Secret Miracle," translated by Harriet de Onis, from Jorge Luis Borges, *Labyrinths.* Copyright © 1962 by New Directions Publishing Corporation. Reprinted by permission of New Directions Publishing Corporation.

Elizabeth Bowen, "Her Table Spread" from *Look at All Those Roses* by Elizabeth Bowen. Copyright 1941 by Elizabeth Bowen. Reprinted by permission of Alfred A. Knopf, Inc., and Jonathan Cape Ltd.

Kay Boyle, "Black Boy" from Kay Boyle, *Thirty Stories.* Copyright 1946 by Kay Boyle. Reprinted by permission of New Directions Publishing Corporation.

Karel Čapek, "The Last Judgment" from *Tales from One Pocket* by Karel Čapek, translated by Norma Jeanne McFadden and Leopold Pospišil. By permission of the Estates of Karel Čapek and Dilia (Czechoslovak Theatrical and Literary Agency).

R. V. Cassill, "Happy Marriage" from *Kansas Magazine,* 1956. Copyright by R. V. Cassill. By permission of R. V. Cassill and *Kansas Magazine,* Kansas State University.

Anton Chekov, "The Man in a Shell" from *The Portable Chekov* edited and translated by Avrahm Yarmolinsky. Copyright 1947 by The Viking Press, Inc. Reprinted by permission of The Viking Press, Inc.

Charles W. Chesnutt, "The Web of Circumstance" from *The Wife of His Youth.* Published 1899 by Riverside Press, Cambridge. Copyright Charles W. Chesnutt, 1899.

Joseph Conrad, "An Outpost of Progress" from *Tales of Unrest* by Joseph Conrad. By permission of J. M. Dent & Sons Ltd. and the Trustees of the Joseph Conrad Estate.

Stephen Crane, "The Bride Comes to Yellow Sky" from The Work of Stephen Crane, edited by Wilson Follett, vol. XII (*The Open Boat and Other Tales*), Alfred A. Knopf, Inc., New York, 1898, 1899, 1926.

Pedro A. de Alarcón, "The Nun" is reprinted by permission of Angel Flores.

Guy de Maupassant, "The Piece of String" from *The Odd Number: Thirteen Tales by Guy de Maupassant,* translated by Jonathan Sturges, Harper and Brothers, New York, 1889.

Fyodor Dostoevsky, "A Christmas Tree and a Wedding," translated by P. H. Porosky.

James T. Farrell, "The Benefits of American Life" from *The Short Stories of James T. Farrell.* Copyright 1937, 1964 by James T. Farrell. Reprinted by permission of Vanguard Press, Inc.

F. Scott Fitzgerald, "The Long Way Out" from *The Stories of F. Scott Fitzgerald,* compiled and edited by Malcolm Cowley. Copyright 1951 Charles Scribner's Sons. Reprinted with the permission of Charles Scribner's Sons.

E. M. Forster, "The Other Side of the Hedge" from *The Collected Tales of E. M. Forster.* Copyright 1947 by Alfred A. Knopf, Inc. Reprinted by permission of Alfred A. Knopf, Inc. Also from *The Collected Short Stories of E. M. Forster* by permission of the Author's Representatives and of the Publishers, Sidgwick & Jackson Ltd.

Graham Greene, "Brother" from *Twenty-one Stories* by Graham Greene. Copyright 1949 by Graham Greene. Reprinted by permission of The Viking Press, Inc. and Laurence Pollinger Limited.

James B. Hall, "Us He Devours" from *Us He Devours* by James B. Hall, New Directions—San Francisco Review, New York, 1964.

Nathaniel Hawthorne, "Young Goodman Brown" from *Mosses from an Old Manse,* vol. I, Houghton Mifflin & Co., The Riverside Press, Cambridge, New York. Copyright 1854 by Nathaniel Hawthorne.

Hermann Hesse, "The Poet" from Gesammelte Dichtungen is reprinted by permission of Suhrkamp Verlag. Copyright 1955 by Suhrkamp Verlag, Berlin. All rights reserved.

from Yukio Mishima, *Death in Midsummer and Other Stories.* Copyright ©
1966 by New Directions Publishing Corporation.

George Moore, "Home Sickness" from *The Untilled Field,* 1903, J. B. Lippincott
Company.

Zsigmond Móricz, "Everything Is Good at the End of the World," translated
by Susan Kun. Reprinted from *Hungarian Short Stories,* edited by A. Alvarez,
published in the World's Classics series by the Oxford University Press.

Slawomir Mrozek, "Check!" from *The Ugupu Bird* by Slawomir Mrozek. Translated from the Polish by Konrad Syrop. Copyright © 1968 by Macdonald &
Co. (Publishers) Ltd. Also to be published by Grove Press Inc. Reprinted by
permission of Grove Press, Inc., and by Macdonald & Co. (Publishers) Ltd.

Strates Myriveles, "The Chronicle of an Old Rose-tree," translated by Em-
manuel Hatzantonis. By permission of Strates Myriveles.

Frank Norris, "A Deal in Wheat" from *A Deal in Wheat and Other Stories,*
The Manhattan Press, New York, 1903.

Flannery O'Connor, "The Life You Save May Be Your Own" from *A Good
Man is Hard to Find and Other Stories* by Flannery O'Connor. Copyright
1953 by Flannery O'Connor. Reprinted by permission of Harcourt, Brace &
World, Inc.

Frank O'Connor, "Christmas Morning" from *The Stories of Frank O'Connor.*
Copyright 1946 by Frank O'Connor. This story first appeared in *The New
Yorker.* Reprinted by permission of Alfred A. Knopf, Inc., and A. D.
Peters & Co.

Sean O'Faolain, "The Trout" from *The Man Who Invented Sin* by Sean
O'Faolain. Copyright 1948 by The Devin-Adair Company. Reprinted by
permission of The Devin-Adair Company.

Edgar Allan Poe, "The Black Cat" from *The Works of Edgar Allan Poe,* A. C.
Armstrong & Son, New York, 1884.

Katherine Anne Porter, "Rope" from *Flowering Judas and Other Stories.* Copyright 1930, 1935, © 1958, 1963 by Katherine Anne Porter. Reprinted by
permission of Harcourt, Brace & World, Inc.

Alain Robbe-Grillet, "The Secret Room" from *Esquire Magazine,* February,
1963, translated by Richard Howard, © Alain Robbe-Grillet, 1963, first
published in *Esquire Magazine.* Reprinted by permission of Editions de
Minuit.

Isaac Rosenfeld, "The Brigadier" from *Partisan Review,* March–April, 1947,
pp. 130–137. Reprinted through the courtesy of Mrs. Isaac Rosenfeld and
Partisan Review.

Jean-Paul Sartre, "The Wall," translated by Lloyd Alexander, from Jean-Paul
Sartre, *The Wall.* Copyright 1948 by New Directions Publishing Corporation. Reprinted by permission of New Directions Publishing Corporation.

John Steinbeck, "The Leader of the People" from *The Red Pony* by John Steinbeck. Copyright 1938, copyright © renewed 1966 by John Steinbeck. Reprinted by permission of The Viking Press, Inc.

Leo Tolstoy, "The Story of Yemilyan and the Empty Drum" from *The Death of Ivan Ilyitch, and Other Stories*, Thomas Y. Crowell & Company, New York, 1899.

Mark Twain, "Jim Baker's Blue-jay Yarn" from *A Tramp Abroad*, Chatto and Windus, London, 1880.

José Vasconcelos, "The Boar Hunt" from *The Texas Quarterly*, translated by Paul Waldorf. By permission of *The Texas Quarterly*, The University of Texas, and Paul Waldorf.

Giovanni Verga, "Consolation" from *The She Wolf and Other Stories* by Giovanni Verga, translated by Giovanni Cecchetti. By permission of University of California Press.

H. G. Wells, "The Lord of the Dynamos" from *Thirty Strange Stories*, by H. G. Wells. Copyright 1897 by Edward Arnold. Reprinted with the permission of Harper & Row, Publishers.

Oscar Wilde, "The Remarkable Rocket" from *The Works of Oscar Wilde*, edited by G. F. Maine, 1948. By permission of William Collins Sons & Co., Ltd., New York.

Virginia Woolf, "The Duchess and the Jeweller" from *The Haunted House and Other Stories* by Virginia Woolf. Copyright 1944 by Harcourt, Brace & World, Inc., The Hogarth Press Ltd., and Leonard Woolf.